MW00574277

# PARALLEL LIVES

# PARALLEL LIVES

## A Story of the Greatest Generation

### Peter Turnham

A doctor and a policeman. Two people,
two lives, a serial killer and the bombing
of London during World War Two

The moral rights of Peter Turnham to be identified as the author of this work has been asserted in accordance with the Copyright, Design and Patents Act, 1988.

All rights reserved. No part of this publication may be reproduced, stored in a retrieval system or transmitted, in any form or by any means, electronic, mechanical, photocopying, recording or otherwise, without the prior permission of the copyright owner.

All the principal characters in this book are fictitious, and any resemblance to actual persons, living or dead, is purely coincidental.

Prominent people from the period are characterised to add historical context to this novel. While their office, rank or position is mentioned in the correct context, all dialogue and narrative accredited to these historical figures is purely fictitious. No judgement or comment of any kind is implied nor intended.

* This book contains Parliamentary information licensed under the Open Parliament Licence v3.0 * A CIP catalogue record of this book is available from the British Library

Cover design and interior formatting by JD Smith Design

Copyright © 2024 Peter Turnham

All rights reserved

ISBN No: 978-1-7399941-5-0 (e-book)
978-1-7399941-6-7 (paperback)
978-1-7399941-7-4 (hardback)

Publisher: P&C Turnham
www.peterturnhamauthor.com

**Also by Peter Turnham**

**None Stood Taller**
From the ashes of the Blitz to the D-Day landings.
One woman's remarkable story.

**None Stood Taller - The Final Year**
From the D-Day landings to the VE Day celebrations.
The final year of one woman's remarkable story.

**None Stood Taller - The Price of Freedom**
(October 2022)
An SOE field agent. Audacious, charismatic,
flirtatious, charming, a ruthless assassin.
Also a woman.

**Autumn Daffodils – Charlie's Story**
We are all the product of the past, but the future is ours.

**Autumn Daffodils – Joanna's Story**
Joanna will break your heart, but you will forgive her.

www.peterturnhamauthor.com
peterturnham.author@gmail.com

## Acknowledgements

To my wonderful band of beta readers

To my wife Carol, my spell- and grammar-checker, my editor
and IT consultant, my indispensable other half.

To Jane Dixon-Smith, my cover designer.

A huge thank you to everyone who helped in
the production of this novel.

# Dedication

## To the Saint Thomas's Hospital staff who were killed during World War Two.

Dr J C Campbell (House Surgeon)
Mss S Dunn (Physiotherapist)
Miss K M Forbes (Student Nurse)
Miss H M Richardson (Nursing Auxiliary)
Miss B Mortimer-Thomas (Physiotherapist)
Robert Tanner (Auxiliary Firefighter)

Miss Doucet (Physiotherapist)
Miss S Durham (Physiotherapist)
Miss G Lockyer (Physiotherapist)
Dr P B Spilsbury (House Surgeon)
Miss C G Walker (Student Nurse)
Evan Morgan Jones (Auxiliary Firefighter)

## To the people killed in the Balham Tube Station bombing on October 14th, 1940.

Ballam, Frances Sarah (Age 55)
Ballam, Percy Frederick (Age 55)
Baxendine, James Charles (Age 26)
Benbrook, Gladys Bessie (Age 42)
Brown, Ada Mary (Age 41)
Brown, Harry (Age 21)
Brown, James William (Age 41)
Brown, Mary Ann (Age 65)
Budd, Olive Hilda (Age 13)
Comben, Alfred Joseph (Age 48)
Cottingham, Elizabeth (Age 55)
Courtney, Bridget (Age 49)
Dibble, Roy John (Age 7)
Dudley, Frederick Arthur (Age 34)
Flack, Winifred Mary (Age 20)
Greenhead, Albert (Age 32)
Harrison, Arthur Edwin (Age 43)
Harrison, Joan (Age 20)
Harrison, Patricia (Age 13)
Heron, Frederick William John (Age 24)
Hyde, George Francis (Age 60)
Lyle, Grace (Age 14)
Mansfield, Iris Audrey (Age 19)
Miller, Caroline Elizabeth (Age 52)
Neal, Marie Clare (Age 16)
Neal, Sidney (Age 19)
Palmer, Thomas Samuel (Age 63)
Ravening, Elsie Mary (Age 35)
Rhind, Daisy Bertha (Age 40)
Sexton, Alfred Robert James (Age 46)
Sexton, Maud Alice Rose (Age 34)
Trudgill, Mornington Sydney (Age 35)
Willer, Mary Helen (Age 50)

Ballam, Margaret Emily (Age 26)
Baxendine, Alice (Age 26)
Bell, Clarence Montague (Age 42)
Boland, Ernest Frederick (Age 27)
Brown, Constance (Age 14)
Brown, Ivy Edith (Age 26)
Brown, Joyce (Age 12)
Budd, Caroline Sarah Hilda (Age 58)
Carey, George Walter (Age 57)
Comben, Emma Emily (Age 45)
Cottingham, Joseph William (Age 53)
Courtney, Mary (Age 26)
Dobbs, Frederick James (Age 41)
Flack, Emily Ann (Age 47)
Graham, Samuel (Age 26)
Hall, Edward John (Age 40)
Harrison, Ethel Olive (Age 46)
Harrison, Kathleen Olive (Age 16)
Heron, Elsie Irene (Age 47)
Heron, John (Age 47)
Hyde, Irene Louisa (Age 37)
Lyle, Margaret Grace (Age 59)
Mansfield, Nellie Grace (Age 5)
Neal, Lawrence Archibald (Age 45)
Neal, Sarah (Age 45)
Palmer, Emily Louisa (Age 37.)
Parrish, James William (Age 54)
Ravening, Michael John Anthony (Age 4)
Rundle, John (Age 64)
Sexton, Arthur George (Age 4)
Shopland, Leonard George (Age 38)
Welsh, Francis Patrick (Age 19)
Wilson, Edith (Age 51)

# Table of contents

# Author's Notes

The books in my "None Stood Taller" series have been successful beyond my wildest dreams. Having a number-one bestseller shortlisted for the self-published Book of the Year has been a daunting challenge. The "None Stood Taller" books opened in March 1941, so I thought it would be appropriate to go back and revisit the Second World War from the outset, in 1939. Six years previously, the people of Germany had stepped blindly into the ballot box. They realised too late that the road to tyranny is not paved with good intentions; it is paved with falsehoods and manipulation. Six years later, faced with the reality of war, the ordinary men and women of Great Britain stood fast, forty-one million individuals united in spirit.

I wanted to tell the story of the unsung heroes, the ordinary people who, against all odds, simply carried on. I didn't have to search far; the unsung hero is to be found everywhere in wartime Britain. My research discovered so many incidents, unimaginable tragedies, and acts of heroism that it was difficult to know where to begin. I decided to tell the story of the greatest generation through the lives of two ordinary people, Doctor Emma Stevenson and Detective Inspector Roger Pritchard. Central to this retelling of history are two life-changing events - the bombing of St Thomas's Hospital, London, and the Balham Tube Station disaster. To complete the scene, a notorious serial murderer, aptly named the "Blackout Ripper", roamed the streets of London.

The tragedy that befell St Thomas's Hospital requires no embellishment from me. Indeed, any deviation from the historical events would be a disservice to the courageous staff of that noble institution. A testament to that courage is that three George Medals were awarded to staff members. The image reconstructed for the front cover of this book graphically depicts an empty space formerly occupied by the nurses' home at St Thomas's Hospital. What that image does not contain reaches out across the ages.

1

The specific events detailed in this book, as well as the dates and times of the bombing and its consequences, are accurate. The same applies to the Balham Tube Station disaster. I urge the reader to do their own internet research. Look at the available photographic images. The sight of the red London bus that fell into the bomb crater in Balham High Street is one of the most iconic images of the Blitz.

The final inspiration for this book was the mass murderer Gordon Cummins, known as the "Blackout Ripper". Cummins served with the RAF at the junior rank of leading aircraftman, although he aspired to be a pilot. In February 1942, Cummins murdered four women and attempted to kill two others. He is also suspected of other killings and was hanged on the 25th of June 1942. His only call to fame in the telling of this book is that he provided the initial inspiration and, of course, the sinister name of "The Blackout Ripper".

Restrained only by the historically accurate details of those events, I let my two characters, Emma and Roger, tell their own stories. They took me back to 1939, and for the past two years, I have experienced what they experienced. It has been a harrowing and often awe-inspiring journey. The realisation that later generations stand on the shoulders of giants has been a humbling experience. It has left me with an overwhelming sense of gratitude to the people of my parents' generation. War is the greatest self-inflicted tragedy that can befall humanity. The wisdom of that generation will die with them, but their message to us is clear. We must never let it happen again. So, dear reader, I invite you to embrace my two characters, step back in time with them to September 3rd, 1939 and share the lives of two of the greatest generation.

Peter Turnham
August 2024

https://www.peterturnhamauthor.com
peterturnham.author@gmail.com

# Chapter One
# September 3rd, 1939

Emma

*"Few people rejoice at the death of a person, much less a thousand, but the entire world rejoices when a single life is saved."*

No one who lived through what I experienced will ever be able to view the past with innocent eyes again. Sunday, September 3rd, 1939, marked the end of the time before - the day when innocence became consigned to the past. I visited my parents most weekends, so that fateful day started like any other, but it would not end that way. It was a date destined to become etched into the nation's memory.

My parents sat in the front room of their little terraced house in Balham, South London. My mother sat in the same armchair she had sat in for decades; the fabric gracefully faded just as she had surrendered the bloom of her youth. She shared her attention between her knitting and listening to my father's laboured breathing. The wireless sat on the sideboard like an uninvited guest about to impose its conversation upon us. Mum pretended everything remained perfectly normal while Dad sat with the expression of a condemned man resigned to his fate. Even then, making them both a cup of tea seemed more important. As I went into the kitchen, I could hear the wireless humming into life, as if the uninvited guest had to draw breath. As I poured us each a cup of tea, Mum called out to me.

"Quickly, Em, Dad says this is important; it's about to start."

My parents sat without saying a word, looking at each other and not at me. The wireless fell silent as the broadcast waited to be connected to the Prime Minister. The gravity of the situation suddenly struck me. I stood motionless in the middle of the room, holding a tray with three cups of tea. The silence coming from the wireless had a presence of its own; it reached out into every corner of the room, a rising tide of cold anticipation. Only the sound of my breathing and the tick, tick, tick of the clock on the mantelpiece broke the silence. At precisely 11:15 am, the Prime Minister, Mr Neville Chamberlain, addressed the nation. He sounded so clear, almost as if he were there talking to me in the front room. For a moment, I marvelled at the technology rather than the Prime Minister's message, but that quickly changed.

*"This morning the British Ambassador in Berlin handed the German Government a final note stating that, unless we heard from them by 11 o'clock that they were prepared at once to withdraw their troops from Poland, a state of war would exist between us. I have to tell you now that no such undertaking has been received, and that consequently, this country is at war with Germany."*

(Neville Chamberlain's address to the nation September 3rd, 1939) *

I repeated his last sentence; my recollection became even more poignant and shocking than the Prime Minister's words. He said this country is at war with Germany. Did he really mean we were at war like last time? I looked towards my father, as always, when I needed guidance and advice. His experience of war lived in his eyes, and they reflected nothing but pain and anguish. My father understood what I could not even imagine. His expression confirmed that something terrible had just taken place.

My mother's eyes instantly filled with fear as she looked at Dad, knowing where his thoughts had taken him. He no longer sat in their front room; he stood in a trench with mud up to his shins, watching a sinister pale cloud of gas rolling towards him across the war-scarred landscape of Ypres. Dad's lung capacity reduced his activity to where his daily ritual comprised reading at least two newspapers cover to cover. He remained nothing if not well-informed, something he impressed upon me from an early age.

He used to say, 'Life is an enormous jigsaw puzzle, and every scrap of knowledge is one more piece of the picture.' I had it instilled in me at an early age. He told me I had to keep searching for those pieces, but

I must never lose sight of the picture. I am nothing if not my father's daughter. He was my mentor and guiding light, the centre of my universe. Only then, after the announcement, when it was too late, did I finally understand. The wisdom of the ages my father carried so heavily upon his shoulders would become my cross to bear. I looked down at the cups. The sudden tremor in my hands sent ripples across the surface of the tea. After a long silence, my mother finally spoke.

"What does it mean, Albert? Will this be like last time?"

He hesitated but then spoke solemnly. "No, my dear, I fear it will be far worse."

"How can it be worse than last time? All those lives lost in the trenches."

"We were like savages killing one another, but it always remained a battle between men. Now, it will be a battle fought with industrial might, and we lag far behind."

"I don't understand, Dad. Are you saying we are in danger here?"

"If what is happening in Poland is any indication, then yes, we are in great danger. If Hitler chooses to, he can send his Luftwaffe here to destroy us. The chemical weapons of the last war will be nothing compared to what is available today. The days when a trench or the English Channel might protect us are gone."

"Oh my God, why didn't I see this coming? I've been so preoccupied with the practice and my patients that I've allowed myself to believe what I wanted to believe. I've closed my eyes to this."

"You're not alone, Emma. There are none so blind as those who will not see. While our politicians squabbled about appeasement, Hitler has been rearming at an alarming rate. We have started preparing, but it's too little too late. We are all guilty of not wanting our lives to change."

"Surely that's apathy by another name."

"It is, and there will be a high price to pay for it."

The wireless broadcast interrupted our thoughts with a series of announcements. We were told not to congregate in large numbers, which meant that all places of entertainment were to close immediately. There would be air raid warnings. We would hear a siren telling everyone to take cover. If anyone had not been issued gas masks, they should immediately consult the local Air Raid Warden. It took a moment to fully comprehend what was happening. One moment, I had been concerned for my patients and the practice, and then everything changed instantly. I looked at my father with eyes that could see for the first time. He didn't say, 'I warned you', he didn't need to. The time had passed for that. Nothing focuses the attention as much as the threat of being killed, but you only realise that when it happens.

"What can I do, Dad?"

"You will do what you have been trained to do, Emma; you're a vital part of the war effort now."

"I didn't train for this, but I suppose you're right; I will have a part to play."

"Not just a part, Emma, a vital part. Think about it. Few people rejoice at the death of a person, much less a thousand, but the entire world rejoices when a single life is saved."

"I've never thought about it like that."

"I've seen men carry wounded comrades across no-man's-land trying to save their life. I've seen soldiers struggle to keep a man alive, and when they fail, I've seen the toughest man cry like a baby. War teaches you that life is cheap. It can be taken for the price of a bullet or a blade, but there is no price high enough for a life saved. This is your moment, Emma."

I had never been prouder to be my father's daughter. He hugged me like he had done a thousand times before, but this was different. I knew better than most that his life hung in the balance ever since the chlorine gas destroyed half of his lung capacity. A single respiratory infection might be the end. The 1918 Spanish flu would most certainly have killed him, as would any number of flu outbreaks since. He had been extraordinarily lucky to avoid a serious infection for so long. Mum and I lived in constant fear for him. The trial that lay ahead would make demands upon the fittest of people.

We drank our tea, thinking it was like no other cup of tea before or since, made in peacetime and drunk during the war. That and many other strange thoughts entered my mind. The time before had gone, and with it, all references to normality and security. We entered the unknown, where normal had been erased and security had been replaced with fear. I left them that evening, wondering if I would drive home safely.

# Chapter Two
# Angela Meadows

Roger

*"Evil resides in each of us. We don't close the door to prevent the Devil from coming in. We open the door to let it out."*

Perhaps the time before was an age of innocence. If so, then I am afraid it's gone forever. Whoever we were before 1939, that person no longer exists; the war changed us all. As a policeman, I saw both the best and the worst of human nature. I saw truly remarkable people who gave everything of themselves, often despite terrible personal tragedy. Selfless acts of kindness and courage on a scale that lifted an entire nation. Some people refer to us now as the greatest generation, and I saw many worthy of that accolade. Sadly, I also saw the other side of the Devil's coin: people for whom the accolade of the greatest generation most definitely did not apply.

There will always be those whose moral compass does not align with the rest of society. I regard them as an aberration, parasites that suck the blood of the very body that sustains them. Some commit crimes out of sheer desperation, people down on their luck or victims of circumstance. I had been known to offer such people a helping hand rather than the handcuffs. People can sink into aberrant behaviour for many reasons. Before the war, I thought a line existed that few people would choose to cross because to do so would require you to leave your humanity behind.

The war changed all that; the unspeakable horrors that the Nazis committed brought with it the most chilling realisation of all. The worst of human nature lives among us. Evil resides in each of us. We don't close the door to prevent the Devil from coming in; we open the door to let it out. The Third Reich didn't have an exclusive pact with the Devil; evil also stalked the streets of London. When people prey on one another, when someone exploits the vulnerability of another, especially if that person is a woman, then for me, a line has been crossed.

My naïve belief that love conquers all lies dead beneath a thousand shattered dreams. At the very moment when the nation needed to stand together, crime increased. Some of it, like the black market in rationed goods, became so ubiquitous we virtually had to accept it. There were more serious crimes that I found particularly despicable. The looting of bomb victims' possessions exposed a disturbing flaw in the human condition. Had looting been confined to a morally corrupt minority, it might have been less disturbing, but it wasn't. Otherwise respectable people, and even occasionally trusted people like ARP wardens and firemen, succumbed to temptation. It laid bare the true nature of what lies behind the mask of civilisation.

Worst of all is the fact that the murder rate increased considerably, especially during the Blitz when the cause of death could so easily be concealed. A series of murders stood out above all others, and the memory of those events still haunts me. Even though we were all traumatised by the falling bombs, a lone individual still created an additional reign of terror. When the bringer of death stalked the streets of London in human form, I knew the Devil had found a willing partner.

I refused to give him the notoriety of a name like Jack the Ripper - Jack implies a human being. The Devil had taken human form, but he ceased to be human. None of us realised then, but it all started for me in the summer of 1939.

A report came in of a young woman who had been attacked in Wandsworth, South London. The injured victim had been taken to St Thomas's Hospital. When our Chief Inspector asked for volunteers, we all put our heads down at Balham police station. Nobody wanted what we assumed would be just another 'domestic'. Anything to do with domestic violence could be notoriously difficult and unpleasant to be involved with. Not that any act of violence shouldn't be taken seriously, far from it. It's simply that domestic disputes are seldom resolved satisfactorily. The couple in dispute often turns their ire towards the investigating officer. Little wonder then that we were apprehensive.

"Well done, Pritchard, that's what I like to see, an eager volunteer," said Detective Chief Inspector Gerry Higgins.

"I didn't volunteer, Guv."

"Yes, you did. I distinctly heard you say how much you wanted it. Be on your way."

Gerry and I got along well; he put his hand on my shoulder as I got up to leave. I'm unsure if he was being friendly or pushing me out the door. The report said the victim had been taken to St Thomas's Hospital, so I would start there. I eventually found a PC standing outside the ward. We had a brief word before a nurse guided me to the bed where the poor woman lay. What greeted me instantly filled me with horror.

The woman's injuries were worse than I expected. She could barely speak, her face swollen with terrible bruising. It was a very difficult interview; I had to ask the most personal questions. This wasn't a domestic case, far from it. The assailant had been entirely unknown to the woman; she appeared to be a random victim. Thank heavens, stranger attacks remain an extremely rare and serious event. I treated the case equally seriously.

I spoke with the PC again, who could add nothing besides where he found her. I felt a deep sense of outrage. I couldn't then, and I still can't understand how a fellow human being can do that to another. My wife Marilyn always said I took these things too much to heart, and I did. I'm a man, and what that monster did reflected upon me personally. When I reported back to Balham, Gerry could see immediately from my reaction that the case was serious. He called those who were available together.

"What's the story then, Roger?"

"This is bad, Guv, about as bad as I have seen, short of murder. The woman, Angela Meadows, had been walking home at night, having attended a local book club meeting, when the attacker grabbed her off the street and dragged her into an alleyway."

"I take it this is a rape case?" asked Detective Constable Jeff Payne.

"She said no, he ripped her clothes off but didn't actually rape her. This poor woman has been beaten senseless. Honestly, it turned my stomach to see her."

"Do we assume he intended to rape her, perhaps he was disturbed."

"That's always possible, Dave, but the violence is totally disproportionate. It looks to me as if that was the prime objective."

"It's not some sort of revenge attack?" Detective Constable David Wheeler asked.

"Angela Meadows is twenty-four years old, an unmarried woman who lives with her parents. The family is well known in the local community and church; they're highly regarded. Nothing singled her out as the victim, except she walked alone at night."

"This begs the obvious question. Why did he beat her up so badly?" asked Gerry.

"This is what's really bothering me, Guv. He's molested her but didn't rape her. What he's done instead is beat the hell out of the poor woman. This is sheer wanton violence for the sake of it. In other words, this bastard enjoys it."

"Is there anything significant about where it happened?" Dave asked.

"No, other than it's very quiet and dark. He obviously chose the location."

"So, a degree of planning?"

"That's what it looks like to me."

At that point, another of our DCs, Detective Constable Bob Hughes, entered the room. We made no pretence about not getting on well together. As far as I was concerned, Bob was the worst kind of policeman. Poacher turned gamekeeper, we had nothing in common.

"What about the woman, Sarge? Does anything single her out?" asked Bob.

"What do you mean?"

"Well, is she a tom for a start? Was she asking for it?"

"It wouldn't matter if she was on the game. No woman asks for it, Bob."

"You know what I mean. Had she been down the pub, had a few drinks, teasing the blokes a bit, you know the type? Probably pissed some bloke off who gave her a bit of a slap."

How I didn't punch his lights out there and then, I do not know. Dave knew precisely how I felt about these things. We were close friends; he raised his finger to me as if to say, don't respond.

"You walk in knowing nothing about the case and then think you can offer us the benefit of your wisdom? Just be quiet, Bob."

"Thanks, Dave. Don't say another word, Bob, alright?"

"Alright, alright, get off your high horse."

"Show us on the map where this happened," said Gerry.

Jeff produced a large-scale local map, and I pinpointed the spot. The alleyway where the attack occurred had been well chosen from the perpetrator's perspective. A long way from the nearest streetlight, it would have been completely dark at night. It was a quiet neighbourhood, with no meeting places like a pub nearby, so there was little chance of the assailant being disturbed. It certainly looked as if it had been a planned attack, which added another level of concern. A door-to-door investigation began immediately. The members of the book club were all women. They could only confirm the time when the victim left the meeting. The usual suspects and informants were questioned, but not a single lead presented itself.

A week later, when the woman had been released from the hospital, I went to see her again. The family lived in a very nice semi-detached house in a respectable area with a car parked outside. That indicated a reasonably well-to-do family. Most people didn't own a car in those days. The front garden was beautifully maintained, and the front door had a recent coat of paint. I knew immediately the kind of people I would be dealing with. A delightful middle-aged lady answered the door. She had salt and pepper hair with glasses that hung around her neck on a gold chain.

"Hello, I'm Detective Sergeant Roger Pritchard, and this is my colleague, Detective Constable David Wheeler. Would you be Mrs Meadows?"

"Yes, have you come to see my daughter?"

"If she feels up to it, yes."

We found the young woman sitting in an armchair, looking, frankly, dreadful. Her bruised face now had every colour imaginable. Dave, who hadn't seen her before, stopped in his tracks.

"How are you, Miss Meadows?"

"How do I look?"

"I spoke to the hospital; they say you'll fully recover. So don't worry about how you look now; in a few weeks, it will look as if nothing has happened. I'm afraid the mental scars will take much longer to heal, but it's over now; you can start to recover. Do you mind if I call you Angela?"

"No, please do."

"I'm Roger, and this is Dave. Do you mind if we go through it all again? I know how difficult and embarrassing it is for you, but every detail can help us."

"I didn't see or hear anything. He just grabbed me around the neck from behind and lifted me off my feet. I couldn't breathe."

"It's alright, take your time."

"The next thing I knew, I was lying down on my back, and he was hitting me. He ripped at my clothes, but he didn't stop hitting me."

"I know it's difficult, Angela. Just take a moment and breathe deeply."

I cupped her hand in mine, and we said nothing until she regained composure. Dave asked Mrs Meadows if we could have some cups of tea. The pain of reliving her experience was plain to see, but she continued.

"When he finally stopped hitting me, that's when I heard him breathing. He was out of breath, almost gasping for air."

"But he didn't rape you?"

"No. He ripped my clothes off, and he hurt me, but he didn't rape me. Then he seemed to go into a frenzy again and hit me until I became unconscious."

I saw Dave clench his fist; he felt exactly like I did. We stopped for a cup of tea and to let her rest.

"Angela," Dave said, "what did he look like? Can you give us a description?"

"No, I couldn't open my eyes."

"Why not, Angela?"

"I don't know. My eyes were really stinging. I couldn't open them."

I looked at Dave in absolute horror. What she just said had enormous significance. I asked her about the stranglehold that he had imposed on her. I demonstrated various holds on Dave. The moment I demonstrated the classic martial arts rear-choke hold where the assailant's arms are interlocked, one around the neck and the other used to bend the victim's head forward, she said, yes, that was it. We continued for another ten minutes, just talking in case anything else came to light, but it didn't. I didn't realise I had taken hold of her hand again until she looked at me and then at her hand.

"Oh, I'm sorry."

"You're a good man, Roger. It's nice to know there are some good men."

"The man who did this to you is an aberration, Angela; he's a solitary monster. That's what makes it hard for us to find people like this. He's one in a million, but I make you a solemn promise. I'll find the monster who did this to you; I swear I will."

"I believe you, thank you."

We left there with grim expressions and even grimmer thoughts. When we sat in the car, Dave jumped on the comment about her eyes.

"I know what you're thinking, Rog. Is this the same bloke who tried to attack Marilyn?"

"It has to be, Dave. Marilyn said the same thing. She had some kind of irritant in her eyes. How can that be a coincidence?"

We both fell silent. The incident Marilyn suffered about a month previously came to nothing when a neighbour disturbed the assailant. No great harm was done, I couldn't establish any intent, so we had little or nothing to go on. But now, the prospect that it might have been the same man sent shivers down my spine. I spared no effort in the search for that monster, but with nothing to go on, no witnesses, and no connection to the victim, the case gradually grew colder. Eventually, with absolutely nothing to go on, Gerry instructed me to wind down the inquiry. It began to look like one more unsolved crime, but one that I couldn't let go. Little did I know that this was just the beginning.

## Chapter Three
# Goodbye To The Children

Roger

*"Hitler created a tinder-dry forest of twisted ideology, only a spark away from a firestorm. It only required good men to do nothing for evil to triumph."*

Before listening to the Prime Minister's wireless announcement, I suppose, in truth, I still held out a naïve hope that we could somehow avoid war. Like so many, I allowed hope to become expectation, and neither triumphed over reality. September 3rd, 1939 is not a date that any of my generation will ever forget. The events in Europe unfolded before our eyes, but we chose to believe what we wanted to believe. Hitler created a tinder-dry forest of twisted ideology, only a spark away from a firestorm. It only required good men to do nothing for evil to triumph.

There had always been the realisation that with modern warfare capability, the nation, and especially the capital, could suffer devastating air raids. Gas remained our constant fear after the terrible experience of the Great War. Following its use in the trenches, we all assumed it was inevitable that the London smog would become something infinitely more deadly, a prospect so awful it was almost unthinkable. Perhaps this was why we chose not to think about it, not until that dreadful day.

Marilyn and I greeted the Prime Minister's announcement with horror, which quickly turned to fear. For any parent, no primordial instinct is more powerful than protecting our children. When the lives of your children are threatened, nothing else exists. That is your only priority.

Plans had already been put in place to evacuate the children and young mothers from the cities. In fact, so great became the fear that evacuation started immediately the day Hitler invaded Poland. Every family suffered the same torment.

"I can't send them away to complete strangers, Roger. How could we?"

"We've held back long enough, Luv. Dave and Jean's kids are already in Sussex."

"Yes, and they don't even know where they are."

"They will do. It's being well organised."

"So you say, but it's our children, it's John and Mary."

"You just heard the Prime Minister; this country is now at war with Germany."

"You don't think they'll drop gas on us, do you?"

"Why else have we been issued these gas masks?"

One glance through the window revealed dozens of families rushing down the road. The moment you see other people panicking, your instinct is to assume they know something you don't. Our moment of mental conflict ended abruptly. That most primitive of instincts took over. Marilyn looked at me with fear in her eyes. We had to protect the children. The moment reality imposes itself upon you, it brings with it a host of additional fears. War had been declared; they might drop gas immediately. The bombers might be on their way as we argued about the children. We panicked like everyone else. John and Mary were six and eight, respectively, both old enough to understand what was happening. For us, they were in imminent danger; the national mood told us we had days, perhaps only hours, to protect them.

Marilyn and I were ready to leave at a moment's notice; we knew where to go and what to do. The kids were told they were taking part in a grand adventure; they had their bags packed and gas masks at the ready. The same fear drove all the parents, and the evacuation itself only confirmed the justification for that fear. We were trapped in a self-perpetuating spiral of anxiety. Families rushed to the collection centres, thinking a gas attack might be imminent. Marilyn ran about the house wide-eyed, checking what she had only just checked. I did my best to calm her down.

"Slow down, Luv, you're panicking the kids. We don't want them to be frightened. If we're calm, they'll be calm."

"I know, I can't help it. My heart's exploding."

"Pick up your gas mask, Johnny, and you, Mary. Do you remember what we practised about going on a holiday? Now put your coats on and fetch your bags. It's time to go."

"Do we have to, Dad? I don't want to go, not now."

"Johnny, we've practised this at the school. You know what to do. Both of you, hurry up."

Marilyn looked on in disbelief, but it was happening. We assembled at the local school in Balham within an hour of the announcement. What greeted us had to be seen to be believed. A writhing sea of humanity had already formed outside the school. The kids were noisy, and the parents were quiet, hanging on to their loved ones with an expression of despair laced with resignation. We had been told to dress them in warm clothes with a good top coat, preferably a mackintosh.

This became everyone's abiding memory - the children all looking the same, each carrying a bag or case and a gas mask. Most surreal of all, each child had a luggage label attached to them. It was an unworldly sight and, in its way, a terrifying sight - the next generation, with their only connection to the previous generation hanging around their necks.

We were parting with our children and entrusting them to complete strangers. We couldn't even be sure we would see them again. The collective fear and anxiety hung in the air like a freezing fog. You could see it in every adult's face. We assembled at the school like so much flotsam being pushed progressively higher up the beach by each incoming wave, each of us powerless to resist the rising tide. I half expected to see hysterical parents and scenes of mayhem. What I saw instead were parents with the courage to suppress their fear and the determination not to frighten their children. On the surface, we remained calm and orderly. The turmoil that lay beneath the surface stayed concealed until we returned to our homes.

The last kisses and hugs were exquisitely precious. The terrible thought lurked in the back of everyone's mind that this hug might be the last. When we finally saw the children on the bus taking them to the train station, I could no longer suppress the tears. We waved with happy smiling faces; shouts of, 'Have a good time, we'll see you soon,' filled the air. The moment the buses drove out of sight, so did the pretence. A deathly silence fell among us as the realisation dawned that we were parted from our children. The silence soon became replaced with distraught voices and tears as couples fell into each other's arms.

I felt an altogether unexpected sense of pride in that maelstrom of emotions. Against every natural instinct, we had collectively parted with our children in an orderly fashion that neither frightened them nor caused any disorder. The outpouring of suppressed emotion as the buses disappeared into the distance was a testament to an act of greater courage.

Operation Pied Piper proved to be an enormous undertaking involving thousands of volunteers. It included teachers, local authority workers, railway staff, and 17,000 Women's Voluntary Service members. Organised on a local level, the children were assembled at their schools, and the volunteers all wore armbands. The crowds were so large during the initial rush from London that normal rail service had to be suspended on Southern Rail. The trains were simply full of children. We had just witnessed the first example of the collective spirit that would defeat Hitler.

# Chapter Four
# September 4th, 1939

Emma

*"The sun rose as usual, but it only peeked over the rooftops*
*as if fearful of the storm clouds that lay ahead."*

That first morning after the war had been declared, I threw back the curtains and looked out the window of my little rented house in Battersea. The sun rose as usual, but it only peeked over the rooftops as if fearful of the storm clouds that lay ahead. The milkman went about his usual business as if nothing had happened. His white coat caught the early morning light as he rushed from house to house, broadcasting his presence with the reassuring sound of clinking bottles. His horse waited patiently, this day like any other for him.

I breathed a sigh of relief that everything appeared to be the same. Suddenly, normality became a precious thing, something we clung to. My beloved old Morris Eight sat by the curb side where I had parked it. Somehow, my father had generously helped me to buy it. While essential for my work, it also gave me a sense of freedom that I didn't have before, freedom that was now threatened.

The delightfully swept-back radiator of the Morris Eight made me smile. It reminded me of Dad's thick silver wavy hair, and the round headlamps, his glasses. I had little time to listen to the wireless; it was all about war preparations and evacuation. After a quick cup of tea, I rushed to the surgery, carrying what would become the ubiquitous gas mask.

Doctor Hamish McPherson, at seventy-five, probably should have retired years ago. He found himself in a rundown general practice in Clapham, South London, a few years after the Great War. He came to the area because of his friendship with my father. They met their prospective wives together, and then, many years later, as war veterans, they shared a close bond that only veterans understood. Dad knew about the practice where the resident doctor wanted to retire, and Hamish was the obvious candidate.

It spoke volumes for Hamish that he turned the rundown general practice into something cherished by the local community. His wife tragically died soon after he took over the practice, and possibly, in response to that loss, he dedicated himself to his work. He had a reputation as something of a saintly figure. He was a wonderful, caring doctor, but he also had a philosophy that patients should only have to pay what they could afford. If that amounted to nothing, then that was also fine.

History has a way of repeating itself, and so it proved to be with the evolution of the practice. It may not have been entirely by chance that I went into the medical profession. My ambition was to become a surgeon, but despite my training, the obstacles laid in the path of a female surgeon were too large and too many. While it may have been a pure coincidence of timing, I needed a medical practice just when Hamish needed assistance. I might have preferred a practice in a more affluent part of town, just as Hamish probably did all those years ago, but I didn't need to think about it when my father suggested it.

Initially, in the eyes of our patients, we must have made an unlikely pair. Hamish spoke with a Scottish lilt, which he occasionally emphasised for effect. Relentlessly upbeat and cheerful, his smile alone made his patients feel better. We were opposites in so many ways. He was a wonderful, larger-than-life character; I'm quiet and reserved. He had a lifetime of experience, while I had none at all in the eyes of our patients. Our age difference amounted to over four decades, so this only made me appear even more junior. Above all, I was a woman in an age when a female doctor remained something of a rarity.

We both knew that being accepted would be an uphill struggle for me. Well, I must have made my mark because, after over four years at the practice, things had transformed. We both shared the same philosophy: I cared about my patients passionately, and they seemed to respond to me. The days were gone when patients refused to see me, and now they asked for me. The local people knew me, everyone knew my name, and

I couldn't walk between house calls without being offered cups of tea or biscuits. I was a part of the local community; it was one of the happiest periods of my life.

When I arrived at the surgery that morning, I found the sick and needy already occupying the waiting room; Hamish never locked the door day or night. Helen manned the telephone and organised Hamish's life, but we didn't operate a booking system. People just arrived. It felt as if Helen had been with Hamish forever. Of a similar age, they behaved like husband and wife in all respects, except for where it really mattered. The three of us were so close, but I never once felt it appropriate to raise the question of the relationship that Hamish and Helen obviously shared but never acted upon.

He would customarily greet me with a smile and one of his tried-and-tested flattering comments about how my arrival had lit up his life. My arrival wouldn't light as much as a candle, but his kind-hearted flattery always made me smile. Few people deserve the accolade of being called saintly, but in my eyes, if anyone did, it was Hamish. I regarded him as a lovely and inspirational man. Hamish often said he learnt a lot from me, and perhaps some aspects of modern medicine had escaped his attention. But I knew in my heart that while he learned something new from me, it paled into insignificance compared with what he taught me.

"Morning, Emma. This is it then; it's another war."

"Yes, Dad says it won't be like last time."

"Let's hope he's right. Dressing wounds in a field hospital with no roof or walls is not ideal. Gas seems to be an enormous concern now. We need to know how to treat the various symptoms."

"You mean I need to know," I replied, attempting a smile.

"Of course, the young, agile mind picks these things up so much quicker."

"I don't know where I can find out about it, but you're right, I will. You must have dealt with a lot of trauma injuries in the first war; I've never really seen that kind of thing."

"The first hundred casualties are the worst, especially those who don't have a chance. After that, it gets easier. You just need a strong stomach and a plentiful supply of artery forceps."

"Is it really going to come to that again? Dad thinks it will."

"Your dad and I go back a long way; have you ever known him to be wrong about something like this?"

"So we have to prepare, then. How do we pay for whatever it is we need?"

"Mrs Bottomly settled her account yesterday and a bit more besides," Helen said. "That means we can pay the medicine bill and the rent and still have enough to buy some tea."

"I don't know how we've survived all these years, Hamish. We need more Mrs Bottomly's."

"You know the people around here can't afford it. They rely on us, Emma."

We were registered with the National Insurance 'panel', which paid for some workers in specific industries. Hamish relied on what amounted to donations from a handful of wealthier philanthropic individuals like Mrs Bottomly, and by going without himself. Like him, I never drew a proper GP's salary.

Initially, we were overwhelmed with helpful advice from all quarters, but it seemed to add to the confusion. The fear that Hitler might immediately deliver a massive attack, especially on the capital, filled everyone's mind. Everybody felt in immediate and ever-present danger. We carried gas masks wherever we went. That undoubtedly added to the sense of urgency among local and national organisations. This was why evacuating children and young mothers became such a priority. I watched them at the local school, wearing coats or mackintoshes and carrying gas masks. The luggage labels around each of their necks or pinned to their clothes made it all so strange and a bit frightening.

Air raid precautions were rapidly organised, and a national blackout was enforced. Distributing Anderson air-raid shelters had already begun. Mum and Dad had theirs delivered free of charge. They told me that my brother Andrew had installed it for them. I understood what that meant; my brother paid someone to install it. For doctors, the Emergency Medical Service (EMS) swung into action, and the Health Ministry took control of the hospitals.

For the medical practice, life quickly became a cocktail of high-intensity planning and preparation mixed with the mundane of Mrs Murray's chilblains and little Johnny's earache. Restrictions dominated everyone's lives. No large social gatherings and a night-time blackout changed everything. Petrol became rationed three weeks after the war had been declared, and although doctors were given a special dispensation, everything became difficult. During the day, people were at work or queuing at the shops. The only meeting places in the evenings were the local pubs that could remain open for business, albeit with reduced hours. Most people lived a dreary life in fear of the unknown. But for GPs, our patients' needs continued much as before.

One afternoon in November, the telephone rang. Helen passed it to me. Betty, one of the local midwives, sounded flustered. Could I come and help with a difficult birth in Wandsworth? I didn't know the patient, but Betty said her local doctor had been unavailable. I knew Betty well; we were friends. She didn't doubt that I would come. When I arrived, I found an unfortunate woman who had been in labour for over fifteen hours. A difficult breech birth ensued, and for a while, the woman's loss of blood worried both me and Betty. In the end, it all resolved itself, and everyone involved sat drinking a very welcome cup of tea while smiling at a beautiful new baby girl.

"You were amazing, Emma," Betty said. "I wasn't confident to do that."

"Neither was I."

"Nonsense, you've obviously done that before."

"That was my first, Bet. I've delivered a lot of breech dolls in training, but that was my first real one."

"What! I can hardly believe that. You were so calm and reassuring; Beth trusted you from the second you arrived."

"Doctor Macpherson taught me that. He told me, 'Confidence is everything - the patient's, not yours'."

"I'm sure he's right, but that doesn't take away from the fact that you have a genuine gift, Emma. Look at Beth; she's convinced you just performed a miracle."

The young mother, Beth, didn't stop thanking me, and then, as if that wasn't enough, she looked at me with tear-reddened eyes.

"What's your name, Doctor?"

"Doctor Stevenson."

"No, what's your Christian name?"

"Emma."

"Emma, I don't think my baby would have survived without you. May I name her after you?"

"I'd be honoured, Beth, that's a lovely thing…" I choked on my words. The woman's husband approached me carrying a biscuit tin containing their savings.

"What do we owe you, Doctor? Whatever it is, it isn't enough."

"What value do you place on your new daughter, Mr Mathews?"

"Everything I own."

"Precisely, and you've named her after me. You've already given me everything."

I left there that night feeling infinitely richer than when I arrived. With everything else that was going on, that beautiful baby represented a reason to be happy. I sat in the car with a smile from ear to ear; only then did I realise it was pitch black dark. The car headlamps were blanked off except for a narrow strip, amounting to almost no lights at all. It had become the new normal, but I never got used to it. Fortunately, the roads were empty as I leaned forward, desperately searching for the way ahead, not looking at the fuel gauge. Within a mile, the car spluttered and ground to a halt in the middle of the road. Someone had syphoned out the petrol. Having just lived through the very best of human nature, I now experienced the worst as I sat with my head in my hands.

# Chapter Five
# Conscription

Roger

*"The warmth of long summer days gradually surrendered to the cold darkness of winter, just as we surrendered to the cold dark prospect of war."*

The summer of 1939 died a little with every autumn leaf that fell to the ground. The warmth of long summer days gradually surrendered to the cold darkness of winter, just as we surrendered to the cold, dark prospect of war. It was a miserable time; the prospect of winter became synonymous with the national mood. None of us knew what lay ahead; some feared the worst, while others chose not to believe it. Few things confirmed the reality of war with greater clarity than when the nation called upon its young men to fight for our freedom.

With limited conscription already progressing, this became a daily topic of conversation at the police station. You didn't have to be a detective to work out what the likely outcome would be. The army reservists were the first to be called up, and the young men aged 20-22. General conscription quickly followed to include all non-reserved occupations between the ages of 18 and 41. Reduction in police numbers over the course of the war would be quite dramatic. A total force of 60,000 in 1939 would be reduced to 43,000 by 1944, and many of those would be older reserve police officers.

I wanted to enlist; I saw it as my duty. At 34 years old, I remained well within the age limit, and the police force was not classed as a reserve occupation. Marilyn hoped I could somehow avoid it, but I felt uncomfortable about that. Dave and I discussed it on several occasions, and we both felt the same. I told the guv'nor as soon as my mind was made up. I knocked on Detective Chief Inspector Gerry Higgins' office door, intending to inform him of my decision; I didn't expect any discussion.

"I'll be adding my name to the list, Guv; they'll call me up, anyway. I thought you should know as soon as possible."

"No, you're not, Pritchard. You're too old, and you're as blind as a bat."

"There's nothing wrong with my eyes, Guv. I can see well enough without the glasses, and I'm only thirty-four."

"Thirty-four? You look more like fifty-four. What the hell happened to you?"

"It must have been my misspent youth, Guv."

"It looks like it wasn't misspent. It looks as if you enjoyed it."

Gerry and I got on well together; we shared that kind of humour and enjoyed a bit of banter. But Gerry had a serious point to make.

"Look, Roger, I'm going to lose all my young men like Bob, and all we can recruit are the old-timers. As painful as it is for me to say it, I need you. We need old, half-blind coppers, and the recruitment people would turn you down at first glance."

"Well, that's the thing, Gerry, they don't call it conscription for nothing. I'll have to go, anyway."

"Maybe not; I can send a request up the chain. I can tell them I need to retain at least a core strength, and I've chosen you because you're medically unfit for service. The army doesn't want an old blind hack like you; besides, you smoke so much you'd be a bloody fire hazard."

"You don't understand, Gerry, I want to. It's every man's duty to serve his country."

"It's you that doesn't understand, Roger. The country also needs a police force, perhaps now more than ever. Besides, I've already made the request. I want you and Dave to stay and help old ladies to cross the road. What's it like to be wanted, Roger?"

"I don't know; it's an unfamiliar experience."

"Well, get used to it. I've already said I need you, and I never want to admit that to another breathing soul."

I laughed. Despite genuinely wanting to enlist, a part of me could also see the need for continued policing. The Force needed experienced detectives like me and Dave. Despite what Gerry said, I assumed the army would take me without question; my eyesight wasn't really an issue.

I didn't wear glasses at all when I first joined the Force, and I only wore them for driving. Several weeks later, in November, I had no trouble at all seeing Gerry marching towards me with a triumphant smile on his face.

"You're going to remain a copper, Roger," he said, waving a form in the air. "I think the doc's report clinched it; the Enrolment Board reckoned you should be confined to a desk. You're too bloody frail to set foot outside, and you've got a promotion, Detective Inspector Pritchard."

"Bloody hell. How did you manage that?"

"Obviously, I must be desperate, and I know how much you need Dave to look after you."

Goodness knows how Gerry pulled it off - he left me with mixed emotions. For all Gerry's good humour, he actually needed me. I had far more experience than my previous rank suggested, and the same applied to Dave, who had also been promoted - to Detective Sergeant. We managed to hang on to Jeff, who was another experienced detective. Bob Hughes went off to join the army, and that suited me just fine. Dave and I made a great team, we were the very best of friends. As much as we both wanted to enlist, I also didn't want to leave the job I cared about. Our experience would be even more in demand as the police force declined in number.

The news came at the start of what was otherwise a long, arduous day. The only highlight apart from Gerry's announcement had been the arrest of a petty burglar who sat in the pub in a drunken stupor bragging about a toolbox he'd stolen. Dave and I had to hold the man up on his feet while the duty sergeant booked the arrest. Needless to say, we became the subject of much ridicule.

"Did you chase him far, Roger?"

"You should have used the cuffs, Dave, a dangerous man like that."

Had the position been reversed, I would have been the first to join in the banter, so we both left the station with a resigned smile and carried on with our day. With little to show for our efforts, it felt like the end of an extremely long day. I dropped Dave off and set off for the car pound to pick up my own car. Driving during the blackout made it even more tiring; I felt bone weary. With just a small patch of road dimly illuminated in front of me, I inched my way along, straining to see. In the distance, I vaguely saw what looked like a vehicle stopped on the road. Approaching cautiously, I saw a person step out and stand at the side of the car.

I pulled in behind, leaving the engine running with the pool of yellow light dimly illuminating what lay ahead. I always carried a truncheon with me, just in case. Truncheon in hand, I looked at what appeared to be a villain, either stealing the car or perhaps the petrol. With a torch in one hand and the truncheon in the other, I stepped out of the police car. The stationary vehicle appeared to be empty, and then my torch revealed a woman standing wide-eyed and looking rather distressed. Hesitating for a second, I dropped the truncheon back into the car. As I approached, I saw what seemed to be a woman in her early thirties. She wore a skirt and jumper with a loose jacket, and dark brown wavy hair, in fact, perfectly ordinary. I relaxed; she didn't look remotely like your average villain.

"It looks like you have a problem, madam."

"Yes, I don't have any petrol."

"It's late to be out on your own, madam. May I ask what's going on?"

"I'm a doctor. I'm just trying to get home after seeing a patient, and I think some bastard has syphoned out my petrol. Oh, I'm sorry, I didn't mean to swear."

"Not at all, Doctor, I would say something far worse, I promise you. When did the doctor become a damsel-in-distress?"

"Ten minutes ago."

"Well, in that case, why don't I drive you home?"

"Would you? I'd be so grateful."

"Detective Inspector Pritchard - it's fortunate I was driving past."

"Doctor Stevenson."

"It's pure chance I came this way; I was taking the car back to the pound; I'm off duty."

"Well, it's very fortunate for me you did. It's unnerving in the blackout."

"There's a lot of petrol syphoning going on now, what with the rationing and all."

"I didn't realise."

"Are you out a lot at night?"

"I try not to be, but patients need a doctor at night as well, you know."

"Take my advice, Doctor Stevenson; don't spend any longer than necessary out of your car."

"Why, what's the problem?"

"I don't want to alarm you, but two women walking alone at night have been assaulted in this neighbourhood recently."

"I've not heard anything about that."

"No, it's not public knowledge, but it was in this area. I just think you should be aware of it."

"Were the women badly assaulted?"

"Let's just say it could have been worse."

"Well, thank you for warning me. Next on the left, just here."

I delivered her safely to the house. She thanked me and hastily got out of the car; she didn't look back until she stood at her door. Seeing my damsel was no longer in distress, I waved and drove off, not giving it another thought. It had been just another day in what had become the new normal. The new normal also included my welcome home from Marilyn.

"It's in the oven keeping warm. I'll leave you to it then. I'm going to bed."

I didn't react; I thought it best to accept the situation. "Okay, Luv, I'll see you in the morning."

# Chapter Six
# November 1939

Emma

*"Indomitable men who would not be defeated during the Great War and who would certainly not be defeated now."*

When I got home that night after the petrol syphoning incident, I felt emotionally drained. I remained unsure what to make of my rescuer; he frightened me with his talk of women being assaulted. I couldn't see him properly in the dark but guessed he might be in his thirties, about five feet ten. Beneath his hat and coat, he wore a suit, a tie, and a waistcoat, but in the reflected light of his torch, he looked dishevelled and reeked of cigarettes. With his tie undone and his collar crumpled, and with more than a day's stubble on his chin, he looked as if he'd slept in his clothes. He wore glasses; I didn't think policemen wore glasses.

Above all, what informed my opinion of him was the way he said 'damsel-in-distress' in his London accent. I initially thought he might be one of those incessantly cheerful people determined to lift my spirits. He wasn't that type of person at all. He was a kind, thoughtful policeman, not the cheeky chappy I expected. The next morning I had to buy a can of petrol, and then the bus conductor complained about it, saying I couldn't take petrol on the bus. Needless to say, my day didn't start well while the needs of our patients mounted.

With nearly all the children evacuated, the only thing we had less to contend with in the surgery was head lice. The old and frail worried me the most. How would they cope if the worst happened? One of my patients, Daisy, typified my concerns for the elderly, a delightful but frail old lady who I visited as often as I could. With Christmas almost upon us, I found her coughing and wheezing.

"Morning, Daisy, it's Doctor Stevenson. All right if I come in, Luv?"

She didn't answer, so I went straight in and found her sitting in her favourite armchair, looking very poorly.

"Hello, Doctor; it's so kind of you to come and see me. I'll make you a nice cup of tea."

Her previous cup sat beside her, as did many other things, and her fire had long since gone out. Daisy's home had changed little from her Victorian childhood. Lace and furniture filled the room in every available space. Usually immensely houseproud, I could see she hadn't strayed far from her armchair for some time.

"I'll do it, Daisy; you keep your feet up."

"Keep what up?"

"Your feet, you keep your feet up."

"No, it's not my feet, dear; it's my breathing."

"I know, Luv; you just relax."

I picked up a bottle of milk from the larder, and it smelt dreadful. "Is this your only milk, Daisy?"

"Yes, that's it."

"It's gone off. Has it been sitting in the larder for long?"

"There's plenty left - that'll last me another two days."

"No, Daisy, it's gone off."

"Where did it go, then? I didn't use it."

Daisy was the sweetest lady, but you needed to be patient with her. I gave up on the tea and listened to her chest. The sound reverberating through the stethoscope was not what I wanted to hear. She had a temperature of 100.6 Fahrenheit. Daisy had deteriorated rapidly from the day before.

"You're not very well, Daisy, are you?"

"I know, it's my age, you know."

"It's more than that, I'm afraid," I had to raise my voice to be sure she heard. "You've got a very nasty chest infection. This could easily turn into pneumonia. I want you to go to the hospital, Daisy."

"No, dear, I don't go to hospital, never have."

"You must, Daisy, I want you to."

"You're a lovely doctor; you're so kind to me, but if it's my time, then I want to be here at home."

"If you stay here, it might be your time, but the hospital can make you well again."

"No, dear; my Herbert didn't come back when he went there. No, I'm staying here."

I couldn't persuade her, but I was determined not to lose her. "I'm going to give you a drug, Daisy; it's called Prontosil; it'll help. What about your neighbour, Mrs Hastings? Will she sit with you while I get a few things from the corner shop? I'm staying with you for a while."

"No, I don't want her."

She started talking about her late husband, Herbert, but she was no longer coherent. Sulphonamide drugs were the only treatment available for pneumonia in the 30's. All I could do was keep her hydrated and comfortable while the drug took effect. With help from the neighbour, I stocked up Daisey's larder from the local shop and made up the fire. Flames danced above the glowing coals, reaching up in search of the chimney.

The fire's flickering light struggled through the maze of Daisy's Victorian furniture. It created a comfort of sorts for the long evening ahead. The crackle of the burning coal provided a distraction from Daisy's hesitant breathing while the shadows played in every recess. I sank into an old Victorian armchair and prepared for a long evening sitting with her. Early the next morning, Hamish woke me up.

"Sleeping on the job again."

"Oh, Hamish, I must have dozed off."

"Mrs Hastings got a message to me; it looks as if you might have saved the day."

"What do you mean?"

"I've looked at your notes and taken Daisy's temperature - it's dropping."

"Oh, thank God. I thought I'd lost her."

Daisy recovered, much to her own surprise. Typical of some of our elderly patients, we worried about them all. I had several veterans from the last war who, like my father, had disabilities. Some had amputated limbs or burns, and some, like Dad, still suffered the effects of gas. Men like 'Nobby' Clarke and the irrepressible Scotty Henderson. Indomitable men who would not be defeated during the Great War and who would certainly not be defeated now. Any one of them could have been my father; I treated them all as if they were.

In normal times, the other vulnerable group were the children, but following the evacuation, we had few left. We had three disabled children whose parents refused to evacuate them. They were each special children in their own way, but little Alma stole my heart with her blue eyes and golden hair. A polio victim, Alma called me Doctor Emma, and her smile would melt an alpine glacier.

With her paralysis confined to her legs, she was less disabled than many of them and making really good progress. I called in on her as often as I could to monitor her progress, but I realised it was as much for my benefit as Alma's. I had never seen such strength of character in one so young, never downhearted, never dispirited. Alma's love of life existed like a presence around her. I soon came to realise if I spent just a few minutes in that presence, it would stay with me for the rest of the day.

# Chapter Seven
# Christmas 1939

Emma

*"There are lessons in life that inform us, and just occasionally, there are lessons that have the power to change us."*

As the end of the year approached, Christmas reminded us that even in war, life goes on. The nation would celebrate the event regardless; anything less would have been a betrayal. We could look back on events and find reasons to be thankful. We hadn't been bombed or gassed. Hope lived in a remote corner of everyone's heart, but there was no prospect of a happy New Year.

My family got together every Christmas; there had never been a Christmas when that didn't happen. Mum and Dad made it clear that 1939 would be no different. My brother's two children hadn't been evacuated. Andrew would, of course, make his own arrangements. I longed to see them; I enjoyed my role as Aunty Emma. The children were adorable, but I hardly ever saw them. My brother and I were not estranged; we just didn't get on well.

Dad was one of the so-called lucky ones. With his lungs irreparably damaged, he came back from the first war a completely different man - his life would never be the same. He rarely, if ever, spoke about it as I grew up, but we saw it in his eyes. A part of him didn't come back at all. Before the war, he enjoyed a glittering career in academia, culminating in what proved to be his true vocation as the principal of a prestigious boarding school in Leatherhead, Surrey. A man for whom the pursuit and propagation of knowledge had been his life.

Before the war, we lived in a fine Georgian house equipped with a cook and housemaid. My parents enjoyed an enviable position in society. Although I was only a child, I still remember the sunlight streaming in through the tall windows and my father's constant good humour that denied the casting of shadows. My memories of that time are bright and happy, a childhood where my father made every day feel like an exciting exploration. The house saw a constant stream of the great and good from the world of education and academia. As a child, I had no doubt about where the centre of the universe lay and in whose hands it resided.

Following his injury, Dad found himself no longer able to work and became reduced to a war disability pension. Without independent means, we were forced to move to a much smaller terraced house in Balham, South London. My mother made light of it, but with me clinging to her petticoats, I could only imagine how hard my mother's life must have become. Their fall from grace must have been a difficult transformation. Eight years older than me, Andrew felt our economic decline far more than I did. Andrew lived there, but at no time did he feel he belonged there. Too old to accept it, but too young to understand it, he didn't appreciate how our parents struggled. We grew up in a working-class area as the children of an impoverished but middle-class family. I walked with a foot on either side of the social divide, but I never once lost my balance.

Our father regarded education as the central pillar of life. He may have lost his income, but his children's education remained sacrosanct. We all wondered where Andrew's insatiable ambition came from. He went to Oxford University, where he soared above the crowd like an eagle in the rarefied air of the academic elite. He made it all seem so easy while I struggled for my medical degree. I had to work hard, sacrificing everything for the career I so badly wanted. I got my degree by the skin of my teeth, while Andrew never once needed to make an effort. Following eight years behind him, I constantly had to look up at the pedestal he sat on. The rarefied air he breathed didn't support a mere mortal like me.

The Prime Minister's announcement on September 3rd did not surprise Andrew in the slightest. As a banker, he was one of the few who successfully negotiated the financial crash of the 1930s. Perhaps less like an eagle and more like a vulture, fallen markets provided easy pickings. The term 'wealth management' wasn't a recognised banking service then; I often wonder if Andrew invented it. As with all things in life, Andrew saw the war as an opportunity.

Being just above the upper age limit, he didn't qualify for conscription, but of course, he didn't see serving his country as the kind of opportunity he had in mind. Having advised his clients to move their money out of prime London real estate, he realised that his house in Kensington fell squarely into that category. An investment in a six-bedroom detached house in the leafy environment of Maidenhead would provide the perfect retreat.

With adjacent domestic staff accommodation and a train service to London, what could be more perfect? An excellent local school would provide for the two children, and while the glamorous Patricia might miss Harrods, Andrew remained sure she would love life there. I only heard about Andrew's triumphant advance through life from my parents. The fact is, I hadn't seen my brother since the previous Christmas. The grandchildren stayed with Mum and Dad on odd occasions, so at least they knew who their Aunt Emma was.

That Christmas felt significant to us all. The prospect hung in the air that this might be the last time, a negative thought that must not mention its name. Mum and Dad looked forward to it each year; for them, it was all about the grandchildren. I looked forward to it because it pleased them. Andrew endured it. To his relief, the house did not have sufficient bedrooms, so he didn't need to make up an excuse to leave in the afternoon. I arrived to find them already there; Andrew probably reasoned that the earlier they arrived, the quicker they could leave.

"Hello, Andrew. Happy Christmas."

"Hello, Em, it's been a few months, hasn't it?"

"Yes, twelve, actually."

The grandchildren, William and Audrey, were only three and four years old, but they were untainted innocents in my eyes and utterly adorable. I loved my role as Aunty Emma; I immersed myself in it. They were immediately scooped up in my arms.

"Happy Christmas, Emma."

"Oh, I'm sorry, Patricia, the little ones have taken me over. Yes, Happy Christmas."

Patricia sat on another pedestal so high that I had to crane my neck to look up at her. Impossibly beautiful and dressed by Madeleine Vionnet, Patricia consumed all the oxygen in any room she graced simply with her presence. I disparagingly likened her to the top prize at the fairground coconut shy. I convinced myself any woman would feel drab next to

Patricia, but that didn't make me feel any less drab. Andrew sat in deep conversation with Dad while Mum smothered her grandchildren. This embarrassingly left me alone in the front room with the lovely Patricia. Other than talking about the children, I never knew what to say; what did I know about fashion, or what shows to see, or where to dine?

"I hear you're moving to Maidenhead, Patricia."

"That's right, Andrew feels it will be safer for the children."

"Yes, of course, for the children. I suppose it's a delightful house, nothing too small, I hope."

"Oh, well, you know Andrew. It's actually rather impressive. You must come."

"Yes, that would be lovely."

"How is your doctor's practice, Emma? It's in Clapham, isn't it?"

"That's right, nearly five years now."

"I imagine you would prefer to move on."

"Well, the way things are going, I might have to."

"Oh, well done. Will that be a relief for you?"

"I think if that happens, it will be one of the saddest days of my life."

"But surely you don't enjoy working in Clapham, Emma."

"I love it. My work colleagues are wonderful, and my patients are … well, they're all special people to me. I can't imagine not being there for them."

"I'm sorry, Emma, I've just made a really crass comment. I've jumped to all the wrong assumptions, haven't I?"

"Yes, you probably have, but maybe we all do that occasionally."

"I'm sorry we're not close, Emma; as sisters-in-law, I sometimes feel we should be, but we aren't, are we?"

"Well, we have little in common, do we?"

"We have this family."

"We do, but I mean us. Take that dress, for example. I bet it cost you more than I earn in a year?"

"What if it does?" she said, slightly wide-eyed. "It's just a dress; you don't have to hold it against me."

I hadn't once had a real woman-to-woman conversation with my sister-in-law; I had to stop and think for a moment. We only ever discussed the children or the weather. It's true that we had little in common, but maybe I'd been guilty of allowing myself to be intimidated by her. Looking at Patricia was a bit like trying to look at the sun. You needed special glasses. I tried to remember that beauty is only skin deep.

"You're right. I shouldn't hold that against you."

"You must have patients who are disadvantaged compared to you. I bet some are not well educated, certainly not compared to you. And yet you say you care deeply for them, and it sounds as though they care for you. Why must you despise me if they don't despise you for your superior education and position?"

"I don't act or feel superior, Patricia."

"But you imagine I do. I'm not as intelligent as anyone in this family. I don't have a university degree. I couldn't do what you do. Everything I have has been an accident of birth, and I've married a very wealthy man. I know how people see me; that's just an image I've cultivated. I had to learn how to be the woman that you see. Of all people, surely my sister-in-law can see through that?"

Wow, I didn't expect that; she dropped the wind out of my sails in one breath. I suddenly realised you can look at the sun if you're very careful.

"I thought you looked down on me as a dowdy frump." The moment I said it, I realised the meaning of those words, but it was too late to take them back. "Don't bother to answer that. I am a dowdy frump, but it would be reassuring if you said you didn't look down on me."

"Oh, Emma. You might be clever, but you couldn't be more wrong. You don't have the faintest idea what it's been like for an outsider to come into this family. Look at these walls. You live in a world of diplomas, certificates, and photographs of esteemed people I haven't even heard of. Andrew talks to your father about something called the Copenhagen Interpretation. Even Schrodinger's cat has some special significance to them. If it's not that, they discuss Keats and Shakespeare or the impressionist art movement. You've got no idea how it feels to be intimidated. I'm scared stiff of your father, and I feel stupid when I talk to you."

There are lessons in life that inform us, and just occasionally, there are lessons that have the power to change us. Patricia gave me such a lesson. I lived with those diplomas and certificates all my life. My bedtime story was often Keats or Shakespeare. It didn't occur to me that anyone would be intimidated by my father, especially someone like Patricia. Our conversation continued until the others returned to the room, whereupon we reverted to talking about the children and their fabulous new house in Maidenhead.

We discussed more than I thought imaginable, and our conversation continued without words when we were interrupted. You can say so much with body language, a look, or a touch on the arm. We had reached an understanding, a mutual respect I didn't anticipate. We continued to live in different worlds; she remained the most beautiful and best-dressed woman I have ever seen, while I remained a dowdy frump, but I began to like her.

## Chapter Eight
# April 1940

Roger

*"Chairs stood where they were last used, retaining memories of another time. Cobwebs hung like buttresses from an old desk, seeming to secure it to the floor."*

L ife didn't return to normal in 1940; how could it? Instead, food rationing was introduced on January 8th. Preparations for war were continuing everywhere. Behind the scenes, government departments and organisations worked tirelessly; bureaucracy was reduced overnight. The speed of change was very impressive; new instructions came down almost daily from the Commissioner.

They told us we had to work closely with all the other services: civil defence workers, ARP wardens, the Home Guard, the fire department, and the ambulance service. Some of it I expected, such as enforcing the blackout and preventing looting, but there were many things I didn't expect. We were instructed to apprehend deserting soldiers and escaped prisoners of war. Together with the ARP wardens, we had to report unexploded bombs and enforce rationing.

The introduction of rationing instantly produced a black market and an impossible additional workload for the police. One of the most serious black market activities went far beyond that; it amounted to straightforward, serious organised crime. Petrol had to be rationed for obvious reasons. The war effort would depend on it. Petrol syphoning began almost as soon as war was declared. Some were unlikely villains who simply wanted a gallon of petrol for their own vehicle. For others, it developed into serious crime. When the London mobsters became involved, it developed into something serious.

We considered petrol so essential for the war effort that the police or the army guarded refineries and distribution depots. The theft of a fuel tanker in transit would have attracted so much attention from the authorities that the well-known gangs didn't become involved. Instead of drawing attention to large-scale activity, they stole petrol in plain sight. They concentrated on syphoning petrol from vehicles at night rather than robbing tankers or refineries. It soon became apparent why.

The mobsters were not about to get their hands dirty; they didn't want to draw attention to themselves. They used small-time villains to walk the streets at night with empty cans. Idiots prepared to risk imprisonment for the sake of a gallon of petrol. Then, they had to store their ill-gotten gains until an intermediary collected them. The organisation behind it collected hundreds of gallons while remaining completely removed from the crime on the street.

They got away with it because we didn't even know it was happening until we stumbled upon a lucky break. The small-time crooks with the syphons represented the lowlife of South London. They mostly spent their meagre reward on beer or fags, usually within half an hour of receiving it. We knew many of them, but they were too frightened to tell us anything. The assumption was that they stole a few cans and sold them to unsuspecting people.

They were not the brightest bunch; one of them didn't even realise that the fumes from empty cans were still very volatile. The idiot stored his cans in a lockup. A nice confined space where the fumes could vaporise into an explosive gas. When the dimwit lit a cigarette, he blew himself up.

The Fire Brigade realised what had caused the explosion, so we were called in. The man hadn't been killed, although he probably wished he had been. When I visited him in the hospital, the doctor told me his burns were so extensive they didn't expect him to survive very long. I felt sorry for the poor devil; however stupid, nobody deserves to go in that way. With nothing left to lose, he told me everything. A large van would collect his petrol at a set time, the collection being organised by an intermediary. In the back of the van was a concealed holding tank. Beyond that, he knew nothing; they paid him cash and made it clear he should keep his mouth shut. I wished the poor sod good luck, but he needed a lot more than luck.

"This isn't a petty crime, is it, Guv?"

"No, this is precisely what the Commissioner told us to look for, Roger. No point picking up the lags who're stealing the stuff, not if we want to find where it's going."

"I agree. We need to find one of these collection vans and watch where it goes. Let's put the word out on the street to look for suspicious behaviour, people storing drums or cans, and above all, the smell of petrol."

Gerry agreed; it took a while, but a bobby on the beat eventually spotted precisely what we were looking for. A neighbour complained to him about the smell of petrol, so he kept his head down, just watching from a distance. Sure enough, a man living in a respectable-looking house in Tooting Beck unloaded a can from the back of his car and did that almost every night. He went down some steps into a basement each time and returned without the can.

Proper surveillance is difficult and requires a lot of men. Gerry had to get permission from above. Surveillance is usually a real bore, and a policeman's greatest challenge can be staying awake. I sat in the car that day with Dave, expecting another quiet afternoon.

"How's Jean getting on with the food rationing, Dave, with your kids being away?"

"Not too good if I'm honest, Rog, and the house seems so empty. We seem to be at each other's throats most of the time. Why do you ask?"

"Well, I wondered if it was just us; Marilyn's changed."

"That attack she suffered last year really shook her up, didn't it? Jean says she doesn't enjoy going out at night, and now what with the kids being away and everything. It's a bad time, isn't it?"

"It is, but Marilyn won't talk about it. I know it plays on her mind. As you say, she won't go out at night, not for anything. I suppose rationing's the last straw."

"Do you still think those two attacks are linked?"

"I'm certain of it, Dave. Thank God he was disturbed with Marilyn. Obviously, I don't tell her, but if that neighbour hadn't come out when she did, well, I hate to even think about it."

"Let's hope you're wrong. The last thing we need right now is a madman on our doorstep."

"Yes, I agree, but ... hang on, what's that?"

"That, if I'm not mistaken, is Christmas coming early."

In the middle of the afternoon, a large van stopped right outside the

building. Two men dressed in brown working overalls entered the basement carrying wooden crates. They left carrying the same wooden crates,
but now they were heavy. It all looked completely innocent as if they were
removal men. A passerby didn't raise an eyebrow. They even returned what
must have been the empty petrol cans back into the basement. Removal
men came and went just as you would expect. It provided the perfect
cover.

"Start the car, Dave, and for Christ's sake, don't lose them."

I threw my fag out of the window, and we followed the van at a safe
distance; it led us to a builder's yard in Camberwell. Dave stopped the
car, and we sat watching. A packet of fags later, and we had seen enough.
Another two vans pulled into the yard, and the double doors were closed
behind them. When they left, the vans were obviously lighter. We'd found
the goose that delivered the golden eggs. Even more telling, we saw no
activity to do with a building business.

"Bloody hell, Dave, this is big, isn't it?"

"This might be even bigger than we thought. We've just seen three
deliveries arrive in the time it's taken you to smoke a packet of fags. Can
you imagine how big this might be?"

"We need more surveillance. We need to know where it goes from
here. It's like a spider's web. All those small-time villains supply a bigger
villain, who then supplies an even bigger one. What we haven't seen is the
end user, where this stuff ends up."

"What do we do now, Rog?"

"The quantity is too large. This must somehow go back into the supply
chain. I can't believe one of the big suppliers isn't involved. Let's go back
and see what the guv'nor says."

Gerry's eyes lit up. It wasn't every day we had a crime of this magnitude
handed to us on a plate. "I've got to hand it to you, Roger, for a half-blind
copper, this is a bit of a triumph. You definitely saw two more deliveries;
it wasn't double vision?"

"If we don't cock this up, we've got these bastards by the short and
curlies. If you can get authorisation for another surveillance, I reckon we'll
have the end user within the week."

"The Commissioner is all over this; he's got pressure from above. They
want this mob put away. You can take it as read. You'll have your surveillance. Start immediately."

It's the only surveillance I've been on that actually felt exciting. We knew the mother goose would bring us another golden egg; we only had to wait. Lady luck shone brightly on us that day, the very first day of surveillance and a fuel tanker arrived. I half expected a nondescript tanker, or perhaps, if we were lucky, one bearing the name of a distributor. What arrived made my jaw drop. A green RAF fuel tanker pulled into the yard. When it left, we followed it all the way to RAF Hendon.

When I reported back to the guv'nor, he looked as amazed as I was. We assumed that His Majesty's armed forces were not in the business of defrauding the state. The driver of the tanker, well, he was obviously involved, but the RAF must be unwittingly treating it as a regular de-livery. That meant that the normal paperwork supplied by a recognised supplier must accompany the petrol. The paper chain would quickly lead to whoever had been involved. I expected Gerry to give me the go-ahead to follow it up.

"You're off the case, Roger, at least that part of it. I'm told New Scot-land Yard has a specialist team on it. We're left with the builder's yard and the people who supply them."

"You mean we aren't considered smart enough to conduct a serious investigation, but we can clean up the rubbish?"

"This is why I need you, Roger; your powers of perception are second to none. You know where the rubbish is. Get yourself a broom and a shovel and clean it up."

"I'll need a big shovel, Guv. This is a serious mob."

We had to wait until we were given the word from on high, but when that word came, I sent in a dozen coppers. Dave and I sat in a plain car waiting for our opportunity while two vanloads of bobbies sat at either end of the road. We were apprehensive. Faced with some serious prison time, the villains on the other side of the fence would put up a fierce resistance. We had seen five of them during our surveillance, but there could easily be more. None of the bobbies were armed other than with truncheons, but Gerry had the Station Sergeant issue Dave and me with a Webley revolver. We had both had a bit of weapons training, but we had no actual experience with firearms.

"You don't think we'll have to use these things, do you, Rog?"

"I certainly hope not. If this mob's tooled up, I'll be keeping my head down. I'm getting too old for this caper."

We were waiting for one of the delivery vans to arrive so the gates would be opened. When one appeared, we all knew what to do. We charged in behind the van, pretending we were the Light Brigade at Balaclava. They had no idea we were coming, so it took them a moment to respond, but when they did, they were more than prepared to take us on. A couple of our uniformed coppers were big blokes - I saw two of the mob knocked to the ground and cuffed in no time. Dave seemed in control of another. I saw one bloke run into the building, and when no one else noticed, I gave chase. He gave me the slip for a moment, and as I searched the building, I could hear Dave coming after me.

I hadn't realised the main building was disused. It had been a builder's yard and office, but now it contained only shadows of the past. Items of office furniture lay around as if the previous occupants had just walked away. Chairs stood where they were last used, retaining memories of another time. Cobwebs hung like buttresses from an old desk, seeming to secure it to the floor. I opened another door, and it announced my presence with a loud creaking noise. I found myself standing in a dark room. The only window had what remained of a curtain hanging across it. I heard someone behind me, but by the time I turned, it was already too late; I didn't see it coming. The lights abruptly went out.

# Chapter Nine
# St Thomas's Hospital 1940

Emma

*"Adversity brings out the very best in people. The strength of
one becomes the strength of the many, and when the many are
the nation, it becomes an unbreakable spirit."*

The new year brought mixed blessings for Hamish and me. Our
patient list had significantly reduced; this did at least give us more
time, which I gave back to my patients. All the young men had
been enlisted, and most of the children and young mothers had been evacuated. Many folks with relatives in the country joined them. That presented a particular problem for GP practices. Many general practitioners were
forced to reconsider their future without the patient numbers to subsidise
the practice. We already operated on a very thin shoestring. With the rent
on the surgery several months overdue and the tea money exhausted, we
both tried to forestall the inevitable. As March rapidly approached April,
it became increasingly impossible for us to continue.

"There really is no option, Hamish. Do you feel you can carry on by
yourself?"

"I know what you're suggesting, and it's unthinkable, Emma."

"We have to think the unthinkable."

"It's time I retire anyway; I'll leave it to you, Emma."

"I'm not sure that will be the best use of our experience, Hamish. A lot
of GPs are joining the armed forces or the hospitals. If this all goes as Dad
keeps telling me it will, then my duty will be on the front line, either in
the forces or in one of the hospitals."

"I know; Albert and I have discussed it."

"You and Dad talked about me behind my back."

"We did. Your father's subsidising you, so he has a say in this because he's also running out of money. I'm content to stand down, but I believe the gift you have with people will be best served in a hospital."

"That's what Dad told me. I really don't want to go, Hamish. Is there any way we can avoid it?"

"I think we both know there's no option."

We discussed it endlessly, trying to find an alternative, but circumstances dictated the decision; I just had to accept it. The next day, I bowed to the inevitable and reluctantly agreed that I should apply for a hospital job. Hamish was my mentor; I treated him like a second father, and my patients were my extended family. I think it would have been an impossible decision in ordinary times, but things were very different during the war. A sense of urgency influenced everything we did, and the feeling of doing our bit for the nation became all-pervasive. When I enquired about a position at St Thomas's Hospital, they almost tore my arm off.

Those five years with Hamish informed the rest of my career. It proved to be an all-consuming experience where everything I gave came back to reward me tenfold. That realisation was never more painfully demonstrated than on my last day, which proved to be far harder than I could have possibly imagined.

Hamish planned a brief farewell in the surgery, just Helen, Mrs Bottomley, and one or two people we worked with, such as Betty. He also said he invited some of my old veterans, like Nobby Clarke and Scotty Henderson. I don't know if Hamish asked them or if they invited themselves. We had sandwiches and cakes, and Helen had tea brewing for anyone who wanted it. Hamish produced a bottle of vintage champagne with an illegible label.

Then it happened: patients began arriving uninvited. Somehow, word had got around, and people wanted to drop off a card or a little present and most wanted to stay. I didn't expect any of it; I didn't know what to say. One after another, they arrived until the surgery was full. With much fanfare and ceremony, Hamish opened his bottle of champagne. Prising the cork out away from himself, we all expected it to produce a satisfying pop, if not a loud bang. Instead, it dropped quietly to the floor amid screams of laughter. The vintage champagne was indeed vintage, an ancient vintage. As a true Scotsman, he had a reserve option, a bottle of single malt whisky.

I hardly ever drank, let alone whisky, but found myself in conversation with a large glass of Balvenie. Two of my veterans made a little speech thanking me for caring for them; they were far too effusive. I didn't recognise the subject of their praise. All the while, the table set aside for my cards and presents became covered. I was already too overwhelmed to speak when Daisy came in, helped by her neighbour, Mrs Hastings. She struggled to look up at me with her stooped back, but nothing was about to suppress her indomitable spirit. She put her arms around me, and all she said was, 'God bless you.'

It was such an emotional moment. Daisy meant so much to me. Hamish could see I was lost for words, so he stepped forward, seizing the moment to make a farewell speech. As he tapped on his glass to gain attention, there was another arrival. It was Mr and Mrs Wilson, Alma's parents, pushing Alma in her wheelchair. She had a box in her lap and a smile that instantly lit up the room. Hamish abruptly stopped his opening sentence and welcomed them in.

"I made this for you, Doctor Emma," little Alma said.

Hamish saw what it was and took hold of one end of a line of bunting. It was a line of paper angels with Hamish on one end and Alma on the other. On each angel, in barely legible writing, she had written, 'Doctor Emma, we love you'. Everyone said how wonderful it was except for me; I felt totally unable to speak. Hamish regained everyone's attention.

"Ladies and gentlemen. I had a little speech prepared to thank Doctor Stevenson on everyone's behalf for what she's done for this community, but Alma has upstaged me. 'We love you, Doctor Emma.' There's nothing I can add to that, is there? A toast to Doctor Emma."

I was more than a bit tipsy and completely overwhelmed, and I didn't know what to do or say. In fact, I wasn't sure if I could say anything. Without thinking, I stooped down to Alma, sitting in her wheelchair and whispered to her. She smiled and nodded approval.

"Doctor Emma says thank you, everyone. She loves us all and will never be far away."

I received a round of applause for saying very little. The war affected us all in so many ways, but above all, it brought us together. Adversity brings out the very best in people. The strength of one becomes the strength of the many, and when the many are the nation, it becomes an unbreakable spirit.

It had been one of the hardest decisions of my life. When the day came, I approached my new appointment with nothing but apprehension. For me, this was much more about letting go of the past than embracing the future. I was no stranger to St Thomas's Hospital; I'd sent many patients there and got to know several of the staff. St Thomas's is a venerable institution, probably the best-known hospital in London.

Standing on the south bank of the River Thames, directly opposite the Houses of Parliament, both buildings defined the London landscape. On that drab morning, the river reflected the grey colours of the sky, but those two buildings stood resplendent, refusing to allow the poor light to diminish their status. Big Ben towered defiantly into the sky, just as its mirror image reached across the river. In the background, barrage balloons floated silently in the clouds, the only sign that we were at war.

As I approached the entrance, the hospital's long history and magnificent Victorian architecture demanded that I stand for a moment, almost in reverence. Standing at the entrance as a new staff member, I felt both daunted and exhilarated at the same time. I arrived on April 10th 1940, the day after Germany invaded Norway. As a GP Registrar, I had the option of a room in the hospital, but I also lived close enough to go home.

They placed me under Doctor Wiśniewski, so I needed to find him and introduce myself. When I asked where I would find him, the nurse directing me seemed almost afraid for me. She ended our brief conversation with 'Good luck'. I'd heard of him before; he had treated some of the patients I sent to the hospital. A Polish national, Wiśniewski, had lived in England for over fifteen years. My impression of the medical notes accompanying my discharged patients could only be described as highly competent. I waited by the entrance of one ward, looking down the long line of uniform beds on either side. Wiśniewski suddenly appeared, marching towards me. As he approached, he looked at me as if I was something he'd trodden in. My first encounter did not go well.

"Why are you out of uniform, nurse?"

"I'm not a nurse, Doctor Wiśniewski. I'm Doctor Stevenson."

"A doctor? Where did you qualify? I assume you are qualified?"

"I qualified at the London School of Medicine for Women."

"Did you indeed? I thought we had stopped the ingress of women into this profession."

"Not entirely, no, you must be thinking of the Westminster Medical School. They closed their doors to women in 1928. That's why I went to the London School of Medicine."

"Westminster has closed its doors to you because you are a distraction, Stevenson. Do not become a distraction in this hospital."

I wanted to scream, but I thought it probably best not to. "I don't have the slightest intention of being a distraction. I'm an experienced GP, and I'm here to help the war effort."

"Be that as it may, Stevenson, the fact remains that women do not fit easily into the medical world. The patients will have difficulty accepting you, and your colleagues most certainly will. This is why I consider you to be a distraction."

I took a slow, deep breath. "That has not been my experience in general practice, I can assure you. I am here and intend to do the very best I can."

"Well, let's hope you're right. Report to ward four, new admissions, and you can join me for my ward round first thing tomorrow morning."

I left him, mumbling under his breath, the first moment I could. I breathed an enormous sigh of relief as I turned away. Walking rather hastily, I almost bumped into the hospital matron, who was another daunting individual. A middle-aged woman, Marion Horworthy, projected an even larger presence.

"Do not run, and look where you're going. Who are you?"

"I'm a new doctor, Matron. I've just introduced myself to Doctor Wiśniewski."

"Have you just left medical school? Are you one of Doctor Wiśniewski's junior doctors?"

"No, Matron, I'm a GP. I decided to join the hospital."

"Well, I'm pleased to hear it. Doctor..?"

"Oh, I'm sorry. Doctor Stevenson, Emma Stevenson."

"Good, well, I am Matron, and I dislike anyone running in my wards. That applies to doctors as well as nurses."

She ruled her nurses like Wiśniewski ruled the junior doctors; they were terrified of her. She maintained a very professional relationship with all the doctors and consultants, but they never got closer than the starch in her uniform. I suppose that being a woman and a doctor, she presented a slightly kinder face to me. In fact, as unpromising as our introduction might sound, we eventually became really close friends. In new admissions I met Frank, a GP the same as me, who also opted for hospital work. A registrar in his forties, he had been with the hospital for two years. He welcomed me warmly, in complete contrast to Wiśniewski.

"They told me we had another doctor coming. Stevenson, right?"

"That's right, Emma Stevenson."

"Frank Cooper. What's your background, Emma?"

"Four years in general practice; well, nearly five, actually."

"Same route as me, then. I've been here a couple of years now, after nearly fifteen years in general practice. When they said Doctor Stevenson, I assumed you were…"

"A man."

"Yes, you're a pleasant surprise."

"That's not a view shared by Doctor Wiśniewski."

"No, it wouldn't be. The chief isn't known for his people skills."

I liked him immediately. Frank had a kind face and a soft voice. Quite a lot older than me, he had one of those smiles that made me feel welcome. Beneath his white coat, he wore twill trousers with worn areas around the pockets and frayed turn-ups. His short-sleeved cardigan had loose threads hanging, a little like his slightly receding hair that needed cutting. Frank obviously didn't care; his relaxed manner was reflected perfectly in his dress. I felt immediately comfortable with him, like an old pair of slippers. We went around the ward together, sharing views about the various patients. He eventually left me to continue alone, but I noticed he kept his eye on me. I called over to one of the nurses.

"Yes, Doctor."

"I've prescribed this gentleman a medication, and I would like him to start it immediately. Will you take care of that and make sure he takes it?"

"Of course, Doctor," she replied with an enormous smile.

"Have I said something to amuse you, Nurse?"

"No, of course not. It's just nice to see a lady doctor around here. Some of our female patients will prefer that."

"I'm Doctor Stevenson."

"Nurse Walters, Janet Walters."

"It's nice to see such a friendly face, Nurse Walters."

I had a good first morning. One or two male patients didn't initially regard me as a doctor, but I'd already learned how to win them around. Despite being nervous, I approached each patient just as Hamish had taught me. Above all else, I had to engender confidence, the patient's, not mine. I diagnosed a few illnesses and made a difference for some of the patients. Above all, I'd found some friendly faces and didn't feel quite so overwhelmed. When Frank suggested we should grab a bite of lunch while we could, I happily agreed.

The staff canteen was the height of luxury to me, the contrast with our general practice could not have been starker. The splendour of the Victorian building seemed incongruous with its use as a canteen. Hanging chandeliers reached down from the ceiling, while tall windows allowed sunlight to bathe rows of tables and chairs. Crisp, white tablecloths covered the tables with perfectly folded corners. Frank directed me towards a table where two other doctors were already sitting.

"This is Kenneth Osborne and Leonard Jordan, Ken's the bow tie. Gentlemen, this is our new intake, Doctor Emma Stevenson."

Anyone who wore a big colourful bow tie like Kenneth's had to be a larger-than-life character. A man in his early thirties, he had a mop of frizzy hair and a smile even bigger than his bow tie. A house surgeon, he had an air of authority about him despite his flamboyant appearance. Leonard introduced himself as Leo. A junior doctor, Leo was a young man who obviously had the knack of looking right. He was a handsome young devil, too, with his blue eyes and blonde hair, and he knew it.

I approached the group cautiously at first, conscious that a female doctor was very much the exception in those days. For their part, they seemed pleased to see me, perhaps Leo, a little too pleased. Ken spoke with the hint of an Irish accent. I got the impression that he used it for effect like Hamish did with his Scottish accent. Ken had the gift of combining conversation with his expressive face and hands. He combined words and gesticulation like a conductor might orchestrate a piece of music. Leo struck me as the kind of young man who expected to be the centre of attention, the one with the brightest conversation. Except he wasn't, that was Ken. Leo appeared slightly bereft as the conductor sitting beside him orchestrated a conversation he couldn't keep up with.

Frank remained the quiet one, but unlike Leo, he obviously didn't care if he stood in the sun or the shade. It would be well-considered if he said anything at all, which was more than you'd say for his dress sense. I'm sure he didn't need to wear worn-out clothes, but he had an understated confidence that I liked. Joseph Conrad's 'Captain Macwhirr' sprang into my mind. Frank's physiognomy was the exact counterpart of his countenance. He and Leo were polar opposites in age and personality, while Ken had the confidence just to be himself.

"Tell us about yourself, Emma," asked Ken. "Which part of the country is now mourning your absence?"

"Clapham, just down the road. I worked there for nearly five years and really enjoyed it. I'm not sure Clapham is mourning my absence, but to be honest, I'm mourning Clapham, well, the people anyway."

"Then I feel sorry for the good folk of Clapham, but to be sure, their loss has become our gain."

"That's not how Wiśniewski regards my presence."

"You've met the chief, and you're still standing," said Leo.

"I've never been spoken to by such a rude man in my life."

"Sounds as if you caught him on a good day, then," Frank replied.

"Honestly, the man is a dinosaur; he thinks a female doctor is nothing but a distraction for you men."

"He does have a point, Emma; have you looked in the mirror recently?" Ken said.

"I hope you're not being serious, Ken."

"Good heavens, no. That was my pathetic attempt at a veiled compliment, using the unsubtle device of humour. A deplorable comment, obviously inappropriate, and therefore a ghastly mistake."

I couldn't help laughing. Ken played with words to such wonderful effect. He was also ahead of his time in being aware of my female sensitivities. Being a woman in that man's world would not be easy, but I was also sensitive about not letting it show.

"Not so ghastly, but maybe you need to work on the humour a bit."

"Message understood, no reference to gender."

I realised I had got off on the wrong foot. "The chief said I would be a distraction, and I'm determined to prove him wrong. Forgive me if I'm being a bit sensitive."

"No, actually, you're right, Emma. I wouldn't make such a comment to Frank or Leo. The thing is, though, it's a bit like opening a door for a lady or offering a compliment about her dress. A gentleman does that instinctively, with only the highest of intentions."

"Yes, I can appreciate that, Ken. So the question for the lady is, how does she know if she is confronted with a gentleman when she has only just made his acquaintance?"

"Good point, Doctor Stevenson. May I assure you that beneath this disappointing exterior, there dwells the heart of a true gentleman."

"Then, in that case, Doctor Osborne, I can accept your frivolous remark as a veiled compliment and accept it in the same spirit. So, thank you, kind sir."

"Looks as if you've met your match, Ken," Frank said.

We all laughed; the ice had been broken, and I liked them. I didn't have the slightest doubt that Ken's comment had been intended as a compliment, but nevertheless, I felt the need to establish our working relationship. If the truth be told, I was not used to being paid compliments, especially not from a man as instantly likeable as Ken. I might easily have shown my ineptitude by blushing and babbling nervous nonsense. Instead, I was quite pleased with my retort.

Our conversation continued over cottage pie, something of a luxury during rationing. We discussed the hospital, but all the while, the war loomed large in our conversation. Hitler's invasion of Norway and Denmark that started on April 9th dispelled any thoughts of a phoney war. I only repeated what my father told me, and my observations met with approval. We shared much the same opinion, but I listened with interest as they debated the subject. Ken's well-chosen words were delivered with a delightful cadence, while Frank didn't say much. When he did say something, it was always something significant and being the oldest among us gave him additional gravitas.

I very much warmed to Leo as well. Typical, I suppose, of a young man, his bravado went ahead of him, and he didn't always manage to catch up with it. I quickly realised his enormous confidence was only for show. As a very junior, junior doctor, everyone knew more about medicine than he did, and we were all older and perhaps wiser. He felt the need to compensate, but he really didn't need to bother. Behind his fashionable, and I have to admit, dashing exterior, he was a sweet and delightful young man. He couldn't perform vocal gymnastics with Ken, and he certainly didn't have the wisdom of age that Frank had. What he did have was a wealthy family background and the world at his feet.

Despite that initially awkward start with Doctor Wiśniewski, when our lunch break ended, I felt I had gained new friends. Frank and I worked through the afternoon together, and he couldn't have been more helpful. Then, in the last hour of the day, Janet Walters came over to me.

"Excuse me, Doctor Stevenson, do you have time to see a patient for me? She has a problem she doesn't want to discuss with one of the male doctors, and well, you're the only doctor I can ask."

"Yes, of course I can. Show me the way."

The patient was in hospital with a pregnancy complication, but she also had a simple case of thrush. I assured her it was common during pregnancy and self-limiting. The woman convinced herself she had contracted a venereal disease which could only have come from her husband. The poor woman had worked herself into a really stressed condition; no wonder her blood pressure was so high. We didn't have effective treatments for fungal infections in those days, but an anti-inflammatory would help. The relief on her face was a joy to see and the highlight of my day.

"The way you approached that patient, Doctor Stevenson, and how she responded to you ... well, it was wonderful." Nurse Walters said.

"I wish all patients were so easy to please. The poor woman has been so worried."

"The thing is, Doctor, without you, she would have gone on like that. Her blood pressure has been sky-high. I'll make sure we keep her closely monitored."

"Do we have many women like this who would prefer a female doctor?"

"Of course, it happens all the time."

"Well, in that case, when the need arises again, make a point of asking for me."

"I will. It's long overdue, in my opinion. We need female doctors, especially doctors like you."

"What do you mean?"

"Not all the doctors approach the patients in the way you do, and I feel comfortable talking to you."

"Well, that's not bad for my first day, is it, Janet?"

She laughed and hesitated for a moment. "I remember my first day; if you ever want to share a table in the canteen or a drink one evening, then that would be nice."

"Thank you, Janet, how kind, I'll take you up on that."

My first day got off to such an inauspicious start with Doctor Wiśniews- ki, but by the end of the day, I felt really happy. I met some lovely people, and there was definitely a space I could fill in the hospital. I couldn't wait to telephone my mum and dad and Hamish.

## Chapter Ten
# April 16th, 1940

Roger

*"When pain leaves you, what remains is a void,
a space you can once again inhabit."*

Waking up in an unknown place and being unable to see is very disturbing. The unconscious state is one of blissful unawareness. When my consciousness returned, it came with pain and anguish and nothing else. I instinctively raised my hand to my face to find a bulky bandage wrapped around my eyes and forehead. Pain distracts the brain like nothing else. I tried to think, where am I? What's happening to me? Then, the first clear thought struggled free of the pain. Something's happened to me. I'm badly injured. Have I lost my eyesight? I remembered the raid and the builder's yard. A hand took hold of mine and removed it from my head. The hand came with a female voice.

"Inspector Pritchard, you're awake. You're in St Thomas's Hospital. You suffered a knock on the head. How do you feel?"

"I'm in a lot of pain; what's happened to me? What's happened to my eyes?"

"A doctor is coming to look at you. I'm going to take this bandage off; it's tight because we needed to staunch the blood flow. You've got a nasty cut on your forehead."

None of what she said sounded true. I thought the worst as she unwound the bandage. As the nurse lifted it from my eyes, I saw light but little else. Pressing against my forehead with one hand, she wiped my eyes with the other. A face appeared among the blur of shapes, a reassuringly pretty face. Another face joined her, and between them, they seemed to be cleaning me up. All the while, my head ached intolerably, as did my neck and shoulder. I desperately wanted them to stop moving me. I heard the nurse discussing me with someone else as if I wasn't there.

"We're going to take you for an X-ray, Mr Pritchard. Nothing to worry about."

The pain seemed to be everywhere, and every movement of the trolley I lay on only added to my torment. Through one blurred eye, I could only see the ceiling moving above me, and each flashing light seemed to deliver a painful blow. Then, more noise, more lights, more strange objects, and more reassuring words that did nothing of the kind. Once again, the ceiling moved above me, and the lights flashed one after another, and then there were no more reassuring words.

Finally, they left me staring at the same patch of ceiling I started with and with the same pain. A single light bulb hung down above me, surrounded by swirls of rainbow colours. I tried hard to focus my one open eye, but I tried in vain. The colours moved like a meandering stream on a misty morning. My despair reached the edge of a precipice; I might have stepped off had it been within my power. I became aware of a white coat standing next to me. In that world of disinfectant and bleach, I noticed she smelt nice. Speaking with a wonderfully soft and gentle voice, her educated London accent flowed over me like a soothing balm. Almost immediately, I felt calm and reassured.

"Mister Prichard, or should I call you Inspector Pritchard? I'm Doctor Stevenson, and I'm going to make you well again. I know why your shoulder is so painful; it's dislocated, but I can take care of that for you. The great news is that your skull is not fractured, and there's nothing broken in your neck. So you see, Inspector, nothing is going to prevent me from making you well again. I want you to relax. You're going to be fine. The first thing I'm going to do is to give you an injection of morphine and trust me, it will take your pain away."

I don't understand how she did it; she told me to relax, and I did. Her voice, her touch, I simply knew I was in safe hands; I believed every word she said. The injection she gave me worked almost immediately. Unless you have experienced great pain for a length of time, you will never appreciate the unbridled joy of its disappearance. When pain leaves you, what remains is a void, a space you can once again inhabit. The joy I felt could not be contained. I didn't have a care in the world.

The doctor and a nurse sat me upright, and the doctor placed my arm into an awkward position. She leant across me until her face was close to mine. She told me to take a deep breath, but it was her breath I felt on my face. A loud pop and a hot sensation ran across my shoulders, but I really didn't care.

"That wasn't so bad, was it, Inspector? Now, I want you to lie back, and I'm going to do some of my finest embroidery on your forehead." My right eye had closed completely, but with what little sight I had in my left, I looked up at her, concentrating. She paused momentarily to look at her handiwork; then she smiled at me. "I hope you won't mind having a scar on your forehead, Inspector Pritchard. I'm using tiny stitches, it takes a little longer, but it will keep the scarring to a minimum. How did this happen to you?"

"I can remember searching a building. We were arresting a criminal gang. Well, that's it really, whatever it was, I didn't see it coming."

"You mean to say someone did this to you? It wasn't an accident?"

"This is no accident, Doctor. I just hope we've caught the bastard who did it … oh, sorry."

"Don't apologise, Inspector Pritchard. I hope you've caught the bastard who syphoned my petrol that night."

"I don't understand, Doctor; who are we talking about?"

"Unless there are two Inspector Pritchard's, I believe you were the one who came to my rescue."

"You're the damsel in distress. I remember."

"And now you're the one in distress, and I can help you. It's a small world, isn't it? Now, then, the nurse is going to bandage your head and put your arm in a sling. You have torn ligaments in your neck, so you'll need to wear a neck brace for a few weeks. I'm afraid you're going to look a sorry sight for a while. Don't worry about your eyes; it's the swelling that's closing them up. We shall have to wait for that to go before we can properly assess your vision. I'm guessing you wear glasses, Inspector. I've taken pieces of optical glass out of your right eyebrow, but I could see nothing in your eye. It's too early to rule out damage to the optic nerve categorically, but I'm pretty sure you'll make a complete recovery."

"Thank you, Doctor, I mean, really, thank you. You've been wonderful."

"I'll come back and see you tomorrow, Inspector. I'm afraid the pain will also come back when the morphine wears off. You've suffered a serious concussion. The nurse will give you something that will help."

I couldn't see her at all by then, but she took my hand before she left and gently squeezed it. I knew she'd gone; I didn't need to see to feel the absence of her presence. The nurse took over and did as the doctor instructed, but it wasn't the same. Although terribly nice, she didn't have the same reassuring way about her that the doctor had. The doc was right about the pain as well; it did come back, but when you know it will improve, it all becomes more manageable. My first visitor arrived in the late afternoon. I couldn't see who it was, but I might have guessed.

"Bloody hell, Roger, you look awful, mate."

"Cheers, Gerry. Tell me you got the bastard who did it."

"Oh yes, Dave got him alright."

"Are they telling us much?"

"Not the feller who clobbered you, he isn't saying anything. Dave shot him."

"He did what? He shot him?"

"Yes, Dave says he stood over you with a cricket bat intending to give you some more, so he shot him."

"My God. You mean the bloke's dead?"

"As a doornail. Dave says he panicked, he just pointed the gun and fired. The bullet went straight through his heart."

"Crikey, I bet Dave's a bit shaken up."

"He is, actually. I told him to go home. He did the right thing; he might even have saved your life."

"Did you say cricket bat?"

"Yes, I suppose it must have been lying around; it certainly knocked you for six, didn't it? The doctor outside told me you should make a full recovery."

"Was that Doctor Stevenson?"

"Yes, that's her. Nice woman, put herself out to come and talk to me."

"What does she look like? I couldn't see her properly, but she sounded really lovely."

"Fairly ordinary, really, brown hair, early thirties, about five feet six. Had a way about her, though: attractive eyes. And talking about attractive eyes, I've sent a car to pick Marilyn up."

"Oh, thanks, she'll be worried. Does she know Dave shot him?"

"No."

"That might be best."

"She's here, I can see her. I'll leave you two alone, mate. I'll pop by tomorrow."

"Thanks for coming, Gerry."

The first words Marilyn said were, 'Oh my God'. I realised I must have looked a real mess, but I thought she would at least be pleased to see me alive.

"You've got to stop doing this, Roger. Leave it to the young lads; you're too old to be fighting villains."

"He caught me unawares, that's all."

"I'll bloody catch you unawares if you go on doing this, you silly bugger. What do the doctors say? You look awful, you're black and blue."

"The doc says I'll be fine. I'll have my arm in a sling and my neck in a brace, but apart from that, you won't know anything happened."

"Thank heavens the kids can't see you like this."

This is how it went on. She calmed down a bit, but everything seemed to get on top of her. The children being away played on her mind all the time, and combined with the fear of what the war might bring, she just couldn't cope with it. I really wanted to lie quietly; the effort of talking had become too much. As soon as Marilyn saw that, she used it as an excuse to go.

The following day, everything felt a little better. Although I still couldn't open my right eye, I could see a bit better with my left. The noise in a ward doesn't allow anyone to sleep on. Even during the night, things seemed to happen. They wake you when you want to be asleep and ask if you slept well. Later in the morning, I had another visitor, Dave, come to see me.

"Hello, Rog. Has anyone told you how bad you look?"

"Yes, Gerry told me; he also told me you shot the bastard."

"Yes, I did. He might have killed you. He had the bat raised above his head. I didn't have time to think about it. I just did it."

"Sounds as though you might have saved my life, Dave, I'm happy about that. Are you okay?"

"I will be. I've not shot anyone before. It's a bit of a shock, really."

"He had it coming, didn't he? If the position had been the reverse, I'd like to think I would react as quickly. You did the right thing, Dave. Thanks, mate."

"We got them all; they didn't put up any resistance after that."

"I'm not surprised. You must have frightened the shit out of them."

"How's Marilyn taken it? I don't suppose she's too happy, is she?"

"You guessed right. She came to see me last night, and I received a bollocking rather than sympathy. It's the kids being away that's doing it."

"That bloke I shot, he just fell down dead. I mean, he didn't move or anything. I thought people asked for their mothers or something."

"Try not to let it play on your mind, Dave. He must have been a draft dodger as well as a potential murderer. If anyone had it coming, he did."

I could tell from his voice that Dave had been badly shaken up by the incident. He was a good friend and a good copper; we were close. When I thought about it, I knew I would have done the same thing had our positions been reversed. When your friend is in peril, you react instinctively. Dave understood that; it just took a little time for him to accept it.

# Chapter Eleven
# Rose Jackson

Roger

*"Any gratuitous violence towards women takes me
back to a time in my life when I was powerless to prevent it,
and my visceral reaction is always the same."*

As soon as the specialist at the hospital confirmed that my optic nerves were not damaged, I was desperate to go home. As the swelling reduced, my eyesight gradually returned. Finally, equipped with new glasses, I could see properly again and read a newspaper. That might have boosted my morale, but it also supported my need to return to work; I'd been away for two weeks. When I telephoned the station, they put me through to Gerry.

"I'm fine now, Gerry. I just need someone to come and pick me up."

"You mean you've still got your arm in a sling?"

"Well, yes, but that's not a problem; I can still work."

"Tell me if my memory is failing me, Roger. Before this incident, you were a half-blind hack who helped old ladies across the road. Now you have your arm in a sling and your neck in a brace. Do you seriously think the old lady wants you to help her cross the road?"

"I've got to come in, Gerry. I'm going mad here; I'll walk if I have to."

"You think we can't do without you, don't you?"

"I know you can't; get someone round here to pick me up."

He pretended to complain, saying nobody could be spared to drive me, but I knew who'd come for me. Dave appeared within the hour.

"Am I pleased to see you, mate. What did Gerry say?"

"He told me to drop everything and pick you up pronto, so here I am."

"Seriously, he said that?"

"He did, the old bugger worries about you."

I'm a detective; you would think I might have expected the reception I received at the police station. In my keenness to get there, I forgot what a complete clown I looked. The moment I stepped through the door, a cheer greeted me, followed by every cricketing metaphor you could think of.

"Were you standing in the slips when the batsman knocked you for six?" said Jeff.

"No, it must have been square leg. He would have dodged it otherwise," said Dave.

"Silly mid-off, more like," replied Jeff.

"I'm concerned about him coming to work with a collar and no tie," laughed Gerry.

I took it all in good humour and even managed to laugh. The piss-taking continued for a while until it suddenly stopped. It said much for the British spirit that we had any humour left at all. They'd been keeping something from me but could keep it quiet no longer. There had been a second victim found lying in a front garden in Clapham. A passerby found the woman the following morning and telephoned for an ambulance. She was so badly injured that the hospital assumed she had been involved in a car accident. We weren't informed until much later that day, and even then, the PC who investigated it accepted the hospital's assumption that it was a road accident. The inquiry started as a hit-and-run case. It was three days before the victim could speak, three days before Dave became involved. He told me how he found her.

"The woman had her arms in plaster, and her head was almost entirely bandaged. Perhaps that was just as well from my perspective. I'm not sure I would have coped seeing what lay beneath the bandages. Doctor Wiśniewski, one of the senior doctors at St Thomas's, came to talk to me, obviously embarrassed about the mixup. He said he was dreadfully sorry about the confusion with the patient. He told me someone said she'd been involved in a car accident, so nobody else questioned it."

"How could they think she was involved in a car accident?"

"Well, the thing is, Roger, she was unconscious for three days."

As soon as he described her injuries, it all became clear. She had a concussion and lacerations to the back of the skull. Both of her arms were broken, as were her collarbone and two ribs. She also had internal bleeding requiring surgery and very extensive external bruising. Events from our past can lay in wait for their moment to torment us. This was such a moment. Any gratuitous violence towards women takes me back to a time in my life when I was powerless to prevent it, and my visceral reaction is always the same. I struggled to remain focused.

"Had she been raped or sexually molested?"

"The doctor said there was no indication of that."

"Will she fully recover from this?"

"The doctor said yes, she most likely will. It sounds bizarre to use the word 'fortunate' when talking about this poor woman, but in many respects, she is. The doctor says she has been struck repeatedly with an object like a rod or metal pole. The injuries to her skull and internal organs could have been fatal. He left her for dead."

"Did the doc say how long it will take for her to recover?"

"Physically a month or so. Mentally many months, if ever."

"Did anyone take photographs of her injuries?"

"No, of course not. So I asked if your pathologist mate, Doctor Bartholomew, could take a look at her."

"Did he agree to that?"

"Eventually, he did. I had to explain that Bartholomew does a lot of forensic work for us."

"I take it you've interviewed her?"

"Doctor Wiśniewski asked me to spend only a minute with her. I understood completely. I asked her just two questions: her name and address and whether was she assaulted. When I got back here, I found her details matched a missing person's report filed by her parents. Her name is Rose Jackson. She's twenty-six years old, has two young children, and lives in Clapham. She was going to pick up the children from her mother's when he grabbed her. I've been back with Jeff and interviewed her again, and it's an exact copy of the last one. Grabbed from behind, and irritant in the eyes. She saw nothing, and he didn't say a word. She described him as being in a rage, but she wasn't conscious for more than a minute."

"What about where it happened? Anything useful there?"

"Just like the last one, quiet and dark during the blackout. He left her in a front garden on Sedgwick Road."

"Did the occupiers of that house see or hear anything?"

"No, the house is empty; they evacuated to the country."

"Are you assuming he knew that?"

"We don't know, but I think it's more than a coincidence."

"So do I. He's a local man, isn't he?"

"We're continuing with a door-to-door, and we've spoken with the local ARP warden and the beat bobby. There's nothing, Roger. It's as if this bloke is a ghost."

# Chapter Twelve
# May 13th, 1940

Emma

*"Like every soldier who enters the battlefield, we were the
invincible ones; we would triumph no matter what. I both curse
and thank God for that delusion. Curse it because, without it,
there would be no wars. I thank God for it because, without it,
none of us would have been able to face the future."*

I occasionally felt the need to escape the hospital environment, if only for the night. So it was on the morning of May 13th when I woke up at my home in Battersea. It may have been nothing more than a little red-brick terraced house in Birley Street, but I'd made it my own. The morning drive to the hospital took just a few minutes. I only used the car in case I needed it with me. That morning, the sun shone through a clear blue sky as if its only purpose was illuminating the power station chimneys.

The two chimneys of the Battersea power station reached for the heavens. They were the first landmarks in the area to be greeted by the morning sun, standing bright against a dark sky. The chimneys and the adjacent gasometer may not have provided the most celebrated view in London, but I looked at it as a Londoner. This was my town, and I wasn't about to let that awful man Hitler take it away from me.

Marion, the hospital matron, was one of the first people I saw that morning. To my surprise, I'd struck up a growing friendship with her. I came to realise that her position as matron can be a lonely one. Protocol dictated the matron should not socialise with the nurses, and she obviously wouldn't socialise with the male doctors. When I came along, I didn't quite fit into either camp, neither fish nor fowl in Marion's eyes.

Spare time was not an abundant commodity for a doctor; I thought of it as something other people had. My social life, if you can call it that, consisted of chatting with various hospital staff members, and so I came to increasingly value my friendship with Marion. Her only other close friend was Evelyn, the hospital administrator. Twenty years older than me, they were almost of my parents' generation.

They kindly took me under their wing; I suppose it was a bit like joining an old spinsters' club, but I just enjoyed their company. We were relaxed together; I didn't say stupid things like I did with the men. That afternoon, Marion waved me over and suggested I go to Evelyn's office with her. The BBC would broadcast Mr Churchill's inaugural speech as Prime Minister in the House of Commons, and she didn't want to miss it. I felt guilty creeping out of the ward, but like them, I wanted to hear the speech.

"Quickly, you two, close the door and sit down," Evelyn said.

Marion and I did as she asked, like a couple of schoolgirls sneaking behind the toilets to have a furtive cigarette. I smiled at the pair of them. In most people's eyes, they were probably the two most intimidating women in the hospital, and here we were, consumed with guilt, listening to the wireless during work hours.

When I entered the hospital earlier, I had no idea that May 13th would be such a very significant day for the country. Hitler invaded the Netherlands on the 10th, and following our strategic retreat in Norway, it provided yet another blow to the morale of the government. Prime Minister Neville Chamberlain's attempts to appease Hitler may have given us some time, but nothing more. The pressure upon Chamberlain to resign became irresistible. He wanted Lord Halifax to succeed him, but when he refused, only one divisive figure stood large enough to gain the overall support of Parliament. Winston Churchill became Prime Minister on May the 10th.

My father often spoke about Mr Churchill, so I knew his history and background. His first act as Prime Minister was to propose a coalition government. I don't think any of us appreciated the significance of that event at the time. With the arrival of Winston Churchill, a Colossus stepped onto the world stage. The moment the broadcast began, it was as if that Colossus stepped into the room with us.

*"I have nothing to offer but blood, toil, tears and sweat. We have before us an ordeal of the most grievous kind. We have before us many, many long months of struggle and of suffering. You ask, what is our policy? I can say: it is to wage war, by sea, land and air, with all our might and with all the strength that God can give us; to wage war against a monstrous tyranny, never surpassed in the dark, lamentable catalogue of human crime. That is our policy. You ask, what is our aim? I can answer in one word: it is victory, victory at all costs, victory in spite of all terror, victory, however long and hard the road may be; for without victory, there is no survival. Let that be realised; no survival for the British Empire, no survival for all that the British Empire has stood for, no survival for the urge and impulse of the ages, that mankind will move forward towards its goal. But I take my task with buoyancy and hope. I feel sure that our cause will not be suffered to fail among men. At this time I feel entitled to claim the aid of all, and I say, come then, let us go forward together with our united strength."*

(Winston Churchill, House of Commons address, May 13th, 1940) *

When I heard the speech he delivered to the House of Commons on the wireless, the hairs on the back of my neck stood up even though the voice wasn't that of Mr Churchill. The BBC reported his speeches, but reporters or actors read the words. We were all aware that Hitler's forces were rampaging across Europe, but none of the fears about gas attacks and bombing of Britain had so far materialised. There were still people among us who regarded it as a phoney war. I suppose, in truth, we all clung to what we wanted to believe. Mr Churchill shattered that delusion. Only then, upon hearing his words, did I fully appreciate what was at stake and what lay ahead. The three of us sat in silence, with his words resonating in our minds.

"Victory at all costs. We only dare imagine what the price of that victory will be."

"I agree, Evelyn," I replied. "I think we are about to enter Hell."

"It doesn't bear thinking about, does it? We can only do our jobs. That's all we can do."

"You're right, Marion, that's all we can do, but that's no small thing. We're on the front line now."

"Rest assured, my nurses will not let us down, Emma."

"Nobody will be found wanting. We can do this."

We left the office, having convinced ourselves we could cope with whatever the war threw at us. Like every soldier who enters the battlefield, we were the invincible ones. We would triumph no matter what. I both curse and thank God for that delusion. I curse it because, without it, there would be no wars. I thank God for it because, without it, none of us would have been able to face the future.

Just about everyone heard or read Mr Churchill's speech. We all went about our work, but the war became very real that afternoon. Everyone wanted to discuss it, each needing our colleagues to reassure us. I noticed on the odd occasion one or two of the staff would go to the local pub together, but despite an invitation, I had never taken part. Ken invited me that evening, probably assuming I would say no as usual. I was becoming conspicuous for continually saying no, so I felt obliged to say yes. I'd never been inside the local pub; I didn't even know which one they considered being the local.

I met them as arranged just outside the hospital entrance: Ken, Frank, Leo, and someone I hadn't met before. They introduced me to Doctor Alexander Bartholomew. An impressive-looking man in his forties, he carried his three-piece suit against an almost statuesque body. Frank, as always, wore his old short-sleeved cardigan with the hanging threads and the worn shiny patches around his trouser pockets. His old tweed jacket had worn-out leather patches on the elbows. I just followed them, not knowing where we were going. We turned left out of the hospital and walked towards Westminster Bridge. I became intrigued as we walked over the bridge. With the hospital on one side and the Palace of Westminster on the other, this is a view to lift the heart of every Londoner.

It was all rather different that evening. With an overcast sky and the blackout in place, I only saw an outline of the buildings in the twilight and just the suspicion of a reflection dancing on the surface of the river. One or two isolated lights crept out from behind blackout blinds or curtains, inviting the air raid wardens to shout, 'Put that bloody light out'. On the far side of the bridge, we arrived at St Stephen's Tavern.

Ken opened the heavy door, and immediately, we were bathed in light and the sound of people talking and laughing. It seems the war didn't exist on the other side of that door. They didn't ask me what I would like to drink, which might have been just as well because I didn't really drink. Ken just returned from the bar with a tray full of pint glasses, mine included. I accepted it as if it were completely normal. In truth, I sat looking at it, wondering how I might possibly drink it all.

"Well, cheers everyone," Ken said. "Did we all hear Churchill's speech on the wireless?"

We had, and they each had an opinion that varied from good to triumphant. We received a slightly more nuanced response when they asked Alexander for his opinion.

"What you just said, Ken, about Churchill's record in Gallipoli is only correct up to a point. What we have in Mr Churchill is a man for the moment. Has anyone not been deeply moved by that speech? Hitler can be in absolutely no doubt. He's awoken a sleeping giant. What we've witnessed is nothing less than the weaponisation of the English language."

"Wow, and I thought it was just a speech," said Leo.

Alexander looked down his nose at Leo. He obviously didn't appreciate his comment.

"What's your opinion, Emma? You're keeping quiet," Ken asked, perhaps assuming I didn't have one.

"I agree with what Alexander said about Gallipoli. Churchill realised our command of the Dardanelles sea passage would mean defeat for Turkey. I think the hesitancy of the High Command when three ships were lost to mines also contributed to the disaster. You can't fault Churchill's strategic objective, but the execution was flawed."

"How do you know all this, Emma?" asked Frank, obviously amazed that I should understand the issue.

"I'm the daughter of an academic and school principal. I've spent my entire life listening to debates like this."

"Well, it seems it was not time wasted, Emma," replied Alexander.

"My father would be pleased to hear that, but in truth, I only quote what I've heard. I don't really understand it. I'm a carrier of wisdom, it's not a condition I suffer from. I've not seen you in the hospital, Alexander; what do you do?"

"You won't see Alex," said Ken. "He's confined to the basement."

"Pathology, Emma; as Ken says, they don't let me venture upstairs."

"Do you do many post-mortems of gas victims from the last war?"

"Yes, I've had one or two. Why do you ask?"

"My father has lost a lot of lung function, chlorine gas. I've researched it as far as I can. I'm obviously concerned for him."

"When did it happen?"

I told them the story that I knew so well. April 22$^{nd}$, 1915, at five o'clock in the morning. It was in a desolate, war-torn field in Ypres,

Belgium, when the customary early morning mist took a new form. A sinister cloud moved inexorably across the war-scarred landscape. My father described the yellow/green mist, silently clinging to the ground, rolling and billowing like a living creature, creeping towards them. It found the unsuspecting British, Canadian, and French colonial troops conveniently standing in the living hell they called the Allied front-line trench.

Heavier than air, the cloud acted as if it were possessed of malign intelligence. It gently spilled into the trench, feeling its way into the lungs and eyes of its victims. Over 1100 troops were killed, and the price of surviving the chlorine gas was permanently damaged lungs. It was a harrowing account that left them glum-faced.

"That's an all too familiar account, Emma. I would be happy to share my notes with you, but it might involve you venturing into the bowels of the hospital."

"I would risk it."

"Enough of this hospital talk," said Leo with his usual mischievous smile. "We come here to forget it."

Apparently, first-class cricket had been cancelled until further notice. Its absence seemed to weigh heavily upon them, especially Frank, who likened it to a death in the family. Not being one of the mourners, I concentrated on the pint of beer in front of me. To my surprise, I quite enjoyed it, but not necessarily a whole pint of it. As the others discussed something to do with the seam of the ball, Ken moved his chair and sat next to me.

"You're not interested in cricket, are you, Emma?"

"I can tell you who won the 1935 series, but no, I'm afraid it leaves me cold."

"Tell me about yourself, not Doctor Stevenson; tell me about Emma."

I didn't expect that; he completely wrong-footed me. I wasn't good at personal conversations, much less with men. By the time I realised it, I had blurted out my entire life history, and it was too late to stop myself. Ken was a good listener; he seemed to encourage me without saying very much.

"Now I understand why you possess all that miscellaneous knowledge," he said.

"It's the environment I lived in; there was always a discussion about something going on."

"Forgive me for asking, but you make it sound as if you didn't do the normal childhood things at all."

"Oh no, I didn't see it that way. I suppose it depends on what you call normal?"

"Well, for me, that meant playing with the neighbouring kids in the street and returning home late with my knees grazed. And then later on, I went to school with those same kids."

"I didn't do that. My parents didn't encourage me to mix with the local children. I went to a private school. But I don't feel as if I missed out on anything."

"I'm sure you didn't. Are you going to finish that pint?"

"You think I've had a strange childhood, don't you, Ken?"

"I shouldn't be prying, I'm sorry."

He looked a bit awkward, which only made me more embarrassed. I'd been a little ill at ease all evening. I wasn't good at those social things, and then I went and embarrassed myself even more by blurting out my life history like that. It would have been even worse had I done so with any of the others, but Ken was so easy to talk to; I was comfortable with him.

"I've surprised myself with this beer. I might even finish it."

"You've surprised many people, Emma. You're an exceptional doctor, which wins you a lot of respect around here."

"That's a kind thing to say, Ken. Are you just trying to make me feel better?"

"I didn't realise you needed to feel better. I'm sorry if that's my fault. I'm a bit insensitive to these things. Now I feel really awful."

"Please don't; it's entirely me, Ken. I'm awkward in situations like this. It's not you."

We said no more about it, and our silence was interrupted before it grew loud enough to stifle us. The others had moved their conversation away from cricket. I suspect talk of the Ashes had been the final straw. As much as we tried to avoid it, we had to share our thoughts and fears about the war. It might have been comforting to pretend it wasn't happening, but we had chosen a very inauspicious day to do that.

"I can't believe how fast the Germans are advancing," said Frank. "At this rate, the Netherlands will fall in no time, followed soon after by Belgium."

"France must hold on at all costs, or Hitler will take all of Europe," replied Alex.

"What happens if France falls?" asked Leo.

"That's the question, isn't it," replied Ken. "Will we be next?"

"None of us should doubt it," replied Alex. "Hitler won't stop at the English Channel … if France falls, we're next."

"What does the carrier of wisdom say, Emma?"

"My father is in no doubt, I'm afraid. France is not prepared and will fall within the month. We'll know when Hitler turns his attention towards us; bombs will start raining down from the sky."

"Can any of us actually comprehend what this will be like?" asked Frank.

"You mean what's it going to be like to see everything we know and love being blown to hell with people being killed by the thousand … no, I can't comprehend that," replied Alex.

Each of our expressions changed immediately, and despite the cacophony of voices in the pub, a pool of silence descended upon us. The prospect lying ahead was so unthinkable that we each had difficulty admitting it, even to ourselves, not even in our darkest thoughts. For a moment, no one spoke until Ken dared to vocalise the unthinkable.

"We're doctors. I think we all know in our hearts what this means. Our job is to save lives, and we'll not be found wanting."

The silence returned.

# Chapter Thirteen
# Dunkirk, May 26th, 1940

Roger

*"The absence of a child is not just an empty space.
It's a vacuum that sucks the life out of those close to it."*

The talk among our neighbours was all about bringing the children home. It started within a couple of weeks of war being declared. No bombs had fallen, and clouds of poisonous gas hadn't billowed along Balham High Street; perhaps it had all been a false alarm. That's what people wanted to believe, the triumph of hope over expectation. When some of the local children appeared in the street again, Marilyn could contain herself no more.

"I'm bringing them back, Roger. I can't go on like this."

"You can't, don't be fooled by what's happening. You can't put them in harm's way."

"You don't know that; you're never here."

"What's that got to do with bringing the children back?"

"It means you're not interested in this family. This is my decision; I don't need your permission."

"That's a terrible thing to say. John and Mary are my life. I would do anything to protect them."

"Anything other than spending time with us."

"What you mean is anything other than spending time with you. Can you blame me?"

"What are you saying?"

"I'm saying you're not the woman I married; you've become something else altogether, and you're wearing me down."

"Why don't you bugger off then?"

"Perhaps I should."

A period of silence followed as we both stood in an atmosphere so toxic I could hardly breathe. This was the first time we had mentioned the possibility of breaking up, and the seriousness of those words had not escaped either of us. She went off and made a cup of tea, pretending everything continued as usual. When she returned, the toxic cloud had at least descended below our heads.

"I didn't mean that, Roger. I shouldn't have said it."

"We're both missing the children. It's making us miserable."

"I need them here with me. I'll wait another week, and then I'll bring them back."

Things were never quite the same after that. When you think the unthinkable, you can't unthink it. You can't wish it away. It has become thinkable. We didn't bring the children back, but almost half of the evacuees were brought back prematurely. Every parent shared the same torment. The absence of a child is not just an empty space. It's a vacuum that sucks the life out of those close to it. Those parents who brought their children home acted out of misplaced love. For some, it would prove to be the most disastrous decision of their lives.

The speed with which Hitler marched across Europe took my breath away. The history of the First World War told us that territorial gains were measured in yards, not countries. It all seemed incomprehensible, but there it was, in the newspapers. The German army appeared to crush everything before it. The Netherlands had fallen, Belgium capitulated within days, and France would soon follow. I didn't doubt it, but in the process, the British Expeditionary Force, in effect, our entire army, was now cut off and at the mercy of the Germans.

I've never felt so powerless or so vulnerable. If we lost our army, then we would surely lose the war. German soldiers would be marching down Balham High Street. I didn't say that to Marilyn, dreading what her reaction would have been. The events in Europe were so dire there wasn't a man in the police station who was not worried sick about his family. It felt almost crass to ask about police matters, but then again, I suspect we all needed a distraction. Small-scale petrol syphoning continued, and the black-market economy continued to grow. It all had the potential to become a serious issue. So far, the British people were stoic; apart from the odd scuffle, things remained orderly, but tensions rose. The last thing we needed was a madman attacking women on the street.

"Do you still think this is the person who tried to attack Marilyn?" Gerry asked.

"It has to be. The stranglehold around the neck and the stinging eyes are the same. If that neighbour hadn't stepped out when she did … well, I hate to think."

"So what are we looking at here, Rog?"

"It's the degree of violence which bothers me the most. It's bad enough that we have women being attacked, but I think we can see where this is going. We're dealing with a maniac; the violence is escalating. Look at what he did to Rose Jackson. She was so badly injured she was mistaken for a road accident. We know what's coming next. He'll progress to killing them."

"He appears to be local. All three attacks occurred within a few miles of each other," Dave said.

"That could be a deliberate deception, but I'm guessing probably not. It's difficult to move around now after dark. I suspect he's here, on our patch."

"The only way we can warn everyone is to announce it in the paper, and then we might add fuel to the fire."

"I'm not sure we have an option, Gerry; we've all told our wives to stay off the streets after dark. Why should they alone have privileged information?"

"You're right, we have to. The trouble is, we know the effect it will have. In next to no time, there'll be talk of the Balham butcher or the Streatham strangler, and our madman will feed on it."

"No option, Guv. I can't live with someone being killed because they didn't know."

We had a new recruit, or rather an old recruit, who answered the call to come back. Alfred Chambers was a good man; he retired early with health issues. Having got over that, we were pleased to welcome him back.

"Alfie," Gerry shouted. "Write me a piece for the local paper, underplay the violence, and don't alarm people any more than we have to. Show it to me or Roger first."

"We can't be sure these are his only victims," I said. "Jeff, can you check records for all attacks on women over the last couple of years?"

"You think he's built up to this, don't you?" asked Dave.

"I do. Monsters like this often progress from lesser crimes."

We knew now that we were looking for the same perpetrator for all three known attacks. While we hoped it might end, the history of criminology told me otherwise. The vast majority of murder victims know their assailant, and a simple process of elimination will often lead us to the murderer. When the three criteria are applied - motive, means, and opportunity - a suspect usually emerges.

Remove the personal connection to the victim, and the assailant could be anyone. We're only left with a pattern of past behaviour to predict the future. Sad to say, luck plays a big part in such investigations. An eyewitness would be very helpful. If the assailant dropped an engraved cigarette case or a calling card, that would be even more helpful, but such clues have never come my way. With our manpower reduced, we were up against it. All our bobbies on the beat were told what to look for, and Dave and I interviewed the women again, including Marilyn. I had to admit we could have conducted a more thorough forensic examination of the crime scenes, but when the priority is to get the victim to the hospital, that's not always possible.

I asked to see the clothing the last victim had been wearing. When I saw how her clothes had been ripped apart in a frenzy, it painted a terrifying picture. We dusted the hard surfaces such as buttons for fingerprints, and then I sent the clothes over to Doctor Bartholomew at St Thomas's. He was the hospital's senior pathologist who, in recent years, had taken an ever-growing interest in forensic pathology. I'd known him for years; we even shared an occasional pint together. He possessed a razor-sharp mind; very little got past him. Only a forensic pathologist can look at a pile of victim's clothes with the eager anticipation of a child at Christmas.

The following days went by rapidly. We did everything we could with the limited manpower we had, but events in Dunkirk dominated everything. To say it amounted to a low point would be to grossly understate it. The German advance was breathtaking in its speed and ferocity. They advanced so rapidly that the British and French attempts to launch a counteroffensive had to be abandoned when the Germans reached the English Channel. The Allied armies were bypassed and effectively surrounded.

We were facing perhaps the greatest military defeat in our history. It looked likely that the entire British Expeditionary Force in France would be killed or captured. The news came to us slightly behind the events, for obvious reasons, but it gradually emerged that an evacuation would be attempted. What happened became known as the miracle of Dunkirk, and it could not be described in any other terms. Between May 26th and June 4th, hundreds of little boats and the gallant sailors of the Royal Navy performed nothing less than a miracle. 338,000 British and French troops were safely evacuated back to Blighty.

The newspapers, Pathe News, and the BBC described it in triumphant terms. We watched history unfold as our defeated army was prised from the jaws of death. I understood why the propaganda was being fed to us; in some ways, Dunkirk could be described as a triumph. The reality, however, was anything but triumphant. It marked our first catastrophic defeat of the war. 40,000 British troops were captured, as were the same number of French. We alone suffered 68,000 casualties, either killed, wounded or captured.

Hitler swept all before him, and no one, including Great Britain, had been able to stop him. It took little imagination to realise what that implied for the future of the British Isles. We were not a defeated nation, but we began to think like one. There were times when my job began to feel futile. What would be the point of maintaining law and order if, within weeks, we were to be subjugated by Hitler's Third Reich?

None of us voiced those fears. These were thoughts we wouldn't even admit to ourselves. We thought about the police response in the event of a panic on the streets. There might be social unrest as people fended for themselves. That moment became known as our country's darkest hour, and it might have been the beginning of the end. What happened instead is a truly remarkable event. Only one giant figure had the vision and ability to unite and empower the nation. Winston Churchill delivered two speeches in the House of Commons on June 4th and the 18th. Together, they make up what are probably the most powerful political oratories of all time.

*'We shall fight in France, we shall fight on the seas and oceans, we shall fight with growing confidence and growing strength in the air, we shall defend our island, whatever the cost may be, we shall fight on the beaches, we shall fight on the landing grounds, we shall fight in the fields and in the streets, we shall fight in the hills; we shall never surrender'.*

(Winston Churchill, House of Commons speech, June 4th, 1940) *

The entire nation listened to those words when they were broadcast on the wireless. We were sitting in the station together, not knowing what to expect. When the Prime Minister came towards the end of his speech and uttered those closing immortal words, we all knew something profound had just taken place. Significant events that turn the course of history are usually only recognised in retrospect, but we lived that history. Churchill's achievement seemed almost miraculous. He galvanised the country; he imbued us with a sense of courage and determination few of us thought we possessed. We were a nation of people who were far greater than the sum of our parts - we would never surrender.

# Chapter Fourteen
# June 18th, 1940

Emma

*"War teaches you that life is cheap. It can be taken for the price of a bullet or blade, but there is no price high enough for a life saved."*

I telephoned Hamish whenever I could; we always had news to share. An outbreak of chickenpox around Clapham had taken its toll on his time; I could tell he was struggling. There isn't a great deal that can be done about it other than calamine lotion, but it can look much worse than it is. Very often, it's the parents who need reassurance rather than the children. When he told me it sounded as if little Alma had contracted it, I worried. As a hospital doctor, I wouldn't normally do house calls, and I certainly shouldn't be seeing my ex-patients. Nevertheless, there were several I worried about, and I wangled a day to see them.

I made a point of going directly to see Alma. I found her with a high fever and covered in painful spots. The poor child had enough to contend with. Having suffered through polio, I knew any infectious illness would alarm the parents and child. Seeing her suffering a high fever, her parents were beside themselves with worry. Despite everything, when Alma saw me, her face lit up.

"Doctor Emma."

"I told you I wouldn't be far away, didn't I, Alma?"

"Will I be alright, Doctor Emma?"

"I'm here, Alma, so of course you'll be alright. You've got something called chickenpox, and it's given you all these nasty spots. I'm going to rub this lotion all over you, and if Mummy does the same thing every day, this nasty chickenpox will go away."

Her eyes were red from crying, but that stopped the moment I arrived. She looked a sorry sight, covered in a rash and her beautiful blonde curly hair knotted and damp with sweat. I dreaded the prospect of Alma one day contracting something that might not go away so easily. The child and her parents had such faith in me it had grown into a daunting responsibility. The prospect of ever letting her down would have been unbearable.

"She will be alright, won't she, Doctor?" asked her mother, Mrs Wilson.

"The polio has left her vulnerable, but this will run its course, I promise. She'll make a full recovery. Cover her in calamine twice a day and maintain a cold compress on her forehead for as long as the fever lasts. If you ever have any doubts about her, and Doctor McPherson is not available, or anything at all, I want you to take her to St Thomas's Hospital; it's not far. Go to outpatients and ask for me by name. I may not be there but tell someone to find me; tell them I told you to ask for me."

"Will it cost a lot of money?"

"I'll make sure it doesn't cost you anything; you just be sure to get Alma there if you need me."

"Alma's right about you, Doctor Stevenson. You are an angel."

"I'm just doing my job, Mrs Wilson."

"You're doing much more than your job, Doctor. Just know how grateful we are."

I left there as I always did when I visited Alma. Even when she was poorly, Alma had the power to lift my spirits. Next on my list was Daisy, who insisted I stay for a cup of tea. Then, I visited Scotty Henderson and two of my other veterans. Perhaps my visits were as much for me as they were for them. Either way, I left them with smiling faces.

When I returned to the hospital, I made my way to the canteen and found it had already started filling up; there seemed to be a rush. With most of the tables occupied, I hesitated, wondering where to go, but then I heard a voice calling my name. The boys had caught sight of me and were waving me over to join them; they appeared to be waiting for me, which I found quite reassuring.

"Why are we all gathered at this end?" I asked.

"Churchill made another big speech in the house this afternoon. It'll be broadcast soon on the evening news bulletin," said Alex.

"Do we know what it's about?" asked Leo.

"How about the fall of France and our response, Leo? That might be relevant," said an irritated Alex.

"I still can't believe it, Germans marching through Paris," Leo replied.

"Well, you'd better get used to it, Leo. This is the shape of things to come," replied Frank.

I sensed they were a trifle irritated with Leo. His continual flippancy at all things in general, and the war in particular, did appear a bit out of step. I think Frank found Leo's youthful sartorial elegance particularly baffling; he obviously didn't agree that clothes maketh the man. On the other hand, Alexander looked down upon anyone whose grasp of current affairs was less than his own. In fact, Alex looked down on most people.

A large wooden wireless set had been installed in the canteen, and this became the focus of attention. None of us associated the wireless with anything other than disturbing news, so the moment it hummed into life, it grabbed everyone's attention. A news announcer said that the Prime Minister, Mr Winston Churchill, had made the following speech in the House of Commons. The actor who now read Mr Churchill's speech on the radio sounded exactly like him. The long speech ended as follows.

* *'What General Weygand called the Battle of France is over. I expect that the Battle of Britain is about to begin. Upon this battle depends the survival of Christian civilisation. Upon it depends our own British life, and the long continuity of our institutions and our Empire. The whole fury and might of the enemy must very soon be turned on us. Hitler knows that he will have to break us in this island or lose the war. If we can stand up to him, all Europe may be free and the life of the world may move forward into broad, sunlit uplands. But if we fail, then the whole world, including the United States, including all that we have known and cared for, will sink into the abyss of a new dark age made more sinister, and perhaps more protracted, by the lights of perverted science. Let us therefore brace ourselves to our duties, and so bear ourselves that, if the British Empire and its Commonwealth last for a thousand years, men will still say, 'this was their finest hour'.*

(Winston Churchill. House of Commons speech, June 18th, 1940) *

Leo responded to the speech with typical youthful insensitivity. "Survival of Christian civilisation - bloody hell."

"Shut up, Leo," said Alex, stern-faced. "You have just listened to one of the finest pieces of oratory you'll ever hear, and all you can say is bloody hell. That speech was breathtaking."

"People will re-read that speech in a thousand years' time," said Ken.

"If that doesn't inspire the nation, nothing will," said Frank. "What do you think, Emma?"

"This is history in the making. The Battle of Britain begins."

"I must say you're very calm about it, Emma," said Frank.

"I'm not calm on the inside, Frank; this is me being calm on the outside. My father told me something I will never forget, and he told me within minutes of the war being declared. He said, 'War teaches you that life is cheap; it can be taken for the price of a bullet or blade, but there is no price high enough for a life saved.' This is our moment. We have a vital part to play in this war. So, in Mr Churchill's words, let us brace ourselves to our duties."

Someone at another table started clapping, and then another, followed by another. I had never made a speech in my life, and if I had known I was being overheard, I would have stopped immediately.

"Well said, Doctor Stevenson," someone shouted, "Hitler will never defeat us."

"Hear, hear," everyone shouted.

"Do you know," said Frank, "I've never been prouder to be British."

"It looks as if you've single-handedly rallied the entire hospital behind you, Emma," said Leo.

"Oh, for goodness' sake, don't be ridiculous, Leo," I replied. "The only spirit I could raise is a glass of sherry. Churchill has done this, and it's not just our hospital. He's galvanised the entire country."

"Yes, shut up, Leo," said Alexander.

Poor Leo, he meant well but seldom thought before he spoke. I felt sorry for him; he looked deflated. He always looked so well-dressed and perfectly groomed. A glum expression didn't suit him. We each sat in our thoughts for a moment, wondering exactly what bracing ourselves to our duty would entail. Frank remained as unruffled as ever, while Ken perhaps wished he hadn't chosen that day's brightly coloured bow tie. Alexander was the senior among us, and he looked and acted the part, but he worried like all of us. They left Frank and me at the table as they went thoughtfully back to work.

"I feel sorry for Leo," I said to Frank.

"He's young with a lot to learn; besides, I've got a feeling he's in love."

"Who with?"

"I've seen him with that gorgeous nurse in casualty. You know, the one with the raven black hair and big eyes."

"That's typical, isn't it; they're the two most attractive-looking people here. I suppose they were meant for each other."

"Looks like it."

"Why are you still single, Frank? You're an attractive man." I hesitated for a second. "I can't believe I just said that. Forgive me, don't answer, Frank, that's none of my business."

"Doctor Stevenson, this is not like you to be so forthright."

"I know, I'm sorry. Blame it on Mr Churchill."

"Don't be silly. We're not all sensitive like you. I suppose some of it is the job. I've always worked long, unsocial hours, and it's not easy, is it? Perhaps if I'd met the right person at the right time, but I haven't. So, of course, I'm going to ask you the same question now."

"Oh dear, I walked into that, didn't I?"

"With both feet. Sorry, I know you're not comfortable with personal issues."

"I'm not. It's just how I am, Frank. Let's just say I haven't met the right person either."

"Have you ever been close?"

"No, I've never been close. Have you?"

"Yes, there was someone when I was at university. We were young, and I thought the world would be full of girls like her, so I let her slip through my fingers. I realise now that the world is not full of girls like her. I probably made the biggest mistake of my life."

"Oh, Frank, I'm sorry."

"It's the old story, isn't it? If I knew then what I know now, but I guess wisdom only comes with age."

"You're very candid, Frank. I wish I could be like you."

I felt the need to tell Frank I had never had a proper relationship at all, but something always prevented me. It's not that I thought he would make fun of me. I knew he would never do that. I lacked the confidence to admit to what I considered to be a shortcoming, an inadequacy if you like. My entire childhood and education were based upon achievement. The Stevenson family simply didn't fail; in this one regard, I was a complete failure. That's a big thing to admit to, and I certainly couldn't admit it to Frank.

## Chapter Fifteen
# July 1940

### Roger

*"It's tempting to view the past through the eyes of today.*
*Opportunities missed can be endowed with perfect endings."*

July is usually a delightful month - long, warm evenings spent watching the kids playing in the garden. Not so in 1940, as the country prepared for what the Prime Minister warned us would be coming. None of us knew what to expect, and the unknown is the worst enemy of all. I persuaded Marilyn not to bring the children home, and that decision now looked well-advised. She agreed with that decision, but accepting it was a different matter.

Dave and I had known each other since childhood. He was the best man at my wedding, as I was at his. Marilyn reluctantly agreed when I suggested the four of us should have an evening in the pub. I simply wanted to unwind with our friends, anything to relieve the tension we now lived with. We were a little late; Dave and Jean were already there when we arrived at the Fox and Hounds.

"Hello, Jean, how are you?"

"I'm fine, Roger. Thanks. How are you, Marilyn? Do you still feel under the weather?"

"Who said I was under the weather?"

"Well, I don't know. It must have been Dave."

"I wish you wouldn't talk about me, Roger. I'm fine; he imagines things."

"This feels strange, doesn't it?" Dave said. "Being able to go out together, with no kids to worry about."

"I still can't get used to it," Jean replied. Marilyn didn't answer.

"Did you hear anything, Dave, about this new spate of burglaries?"

"I spoke to one of my old lags, and he says they're not local. He said they were from north of the river."

"What did I tell you, Dave?" said Jean.

"Yes, sorry, Luv, I didn't see Roger this afternoon."

"He brings it home to me every night; I'm sick of hearing about it," Marilyn said.

"I give Dave half an hour each evening to get it off his chest, and then we talk about something else. It's most often the kids, but lately ... well, times are different, aren't they?"

"What on earth do you find to talk about if it isn't police work or the kids?" asked Marilyn.

"I grumble about how difficult it is to buy anything with the rationing, don't I, Dave? We talk about what's happening with the neighbours. You know, normal stuff. These days, of course, we discuss what's in the papers about the war. It's all about to change, isn't it?"

"Yes, it sounds like it," I said. "Hitler's poised and ready on the other side of the Channel."

"Why, then, are we sitting here pretending everything's normal when this pub might be full of German soldiers next week? This is why, isn't it; you think this might be the last time?"

"Don't get hysterical, Marilyn; we're a long way from that."

"Yes, twenty miles across the Channel."

"Roger's right, Marilyn. It might only be twenty miles, but we've still got the most powerful Navy in the world. Hitler isn't marching across the Channel anytime soon."

"And what makes you the expert, Jean?"

"I read the newspapers, Marilyn. I know what's going on. You should try it rather than sitting around feeling sorry for yourself all day."

"Stop it, Marilyn, it's bad enough at home. Jean's right: there's no way Hitler's just going to march into Britain. He can't launch an invasion force across the Channel as long as the RAF still operates. We have to assume the Battle of Britain means the battle for air supremacy. So yes, I suggested we go out together tonight because it might be the last time for a while. This isn't all about you, Marilyn; we must stand together as never before - we depend on each other."

Jean picked up another crisp from the bag, trying to look unconcerned. "Is that how you see it, Dave?"

"It is, Luv. I don't think any of us can imagine how bad this is likely to be. Look at Poland; thousands have been killed. It's no good pretending this isn't happening. At least the kids are all safe in the countryside."

"So you're both smug about that because I wanted them back. I can't help it if I miss my children, Jean, and you obviously don't."

"Don't answer that, Jean, it's not worth it," I said, but it was too late.

"How dare you. You moan and complain all the time. I don't know how Roger puts up with you. Complain all you want to him, but don't you dare tell me I don't care about my children, or so help me ..."

"Perhaps it's best if we go, mate, you stay and enjoy your beer. I'm sorry, Jean."

"It's not your fault, Roger, don't go."

"I think it's best, Jean."

Marilyn stood up, almost knocking her chair over. "I'm not staying here. You stay with Dave and your girlfriend. Don't wake me when you get home."

With that, Marilyn stormed out, leaving an awkward atmosphere around the table. She had done similar things before, but nothing that embarrassing. A part of me wanted to follow her, but it would be pointless and only prolong the argument.

"What the hell does she mean, 'your girlfriend'?" Jean asked.

"She doesn't know what she means, Jean, forget it. She accused me of making eyes at that ghastly woman in the bakery last week."

"You're joking. She's an awful woman.

"Look, this is all very embarrassing; can we just pretend it didn't happen?"

There was a long silence before Dave finally smiled.

"I secretly fancy that woman in the bakery - you can't blame Roger."

I nearly choked on my beer. We laughed; in fact, we each fell about laughing. Dave had broken the ice. Nothing would ever come between Dave and me, and he and Jean were inseparable. We met our future wives together at the Hammersmith Palais. It seems like only yesterday; they were sitting together at a table when the pair of them caught our attention. We had that brief discussion that blokes have at such times. I would head towards the brunette and Dave, the blonde. It's amazing how a decision that might affect the rest of your life can be taken with such little regard.

We met them again a few days later, and Jean and I looked at each other with an expression that posed a question. There was an undeniable spark between us, but it was already too late as if our decision had been cast in stone. Dave didn't want to admit it, but he'd fallen head over heels in love with Jean. He'd written his own script, and I was not about to challenge it. A few weeks later, he broached the subject over a pint after work.

"I'm seeing Jean again tomorrow; do you want to arrange something with Marilyn?"

"Yes, that sounds good, I'll ask her. You're seeing a lot of Jean, aren't you?"

"I'll be honest, Rog, it's getting serious between us. Do you think I'm being daft?"

"Are you kidding? I don't know what she sees in you, mate, but if I were you, I would never let her out of my sight."

I sat for a moment, pondering my impromptu response all those years ago. I said it without thought and realised immediately that I meant every word. Now, don't think for a second that after all the intervening years, I coveted my best mate's wife; it's nothing like that. What I coveted was their relationship. Jean is a lovely-looking woman, but much more than that; she's a delightfully warm, outgoing person who is just lovely to be with. It's tempting to view the past through the eyes of today. Opportunities missed can be endowed with perfect endings. I never mentioned it; I rarely allowed myself to even think about it. But there were just a few occasions when Dave and Jean reminded me of what I missed. It's the warm smile and the gentle touch of a woman. I missed that.

They were both such good friends and conscious of my embarrassment, and they did their best to lift my spirits. We walked on eggshells for the rest of the evening. Jean treated me as if I'd suffered a terrible family bereavement without ever mentioning why. The only time she mentioned the subject was when we left. I shook hands with Dave, and Jean put her arms around me.

"Marilyn will be fine, Rog. When the kids come home, you'll be back to normal."

Dave and I continued as usual the next morning at work, saying nothing about it. He wanted to follow up on his contacts concerning the new spate of thefts, while I needed to see Doctor Bartholomew, the pathologist. He'd left a message to say he had a report for me about the latest victim's clothing.

I had many dealings with Bartholomew over the years; I found him to be a most interesting man. Initially, I found his appearance and manner daunting. Obviously incredibly intelligent, he carried himself with an air of superiority. When we first met, I had the impression that I fell into the category of lesser mortal. He worked on many of my cases, and gradually, I commanded his respect. One evening, he took me by surprise when he suggested we go for a pint together; we had been friendly ever since.

"Come in, Inspector, how are you?"

"I'm fine, Doc, thank you. What have you got for me?"

"Not a lot, I'm afraid, but there are one or two small clues."

"Such as?"

"The clothing has been ripped apart in a frenzy. There's nothing methodical about it. The victim said she wasn't raped, but he felt the need to expose her body."

"Is there any trace of semen?"

"We don't have a conclusive test, but I would say not. This is all about domination. He wanted to defile the victim. Above all, his gratification is all about violence."

"So, in my language, I'm dealing with a madman, a sadistic monster."

"That would be a fair assessment, Inspector."

"What about the injuries?"

He reached for his notes and his pipe. I had to wait while he pressed fresh tobacco into the bowl and struck a match. It hissed and burst into life until he drew the flame down into the pipe.

"Yes, I've seen the victim and read the notes. I agree with the suggestion that she's been beaten with a rod or pole. All the injuries are to the front of the body. That suggests he inflicts them with the victim lying on the ground on her back. I would say he knelt between her legs and inflicted the injuries from that position."

"You paint a horrifying picture, Doc. Anything else?"

He casually blew smoke into the air. I could tell he had something interesting to tell me.

"Yes, one interesting finding. You mentioned each victim suffered from stinging eyes, so I looked for traces of irritants. I found a bioactive compound called piperine."

"What's that?"

"Pepper, just ordinary pepper, almost certainly black pepper. I found traces on parts of the clothing that the perpetrator would have gripped in his frenzy. So, I conclude he had it on his hands. The interesting thing is, I doubt he would want to risk touching himself, so he must have worn gloves."

"Now that is useful, Doc. So why pepper?"

"He doesn't want to risk the victim seeing him, which shows he didn't intend to kill them. It's premeditated, which confirms this is certainly not random. Pepper is ubiquitous and untraceable. The violence has increased with this last victim; does this indicate a pattern to you? Another increase in violence will almost certainly result in death. Do you think this is where he's going?"

"When you study serial killers as I have, Doc, one thing is constant: their behaviour is progressive. It starts with antisocial behaviour, which often involves things like brutality towards animals. There seems to be a point when their violence crosses a boundary, and from that moment on, it becomes progressive. We'll know when he crosses that boundary because he will abandon the eye irritant."

"That's a very chilling assessment, Inspector. I have to say you confirm everything I've read. The case files also tell us these people are notoriously difficult to track down at the best of times."

"Will you keep me informed, Doc?"

"I certainly will, Inspector, and I hope you find him."

As soon as I got back, I called a meeting at the station. I had already assumed most of what the doctor had told me, but the pepper and the gloves were a potential breakthrough.

"We must interview the women again with particular reference to gloves," said Dave, "and we must search the crime scenes again."

"I agree, Dave. It's not much, but it's something. Is there any point asking grocers and barrow boys about pepper?"

"What's the chance of a sinister-looking man being remembered for buying pepper?"

"None at all, Dave, but let's do it anyway."

Two women, including Marilyn, agreed the attacker might have been wearing gloves. Our search of the crime scenes found nothing, and the pepper enquiry predictably got us nowhere. We were into August, and Hitler had amassed an invasion force on the other side of the Channel. The mood in the country was one of foreboding. The only thing standing between us and an invasion was the RAF. We did the very best we could with the limited resources we had at our disposal, but maintaining our sense of purpose became all but impossible. Against us, we had to contend with the North London mob, who were conducting an increasing number of burglaries. They seemed undaunted by the prospect of an invasion; they went about their business as usual.

## Chapter Sixteen
# The Battle of Britain, August 5th, 1940

Emma

*"All that stood between us and defeat were those young pilots flying their Spitfires and Hurricanes. They faced overwhelming odds, but the spirit of the nation flew with each and every one of them."*

The 5th of August saw the start of the Battle of Britain. We saw the fighter planes above our heads daily; the ever-present drone of the Merlin engines in the Spitfires and Hurricanes became our daily companions. Newspapers and news broadcasts on the wireless provided us with the only news. We voraciously consumed the daily gruel of information, searching for any appetising morsels. Hundreds of German bombers and fighter planes were crossing the Channel every day, their mission to destroy the RAF. Everyone knew what was at stake - Mr Churchill had told us.

All that stood between us and defeat were those young pilots flying their Spitfires and Hurricanes. They faced overwhelming odds, but the spirit of the nation flew with each and every one of them. The national mood might have been described as apprehensive, but in reality, the chill wind of fear made us all tremble.

"Do you think we can believe the figures in the reports?" asked Ken.

"Probably not," replied Alex, "but maybe we can believe the message."

"Well, if the Germans are losing planes at anything near the rate they tell us, it can't go on, can it?" said Frank.

"You're not eating, Leo," I said.

"No, I don't seem to have much appetite these days. There's just a handful of pilots up there fighting to save this country, and we just carry on as usual."

"That's very profound for you, Leo," said Alex.

"One of the nurses asked me yesterday what would happen if the RAF lost this battle. I said we'll lose the war and be subjugated by Hitler's Third Reich. She burst into tears."

"That sounds a sensible reaction to me," I said. "If the RAF loses, she won't be alone."

"Churchill got it exactly right," said Alex. "He didn't say we had to do our duty. He deliberately used the term 'brace ourselves'. We go about our work because this is what holds the country together. We're what the RAF are fighting for."

"I know you're right, Alex, but I don't mind admitting I find it hard."

"We all do, Leo, but you're the one with the courage to admit it," I said.

"That's true. I think it, but I don't admit it, but that doesn't make it any less real," admitted Frank.

"Is that nurse the one I saw you holding hands with, Leo?"

"Oh, you noticed, Emma. Yes, I've been keeping it quiet."

"Why would you do that?" said Frank. "With an uncertain future, we all need to cling to the present."

"Or better still, cling to a nurse," laughed Ken.

As we laughed, I looked up, and through the tall windows, I could see a Hurricane flying over us with dense smoke trailing behind it. The whole canteen stood up and looked at it as a lone pilot struggled to get his plane home right above our heads. Perhaps he was injured; perhaps this proved to be his last struggle. Everyone in the canteen wished him a silent Godspeed.

I felt a terrible helplessness. Alex was right. We braced ourselves to our duty, but seeing that pilot, my duty seemed woefully inadequate. None of us said a word. We each sat in quiet contemplation. The sight of stricken pilots struggling with their burning fighter planes became an all-too-common sight. It never got any easier. A part of each of us reached up to every pilot. Hitler unleashed that mighty spirit; I felt it everywhere I went. Mr Churchill's words echoed in our ears: we would never surrender.

The next afternoon, Frank waved to me across the ward. Thinking it concerned a patient, I walked over to him.

"What are you doing tonight, Emma?"

He caught me totally by surprise; I expected something completely different. With nothing to qualify his question, it sounded as if he was asking me out. I had already demonstrated to Frank how hopeless I could be in social situations. Why would he ask me out? He obviously recognised my embarrassment.

"It's Leo. The boy wants to introduce his girlfriend to us. He asked me, but I would find it awkward. I need your support, Em."

Frank never called me Em. That's something my parents called me. My head spun. This all felt like a social disaster for me, but I would look foolish if I said no.

"Where are you going?"

"Only the pub. I'll give your door a knock at about seven. See you then."

With that, he walked off, leaving me to wonder what just happened. I didn't agree to anything. An hour later, I found myself changing my clothes and worrying about makeup. I seldom wore makeup, very seldom, but suddenly, I thought about it. I changed my clothes again, this time from a dress suit back to my first choice of a black dress. Then I decided on some lipstick. As the time approached seven o'clock, I removed the lipstick. When the knock on my door came, my heart jumped.

"Are you ready?"

"Yes, Frank."

I stood there, having obviously made some effort with my clothes, and Frank arrived in his usual threadbare cardigan. Feeling ridiculously overdressed, I gratefully put on a coat over my black dress.

"Well, come on then. I wonder how serious this girl is to Leo; I suspect it must be very serious."

"I've seen them together. I'm no expert with these things, but I would say he's besotted with her."

"Well, good for Leo. He's such a good-looking sod, I'm surprised it's taken this long."

We walked side by side out of the hospital, and I felt very conspicuous out of my white coat. British fighter planes and German bombers had filled the sky that day with the sound of their engines and the sight of their condensation trails. Now they had all returned to their bases; the evening air remained unusually quiet after the German bombers returned home for the night and the RAF had stood down. Our view from Westminster

Bridge was breathtaking. The late evening sun dipped into the western skyline, painting the underside of the clouds with a palate of pink and gold. The river mirrored it perfectly, adding its sparkling magic. To my right, Big Ben glowed in the soft light, as defiant as ever.

"Isn't it wonderful, Frank - this is what we're fighting for, isn't it?"

"I hadn't looked at it that way, but when you say it - yes, it is."

We walked on towards St Stephen's Tavern, and the war seemed to exist in a different place and time. Leo had already commandeered a table where he sat with his young lady. I recognised her immediately; I'd seen her around the wards on many occasions. Not knowing her name, I had only addressed her as 'nurse'. She always caught my eye because she was blessed with a face that you couldn't look away from. Her ebony hair and large brown eyes were captivating. Her hair, usually tied up in a bun, this evening hung down below her shoulders. I couldn't help thinking what a handsome pair they made as we walked towards the table.

"Evening, Leo," said Frank.

"May I introduce Gloria? This is Emma and Frank."

"Hello, Doctor Stevenson, Gloria Cummings. We haven't been introduced before, and Doctor Cooper."

"It's Emma and Frank, please."

"I'll try, but you get used to calling people by their title. Have you and Doctor Cooper been going out together for long?"

"Oh, no, we're work colleagues, that's all."

"Well, it's nice to meet you outside of the hospital. Actually, I wanted to talk to you. I'm just curious, really, you're the one some of the patients call Doctor Emma. They come into outpatients, and they ask for you."

"Yes, I'm sorry about that. I made the mistake of telling one or two of my former patients, and well, they've rather taken me at my word."

"I wanted to meet you; they speak so highly of you; it's lovely. We had an old gentleman come in the other day, a veteran of the last war. He asked if he could see the Angel of Balham."

"Yes, I saw him, Scotty Henderson. I'm sorry about that."

"We almost dismissed him; Sister thought he was being delusional."

"That delusional old man has more medals and awards than can be mounted on his chest. He's a veteran of Verdun and the Somme; a part of him has never come home. Your ward sister has probably never spoken to a greater man."

"I'm sorry, Doctor. I didn't mean to be disrespectful."

"Not your fault, Gloria. I get a bit emotional when I speak about Scotty and men like him. Call me Emma and tell us about you and Leo."

"The first time I saw Leo, I think I fell in love with him. It was just a fantasy, of course. I wasn't the only nurse to think the same thing. Then, when I noticed him looking at me, I dared to dream a little bit more. And then, about a month ago he walked up to me in the ward and said, 'Nurse Cummings, will you do me the honour of having dinner with me one evening'?"

"And what did you say?"

"I'll tell you what she said," replied Leo. "She said, as calm as you like, 'I thought you'd never ask'."

"That was a bit forward, Gloria," said Frank.

"I know. I was terrified of saying something ridiculous, so I blurted that out."

Leo sat with the smile of a Cheshire cat, and Gloria's brown eyes sparkled. I looked at Frank, and we shared the same expression. I knew nothing of these things, but I instinctively recognised the love between them, and it made me smile. The barmaid appeared with two more glasses of beer.

"I ordered these for you," Leo said.

I warmed towards Gloria; she was bubbly and outgoing, and she had something interesting to say about most things. Without her I would have struggled to make conversation with the men, but she made it all seem so easy. A part of her charm was looking so lovely; I noticed Frank swooned every time she smiled at him. What impressed me most about her was that she behaved as if her looks were not a part of who she was; she had greater confidence. I wondered if she would have that same confidence if she looked like me. The more I saw past her face, the more I realised she probably would.

We talked about the war, of course, but we also talked about our lives before the war, a time that had not yet been erased. Frank spoke about his childhood in Bedford and how he was the only kid in the street who went to university. He must have had a driving ambition to rise above his background and create such a successful career. None of that was reflected in the Frank I knew. Leo, on the other hand, came from a wealthy back-ground with every advantage family and status could provide.

I'd only seen the privileged and spoiled Leo, the Leo who would say flippant things that antagonised Alex. He was all those things, and his good looks gave him an even greater swagger. But that evening, I saw what lay behind the facade: a young man who didn't have the confidence of his bravado. It took something exceptional to make him step out from behind that facade. We didn't have to look far to realise what, or rather who, that was.

Two airmen walked into the pub looking tired and haggard. The moment they entered, the RAF's blue uniforms were a signal to the entire pub. A path to the bar cleared immediately, and each pilot received a hand on the shoulder or a touch on the arm; people further away clapped. Needless to say, they were not about to buy their own pints. The entire pub, us included, treated them as heroes, which, of course, they were. They needed a quiet pint, but instead, they were inundated with questions.

It was August 15th; what we didn't know was that Germany had just launched the largest attack on RAF airfields of their campaign. It became known as Eagle Day. Over 1000 German aircraft flew 1790 sorties. Those two pilots had probably been in the thick of it. I can't even imagine what they had been through or the memories tormenting them. They were prepared to say very little other than the Germans were suffering huge losses. When asked about our losses, they were more guarded. The pub fell silent as the pilots' thoughts turned towards their fallen comrades. Out of the silence, someone asked if we could win this battle, the Battle of Britain.

One pilot soberly looked up and spoke. "There isn't a pilot in the RAF who thinks otherwise."

A muted cheer came from the crowd as the two pilots raised their glasses. The people dispersed and left them to enjoy their beer. We looked at each other, and the pilots' presence seemed to put everything into perspective. Frank peered into his glass while Gloria and Leo looked towards each other for strength and found it. As Frank and I walked home that night, he said something that expressed exactly what I had been thinking.

"I've never seen Leo like that before; the two of them seem to be greater than the sum of their parts."

"I agree. That was a lovely evening, Frank."

"I've not seen you look so relaxed before, Em."

"Yes, they were easy to get on with. What's your opinion of Gloria?"

"Lovely, I mean a lovely person."

"She is, isn't she? The only other really attractive woman I know is my sister-in-law, and we hadn't got on together until recently; her looks intimidate me."

"I got to know you better tonight, Em, and I can't imagine why you would be intimidated by anyone."

"Then you don't know me at all, Frank. I'm socially awkward, I've no real-life experience, and I babble when I'm nervous."

"I don't recognise that person. You didn't babble tonight."

"I impressed myself, Frank. I got on well with Gloria; she didn't intimidate me, and I'm okay with you."

"That's good to know, Em."

"Only my family calls me Em."

"Oh, I'm sorry."

"No, I like it."

"Do you think we should do something like this again, Em?"

"What with Leo and Gloria?"

"Well, yes, but maybe also just us."

"I'm not sure, Frank. It would be different if we were alone."

"Of course, stupid thing to suggest, very unprofessional."

"It's not a stupid thing to say at all. I can say things to you, Frank. I'm just not used to that. Ask me again when I haven't drunk a pint of beer."

"Don't make a big thing of it, Em. I'm only suggesting a drink and a chat."

"It's a big thing to me, Frank."

"I would have thought all things would be possible for the Angel of Balham."

I playfully whacked him on the arm. "You promised you wouldn't bring that up."

"It's those wings. I couldn't resist it."

He hastened away from me, and I gave chase. The pair of us ran over Westminster Bridge laughing. It might have been a simple act of fun for some, but for me, this was something far more significant.

# Chapter Seventeen
# Joey Katz

Roger

*"Marilyn said more than once that I lived in a sewer and I came home smelling of it. I confess sometimes I didn't know where the sewer ended and the moral high ground began."*

The North London mob conducting the burglaries and robberies had trodden on several toes. Criminals have a strong, albeit misplaced loyalty. With most of the younger villains now being taught a different kind of loyalty, the old lags held sway. While one old lag would never be seen to grass on another, a casual hint was not unheard of. The North London boys stepped on the wrong toes when they entered Joey Katz's patch. Joseph Katz's family came to Britain as Jewish immigrants fleeing Russia in 1910.

In the perverted world of criminality, Katz sat at the top of the pile. In his South London 'thiefdom', nothing happened that he didn't know about, and nobody trod on his toes. Katz lived by old-fashioned values; in his world, the term 'honour amongst thieves' still applied, provided it accorded with his interpretation. He ran a legitimate and prosperous family business in the rag trade, and we could pin nothing on Katz. He skilfully hid behind his legitimate business, delegating his nefarious activities to underlings. Principal among those were his two sons, one of whom was rapidly gaining prominence, while Katz preferred a trouble-free life.

On August 18th, two men in the 'Kings Head' pub in Balham were badly beaten. Both were taken away in an ambulance. The local bobby on the beat knew his patch well and told me Katz ordered the beatings. I knew Joey Katz, professionally, that is; this is the world I inhabited. I had a simple choice with people like Katz - treat them as the villains they are or develop some kind of understanding. There are very few low life's who I am prepared to share a pint with, but Katz had the dubious honour of being one of them. He never crossed the red line; I had no option but to respect that. I had little doubt that the two men in the pub were a message. I called on Joey that same afternoon.

"It's been a long time, Inspector; I've missed our little chats."

"I was so sorry to hear about Eva, your wife, Joey. You must miss her terribly?"

"Grief is an exquisite pain, Inspector; you only realise that when you experience it."

"Have your boys been called up?"

"Yes, the older one, Aaron has; he's doing his bit for King and country. How's that lovely family of yours? Boy and girl, isn't it?"

"Evacuated, so at least they're out of harm's way."

"It's a bad time, Mr Pritchard. I didn't think I would ever see it again."

"This is not going to end well, is it, Joey? I hate to think about what the future holds. All we can do is muddle on, I suppose."

"That's what I say; I'm buying cloth in the hope there'll be a market for it tomorrow. Anything else would amount to surrender, and that's not going to happen."

"That's why we all muddle on. The reason I called is to do with that calling card you left me, Joey, in the 'Kings Head'."

"What calling card would that be, Mr Pritchard?"

"You know the one, those two toe-rags from north of the river."

"Oh, that calling card. I heard about that."

"Yes, that's the one. You see, it looks to me as if those boys might have trodden on someone's toes."

"That's what I heard, Mr Pritchard. I heard they overstayed their welcome."

"The trouble is, Joey, that might not be the end of it; they might not take kindly to that little disagreement - with whoever it was."

"I imagine that might be the case. Now you know me, Mr Pritchard, I would want nothing to do with that kind of thing."

"No, of course not, I understand that."

"It's probably best your lot remove that little problem, don't you think, Mr Pritchard?"

"I agree, Joey. I don't suppose you've heard anything that might help me do that?"

"Nobody in the rag trade would be involved in anything like that, Mr Pritchard. I could ask around though, you never know, do you?"

"You never do, Joey. I'll be off then; give my best to Aaron when you see him."

"And to yours, Mr Pritchard; don't leave it so long next time."

In Joey's world, we had just struck an unspoken agreement. He wanted the North London mob out of it as much as I did. If we didn't do it, he would, and that had the potential to become really ugly. Joey Katz was a pragmatist; he did nothing that wasn't in his own best interest. I had to create mutual understanding and trust with people like Joey; if it involved concession on my part, then so be it.

More than ever, it reminded me of the grubby world I inhabited and the people I had to associate with. Marilyn said more than once that I lived in a sewer and I came home smelling of it. I confess sometimes I didn't know where the sewer ended and the moral high ground began. I worried I carried the stench with me, regardless.

A few days later, the local bobby came by the name of a warehouse. He didn't initially connect it with anything important, but when he reported it to Dave, he spotted the connection immediately. The information came from a homeless man standing in the soup queue at the local volunteer centre. Except he wasn't homeless and he didn't wait for the soup.

We put the warehouse under surveillance, and what do you know, like a well-tended hive, the worker bees provided it with pollen nearly every day. I expected to see household goods from burglaries; I didn't expect black market produce, including dozens of cases of Johnny Walker Red Label whisky. We hadn't realised the gang was involved in the black market, not on such a large scale. With memories of the builder's yard raid fresh in my mind, Dave and I watched from a distance as the uniform bobbies went in.

When we entered the building, we found a treasure trove, including the gang, safely in handcuffs. It's rare in a policeman's life when a caper of such a size falls into your lap like that. Dave and I looked at each other in amazement. The local crime rate would plummet as a result. We expected to be welcomed back at Balham as triumphant heroes.

"Joey came up trumps this time, didn't he, Dave?"

"I can hardly believe it, he's just saved us goodness knows how many months' work. He could have taken the lot himself."

"I know him too well. Had his boys robbed that warehouse, the North London mob would have retaliated in a big way; we'd be looking at a gang war. For Joey, that would be bad for business. One of these days he'll cross the line, and I'll be there waiting, but until then, he knows which side his bread's buttered."

"Why don't we arrange for one of those cases of whisky to go Joey's way, kind of a little thank you from us?"

"I thought about that too, but it would put us on the wrong side of the law, Dave."

"Come on, Rog, you were thinking the same thing. Information like that's priceless, I reckon it's a small price to pay. Tell you what, why don't we ask Gerry - try to make it an official greasing of the wheels?"

"Good idea, mate. I'd like to see the bastard behind bars, but I would sooner have his cooperation than his opposition."

"I reckon Gerry's probably organising a celebration at the station right now."

"It's certainly worth celebrating; we haven't pulled off something such as this since I don't know when."

# Chapter Eighteen
# Mary Thompson

Roger

*"Death never takes a single life; it also steals the
lives of those the departed leave behind."*

In the middle of the Battle of Britain, with the future of the country
hanging by a thread, all Dave and I could think about was our triumph.
We entered the station expecting bunting around the incident room
and bottles of whisky. Imagine our amazement when we found Gerry
looking decidedly concerned.

"Well done, you two, but I've got bad news, it looks like he's back."

"Who's back?"

"You might be right about our night-time attacker, Roger. If it turns
out to be him, then he has crossed the line. There's a dead woman in
Clapham, on the Common."

"Oh, Christ, no. Do you think it is him?"

"Too early to say; get over there, Roger, now."

The euphoria of an hour ago evaporated like an early morning mist
and left that same chill in the air. Dave and I jumped in the car and rushed
over to Clapham Common. We hardly spoke on the way. A crowd had
gathered and the local bobbies were busy keeping the scene under control.
What greeted us turned my stomach, I had never seen so much blood
from one individual. She lay partly concealed by undergrowth and had
been there from the night before. The police photographer had done his
job, as had the local doctor.

I instigated a detailed search of the Common and called in more uniform coppers. The local doctor confirmed the time of death which placed the murder at about 11 pm the previous evening, but I needed a detailed forensic report and an identification. Dave and I combed every inch of the crime scene and I asked the photographer to take more photographs of some footprints we found. They could have been anyone's footprints, perhaps just a dog walker. Alternatively, they were close to the crime scene in some soft ground, so they could be our man; I asked for some plaster casts to be taken.

We'd done everything we could by the time the light faded, so I had the body moved to St Thomas's. A frantic mother had already reported her daughter missing and the description of her clothing matched, so it sounded as if we had our identification. Her name was Mary Thompson. Someone had the unenviable task of dealing with the family until a formal identification could take place. I could do nothing more until Doctor Bartholomew had seen the body. When Dave and I finally left the station late that night, we stepped out into the cool night air, hardly able to put one foot in front of the other. Fatigue inhabited every part of us.

Neither of us had any feelings left, our emotions stretched and frayed like the sails of a storm-tossed ship. We stared vacantly into the distance, as we walked away from the station. Neither of us had the strength to speak. We went our separate ways, both heading towards a bottle of whisky. I arrived home just before midnight to find Marilyn pacing the kitchen, her expression saying it all.

"What bleeding time do you call this?"

"I know, it's been a really long day."

"Yes, well, I have long days as well. I queued all bloody day for two miserable sausages and now look at it. Why should I bother when you don't give a shit?"

"I'm sorry, I should have telephoned."

"Yes, that's it, reach for the whisky bottle; that doesn't care when you arrive."

"Shut up, Marilyn, please, just shut up."

"I should shut up? You're the one who doesn't give a shit, don't you tell me to shut up. What have you been doing, who've you been with all this time? If you've been with another woman, Roger, so help me, you can get out right now."

"Yes, I've been with another woman, a dead woman. The man who attacked you probably murdered her. I've had enough, and I can't cope with anything else. Just leave me alone."

"All right, don't shout at me; why didn't you say?"

"I've just told you, but don't go repeating it."

"Where did it happen?"

"On the Common."

Marilyn slumped into a kitchen chair and poured herself a glass of the whisky. Neither of us said anything. I stared into the bottom of that glass until I could no longer focus on it. When I woke in the morning, I found myself sitting in the same armchair with a blanket over me. A full ashtray lay scattered on the floor. Marilyn appeared with a cup of tea, and neither of us said very much. Regret isn't like revenge; it's not best served cold.

"I should have phoned you yesterday, I'm sorry, I just had so much going on."

"I'm sorry about saying those things about another woman, I know you wouldn't do that. I just sit here getting more and more stewed up, and then when I let it all out, I don't even know what I'm saying half the time."

"I deserved it, you must have been worried sick."

"You did deserve it, but I wish I hadn't said it."

I looked at the clock and at Marilyn; she knew I had to go. She handed me a sandwich to take with me. Anything made with the so-called national loaf would not be very appetising, but I could see Marilyn had made an effort.

"Take this with you, it's better than nothing. Catch the bastard, Roger, I don't care if you have to come home late, just catch him."

"I will," I said as if I had command of the situation.

She put her arms around me, and we stood in the kitchen hugging each other. I left and went straight to St Thomas's and down into the basement where I found Bartholomew standing over the body laid out on a dissection table. It's not a sight you ever get used to, or want to get used to. With the body cleaned of blood, the extent of her injuries was immediately obvious. I mumbled something to the effect of 'good morning' but beyond that, we didn't exchange any pleasantries; I simply asked - how many times?

"She's been stabbed 39 times. There are entry wounds on almost every part of her body. Some wounds are extended, indicating he exerted considerable lateral force."

"The weapon?"

"A long single-edged blade, an inch wide and at least seven inches long. Could be a kitchen filleting knife."

"Left- or right-handed?"

"Right."

"How did he hold the knife?"

"Thumb at the top of the handle. He stabbed downwards; all the entry wounds extend in the same direction."

"Can you determine his position relative to the victim?"

"Yes. The victim would have been flat on the ground; he would have been kneeling between her legs. All the wounds radiate from that position, the same as the previous victims."

"Strangulation marks, as before?"

"Yes."

"Cause of death?"

"One of the stab wounds penetrated the heart. The blood loss indicates at least some wounds were perimortem."

"Sexual assault?"

"Her clothes were partly removed, but she hasn't been raped and I can find no trace of semen."

"He didn't rape her, so once again, this is pure sadistic violence?"

"There is a sexual element, but it's about defiling the victim. So yes, this is sadistic violence."

"This is him, isn't it?"

"There's no evidence that it is, but the way the attacks have progressed and the location, I would say almost certainly, yes. There's one more thing, there's no irritant in the eyes. Either this is another man, or he deliberately set out to kill her."

"So, assuming it's him - he's crossed the threshold; he's become a fully-fledged monster."

"It looks like it, yes. Morning, Inspector."

"Yes, sorry. Morning, Doc."

"Inspector, I've had corpses in here that look better than you. Have you had any sleep?"

"Not really."

"Look, I've been up most of the night as well, I've done all I can here. You look as though you need breakfast."

"How can you eat breakfast after this?"

"You get used to it, I promise you."

"But she was a lovely young woman with all of her life ahead of her. Does this not fill you with rage and horror?"

"If it did, Inspector, I couldn't do my job, and the same applies to you. I'll take you to the canteen."

We left the mortuary attendant with the unenviable task of preparing the body for identification. I wanted no part of that harrowing experience. Death never takes a single life; it also steals the lives of those the departed leave behind. For the woman's loved ones, life would never be the same.

Bartholomew returned minus his white coat, wearing a Savile Row three-piece suit. I had to wait while he went through the ritual of pressing tobacco into the bowl of his pipe and then the ritualised lighting with a match. He then pointed the way forward with the pipe stem, using it as an army officer might use his swagger stick. As we walked towards the canteen, he looked like something out of a tailor's shop window, while I looked like something out of the tailor's dustbin.

I couldn't face anything to eat after what I'd just seen, but he insisted, and I soon found myself standing in line with a tray. The canteen heaved with doctors and nurses, a sea of white coats and uniforms ebbing back and forth between the tables. I felt decidedly conspicuous in my crumpled suit, while I got the impression that Bartholomew enjoyed being conspicuous in his tailored masterpiece.

Marilyn had queued all day for two sausages and here there were trays of them. I couldn't believe my eyes as one was placed on my plate, together with an egg and a rasher of bacon. A large mug of tea followed. Bartholomew marched towards one of the few vacant tables, tray in hand. I walked behind, enveloped in a trail of his pipe smoke. An unfortunate person seemed to be heading towards the same table. Bartholomew looked up imperiously, and following an imperceptible movement of his head, the junior doctor quickly stepped aside subserviently.

Once seated, I looked down at the plate before me with eyes that strained to focus. He placed his pipe to one side as if parting with it amounted to an emotional farewell. Then, oblivious to the horrors he'd just witnessed, he plunged a fork into the egg. I tried to do the same but couldn't remove the image from my mind.

"Close your eyes, Inspector. Concentrate on what your taste buds tell you and imagine what it looks like rather than looking at it."

It worked to a degree. Anything to banish the image in my mind.

"Anything you can add, Doc?"

"I've taken samples and will continue testing, but at this stage, I can't offer you much more than you already know. She was murdered where you found her and the local doctor's estimate for the time of death is accurate. So far, I've found nothing on the body nor the clothes that might help you, but that work will go on. If the killer has left traceable evidence of himself, such as clothes fibres, I will find them."

As I struggled to continue, I heard a familiar voice from behind me. "Morning, Alexander, don't often see you here for breakfast."

"Morning, Emma, this is Inspector Pritchard."

"Inspector, we meet again."

"Do you two know each other?"

"Let's just say we've bumped into each other. How have you recovered from your injuries, Inspector?"

"Thanks to you, Doctor, I'm fine."

"What are you doing here?"

"Police business, I'm afraid."

"Oh, I see. You've been down to the dungeon with Doctor Bartholomew."

She sat with us and chatted to Bartholomew about a patient. I felt like a spare part in a repair shop waiting to be useful. She glanced at me and then at him, no doubt noticing the contrast between the tailor's shop window and the tailor's dustbin. I hadn't shaved or changed my clothes that morning; only then did I appreciate how awful I must have looked to her. She spoke with that warm soft voice of hers, while he obviously tried to impress her. It's my job to notice these things; people give away a lot about themselves without intending to.

He straightened his tie and looked her in the eye with a smile, attentive to her every word. She seemed indifferent to his attention, neither flattered nor impressed, perhaps just oblivious. Her interest centred on the patient she wanted to discuss. I could sense her deep concern. She wanted advice about the patient's condition, so I decided it would be better for me to leave. I had what I came for and sitting next to Bartholomew, I now felt less like a spare part and more like a broken part. I stood up, making my apologies.

"Don't leave because of me, Inspector. You came to see Doctor Bartholomew, and I've monopolised him with my concerns for my patient. Your concerns will be just as important; I bet it's something really interesting. Forensic pathology has always interested me; I must leave you two alone."

She stood and gestured for me to sit back down by touching my arm. Having graciously walked away a few paces, she half-turned and gave us a wave and a smile. It seemed an almost childlike gesture, immediately reminding me of my daughter Mary.

"She's something, isn't she?" Bartholomew said.

"I don't know her, but she made an impression on me when I was a patient here."

"Yes, a lot of patients say that. I can't pin it down; she's very reserved and difficult to get close to. I suppose that's the challenge really; we always want what we're not supposed to have."

"What do you mean?"

"Oh, nothing. Eat your breakfast, Inspector."

I knew precisely what he meant, and I didn't care for it. Choosing not to comment, I looked down at my breakfast, but I couldn't face it. Professionally, I had to admit Bartholomew was brilliant, probably the sharpest man I have ever known. Personally, I began to find him ever more arrogant. I got the impression that he expected women to swoon at his feet, but if like Doctor Stevenson, they didn't, then he regarded that as a challenge to be overcome. In my job, you need to detect those character traits that people often let slip. Bartholomew had just done exactly that. His attitude towards women concerned me; he didn't just have an excess of male bravado, there was something of the predator about him.

The little I knew about Doctor Stevenson told me she may well have been reserved and difficult to get close to. She dressed plainly and didn't exploit her femininity at all, but I found her to be charming. The little wave she gave us spoke of a child-like innocence, and I had no doubt that had become the object of Bartholomew's challenge. Perhaps I misread the situation, but if I hadn't, then that would cross a red line for me. I can tell you, the way he looked at her made me feel uneasy. I thanked Bartholomew for his initial report, but as I left to go back to the station, I couldn't help wondering if my concerns about him were genuine or unfounded. Either way, it had nothing to do with me, so I dismissed it. I had enough to worry about.

# Chapter Nineteen
# August 20th, 1940

## Emma

*"We clung to what we cherished most in the here and now
and abandoned all hopes and dreams that dared to exist
in that most uncertain of places - the future."*

For months, our daily gruel of news contained nothing to sustain either mind or body. The prospect that German forces were preparing to invade us affected us all the same. We clung to what we cherished most in the here and now and abandoned all hopes and dreams that dared to exist in that most uncertain of places - the future. It reflected in our faces, not least among those already weakened by illness.

During August, our daily gruel contained some crumbs of sustenance. The RAF had not been defeated. German losses were considerable; the Battle of Britain seemed to swing in our favour. Even a single candle brings light into the darkness, but the Prime Minister's announcement on August 20th brought the blinding light of salvation into our lives.

*"Never in the field of human conflict was so much owed by so many to so few."*

(Winston Churchill, House of Commons speech August 20th, 1940)*

I can't imagine a form of words that could better express the nation's gratitude than those expressed by Winston Churchill. The German Luftwaffe could no longer sustain its enormous losses. The Battle of Britain had been won. Among the patients in the hospital wards, the atmosphere reflected that of the nation.

"How are you feeling today, Mr Williams?"

"Bloody marvellous. I got out of bed for the first time this morning and managed to go to the toilet by myself. What a treat that was, I can tell you."

"I'm delighted, Mr Williams; going to the toilet by yourself shouldn't be underestimated, should it?"

"Too right, Doc."

"You've suffered a nasty infection, Mr Williams, and we still have to deal with your blood sugar. You must change some aspects of your diet, and I want you to cut down on the amount of beer you drink."

"I know, Doc, you already told me."

"So will you do it, Mr Williams - I mean, really do it?"

"My missus tells me I have to do as you say; she thinks the sun shines out of your - well, you know."

"I shall be keeping an eye on you, Mr Williams. I promised your wife, Rose, I would get you through this, and I'm not about to let her down. If I find out you're still drinking pints of beer every night, you'll have us both to contend with, okay?"

"Cor blimey, what's a bloke to do with a doctor like you and his missus watching over him?"

"Best do as you're told, I'd say."

"What are you doing here, Doctor Stevenson?" asked Doctor Wiśniewski in a raised voice.

"I looked in on this patient. Why - is there a problem?"

"Yes, there is a problem. This is not your patient."

"I'm just taking an interest. I know this gentleman."

"You know him. This is totally unprofessional. I've told you about this before. You cannot give preference or have preferred patients - what on earth are you thinking? This is precisely what I warned about when you imposed yourself upon this hospital. You are a distraction, Stevenson."

"Oi, don't you talk to her like that," shouted Rob Williams. "If you gave us patients one-tenth of the care she does, we'd all be better off."

"Be quiet, Mr Williams. This does not concern you."

"You what? I'm the flipping patient you're talking about."

"Exactly, Mr Williams, you are a patient. Leave these matters to people who know best."

"Right! Why don't you ask some people in this ward who they think knows best, and I can tell yer it won't be you, mate."

"That's enough, Mr Williams," I said, "Doctor Wiśniewski is quite right. You aren't my patient and I shouldn't be interfering. I apologise, Doctor. I'll leave Mr Williams in your capable hands."

Rob Williams protested again, so I gave him a knowing look and a wink. He smiled and finally shut up, much to my relief. I knew how to handle Wiśniewski by then. Given a sufficiently large piece of humble pie to gloat over, he usually let me be. He would be content for the moment if I'd been put in my place and adequately humiliated. As I hastily left the ward, nurse Janet Walters spoke to me.

"I was going to ask you to look at Isobel Armstrong, Doctor Stevenson. She isn't responding to treatment, but it's probably not the right moment."

"No, it's probably not, Janet. I'm in enough trouble already. Tell you what, when he's gone, I'll come back to look in on Isobel."

"She keeps asking for you; that's the trouble."

"Isobel's an incredible lady, isn't she? Did you know she served as a nurse in the last war? There are many veterans of Passchendaele and the Somme who owe their lives to Isobel."

"No, I didn't realise that. Oh, good heavens, I feel awful that I didn't know."

"Talk to her, Janet, ask her about it. I don't doubt it was the most rewarding time of her life, but it was also the worst. To recall the one is to recall the other, and so for years, she's never spoken of it - it remained locked in her memory like a rotten apple. She'll be reluctant to speak of it, but you watch the weight lift from her shoulders if she does. If you want to see Isobel recover, get her to talk about it."

"How do you do it, Doctor? How do you know all this?"

"It's like I know you're preoccupied with something else; something's troubling you, isn't it?"

"I didn't realise it showed. I'm sorry."

"Do you want to talk about it sometime?"

"I can't believe I'm saying this, but alright, I will."

"I'll meet you in the canteen tonight, about 7.30. Will that be okay?"

"Well, yes, if that's alright with you."

Marion caught sight of me delaying one of her nurses, and she gave me one of her looks. I gave her a wave, and she beckoned me over.

"Sorry, Marion, I got chatting."

"No, that's alright. I wanted to mention dinner at Evelyn's on Friday."

"She already mentioned it to me. Yes, I'm looking forward to it."

"Good. I saw Wiśniewski giving you a hard time again. I don't know how you put up with it, Emma."

"I don't have an option, Marion. He's my superior, and I need to keep him sweet somehow."

"Well, credit to you; if he spoke to me that way, I'd give him a piece of my mind."

"Now that I would like to see. I'm off to talk to Doctor Bartholomew in the dungeon. Perhaps a spell in the mortuary will lift my spirits."

She laughed and wished me well. I gave Janet a wave as I made my way into the bowels of the hospital. People think the mortuary smells of dead bodies, but mostly it doesn't. You're much more likely to find the smell of Formalin and disinfectant. I wanted to go down to the basement and talk to Alexander about chlorine gas, but I kept putting it off. Silly, really, because I found him to be a most engaging man. That might, of course, have been the reason for my hesitancy. He could be insufferably superior at times, but never with me. He always showed me respect, something that could be sadly lacking in other quarters.

The bowels of the hospital reflected their Victorian heritage the further down you went. The white tiles had decorative mouldings and freezes; all felt very clinical. As I walked down the steps, my low heels echoed back and forth between the tiled surfaces. Having already announced my presence, I breezed in as if it had been a spur-of-the-moment decision and not something I had been building myself up to for days.

"Hello, Alex. Can I come in?"

"Emma, how nice to see you - you've dared to enter the catacombs."

"Yes, they really do keep you in the cellar, don't they?"

"I found the autopsy notes you wanted on those two gas victims."

"What I'm interested in is the specific causal agent of the permanent damage. The initial pulmonary oedema wouldn't cause such extensive damage; men like my father never recover their lost lung function."

"When you look at the lung under the microscope during an autopsy, I'm afraid it's all too obvious. The alveoli are destroyed."

"But some victims make something of a recovery?"

"I presume it depends not only upon the concentration of gas inhaled, but the duration is also probably important. The sinister thing about chlorine gas is that it undergoes chemical reactions while in the lungs. It transforms into hydrochloric acid."

"Oh my God. No wonder the damage is permanent. My poor father. So once that occurs, there's obviously no chance of the damage being repaired."

"None at all. The worst of it is that so many of those victims continue to smoke, which then destroys the function of whatever lung capacity they have left."

"How serious is smoking then?"

"Oh, be in no doubt, Emma, it kills you. Come and look at some specimens."

He took me into a back room where the walls were lined with shelves, and those shelves were full of glass jars of every conceivable shape and size, each one a triumph for the glass blowers who produced them. Those jars contained all kinds of anatomical specimens preserved in formalin. Undoubtedly macabre, but for someone like Bartholomew, and I confess for me, they were fascinating. Without a moment's hesitation, he directed me towards the lung specimens; he knew precisely where to find them. A pristine lung from an otherwise healthy individual who never smoked sat there next to the lung of a smoker who died of lung cancer. It was horrific.

"Need you ask if smoking kills, Emma?"

"This is something I've never seen before. As you say, the evidence is obvious."

"What you can see is the buildup of tar, but it's not only what you can see, Emma. We're discovering new chemical compounds in the tar every year, and all those chemicals are being absorbed through the lungs, potentially causing serious effects."

"I told my father to stop smoking even before I qualified; it seemed an obvious thing to do. Thank heavens he listened to me."

"You had a good instinct, Emma."

"I have to ask, Alex. What are you working on for that police inspector?"

"It's a murder victim, a young woman."

"Oh my goodness - you mean someone has been killed around here?"

"Yes, Clapham Common. A vicious attack, she was stabbed many times, an awful business."

"That's terrible. Do the police have any idea who's behind it?"

"No, but Inspector Pritchard is a good man. He's not like the others I work with; they're not just victims to him - he seems to take it all personally. If he can't find the murderer, it won't be for the want of trying."

"I'm pleased to hear it."

"Look, Emma, it's a bit forward, but would you have dinner with me one evening?"

I froze. He just said it out of the blue. I didn't have time to think. He caught me by surprise. I never thought for a second he would ever suggest such a thing. I didn't know what to say or how to react. In my panic, words came out of my mouth that didn't seem to belong to me. Silly things about how busy the next few days were going to be, and anyway, I already had a dinner engagement at the end of the week. Perhaps I expected him to ask if I intended to dine anywhere exciting. To which I would say, 'Oh no, nothing exciting, it's just a meal at home with Evelyn and Marion.' But he didn't say that.

"Oh, what a shame, Emma. I shall have to take the view that my disappointment is someone else's good fortune. I presume I may ask again at a more opportune time?"

"Yes, well, that's ... a shame."

I remember thinking, 'Shut up, Emma, don't make it worse.'

"I must call in again, Alex."

"Indeed, you must, Emma; my door is always open, as they say."

As I walked back up the stairs, I felt utterly ridiculous. He would have seen my face flush and listened to my nervous babble. What must he have thought of me? I noticed that the nurses' heads would turn whenever he appeared, and he had a way of acknowledging their attention without appearing obvious. Most women would undoubtedly consider him a very attractive older man, but I found that intimidating. If I could exclude all the relationship stuff that frightened me, I might even have enjoyed sharing dinner with Alexander. I chose instead to dine with two middle-aged women.

I hadn't forgotten about meeting Janet in the canteen that evening. I enjoyed not having to consider my appearance or worry about what clothes to wear. I changed out of my dress suit and put on a simple dress, the first one that came to hand. Most of the staff wore uniforms to the canteen, which always provided anonymity, so I put my white coat back on over my yellow dress. Only as I walked towards the canteen did I question what Janet might want to discuss with me, and it immediately became blindingly obvious. Janet was a nice girl in her mid-twenties and quite pretty, but above all else, she had an outgoing, engaging personality, all the things that I'm not. If she had a problem, then no doubt it concerned a man, and who was I to advise on such matters? It occurred to me that I should ask for her advice.

"Hello, Doctor Stevenson, this is kind of you to give me some of your time."

"Nonsense, Janet, it's a pleasure, but I'm not sure if I can advise you."

"I can't think of anyone else I'd feel comfortable to talk to, Doctor Stevenson."

"That's a kind thing to say, Janet. So, first thing, when we're not in the wards, call me Emma, please."

"That would be nice, thank you. I'll get straight to the point, Emma. My boyfriend has proposed to me."

"Well, congratulations, Janet, what's the problem?"

"It's simple: I won't be able to work as a nurse if I'm married."

"Oh, I see. I'm not sure that's a strictly enforced regulation, but it is customary for nurses to leave the profession when they marry. So your dilemma is that you want both?"

"I love him, you see, but I love my work as well. I just don't know what to do."

"Does he understand your dilemma?"

"No, he doesn't. Barry thinks I should put our marriage first. We had a row about it."

"Now I understand why you're distracted. Is Barry in the forces?"

"Yes, he's an engineering officer in the RAF."

"I can't advise you about your relationship with Barry. I don't understand these things myself, let alone advise someone else. But what I can tell you is that you're a superb nurse, Janet. The war is going to get considerably worse as time goes on. This hospital is likely to become full of war victims, broken and bleeding people who will desperately need our help. We will be all that stands between life and death for hundreds, perhaps thousands, of people. Terrible decisions will have to be made, decisions that should only be asked of God. This is what we trained for, Janet; this is our moment to serve the country.

There's something my father told me the day war was declared. He said the whole world rejoices when a single life is saved. To save a life is the greatest gift anyone can possess. You have that gift, Janet. You have the power to make the whole world rejoice. You mustn't abandon it, Janet. So many people will need you."

She looked me straight in the eye, and tears rolled down her face unashamedly. "I've never considered it in those terms before; you're right. It's what I must do. I don't have a choice."

"Yes you do; explain to Barry that just as he has his duty to perform, so do you. When you both understand that, then you can talk about your relationship together. You've been having the wrong discussion. This isn't about your future as a nurse; it's about how you and Barry work around it."

"Barry did once suggest that we move in together, but I can't imagine doing such a thing. My mum would never speak to me again."

"This is where I can't advise you, Janet. I'm hopeless at relationships, but I must admit, moving in together before you marry does sound rather scandalous. I'm sure your mum would disapprove."

"Oh, Emma, you must know what it's like. I long for him all the time. We have days apart now, sometimes weeks. When we meet, nothing else in this horrible war-torn world exists; it's just me and him. I feel we're two halves of the same person, and I'm only a whole person when there's no space between us. I can't live without him, Emma."

"I've never heard love described that way before; what you describe sounds truly wonderful."

"Have you never felt like that?"

"No, I haven't, but I've never missed it before, not until now."

"I'm sorry, I shouldn't be asking you that. I just assumed you'd understand."

"You understand a lot more than I do, Janet."

"Has the right person simply not come along for you?"

"I suppose that's it, although I'm not sure if I would recognise that person if he came along."

"I don't understand, Emma, you're a really lovely person - you must have offers all the time."

"Funnily enough, Doctor Bartholomew just asked me to go to dinner."

"What did you say?"

"I made excuses."

"I must say, for an older man, he's quite a dish, isn't he? But I think you should look for someone younger."

"To tell you the truth, I don't actually look for anyone. I suppose I'm a bit frightened and intimidated by the whole thing, really."

"Well, I can't think why, I'm sure. You have a wonderful way with people; the patients love you."

"I'm fine with patients, including the men; it's relationships. But look, we came here to talk about your problems, not mine."

"Yes, of course, I'm sorry. What you said, Emma, leaves me with no decision to take. I think in my heart I always knew, so thank you."

"Will Barry accept your decision?"

"You're so right, Emma; we've been having the wrong discussion. It's not about whether I stay as a nurse but what we do because I'm a nurse. He will have to accept it - we'll have to delay getting married."

"I never thought I would suggest such a thing, but if you can't bear to be apart, don't be. These are not normal times, Janet; make your commitment and live together."

"Emma, I'm shocked. But I agree, we must be together and to Hell with anyone who disapproves, including my mum."

"Before this evening, I would never have suggested such a thing, but what I saw in your eyes has taught me something, and you've changed my mind."

"What did I do?"

"You were honest. When you speak about Barry, your eyes well up; if that were me, I would hide my face, but you don't."

"I didn't realise I do that."

"That's the point; what you feel for Barry is such a part of you; it would be like concealing your breath. I need to thank you, Janet. I think you've helped me far more than I've helped you."

"I don't want to say the wrong thing, Emma, and I would hate to say anything that might cause you offence. But can I say I hope you find what I have with Barry? It's the most wonderful thing I've ever experienced, and I wish it for you."

I quickly realised that Janet was outspoken and happy-go-lucky, but I hadn't expected her to be so perceptive. She blew into my world of quiet reserve as a breath of fresh air. I'd never had a close friend I could confide in; Janet made that role her own.

# Chapter Twenty
# The Blitz, September 7th, 1940

Roger

*"Fear has a presence of its own. It inhabits you,*
*a malign entity that takes control of every function."*

The dead woman, Mary Thompson, was a twenty-five-year-old young woman from Clapham who had been walking home from a friend's house. Her regular route took her along Windmill Drive, next to the Common, at about 9 pm. We could be reasonably sure that the assailant walked up behind her and grabbed her round the neck with a stranglehold, dragging her onto the Common. We sat in the station, trying to fit the pieces together.

"There must be something these women have in common; a reason he chose them?"

"The trouble is, Dave, it might just be that the common factor is - they're all young women."

"Roger's right," said Gerry, "they were all in their twenties."

"Perhaps we're missing the obvious," said Jeff. "The victims were all out at night after dark, and in each case, they were going home."

"Yes, but we found no connection between where they'd been," said Dave.

"Correct, but I can see what Jeff means," I replied. "The connection isn't the activity; it's the fact that they each did it regularly. Marilyn visited her parents every Thursday evening. Angela Meadows' book club was every Tuesday evening. Let's check to see if the other victims had regular engagements."

"What can we say about the perpetrator, Roger?" asked Gerry.

"The stranglehold tells us something. Most people are unfamiliar with that type of hold; it closes the throat and shuts off the carotid artery immediately. It implies some kind of training. He also lifted Angela Meadows off her feet, which takes considerable strength, and it tells us he's probably quite tall."

"What about the man himself, Guv? You've studied these things," asked Alfie.

"If he becomes a serial killer, and I think he will, there are traits these monsters share. He will be psychopathic, he'll have no empathy, no remorse, and he'll be impulsive. To outsiders, he'll appear to be charming, but inwardly, he's likely to be narcissistic and manipulative. The fact they're addicted to their perversion tells us they may have other addictive traits."

"I thought you only helped old ladies across the road, Roger. How the hell do you know all this stuff?"

"I went through Hendon College, and I read, Guv. I study these things; we're detectives, remember?"

"So this is why you're sure this is the same bloke. You can see a pattern?"

"That's right, Alfie. The irritant in the eyes shows it's obviously the same man. The only doubt is this killing, but it fits the pattern of progression. This bloke didn't just wake up one morning and decide to attack women. He has built up to this. If you look at infamous cases like 'The Ripper', it seems likely he committed offences before his attributed murders and probably even committed previous murders. The murder victim Martha Tabram might well have been one of his, and an earlier survivor, Annie Millwood, may have been a Ripper victim.

I suppose in their perverted minds, as they gain experience and confidence, they need to progress onto what, for them, are more fulfilling achievements. If you look at the Ripper's known murders, they became increasingly more grotesque until he reached what for him was the climax of his reign of terror with Mary Jean Kelly. What he did to her body creates a picture of someone who we would be frightened even to imagine."

"Are you sure you're not getting ahead of yourself, Rog?" said Dave. "He's not exactly Jack the Ripper."

"I agree, but the pattern of events is troubling me. I've dealt with murderers and rapists in the past, but they nearly always commit similar crimes. This bloke has built upon each event progressively with more and more violence. We know he set out to kill her because he didn't use the pepper. That means this is pure sadistic violence. He's on a path that will only stop when we stop him. If I'm right, he'll probably have a serial killer in mind that he wants to emulate and show us how much better he is."

"This is all just speculation. He's killed once; we have no real reason to think this is the start of a series of killings," said Jeff. "This is nothing more than your gut feeling, Guv."

"I agree, Jeff; perhaps I'm worrying unnecessarily, but I feel I'm right."

"What's that noise I can hear?" Dave said.

"It sounds like the air-raid siren," replied Alfie.

"It is the siren; it must be a test or something," Jeff said.

"Nobody warned us," Dave replied. "Perhaps I'd better ask the sarge, see if he knows about it."

The siren started slowly and then gradually wound up into that awful wailing sound. It was 4 o'clock in the afternoon, and we didn't know what to make of it. We looked at each other incredulously, convinced it must be a drill or perhaps just a test. Our ambivalence came to an abrupt halt when Dave returned with Jack, the station sergeant, who announced that this wasn't an exercise. German bombers were flying over London.

"Are you sure? I can't hear anything," I asked.

Jack had been a sergeant major in the last war; he ruled the station with reassuring authority. He stood to attention, his back as straight as a board, no doubt thinking we looked like a bunch of bewildered schoolboys.

"Yes, quite sure, a message from Civil Defence. Perhaps we should make our way down to the detention cells, gentlemen, and in an orderly fashion if you please."

Dave said he'd quickly go outside to have a look, so I went with him. The siren had just wound down, leaving a ghostly echo reverberating among the buildings. One or two people hurried about, but apart from that, the streets of Balham remained unusually quiet. It seemed almost incomprehensible that German bombers would drop high explosive bombs on London. The destruction would be devastating. Surely it couldn't happen? We both clung to that comforting delusion until we heard the distant sound of aeroplanes.

High in the southern sky, the unmistakable sight of two fighter planes rapidly approached us. This had become such a common sight and sound during the Battle of Britain that we no longer reacted to it until that moment. The two Hurricanes sped over us, silhouetted against the high white clouds. The notion that two Hurricanes might halt the advancing

German bombers made an appealing narrative we both embraced.

Dave and I looked at each other, desperately wanting to dismiss the whole thing as a false alarm. The unthinkable is precisely that. When something truly awful threatens you, it simply doesn't conform to your worldview. When that terrible moment arrives, and the unthinkable happens, it does so abruptly. One second, all is well; the world appears exactly as you imagine it should. The next second, reality rolls over you like a tidal wave. Dave saw the approaching bombers a second before I did, and the realisation of what was about to happen caused us both to stare in numbed silence.

Initially, they were only specks in the sky, hundreds of them, like a swarm of bees approaching from the east. The sound belatedly followed the vision. Beneath the distant drone of engines, flashes of light illuminated the eastern sky, and billows of black smoke rose in the distance above the rooftops. Seconds later, the sound of explosions filled the air. Reality makes a cold companion when it's thrust upon you with no warning.

"Fuckin' hell!" shouted Dave, with eyes as wide as saucers.

"Run, mate, down to the cells."

We ran into the station like frightened rabbits, crashing the doors against the walls. We ran as if the swarm of bees was three feet behind us, biting at our heels. The boys were all standing in the two largest cells, not knowing what to do. Everything changed as we burst through the doors. Fear has a presence of its own. It inhabits you, a malign entity that takes control of every function. Dave and I didn't need to say a word; our worst imaginings went before us. We stood clutching our gas masks, each of us alone with our darkest thoughts, when a single moment of clarity sprang into existence.

"Oh God, what if our wives and families aren't in shelters?" Alfie said.

The anxiety rose into my throat. I almost welcomed the approaching German bombers; I could replace my fear of the unknown with a real and present danger. It seemed to last forever, one wave of bombers after another. It didn't matter if I stood or sat; the tension made my back and shoulders ache. We each tried to remain calm. Nobody wanted to appear afraid, but in truth, we were terrified.

All the while, the sound of exploding bombs remained exactly that, just distant sounds. It lasted for two hours, and when finally it came to an end, a deathly silence filled our senses. We looked at each other, daring to believe that our worst fears had not come true. The pendulum of fear swung in the opposite direction to be replaced by its alter ego. One by one, we laughed and made jokes. Nonsensical involuntary humour filled the air as the tension drained from our bodies.

The detention cells had no windows, and so none of us knew what horrors existed in the world outside. Nobody said, 'Let's go outside'; it just happened spontaneously. We stepped through the door, almost afraid to look. The evening sun had dipped below the rooftops, but rather than the western horizon reflecting shades of red and gold, the east of London was glowing against the smoke-filled sky. Smoke and the residual smell of high explosives filled the air. The unearthly sight of London burning sent a chill down my spine, but Balham remained unscathed as far as we could see.

People emerged from their garden shelters or even from beneath their staircases, and one by one, they gathered outside. My abiding memory is silence; no cars or lorries were moving. The people just stood, speechless. The local area appeared to have been spared, but the silence reflected the obvious fact that just a short distance away, hundreds of people must be dead or dying, and many more homes razed to the ground.

When the intoxication of simply being alive subsided, our thoughts turned immediately to our families. I wanted to go home as quickly as possible, but as we filed back inside the station, Jack had already collected his uniform bobbies together to give them a lecture. Dave and I had no option but to stand and listen.

"Well done, gentlemen. We've all remained calm, and we shall continue to do so. I would remind you we are public servants; we remain on duty, and the great British public needs us now more than ever. I know some of you fear for your families, but I don't need to remind you where our duty lies. We all know what that horrible little man Hitler is trying to do; he's trying to inconvenience us. I want you all out there on the street to ensure that doesn't happen."

The boys greeted his words with a chorus of 'Yes, Sarge'. They filed out onto the street as if it were a normal evening. I turned towards Dave, who calmly placed his jacket over the back of a chair. We weren't going home; we would wait until the reports came in. There would be work for us to do that evening. When the room had cleared, I had a word with Jack.

"Well done, Jack; for just a moment there, I think we might have lost our heads."

"This isn't the end, Roger. This is just the beginning. That little shit is going to test us to the limit, but my boys will not be found wanting."

Jack was the toughest man I ever knew. I'm not sure he even understood the meaning of fear. Forged in the hearth of the Great War, his experience shaped him like the folded patterns of the finest Damascus steel. When Jack said Hitler wouldn't be allowed to inconvenience us, he meant it. More to the point, the entire police station knew he meant it.

Dave and I made one concession; we both made a phone call home. Marilyn had just returned. She had taken refuge in the public shelter close to our house. She saw no local damage, but smoke rose into the air just a few streets away. To my surprise, she remained relatively calm; the people's attitude in the public shelter had lifted everyone's spirit. Dave said Jean also sounded stoical about it, so that did a lot to raise our spirits.

The phone calls started to come in thick and fast, reports of damage and injured people, and then, to my profound disbelief, someone reported a looter. We had emergency plans in place for precisely this eventuality. The cooperation between the emergency services proved to be well organised. As our response moved up a gear, the warning siren started to whine again. I could hardly believe it. Dave and I looked at each other in disbelief for the second time. Jack put the telephone down and nodded his head; we needed to go back down to the cells. Jeff and Alfie had gone out in response to calls about looting and a burglary. All of Jack's boys were out on the street.

We went down to the cells with Gerry while Jack stood at the door, hoping beyond hope to see some of his boys return. It soon became apparent that this had been the Germans' intention all along. The first raid created enormous destruction, but crucially, they dropped thousands of incendiary bombs, effectively lighting up the capital in preparation for a night-time raid. Jack calmly walked down to the cells as the bombs started to fall. Our previous experience hardly prepared us for this onslaught. Bombs fell much closer to us, the building shuddering on several occasions. We flinched and cowered while Jack just stood defiant.

"You eventually get used to it," he said. "The fact is, if one of these bombs has our name on it, then no amount of hiding in the corner is going to save us."

He was right, of course, but your physiological response is automatic. My heart raced a little faster with each explosion, and my breathing became erratic. I sat with my fists clenched, grinding my teeth. A bomb landed just a hundred yards away, though it felt as if it were much closer. The building shook violently, the lights momentarily went out, and the shock wave found us cowering on our haunches. It hit my chest and made my ears pop. I wanted to be as brave as Jack, but we were cast from different moulds. The bombing went on right through the night until 4.30 the following morning. September 7th became known as Black Saturday, the first day of the Blitz.

## Chapter Twenty-One
# September 7th, 1940

Emma

*"In amongst the senseless death and destruction of war,*
*I had been blessed with a reason to rejoice."*

I will never forget the first day of the Blitz. Until that awful day, our armed forces had fought the war; the staff of St Thomas's Hospital had been spared that onerous duty. The people of London had no idea what lay ahead; you can't prepare yourself for the unknown. Until 4 o'clock in the afternoon on September 7th, our lives continued relatively undisturbed. My life, and everyone else's, changed forever that day. Hell visited itself upon us. When it came, it did so with no warning other than the dispassionate wail of the siren.

Unsure what might happen, several of us went up to the balcony on top of the hospital, clutching our gas masks. From our high vantage point, we expected to see the usual magnificent view across London. The vision of Hell that greeted us instead will haunt me for the rest of my life. In the distance, I saw hundreds of German bombers, with smoke and fire rising from the streets of London beneath them. I gasped aloud as my breath caught in my throat; the shock reverberated right through me. They were destroying London in front of my eyes; it violated my every sense. We watched in utter disbelief, standing with our mouths open, incapable of expression. The sound of approaching explosions finally jolted us back to life.

"God Almighty, this looks like Armageddon," yelled Ken.

"Fuckin' hell, the bastards are destroying London. Oh, I'm sorry, Emma."

Even in that moment of existential crisis, Frank reverted to his usual polite self. He actually apologised for swearing. I neither acknowledged his apology nor made any comment at all, remaining speechless. I remember withdrawing into myself as if I could stand apart from what was happening before me. Frank looked furious. He would have thrown his stethoscope at the distant bombers if he thought it might help. Leo, like me, appeared terrified, unable to comprehend what he saw, incapable of doing anything.

It became immediately apparent that the docks were being targeted as successive waves of bombers were progressing west, following the river. It should have been obvious to me that the hospital sitting on the south bank of the Thames directly opposite the Houses of Parliament would be directly under the flight path, but that would have required rational thought. Alex, the last to join us, calmly assessed the situation and suggested we might be safer to go down to the basement. Ken eagerly agreed and followed Leo, who had already taken steps towards the stairs. Frank had to be persuaded. Perhaps we were in shock or sheer bewilderment, but I understood Frank's reluctance to go.

Reality can be so far removed from any previous experience and so abhorrent that we refuse to accept it. We had a view across our great city, and the German Luftwaffe were defiling it right before our eyes. We saw it, but we just couldn't believe it. I felt that turning our backs on London would be like abandoning a patient in their hour of greatest need.

The others hastily left, and we said we would follow. I looked at Frank and found his grim determination not to turn the other cheek strangely comforting. As the bombers and their attendant destruction drew closer, we could see the bombs cascading from the bellies of the aircraft. The sight and sound filled my mind to the exclusion of all else. I reached out and took hold of Frank's hand without realising I had done it.

We might have continued to stand there had it not been for the sight of German bombers flying directly above us. Neither of us had the sense to realise those planes had empty bomb bays, but the perceived danger shook us out of our malaise. Frank refused to run, and so the pair of us walked away down the stairs towards the basement.

"You realise we're heading towards the morgue, don't you?"

"Let's hope we're just visitors. I'm not ready to be a resident yet, Frank."

I had just had my first real lesson of the war. I thought when faced with danger, I might run and scream hysterically, but when that moment came, I found myself taking comfort in humour. My heart raced, and my body flooded with adrenaline, but something essentially human remained. Only when we were relatively safe in the basement did I start to tremble and flinch at the sound of the bombs. We were all petrified human beings in the basement; on the balcony, we were someone else.

After two hours, it finally stopped. I might have expected us to celebrate being alive, but that proved to be short-lived. Something unexpected happened. We were all medical staff and we instinctively knew our moment had come to serve the nation. Our only concession was to look outside to confirm that London still stood. The scene greeting us defied belief; the sight of London burning sent a chill down my spine. A vast cloud of black smoke hung over East London. I had no experience of war, but I knew death and destruction lay beneath that cloud.

I worried about my family, but my concerns had to be directed towards the casualties that I knew would soon pour through the hospital doors. We had a well-rehearsed procedure in place for precisely this eventuality. As Frank and I walked together towards the casualty reception area on the ground floor, I felt strangely calm and empowered. I didn't think about myself or Frank; injured people would need me - my moment had come.

The first to appear were the walking wounded. Most of them had open wounds caused by flying glass or shrapnel. They arrived with their wounds wrapped in tea towels or anything they could lay their hands on. I knew what to do; I knew who to prioritise. I also knew far worse would soon arrive in the ambulances. We worked as fast as we could; I sent the eye injuries to ophthalmology and the broken bones to orthopaedics; the rest we cleaned and stitched.

I glanced across the hall to see everyone working together like a well-oiled machine. Basic first aid was not beneath any of the seniors. Alex worked on cuts and contusions, just as Doctor Wiśniewski did. Marion helped the nurses with patients, and surgeons like Ken applied bandages. Among the nurses, one stood out. Janet Walters had an air of confidence about her. The other nurses looked towards her for advice whenever the ward sister or matron was unavailable. As soon as the more serious cases started arriving, I beckoned her over to work with me.

"Thank God you're still with us, Janet. We need you, and right now, I need you."

"After our talk the other week, I knew you were right, Doctor Stevenson. This is my calling; I'm not going anywhere."

"Thank heavens. Work with me, Janet. We'll make a good team."

We were a good team, and we needed to be. Our training taught us what to expect, but nothing could prepare us for the horrendous injuries arriving in the ambulances. Blast injuries, major broken bones protruding from gaping wounds, crush injuries, and burns. A virtual sea of humanity, many in agony, some clinging to life in silence. It could quickly become overwhelming. I remember Hamish telling me about his anguish when confronting this same scenario. His advice was to see past the blood and the pain, stop arterial bleeds, and check the airways and vital signs. Only try to save those who can be saved. Above all, he said, be decisive and act quickly.

I tried to do as Hamish told me; I clamped the arterial bleeds while Janet checked the vital signs. We gave them pain relief and IV infusion where necessary, moving from patient to patient, only attempting to stabilise them. Janet pronounced one injured man dead as I tried to save him. That hit me really hard. I held that man's hopes and dreams in my hand. Despite everything I tried to do, I failed that poor man.

"Not your fault, Emma, move on," Janet said.

I marvelled at her stoicism and drew strength from her. I moved on, but now, with an even greater determination not to lose another soul in my care. Gloria Cummings shouted to Janet, her voice rising above the cacophony of sounds. Sensing the urgency, Janet ran to her. Marion would normally scold one of her nurses for running anywhere, but not that day. Gloria and Janet waved frantically for me to come immediately, but the patient in front of me also needed my help. Gloria's expression told me I had to go, and so I ran towards the injured woman.

She had the most horrific crush injury I had ever seen. Blood gushed from somewhere in the top of her left leg. The leg would have to be amputated, but amongst the mess of bone and flesh, her femoral artery pulsed blood at an alarming rate. I didn't know how long she had been bleeding. She might die at any moment. With barely a pulse and with her unconscious face chalk white, I could see the bringer of death reaching out to her. The woman was in hypovolemic shock, and Gloria shook her head.

"No, no, no, I can't lose her. I won't give up. Get a saline drip into her immediately; I have to try."

She hardly had enough leg remaining to apply a tourniquet, but

I managed to reduce the blood flow. With the victim's femoral artery crushed and severed, I couldn't even find where to apply artery forceps. The leg would have to be amputated above the wounds immediately. I looked around for Ken or one of the other surgeons, but they had moved on to the operating theatres. Grabbing the nearest surgical instrument trolley, I had to do something I had never done before with a live patient. Despite not being a qualified surgeon, I knew how to amputate a limb; this is what I trained to do. Before the days of anaesthetic, to reduce blood loss and shock, a surgeon could amputate a leg in under three minutes. They prided themselves on their speed. For my patient, three minutes might be all she had left.

Janet and Gloria didn't hesitate to assist me. I set about amputating the woman's leg as quickly as I could. With all the blood vessels finally tied off, I closed the wound back over the severed bone as neatly as I could, the crushed leg still lying on the stretcher beside her. I looked up at Gloria, and she said the one thing I wanted to hear. "She's still alive." She would need a massive transfusion of blood as quickly as possible, but we had given her a fighting chance of staying alive. Her life sat in the palm of my hand, and I refused to let go.

As we moved about, we left footprints of blood in our wake. The entire hall resembled a battlefield. A woman with a collapsed lung received our attention, and then another bleeder required immediate lifesaving treatment. We were not halfway through treating them when the air raid warning siren sounded again. For a moment, everyone stood in silence with their mouths open and eyes that could only stare towards the heavens. Doctor Wiśniewski stepped forward and calmly announced that all patients must be transferred to the basement.

"There are casualties here who we dare not move until we have stabilised them. I'll stay with them; you go ahead to the basement, Janet."

"I'm staying with you, Emma."

We didn't discuss it. We just attended to those patients. I noticed Leo left with a patient going to the basement, and I saw Gloria give a sigh of relief. The connection between them across the hall felt almost tangible. Gloria didn't worry about her safety, provided Leo remained safe. I smiled, we understood each other. The second wave of bombers started at about 8 pm, and it proved to be far worse than the first wave. Bombs fell quite close, shaking the building, and each time, we looked at each other as if to say, 'We survived that one'. Frank and another doctor, Maurice, worked alongside us, as well as two other nurses. We continued until all the patients could be moved to the basement.

The bombing continued until 4.30 the following morning. All of us were utterly exhausted. We ventured up from the basement just before dawn, happy to be alive. Too weary to place one foot in front of the other, I sat on a chair next to Frank and Ken. Elbows on knees with our heads in our hands, we just sat without a word being spoken. Leo and Gloria joined us, our blood-stained coats and aprons testament to what had gone before.

"We did well last night, didn't we?" said Frank.

"I believe we did," Leo replied. "I didn't think I would cope, but somehow we all did."

"We did more than cope," said Ken. "I saw that patient whose leg you had to amputate, Emma. You did an outstanding job, yet I understand you've not done that before, not on a live patient. Thanks to you, she will survive."

"Oh, thank God, I prayed we wouldn't lose her. I didn't do it by myself. I couldn't have done it without nurses Walters and Cummings. We worked together all night."

I looked at Gloria, and somehow, we both managed to smile. Janet saw me and walked over to us, her eyes hardly able to focus. We saved lives that night, and that single fact displaced all the horrors we had witnessed. For an indulgent moment, I allowed myself the satisfaction of knowing that we had given people a future where none existed before. Janet could feel it, too. With a slight nod of the head, she acknowledged what we both felt. Leo squeezed Gloria's hand; they no longer felt the need to conceal their relationship. As much as the air raid had brought us together, we all wanted that to be the end, but of course, this had been neither the beginning nor the end. We sat during a brief interval between the influx of victims.

At first light, casualties started appearing again, and we were there for them. Once again, the reception hall resembled a battlefield, and once again, we were steadfast on the front line. What followed was the longest day of my life. Had you told me then that this would be just another day during the Blitz and far worse would come, I wouldn't have believed it possible. I saw some terrible things on the first day, things that heaven forbid we would become accustomed to. With no sleep, fatigue and stress pulled in one direction while the patients' needs pulled in the other. One thing above all else gave me the strength to continue. My father's words echoed in my mind. The whole world rejoices when a life is saved. In amongst the senseless death and destruction of war, I had been blessed with a reason to rejoice.

## Chapter Twenty-Two
# September 8th, 1940

Roger

*"We entered a new kind of war where unarmed civilians were on the front line, and the slaughter of the innocent became the measure of success."*

Everyone expected the bombing to continue, but none of us expected the Blitz would go on for another 57 consecutive nights, not stopping until May 11th, 1941. Had we known that, I'm not sure how we would have coped. Everything changed that day; London looked and smelt different. We entered a new kind of war where unarmed civilians were on the front line, and the slaughter of the innocent became the measure of success.

We were lucky on that occasion. All of our boys at Balham police station reported back safely, bringing horrific descriptions of what they'd seen. Gradually, a picture of the aftermath emerged. The bombing had been concentrated around the docks, but few areas of London escaped completely unscathed. That first day claimed the lives of 420 people. 1,600 were injured, and countless homes lay in ruins. Our contingency plans were well rehearsed, but this felt like a giant step into the unknown. The emergency services, of which we were just one part, swung into action. We were charged with maintaining order in a city now defined by disorder.

With no food or sleep, even Jack had to admit that Hitler had temporarily inconvenienced us, and so we agreed we would have to regroup, go home and rest. Dave and I decided we should first get some sleep, but then we should meet with Marilyn and Jean to discuss what we should do. When we last met, Marilyn created quite a bit of tension between the four of us, but we had to put that behind us. Dave and Jean were our longest-standing and closest friends. In times of trouble, you need your friends near you.

Dave drove me home the short distance to the other side of Balham. Each corner we turned came with the expectation of seeing evidence of the bombing. These were roads we knew well, with each one getting closer to home. An ambulance passed us at great speed, its bell ringing. When it stopped some distance ahead, Dave and I looked at each other. Smoke rose into the sky as the firemen damped down the fire. The ambulance crew threw open the doors of the ambulance. A police constable we knew directed the traffic and held the local people at bay.

Neither of us had seen what a 500-pound bomb could do to people and property. The sight confronting us seemed to be of another world, a place you could only describe as Hell. What once had been three terraced houses now lay in a jagged heap with bricks and masonry spread far and wide. Two bodies lay beneath sheets in a space cleared between the debris. A river of blood joined them in death, as perhaps they were joined in life. I wound the window down to speak to the PC, and that's when I heard the awful cry of a woman who the bringer of death had chosen to suffer in this life.

Injured and in shock, the poor woman screamed, 'No, no, no', over and over again. I felt her pain as if it were my own. We understand now what a bomb does when it falls blindly into people's lives. Broken homes mean broken dreams and memories. Only the dead are at peace; the human tragedy for those left behind is incalculable. I asked the PC if there was anything we could do. When he said the situation had been brought under control, I looked at Dave, and we breathed a collective sigh of relief. We would have done anything to help the trapped or injured, but that poor woman wanted what no mortal could offer. We drove on.

"If that's what one bomb can do, can you imagine what the future holds for us?"

"Doesn't bear thinking about, does it, Rog?"

"No, it doesn't. But somehow, we have to cope with this."

Neither of us said much after that, both retreating into our thoughts. The woman's grief that I had just witnessed tormented me. There, but for the grace of God go any of us; she foretold the future. When we arrived, we sat for a moment outside my house. Dave said he and Jean would return after a few hours of sleep. I only answered, "Okay, mate."

Despite our recent differences, Marilyn greeted me with an enthusiasm that bordered on desperation. The new reality made our petty squabbles seem rather ridiculous. She looked pale and shaken; I could see the fear in her eyes. Marilyn finally accepted that evacuating John and Mary had been a good idea. Your priorities change dramatically when your life is threatened.

Everything felt different that morning. Suddenly, everything we had became precious. We had our trials over the years; we were never that most elusive of dreams, the perfect marriage. The augments about my long working hours and Marilyn's many obsessions were all vastly preferable to what the future might hold in store for us. We sat eating the little that rationing allowed us, and finally, we fell asleep in each other's arms. Dave knocked on the door about 3 o'clock in the afternoon.

"Come in, mate. How are you, Jean? Are you alright?"

"Yes, I'm okay, Roger. I was a bit shaken up while it went on, but we came through it, didn't we?"

I usually avoided hugging or kissing Jean with anything more than a perfunctory peck on the cheek; it only antagonised Marilyn. That day, things were different; we hugged each other tightly, and Dave put his arms around Marilyn. Jean and I liked each other; we always had, but it was never anything more. Dave and I never discussed such things; he rightly knew we didn't need to. Unfortunately, it had been one of Marilyn's obsessions right from the start, just one of the many things she obsessed about. Now, we all had something far more important to be concerned with.

"I'm sorry about what happened in the pub the other week. I didn't mean those things I said, Jean."

"Don't worry about it, Marilyn. It doesn't seem important now, does it?"

"No, nothing else seems important now. The attitude of the people in the public shelter surprised me," Marilyn said. "We were all frightened, but everyone kept their spirits up; no one wanted to let the side down."

"I wish I'd done that," Jean replied. "I went into the Anderson shelter next door with old Mrs Steddings."

"We were safe enough in the cells," said Dave. "The worst part was worrying about you two."

"Will they be coming back?" Jean asked.

"Yes, we can safely assume they will," I said. "We must be prepared. The reports we've seen assume they will adopt night-time bombing - the

RAF are shooting down too many of their daytime bombers. If me and Dave are not here, you two should always be together in the evenings to look out for each other."

"What about you?"

"Don't worry about us, Marilyn; we've been looking out for each other for years," Dave said.

"That's true," Jean replied, "there are times I think they're married to each other, not to us."

"What's going to happen to us, Roger?"

"We'll be okay, Marilyn. We'll get through this."

"No, I didn't mean us, I mean all of us, I mean London. They killed hundreds of people last night and destroyed goodness knows how many houses, and we couldn't stop them. That's just one night. We can't go on this way."

"The advice is that we'll be safe in the shelters from anything other than a direct hit. We've just got to keep our heads down."

"Roger's right, Marilyn," said Dave, "we'll get through this."

"Get through it for what? There will be nothing left outside the shelters."

"Calm down, Luv, this is what the Germans want. Hitler's trying to break our spirit. They think if the people throw in the towel, Churchill will follow. They don't know the British people, do they?"

"We don't know how bad it will be, do we? This is just one night."

"I'll be honest, Jean," Dave said, "we can't even imagine how bad this is going to be. Life as we know it has gone, but as Roger says, they're trying to break us, and we mustn't ever let that happen."

"What about all the basics, food and water, and the buses and the underground?" asked Marilyn. "We can't manage without those things."

"This is the basis of all the training and organisation that's been going on," I said. "One way or another, those things have to continue because, without them, we'll be defeated. Remember what Churchill said, 'We must brace ourselves to our duties - we will never surrender.' However bad it gets, we keep going. Even if there's not a house standing, Dave and I will continue to police the streets, the milk will be delivered, and the postman will deliver the mail. This is how we fight back. This is what 'never surrender' means."

"Bloody hell, Roger, you really mean that, don't you?"

"I do, Jean, and you must be the same. Our sergeant at work, Jack, says

Hitler's trying to inconvenience us, and he's not about to let that happen, so neither are we."

"If me and Roger can be home before dark, then all well and good, but if we can't, we need to know that you two are together, looking out for each other. You must be in a shelter in good time with your gas masks. The worst thing would be us worrying about you two."

"I was terrified in the Anderson; I don't want to do that again. We will do as you say. We'll have an arrangement every evening: either I'll come here, or you come to my house, Marilyn."

"And promise us you'll keep safe," said Marilyn.

"We will, and we will come through this. Just remember, Hitler can only win this war if he breaks us. If he fails, then he'll lose everything. He's sown the wind, and he'll reap the whirlwind."

Chapter Twenty-Three

# The Nurses' Home, September 9th, 1940

Emma

*"He gasped for air until finally releasing the primordial cry of those that love leaves behind. No, no, no."*

The future stared us all in the face; we knew we were very much on the front line. When the initial emergency with the patients calmed down, the need for self-preservation manifested itself in what felt like a bizarre ritual. Many of us who had rooms in the hospital physically dragged our beds down into the basement. The nurses had their block with its own basement, so just a handful of us women shared a storeroom while the men were packed together in various convenient places. The entire process provided a strange boost to morale; we felt as if we were being proactive.

I grabbed what little sleep I could during the day in anticipation of another long night. Little did I know just how long that night would be. It started again at 7 pm, halfway through my first proper meal in two days. The siren sounded, but this time, we knew what would follow. I gulped a last few mouthfuls of food and pursued the boys out of the canteen. Within minutes of our arrival in the basement, we felt and heard it start again. Distant explosions made their presence known by a seismic shock wave that we could feel reverberate through the basement floor. Once or twice the building shook as the bombs fell closer.

When it stopped, we were informed that the raid had dropped mainly incendiary bombs, and hundreds of fires now raged across London. The

Germans adopted the same tactic as the night before, lighting up London to prepare for a devastating night raid. Fires raged close to the hospital, which left us with the uncomfortable realisation that each fire acted as a beacon for the next wave of bombers.

The first casualties soon started arriving, and we knew from experience that we should move as many as possible directly into the basement. We received fewer casualties than the night before, or perhaps we were better organised. When the night raid began at 9 pm, most of us were already in the basement, and with our level of sleep deprivation, many even went to bed. I felt too nervous to sleep, but I sat on the mattress next to my two female colleagues. They were good company, and both of them were cheerful, capable women determined to make the best of it.

Neither of them was a resident in the hospital; they just wanted to do whatever they could. Sheila had a big personality and a big smile; in fact, everything about Sheila was big. As a physiotherapist, she would normally see patients in a day clinic. Doreen worked as an assistant in radiology; she said she simply found herself trapped in the hospital, but as with Sheila, I suspected she intended to be there.

The bombing continued right into the night, and each time we relaxed just a little, another bomb fell close by. Sheila seemed to be undaunted by any of it, remaining relentlessly upbeat. Doreen didn't have Sheila's outgoing personality; she didn't make light of it - when the bombs fell close, she flinched like I did. I sat with my knees up under my chin, grasping the bed sheet.

We were strangers thrust together into circumstances that, a few weeks ago, we couldn't even imagine. I didn't cease to wonder how the normal social disciplines had vanished. The protective veneer that we usually present to the world no longer existed. Doreen didn't make light of our circumstances because she accepted we were in a perilous situation. Sheila didn't acknowledge the danger. Her positive approach to life only allowed for one outcome. They both displayed enormous courage and self-determination, albeit in totally different ways. I drew strength from both of them.

At about 2 am, the bombing became particularly intense. Bombs fell close to us; I reached for Doreen's hand, and the three of us looked at each other with wide eyes. Then it happened. A tremendous explosion rocked the building. It almost threw me off my bed. Instantly, a shock wave hit us, taking our breath away. Dust fell from the ceiling just before the lights went out. A chorus of screams disguised themselves as a sharp intake of breath. The light quickly returned to reveal three terrified faces, each covered in dust. It took a moment to realise that not one of us was injured. We had been very lucky; we also knew our good fortune had been someone else's misfortune.

The bombs were still falling, but we knew a part of the hospital had been hit. We knew we had to help. The moment we stepped out of the storeroom, we entered a world of panic and confusion. People quickly appeared from all around, hurrying towards the scene of the explosion. None of us knew what had happened or what to do about it; we only knew we had to get there. St Thomas's comprised nine blocks, and smoke and fumes quickly became more intense as we moved from one block to the next. I met with Leo and Frank along the way. People ahead of us moved debris away from the corridor. Finally, we came face to face with the most horrific sight I had ever seen. The block directly opposite Big Ben lay as a tangled mass of smoking debris; it no longer existed.

I struggled in the dark to comprehend the scene in front of me. The air resounded to the sound of exploding bombs, and I looked up at search-lights combing the sky where once a building had stood. None of it made any sense, not until the realisation dawned that the devastation in front of me had just a few minutes ago been the nurses' home. With my heart wedged so firmly in my throat I could hardly breathe, I just stood frozen in shock. Our friends and colleagues were in that building. People swarmed over the debris, including Leo, desperately moving broken timbers and masonry, hoping beyond hope to find survivors. I instinctively stepped forward to help, but Frank stopped me.

"Stay here, Emma, keep yourself clean. We might need you."

I did as he said and watched as more people arrived with torches. With no equipment, they manhandled the rubble as if they were human ma-chines, frantically trying to find survivors. The knowledge that our friends and colleagues lay beneath the ruins filled every one of us with a toxic mix of desperation and fear. Desperation to find survivors, and fear that we might not. I didn't think it possible to feel more anguish, not until I saw Leo. He tore at the rubble, moving pieces of masonry no human should have been capable of lifting.

Then, miraculously, they found a survivor. A nurse, grey with dust, was helped away. Then another emerged, apparently unscathed. It felt like a triumphant moment, but it didn't last. They recovered a body and then another, followed by another. What followed remains one of the most harrowing experiences of my life. Leo, the poor man, was so desperate to find Gloria that his hands and arms were bleeding. Frank went to him, attempting to calm him down, but he stopped dead in his tracks. Leo had found a body crushed beneath the rubble.

Unrecognisable to all except the bringer of death, the victim lay more a part of the rubble than of this world. A pool of light from a torch revealed nothing more than a shape with the bright glistening colour of life being consumed by the unforgiving grey dust. Leo desperately went straight to the arm and to the bracelet that he had recently placed on her wrist. He had found Gloria! I saw Leo suddenly become motionless. He seemed not to breathe as reality fought against denial. When reality finally forced itself upon him, I, too, realised what he had seen. He gasped for air until finally releasing the primordial cry of those that love leaves behind. "No, no, no."

I felt as if my heart had been ripped out; I had never seen a man in such distress. Frank tried to console him while I stood helpless, trembling from head to toe. My eyes were consumed with the carnage before me, but for me nothing moved. The entire world stood still, locked in that awful moment. Ken appeared and, realising what had happened, held me in his arms. Only then did time resume, time without Gloria. Eventually, Frank dragged Leo away from the terrible sight lying beneath them. He could hardly move, his body in one place and his mind lost in another. He fell into my arms, and we both cried uncontrollably. I wanted to comfort him, but I had nothing left to offer.

Frank and many others continued to search for survivors, but it seemed impossible that anyone else could have survived. It was impossible until it happened. A nurse crawled out from beneath the rubble, seemingly uninjured. Rescuers rushed to help her, but she stood unaided, resembling a phoenix rising from the ashes. Covered in dust, she stood there, bewildered but alive. We all stood motionless like her, equally bewildered, unable to believe what our eyes could see. Everyone looked on in complete amazement. It seemed to be so unlikely, so incredible; it had to be a miracle. I think for a strange moment, we thought if we acknowledged the miracle, it would become a mirage, a figment of our collective hope.

She regained her senses sufficient to speak and simply said, "That was a close call. Is anyone hurt?"

The spell was broken; everyone cheered and clapped. If she wasn't a miracle, then she was certainly a gift from God, and we treated her as one. The message was unmistakable. Where the human spirit is concerned - hope springs eternal. The rescuers went back to their task with renewed vigour. Within five minutes, a rescuer shouted for help, and everyone frantically moved masonry and timbers. A body lay in a contorted position beneath a large slab of concrete. When Frank found a pulse, it was as if the entire world rejoiced. It was another miracle and one that deeply affected me. They found Janet Walters alive.

I ran to her as they laid her on a stretcher. Frank and I examined every inch of her as quickly as we could. She had multiple minor cuts and abrasions and a broken arm, but unless she had internal injuries we couldn't see, she would survive. As I wiped the dust away from her face, she opened her eyes.

"Emma."

"I'm here, Janet. I've got you; you'll be alright."

She attempted a smile and mouthed the words, 'Thank you.' I could see the anxiety drain from her body as she relaxed, placing herself in my care. We lost six women that night, including Gloria. It seemed incredible to us that 'only' six were killed. Each survivor recovered from the rubble represented another triumph for the human spirit and another reason for the world to rejoice.

I didn't see how we could continue that night; I remained in shock, and poor Leo was irreconcilable. When nothing more could be done, we made our way back towards the wards. Most of us were black and grey with dust, and some of us carried the blood of the victims with us. Doctor Wiśniewski addressed us all in the corridor. He too had been covered in dust.

"We have suffered a terrible blow tonight. We have lost six of our own. I, for one, would like nothing more than to drown my sorrows in a large glass of whisky. But we have a duty to all the unfortunate victims who will shortly arrive here. I would remind you all that we also have a duty to those we have lost tonight. Every one of them dedicated their lives to helping others in need. They did not falter, and we will honour them by continuing in their footsteps. We all need to clean up, and I expect to see everyone back on duty within half an hour."

Several doctors said in unison, 'Yes, Chief.' I never got on with Wiśniewski, but he had tears in his eyes that night, and he went up in my estimation considerably. My grandparents died when I was very young. I have little memory of their death. They were there as a constant presence until they weren't. My parents hid their grief from me, and so nothing equipped me for that terrible night. It is the unfathomable nature of it that eats into you. Gloria was such a beautiful person; how can a light so bright suddenly just vanish? Denial offered a temporary haven, but even that illusion shattered when I looked at Leo. I had never seen a man in such pain. His agony had no boundaries. Frank and I tried to console him, but no amount of my tears could bring Gloria back.

Frank and I tended to him in his room, but he remained incapable of doing anything. We gave him a sedative and left him free from pain for a few hours at least. We all reported for duty early that morning, all except for Leo. That night had been a devastating blow for the hospital. Six women, each with a life ahead of them, each with dreams and hopes for the future. As for those that death leaves behind - they never forget, they never recover. The departed live on for as long as they are alive in the minds of those they leave behind. Leo's last vision of his loved one will haunt him until they are reunited. Me? Yes, Gloria visits me whenever I am feeling low. She still has the power to make me smile, but she is no longer alone; she is one of many now.

# Chapter Twenty-Four
# Irene Newnham

### Roger

*"Traumatised people everywhere were still climbing over rubble, searching for lost possessions, or perhaps lost souls."*

D ave and I drove to the station through a changed landscape. Not only did London look different, it smelt different. The expressions on people's faces had changed. Like the smell in the air, you couldn't pin it down to any one source; it permeated every aspect of life. Jack greeted us with something of a smile - to his evident relief, everyone had reported for duty. It seemed strange to me that we treated the day as if it were the same as any other. We had the morning meeting as usual, but inevitably, we only had one topic of conversation.

"The house at the end of my road bought it," said Jeff. "Nothing left. I mean absolutely nothing; it's just gone."

"Were people in it?" asked Garry.

"No, they came back from the public shelter and just stood there. They were like two pillar boxes standing with their mouths open. They couldn't take it in."

"My Pam looked out of the shelter to find the building opposite flattened," said Alfie. "The blast really shook them up, but when they went outside, they found people lying in the street. Well, not even people really."

"How is she, Alfie?" I asked.

"She's in shock; she's hardly spoken since."

"What are you doing here, mate? You should be with her."

"Her sister's with her. We can't start taking time off, not now; this thing's only just starting."

"Tell Pam we're thinking of her, Alfie. What she saw is going to haunt her for a long time."

"I will, thanks, Roger."

"Do we know of any disorder? What about looting?" asked Gerry.

"No reports of disorder on our patch, Guv," replied Dave. "I'm amazed how well people have reacted. Looting is going to become a problem, though."

"You can't believe it, can you?" I said. "How on earth can someone inflict even more grief on a bomb victim? Isn't it bad enough that people lose the roof over their heads without some bastard stealing possessions?"

"After what I've seen already, I can tell you, if I catch one of these bastards, I'll knock seven bells out of them."

"We all feel that way, Jeff, but take it easy. We can't have the public taking the law into their own hands. That's the definition of disorder."

"I know, Guv, but let's hope they resist arrest."

"Gerry's right though, Jeff; we need to keep a lid on it," I said.

During the meeting, one of Jack's uniform boys reported in by telephone. I noticed Jack out of the corner of my eye through the window of the door. When he sprang to his feet, I knew something was up. He reported to Gerry, who promptly reported to the rest of us.

"We have another murder victim," he said solemnly.

"A young woman?" I enquired. "Are we talking about the same killer?"

"Yes, it's a woman, but this sounds different; she's been killed in her home in Wandsworth; that's all we know."

"Is the PC sure it's a murder?" asked Dave. "The woman might be a bomb victim."

"He says it's definitely a murder, so it's a job for you, Roger. You and Dave better get over there."

Dave and I left immediately to drive to Wandsworth. For the first mile, neither of us spoke, sitting quietly with our thoughts.

"Is it just me, Rog, or does this all seem surreal? Here we are going to investigate a murder when all around us, the Germans have just murdered hundreds?"

"Yes, I'm thinking the same thing. I suppose we just have to maintain law and order because now, of all times, we can't allow a breakdown of society. If things fall apart, Hitler has won."

"I know you're right, but in reality, it's just one more unlawful killing."

"I guess so, but it's a killing we can do something about."

Typically, a murder scene would attract a crowd of nosy onlookers, but not this murder. We arrived at an ordinary terraced house in a row of similar homes to find a couple of PCs standing outside talking to a neighbour. One or two people peered out from behind curtains, but most people had far more important things to be concerned about.

"Morning, Constable, what have we got here then?"

"Morning, Sir, it's obviously a murder. I've seen nothing like it; it's awful, what's happened in there. She's in the kitchen."

"What do you mean?" asked Dave.

"I don't want to describe it; it's turned my stomach. I only know the woman in passing, but we chatted occasionally. She impressed me as a fine woman; her kids were always well-dressed. Her name is Irene Newnham."

Dave and I looked at each other, not knowing what to think. We entered the house cautiously and found the kitchen. Unlike the constable, I investigated many murders; I had seen some gruesome things, but what we saw that day turned my stomach as well. The victim, a woman probably in her late twenties, had been positioned on a kitchen chair with her throat cut right back to the spine. Her clothes were ripped away from her torso, displaying numerous wounds, including a gaping wound across her abdomen where she had been disembowelled. I stood speechless while Dave put his hand over his mouth and puffed up his cheeks. Neither of us had seen anything like it. We were both thinking the same thing, but Dave said it first.

"What kind of person could have done this?"

"Someone mad or evil, or both. A monster."

There were signs of a struggle, but nothing more than a broken plate and a cup on the floor. Blood covered the floor with splatters over two walls. The house was clean, well-kept, and almost obsessively tidy, which made the kitchen scene even more gruesome. In all of my years, I had never attended a more gruesome crime scene. Despite our revulsion, Dave and I knew our business; we searched every corner of every room. We checked the doors and the windows, and we combed every inch of the small back garden. I stood silently in that kitchen, just looking at every detail, absorbing the evil presence that the murderer had left behind.

Eventually, the police photographer arrived, and a doctor followed by a fingerprint expert. We avoided walking in the blood, so the photographs captured an undisturbed scene. When we had done everything we could, I left instructions that the body should be taken to the mortuary at St Thomas's. We stood for a moment outside and drew a deep breath of untainted air. We both felt contaminated by that house, as if an evil, malign presence had attached itself to us. We gathered the statements the neighbours had given the PCs and slowly made our way back to Balham.

We said very little; with hindsight, I realised we were both in shock. Bombed houses lined our route back. Ambulance drivers were still loading recovered victims into the ambulances. Traumatised people everywhere were still climbing over rubble, searching for lost possessions or perhaps lost souls. The murder we had just witnessed was more gruesome than any I had seen before, and the carnage in the surrounding streets defied belief. We were living in a world that neither of us recognised. When we arrived at the station, Gerry lost no time requesting the details. It provided a harsh reminder that the world we had come from still existed.

"It looks to me, Guv, as if the murderer selected his victim. The neighbours tell us she was a fine woman with two children. There is a husband who we were told is away in the army. If that's true, it counts him out. She's known to the local bobby who found her; he says her children went to the same school as his kids until they were evacuated."

"Why do you say the murderer selected her?"

"She was an easy target, husband away, alone in the house. It was pure luck that she was discovered when she was."

"If the time of death confirms what we expect, then she was murdered during the bombing raid in the middle of the night. I think he used the raid as cover and just walked in."

"It certainly looks like that, Dave, but it begs the question - how did he know she was alone in the house? He must know the area, and he must have watched her to know her movements."

"Let's face it, with nearly all the young men enlisted, there are no end of single women alone in houses. It might just be chance," Dave said, "but I'm inclined to agree; I think he watched her."

"Do we have anything to go on?" asked Jeff.

"Just one thing, we have his footprints in the blood. He also didn't disguise the fact that he sat down at the kitchen table and wiped the blood from himself, including his shoes."

"How do you know?" asked Gerry.

"He left the towel there, with marks on it that could be dirt from the sole of the shoe or even boot polish."

"So he commits this horrendous murder and then calmly sits down to clean his shoes while the bombs are falling. What sort of man are we looking for now, Roger?"

"We're looking for a veritable monster, Guv."

"You don't think this is connected to the murder on Clapham Common, do you?"

"This is different, but it could still be the same man. In fact, I've got a hunch it is. If the footprint matches the Clapham Common print, that supports the possibility. Above all, it would fit the pattern of progression. I'll see what Bartholomew says when he carries out the autopsy."

"We could call in this new police laboratory they have at Hendon to look at the scene."

"I thought about that, Guv. How many staff do they have - six, isn't it?"

"Yes, you're right, Roger, it's down to us."

"It's probably just a coincidence," I said, "but it occurred to me that the method of killing and mutilation match those of Jack the Ripper."

"Are you sure that's not just your obsession with Jack the Ripper?" asked Gerry.

"I'm not obsessed about it, Guv; it's just something I've studied. It's probably just a coincidence, but the Ripper's first known victim suffered exactly the same injuries. I mean identical injuries, as far as I could see."

"When will Bartholomew have a report for us?"

"A couple of days for the official autopsy report, but I know him; he'll have something for me tomorrow."

"From what you describe, this bloke must have been covered in blood," said Jeff. "How does he walk away without being noticed?"

"Good question," replied Dave. "We don't think he could risk walking the streets covered in blood, even at night; we think he must carry some kind of overall with him."

"So we're looking for someone carrying a bag or case."

"That sounds logical, Jeff."

"Not much to go on, is it?"

"It's bugger all," I replied. "We have a shoe size and a few guesses. We need solid evidence."

"I might have something," Alfie answered. "I did as you asked, Guv. I looked again at all the attacks in our area for the last few years. After reading the files, three of them sound as though they might be connected.

One in 1937 and two in 1938. A stranger committed each of them, and they each showed a degree of unnecessary violence."

"You and Jeff interview these women; find out everything you can, especially if they suffered any eye irritation."

"Just make sure the papers don't get hold of it," Gerry said.

## Chapter Twenty-Five
# September 10th, 1940

Roger

*"Something remarkable had just taken place. None of us knew what it was, much less had a name for it. I now realise we had witnessed the birth of what came to be called 'The spirit of the Blitz'".*

We achieved little else that day despite seemingly working hard. It became almost impossible to conduct business as usual. The bombing disrupted not only our infrastructure, it disrupted our ability to think about anything else. During those first days of the Blitz, we existed in a state somewhere between shock and denial. It just seemed incomprehensible that German bombers would rain death down upon us, and all we could do was hope the bombs didn't fall on us. Every Londoner now had two things in common: fear and bewilderment.

Dave and I both got home before dark that night. We arranged for Dave and Jean to come to us, and we would walk down to the public shelter together. Neither of us wanted to go through that ordeal alone, much less for our wives. That we now expected a raid and had plans in place made an enormous difference. The bombing might have been terrifying, but fear of the unknown is even worse.

Marilyn had some blankets and provisions ready, and I could see her level of preparedness reduced her anxiety. We had our evening meal, the best scraps rationing could offer, and neither of us complained once. Instead, we talked; we didn't shout or argue; we just talked. It amazed me how an existential threat could focus the mind. Dave and Jean arrived with smiling faces. They weren't happy smiling faces but an attempt to make light of our circumstances. We immediately lifted each other's spirits with a bit of banter, attempting to dismiss the threat as nothing more than an inconvenience.

"You're not taking all that with you, are you, Marilyn?"

"I am, Dave; it's better to be prepared."

"Looks like you've got the kitchen sink in your bag, Jean."

"I have, Roger; I would bring the flipping toilet with me if I could."

"What are the arrangements for that kind of thing?" asked Dave.

"I imagine a bomb falls close and you piss your pants," I said.

"Don't laugh about it," said Marilyn. "I nearly did that last night."

"Only nearly. Lucky you weren't in the Anderson with me the other night, Marilyn."

We laughed; not a nervous laugh - we really laughed. Being together was obviously a good idea; we immediately cheered each other up. All in good time, and well before the siren sounded, we made our way to the public shelter just down the road from us. Built on a small area of open ground, it didn't amount to much. Its red bricks inspired little confidence. The thick concrete roof looked substantial, but none of it would survive even a close hit, let alone a direct hit. Inside, the shelter comprised a single long rectangular room with wooden bunks four high along the sides. It had no windows in the brick walls, and the concrete floor and ceiling offered no more comfort than a couple of hanging light bulbs. We saw the answer to Dave's question in the far corner, with a thin curtain around it for modesty.

The people arrived in an orderly fashion, everyone attempting to make light of it. I marvelled at the stoicism and goodwill shown by just about everyone. Few people grumbled or complained; the vast majority laughed and joked, albeit mostly a contrived gallows humour. We made ourselves comfortable sitting on the bunk beds as the last of the people arrived. A man with an accordion appeared, and then another walked in with a ukulele under his arm.

When the siren began to wail, the heavy door was closed by the air raid warden. It made a jarring scraping sound, followed by a loud bang that echoed around the shelter. For a moment, it felt as if we were all there to escort an Egyptian Pharaoh into the afterlife, the great stone rolling across the entrance sealing the tomb for all eternity. The lighting cast sharp shadows, making our tomb feel even more claustrophobic. I didn't doubt that many probably wanted to panic and run back outside into the open air, but to everyone's credit, an air of calm resolve pervaded the shelter.

The first bombs started falling at about nine o'clock. At first, we felt nothing, just that distant sound. One dull crump followed another until they merged into a cacophony of increasingly louder noise. Everyone must have been aware that each bomb brought death and destruction to some poor devil. That sobering realisation came with one inescapable caveat. If our names were not on those bombs, then it had to be someone else's. The reality of our situation could be summed up in one time-honoured expression. There, but for the grace of God, go I.

As the bombs fell closer, so our tension grew, and in response, the collective spirit of the people grew. Inevitably, the bombs started to fall close enough to shake the shelter. Shock waves penetrated around the heavy door and through the air vents, reaching in and pressing against our chests like an unseen presence. Dust fell from the walls and ceiling; it even seemed to jump up from the concrete floor. The hanging light bulbs swayed above us, and the flames in the two oil lamps danced back and forth above the wicks. The laughing and merrymaking subsided as people gripped the wooden frames of the bunk beds like mariners in a storm-tossed sea.

Then, just as we seemed to be in the greatest danger, something quite extraordinary happened. The accordion started playing 'Down at the Old Bull and Bush', immediately joined by the man with the ukulele. Another man produced a mouth organ and promptly started playing and shuffling his feet in time to the music. A woman with a fine voice and a broad Cockney accent stood up and sang the words. Something remarkable had just taken place. None of us knew what it was, much less had a name for it. I now realise we had witnessed the birth of what came to be called "The spirit of the Blitz".

I don't suppose any of us attempted to understand what we experienced, but we all felt it. We were in imminent danger of being blown to kingdom come, but instead of fear and panic, our hearts swelled with patriotic fervour. Everyone knew the popular Vera Lynn song 'There'll be Bluebirds over the White Cliffs of Dover'; even I joined in. Like many other friends and families, the four of us held hands, swinging in time to the music. Marilyn smiled at me, and I squeezed her hand tighter. With Jean holding my left hand, the bond between the four of us felt unbreakable. We all knew the words, but I suddenly realised we hadn't fully appreciated their meaning, not until that night. 'There'll be love and laughter and peace ever after, tomorrow when the world is free'.

It finally ended during the small hours of the morning, and none of those bombs had our names on them. The music gave way to tiredness as the tension drained out of our bodies. Marilyn and I cuddled together on the bunk, not that there was room to do anything else. Holding her in my arms, something sparked between us, something that we hadn't felt for a long time.

"I do love you, Roger. I'm sorry I don't always show it."

"Isn't it strange that it takes all this for us both to realise how lucky we are to have each other?"

"Go to sleep, you two," said Jean.

We woke in the morning to welcome another day, except, on that day, we really did welcome it. The heavy door swung open, and the day burst through in all its iridescent glory, making everybody cover their eyes. Bombs had fallen quite close, so we knew there would be damage, but none of us knew what might confront us outside. However bad the destruction, our lives existed outside, not in that tomb. The people about to leave that shelter were not the same ones who entered it. The experience changed us all.

I stepped outside, almost afraid to look. Marilyn gripped my hand. The four of us stood together, casting long shadows as the early morning sun looked down on us. It seemed almost inappropriate that the sun should shine warmly upon us. The air hung heavy with the smell of smoke and strange, unaccustomed fumes that caught in the back of your throat. Exhausted firemen gathered together after fighting fires for most of the night.

Not even a hundred yards away, a terraced house had been completely destroyed; it lay on the ground as a pile of smoking rubble. Beyond it, several columns of smoke rose above the rooftops. An ambulance stood by as rescuers searched frantically beneath the debris. The two houses on either side remained standing, but each of their interiors was exposed for everyone to see. On one side, someone's bedroom remained relatively intact, albeit with its bed perched precariously on the edge of oblivion. In another room, a large part of the ceiling hung down, refusing to join the debris on the floor beneath. On the other side, a kitchen table still stood upright, but instead of plates, bricks were strewn across it. A single chair stood by the table awaiting its usual occupant while the others lay smashed around the room.

"This was someone's home," observed Jean. "Can you imagine losing everything like this?"

"It's not just possessions, is it?" Dave said. "It's memories."

"They must think someone was in there. I'll ask that ARP warden." I walked over to the warden, who looked grim-faced. "Was someone in there?"

"Yes, I think so. It's an old lady. I tried to persuade her, but she refused to leave last night, so I can only think the poor old girl is under that lot."

"Have you been out here all night?"

"Yes, I've been doing what I can for most of the night. I might go home and get a bit of shut-eye now."

He had obviously been in the thick of it. The soot and dust on his face and uniform spoke of heroic efforts to help victims during the raid. The firemen shared the same expression; their faces spoke of grim determination. We walked on towards our own homes without voicing our one overarching concern. As we approached the junction of our road, we could see smoke rising above the rooftops. Marilyn said nothing, but her grip on my hand became tighter. Seconds later, our road came into view and a column of smoke rose into the air from a house on the opposite side of the road.

A bomb had not destroyed the house; it resulted from an incendiary falling through the roof. We knew the family who lived there; they walked not far behind us, having come from the same public shelter. So, at least we knew they were unharmed. Other neighbours stood by, ready to help as the firemen damped down the last of the fire, and so we continued on our way. I realised we were prepared to walk away because, in our strange new world, the scene before us was not unusual.

"We're okay, Luv, not even a broken window," I said.

"Oh, thank God. I can't even imagine what it must be like to lose everything. What do people do, where do they go?"

"They initially go to rest centres," replied Dave, "but longer term, we seem to make it up as we go along."

"Come on, Dave, I've got to know if we're okay."

"I'll see you back at the station later then, Roger."

"Yes, okay, mate. As soon as I've seen Bartholomew at St Thomas's, I'll come straight back."

Dave and Jean left us, obviously eager to find out if their house was still standing. They gathered pace as they walked away. That became another part of our new life, the constant fear and need to know if we had lost our homes.

"I'm desperate for a cuppa, Luv. Can you put the kettle on while I quickly wash and change?"

"Yes, I'm gasping. What are you going to St Thomas's for?"

"I want to see the pathologist; it's about that last murder victim."

We both needed a cup of tea and to wash and change, and then I wanted to go straight to the hospital. Marilyn didn't question it, and apparently, neither did Jean. Our world had been turned upside down, and we were going to work as usual. As I drove away, the firemen were returning to their station. The milkman had almost completed his round, and the postman delivered the post as if absolutely nothing had happened. I allowed myself a brief smile.

In our strange new world, life as we knew it became but a memory. Faced with unspeakable suffering, the very fabric of society could be in danger of collapsing, except it didn't. It's only when you risk losing something that you realise its true worth. Each and every one of us is the fabric of society; we are the sum of our collective parts. As I drove to work, I realised that as long as the milkman delivered the milk, the postman delivered the post, and my colleagues maintained a police force, then we had a chance of holding our way of life together.

On my way to St Thomas's, I encountered numerous bomb-damaged buildings and closed roads. The news that the hospital had been hit by a bomb hadn't filtered through to me, and so the moment I realised it came as a shock. St Thomas's Hospital was such an iconic London landmark it seemed incomprehensible that one of the nine blocks lay in ruins. Workmen were busy clearing the rubble and loading it onto a lorry. The road and pavement outside had already been cleared.

I stood in shocked silence; I could hardly believe the sight before my eyes. A London landmark had been erased, but most shocking of all was what had replaced it. I looked across to where the building once stood, but what I saw instead was Big Ben and the Houses of Parliament on the other side of the river. The vision before me was not so much one of Hell; it felt like the door to Hell. The local constable approached me.

"Morning, Sir, this is a terrible business, isn't it?"

"That doesn't quite express it, does it, Constable? Do you know what this block was used for?"

"I'm sorry to say it was the nurses' home."

"Oh, good God. How many were killed?"

"Six killed and dozens injured."

"Only six? You mean women got out of that alive?"

"I know, it seems like a miracle. I was here soon after the first light and helped in the rescue. One woman simply got up and walked away; we couldn't believe our eyes."

I commended the PC on his efforts, but his description of events made me think. Our values and sense of normality had changed irrevocably. Six people had been killed, and immediately, we regarded that as a reason to be grateful. 'Only' is a dangerous word when it applies to loss of life.

I walked on, and as I approached the main entrance; I realised I had made a mistake coming that morning. Bomb victims were arriving in ambulances, and walking wounded were everywhere. It instantly looked like a war zone, and I almost left rather than find myself in the way. I assumed Bartholomew would be in the pathology department rather than tending to patients, and desperate for information, I disregarded my instinct and continued on.

Inside the hospital, the war zone extended into every hallway and corridor. White coats and uniforms rushed about every which way, and in every direction broken and bloodied people sat or lay in various states of distress. Dead bodies lay on trolleys being transported down to the mortuary, down to where I intended to go. I realised all too late that the victim I was interested in was just one more lost soul in this sea of lost humanity. Having second thoughts, I turned to leave, and the mortuary attendant caught my eye.

"Are you looking for Doctor Bartholomew, Inspector?"

"Well, yes, I was, but I'm sorry, I didn't think. I shouldn't be here now."

"He isn't here; he's helping with the live patients upstairs. I know why you're here, Inspector, and I know he made some preliminary notes about your victim during the night. He'll give you the finished report anyway, so I can see no harm in you looking at his notes."

I thanked the man; I had seen him before but didn't know his name. His vacant expression looked not dissimilar to the many victims he escorted into the mortuary. I can only imagine the psychological impact of what he had to deal with. When I thought about the many distressed family members who would besiege him for news of their loved ones, I viewed his job in an entirely different light. He was very articulate, obviously an intelligent, educated man, but he remained a man without a name, unknown and unseen by most people, yet another vital part of our fabric of life.

He didn't have time to show me the body, but I did read Bartholomew's initial notes. I struggled to read his awful, almost unintelligible handwriting, but he had taken the trouble to write one sentence in capital letters. 'The size and type of knife used, the angle of wound entry, and the shoe prints all present close correlation with the Clapham Common murder.' The shoe prints were not only the same size, they were also the same shape. He even found black shoe polish on the towel. I had read enough; a part of me wanted to leave that place as quickly as possible. I called out to the attendant as I went.

"Thank you, this has been really helpful. I didn't catch your name."

"George Rawlings, Inspector."

"Thank you again, Mr Rawlings. You and your colleagues are doing vital work down here. I commend you."

"That's kind of you to say, Inspector. Would you do something for me?"

"If I can, certainly."

"Find the monster who killed that woman."

"I intend to, Mr Rawlings, but I'm surprised you have time to give her your attention. She's only one of many you have to deal with."

"She's not the same as these bomb victims. The bombs are blind assassins. They don't discriminate; it's not the bombs that are evil. Death gratefully accepts any innocent soul the bombs offer. The bombing is an evil not of our making; it's being imposed on us by an enemy beyond our shores. Hitler's bombs question his evil intent, not ours. These killings are different - this is an enemy from within; this is a reflection upon our society, our way of life."

I misjudged the mortuary attendant completely. I didn't expect him to offer such a well-considered and erudite opinion. He expressed my view precisely, but he articulated it infinitely better than I ever could.

"That is a profound assessment of our situation, Mr Rawlings. I couldn't agree with you more." I formed an immediate opinion of Mr Rawlings and decided to explore it. "Tell me, Mr Rawlings, what's in your background that has enabled you to articulate such a well-considered opinion?"

"I am a Professor Emeritus of psychology, Inspector."

"It's none of my business, Mr Rawlings, but I have to ask, why is a professor of psychology working as a mortuary attendant?"

"If I answer you, Inspector, will you assure me it will go no further?"

"You have my word."

"As a person who has studied the meaning of life more than most, I cannot possibly condone the taking of life, and so I cannot actively support the war effort. I have struggled with that position because a pacifist can also be a patriot. If I were younger, I would undoubtedly be a conscientious objector, but I still want to do whatever I can for my King and country. If, like our doctors and nurses, I could save lives, then I would. Regrettably, psychology has not equipped me to help the living in that context, so I volunteered to help the dead. There is an enormous demand for this work, Inspector; I am making a contribution."

Standing there among the dead, that man single-handedly lifted my spirits. It didn't matter that I disagreed with his pacifist stance; I respected his decision enormously. That he volunteered to do work which few of us would even consider spoke volumes. He impressed me immensely.

"Does Doctor Bartholomew know about this?"

"No, I didn't feel the need to tell him."

"It has been a pleasure, Mr Rawlings, and that's not something I ever thought I would say standing in this place. I think you should be proud; this is no small contribution you are making here."

I left him, deep in my own thoughts. Bartholomew's notes confirmed my hunch and Rawlings' observations added additional gravitas to an already grave situation. As I headed up the stairs towards the land of the living, those who had departed that land came down in the opposite direction, a terrible reminder of our new reality. With people rushing about in all directions, I hurried to get out of their way. At the hospital entrance, ambulances disgorged yet more victims, some of whom looked to be in a terrible way. It appeared to be chaotic, but I could see order beneath the chaos; they worked with speed and purpose.

As I drove away, I passed the open space where the hospital building once stood. In its place, our accustomed London landscape had been replaced with a view across the river. A solitary tree stood in the foreground, its bare skeletal branches a memorial to the twisted wreckage beneath it. Big Ben stood defiantly on the other side of the river; not only the seat of government but a symbol of British resilience, but for how much longer? I couldn't help wondering what would happen to our British resilience if that magnificent building also lay in ruins.

## Chapter Twenty-Six
# September 13th, 1940

Emma

*"Grief takes you to a place where no human wants to go.
The great divide is where all understanding ends, and eternity beckons.
It is as incomprehensible as life itself. We can still see their faces
and hear their voices, but they are no longer with us."*

Following that awful night, we had to evacuate 76 of our patients to other hospitals while the basement was prepared for emergency cases. It seemed like a defeat, but we had no other option. New victims would be directed to other hospitals, and so for a while, at least, we could regroup. Needless to say, my dinner arrangements with Marion and Evelyn came to nothing.

Marion had the reputation of being quite fearsome. She was always in control with only a nod or the wave of a finger. She ruled her nurses with apparent ruthless efficiency, but beneath her austere exterior, she was as soft as butter. I marvelled at her ability to maintain the facade she had cultivated. On the night of September 13th, Marion and five other women shared the basement store room with me. With the nurses' home destroyed, we were all sharing the basement together. It had to be seen to be believed, people laying claim to every conceivable space.

"This is an appalling state of affairs; what on earth are my nurses going to think seeing me like this?"

"Exceptional times call for exceptional measures, Marion. Besides, we're all in the same boat. I saw Doctor Wiśniewski in his pyjamas yesterday. I don't think he lost any credibility; he's still a tyrant in my eyes."

"So you think my nurses see me as a tyrant?"

"No, I didn't mean that. We're all the same down here; I'm joking about Wiśniewski. Your nurses respect you enormously; they might live in fear of being told off, but that doesn't change their respect."

"After what's happened, we need to maintain morale, but it's difficult, isn't it? Two of my nurses and four of our physiotherapists are dead, and even more are injured. I can't stop seeing their faces; I know them all. Nurse Walters will make a full recovery, I am pleased to say. I didn't know about the relationship between Nurse Cummings and Doctor Jordan. How is he taking it?"

"You wouldn't have approved, would you?"

"I certainly wouldn't, but I confess I had a soft spot for Gloria Cummings; she was a lovely girl."

"I know what you mean; I can't get her out of my mind. As for Leo Jordan, it just breaks my heart to see him. The poor man is completely broken."

As we spoke, the bombs started falling. We were not surprised; this had become our life. The younger nurses looked terrified, and after what happened to the nurses' home, who could blame them? Several bombs fell close, and one nurse screamed aloud. Marion, who had tried hard not to let the nurses see her out of uniform, calmly stood up and took the woman in her arms. It seemed to be so totally out of character it took everyone by surprise.

"Don't be frightened, my dear," she said, "they will have to go through me first."

When faced with high-explosive bombs, it might have been absurd to say, but her meaning was clear to everyone. The other nurses came together with their arms around Marion, and without thinking, I did the same. I doubt Marion would have been able even to imagine that situation a few weeks before; I don't suppose anyone would. It seems I wasn't the only person who knew the real matron.

"I'm sorry, Matron. I lost control for a moment. It won't happen again," the young nurse said.

"You didn't lose control; you simply did what we would all like to do. You're not alone, Nurse Roberts; we all face this together."

"How can you be so calm, Matron? You and Doctor Stevenson seem to take it all in your stride?"

"If you took my pulse, you would find it's racing the same as yours.

I'm just as terrified as you are, but I have to remain calm. While you're in this hospital, I am responsible for you, and I will never let you down, any of you."

Nothing more needed to be said, but what we didn't say spoke volumes. The bombs continued to fall around us, but we all remained calm, outwardly at least. Then at about 3.15 am, it happened again. My eyes were closing when a terrifying explosion shook the building. When the shock wave hit us, we knew it must be close. As I sat up, another explosion made the store room shudder, and a part of the ceiling fell down, filling the room with dust.

"Is everyone alright?" I shouted.

It seemed that we were; the section of the ceiling fell onto a filing cabinet, and we were only covered in dust. Marion gathered her nurses like a mother hen gathering her chicks. I knew what had happened; the hospital had been hit again - twice. My heart raced; what lay beyond our door? How many had been killed this time? Marion stood with her hands raised in front of her, her fingers apart.

"Put your uniforms on, ladies," she said, indicating calm with her hands. "We shall look like nurses, and we will act like nurses. There will be people out there who need us."

If Marion told us to remain calm, then that's what we all did. Some people have the ability to inspire and raise others up. Marion had it more than most. We soon joined the rush of people heading towards the scene of the explosions. Everyone shared the same crushing anxiety: how many of our colleagues had been killed this time? Another of the hospital blocks had been hit and partially destroyed. A part of me wanted to close my eyes, but my duty as always remained with the injured.

It took time in the confusion of darkness and falling bombs to assess the situation. Someone said the block was mainly administration, and apart from those sleeping in the basement, it remained unoccupied. The rescuers scrambled to clear the basement staircase. Finally, a way through was found, and people emerged up into what must have felt like the afterlife. One by one, doctors, nurses, and all manner of people couldn't believe their good fortune. The hospital had suffered another devastating blow, but as the people emerged unscathed, we stood in celebration. I didn't expect to see Janet Walters there, but I should have known she wouldn't stay long in her sickbed. She came and stood next to me. Her arm remained in a sling, and she had a bandage around her head; in every sense, walking wounded.

"Isn't it wonderful, Doctor Stevenson? I don't know whether to laugh or cry. I thought so many would have been killed." She looked at me and paused. "Oh, I'm sorry, Emma, you're crying. Has someone been killed?"

"No, not at all. It's just as you said, I didn't know whether to laugh or cry, so I cried."

"I don't blame you. It's just as you said, it's as if the whole world is rejoicing."

Not a single person died that night. We lost even more of our hospital, yet we rejoiced. Marion joined us. She smiled a motherly smile at Janet, which is something she would never usually do, but this was not an ordinary time.

"Is there anything I can do, Matron?"

"You have your arm in a sling, Nurse Walters. I think you have done enough."

"What will happen now that we've lost this building?"

"Well, I can tell you one thing. Evelyn will be looking for a new office," replied Marion with a smile.

"She'll get a shock when she comes in tomorrow," I said.

"We'll manage, won't we," Janet said, "everyone feels the same; we won't be beaten."

As we talked, the long line of people coming out of the basement continued one at a time, and then Ken appeared, followed by Frank. I didn't know they were there. In response to the shock of seeing them, I rushed over without thinking and hugged and kissed Ken. Then, when Frank approached me, I threw my arms around his neck and hugged him. I didn't think; I didn't intend to do it - it just happened. The moment I realised, I stepped back and felt the dust and grit on my lips. Ken stood bewildered, his lips exposing the only colour on his dust-covered face. I felt ridiculous with everyone looking at me.

"That's a nice welcome back from the dead. I must do it more often," he said.

"Don't you dare. If I had known you two were down there, I would have been beside myself."

"If we knew you were up here, we would have come out sooner," said Frank.

We had grown so close together, my friends and I, but never more so than that night. The war did that to people; we were thrown together, and we left our cares and inhibitions behind. It was certainly true for me, and I had more cares and inhibitions than most.

"I don't know about you, but I need a large Scotch," said Ken. "If my room is still here, I've got a bottle of single malt. Will you all join me?"

I thought he meant me and Frank, but then he surprised me. "And you and Janet, Matron."

"Nurses do not frequent doctors' rooms," she replied sternly.

"That would be inappropriate, of course, but not if the Matron accompanies the nurse."

I could see Marion had been completely taken aback. "Of course, we shall all come, Ken," I said. "We all need a drink, don't we, Marion?"

She didn't know what to say, but these were unusual times. Having a drink in a doctor's room was not unheard of as far as nurses were concerned, but it certainly was for the matron. It says much about the camaraderie the war created because Marion agreed. We did indeed live in strange times. Our hospital had been bombed again, but we were celebrating.

We all squeezed into Ken's room, each covered in dust. Only then did we realise we were three glasses short. Frank rushed out to his room as if it were a national emergency. He quickly returned with three glasses and a lovely smile directed at me. As Ken filled the glasses with twelve-year-old Bowmore malt whisky, his lovely wavy hair looked undisturbed, albeit grey with dust. He still wore his brightly coloured bow tie.

At any other time or place, this might have been a conventional scene, but at five o'clock in the morning, with each of us bedraggled and covered in dust, we must have looked the most improbable sight. Marion maintained her matronly persona, referring to Ken and Frank only as Doctor. Despite her reserve, I could see she was enjoying this novel experience and the whisky, which, frankly, even I needed.

"Was it bad, Ken?" I asked.

"If you mean, was it bad being buried alive, then yes, I can say categorically that it's a bloody awful experience."

"I thought we'd bought it, Em," Frank said. "I don't know what the human body limit is for pressure wave damage, but it really hit us."

"Several people are hurt," Ken said. "They haven't got a mark on them, but they are suffering from chest and abdominal pain."

"Will they be alright?"

"We really don't know, Matron; we're not exactly experienced in this field, but they walked away," Ken replied.

"Are you sure you are both alright?"

"We're still standing, Em; that's a good sign."

"We felt the same thing in the nurses' home," said Janet. "It all happens so fast; you don't have time to be frightened. I don't even remember being buried under the rubble."

"You were on the south side, Janet, weren't you?" asked Frank.

"Yes, most of the dead, including Gloria, were on the other side. They didn't stand a chance."

"I can't believe no one has been killed tonight," Marion said. "They say two bombs hit us."

"I can only think they were smaller bombs. How else can you explain it?"

"I don't think we can explain any of it. My father said the same thing about the shells randomly falling into the trenches. Either they have your name on them, or they don't."

"Look at us," said Ken, "we're all lucky to be alive. Janet's covered in cuts and bruises with her arm in a sling. We're all covered in dust, and six of our colleagues have already been killed."

"I keep seeing Gloria in my sleep, and I can't forget that moment when Leo found her."

The room fell silent the moment I said it. We all knew the women who had been killed, but Gloria was such a special person to us. The boys were probably still in shock, and I suspect we were all still in denial about Gloria and the other five women. Reality is a cruel master; it's always there waiting to visit itself upon you, and that night became its opportunity. The coldest of all human despair entered the room and reached into each of our hearts. Grief takes you to a place where no human wants to go. The great divide is where all understanding ends, and eternity beckons. It is as incomprehensible as life itself. We can still see their faces and hear their voices, but they are no longer with us.

I looked at Janet, and her eyes welled up. Marion bit her bottom lip and half closed her eyes. Both Frank and Ken put their glasses down and looked at their shoes. Three doctors, a nurse, and a matron, and we each felt it simultaneously. Collective grief comes with an understanding; it becomes your most private emotion laid bare. Without a word being spoken, we hugged each other. We felt no barriers and no shame; we each carried the same burden. Ken picked up his glass and raised it high into the air, looking towards the heavens.

"To our friends and colleagues, Godspeed."

Marion hesitantly recited each of their names and I saw instantly the depth of her pain. We attempted some small talk, but in reality, we had nothing else to say.

"If we hurry, we might get two hours of sleep before we're all on duty again," Marion said.

"I agree; we must go. Two hours of sleep is better than nothing," I replied.

We left together but the memory of that night never has. I didn't think for a moment that I would sleep, but I underestimated the effect of sleep deprivation and the whisky. I washed the dust away as if the memories would go with it, and as I lay my head down, sleep granted me two hours of peace. If Frank had not knocked on my door, I would have stayed asleep.

"I'll see you in the canteen, Em; we need a quick bite to eat."

"Okay, Frank, save me a chair."

Desperately tired and with legs like lead, I struggled down to the canteen to find business as usual. Two of the hospital blocks had been bombed, and yet the routine continued as if nothing had happened. Frank had dragged Leo out of bed, and he sat at the table, or at least what was left of Leo sat at the table. I saw Janet and beckoned her to come and join us. I needed her cheeky, irrepressible personality to brighten my day. Everyone looked jaded, but the attempt to simulate normality seemed all-pervasive. The canteen staff smiled as we queued with our trays, and colleagues politely said good morning. It was a strange normality but one that we each embraced. Janet and I sat together.

"How are you, Leo; have you eaten anything?" I asked.

"No, I can't eat or sleep but maybe I'll try some breakfast."

"You don't need us to tell you that you must eat."

"Yes, I know. Thank you all for the other night. I don't know what I would have done without you."

Leo looked awful, but a part of him was attempting to claw his way back. We didn't mention Gloria; instead, we made light of the latest event. It became the universal antidote to adversity; we joked and made light of it. Towards the end of our breakfast, Janet took me completely by surprise. I had long come to realise that natural reserve did not apply to Janet. Even in normal times, she seemed to have a special exemption. Frank returned for another cup of tea, and she whispered in my ear.

"I didn't know you and Frank were close, Emma. You kept that quiet."

"We're not, not really."

"But you kissed him last night."

"I did, didn't I? I can't believe I did that."

"I've seen how he looks at you. Why do you pretend it's not happening?"

"Is that what I'm doing? Perhaps I am. I'm not good with things like this," I whispered.

"Well, if you want my opinion, Frank is the nicest one of the lot. I always feel comfortable with him, which is more than can be said for Doctor Bartholomew."

"What do you mean?"

"He's always brushing past you or putting his arm around you. I don't enjoy being in the same room with him."

"Oh, my goodness. I didn't know that; he's asked me to have dinner with him twice now."

"It wouldn't only be dinner, Emma. What did you say?"

"I said no, but only because I didn't have the confidence to say yes."

"I don't understand why you lack confidence, I'm sure, but you made the right decision."

Frank came back with his tea. "What are you two in deep conversation about?"

"Janet has been telling me about Alex; did you know he has a reputation among the nurses?"

"That depends on what kind of reputation you mean."

"He's a womaniser, Frank, didn't you know?" Janet said.

"No, I didn't, but I suspected. He's also a brilliant man."

"He asked Emma out to dinner twice."

"Janet!"

"Well, he did. I'm glad you didn't have the confidence to say yes, Emma."

"Janet, Frank isn't interested in that."

"Oh, but I am."

"And so are we," said Ken.

"And so you should be. You should ask Emma out, Frank."

"As it happens, I have."

"Don't tell me you said no, Emma."

"Janet, really."

"You did, didn't you? You both want to be together, so why don't you?"

"Janet, that's enough, please - don't embarrass me even more."

"I don't mean to embarrass you; I just want to open that door between you."

I wanted the canteen floor to swallow me up. Janet had become such a good friend. I knew she meant well, but her boisterous personality made me feel so embarrassed. Frank offered me a lovely smile, and I tried and failed to do the same. Ken could see my flushed cheeks as I looked down at the chair legs. Even Leo managed a half smile.

I seemed to have become the centre of attention for all the wrong reasons, and the more they smiled at me, the more I thought they felt sorry for me. Then, to complete my humiliation, Marion approached our table, looking every bit the hospital matron in a freshly starched uniform. Even after sharing drinks together a couple of hours earlier, she still frowned to see Janet sitting at a table full of doctors.

"Good morning, Doctors. Good morning, Nurse Walters." She emphasised the words, 'Nurse Walters'.

"Morning, Matron," Janet replied, still retaining her infectious smile.

I could tell Marion sensed Janet was up to mischief. I also knew Janet could not resist continuing with her matchmaking campaign. Having finished our breakfast, I intervened in an attempt to reduce my embarrassment.

"I must be off then, plenty to do."

Janet took hold of my hand just for a moment as I stood up. "I'll see you on the ward, Emma."

I would never have done that. For me, reaching out and touching another person, even in the most innocuous way, would be unthinkable. When Janet did it, it became something entirely different. It meant I'm your friend, I really care about you. I held her hand for a second longer. If I had the courage, I would have said, 'You're my friend; I really care about you as well.' I didn't, of course, but I attempted a smile. With a last glance towards Frank, I left with Marion.

"What's Janet been up to, Emma? I sense mischief."

"You don't miss much, do you? She's trying to encourage Frank Cooper and me to be together."

"You and Doctor Cooper? Well, why not? You would make a lovely couple."

"Not you as well, Marion."

"No, you mustn't allow anyone to pressure you, Emma. You have every right to stay in your own comfort zone."

"I've been there all my life, Marion."

"You'll know when to step outside; you don't need kind-hearted people to tell you."

"What if Janet's right, and I need pushing?"

"Then you will know, but not before."

"You make it all sound so simple, Marion."

"No, it's not simple. I know what you're thinking: if it were so simple, why am I a middle-aged spinster and not happily married with a family?"

"No, really, I wasn't. Well, I suppose I might have wondered."

"Of course, you did, just as your friends wonder about you and Doctor Cooper. I know it's not a simple matter to understand because I've had plenty of time to think about it. I dedicated myself to my work, and I suppose the right man has never come along to distract me. Now I'm middle-aged, overweight, and out of luck as far as that kind of thing is concerned."

"Do you ever regret it?"

"Well, sometimes I've wondered what it might have been like. So, if I'm being completely honest, maybe there have been regrets, but it's not something I dwell on. I have my friendship with Evelyn. We're two old spinsters who found ourselves in the same boat, and so we thought we might as well row together."

"That's a lovely way of putting it."

"We are just friends, nothing more, but we've come to rely on each other."

"Well, I think that's very nice."

"We do all need someone, Emma."

"I know. I have my family, and that's really important to me."

"Your father will not always be there, Emma. Don't leave it too late."

We reached Marion's office and parted company, but before parting, I did something I had never done before. I reached out and held her hand for a second. She smiled at me, and our unspoken conversation said precisely what I wanted it to say.

Chapter Twenty-Seven

# September 14th, 1940

Roger

*"Hitler lit the match that started Kristallnacht in 1938 with an ember no hotter than your boy holds in his hand right now."*

On my way to work, I stopped as I approached Stockwell Underground Station. A large crowd had gathered outside, protesting to officials. Tempers were frayed, and a lone PC had lost control of the situation. The protest was in imminent danger of turning into a riot. With my mind full of Bartholomew's notes, I wanted to get back to Balham as soon as possible, but I could see that the PC needed help. The crowd wanted to use the underground as a shelter at night, but the government decided that the smooth running of the trains should take precedence. The gates were being locked each night, denying the public access. We were aware of the unrest, but this was the first time I had seen it myself.

I reluctantly parked the car and lit a cigarette before approaching them looking like another protester. These were ordinary people who were fearful for their lives, and even ordinary people do extraordinary things when their lives are in danger. Otherwise law-abiding people were behaving in ways that, in ordinary times, they would have found reprehensible. This was precisely the kind of civil unrest that we had been told to guard against. With the brim of my hat pulled down, I mingled with the crowd just long enough to pick out one or two ringleaders. When they started to manhandle the PC, I had to intervene. I approached the constable, waving my warrant card.

"Okay, everyone, let's all calm down," I shouted.

Nothing happened, they just ignored me, so I shouted again at the top of my voice. "Quiet everyone, listen to me."

"Who are you then?" someone shouted back.

"I'm a police detective inspector, and I would like my family to shelter in the underground, the same as you."

"Why don't you do something about it then?"

"I will, but this is not the way. This is exactly what Hitler wants. He wants to break our unity, to destroy our spirit. If we riot on the streets, if we turn against ourselves, we might as well surrender now."

"I've got friends who were killed in their Anderson shelter," one man shouted. "What do you tell their families?"

"This is what 'never surrender' means. What's the point of all this sacrifice if we end up under the boot of the Third Reich? You're right about the underground stations; I'm just a copper, but I can promise you that the Commissioner will be told about public opinion, and the Government will have to change its mind."

"What are we to do in the meantime?" the man replied.

"Make your protest known, march outside the Houses of Parliament if you wish, but always remain peaceful and orderly. United we stand and divided we fall; don't be the person trying to divide us."

These were not hoodlums; they were just people too frightened to think clearly. The moment ordinary, decent people calm down, they look at what they're doing and see it for what it really is. The majority obviously felt ashamed while the hotheads still simmered. I addressed one in particular.

"Don't be the one to divide us. I want to support you, but I can't support anyone who furthers Hitler's war effort."

I was being grossly unfair, but by effectively branding the man a potential traitor, I left him few options in front of the crowd. He just stood there, unsure what to make of me, so I pushed up the brim of my hat with the finger of one hand while I reached into the pocket of my overcoat with the other. When I offered him a fag, he decided that discretion was the better part of valour. The moment he took the cigarette, the tension eased.

I asked him about his friends who had been killed in their Anderson shelter, and he told me the most harrowing story. My sympathy and anger were shared in equal measure. He had good reason to be angry about being denied access to the underground station. When the crowd dispersed, the PC came and stood next to me.

"Well done, Sir; I don't know how you did that. I thought they had gone past the point of no return."

"Yes, it was getting ugly, wasn't it."

"This is going on all over; the Government has to do something."

"It's obvious to you, Constable, and it's obvious to me and that crowd. So why the hell is it not obvious to the Government?"

"After that little speech you gave to the crowd, Sir, maybe you should be a politician. I reckon you'd get it sorted."

"I suppose Churchill has other things to think about."

With that, I left him to oversee the dispersal of the crowd as I headed back to my car. The sight of a potential riot on the streets of London really did alarm me. Civil unrest had always been high on the list of government concerns. I could see police resources would be stretched as we were tasked with the job of maintaining order. I thought about the hospital that had been extensively damaged and how the staff continued as if nothing had happened. That alone gave me hope that we could take it. I arrived at the station and found Dave and Jeff waiting for me. They were desperate to hear what I had learned from Bartholomew.

"The hospital has been bombed again. I didn't get to see Bartholomew, but I've been able to read his initial notes."

"We can't afford to lose hospitals," exclaimed Dave. "How bad is it?"

"Oh, it's bad, but somehow they're carrying on; don't ask me how."

"What does he say then, Guv?" asked Jeff.

"He suspects this is the same man. The footprint is identical in shape and size to the Clapham Common print."

"But this is so different; this is off the scale."

"It is, Dave, but he says the knife used is the same or very similar. All the cut marks radiate from the same position. He also confirms the time of death at 2 am."

"So you think this fits with your theory that he's progressing?"

"Evolving is perhaps a better description, Jeff."

"But it can't get worse than this - can it?"

"No, in his twisted mind, he has evolved into what he thinks is his perfect form. He can only kill his victims and defile their bodies, but now he wants more of them."

"I've got chapter and verse on the victim," said Dave. "Irene Newnham, twenty-eight years old, married with two young children, both evacuated. She worked as a press operator in an engineering factory. Her husband's in the army, currently based at Colchester."

"So she was alone?"

"Yes, but it doesn't explain how he got into the house in the middle of the night," Dave said. "Not unless she knew him, of course."

"There's no sign of a forced entry, so either she didn't lock the door, or she let him in," said Jeff.

"There's another possibility," I said. "There's an Anderson shelter in the garden."

"Of course," said Dave. "He grabbed her there, or when she went in or out, and then took her into the house."

"That would also fit if he grabbed her with that same stranglehold. Bartholomew couldn't be conclusive about the bruising around the neck because he'd cut her throat so badly, but he thinks it's likely she was strangled first and then killed by the cut-throat. Then there's the question of the blood," I said. "He must have blood on his clothes, and he couldn't possibly risk being seen like that. So, as we said before, he must carry some form of protective clothing."

"The fact is," said Gerry, "we have nothing to go on other than a size ten footprint. So far, we haven't found a single fingerprint in that house that we can't account for."

"You're right, Guv," Jeff replied, "he must wear gloves and protective clothing. He sets out methodically to kill his victims, making sure he leaves no trace, but then he carelessly leaves a footprint."

"That's a good point, Jeff," replied Dave.

"I hadn't thought of that," I said. "It's almost deliberate as if he wants us to know the Clapham Common murder and this are connected. If that's true, it also implies he needs to be recognised. That might just lead us to him. All we can do now is put the word out there, ask our boys on the beat to look out for any signs, and ask the ARP wardens and firemen to be especially vigilant at night."

"What if it's one of them?" asked Gerry.

"Don't you think I've thought of that, Guv? What options do we have? As you said, all we have is a shoe print."

Alfie entered the room looking as if he'd slept in his clothes, which he probably had. He looked harassed.

"What's up, Alfie?" I asked.

"Sorry, Guv. I've been sorting out a bit of a disturbance on Joey Katz's patch."

"What's Joey up to?" I asked.

"It's not so much Katz, a member of his family got thrown out of a shop, and the crowd got very unpleasant."

"Why, what did this person do?"

"She did nothing, as far as I can see, other than being a Jew. There are a few people who blame the refugees for everything. Poles and Jews especially are being victimised."

"I know what you're going to say next, Alfie. Joey's boys will take matters into their own hands."

"You got it in one, Guv, but it's even worse than that. The woman involved is Rachel Katz."

"That spells big trouble," replied Dave.

"Who's Rachel Katz then, Guv?" asked Jeff.

"She's Ezra's wife, Joey's son," I said. "Of all the people to pick on, the crowd has to choose Ezra's wife. He's just about the nastiest human being I know. I've just come from a disturbance outside Stockwell Tube Station, and now you tell me people are blaming the refugees for all our troubles. The bombing has only just started, and already we've got civil unrest."

"We need to keep on top of this," said Gerry. "If we can't protect the public from criminals and civil unrest, this could quickly get out of hand."

"Joey Katz and I go back a long way, Guv," I said. "I'll go and see him. I'd better go now before Ezra kills someone."

I spoke to Dave before I left. "Stay on the murder case, Dave. Can you and Jeff interview the local ARP and fire brigade?"

"Yes, that's what I planned to do. Be careful with Katz, Rog; you're skating on thin ice with him."

"I know, but it's probably worth the risk."

"Let's hope so. Why don't we meet up a bit early tonight and have a drink in the pub before we go to the shelter?"

"Good idea, mate. What shall we say, about six o'clock?"

"Yes, see you then."

I had a quick word with Jack as I left the station, hoping he could spare more men to police Katz's patch.

"I've already got every man I can spare guarding bloody tube stations. What the hell is going on, Roger? We've got better things to do than stand guard at underground stations."

"This is exactly the problem we were told to watch out for, isn't it? We really have to keep a lid on it, Jack."

"The Government could solve this underground shelter issue in one stroke; why the hell are they delaying?"

"It's a mystery to me, Jack. I didn't see this backlash against the refugees coming either, did you?"

"I'll try to find someone; at least it will be a uniform presence."

"I'm just off to see Joey Katz. Wish me luck, Jack."

"Watch it, Roger, you know what they say about playing with fire."

With that thought in mind, I set off. Katz had mellowed considerably in his old age; I no longer regarded him as a threat, but his son Ezra was a different matter entirely - he was pure evil. Nothing changed the fact that Joey was the head of an organised crime family, but he had always been a man of principle. Beneath it all, Joey lived by a code of conduct that mostly I would approve of. It was that other part that troubled me, the part that 'most' doesn't include. We shared one thing in common: he wouldn't tolerate the slightest mistreatment of women. If someone had hurt his daughter-in-law, we really were in for trouble.

His shop front was exactly that, a front onto the High Street where he sold fabric and haberdashery to the public. Behind the shop lay a large warehouse stacked from floor to ceiling with roll upon roll of cloth. He ran a legitimate business, and we could never prove that he had his hands soiled in the underworld. If there is such a thing, Joey was a gentleman mobster. I knocked on his office door and found him, as usual, sitting surrounded by his orders and accounting books. Whenever I called on Joey, he made a point of welcoming me. A policeman arriving unannounced might alarm most criminals, but Joey was not most criminals.

"Mr Pritchard, what a pleasure. What can I do for you?"

"Have you got a cup of tea, Joey? I'm parched."

I placed my hat carefully on some cloth samples and then hung my coat on his coat stand. We were playing out a ritual; by parting with my hat and coat, I signalled that this was not official business, and if he agreed, it might take some time. If he offered me a cup of tea, then he agreed to our terms. In truth, I think we had passed the ritualised welcome stage. Joey and I went back a very long way. He shouted out to his assistant and asked for two cups of tea.

"I'm pleased you've dropped by, Mr Pritchard. I wondered if you knew anything about a case of Johnnie Walker Red Label that someone delivered to my shop."

"Do you mean just after we found all that stolen whisky in a warehouse?"

"It might have been around that time, yes."

"I've got no idea, Joey."

"No, nor have I. Strange business that."

"We've got a problem, Joey, and when I say 'we', I mean both of us."

"If you mean what's happened to my daughter-in-law, Mr Pritchard, you would be right."

"We mustn't let this get out of hand, Joey. I deplore what's happened, but if your son Ezra does what I think he might, then he will start something bigger than all of us."

"We're Jewish, Mr Pritchard; do you think for one second we're not used to persecution? I know where this could lead, just look across the Channel."

"How can we stop it, Joey?"

"I've spoken to Ezra, he is ... he's not everything I would want him to be. I have one son in whom my pride knows no bounds, and I have another who dishonours me."

I had never heard Joey Katz say anything remotely critical about a member of his family before. To confide such a thing to me, a policeman, took considerable courage. It told me he must be at his wit's end. As far as I could tell, his son Aaron had turned away from the family business. He was a pilot in the RAF, now a wing commander awarded the DFC during the Battle of Britain. The contrast between his two sons could not be starker. One a war hero serving his country, the other a sociopath.

"Can you prevent Ezra from retaliating, Joey? Do you have any control over him?"

"My sons have been brought up to understand the ways of our people. The Talmud states that 'A man without a wife lives without joy, blessing, and good. A man should love his wife as himself and respect her more than himself.' That applies to all women, Mr Pritchard."

"I couldn't agree with you more, Joey. So whoever has abused your daughter-in-law has, in Ezra's eyes, broken your code of conduct."

"They have. Ezra demands an eye for an eye."

"You know better than me, Joey, Judaism does not apply Lex Talionis literally; it applies more to financial compensation rather than retribution."

"You never cease to amaze me, Mr. Pritchard. You are well-read. I'm sorry to say my son has his own interpretation of retribution."

"What can we do, Joey? We're both fathers of sons; we both know they will go their own way, but Ezra's way could lead to racial riots. Hitler lit the match that started Kristallnacht in 1938 with an ember no hotter than your boy holds in his hand right now."

Joey sat motionless; I could almost see the conflict in his mind. "You have a very persuasive way with words, Mr Pritchard. I know we don't always see eye to eye, but you're a man of great integrity; you command respect, and I give it freely. We share more in common than I think you realise. Leave my son to me, Mr Prichard; I'll deal with him in my own way."

I had to resist liking Joey - he was right; we shared a lot in common. He never admitted it, but I think as he grew older and wiser, he turned further away from his previous life of crime simply because it no longer conformed to his sense of values. I doubt it was ever a road to Damascus moment, but I had to admire the Joey Katz in front of me. I could also never forget about the Joey Katz who built his reputation in gangland upon his ability to intimidate people. Rumour had it that he once gave the order to have a man nailed to his front door.

"This is difficult for you, Joey, I know that, but you're too wise not to see the danger."

"I've seen it all before, Mr Pritchard; it's what my family ran away from in Russia in 1910. We can't have it here on the streets of London."

"We have limited resources to deal with things like this, Joey; I won't tell you otherwise. But I give you my word that whoever abused Rachel will incur my personal displeasure."

"You're a man of your word, Mr Pritchard, and your word is good enough for me. I just hope my son will agree."

"That's all I can ask. There's something else, Joey, something where we will be in complete agreement, and just maybe you can help me."

"What is it, this thing we will agree on?"

"We've got a serial killer stalking women right here in our part of South London. This is no ordinary killer; this man is the Devil incarnate. I can't give you the details, we have to keep that quiet, but he killed the last victim in her house during the night, during a bombing raid. If you hear of anyone being seen at night, possibly carrying a bag, possibly with some blood on him, will you tell me?"

"Is this your way of saying you suspect my son, Inspector?"

"No, not at all. No, that's not what I meant. I know you have a lot of contacts; if this man has any connection to the underworld, then I'm hoping you might get to know about it."

"If I hear about someone killing women, Mr Pritchard, then God help him."

"I don't want this to be public knowledge, Joey, but I need all the help I can get."

"You have it."

We drank our tea and talked about the bombing and the rationing just like anyone else, and Ezra wasn't mentioned again. I admit our informality had probably become too informal, but there was a question I had always wanted to ask. What I didn't expect was an honest answer.

"I've always wanted to ask, Joey. That story about you nailing some poor sod to his front door, is that true?"

"It's true about the story."

"Yes, but is it only a story, or did it actually happen?"

"What do you think, Mr Pritchard?"

"I don't think you would want to be a part of something like that. I've always thought you manufactured the story."

"Keep it under your hat, Mr Pritchard - I have an image to maintain."

We laughed like a pair of old friends, but all the while, I could see the concern in his eyes. What he said about me suspecting his son really played on my mind. I hadn't thought about Ezra, certainly not in that connection. Something had caused a rift between them, and it left me wondering. It was only a matter of time before Ezra fell foul of the law and made an appointment with the hangman or, at the very least, spent a long time at His Majesty's pleasure. In my opinion, the sooner, the better.

I had mixed thoughts as I drove away; I had sympathy with Joey as a father. He was perhaps the last of a long line of his kin where their sons would obey their father's word to the letter. For Joey, a wayward son is as unconscionable as it is incomprehensible. He couldn't hide his conflict, and rightly or wrongly, I found myself sympathising with him. Above all, I took Joey's words with me; did I suspect his son? I didn't when I arrived, but I did when I left.

# Chapter Twenty-Eight

# September 15th, 1940

Emma

*"That's the wonder of it, Emma. The butterfly has no idea
how the light reflects from its wings. It simply does what the
butterfly does, but believe me, I'm dazzled."*

E ven with most casualties being taken to other hospitals, we still
struggled to clear the backlog. Ken invited me to help him with
surgery in the operating theatre. It was what I always wanted; it was
what I initially trained for. Admittedly, I had only ever dissected cadavers
and witnessed other surgeons' operations, but I had the knowledge. Most
casualties required surgical intervention. It might just be wound closure or
bone setting, but more often, it involved internal injuries requiring direct
intervention.

Doctor Wiśniewski disapproved, but he was overruled. We needed
more surgeons, and I was keen to learn. We also needed more theatre
nurses, and the fact that I immediately got what I asked for showed how
desperate we had become for personnel. Janet joined me in surgery. We
both learned quickly; we had no option. The last surgical patient was
wheeled out of the theatre late in the afternoon of September 15th. Ken
congratulated me and Janet; we shared a successful day.

"Why don't we go down to the pub for an hour before it gets dark?"
suggested Ken.

"You mean to have time off, relax?"

"Yes, Em, why not? God knows we deserve it."

"Come on, Janet, we're going to the pub for a drink."

"I'm meeting Barry at Charing Cross. It's his first leave in ages."

"I know how much you want to be together, but could you spare an hour? I'd love to meet him."

"I'd like to show him off, Emma; you'll love him, I know you will. Only an hour then. I haven't seen him for weeks, and well, you know."

"We know," said Ken with a grin.

"One condition, Emma. You bring your boyfriend."

"My ... boyfriend?"

"Yes. Frank, he's your boyfriend, right?"

Then she did what Janet does, she put her arm around me and gave me a hug. She then breezed out of the operating theatre as if she owned the place, saying, "See you later, Ken."

He initially looked at me with a sad expression that I was slow to interpret, but then he laughed. "That woman is something else, isn't she? I remember when nurses used to call me Doctor, not Ken."

"I know, these aren't normal times, are they? Janet's not an ordinary nurse, is she? I'm getting used to her now; I even begin to wonder what we would do without her. If anyone can lift our spirits, she can."

We agreed that you need people like Janet when times are tough - someone who can make you smile, however difficult the circumstances - someone with the gift of bringing people together. I felt completely exhausted, but Ken was right; we needed a break, and an hour of normality would do us a power of good. With little time, I rushed off to change, but first, I found Frank on one of the wards.

"You're going to the pub for an hour, Frank. Can you be ready in fifteen minutes?"

"Are you asking me out, Em?"

"Yes, I suppose I am."

"Then I'll be ready. Shall I ask Leo?"

"Yes, he needs a beer more than any of us; do you think you can persuade him?"

"I'll try."

Fifteen minutes later, there was a knock on my door. I opened it to find them both standing there. Poor Leo looked a shadow of his former confident self, but at least he'd made the effort. Frank looked like - Frank - standing there in the same threadbare woollen waistcoat and twill trousers. It struck me for the first time that despite his indifferent dress sense, Frank always looked presentable in a relaxed kind of way. He rose above sartorial elegance with his understated self-assuredness; he didn't need to worry about looking good; he just did.

I suddenly realised what a lovely face he had; it seemed to belong to a man much younger than his forty-seven years suggested. Perhaps it was his almost perpetual smile, an attribute ably enhanced by the sparkle in his eyes. Leo stood in stark contrast; the twinkle in his eyes died with Gloria. He dressed the same and combed his hair the same. He would still grab the attention of the casual observer, who would only see the fashionable, handsome young man he used to be. I saw the real Leo, the remains of a once beautiful man whom death had destroyed in life.

"Hello, Leo. I'm so pleased you're coming with us; you need a drink more than any of us."

"Frank didn't give me an option."

"Well done, Frank. You need it, Leo."

Frank took my arm, and then to my surprise, Leo took the other. They walked me down the stairs towards the entrance, making me feel like Rita Hayworth. When Ken appeared standing in the central hallway, he looked up at me coming down the stairs as if I really was Rita Hayworth.

He momentarily greeted me with the same expression I had seen in the operating theatre. Then again, like a wind vane, he changed direction. A smile appeared on his face that seemed even more enthusiastic with his brightly coloured bow tie beneath it. The picture was complete with a striped boating jacket and Panama hat. Ken always dressed to make a statement, and that night he said: look, I'm here. I'm out to impress you.

We had only parted company twenty minutes ago, but when our eyes met, he looked at me as if he hadn't seen me before. We shared a mutual gaze; what we were saying with our eyes, I wasn't sure, but I enjoyed it. Usually, any attention from a man would make me feel awkward and self-conscious, but for the first time in my life, I not only felt comfortable in the presence of men, but I truly welcomed their company.

We hadn't set foot outside the hospital for days. It began to feel like the forbidden land, with us being the Morlocks daring to enter the world of the Eloi. The London that greeted us when we set foot outside had changed profoundly. We stepped into another time; it would have been no more incredible had H G Wells' time machine transported us there.

Surrounding buildings lay in ruins, not to mention the terrible damage to the hospital. Our memory prepared us to see the nurses' home, but in its place, we saw Big Ben on the far side of the river. It created an unworldly image that violated our senses. The entire block had been razed to the ground. The buildings on either side stood in proud defiance, the remaining books on a bookshelf with their continuity broken by a yawning gap. Those irreplaceable lost volumes contained the lives of generations past, and the most recent still echoed with the youthful sound of our fallen colleagues. A single tree continued to reach towards heaven with its broken branches. It was all that remained between us and the Palace of Westminster. If that sad and broken tree could speak, it would only have one word to say - 'why'?

It might have been a scene from Dante's Inferno, except people went about their business as usual. We walked past another tangle of masonry and rubble, another building that had previously witnessed a lifetime of human activity. Wafts of smoke still rose from deep within its remains. Each ribbon of smoke was the final dying act of the collective memory of generations being scattered to the four winds. We walked past the desolate scene as if it were an everyday sight. War quickly does that to you. To become accustomed to destruction is to become dehumanised; you have no other option.

For a moment, I worried that the Tavern may have suffered the same fate, but we came to realise that our oasis in the desert of war remained precisely that, a shimmering mirage existing in another time and place, immune to the ravages of war. Janet and Barry arrived breathless at almost the same time, having rushed from Charing Cross Station. Janet took a deep breath and proudly introduced us, and all the while, her blue eyes didn't stray from his. I must say he cut an impressive figure in his RAF Warrant Officer uniform.

I knew he was twenty-eight years old, Janet had told me, but he looked much younger. He wore his dark wavy hair slightly longer than the accustomed norm; he combed it back from his face except for the little bit that hung down his forehead. This, combined with his cheeky smile and thick eyelashes, gave him a boyish appearance that seemed at odds with his highly responsible position in the RAF. Barry shared something in common with Leo, that indefinable ability to look effortlessly perfect. He looked straight into my eyes and held my hand for a moment before formally shaking it. Only then did he say hello in an educated London accent. I decided, even without Janet's encouragement, that Warrant Officer Barry Roberts was absolutely lovely. She introduced me as her best friend.

"Good to meet you, Barry," said Frank. "What would you prefer - a beer?"

"No, let me," he said.

"Don't do that," said Ken, with a hint of seriousness, "you might cause offence in this pub; RAF personnel don't buy their own drinks in here."

Barry offered a coy smile of appreciation and sat back down at the table, seemingly without a crease appearing in his uniform. Frank returned from the bar with five foaming beer glasses, carefully balancing them on a large tray. I reached for mine like a veteran beer drinker. The glasses were full and overflowing, so I quickly drank a mouthful before it spilled. I looked up at the more experienced beer drinkers to see them all smiling at the froth on my nose. Ken offered me his handkerchief, and I laughed along with them. Within moments the men were talking about the war, and Janet quietly asked me what I thought of Barry.

"I've only just met him."

"That's what I mean, first impression?"

"Before I met you, I might have said he seems like a nice man, but you're having a bad effect on me, Janet. I think he looks absolutely adorable."

"He is, isn't he, he's gorgeous."

"Oh, you're so lucky. You have that same look Gloria had with Leo."

"I don't know how Leo will ever get over losing Gloria. We were good friends. I know how much she loved him; I can't bear to think about it."

"Let's not, not tonight, Janet."

We turned our attention back towards the men who were asking Barry about the war. Barry said we had been possibly only days away from losing all of our operational airfields in the southeast. The Battle of Britain was Hitler's attempt to defeat the RAF by destroying its planes, but crucially, also by destroying its airfields. None of us realised how close the Luftwaffe had come to achieving its ambition.

Barry graphically described how they survived the air raids but then immediately had to work to repair the runways and infrastructure. Ground crew worked tirelessly to keep fighter planes in the air and to keep the airfields operational. Had the Germans continued bombing the airfields, it might have been a different outcome. When Ken asked what that meant, Barry shocked us all.

"It might have been the end. Without operational airfields, we had to use aircraft from further north. There were fewer of them, and it took them longer to get here. Every day the Luftwaffe could fly unopposed, the more they would have established air superiority. We might have lost the war."

"So bombing London has saved the war?"

"As crazy as that sounds, it might be true."

"So how are we placed now, Barry, are you getting planes back in the sky?"

"Anything we can repair, we do; we're working day and night. But the best thing is the rate of production. Spitfires, Hurricanes, and Lancasters are rolling off the assembly lines quicker than ever before. We've got more fighters now than we had at the start of the battle."

"That's bloody marvellous news," said Frank.

"I shouldn't really be telling you that, so don't repeat it. Janet told me about what you're all going through at the hospital. I figured you've earned the right to know."

"No one needs a bit of good news more than us," Leo said.

"Why don't the Spitfires shoot down the bombers?" I asked naively.

"They can't, Emma, they're a day fighter, same as the Hurricane. We can't see them in the dark. We're developing night fighters for the task. Trust me, it's got priority."

"We've lost a lot of pilots, haven't we?" Janet said.

"Yes, it's been awful to witness; every day, some of them don't come back, and the rest just continue as if nothing has happened. Our Wing Commander at Hendon, Johnny Albright, has shot down over five enemy fighters, so he's won the fragile accolade of fighter ace. After nearly every sortie, we have to repair damage to his Spitfire; how long can pilots like that continue?"

"When Churchill gave that speech in the House, he said exactly what the nation couldn't find the words to express," commented Ken. "He said 'Never have so many owed so much to so few'."

"Yes," said Barry, "that speech did more for our morale than a thousand new Spitfires. But never underestimate what you're doing. You're as much on the front line as we are."

"We are," said Janet, "but we've got an advantage over the RAF. Do you ever celebrate when a German pilot is killed?"

"No, not really; it's all the same if they bail out."

"That's the difference Emma taught me. We celebrate what we do. The whole world rejoices when we save a life. I've never been so proud to be a nurse as I am now. We save lives, Barry, and I have to go on doing it for as long as it takes."

I saw Barry's expression; Janet had jumped in with both feet as she always did. She told him in no uncertain terms that she would remain a nurse. I also knew she'd decided they should live together instead of getting married, but she kept that to herself until they were alone. Barry must have suspected the same because he just sat smiling at her.

Ken didn't know that Janet wanted to get married and would therefore have felt obliged to leave nursing. He just saw the two of them, like Leo and Gloria had been just weeks before; two people in love. I didn't understand it, but I intuitively embraced the joy surrounding them. I noticed Frank had a beaming smile, as did Ken, but I also sensed the couple's joy was a painful reminder for Leo. Then I noticed Ken turn away with a hint of sadness in his eyes.

"It's like when someone laughs, isn't it, Ken? It seems to be contagious."

"Oh, it certainly is."

"Who are you thinking about, Ken, when you look at them?"

"How did you know I was thinking about someone?"

"I don't know how I know; I can just tell. There is someone, isn't there?"

"It's just the past coming back to haunt me, that's all."

"Love lost, or opportunity lost?"

"You're fishing, Em. For someone who repeatedly says she doesn't understand these things, you understand a lot."

"Well, come on, share it with me."

"You've changed a lot since you've been with us, do you know that? What happened to the woman who wouldn't come to the pub with us and only spoke if she had to?"

"There's a word for what you're doing, Ken - obfuscation."

"You're right; I often do that. I'm not the only person who's given up a lot for my career; the hospital is full of us. There was someone once, and when I look at Barry and Janet, I see myself. I obfuscated then, just as I am now. When decisions are difficult, it's easier to do nothing and let fate decide. Well, that wonderful and amazing woman who I might have spent the rest of my life with decided she needed a decision, and so she took her own."

"She left you."

"She did - she married, of all people, another doctor. I bitterly regret losing her, but even more, I regret being indecisive."

"That's not the Ken I know. In the operating theatre, you make split-second life and death decisions every day, and you're brilliant at it."

"I don't have to think about that, Em, I just react. It's the decisions that involve a step into the unknown where I flounder."

This was not like Ken at all. He usually projected an air of confidence right down to his flamboyant bow ties. He looked at me with an expression that said he was trying to tell me something.

"What is it, Ken, tell me what it is you want to say?"

"I've only been lucky enough in my life to meet two truly exceptional women. On both occasions, I didn't act soon enough and coming second doesn't count, does it?"

I had grown very close to Ken; I worked closely with him all day. I realised that perhaps, like all of us, he presented one face to the world and another that smiled beneath it. I thought his brightly coloured bow ties reflected his extrovert personality, but I had seen another Ken, the sensitive one that his bow ties were designed to protect. He reached out to me, and so I knew he had something important to say.

"You said you've only ever met two truly exceptional women, and the first one married another doctor, so what happened to the second; tell me about her?"

"I can't believe you're asking me that, Emma. You're supposed to be the shy little lady without an opinion of her own. You don't delve into other people's private lives; you profess not to understand these things. I've never believed a word of it, Emma. I have instead observed you patiently like a lepidopterist expectantly watches a chrysalis, anticipating the miraculous moment of metamorphosis when the butterfly emerges to dazzle the world."

"I'm not about to dazzle anyone, Ken."

"That's the wonder of it, Emma. The butterfly has no idea how the light reflects from its wings, it simply does what the butterfly does, but believe me, I'm dazzled."

Ken always enjoyed playing with words, but this was something more; he was playing with me but in the nicest possible way. Did he really see me as someone with the power to dazzle? Only Ken would use such a word. Of course, I didn't dazzle anyone, but if he said I did, then in his own inimitable way, he was paying me the nicest compliment I had ever received. I would have found it easier to respond had he made light of it, but he didn't; he was being incredibly serious. I found myself speechless. Frank unwittingly joined our conversation at that very moment.

"How's Emma doing in surgery, Ken?"

"She's a natural; you really have a gift for it, Em."

"I have a good teacher, Frank. It's what I've always wanted to do, and I suppose I'm good with my hands. My dad always says I'm the only one in the household with any dexterity. No one in my family can change a light bulb."

"Well, you're certainly the exception, Em; you should stick with it."

"I would like to, Ken, but it depends on what Wiśniewski says. I think he still regards me as a distraction."

"I can't believe that's true any more," said Frank. "I think it's us who've been distracted, have you seen the time?"

"Oh, good heavens, it's nearly 8 o'clock; we must go immediately."

Outside, the sun had already set beneath the horizon. There were only one or two anxious people about, and like us, they hurried on their way in the dwindling twilight. We had all become troglodytes, escaping the dangerous world above in favour of our subterranean utopia. The walk over Westminster Bridge took only minutes, but it felt much longer as I relived Ken's words, searching for their hidden meaning.

We arrived at the hospital to find it deserted. Everyone had already taken their places in the basement underworld. Conscious of the time and a little anxious, we all had to rush to our rooms and grab our night things. When we came to where we would each go our separate ways, we stopped for a second. Frank looked first at Leo and then at Ken before he looked at me. Ken shared his awkward expression. Leo appeared to be as much in the dark as I was. I got the distinct impression that either Frank or Ken wanted to say something, but whatever it was, the words proved to be too precious for them to part with.

In normal times, I might have asked what bothered them, but these were not normal times. With far more pressing things to worry about, we parted company, but we did so like children forced to leave a toy shop. Nothing more was said, but I couldn't stop thinking about it.

## Chapter Twenty-Nine
# September 16th, 1940

Emma

*"What greeted me was a vision from hell. It was not the hell of fire and brimstone; this was the hell of a thousand nightmares, the place where the damned cry in terror for all eternity."*

Having grabbed my things, I made my way down to the small basement storeroom just before 8.30 pm. Marion and the nurses were there waiting for me.

"Where have you been, Emma? We were worried."

"You won't believe it, Marion, I've been having a drink across the river."

I realised my comment must have sounded out of character when Marion looked at me slightly askance. My smile reflected the fact that I felt quite chuffed with myself, as if I had scrumped a handful of apples and got away with it. In a time when high spirits were as rare as hen's teeth, I wanted to share my glimpse of normality, but it was not to be.

The bombs had already started falling, but there is a moment when you cling to the time before. You refuse to accept reality until reality is all there is. The cherished memory you had before is torn from your grasp; you can reach out, trying to reclaim it, but it's no use, it's gone.

"They're early tonight," one of the nurses said.

No sooner had she said it than the most terrifying explosion blew us all off our feet. The shock wave literally knocked the air out of my chest. I felt as if a giant unseen fist had punched me. What remained of the plaster ceiling fell down on us in a thick cloud of dust, taking the lights with it.

A deafening roar immediately followed the explosion, and the store room shook violently as the building collapsed above us.

Dazed and in shock, I lay on the floor, not knowing if it was me or the building that was trembling. All the while, the building above us groaned in submission. I braced myself for what I thought would be the inevitable; I felt sure we were about to be crushed beneath the entire weight of the hospital. The inevitable didn't happen. A torch beam appeared in the eternal blackness, a shaft of light so clearly defined in the dust it could be mistaken for a solid object.

"Emma, are you alright?"

"Marion. We're alive."

"Shirley, are you alright?" Marion shouted to each of them. "Joyce, Beverley, Alice, Catherine."

They all responded. One by one, we freed ourselves from the plaster debris that had once been the ceiling. We struggled to our feet, each of us coughing and gasping in the thick dust. Miraculously, nobody had been badly injured. Seconds passed, and we looked at each other in stunned disbelief. We all instinctively covered our noses and mouths with whatever fabric was to hand, trying to evade some of the dust. It caught in my throat and crunched between my teeth. I set about quickly examining everyone with the aid of a torch. We shared minor head wounds inflicted by the falling ceiling and various other abrasions, but not one of us suffered as much as a broken bone or a concussion. The floor above us had mostly remained intact.

"I think the building has collapsed around us," I said. "Let's try to get out of here."

To my amazement the door opened, but just a glimpse with the torch revealed the corridor to be completely collapsed and blocked. Then, I saw the frightening sight of smoke rolling along the ceiling towards us. Joyce saw it too, and we looked at each other, frozen in fear.

"What do we do?" she said.

"Back in the storeroom, quickly."

"Can we get out?" asked Marion.

"No, and there's smoke filling the corridor."

"You mean it's burning, and we're trapped," screamed Shirley.

"Calm down, everyone," said Marion. "Let's not panic and make matters worse."

"Matron's right, Shirley," I said, "they'll come for us, and we'll be out of here in no time, but we need to keep the smoke out of this room. So let's put a blanket over the door and close it onto it, and then we can block the bottom with more blankets."

Within a minute, the door had been sealed as much as possible, but the air had already become laden with smoke and fumes. I shone my torch up to the floor above us. In the absence of the plaster ceiling, the wooden joists and floorboards were exposed. I didn't know how large floor joists would normally be, but these looked huge. Big enough, I hoped, to stop the floor above from falling down on us. We could see smoke creeping through gaps in the boards. It only appeared in the torch's beam. Perhaps it would cease to exist if I switched the torch off.

While we were actively doing something, time seemed to speed by us, but the moment we stopped and just waited, time stood still. For us, time had stopped. We were trapped in a tiny storeroom while the building above us continued to collapse and burn. I had never experienced such complete helplessness. The stultifying effect of submission leaves only hope to cling to. Hope that the building didn't collapse further, hope that the fire wouldn't reach us, and hope that the rescuers would find us in time.

We sat in a huddle on the rubble with the light of a single torch to remind us we were still alive. Our world had been reduced to a single pool of light. The shadows we cast upon the walls were as fleeting as we were. My eyes stung from the effect of the toxic smoke and dust. My lungs heaved.

"Are we going to die here?" said Shirley.

"Doctor Stevenson's right, Shirley; they will rescue us," replied Joyce, unconvincingly.

"We must all stay calm," said Marion. "We have limited air in this little room. Let's not use it up discussing what we have no control over. The rescuers will find us in due course."

Marion's reassuring authority spread like a soothing balm. If she said the rescuers would find us, then that is precisely what would happen. She sat with her hands on her knees, looking at each of us with a warm but demanding expression. In Marion's eyes, we were on parade; she inspected us for any sign of weakness or panic, and when she found none, we were rewarded with a slight nod of the head.

I marvelled at her ability to exert effortless authority, and like the rest of us, I drew strength from it. We remained calm, but with every creak and moan of the timbers above us, our eyes followed the torch beam looking for the source of the sound, but all the while hoping not to find it. Shirley flinched at every sound, pulling her head into her body in a tortoise-like fashion. Beverley simply raised the corner of her mouth, a gesture of defiant acceptance. Joyce closed her eyes tightly, a moment with God or perhaps just contemplation. Each of us withdrew into the sanctuary of our own thoughts.

Another crash made the floor above us moan in response. Like people fighting for their lives, the floor timbers called upon all their reserves of strength to resist the ever-increasing threat to their existence. The floor strained every fibre of its being, every muscle and sinew, until, like a dying person, it simply accepted the inevitable. It started with a creaking sound, like the loose floorboard you try to avoid in the middle of the night. But that floorboard only creaked louder until its cries of submission turned into the floor's equivalent of a scream. Each fibre broke with its own splintering cry for help, imposing an ever greater burden upon the beams that continued to resist.

For the condemned, that last second became a lifetime. I looked up like a casual observer from the safety of another dimension. The floor beams above us finally submitted to the inevitable. The entire floor above one side of the storeroom snapped like so many matchsticks. Its submission sounded like an exploding bomb. It happened so quickly we had no time to react. Our world crashed around us with a terrifying ferocity.

One moment we were sitting in a huddle at the bottom of an open grave. The next moment, the grave was filled in. It took many seconds, perhaps many minutes, to realise what had happened. I remember opening my eyes and seeing nothing. I could hear nothing other than a constant hissing sound in my ears. My external sensory world had gone. I felt nothing at all, no connection to the terror I'd left behind. I existed in a place where the conscious mind had nothing to react to. For a moment, I thought I was asleep, in that sublime moment between sleep and wakefulness, a part of one but also a part of the other. I resisted the waking moment, but that all changed abruptly when I became aware of the pain rushing up my legs. Disorientated and confused, I had only the pain to tell me I was alive and not dead. A lifetime flashed before my eyes before I realised where I was and what had happened.

"Is there anyone there?" a weak voice asked.

"Yes, it's Emma, I'm alive."

"It's Shirley, Emma. Can you reach your torch?"

I groped in the darkness and found my torch only inches from my hand. For a second, I hesitated to turn it on. I dreaded what I would see. What greeted me was a vision from hell. It was not the hell of fire and brimstone. This was the hell of a thousand nightmares, the place where the damned cry in terror for all eternity. We were buried alive in a grave. I lay flat on my back with my legs trapped beneath heavy timbers. I could hardly move. I shone the torch and tried to move my head in search of the others as best as I could. A small vertical space remained on one side of the room about two feet high. The remaining triangular space quickly diminished into nothing.

Joyce sat next to me with her legs straight out in front of her. She was bent over double in the thin end of the space. Her head rested on her chest at a grotesque angle, her arms limp at her side. The only colour existing in that grave of dust ran down her chest and pooled between her legs. Joyce was dead.

Shirley screamed when she saw her friend in the torchlight. Unable to move, I could only listen in horror. She would have continued screaming if she had the breath, but she was quickly reduced to sobbing. I looked at those I could see. Shirley lay beneath timbers the same as me, but she had the strength to scream. Alice raised her hand but said nothing. Beverley looked to be relatively unharmed; she could move. I couldn't see Catherine or Marion.

"Marion, Catherine, can you hear me?" I said, but there was no reply. "Beverley, can you see them?"

"Yes," she replied in a thin rasping voice. "Catherine is not moving, but I think she's alive."

"Can you see, Marion?"

"Don't shine that torch in my face," a weak voice said.

"Matron's alive," Beverley said. I heard the relief in her voice.

The smoke rapidly became thicker until it combined with the dust in our lungs, causing involuntary spasms. Choking became the only sound any of us could make. Beverley remained the most able of us. Somehow she found the breath to say a last word.

"Goodbye, everyone. We did our best, didn't we? We'll not die for nothing."

I desperately wanted to say something significant. It seemed only right that the last thing you say should be something important. The only thing any of us would leave behind would be our achievements in the hospital. I'd saved lives, we all had, it was a fitting epitaph that we all shared. People were alive because of us; we had given our lives in the service of our patients. In that last moment between worlds, I felt immensely proud. As my lungs convulsed, I wanted it over before the flames reached us.

I lay waiting for the bringer of death to take my hand. I had seen so many people die; I knew that when the last moment comes, we instinctively know. We cling to life until all hope is gone. Fear and terror belong to this world, but in that last moment, when you submit to the inevitable, you leave fear behind. I realised our last second in this life is our most precious second. In the emptiness of complete darkness, I knew my journey had begun. I submitted to the inevitable as I waited for my last second to relieve me of my pain and suffering.

In the far reaches of my mind, I could feel the flames as they reached out for my face. I lay there resembling a spectator, still there but no longer a part of it. First, a single flame licked my face and then another brushed my chin before it continued down my neck. More flames reached out to me. I felt them penetrating my clothes. I clung to my grateful oblivion, but the more the flames engulfed me, the more I had to struggle to resist them until I could resist no more. Consciousness returned uninvited and thrust me back into that place of pain and horror. I panicked and struggled as the flames spread further over my body, but this was not to be my final second. The flames were not fire; they were water.

The smoke increasingly turned to steam, and the water washed the dust from my eyes and mouth. I reached again for my torch, and I could just see Beverley trying to wash the dust from her eyes as she lay in the tiny space between the timbers.

"Check the others, Beverley. Make sure they can breathe. It would be silly to drown now, wouldn't it?"

"I will. What's happening, Emma?"

"It must be the firemen putting out the fire. That means the rescuers are here."

She crawled between us as best as she could, making sure each one of us could breathe. Marion said she was alright, to tend to the others. Catherine remained unconscious, while Shirley no longer stared into oblivion. Alice grimaced in pain but raised a clenched fist. Something truly remarkable had happened. When all hope is gone, it takes you with it, but the reverse is equally true. Offer hope to those resigned to their fate, and you offer them the gift of another life. Those of us still alive seized that gift with every fibre of our bodies.

Water continued to pour through the rubble, and we could hear something happening. Whenever we heard something, Beverley boosted our confidence, saying they were getting closer. She crawled between us, maintaining our spirits. Where she could, she applied rag bandages to stop bleeding, and it always came with words of encouragement. It seemed to take forever, but eventually, Beverley shouted.

"We're here, down here, we're alive. I can hear them," she shouted. "They're coming for us."

However desperate our situation, here, at last, hope had become salvation. I tried to assess how badly injured my legs were, but I could see nothing beneath the timbers. The pain was as nothing I had ever experienced, intense like a cramp in every muscle. Then I realised that with effort, I could still move my toes. That told me my femoral nerves were unbroken, and the pain told me my legs were still fully attached to my body.

The water pooled around us. We were at the lowest level of the hospital. There was nowhere lower for the water to go. When it rose around our trapped bodies, a new terror entered our minds. Nobody said anything, it was vastly better than the fire, but we each now shared a new fear. We knew the rescuers were desperately trying to get to us, but what we didn't realise was how dangerous and nearly impossible those attempts were proving to be. Lying there in such pain, those hours were the worst hours of my life. I thought it would never end, but finally, I heard voices. The voices became louder until a shaft of light appeared above us. That single shaft of light grew until it was just large enough for a fearless and determined man to speak to us.

"How many of you are there?" he asked.

"Six," Beverley replied, "five alive."

The man struggled closer to us, endangering himself and us. Finally, I could see his head and shoulders as he calmly assessed our situation with a powerful torch.

"Emma," he shouted, "are you hurt?"

"Leo," I screamed, "I'm trapped. We all are."

"We'll get you out of here, I promise you, but first, we need equipment to move these heavy timbers. So, don't go anywhere, ladies; I'll be back."

His confident humour belied the fact that he appeared to be only slightly less injured than we were. We waited as reassuring voices tried their best to maintain our spirits. Then another voice we all knew shouted down to us. It was Doctor Wiśniewski.

"Who is down there?"

Beverley gave him our names, and he wanted to know the extent of our injuries. She told him what she could see and that we were all but one fully conscious. He had the unenviable job of trying to assess our condition ahead of the attempted rescue. We had all experienced a rescue before; we knew the rest of the building might collapse at any moment. Those most likely to survive must go first. Any of us with crush injuries might require amputations before the rescuers could release us.

Gradually the rescue tunnel became larger, but as they removed timber and masonry, more rubble collapsed around us. The measure of our plight suddenly became horrifyingly clear when the huge timber joist trapping Alice suddenly gave way. With no more than a final gasp of air, her head rolled to one side, and her arms fell limp. Our grave filled with cries of "No, no, no," until they subsided into yet more uncontrolled sobbing. Alice, like each of us, had been offered renewed hope, another life, only for it to be brutally snatched away. It seemed so unbelievably cruel. Our tears were shed both in grief and anger. Who or what we were angry with, we didn't know, but at that moment, we demanded that fate should have a face.

A fireman appeared, closely followed by Leo. We had no option but to be there, but they were putting their lives on the line for us. They pulled Beverley free and physically pushed her into the tunnel. She had sufficient strength remaining to climb her way out. The fireman looked at the timbers trapping us and decided which one would be least likely to cause a collapse. It would release Marion and Catherine. Marion was adamant the fireman would release her at his peril.

"This lady is unconscious, and as I am the oldest. I will be the last to leave, God willing. Save the others first."

Leo crawled over to Catherine and agreed with Marion. It would be very difficult to get Catherine out. Shirley didn't appear to be badly injured; Leo said her vital signs were good; she could help herself if she were freed.

The fireman placed the hydraulic jack beneath the beam trapping her. With each push of the handle, the beam relinquished its grip on Shirley. With only inches to spare, they dragged her out. Somehow in that tiny space, they dragged, pushed, and moved her into the tunnel where eager hands were waiting to pull her to safety. Leo crawled towards me.

"How bad is it, Em?"

"It's my legs. The pain is terrible."

"I'll give you some morphine. Can you move your toes?"

"Yes, I can feel both feet, but I think I'm bleeding."

"Broken bones?"

"Not sure."

Every part of me wanted to scream both in pain and terror. The awful feeling of claustrophobia combined with the imminent possibility of death is a powerful incentive to let go of your grip on reality. Leo remained both calm and reassuring; his grip on reality became my strength. The fragile timbers above us might collapse further at any moment, but Leo ignored the imminent danger. He acted as if examining me while laying flat on his stomach was perfectly normal.

The fireman inched his way through the labyrinth of twisted timbers and masonry, struggling to move the hydraulic jack. With one final Herculean effort, he placed it beneath the larger of the beams that lay across my legs. As he pumped the handle, he looked at Leo as if to say, 'Good luck'. He could only move the handle a few inches at a time, and then slowly but surely, I could feel the pressure on my legs easing. Small pieces of debris fell down, and the combination of timber and concrete above us creaked and groaned in response. Catherine remained unconscious, and whatever fear Marion felt, she courageously suppressed. Incredibly, our claustrophobic tomb echoed with words of hope and optimism.

The morphine acted almost instantaneously. The pain tormenting me for so long became just a bad memory. The abject terror that I struggled to suppress joined my pain in some distant place beyond my concern. Leo constantly reassured me, saying, "I'm here for you, Em. I'll get you out." I remember them pulling and pushing me, and finally, the hands that reached down to me from the world above. I remember those last moments as if recalling a bad dream, too real to ignore but too awful to relive.

I don't know how much morphine Leo gave me, but I have little recollection of my rescue. My next clear memory is lying in a bed in a makeshift ward with a soft voice waking me up.

"I've got you, Emma, I've got you. You're safe now; you can open your eyes."

"Janet, is that you?"

"Of course it is. When I was injured, you took my hand, and you said, 'I've got you; you'll be alright'. Well, it's my turn now."

"Am I badly injured, are my legs okay?"

"Your legs are fine, a funny colour, but fine. Considering what you've been through, I can't believe how well you've come out of it. You've got a lovely, neat row of stitches down your right shin. I think they're the neatest I've ever done. Oh, and while I was about it, you've got more stitches further up your leg. You're sitting on them. I saved you the piece of wood I pulled out as a souvenir."

"When did you get here?"

"I was at Barry's. I came the moment I heard. Doctor Wiśniewski checked you over, and then I took over. I've been with you every minute."

"Bless you, now I feel safe. You have to tell me, Janet, did Matron and Catherine get out?"

"Thanks to Leo and the fireman, yes, they did. Leo and that firemen are being treated as heroes by everyone."

"Are Matron and Catherine alright?"

"Matron has a broken leg and a multitude of cuts and bruises, but she'll be alright. Catherine remained unconscious. She had a bleed on the brain; they needed to operate. Her other injuries are serious, she will need weeks of hospitalisation, so she has been sent home to Edinburgh. They put her on a train this morning."

"Did Ken operate on her?"

"No, it was … someone else."

"Is Frank alright?"

"Yes, he's been here with me, but you were out of it. He was very lucky, it's the second time he's been rescued with only a few cuts and bruises. There's something else, Emma. I'm really sorry, but I can't hide it from you, Ken's dead."

There are words in this life that bring so much pain we try to reject them but we can never evade them. I stood before the avalanche in complete denial … until it hit me. First, my heart pounded, and then it felt as if my blood had been replaced with ice water. It ran to the tips of my fingers and down to my toes. I started shaking.

Janet reacted immediately. She raised my feet with pillows and forced an oxygen mask onto my face. I tried to struggle, but she was forceful. A part of me knew what was happening. Shock can be a serious medical condition if it's not treated. Shock and grief are a toxic mix, add a broken heart, and you have a combination so corrosive it can quickly destroy you from within. I fought against it as best as I could, but the connection with my previous self and the trembling woman who lay on that bed hung by a thread.

Janet saved me that awful day. She did everything medically possible, but she did so much more. What other people must have thought, I can't imagine, but Janet understood what the medical profession didn't. She took me in her arms and didn't let me go until I stopped shaking. When your heart is broken, there is no medication that can help you. It takes an extraordinary person to fill that void. They have to give something of themselves, something so generous and so wonderful that it gives you a reason to continue, a reason to believe.

The following morning, I woke with what felt like the worst hangover imaginable. I found Janet slumped in a chair next to me, asleep. I had stopped shaking; I had been reduced to yet one more grieving woman in that war of broken hearts. As I moved, Janet woke up with a start.

"Emma, how are you?"

"I'm still here, thanks to you."

"You've been to hell and back, I'm pleased you've made it."

"Anyone who's not been trapped in that way could never understand."

"I know what you mean. We have our own unique club that no one else wants to join."

"Do you ever close your eyes without thinking about that awful feeling of entrapment?"

"Honestly, no. It haunts me every night. I wonder if it will ever go away."

"Even the weight of these blankets makes me feel trapped; I want to scream."

"Don't worry, I've got you, you'll be alright. I knew the awful news about Ken would be a terrible shock, but I didn't realise how close you were to him."

"We were friends, really close friends."

"I think you were more than that. I've seen how he looked at you, and I've seen how you looked at him. I should have realised."

"Don't make it worse for me, Janet. He's gone, is that not bad enough?"

"No, I don't think that's right, I saw how you reacted. There was something special between you. I don't think you should deny it. We have to keep our cherished memories."

"I'm really confused about it. I only know my heart's broken."

"You're not alone. There are a lot of broken hearts today; that bomb caused some terrible damage. It hit the main corridor. We've lost the out-patient department, and the resident staff quarters are gone, as are several of the wards. The dispensary and the X-ray department are both damaged. We've even lost the medical school."

"How many people have we lost, Janet, tell me?"

"It's not just Ken. We've lost Joyce and Alice and that auxiliary fireman who helped to rescue you."

"Oh no. Oh, Janet, I'm to blame for his death - he died saving me."

"No, you're not to blame; it happened after you were rescued. It's the bomb that killed him. It's the bomb that killed all those people."

The magnitude of the damage and all the people it had killed over-whelmed me. It didn't seem right that all those people had risked their lives to get me and the others out, only for one of the rescuers to be killed. I struggled with a maelstrom of emotions, guilt, anger, sorrow, and all the while, Ken loomed large in every aching thought. The burden of so much grief and heartache became increasingly impossible to bear.

How Janet found the strength to support me, I do not know, having suffered every bit as much as I had when the nurses' home was bombed. What happened to the hospital and our friends and colleagues was truly awful. The enormity of those events was beyond anyone's capacity to cope. I tried so hard to be brave, but I knew eventually my frailty would overwhelm me.

# Chapter Thirty
# September 18th, 1940

Roger

*"The means is always aggression, the spawn of ignorance.*
*The end is a scapegoat, a substitute for genuine introspection."*

Dave knocked on my door at precisely 6.30 that evening. He was nothing if not punctual. We had only parted company a couple of hours ago but shook hands as we always did. Then, more than ever, those seemingly pointless rituals took on an even greater significance. Dave hugged Marilyn, and Jean pulled me towards her. Long-standing true friendship has only two weaknesses. One is over-dependence; the other is taking it for granted. Dave and I were guilty on both counts; we relied upon each other implicitly and never once doubted one another.

Marilyn and Jean had a different kind of friendship. Marilyn's long-standing obsession that Jean and I had some sort of unfinished relationship had always been there bubbling somewhere deep beneath the surface like a toxic fermenting brew. On the odd occasion when it bubbled to the surface, Jean usually just ignored it. It said much for our friendship that we managed to ignore such a potentially divisive obsession. Even though they were lifelong friends, Marilyn didn't depend on Jean as I did Dave. I suspect all four of us were guilty of taking our friendship for granted, but the Blitz changed everything.

The once important things in life, like your neatly trimmed privet hedge, became inconsequential. When your way of life is threatened, you quickly formulate a new set of priorities. The things we took entirely for granted, such as a really good cup of tea, suddenly became a valued commodity. One thing above all else became our most treasured possession. Only one thing in life is truly irreplaceable - your friends and family.

We set off towards the pub, together in every sense of the word. Our local pub, the 'Fox and Hounds', went back a long way. It didn't take a couple of police detectives to work out that it had been a long time since the streets of Balham echoed to the sound of fox hounds. The pub was another place we used to take for granted. Its seamless link with past generations was also something we couldn't replace.

We sat in the corner at 'our' table, and I thought of previous generations who had sat in that same corner and called it their own. What price can you place on such a connection with your heritage? Dave came back from the bar with two beers, and to the surprise and delight of the girls, two gin and tonics. The pub had kept some bottles of gin, but the tonic was in very short supply. We raised our glasses in a toast.

"To us," Dave said.

"To us," I replied, "and the future."

"You mean a future without this awful war."

"That's what the future means, Jean. Anything else isn't much of a future, is it?"

"If the bombing carries on like this," Marilyn said, "what sort of future can there be? This pub will be gone. Our homes will probably be gone."

"As long as there's the will, there'll be a way. Hitler can destroy our buildings and kill our people, but the spirit of the nation lives in every building and every person. For as long as someone remains who can call themselves British, Hitler has not defeated us."

"Bloody hell, Roger," Jean said, "you should give a speech like that in the House of Commons. I always said you should have been a politician."

"We could do with someone in charge who actually knows what's going on," Dave replied. "Look at this nonsense with the tube stations. We've got perfect underground shelters, and the authorities charge us with the responsibility of keeping the people out of them at night."

"I'm not surprised there've been protests. We keep hearing about people being killed in their Anderson shelters - and the public shelters, for that matter."

"They're a lot better than nothing, Marilyn," replied Dave.

"I've sent another message to the Commissioner about it via Gerry. The tube stations should be opened to the public as a matter of urgency.

Any delay will cause additional deaths. I also pointed out that by making us responsible for enforcing the ban, we're inviting the public to blame us for the decision."

"Is the Commissioner going to listen to you, Roger?"

"I'm sure he will, Jean. It's not his decision, but I know he'll make our views known to the Home Secretary."

"What's happening about the murderer who's been killing local women? Roger never tells me anything."

"We've got next to nothing to go on, Marilyn. There isn't much to say."

"They know more than they're telling us, Marilyn. I know Dave's worried about it."

"We are worried about it," Dave said, "this is the worst possible kind of murderer. Most murderers have a motive that we can at least understand. That's usually what leads us to them. This man does it because he enjoys it, making him uniquely dangerous."

I didn't like talking about the serial killer because I didn't want to worry them, but I also didn't want a word of it to be mentioned at the baker's or grocer's shops. The one thing our killer wanted was notoriety, and I didn't want to give it to him. I delicately changed the subject by suggesting another round. As I stood at the bar, I suddenly noticed who was sitting at a table on the far side of the pub. It was someone I had never seen in the 'Fox' before and didn't want to see. I quickly turned my back, carried our drinks back to our table and immediately took Dave to one side.

"Don't look over there, but I've just seen Rachel Katz sitting on the other side."

"Don't tell me Ezra's with her."

"I didn't see him; she's sitting with another woman. I pray to God he isn't here."

"Will he recognise you if he's here?"

"Most probably, and that could be big trouble. I've only seen Rachel from a distance; she doesn't know me or you."

We both had a surreptitious look towards Rachel, who was impossible to miss. She was absolutely exquisite. Her raven black hair was always pulled back from her face, revealing her perfect bone structure. Her big brown eyes could stop a man in his tracks. At only twenty-two years old, she appeared little more than a child to me and far too young to be so conspicuously wealthy. With a father-in-law in the rag trade, she wore only the finest haute couture, which stood out like a pork pie at a bar mitzvah in that time of rationing. Rachel was something, I can tell you. I had never seen a young woman like her; she was bewitching.

I can't imagine why she married Ezra. Sure, he brought his father's wealth with him, but the man was a low life. Rachel traded in style and sophistication, while Ezra traded in violence. She had an intellect born of a fine education; the best you could say for him is that he was streetwise. I could only speculate that she mistook the respect and privilege demanded by mobsters for actual status.

With no sign of Ezra, we ignored her and continued chatting between ourselves. The girls talked about the children, and I confess Dave and I discussed the serial killer when they weren't listening. We were enjoying a rare moment of relaxation when it all came to an abrupt end. An elderly couple were leaving the pub, and the woman couldn't resist a comment about Rachel as she walked past.

"Fine for you in your posh clothes, thinking you're better than us. Don't suppose rationing means anything to you, does it? Your lot is a bloody disgrace."

The couple left unaware that they had left a time bomb ticking on Rachel's table. The Fox and Hounds is a fine pub. It didn't attract low-lifes, that's why we frequented it. That evening of all evenings, three louts were drinking more beer than they could afford. The woman's comments were manna from heaven for those who make a virtue of bigotry. It was too much for those idiots to resist. It started with nasty comments picking up on the previous topic of rationing, but it quickly escalated into racial hatred.

Rachel was Jewish, and she did not attempt to hide the fact. There had been an influx of European refugees escaping the Nazi persecution. That they also found persecution in this country appalled me. It might have been perpetrated by an ignorant minority, but for me, one would be too many. Dave and I listened with growing concern as the verbal abuse escalated ever closer to violence. Bigotry is a blind master, and Rachel Katz represented nothing more than the means to an end. The means is always aggression, the spawn of ignorance. The end is a scapegoat, a substitute for genuine introspection.

"What are we going to do, Rog?"

"Don't you do anything," Marilyn said, "there are three of them."

"We can't sit by and watch this, Marilyn. This is way out of order."

"You're both off duty," said Jean, "it's not your responsibility."

"That's exactly what the decent people of Germany said."

"Why do you do that, Roger; why do you always have to make us see the awkward truth?"

"Because there is only one truth. I'm sorry if it's awkward."

"Roger's right, Jean, someone has to intervene, and it's our job."

Jean was about to argue, but Dave was already on his feet. I wasn't good at strong-arm tactics, but it's one of those things that made us such a good team. Dave was the gentlest, kindest bloke I ever knew; it completely belied the fact that he had been a very accomplished boxer. If ever we needed to deal with ruffians, I relied on Dave. He had a physical confidence about himself that either intimidated people or antagonised them. I desperately hoped our three idiots would be intimidated. One of them dragged Rachel from her chair. I assumed he planned to throw her out of the pub. We rapidly approached them.

"What the hell do you morons think you're doing?" Dave said. "Let that woman go immediately."

"What the fuck has it got to do with you?" came the reply.

I waved my warrant card, but the response was, "Piss off, copper."

Dave grabbed the arm of the man manhandling Rachel, and he instantly took a swing at Dave. That was a big mistake. When a drunken man takes a swing at a one-time boxer of some repute, there's only ever going to be one outcome. Dave swung his right shoulder back, transferring his weight onto his right leg. He sidestepped the blow with consummate ease, but that also placed him in the perfect position to launch a formidable right cross that caught the man square on the nose.

It was one heck of a punch; the impact seemed to echo around the pub. He might have punched him on the chin or the stomach, but the nose is by far the most disabling. I realised Dave's tactic immediately; he didn't want to start a fight with the man; he wanted to end it immediately. The man on the receiving end dropped like a felled tree, with his heels seemingly planted to the floor.

He just lay there out cold with his nose spread across his face in a stream of blood. The sight of blood can be very arresting, even for those who think themselves to be tough guys. The other two froze in their tracks, realising the demise of their fellow idiot could just as easily be theirs. A crowd quickly gathered, and for a small minority, their sympathies were mixed. I stepped in before it could escalate further.

"Have you people learnt nothing? Hitler led the German people into this war by exploiting exactly this kind of ignorant bigotry. You, madam, how would you like your husband dragged off the street and shot simply because he has dark hair? You, sir, would you want your entire family sent off to a concentration camp because you're seen to be a troublemaker? We have something the German people have lost; it's called freedom, and it's not a right; it's a privilege. Our armed forces are giving their lives in defence of that principle. How dare you defile their sacrifice by bringing Hitler's twisted ethnic ideology into this pub? Anyone who wants to espouse that ideology, say so now, and so help me, I'll arrest you as a traitor."

I admit it; I lost my temper. Shouting at people usually means you've handed the initiative to the recipient of your anger. They touched a raw spot that evening. I cannot abide abuse of women in any guise, and I cherish freedom in all its incarnations, including Rachel Katz's freedom. Despite my outburst, I must have made an impact because the entire pub fell into a deafening silence. They looked into the mirror as lone individuals and not as a crowd. Racism is a bitter fruit when eaten alone. The two idiots knelt over their fallen comrade, stripped of their bravado and looking crestfallen. Dave stood over them, but they had no fight left in them. We didn't want to arrest them on our night off, so I adopted another tactic.

"Do either of you idiots know who that woman is that you just intimidated? No, I didn't think so. You've just insulted Ezra Katz's wife."

"Oh, fuck!"

"Yes, precisely; if I were you, I'd keep my head down. Now pick your mate up and clear off."

They were only too pleased to go. For people like that, losing face and credibility leaves them with nothing. They left as men of straw, the same as when they arrived. One or two others tried to step back while retaining face, but the vast majority of the crowd agreed with me, and the displeasure of a crowd is a force to be reckoned with. A lone individual started clapping, and then another, and the entire pub echoed to the sound of raised spirits. Only then did we notice that Rachel Katz was in floods of tears, being comforted by her friend. Being very aware of her connection to Joey, I would probably have reluctantly turned away, but not Dave.

"I'm sorry, Mrs Katz; those people are not representative of this country. I apologise on their behalf."

"How do you know who I am?"

"We are aware of your father-in-law."

"And you still help me."

"Of course, what my colleague said is absolutely right. We can never stand by and witness that kind of ignorance."

She remained in quite a state, and I should have guessed that Jean would step forward to help reassure her. Jean is that kind of woman, compassionate and caring - she couldn't see a woman in distress without helping. Typical Jean, she did no more than walk over and put her arm around Rachel. In truth, I wanted to do precisely the same thing, but instead, I glared at Marilyn, trying to ask her not to go. She joined Jean anyway, and so, completely outnumbered, I had no alternative but to join them.

"I was so frightened," she said. "To know that people hate you is just the most awful feeling. I was terrified. What have I done to them?"

"Mrs Katz, you've done nothing," Dave said. "The blame is entirely theirs."

"You're all so kind. I can't thank you enough."

"What's your name, Luv?" asked Jean.

"Rachel, Rachel Katz; this is my friend Elizabeth."

"I'm Jean, and this is Marilyn. And I'm proud of these two men. This is my husband, Dave, and this is Roger."

"I think you should be proud of them. You were magnificent; I can't thank you both enough. What you said to these people, Roger, was wonderful. You're policemen, and you know who I am, and yet you not only defended me, you're all being so kind to me."

"How do you know Rachel then, Roger?" asked Marilyn.

"Let me answer that," Rachel said. "My husband is a criminal; they know this. They also know my father-in-law, Joey Katz, who heads a crime family. This is why your kindness overwhelms me."

"Is this true, Roger?"

"Yes, it's true, but we don't regard Rachel as a criminal. Even if she were, we wouldn't stand by and see her mistreated that way."

"I've never spoken to a policeman before; you're nothing like I was told to expect. I promise you, I'm not a criminal."

"You're a lovely, intelligent woman," I said. "How did you get involved with Ezra?"

"Roger, you can't ask her that."

"It's alright, Marilyn, many people ask me that. It's no secret I made a mistake. I met Joey through my family long before I met Ezra, and Joey can be charming. I've never seen the Joey that I now hear about. Have you ever spoken to my father-in-law?"

"I know Joey well," I said, "and I've never seen the Joey that I hear about, either."

"This is difficult for you, isn't it? You stand on one side of the fence while Ezra and his father stand on the other, and I'm sat in the middle."

"Yes, this is awkward, Rachel; we have to be careful what gets back to Joey and especially Ezra. We're policemen and can't be seen collaborating with known criminals."

"I'm not a known criminal, Roger."

"I didn't think for a minute that you were."

"What's going to happen to Ezra?"

"When do you mean?"

"I mean in the future, in my future."

"Do you want me to be brutally honest?"

"Yes, I need to know."

"He'll go too far one day, and well, it could end with the hangman."

"That's what I thought; thank you for being honest with me."

I couldn't help but like her. Clearly, she had made a mistake with Ezra; her decision was the product of innocent youth. I likened her to a flower in an exotic greenhouse collection - the flower that captures everyone's attention because not only is it the most beautiful, but it's also the only flower with poison petals.

"Can I give you some advice?" asked Jean.

"I'd welcome it."

"What that ghastly woman said about your clothes, she's right, you know. Life would be simpler if you didn't draw attention to yourself."

"I know, it's just me being proud and defiant. I intend to continue being proud and defiant, but I'll also be more sensible in the future."

I sat back and listened to them chatting away with Rachel and her friend as if they were old friends. The whole situation had taken on bizarre proportions. We were two policemen chatting with a gangster's moll, except she was no moll that I could ever imagine. It was very easy to be seduced by her; she had the key to every man's vulnerability. One smile from her and your commonsense flew out of the window. It may have resulted from her seduction, but I ended the evening thinking she was exactly what she appeared to be - a beautiful young woman who regretted her choices in life. She captivated us all to the point where we lost track of time. The pub was empty, and the landlord had to remind us of the time.

We rushed outside into the pitch-black darkness of night. The clear sky gave us some moonlight. The blackout divided Balham into a black-and-white mosaic of cold light and dark shadow. We had experienced a couple of hours where the war didn't exist - in that world, we would have stepped out onto a street with lighting and people going about their business. The sudden intrusion of our new dark reality came as a shock, as our relaxed emotions turned immediately to fear.

"Look at the time," said Marilyn, "we'd better run."

"Have you got a shelter to run to, Rachel?" asked Jean.

"Not here, no; we should have left ages ago."

"Come with us, then."

As we began to run, the siren started wailing. A part of you says the bombs will fall anywhere but on you - you cling to that belief until you hear the first explosions. It started further east as it always did, but with every second, they drew closer. When you can hear the drone of the bombers and the whistle of the falling bombs, that's when the fear knots your stomach and takes the breath from your lungs. From the pub to our local public shelter was only about a mile, but it felt like a thousand miles.

A bomb fell not more than seventy-five yards from us. It landed in one of the terrace houses on the other side of the road. A flash of light was followed almost instantly by a deafening shock wave. The house expanded like a balloon. Its slate roof offered no more resistance than wedding confetti as the slates flew high into the night sky. The glass windows shattered into a thousand lethal projectiles searching for victims. The brick walls expanded like a middle-aged waistline before slumping down onto the road. In just a few seconds, someone's home had gone forever, reduced to a pile of broken memories.

At seventy-five yards, the blast wave knocked the wind out of our lungs and threw us to the ground. Pieces of debris rained down on us. It took a moment to process what had happened. Unless you have stood in front of an exploding bomb before, you have no reference point. All six of us struggled to our feet in shocked silence. Dave was the first to regain sufficient composure to speak.

"Is everyone alright?"

"I think so," replied Marilyn, a response we each echoed.

"That was a close one," Dave said.

"Close!" Marilyn replied. "What if we'd walked fifty paces further down the road?"

No one answered. The frigid chill of reality made a terrifying companion. Everyone in and around London knew that life had become a lottery, but understanding and accepting that reality are entirely different things. Not allowing the evidence to affect our judgment is one of our most dangerous human weaknesses. The inconvenient truth is always exactly that. We cling to what we want to believe, and nothing is more appealing than confirmation of our own opinion. Our close encounter with death shattered any misguided illusions of immortality we might have clung to.

Another bomb fell a few streets away, and then another. Our state of shock turned to panic as we realised we remained in imminent danger. We took to our heels but had to negotiate our way slowly through the remains of the fallen house. A sudden realisation struck every one of us as we clambered over the rubble. Had we arrived just a minute sooner, this is where our bodies would have lain, crushed beneath the debris. That thought didn't escape any of us. Not one of us mentioned it, but whatever misguided thoughts of invulnerability we clung to were left beneath the rubble. We ran for the shelter, terrified of our own mortality.

## Chapter Thirty-One
# October 1940

Emma

*"The tears running down our cheeks joined the increasing sea of sorrow that flooded across the country, pooling ever deeper over the East End of London."*

I recovered from my physical injuries quickly enough, but the trauma of that day, the 15th of September, never goes away. The same applied to the hospital, it would never fully recover either. Janet nursed me, not in a ward but in a basement room that had been a part of the laundry. All our wards were damaged or no longer safe to use. I had so many questions when Frank and Leo visited me. They were both working every hour they could stay awake. They arrived looking tired and haggard.

"How are you, Em?"

"Never mind me, look at you two."

"It's been tough," acknowledged Frank, "we've evacuated most of the patients to other hospitals."

"We're not closing down completely, are we?"

"No, never. We're going to soldier on with casualties as best we can, but it'll be limited numbers."

"Oh, Frank, I'm pleased. I don't want to give in."

"None of us does," said Leo.

"I've been trying to find the words to thank you, Leo, but words are simply not enough. You placed yourself in so much danger to save us; there's no greater sacrifice. It's the bravest thing I've ever seen. Come here, let me put my arms around you."

My usual reserve had been subverted by a rush of emotions I neither recognised nor understood. I hugged him for ages; I didn't want to let him go. Janet came into the room to find Leo more or less in bed with me, and Frank sat on the foot of the bed.

"Oops, should I come back at a more convenient time?"

"No, it's okay, Janet. I'm just thanking Leo for saving my life but holding him close hardly seems adequate."

"Perhaps if I hug him as well, then."

We laughed; we actually laughed. They were my dearest friends; I drew strength from each of them. Janet told me I was to be moved into a larger basement room with the other casualties, and she had to prepare the room. Leo went with her, leaving me alone with Frank.

"I've been so worried, Em. I've been bombed and buried alive for the second time, and then I'm told you were trapped beneath the fire. I know which was worse; please don't do that to me again."

"I'll try not to, I promise."

"I still can't believe Ken is gone. I expect to see him walk through the door at any moment."

"I've thought about nothing else. You have to tell me, Frank, you know something about Ken; I know you do."

"It's been both the best and the worst kept secret, Em. Ken was crazy about you. Surely you knew that?"

"Oh, Frank, I must be so stupid. I didn't know."

"He said you always held him at arm's length. That didn't change how he felt about you, but it prevented him from doing anything about it. He thought your affections were for me, that his opportunity had gone by."

Every word Frank said seemed to thump against my chest. I had to catch my breath. I thought about Ken all the time; how could he think I held him at arm's length? How could he not know that I really ... cared about him? Janet could see it; why didn't Ken? When he said he'd only ever met two truly outstanding women, he must have meant me. When he said I dazzled him, he actually meant it. Now I went from understanding nothing to realising everything, and it was the most painful awakening of my life. My age of innocence died with Ken.

"My naivety is embarrassing. I've never professed to understand these things, Frank, but I didn't realise the extent and consequence of it. How can I live with myself knowing what you've just told me?"

"It's been difficult for me too, Em. I don't profess to understand these things either. I should have talked to Ken about it, but more importantly, he should have talked to you."

"He tried to, that last night."

"What did he say?"

"He told me about his lost love from the past and his regrets. Then he said he'd only known two truly exceptional women and regretted his obfuscation, past and present."

"He was talking about you."

"I think he was, but I'm not truly exceptional. I told myself he couldn't mean me."

"There are a great many people in this hospital who would use those same words to describe you, Em, including me. Life would be much more straightforward if we didn't hide behind our words, wouldn't it?"

"It would be for me."

"So, I'm wondering, what would you have done had Ken made his feelings for you abundantly clear?"

"This is when I want to hide behind my words."

"I think I already know the answer to my question."

"I don't know what to think, I really don't. After what's just happened, all I can think about is being trapped, and I can't get the image of Joyce and Alice out of my mind, especially Joyce. She just sat there crumpled over like a rag doll. When Janet told me about Ken, it was the final straw."

"Of course, we all need time."

"The terrible thing, Frank, is that there's no normal time to return to. We don't know what the future holds. I just pray it doesn't look like this."

At that point, a nurse rushed into the room, looking for Frank. Yet another emergency required his attention. I confess his departure came as a relief. Even me, in my naively stupid way, understood what Frank wanted to ask me. He wanted to know if we had a relationship, and I couldn't answer him because I didn't know. He also wanted to know what I would have said if Ken had been open with me. After all that had happened and all I had been through, I couldn't think clearly about anything except Ken. It's easy to be wise after the event, but if Ken had still been there that day, I would have told him I felt exactly the same way he did.

The same afternoon, Janet moved me into a larger makeshift ward. Before the bombing, I hardly knew the women I met in our storeroom shelter. After that awful night, it was as if I had known them all my life. We shared something we could share with no other living soul. That event united us in a way a lifetime together never could. Janet told me they were putting us all together.

I managed to smile as they pushed me into the room. Beverley, who had been sitting on the side of her bed, immediately stood up and hobbled towards me. Shirley sat propped up against several pillows, but beneath her bandages, her face lit up. Poor Marion had her left leg fully plastered and raised up, with her left arm also in plaster, resting in a sling. She resembled a caricature of a patient from a children's comic. It looked as if hardly any part of her had escaped injury, but her indomitable smile beamed across the room despite it all.

I thought our reunion would be something to celebrate, a joyous occasion, and for the first minute, it was. Individually, each of us had called upon our last ounce of courage; not one of us had submitted to the horror of those memories. Janet understood better than anyone as she closed the door behind her and looked at me. Whatever was in that room with us would stay with us. Individually, we needed to be strong, but the moment we came together, we no longer had anything to be strong for.

We had each experienced that precious last second. We had been to the place from where few returned. Where the hopes, fears, dreams, and ambitions dwelling in the darkest recesses of our minds surrender to the light, and the unfathomable becomes clear. I saw it in Beverley's eyes. Our emotions struggled for expression, words that did not exist. I bowed to the inevitable; we all did. In the privacy of that room, we shared an experience only we could share. There is comfort of a kind in tears; we knew we were not alone. The tears running down our cheeks joined the ever-increasing sea of sorrow that flooded across the country, pooling ever deeper over the East End of London.

Chapter Thirty-Two
# October 2nd, 1940

Roger

*"Just as reality is a cruel master, so self-deception is an enticing seductress."*

We didn't part company with Rachel and her friend until the early hours of the following morning. The six of us left the shelter with a shared experience that changed our relationship completely. However much I resisted it, Rachel ceased to be a gangster's moll. She was impossible not to like; when the time came for her to go her own way, she put her arms around me and kissed my cheek. Only when her spell had broken did Dave look at me with an expression, asking, what if?

Every morning, the walk from the shelter brought with it fresh horrors. Smouldering buildings became like theatre staging, the backdrop for a human tragedy playing out before it. A shopkeeper swept the broken glass out of his shop window. He didn't speak, his thoughts shared between how to survive and anger. A couple stood looking at the shattered remains of their home. They didn't speak either. Still in shock, all the practicalities of how to survive awaited them. Another woman screamed in pain and anguish as she knelt beside the body of a loved one. She was but one more agonised voice in an ever-growing chorus of misery.

A few days later, Marilyn and I were getting ready for the usual evening in the public shelter when I heard a timid knock on the door. I expected to see Dave and Jean, but to my surprise, a very smart gentleman stood there looking rather meek and bothered. He wore a bowler hat above round wire-rimmed spectacles and carried a briefcase. My immediate assumption suggested a bureaucrat of some kind, a man from the council, perhaps. We were in a rush and not wanting to get involved with some sort of bureaucratic nonsense, so I might have been a little brusque with the man.

"Yes, what is it?"

"Mr Pritchard?"

"Yes, what do you want?"

"My name is Hewitt, sir. I'm from Slater and Fenwick of Savile Row."

"Savile Row, what - are you a tailor or something?"

"Precisely, sir. I'm here to measure you for your suit."

"What suit? What are you talking about?"

"Yes, indeed, my instructions are to measure you for a three-piece suit, and the specification is to be the finest we can offer. I would point out, sir, that we have the Royal patronage of the King, and as such, the finest we can offer is the finest there is."

"What!"

"Yes, that's right, sir, the finest there is."

"I don't doubt your tailoring is excellent, but I haven't ordered a suit, and I certainly can't afford one, so I'm afraid you have made a mistake."

"It's no mistake, sir, I can assure you. My instructions come from one of our most esteemed suppliers, Mr Katz. He is absolutely insistent that you should accept our services."

"No, I'm sorry. I have no doubt you're unaware of the circumstances, but I cannot accept your offer."

"Mr Katz asked for me personally and gave me explicit instructions. He said you might be reluctant to accept his gesture of gratitude. My instructions in that eventuality are to give you this letter."

He handed me the letter. I looked at him and then at the letter. I knew if I opened it, I would immediately become further involved, but like the cat, curiosity got the better of me. The letter read. 'Dear Mr Pritchard. I beg you not to refuse the service offered by Mr Hewitt. I love my daughter-in-law as if she were my own; there is nothing I wouldn't do for her. When she came to me and told me about your kindness, I told her you would consider any gesture I might want to make inappropriate. She pleaded with me, 'Please, Papa, do this for me.' To break her heart would be to break my heart, so please accept our gratitude and give this old man his moment of happiness.'

What could I say? This was not a bribe. Joey wasn't trying to curry favour. He could no more resist Rachel's charms than I could. It went against my better judgment, but I invited Mr Hewitt into the house. It took a bit of explaining, but Marilyn quickly decided that Joey's generous gift was a wonderful gesture of gratitude that I deserved.

The situation rapidly got out of control the second that Dave and Jean arrived. Marilyn effused about the generosity of a man she had never met while I continued to struggle with the ethical considerations. Those concerns suddenly compounded when the terribly polite Mr Hewitt turned his attention towards Dave.

"This is very fortuitous, Mr Wheeler. My instructions were to visit your home address, but Mr Katz found himself unable to provide me with that detail. Perhaps if you have the time, sir, you might allow me to take your measurements now?"

Dave, like me, hesitated, but Jean responded to Marilyn's enthusiasm and accepted Mr Hewitt's services on his behalf. He had to stand in front of three smiling onlookers while his inside leg was measured. I didn't question Joey's good intentions, but the broader considerations niggled in the back of my mind. In its own bizarre way, that evening remains a happy wartime memory. We both accepted an extremely generous gift from a notorious villain and smiled about it. Accepting a suit of clothes from the King's tailor was one thing, but wearing it would be another.

We reconciled the contradiction by telling ourselves that while we accepted the gift, the transaction would only be complete if we wore the suits. I'm not sure how we convinced ourselves of that elaborate self-deception, but as with a tailor-made suit, it fitted perfectly. Just as reality is a cruel master, so self-deception is an enticing seductress.

# Chapter Thirty-Three
# October 5th, 1940

## Emma

*"Words can float by you like paper boats on a stream or be carriers of wisdom and emotion, informing and seeking a response. They can change the past and influence the future; they can change who you are."*

My first walk away from our basement 'ward' came as a terrible shock. Frank came with me, holding my arm. The destruction of the hospital had to be seen to be believed. When I saw the charred remains of where we had been buried, the enormity of our rescue became self-evident. Just the sight of it started my heart racing and my head spinning. The feeling of panic became overwhelming. I had to get away immediately, but I left with unanswered questions. Frank took me to our new makeshift canteen for a welcome cup of tea. I sat there, conscious that I needed both my trembling hands to steady my cup.

"How did Leo get us out? It looks impossible."

"I didn't arrive until he'd already found you, but I couldn't believe it either. Everyone said the same thing. They said the fireman tried to stop him because of the fire, but he went anyway. No one can understand how he managed to get to you. They talk about it as if it were another miracle."

It was no miracle. Leo and two other members of staff risked their lives to such an extent they were later awarded the George Medal for gallantry of an extremely high order. There's no higher civilian award. They say you can't tell a book by its cover, and so it proved. Leo, who we berated for his youthful impetuosity and carefree attitude, had the heart of a lion.

To know that Leo and the fireman granted me another life at the risk of their own is indescribably humbling. Had it not been for Leo and the auxiliary fireman, I would not have been sitting in the canteen, looking at my trembling hands.

It brings to mind something that Franklin D. Roosevelt said. *"Courage is not the absence of fear, but rather the assessment that something else is more important than fear."*

For Leo, my life was more important than his fear. I vowed then and there to repay that debt with the only currency I had. I would devote my life to saving the lives of others. If Leo had been prepared to risk his life for mine, then I had to be worthy of his sacrifice.

Physically, I felt fine; my backside hurt when I sat on the stitches, but the real pain lay in the memories. Flashbacks would come without warning during the day. The silliest of things might trigger it, and each time they transported me back to my smoke-filled grave. Nights were the worst, my mind contriving to torment me with illusory demons so real I could touch them. The swirling smoke took form around me. The tortured faces of my friends appeared and disappeared. Worst of all, a cold hand would clasp mine, drawing me into oblivion pulling me away from life. I only felt comfortable with my fellow survivors. I didn't have to pretend with them.

The moment my legs could support me, I visited my parents. I assured them over the telephone that I had been unhurt, omitting the fact that I was speaking from a wheelchair. It coincided with a Sunday, so Andrew, Patricia, and the children were there. I can't tell you how much I looked forward to it; the hospital had been my only environment for so long. I knew I also needed my family, the sanctuary of home.

The short drive to Balham felt like a novel experience, as if it were the first time. I viewed everything through the eyes of someone who had looked but not seen before. The familiar sights provided fresh nostalgia from the past, while the bomb damage held me firmly in the apprehension of the here and now. To my immense relief, my parents' road remained untouched by the ravages brought upon us by the Luftwaffe. My mum greeted me at the door, immediately putting her arms around me as if I might blow away in the wind. She just held me; neither of us spoke. Eventually, she held me at arm's length and looked at me.

"Thank God, you're alright. I've been worried sick."

"I'm fine, Mum, really. This is all I need, to be home again with you and Dad."

It had only been a matter of weeks since my last visit, but those weeks had taken their toll. Mum looked more broken than tired. Her eyes had lost their sparkle, her face pale and drawn. Andrew bounded down the hallway and greeted me as he'd never done before. My self-centred brother was actually concerned about me. I couldn't remember a single occasion when I stood in his arms before. To my amazement, he seemed a bit lost for words; it made a deep impression on me. So many years had passed since I looked up to him as a child - I suddenly realised I'd missed him. The children saved him from the embarrassment of trying to find the words to express his feelings when they erupted on the scene.

"Aunty Emma, Aunty Emma."

I scooped them up and squeezed the breath out of them in my enthusiasm. Here, at last, in my arms, those innocent, carefree bundles of joy reminded us all that life continued. The war didn't exist in their little lives, so for a moment, I entered their world and left it behind. Patricia greeted me next. She appeared at the front room door looking as radiant as Patricia always did, but now those years of cold detachment were behind us. Her perfectly applied mascara became smudged with tears that she immediately deposited on my face. We had wasted so much time not understanding one another. Patsy, as Andrew called her, clearly wanted to make up for lost time; for my part, I welcomed her with open arms.

Then, finally, I stepped into the front room to be greeted by my dad. Slowly and with some effort, he pushed himself up from his armchair. The rest of the family stood back, not wishing to come between us. We never spoke about it as a family, but I think we all understood that he was the centre of my universe and that I was the moon to his earth. I stood in his arms, finally safe from the outside world. This was my family - I realised then more than ever how much I loved and needed them.

The news about the hospital bombing had become common knowledge; newspaper photographs appeared. Desperate for every shred of news, they bought every newspaper covering the story. The pictures they showed me sent a chill down my spine; no wonder they were all so worried. They went to the hospital after the last bombing, desperate to see me, but in the chaos, were turned away.

"Are you sure you're alright, Em?" asked Dad.

"Yes, look at me, I'm fine."

"The damage looks so bad," said Andrew, "how did you escape serious injury?"

"I suppose I was lucky."

"This photograph, Em, where you can see the firemen putting out the fire - it says people were rescued from beneath that burning rubble. This isn't where you were, is it?"

"No, of course not, Mum; I was on the other side of the building. It wasn't so bad there."

"The lady on the telephone told us you had been trapped beneath the collapsed building, but they managed to rescue you."

"Well, that's true; I was trapped for a little while."

"The lady on the telephone made it sound much worse than just a while. It must have been awful."

"I think you must have spoken to Evelyn, Dad; she exaggerates a bit. I was trapped in a basement room with some other women, but a friend of mine got us out alright."

"But you were injured. What happened to you?"

"Oh, it was nothing, Mum; I had a splinter of wood in my leg, that's all. I've got a lovely, neat row of stitches."

My mum appeared to accept that, and I felt sure I had put their concerns to rest. I told them all about the hospital and how we were trying so hard to continue. All the while, Dad remained quiet, which was unusual. He just sat looking at me. When Mum and the others went into the kitchen to prepare lunch, he took me to one side.

"You can fool the others, Em, but you know you can't fool me. Tell me what really happened."

"I knew you'd see through me. I'm sorry, Dad. I didn't want to worry Mum."

"How bad was it?"

"It was terrible. The building collapsed on us. We were all trapped. My legs were trapped, and I couldn't move at all. I've never been so frightened in all my life."

"That's what I thought; I can see it in your eyes. I saw it in the trenches; men who stared death in the face all had that same look in their eyes. It's as if you can still see the hand of death reaching out for you."

"Did you see that?"

"I did. I know what you've been through, Em."

"Did you keep seeing it afterwards - will it go on forever?"

"I know some for whom it did. I've seen lives that never recovered, but that's not you, my darling Emma. I know you; you didn't cheat death. You fought against it and won. Now, we both view life as only those who know death can view it. For you, this is a gift that will make you even stronger, and you'll do all you can to be worthy of this life you've been given."

"That's exactly how I feel. I have to be worthy of this second chance. Oh, Dad, you know everything. I love you so much."

Despite his increasing frailty, my father's strength of character had not dimmed. He remained the same man who stood in a desolate trench in Ypres all those years ago. The intervening years and the chlorine gas conspired to diminish him physically, but despite the best efforts of those malign forces, his wisdom grew with every passing year. He feared the worst had happened to me from the moment they heard the news, and yet he remained the rallying point for the rest of the family. For him, like Leo, there was something more important than fear.

Not only had I been granted a second life, I had also been granted a family that I saw with fresh eyes. I had never felt close to my brother, Andrew. The age difference to me as a child seemed immense; our maturity gap was more of a yawning chasm than a mere bump in the road. As that chasm filled with the residue of the years, another opened as our life choices diverged. We didn't dislike each other; it was more a case of maintaining our distance. It's true I didn't approve of his selfish pursuit of wealth and status. The contrast with our father, who dedicated his life to the education of others, could not have been starker. Perhaps that, more than anything, influenced my opinion. Now I looked at that situation afresh, I realised blood is always thicker than water. It all came to a head when Patricia, of all people, intervened.

"There was a moment there, Emma, when I thought I'd lost you, and it was one of the worst moments of my life."

"Oh, I'm sorry, Patricia, I wish Dad hadn't found out about it so quickly. But what you just said, well, that was a lovely thing to say."

"I mean it, Em; I feel we're sisters now."

"So do I. I'm so sorry for all those lost years."

"That's something else I wanted to talk to you about. Isn't it silly how people can get hold of the wrong end of the stick and beat you with it? Look at us; we didn't understand each other, did we? It's the same with you and Andy. You don't really get on, do you?"

"Well, I wouldn't say that."

"I would. Whenever he talks about you, it's never been with affection, and that's not right. It's the same when you talk about him. This terrible incident has made us all realise how much we love and value each other. When I told Andy what your father said about the bombing, I've never seen him react like that before. He just broke down and cried, and then over the course of the next hour, he poured his heart out to me."

"He cried about me?"

"He did; he told me everything."

"Told you what? What did he say?"

"I told him he must tell you himself. I forced him, really. I said if he didn't tell you, I would."

"I'll talk to him now - I need to know what's going on."

"It's deeply personal, Em; it's very difficult for him. Be kind to him."

"I couldn't be anything else; he's my brother."

I didn't know what to think. This didn't sound like Andrew at all. Mum and Dad were engrossed in their grandchildren, so I grabbed Andrew by the arm and escorted him into the kitchen. He saw Patsy and me exchange a knowing smile, and his face went pale. He followed me like a lamb to the slaughter, unaware of the outcome but fearful of the journey.

"Patsy's spoken to you?"

"She has; we've had a lovely talk together."

"I love the way you two get on now. She worships you, you know?"

"When you discover a sister at our age, it's kind of wonderful. We both feel the same, but what about you, Andy? What have you discovered?"

"She hasn't told you?"

"No, but you're just about to."

"It's difficult, Em, it's really difficult."

"Just take a deep breath and start at the beginning."

"Before you were born, I was the golden boy; I thought everything revolved around me. But then you came along, and everything changed."

"Well, that's perfectly normal between siblings, isn't it?"

"Not for us, no, I don't think it is. Dad idolises you to the exclusion of all else, including me. As you grew up, that bond between you just grew stronger. Mum could see it, I'm sure she tries to compensate, but a boy needs his father. Why do you think I worked so hard at school and then at university?"

"I thought you were simply obsessed with getting on in life."

"I was, but it had nothing to do with getting on in life; I wanted to impress Dad. I wanted him just once to praise me."

"He did; he constantly praises your achievements."

His eyes welled up, and so did mine for reasons I didn't understand. I instinctively hugged him, and it felt wonderful.

"I wanted to be loved, Em, like he loves you."

Those words were the gale that blew the mist from my eyes. I had spent my life not seeing through the impenetrable mist hanging between us. Only then, in its absence, did I see my brother as if for the first time. I clung to him, not wanting anything to come between us again. The memories came flooding back: those special occasions, school presentations, and Christmases past when Andy treated me unkindly, and I despised him for it. I suddenly realised he felt unloved as I basked in the reflected light of our father's adoration. Of course, he loved Andy, his only son, but the painful truth is that I acted as if he loved me more, and perhaps he did.

"You're wrong to think he doesn't love you, Andy; I know he does. In so many ways, he's still that soldier in the trenches; he had to be strong for all of us. Beneath that gentle exterior, he's as tough as old boots - he had to be, to survive what he's been through. He doesn't know how to express his love for you; it's that silly masculine thing you all have."

"Do you really think so?"

"I know it."

"You can't deny there's some kind of special connection between you. It's so obvious."

"I know there is. He means everything to me, but that doesn't mean he doesn't feel the same about you. Neither of you expresses your feelings towards the other. You can be a bit detached when you want to be."

"I suppose you're right."

"When did you last give him a hug?"

"I can't remember, probably thirty years ago."

"Do you seriously think if you gave him a hug, he wouldn't welcome it?"

He didn't answer. Words can float by you like paper boats on a stream, or they can be the carriers of wisdom and emotion, informing and seeking a response. Words can change the past and influence the future; they can change who you are. I don't know which of us changed the most that day, but our past no longer clouded the future.

We returned to the front room together and joined the noise and excitement the children were creating. Only Patsy had any inkling about what had been said between us. She looked at us with all the expectation of a child about to open a Christmas present. My expression must have answered her question because her face lit up the room. I savoured every second of that afternoon; I wanted it to continue forever. Andrew usually found a reason to leave family occasions early, but not that day.

We ignored the time until the impending blackout forced us to delay no further. We said our goodbyes with the usual hugs and kisses, except this time was different. Andrew put his arms around Dad, and they stood in each other's arms. I reached immediately for Patsy; we didn't need to say anything. I didn't know it at the time, but that family gathering has become the most important family occasion of my life. It was to be the last time when we were all together.

## Chapter Thirty-Four
# The Balham Tube Disaster, October 14th, 1940

Roger

*"In the absolute darkness of the grave, this had to be the final judgment: drowning people screaming at the gates of hell. I thought I had entered the hinterland. A place between life and death - a place where life's hold weakens, and death's hand reaches out."*

October heralded the beginning of autumn and a reminder that despite the destruction raining down upon us, the seasons remained immutable. As the days became shorter, so the nights became colder. The prospect of another cold, dark winter only added to our misery. The government's decision to open the underground stations as night-time shelters came only just in time. Public morale was undoubtedly sinking - surface shelters like the local one we had been using proved to be inadequate at best. People rightly didn't believe the government's assurances that they were safe; several had been badly damaged and people killed.

The tube stations rapidly became a rallying point for Londoners, us included. Our night-time routine changed on the day of the announcement, and by the middle of October, the underground culture had become well-established. Initially, conditions were grim. Stations like Balham obviously had no facilities for people to sleep overnight. Strange as it may seem, we instantly overcame our revulsion; the smell of sweat and toilet buckets can be tolerated if peace of mind accompanies them.

"Evening, Jean. Crikey, you smell nice. What's that perfume you're wearing?"

"You know full well that's not perfume, Roger. It's Dave's Old Spice aftershave. I'm not wasting my expensive perfume in that stink hole."

"That's a good idea," replied Marilyn. "I should've thought of that, anything to smell sweeter."

"Does anyone want a quick drink before we head off?"

"Is the Pope a Catholic?" replied Dave.

We probably didn't notice it at the time, but like everyone else, our spirits had lifted. In normal times, the absence of fear is a condition we take entirely for granted. During the Blitz, the absence of fear suddenly became a rare and precious commodity. The station platforms at Balham sat 42 feet beneath the ground. We were happy to suffer all the indignities for the security we thought it offered. A glass of something before we left would ease our transition into the underworld. I reached for the bottle of Johnnie Walker Red Label I had waiting on the sideboard.

"Here's to another joyous night in the underworld."

"And God bless all who stink in her," said Dave.

That evening came close to being a pleasant occasion. We laughed and joked as if spending the night in an underground station constituted an enjoyable evening. We drank our whisky and a little more besides, and why not? Pleasures had become few and far between. The four of us left our house in fine spirits, walking arm in arm with a smile on our faces. We carried our bedding and provisions under our arms or on our backs, and nothing was about to remove the spring in our step. As we got closer to the station, we joined the general tide of people, all heading in the same direction. About 600 of us entered the tube that night, and with very few exceptions, it remained orderly and good-natured.

People tended to occupy the same pitch they had previously occupied, so a kind of orderliness pervaded proceedings. Our pitch resided on the northbound platform, enjoying a superior view of the railway track about halfway along. By then, we all knew the drill: stake your claim with your bedding and make yourself at home. The fact that home had become a section of filthy concrete platform mattered less than the peace of mind it offered. We enjoyed every luxury an underground station could offer. Blankets to keep us warm, a flask of hot tea, and a corned beef sandwich made with the delightful 'national loaf'. With our spirits raised by Mr Johnny Walker, we were not about to be deterred by any minor inconveniences.

The bombing started predictably on time, but for the occupants of the underground stations, the war belonged to the world of open space and fresh air. It need not affect us in the bowels of the earth. The ground would occasionally shake, a reminder that above us, high explosive bombs were destroying London. We would face the damage another day.

The station clock in our subterranean world showed 8:02 pm. Above us, a German bomber, possibly a Heinkel HE 111, or perhaps a Junkers JU 88, opened its bomb bay and released a 1,400 kg semi-armour piercing fragmentation bomb. The bomb fell into the darkness, a blind assassin content to fall wherever chance dictated. This is when the hand of destiny intervened.

That bomb could have landed anywhere, but destiny pointed its finger towards Balham High Street, right outside United Dairies. It penetrated the road at two minutes past eight and exploded deep within the ground with devastating effect. Destiny must have conspired with the bringer of death that night because the bomb penetrated first, then exploded in one of the side tunnels joining the two main tunnels leading into Balham Station. Not only did it find the tunnel, but it also dropped with unerring accuracy onto a major South London water main and sewer pipe.

We had no warning. Everything remained perfectly normal one moment, and then the blast hit us. The shock wave blasted down the tunnel and erupted into the station. It hit us one way, and the vacuum it created caused another reverse shock wave. We would have been thrown about like so many rag dolls had we been standing. The people closest to the tunnel entrance must have been killed immediately before the blast dissipated into the station. My head hurt, and my lungs ached. I wiped blood from my eyes. The shock left me completely stunned and disorientated. I reached for Marilyn and clasped her hand in mine.

As the tremendous sound of the blast echoed down the tunnel, another roar replaced it. It sounded as if an approaching train was speeding towards us. The terrifying roar collected my senses. It happened so quickly I had no time to do anything other than stare into the tunnel. It appeared like a monster from its lair. A tidal wave of mud, sand, debris, sewage, and water erupted from the tunnel. I looked at it, frozen in fear, powerless to resist it. It took just two seconds to reach us, but those seconds provided a vision of hell I can never forget. It filled the tunnel almost to the top with a fast-flowing river. People were either consumed instantly or washed away like confetti in the wind.

I gasped a deep breath before it hit us. The impact instantly tore my hand from Marilyn's, sweeping me along the platform. Nothing more than luck kept my head above it. Along every inch of the platform, I hit another person. We collided with each other and with whatever else we came into contact with. For those unfortunate enough to become entangled, the flood of mud and water simply dragged them under. I reached out to some pipework high up the wall of the tunnel and hung on to it with every ounce of strength I had. A man desperately grabbed hold of me, and then another.

I couldn't support us all, and my grip quickly failed. I submitted to the water, expecting it to pull me down into breathless oblivion, the same fate that befell my uninvited companions as they slipped beneath the surface. I kept my head above water just long enough to see the lights suddenly go out. We were at the mercy of the torrent in absolute darkness.

As the seconds passed, I no longer knew where I was, how deep the water was, or when that living death would end. I crashed blindly into an obstacle. That obstacle was a tangle of bodies, lost souls who, in death, offered me the gift they were denied. I clambered over them, reaching out into the darkness. When I touched cables high up the tunnel wall, I grabbed them, and this time I didn't let go.

The terrifying roar of the torrent gradually subsided to be replaced with something even worse. Desperate people thrashed in the water; their final cries echoed through the tunnel. In the absolute darkness of the grave, this had to be the final judgment: drowning people screaming at the gates of hell. I thought I had entered the hinterland. A place between life and death - a place where life's hold weakens, and death's hand reaches out.

I could hardly breathe with mud and goodness knows whatever else was in my eyes, nose, and mouth. I coughed and choked, only half conscious. My hold on the tunnel wall grew weaker. When I could hold on no longer, I once again submitted to the inevitable as I slid back into the water.

In the absolute blackness, time lost all meaning. I didn't know what was happening to me. Whatever it was, I had already surrendered to it. The sound of flowing water continued, but I stopped moving. I became stuck in thick mud and debris close to the tunnel wall. Beyond that, I knew nothing. The sound of people shouting for help brought me back to my senses. Their cries were no longer the desperate pleas of poor souls fighting for their last breath. These were dazed and bewildered people like me reaching out in search of a fellow human being. None of the survivors knew what had happened; we were all just bewildered victims trapped in a subterranean hell.

It took several minutes for me to rationalise where I was and what had happened to me. My first clear thought was Marilyn, Jean and Dave. Where were they? I called out, "Marilyn," in a weak voice. I called again and again. Other people did the same. They called out for their loved ones. What remained of the tunnel echoed to the sound of lost souls. A lucky few were greeted with the response they prayed for, but many were not. When the calling out subsided, the silence that replaced it was like no silence before or since. It was the silence of the dead.

I struggled to free myself; perhaps I could save Marilyn and the others. I must do something. Trying to do something means not admitting defeat, not accepting the horror of your worst fears. Buried below the waist in mud, I struggled to free myself, and all the while, I kept calling Marilyn's name. They were desperate moments made ever more desperate by the lack of Marilyn's voice.

"Roger, is that you?" a weak voice called somewhere in the distance.

"Jean, I can hear you." My voice joined with several others in a similar chorus. "Are you alright? Are you hurt?"

"I can't move, Roger, I can't move."

"Is Marilyn or Dave with you?"

"No."

The way she said no confirmed everything I didn't want to hear. The sound of trapped people calling to their loved ones decreased by the minute as the cold drained our will to live. I struggled to free myself with every ounce of strength I had left. Slowly, I clambered free, allowing the water to come between me and the mud.

"Keep talking, Jean. I'm trying to find you."

"I'm here, Roger, I'm here, over here."

I followed the tunnel wall where heavier debris had settled, crawling along an inch at a time. Following her voice, I found her. I actually found her in absolute darkness. It was so improbable that, to this day, I can only describe it as divine intervention. We clung to each other as if we were the last two people on earth.

"When did you last see Marilyn and Dave?"

"I don't know. I remember nothing until I heard your voice. Where's Dave - oh God, where is he?"

She wanted to scream and shout, but the cold had all but silenced her. I held her, saying things such as, "Don't panic; they'll be safe somewhere," and, "Keep calm; we'll find them." I wanted to believe it, but the same dread inhabiting Jean also consumed me. We fought against that dread by trying to free her, and eventually, we succeeded.

"Are you sure you're not injured, Jean? Nothing broken?"

"I don't think so. We have to find Dave and Marilyn."

"I know, but how? We can't move, and we can't see."

"Don't let me go, Roger. I'm so cold. Keep hold of me."

"We've survived, and so will they. All we can do is wait for rescuers."

"Will they come?"

"Of course they will."

They did come, but it took hours. It was hours that many people didn't have. A torchlight appeared in the far distance. It was only a speck of light further down the tunnel, not near enough to help us but enough to raise our spirits. A loud voice shouted, saying he was getting out and rescuers would be on their way. That voice belonged to a train driver who, knowing the underground, led some people to safety through a service entrance. He did more than lead those people out; he gave us our first glimmer of hope.

Time is not on your side when you're wet, cold, and in shock. I could feel Jean's head loll from side to side as she said less and less. The terrified voices that had filled the tunnel were now virtually silent. People who survived the torrent were now submitting to the cold.

"Keep talking to me, Jean, keep talking."

"Am I dying, Roger?"

"No, you're bloody not. We'll find them, and we'll all walk away."

"You promise?"

"I'm not leaving here without you; I can promise you that."

Hypothermia sapped the life out of us, and the absolute darkness diminished the will to live. The worse it got, the more determined I became to save Jean and the others. I don't know where that determination came from, but we would not die in that tunnel. When a shaft of dazzling light appeared midway along the tunnel after several hours, I knew salvation had arrived. Within a few seconds, the tunnel came into focus, and the scene before me took my breath away.

Debris filled the far end of the platform to the roof of the tunnel. It buried the entire platform. Then, to my horror, I could see arms and legs protruding like weeds growing on the ashes of a funeral pyre. Some arms and legs had faces, but they didn't blink at the light. There were more survivors than I dared to imagine, but nobody spoke. We were buried in a mass grave, and the horror of that realisation did not escape anyone.

The rescuers went about their work equally horrified; they could no more believe their eyes than we could. Firemen started pumping the water away, and the men cleared a path towards us. They ignored the dead; the rescuer's mission was to save the living. I still clung to hope; Marilyn and Dave might have been washed away; they could be anywhere - they might be waiting for us above. For the other lost souls searching for loved ones, hope dwindled, and the pain was awful to witness.

Jean became so cold her face turned blue, but she was still alive. A rescuer crawled over to us and said calmly, "Come along now, madam, let's get you a nice cup of tea." With the help of rescuers, I joined her on the next level, where the walking wounded were being wrapped in blankets. The answer to any crisis is always a cup of tea; somehow, that essential requirement appeared in my hand. It was manna from heaven. Jean sipped the tea with her trembling hands clasped around the cup as the pain and sorrow reflected in her eyes expressed the words neither of us could say. I knew what I had to do. I went back down with the rescuers to look for Marilyn and Dave.

More and more rescuers arrived, including some doctors and nurses from St Thomas's who tended to the badly injured. I struggled over the mud and debris, helping the living and looking for the dead, not wanting to find them. Each body that was not Marilyn or Dave gave me a macabre hope. The tunnel became strangely quiet. The living didn't celebrate being alive, and the rescuers no longer celebrated rescuing them. We just went about our task with grim determination.

A mop of what had once been blonde hair caught my eye, lying in the mud. It was a child, a girl with her face to one side, her mouth just above the water. I assumed she must be dead because the body remained motionless, but something made me crawl over the debris and try to reach her. When I found her unresponsive but alive, the realisation made my heart soar. I cleared the mud from her cold, lifeless face, and she coughed and struggled for breath. When I pulled her away from the mud, I found she had callipers on her legs. The poor child was helpless.

I held her in my arms as I crawled towards help. The moment I reached relative safety, a fireman offered to take her from me, but I wanted to see the job through, to take her up where the doctors were. The concourse was full of people. ARP wardens and firemen shouted orders; rescuers rushed about everywhere. Walking wounded wandered aimlessly, searching for loved ones. Doctors and nurses tended to the seriously injured as they lay on the ground. I shouted for help, but no one could hear me in the noise and chaos. Then, out of nowhere, I heard a scream so desperate it rose above the cacophony of voices and sent a shiver down my spine.

"Alma!" The voice screamed.

A doctor ran towards me, her white coat flailing behind her. Despite the chaos of the moment, I recognised her. It was the doctor from St Thomas's who had treated me. It was Doctor Stevenson.

# Chapter Thirty-Five
# October 14th, 1940

Emma

*"I was neither in this world nor the next. Only when time begins again do you realise it's time without them."*

The Blitz continued relentlessly every night following the 7th of September. I thought I had seen and suffered every tormenting horror that the bombing could throw at me. I was wrong. October 14th became the most painful day of my life. As usual, we made our way down into the hospital basement and waited for the bombers. When they arrived, my heart raced. I relived the trauma of being trapped with the sound of each distant explosion. I doubt I could have coped by myself, but together, we women were stronger than each individual. Janet became my life support in more ways than one, and Beverley had the strength to unite us all.

Shirley flinched every time the building shook. She sat gripping her knees with eyes like saucers. She didn't have Beverley's forceful character or Marion's stoicism. What she had instead was the courage to overcome her fears and never submit to them. I admired every one of them; this is why we were stronger together. After everything we had been through, we knew we faced each night together.

The bombing started at about 8 o'clock and just continued relentlessly. Wave after wave flew over us, but our luck held out. We were just beginning to relax when we heard movement outside our room. Beverley went to look and returned with the news that would change my life.

"They've hit Balham Tube Station. The warden says it's an absolute disaster. They need someone there to tend to the seriously injured."

"I thought the tube was safe," said Shirley.

"What's the matter, Emma?" asked Janet.

"That's where my parents are sheltering."

"Oh, my God. Then we answer the call and go now," said Janet.

We assembled in a matter of minutes. With our staff so reduced and the pressure intense, I worried we might not find another doctor quickly enough. I needn't have worried; Frank volunteered immediately. We also had to man the hospital, so Leo and his junior doctor friend, Maurice, said they would stay by the phone if we needed more help. I couldn't think; I just had to be there. The others organised our emergency medical supplies. All the while, the ARP warden who had run for help told us what he knew.

"I'm not sure what's happened," he said. "There's a bloody great crater in the road outside. It's flooded down below. I've seen nothing like it. It's as if the station has been filled in; it's terrible."

"Are there many casualties?" asked Frank.

"Hundreds. I've never seen so many casualties."

"Does that mean many people have been killed?" I asked, fearing the answer.

"They're not bringing out bodies; it's only survivors."

"What does that mean?"

"It means there must be too many to recover. They have to concentrate on the living."

Janet told Frank and Leo about my parents, and they all closed ranks around me. With no ambulance crew available, we used my Morris and Frank's Wolseley. It didn't even occur to us that the bombers would likely return. Except for firemen and wardens who braved the bombs night after night, the short drive to Balham remained deserted. The sky was aglow with countless fires, some very close to us and many more in the distance.

The night sky glowed red and orange to the east of London. The sharp beams of searchlights combed the sky like fingers, feeling their way through the patchy clouds. Every so often, strange ghostly objects appeared in the sky as barrage balloons became silhouetted by the searchlights.

The colours in the night sky presented a strange beauty that belied their true nature. As soon as we entered Balham High Street, any such thoughts vanished like the wisp of smoke from a snuffed candle. The image before us defied belief. Vehicle headlamps and people with torches illuminated the scene. We looked in complete shock and astonishment. Close to the station, an enormous crater spanned the entire width of the road. I couldn't imagine the bomb that had created such destruction. What confounded us even more was that a red London bus had fallen into it, and the enormous crater had swallowed it whole.

Such an unworldly sight stopped us in our tracks. We just stood there holding our bags and boxes of medical equipment. The walking wounded emerging from the station shook us back to our senses. A solid mass of casualties greeted us the moment we entered the station. We were used to dealing with large numbers of casualties, but at the hospital, they came from all around - none of us had seen a single incident of this magnitude. Firemen and ARP wardens greeted us with open arms. They directed us towards what they thought were critical injuries.

I expected to see the usual blast injuries, but there were none. We realised that anyone with a blast injury had drowned. What confronted us were impact injuries, lacerations, and broken bones, and there were hundreds of them. We had gained a lot of experience dealing with large numbers of casualties. Acting as a coordinated team, we set about identifying those most in need of help. They were all soaked and suffering from hypothermia and shock. Somebody told us the water they had been immersed in contained sewage from a drainage pipe. This meant that open wounds would likely become infected. A warden took me to a man who had lost an enormous amount of blood. He said he knew the man.

"Can you save him, Doc?"

"No, I'm sorry, there's nothing I can do. I'll give him morphine to ease his pain, but I can't save him; I'm so sorry."

"But you haven't even tried; how do you know you can't save him?"

"I do this every day, trust me; I have to move on."

The poor man was beside himself, pleading with me. I tried to find the strength to push him aside, but I knew his pleas would come back to haunt me.

"There are people here I can save; I have to go to them. Who is this man to you?"

"He's my brother."

I took a moment to hold the man. It was a moment that might have made the difference between life and death for someone else, but what price can you place on humanity? I looked again at his brother, and he was gone. I rushed from casualty to casualty. The priority was to stop blood loss and keep them warm. We had to stabilise those we could; anything else would have to wait until we got them to the hospital. Several needed surgery and there were many broken bones. We followed the usual procedure of attaching a parcel tag to each casualty. X for internal injury, T for tourniquet, and M for morphine.

When I looked up, I could see every member of our team working on a casualty, and then I could see more being carried towards us. Additional help arrived every minute. Women from the local voluntary organisations brought more blankets and set up a table to produce an endless supply of tea. I felt an overwhelming sense of pride. Faced with that terrible disaster, everyone came together to help those in need. Hitler wanted to bomb the civilian population into submission by stripping us of our humanity. We responded with human kindness, and it was human kindness that ultimately defeated him.

Each new casualty I tended, I wanted to be my mother or father, but none of them were. In my heart, I knew my father could not have survived in the water. I also knew equally well that my mother would not have left him. Each coherent victim I tended to, I asked the same question. Had they seen an elderly couple, and I described them? With every negative response, the hope in my heart dwindled. As I left one victim for another, a dreadful fear welled up from my stomach.

My colleagues were also looking and asking. Janet looked in my direction to be sure I was coping. I coped, but I would have struggled without them. I refused to accept the worst; it was such an agonising prospect I felt incapable of even considering it. Just as I finished closing a horrible head wound, I heard a man calling for help. One of the walking wounded staggered towards me. His hair was red with blood, but despite his injury, he carried a child in his arms. Initially, he was just one of many, but then I recognised the child. How could I not? It was Alma.

I reacted without thinking; I screamed her name out loud and ran towards her. The man was so relieved to pass her over to me; he looked as though he couldn't take another step. I could see he had a head injury; his face was covered in blood and mud, but I confess my attention went immediately towards Alma. Having laid her down, I turned to thank the man, but he had gone. Alma felt desperately cold. Holding her close to me, I wrapped us both in a blanket. With my face close to hers, I could hear her breathing in short, shallow breaths. She had some minor cuts and abrasions, but I knew that shock and hypothermia were closing her body down.

The signs were obvious; she was close to death. I had a special relationship with that little girl; if she died, she would take a part of me with her, and the prospect terrified me. My thoughts went back to when Leo saved my life and my pledge to be worthy of his sacrifice. Irrational thoughts enter your mind at such times. Had I been saved for this very moment? Was this a life in exchange for my parents? I recoiled against such nonsense, but something remained. I would have agreed to a pact with the Devil to save Alma.

I could only warm her up, so I asked Beverley to tie the blanket around us both. With Alma held securely against my chest, I could still just about work. I could continue to tend the injured. All the while, I worked on other casualties, and I kept talking to Alma. One poor woman looked at me as if I were mad.

"Don't leave me, Alma; stay with me, Alma; it's Doctor Emma."

"My name's not Alma."

"Yes, I know, I'm sorry. I've got a child under this blanket."

Carrying Alma's weight, the blanket and all the rushing about made me sweat. I suddenly realised what an asset that was. Alma was six years old, and although she was tiny for her age, she was still a weight to carry. Exhaustion nagged at every fibre of my body, but I carried on. Janet said she would take Alma from me to give me a break, but I couldn't be parted from her. The more I overheated, the more warmth I gave her. After nearly two hours, her breathing finally became more regular. I knew I had saved her. I laid Alma down in a cradle of blankets and accepted the cup of tea that Shirley insisted I should have. I looked up as I sipped it, to see the man who had brought her to me. An ARP warden was almost carrying him, with the man's arm over his shoulder. The poor man must have been so exhausted he could hardly move.

"What's happened to this man? I saw him two hours ago."

"He's been searching for his wife; no one could stop him. The man's a bloody hero; he's saved several people. Looks as though he's lost a lot of blood."

"Sit him down here; I'll take care of him."

I wiped the blood and mud from his face, and I recognised him immediately. It was the police inspector, Mr Pritchard. When he opened his eyes, they reflected a sorrow that seemed to fill the concourse. Not since Leo had I seen a man visibly express such grief; it washed over me like iced water.

"Is it your wife?"

"She's gone, I've lost her. And my friend, my best friend, I've lost them both."

"How can you be sure? They might still be alive."

"There's no one left alive down there. Anyone who is still there is ... dead." He hesitated to say the word, but when he did, it went through me like a knife. "Have you lost someone too?"

"My mum and ... dad."

Those words fell out of my mouth; I said them before I accepted their meaning. What I feared the most, what I refused to believe, had suddenly become reality. There is a moment when an event is so terrible that your brain cannot accept it. Denial allows you to cling to your loved ones, to keep them in your life. You desperately want to stay in that time. The past has gone, and the future has no meaning, so for you, time stands still. I knelt next to Pritchard, clinging to the vision of my parents. Unable to go back and unable to accept a future without them, I was neither in this world nor the next. Only when time begins again do you realise it's time without them.

When that time came, my heartache had no beginning or end; it became all of me. I remember little more of that dreadful moment other than crying uncontrollably and repeating what I had heard so many others say in their hour of need. "No, no, no."

My next memory is being held in Pritchard's arms as we tried to console each other. I didn't really know the man, but his pain was as great as mine, and it was a pain we shared. Another woman who seemed to know Pritchard joined us. Whoever she was, her pain was self-evidently no less than ours. Janet and the others looked on, desperate to console me, but we were three people consumed in a very private grief. Just as we were stronger together in adversity, so we were stronger together in grief. Then I left Pritchard and the other woman to console each other while I cried in the arms of my friends.

They spent time with me, time that might be precious to the casualties. First, Frank had to rush to help a critically injured woman, and then Shirley, quickly followed by Beverley. Janet, who I depended on so much, stayed with me as long as she could. When she had to go, I stood alone. In every sense of the word, I stood there alone. Alma cried, and the casualties still needed me. This was the reality of a future without my parents. Perhaps the hardest lesson of all for the bereaved is that life goes on all around you.

# Chapter Thirty-Six
# October 15th, 1940

Roger

*"Our loved ones do not leave this life in an instant. They walk a little farther away with each passing day, but when you reach out a hand, they will always be there to take that hand in theirs."*

Jean and I needed each other that awful night; I can't imagine how I could have got through it alone. Being with someone who feels your pain is everything at a time like that. I felt so sorry for Doctor Stevenson; when I told her there were no more survivors, the poor woman appeared utterly broken. She poured her heart out on the shoulder of a virtual stranger and invited me to do the same. This was something happening repeatedly between strangers that night. The bereaved needed the comfort of a kind-hearted soul, and there was no shortage of either. There is just one chink of light in what is otherwise the darkest night of my life. The survival of the little girl I found.

When the nurse patched up the cut on my head, I had only one desire: I had to get out of there. Jean felt the same; we were in a place of misery and pain. We thought if we left, we would leave it all behind. We stepped outside the station entrance and looked up at the first light of a new day. Jean stood rooted to the spot, as did I. Our need to get away didn't include a new day, and it didn't include leaving Marilyn and Dave behind. To walk away would be to walk away from them. But we had no other option but to walk into that new day without them, a day they would never see. It was as if they died a second time. Jean broke down in tears again, and I struggled to be strong for her sake.

"We can't stay here, Jean; we have to leave them."

"I know, but it's so hard. Why us, Roger, why does this have to happen to us?"

"I wish I had the answer to that. We have no option; come on, let's go."

With the first light, more ambulances were arriving. It was as chaotic outside the station as it was inside. We had no option but to move on. That's when we saw the crater in the road with a red London bus in it. We couldn't believe our eyes, but it explained much about what happened in the underground tunnels. A crowd was gathering to view the spectacle; some, like us, were survivors, and others were just onlookers.

"They have no idea, do they?" said Jean.

"No, and how can they? I can't believe it myself."

And so, on the morning of the 15th of October, we walked away. Too numb to rationalise anything; it felt as if we were walking into the unknown, which is precisely what it was. Every part of my body hurt, but both of us could walk. We said nothing until we were nearly home.

"What do we do now, Roger?"

"I suppose one step at a time. The first step is to clean up and maybe eat something. Then I just want to close my eyes."

"You're right, but I don't want to be alone, not today."

"You can stay with me - have the kids' room."

"I'll bring whatever I've got in the larder to eat."

"I hoped you'd say that; I can't face being alone either."

I left Jean at her house and continued on to mine. I walked into the empty house, and Marilyn was there to greet me. Her voice filled every room; she followed me everywhere. I could see her, I could hear, smell, and feel her presence in every corner of the house, but I couldn't touch her. It was just the start of the agony. Our loved ones do not leave this life in an instant. They walk a little farther away with each passing day, but when you reach out a hand, they will always be there to take that hand in theirs.

It was to be the first of many such steps. I experienced the second when I telephoned the station and spoke to Jack. Without going into detail, I just told him what had happened and that I would not be coming in. Two steps behind me, how many more steps to go. I couldn't even bring myself to think about telling the children.

You learned during the war that grief was a peacetime luxury. We all had to carry on regardless; anything less would be admitting defeat, which could never happen. The 'Spirit of the Blitz' told us that no sacrifice was too great, and no one made a greater sacrifice than the bereaved. The departed left with little ceremony, and the living carried on, regardless. There was no shortage of heartache, it wasn't rationed, you could find it almost anywhere. We just chose not to look.

Jean stayed for two days; neither of us could face the memories alone. Despite my aches and pains, I knew I had to return to work, and we both knew we couldn't hide from the future forever. So, the 17th of October felt like day one of whatever the future held. Jean went to work for the WVS, and I went to the station.

"Morning, Roger. I'm so sorry, mate."

"Thanks, Jack, what's been happening here?"

"One of my constables was in Balham station, and he didn't make it either."

"Who was it?"

"Sidney Halstead."

"I know Siddy; his kids go to the same school as mine. I didn't see him there."

"They say it'll take weeks to recover the bodies. I'm really sorry, Roger."

"Do you know how many have been killed?"

"It's sixty-six dead or missing, presumed dead. Goodness knows how many are injured."

"How are the locals dealing with it?"

"There's not a person in Balham who hasn't lost someone or knows someone who has. We just have to carry on."

"That's all we can do, Jack, carry on."

"How long do you think the people can stand it? It's relentless."

"I'm here, you're here. What did Churchill say - 'We shall never surrender'."

They didn't come any tougher than Jack; I left him with a look of grim determination on his face. Gerry put his arms around me, which was as unusual as a crocodile wearing lipstick. Jeff and Alfie put a brave face on it. Dave loomed large in the room; whenever a door opened or we heard a voice, one of us would look up with an expectation that would not be met. That first morning was the most difficult, but I got through it; we all did. I needed some proper work to occupy myself.

"Are there any advances with the murder case?"

"You mean the 'blackout ripper'?"

"I didn't want to call him that, Jeff. We can't give him any notoriety."

"After the last one, what else can we call him?"

"I suppose you're right, but for goodness' sake, that's only between us."

"There's nothing to report. Alfie and I interviewed every warden, fireman, and ambulance crew member in the area that night. No one saw anything."

"I suppose with bombs falling, that's not surprising. Did any of them raise your suspicions?"

"Not really; they all seem to be good men."

"The neighbours?"

"It's the same. Who stands at their window during the bombing?"

"So all we have is a couple of footprints. In other words, we just wait for him to do it again."

Those are not words a detective wants to think, let alone say; they meant failure. We had so much else to deal with. Crime increased during the Blitz. Some of it was petty, such as minor rationing violations—we turned a blind eye to that. Petrol syphoning continued, but organised crime was no longer involved, so at least we had one major success.

Looting became an enormous issue. For many, it was the most insidious crime a person could commit. Public outrage became so intense that some newspapers even called for the culprits to be hung. Yet, despite the outrage, looting became virtually ubiquitous.

Worst of all, the murder rate increased. Not murderers like the ripper, but domestic murders, invariably disguised as bomb victims. This was my department; here at least I could conduct proper investigations. That first day back at work, I understood why we all carried on, regardless. I needed to carry on; work gave me purpose and order in my life. Perhaps the spirit of the Blitz was not so much national defiance as self-protection.

A potential case had come to light a couple of days earlier. The local bobby was suspicious, and when Jeff went to investigate, he agreed with him. He found a woman in her early fifties in the remains of her own house. She had suffered various injuries, but neither the constable nor Jeff thought they looked consistent with a bomb blast. The body had been taken to St Thomas's for a postmortem. It sounded straightforward, the kind of case becoming all too common. I told Jeff I would talk to Doctor Bartholomew at the hospital the following day.

Jean and I had to find somewhere else to shelter, so we adopted Clapham South Underground Station as our night-time shelter. Just walking into the station filled us with terrible memories. The Clapham underground became the place where the past met with the future. We both dreaded the nights. We relived the Balham disaster with every waking moment, and every sleeping moment was worse.

We went home to our respective houses the next day, and I washed and shaved. I then went through the usual ritual of leaving the house. I put my overcoat on, leaving the buttons undone. My keys were in their usual place, and I picked up a packet of fags and a box of matches. The image in the hall mirror looked like a sorry figure. I ignored that and straightened my tie despite my shirt being crumpled. Last but not least, I placed my hat on my head and settled it into place.

I drove to the end of our road and turned left. I realised I was driving to Dave's house when I reached the next junction. I stopped, leaned forward with my hands on the steering wheel and slumped my head on my arms. Dave and I had a little conversation together. I told him what he knew anyway; he was the best friend a man ever had. I told him he would live forever in my memory and that I would always be there for Jean and his kids. He looked at me with his usual smile as if to say, 'Thanks, mate.' Then he was gone, and I never saw him again.

When I arrived at the hospital, my heart sank. I found another of the blocks had been hit. The damage was extensive. I wondered if Bartholomew was even there - was anyone there? To my amazement, one or two ambulances were still delivering casualties. I entered with some trepidation, not knowing what I might find. What I found was a handful of doctors and nurses still doing their best for the casualties in the most appalling conditions.

Doctor Stevenson was there with a nurse beside her, running between patients. She directed them left and right with a gentle touch or a kind word for each of them. When the porter rushed in with what they described as a bleeder, she pounced on the man. They didn't hesitate for a second. I had not the slightest doubt that they would save that man's life. It was a reenactment of what I saw in the Balham tube station, and I realised she did that all day, every day. I asked the porter if the pathology lab was still operating in the same place, and he confirmed it was.

The usual route no longer applied. Corridors and hallways were closed. Some of the bomb damage had been cleared and even restored in places. In others, it looked as if the bomb had just exploded. Eventually, I found pathology down in the bowels of the hospital. Bartholomew and the attendant, George Rawlings, were there. I had immense respect for that man Rawlings; I shook his hand.

"When do you think the good doctor will be free?"

"I know he wants to talk to you, Inspector, so I imagine quite soon."

Bartholomew looked drawn and haggard. I wondered when he last saw daylight. For someone who usually looked immaculately dressed, he looked more like me, which made me feel a little less intimidated.

"Inspector Pritchard, just the man I wanted to talk to. How are you?"

"Well enough, thank you. I need to know about the potential murder victim, Mrs Fletcher."

"Straight to the point, Inspector, I like that. You want to know about the deceased lady with the skull fracture caused by a ball pein hammer."

"Do I?"

"Well, unless the Germans are dropping ball pein hammers on us, then yes, I'm sure you do."

"How can you be sure about that?"

"I jest, Inspector, but only slightly. The woman has numerous skull fractures, but they appear to be postmortem. An interesting one is a perfectly round depression in the occipital bone."

"The back of the head."

"You've been paying attention, Inspector. Yes, indeed, she was knocked unconscious and possibly killed by that very blow. So, you need to look for a ball-shaped object, presumably metal. I can't think of anything that fits the bill more readily than a ball pein hammer."

"What would I do without you, Doc?"

"Pleased to be of service. Now tell me, Inspector, what news do you have about our serial killer?"

"I hate to admit it, Doc, but all I have are two footprints."

"That's all?"

"That's it. This man leaves no trace of himself. He's either very clever or very lucky."

"He'll make a mistake, they all do."

"I can assure you of one thing. When he makes a mistake, I'll be there."

He wished me good luck in that undertaking, as did Mr Rawlings. As I left, I saw Doctor Stevenson sitting with a cup of tea, looking exhausted. I didn't know if I should interrupt her, but I really wanted to talk to her. She sat with another doctor and a couple of nurses, so I felt a bit out of place and thought better of it. Just as I turned away, she saw me and caught my attention. The blood on her coat and apron contrasted with her pale, drawn face. She hardly had the strength to stand. She approached me, looked over the top of her half-rimmed glasses and smiled. The woman looked so exhausted even a smile must have taken some effort.

"It's Inspector Pritchard, isn't it? How's your head?"

"I'm fine. A little blood and water goes a long way; I don't think it was as bad as it looked."

"I hoped I would see you again; I wanted to thank you for the other night."

"Thank me? Why would you thank me?"

"I needed a shoulder to cry on, and you provided it."

"As I remember, it was the other way around."

"That was the worst moment of my life ... I think yours as well." She struggled to speak to me. "I know we don't know each other, but we shared something really important to me. I can't explain it, but can we talk about it? Perhaps I could meet you one day?"

"Actually, I've been dithering about here, hoping I might talk to you. I'm still reliving that night and feel the same way you do. I need to talk about it."

"Is there a telephone number I could ring? I never know when I can take an hour away."

"Of course. This is my home number, and this is the police station. You can leave a message there if I'm not available."

"Thank you, Inspector. I just need to talk about it; I hope you understand."

"I think we both need to talk about it, Doctor; I look forward to it."

I left her looking very sorry for herself, and I suspect she felt the same about me. When her smile dropped, her eyes looked far away, as if she couldn't be bothered to focus on this world. I recognised that look; it greeted me each morning in the mirror.

# Chapter Thirty-Seven
# October 17th, 1940

Emma

*"If I closed my eyes, I could see the Fighting Temeraire's last journey as it sailed into the sunset. But not even a Turner painting could capture the hell that was London burning."*

I awoke on the afternoon of the 15th to find myself in my own bed in Battersea. Still half asleep, it took several seconds to realise where I was. When that realisation came, I woke up with a start. A confused memory of one of the girls driving my car drifted into my mind. Then I remembered when I broke down at the underground station and how they rallied around me. I sat up to find I was still dressed in my underwear, but I couldn't remember how I got there.

Then I saw a note on my bedside table. I should have guessed - Janet placed it there. It said, 'You couldn't continue, Emma. Frank put 200mg of Tuinal in your tea, and I put you to bed.' Tuinal is a strong barbiturate; no wonder I didn't remember going to bed. The drug left me still slightly sedated, but nothing could separate me from the grief inhabiting every part of my body. It still didn't seem real - how could they be gone? My father was the centre of my universe; without him, I had no reference point. I had been cast adrift. Confusion, fear, and incomprehension; these are the constituent parts of grief. Confusion that your world is no longer what it should be - fear of the unknown and the incomprehension of mortality. Grief is an empty room where love once lived, a place where memories echo against bare walls.

My bedside clock showed 3:15 pm; I had slept many hours. A large part of me wanted to stay there and surrender to the darkness, but I knew people needed me. I had just enough sense to realise that my salvation lay in helping others. My car keys were next to Janet's note; I knew what I had to do.

I arrived at the hospital at 4:30 to find them still tending to casualties from the station disaster. Everyone greeted me with hugs and sympathy, while many people around me were in the same position. Nothing puts your suffering into perspective more than seeing that you are but one of many. I realised I had no more right to sympathy than anyone else; I had a duty to my patients to rise above it. Walking toward Frank, I bumped into Doctor Wiśniewski; I didn't know what to expect.

"I'm terribly sorry for your loss, Doctor Stevenson. I've been told about the heroic work you and your colleagues performed last night. We don't always see eye to eye concerning procedural matters, but I have to tell you, Doctor, you're a credit to this hospital. It should be a comfort for you to know that your parents must have been enormously proud of you."

He didn't just take the wind out of my sails; he capsized the boat. He was right, we didn't see eye to eye, and this was the last thing I expected. Words failed me, I stood for a moment in an embarrassing silence.

"Thank you, Doctor Wiśniewski. That means an enormous amount to me; I'm really ... thank you."

I ran out of words; Wiśniewski was human, after all. Having said his piece, he left, probably not realising what his words meant to me. Frank came over smiling.

"Wow. You've even worked your magic on Wiśniewski; good for you."

"I'm sorry I broke down last night; I let you all down."

"The chief got it right, Emma, you're a credit to this hospital. You didn't let us down - quite the opposite; you inspired everyone last night."

"You sedated me, Frank."

"For your own protection. No matter how many you save, you push yourself to save more. After what happened last night, I had to protect you from yourself."

"I suppose I should thank you, then."

"It was self-interest, Em, we can't afford to lose you."

I would trust Frank with my life; a part of me knew he would only ever act in my best interest. The prospect of having to be sedated for my own protection frightened me; perhaps I did push myself too hard. I wondered, as I always did, what my father's advice would be. I knew in an instant that he would say - listen to trusted advice and never reject an opinion just because it didn't agree with mine.

He would also tell me that my indignation was the product of pride and embarrassment, what he would call 'the fog that stops us seeing clearly'. I thanked Frank; I thanked them all, and finally Janet. She appeared with her huge smile and greeted me as if we hadn't seen each other for months.

"Thanks, Jan. It seems that you, Frank and the others saved me."

"You're not cross?"

"It is a bit embarrassing. Whose idea was it to drug me?"

"It was Frank's idea, but I agreed. You lost control; you were grief-stricken and working twice as hard at the same time. I wasn't about to let you have a breakdown."

"I feel stupid, but I'm really grateful, Jan. Thank you."

"It's not a big deal, is it? I had to put Shirley to bed once when she was rolling drunk."

"What would we all do without you, and me especially?"

My next task had to be to telephone Andrew, my brother. I could put it off no longer. I borrowed Evelyn's office, and my hand shook as I dialled the number. It was as if they died all over again. Andrew took it badly, and I found myself in the unaccustomed position of trying to be emotionally strong for him. That their bodies had not been recovered and might not be recovered for weeks only added to the pain. In some regards, it was a cathartic moment - for the first time, I spoke about them in the past tense. It meant time had elapsed; I entered a new time, the time without them.

I tended to some patients in the early evening and welcomed having a purpose. One of those patients was Marion. Her injuries were healing well, but she remained confined to bed. We had her in one of the basement wards, and she longed to see the sun again. Janet had already told her about my parents, and of course, she had long experience of dealing with the bereaved. In a world of disorder and chaos, I needed her calming influence. I increasingly relied upon her advice and experience.

The canteen that evening proved to be the final hurdle as far as entering the new time was concerned. It seemed all the staff knew about my parents. There were kind words and an inescapable sense of support. When our little group of women retired to the basement that evening, I did so, hoping I was returning to what now passed as normal. I calculated the odds and concluded that we were unlikely to be bombed again. Four bombs had already hit us on three occasions, at the loss of many lives. Following the Balham disaster, it seemed incomprehensible that we would be hit again.

All of that proved to be wishful thinking, yet one more occasion when hope triumphed over expectation. At 9:15 pm, a big 500lb bomb struck the hospital. We were huddled together in our basement room when the bomb exploded. Once again, the blast threw us to the floor, the lights went out, and we relived every second of our entrapment. Once again, our hearts raced, and our hands trembled. The block we sheltered beneath had been spared, but another suffered terrible damage. One of our wards and the telephone exchange had been destroyed. Yet more destruction, yet more casualties. We were better equipped this time with lamps and torches. However traumatised we were, we were spared, and our thoughts turned to those not so fortunate.

We searched through the debris, with the bombs continuing to fall all around us. Fire engines rushed past with bells ringing. In the distance, silhouetted against a raging fire, we could see water jets rising high into the air from fire hoses. Fireboats pumped water onto another inferno next to the river as flames danced across the water. Everywhere, the glow of fires lit the sky in orange and yellow. The latent boom of explosions followed distant flashes of light. The bombs falling nearby announced their presence almost immediately. Pressure waves filled the night air; some buffeted us as a gentle breeze, and others hit us like an unseen fist. All the while, the acrid smell of smoke filled our lungs. One minute, it could be the smell of burning timber. The next could be toxic fumes from burning chemicals and materials, all laced with the smell of oxidised explosives.

Bombers flew overhead, the drone of their engines filling the night air. Occasionally, searchlights would capture one, exposing it to the relentless ack-ack guns. Puffs of white smoke would silently appear in the beams of light before a bang followed its way towards us. Every so often, a flash of light or a sudden rush of flame illuminated the Palace of Westminster, just over the river from the hospital. The tower of Big Ben would be silhouetted against the palette of colours, its reflection dancing on the river like a thousand separate fires. If I closed my eyes, I could see the Fighting Temeraire's last journey as it sailed into the sunset. But not even a Turner painting could capture the hell that was London burning.

That night proved to be particularly awful for the local residents and the hospital. Two surface air-raid shelters were hit, with devastating results.

It became difficult to know when dawn had risen; the eastern sky already glowed with all the colours of the rainbow. As the shadows shortened, the damage became ever more apparent. Smoke rose from yet another of our hospital blocks. All across London, columns of smoke reached up into the sky, searching for salvation.

The surrounding damage was the worst so far. Our thoughts went beyond our own injured; they turned towards the inevitable influx of casualties. We had no idea that two public shelters had been hit and that a tide of human misery was on its way. The ambulances started arriving, and the broken remnants of humanity spilt out of the back. Many had to be sent to other hospitals because we had become so diminished, but many were not.

Some arrived with luggage tags attached: tourniquet, internal injury, and morphine. Some came with missing limbs or gaping wounds. One poor man had suffered extensive burns; his hair was singed and unrecognisable. The smell of burnt hair filled the room as if he had brought the night air in with him. It was business as usual. When the backlog of internal injuries mounted, I would leave admissions and rush to surgery. I now thought of myself as a surgeon. I didn't doubt that the entire world rejoiced at the dozens of lives we saved, but we were too tired to hear the chorus. We suffered the Balham tube disaster one day, and then two public air-raid shelters were destroyed the next. If there was ever a day that appeared to be beyond us, it was that day. Somehow, with cups of tea and Janet's perpetual smile, we got through it.

The night of the 17th/18th of October was considered a light bombing raid. In our macabre world where normality had no meaning, twenty-one casualties, mostly walking wounded, was considered a 'good day', something to be pleased about. We were relieved, almost happy, that 'so few' injured came to us. Tiredness and fatigue had already taken us to the limit of endurance. With the last casualty wheeled away, we sat with a cup of tea.

I hardly had the strength to raise the cup to my lips. My gaze fixed on a point ahead of me, and I didn't move. A volunteer topped up my cup and caused me to look in the other direction. I caught sight of Inspector Pritchard in the corridor. I really wanted to talk to him. We shared something that night in the tube station that I will never forget. It was immensely significant, but inexplicably, I couldn't explain it.

He appeared hesitant, looking out from beneath the brim of his grey trilby hat crumpled down on one side. He looked much better than the last time I saw him but was still bedraggled in the shabby overcoat hanging from his body like a cheap curtain. I caught his eye, and he seemed pleased to see me. If I looked as bad as I felt, then I probably also looked a sorry mess. None of that bothered me any more. I walked over to him, and it became apparent he felt the same as I did.

That terrible night in the tube station, I saw a man whose humanity went before him - a man who had lost everything but still had the compassion to share my pain. The man before me looked very ordinary, not the profoundly compassionate man I'd seen before. He had the vacant look of a lost soul, much like myself. Having kindly given me two telephone numbers I could ring to contact him, he left. The smell of cigarette smoke hung in the air.

# Chapter Thirty-Eight
# Alice Cox

Roger

*"Memories of better days only serve to remind us
of the people who made them better."*

Doctor Bartholomew's analysis of the head injury of my murder victim was priceless. Following the bombing the drive back to work from the hospital was challenging, to say the least. Some roads were blocked, so I had to take several diversions. Fire crews were still damping down the fires, and one or two walking wounded were wandering around like lost souls. Every image brought back memories of the tube station; I had to keep looking away.

I had my day mapped out ahead of me. Jeff or Alfie would come with me, and we would quickly put our latest murder case to bed. Find the hammer, and we would find the murderer, who we assumed would be the husband. When I finally arrived at the station, I could tell by the look on Jack's face that all was not well.

"Morning, Jack, how's things?"

"Bad morning, Roger. One of my boys was badly injured last night. We won't see him back on duty for weeks, if ever. And your killer has struck again."

"Are you sure it's him?"

"It sounds like it. One of the retirees phoned it in first thing this morning. You know PC George Winston; he's got years of experience. He said it's definitely your man."

"Yes, I know George, a good copper of the old school. So he's struck again. Our monster is back."

"You don't sound surprised, Roger."

"No, it's only been a matter of when. I'll speak to the DCI and get over there. Where is it?"

"Battersea, very close to home, if you ask me."

"Which of your PCs was injured, Jack?"

"Robert Jenkins. His wife is injured, too; they were both in a public shelter. The Jerries hit two public shelters last night."

"I saw the casualties at the hospital; it's been an awful business."

I rushed through to Gerry's office to find them all waiting for me.

"You've heard?" asked Gerry.

"The two public shelters?"

"Well, yes, and the latest murder."

"Jack told me, Battersea."

"How do you want to handle it, Roger?"

"Jeff, do you want to team up with me, and we can go straight there?"

"Yes, Guv, I'll get my hat."

"Alfie, the murder in Haslemere Road. Doc Bartholomew is adamant that someone killed her with a ball pein hammer. Go over there and search what's left of that building for a hammer. If the husband owns it, then we've probably got him. Failing that, find out where they sheltered that night and when they left."

Within minutes, Jeff and I left the station en route to Battersea. It felt utterly wrong that it was not Dave sitting next to me. I would occasionally glance to my left and expect to see him. Jeff was a good man, but nobody could replace Dave. We arrived at the scene to find PC George Winston standing at the front door of a terraced house. Several curious people had gathered outside.

"Morning, George."

"Morning, Sir. This is a nasty business."

"Well, I'm pleased you're here, George; glad they dragged you out of retirement. What are we going to find in there?"

"Her name is Alice Cox - a respectable married woman in her twenties. Husband's away in the army. I can't describe what's happened to her. I only looked for a second, and it was just too awful. She's in the upstairs bedroom."

"Who found her?"

"Her sister. The poor woman's being taken care of by Doc McPherson."

"Okay, thanks, George."

I had an inkling about what we might find in there, but Jeff didn't know what he was walking into.

"Brace yourself, Jeff; I've got an idea this might be pretty awful. Don't disturb anything."

We walked in cautiously. The house looked clean and tidy, nothing out of the ordinary. We made our way upstairs to the open door of the bedroom. Nothing, absolutely nothing, could have prepared me for what greeted us. We found a woman laid out on the bed, mutilated so horribly that she was virtually unrecognisable as a woman. The copious amounts of blood spreading over the white bed sheets made the visual image even more stark. It completely violated the senses. Jeff took one look and walked away, holding his mouth.

This was very much like the last victim, Irene Newnham. Her throat had also been cut, almost to the point of decapitation, and there was extensive disembowelment. It was similar to the previous murder, but the mutilations were taken even further. Aspects of the mutilation and the arrangement of the body meant that vital evidence would be lost by moving the body. I decided Bartholomew needed to see this for himself.

When Jeff recovered, we searched the entire house from top to bottom. Then we searched the back garden, where I noted an Anderson shelter. Inside, it was self-evidently in daily use. All the requirements for nightlife were there: oil lamp, tinned food, bunk beds. I got the police photographer to capture everything from every angle. This was the most horrific murder scene I had ever attended, and I had seen many. The nature of it, a young woman, the mutilation, the arrangement of the body, it was the work of the Devil. I tried to convince myself that it was all in my mind, but I swear I could feel the presence of evil in that bedroom. Jeff said the same thing. A presence hung over that house; you could almost touch it.

Back at the police station, we had to describe to Gerry what we had seen. He just shook his head in disbelief. We went through every scenario we could think of. It seemed pretty certain to me that the victim had been killed on the bed where we found her. We found no sign of blood anywhere else. The rest of the house remained undisturbed. Our hypothesis that the previous victim had been overpowered in or near her Anderson shelter also fitted this crime scene. It certainly seemed to be a plausible possibility.

"The question remains, how does he select the victims?" asked Jeff.

"We don't know for sure that he does. He could just be an opportunist."

"That's possible, Alfie," said Gerry, "but I think you're right, Roger. He needs to know the women are alone in the house."

"So he watches them."

"He must do, Jeff; he must know their movements. We have to question everyone who was out and about during the bombing. Someone's seen this monster."

"They may well have, but if he looks ordinary, who takes the time to notice during the bombing?"

"Nobody, you're right. He's chosen the perfect cover. This is why we've absolutely nothing to go on."

"There's another reason, Guv. This bloke plans it meticulously. I hate to say it, but he's very clever at what he does."

"He is. That tells us something about him. We're looking for an intelligent person who also enjoys the meticulous nature of his crime. We have to assume he selects the victims. We need every bobby on the beat to keep an eye open for someone standing around, someone who appears to be observing."

"This case is growing in importance with each day. When this latest murder becomes known, Scotland Yard will want to take over. At the very least, they will send over a team of specialists."

"Yes, I've thought of that, Guv. The thing is, I was a part of one of those teams for several years; I'm a murder specialist. I don't want this taken away - I want this monster."

"I'm inclined to agree, Roger. This is happening on our patch. Leave it to me, I'll have a word. The Commissioner will need to be involved. We could do with more men on the ground, so I'll pre-empt it by asking for help, but below the rank of DI."

As I expected, Bartholomew didn't need to be asked twice to visit the crime scene. He arrived that same afternoon and later arranged the body's transportation to his pathology department. Meanwhile, we went about interviewing the firemen, wardens, and whoever else was about during the night of the murder. Over the course of a couple of days, we interviewed dozens of people, and nobody saw a thing - except one.

"When you saw this man, Mr Fuller, what made you notice him?"

"During the bombing, people are wary - you always look up and over your shoulder. This man walked along, keeping his head down. He didn't look around him. I might be imagining it, but he didn't look right."

"What time was this?"

"About 1 o'clock."

"Can you describe him?"

"Tall man, six feet, I would say. Other than that, nothing, I'm afraid. He wore a hat and a long coat with the collar turned up."

"What sort of hat?"

"A trilby, I think."

"Colour?"

"Couldn't tell in the dark."

"This could be very helpful, Mr Fuller, well done. Keep your eyes peeled, will you?"

Until I could see Bartholomew, that was the sum total of our efforts. We may or may not be looking for a tall man who wears a hat. That applied to half the men of London. I threw myself into the case, needing to remain fully occupied. I sifted through all the statements and pinned their location on a large local map on the wall. When the warden saw our only possible suspect, he could have been en route from the crime scene. The other people in the same area saw nothing. I went home to my empty house feeling low that night.

On the evenings when I could get away, Jean and I got into the routine of having a meal together either at my place or hers. Afterwards, I drove us to Clapham Junction underground station, where we spent the night. It was difficult for both of us. We were such good friends, but things were different now. Both of us needed to find our own way, and in some ways, our friendship perpetuated what had gone before. We were synonymous with Marilyn and Dave.

"You seem glum tonight, Roger. Is it work, or is it ... you know?"

"It's everything, but especially work. This murderer I'm after, I suppose it's getting to me a bit. I just have nothing to go on."

"You're good at what you do, Roger; Dave always used to say so. You'll catch him, I know you will."

"Let's hope you're right, Jean. You look brighter tonight. What have you been doing?"

"I've got a job. I signed up for the mass observation programme. I'm working for the Ministry of Information."

"You're spying on us then?"

"I suppose I am. I have to keep my eyes open and keep a diary of anything of interest that I see."

"You know it's really all about public morale. The Home Intelligence people are obsessed with maintaining morale."

"Do you mean the posters and all that stuff?"

"Yes, it sounds a bit sinister, I suppose, but they manipulate much of what goes on for 'the public good'."

"And who decides what's in the public good?"

"The Home Intelligence Division does."

"Well, all I'm doing is keeping a diary, and they pay me a bit for doing it."

"Good for you, Jean. What you're doing is important, you know. If we lose public morale, we lose the war."

As we were talking, there was a knock on the door. I opened it to find someone I had completely forgotten about. It was Mr Hewitt.

"Mr Pritchard, sir, good evening. I have the first fitting for your suit, sir. I do hope it's convenient."

"First fitting?"

"Yes, sir, if I may."

"Well, yes, I suppose so. Come in, Mr Hewitt."

"Thank you, sir, and will Mr Wheeler be available as well?"

His question stopped me in my tracks. "I'm sorry, Mr Hewitt. Mr Wheeler is no longer with us. Please don't mention it again in front of Mrs Wheeler."

"Oh, my goodness. Oh dear. I'm most terribly sorry to hear that. I understand, sir, yes indeed, terrible business."

"Come through, Mr Hewitt."

All I could think about was Dave and his damn suit. It just seemed to bring everything back. Memories of better days only serve to remind us of the people who made them better. I stood there in that wretched suit, feeling bloody awful. He picked and poked about, marking lines with his chalk. The awkwardness of the situation didn't escape Jean, either. I'm not sure the fitting would ever have been fun, but I just wanted him gone. I wished I had never got involved.

# Chapter Thirty-Nine
# November 8th, 1940

Emma

*"Committing to a relationship should be like a fledgling bird taking to the wing, an instinctive step into the unknown."*

Following the bomb on the 15th of October, we spent every night in varying degrees of terror. They hit us so many times; we expected it again every night. Shirley especially developed a nervous reaction to every bang or loud noise. She would flinch if we dropped a fork onto a plate. Beverley remained outwardly strong, but I saw her most nights lying on her bed with her eyes wide open, staring at the ceiling. None of us was immune to the stress. Even Janet lost some of her sparkle. We entered November without another direct hit. As the uneventful nights mounted, so did our morale. We were spared, but those around us were not; bombing continued relentlessly, night after night. The casualties arrived every morning; the wave of human misery became as reliable as a tide table.

War teaches you that people are resilient; we adapt to whatever adversity befalls us. As the bombing continued, so the people adapted their response. Life in underground stations, shelters, or basement rooms became exactly that. The unthinkable progressively became everyday life. The unimaginable had become the new reality. More than any other, one salutary event showed me how habituated to the misery of war we had become. One morning, during a particular rush of casualties, the ambulance crew momentarily left a body lying on the pavement outside the hospital. Several people walked by without even giving the unfortunate woman a second glance. We entered a world where the dead attracted no more attention than the living.

In our new world of hitherto unimaginable normality, we started to think in terms of making the best of it. Sunday with my parents had always been an integral part of my life. I had nothing to replace it with. Frank obviously realised that and asked me out for Sunday lunch. Initially, such a suggestion seemed incomprehensible. Sunday lunch belonged to a previous time, not today's. I knew he wasn't just being thoughtful; I knew Frank wanted a relationship; he'd made that clear. His proposal surprised me; I babbled as I always do when I'm flustered, replying with a half-truth.

"Let me see if I have time."

Janet, who misses nothing, noticed Frank talking to me and made assumptions. That afternoon, when I went to the canteen for a cup of tea, she quickly joined me.

"I hope you said yes."

"Yes, to what? What are you talking about?"

"Frank asked you out, didn't he?"

"How do you know that?"

"When a man asks a woman out, and he isn't sure of the reply, they always adopt that little schoolboy lost appearance. He did, didn't he?"

"Well, yes, he did. He asked me out for Sunday lunch."

"See, I told you, I know these things. And you're going, right?"

"I'm not sure."

"Oh, Emma, you should be sure. You need a life like anyone else, and Frank's lovely. You would have said yes to Ken, wouldn't you?"

"I would. I wish I had now."

"This is why you're not sure about Frank, isn't it?"

"Maybe it is, I don't know. Shouldn't I know first if I want a relationship? Isn't that how it works?"

"No, of course not. First, you get to know the man, and then you decide if you want a relationship. You don't decide first, do you?"

"But I already know Frank; I know him very well."

"No, you don't; you know Frank, the doctor; get to know Frank, the man."

"They're one and the same, Jan; I do know him."

"Well, get to know him some more."

"Why are you always pushing me into a relationship?"

"Because you're a lovely person, and I want you to have what I've got with Barry."

"Do you know, Jan, you're a wonderful influence in my life? I see something in you I've never seen before. I see it in your eyes every time you mention Barry. I can see how happy he makes you, and you've made me realise."

"What, realise what?"

"I want what you have. I want to be as happy as you are."

"You will be, Em, you will be. Say yes to Frank."

"I will."

Janet just kind of crept up on me. Her wonderfully extroverted personality is the opposite of mine. For some reason, we just gelled together, perhaps the coming together of yin and yang. I valued her as a confidant, as an intimately close friend. Inspired by her, I went straight to Frank that same afternoon.

"Unless we have an influx of casualties, this Sunday should be fine, Frank. Do you think Leo and Maurice will stand in for us?"

"I'm sure they will."

"Where are we going?"

"We don't want to travel far, so I thought I would treat you to lunch at one of the posh hotels on the other side of the river."

"That'll cost a fortune."

"We haven't exactly spent a lot of money dining out recently, have we?"

"It hardly seems fair when food is rationed."

"Emma let's just enjoy it. Don't you think we've earned it?"

I'm not sure who was looking forward to it more, Janet or me. She spotted an obvious problem before I did. I only had one really nice dress. It was black with a bit of lace, but it disappeared along with all the rooms in the residential accommodation. I looked at Janet with a blank face. She just smiled back, saying she would find something. She didn't tell me where she found them, but on that Saturday evening in our basement room, she arrived with a coat and dress. I think Beverley and Shirley also had something to do with it because it came as no surprise to them. Out of the bag came a beautiful iridescent blue cocktail dress.

I would never choose to wear such a fashionable dress but Janet held it up, and we all looked in amazement. It had square shoulders, with finely gathered smock stitching. Short sleeves and a bow waist with pin tucks around a flared skirt. I looked in disbelief. The other bag contained a coat made from black and white herringbone wool. It had a lapel collar, turned-up cuffs, three large buttons towards the top and deep slanted pockets. An air raid started as I stood looking at it, but we all just ignored it.

"Well, put it on. We all need to see it."

"I can't wear a dress like this."

"Of course you can; let's see if it fits."

What followed was one of those bizarre experiences that punctuated the war. I had to stand there, in a hospital basement during an air raid, wearing a glamorous dress, the likes of which I couldn't even imagine. They thought I looked wonderful. I thought I resembled a cross between a carnival queen and a circus clown. They won the argument.

"Honestly, Emma, you look incredible. Do you have to wear your glasses?"

"They're only for close vision. I'm long-sighted."

"Then leave those behind. Wear the coat until you're in the restaurant, and only then reveal the dress."

"Where did it all come from; how have you got it, Janet?"

"Let's just say I know people, but it has to go back tomorrow, so you're a bit like Cinderella."

That was the first time we laughed and joked during an air raid. A bomb that night could have put an end to my fairytale adventure, but fate must have played a hand because we remained unscathed. If I had anything else remotely suitable to wear, I probably would have worn it, but I didn't. So, Sunday lunchtime, Janet got her wish. I felt incredibly exposed and vulnerable. I confess I tried to feel feminine, and dare I say, glamorous, but those things were completely alien to me. I met Frank in the reception area wearing the coat and a hat which he had seen before. His eyes lit up.

"Emma, you look wonderful. What a beautiful coat."

He seemed genuinely impressed, which helped my confidence. I wondered if he would wear his ubiquitous frayed woollen waistcoat, but he didn't. He wore the same old jacket and trousers, but he wore a bright mustard yellow waistcoat. For once, Frank looked quite fetching. We debated walking or driving to the Sunderland Hotel because it wasn't far. My only suitable shoes had relatively high heels - I didn't want to walk that far, so Frank drove us there.

Over the bridge, along Parliament Street, then Whitehall, and finally down the Strand. We were there in no time. It only took a few minutes to observe the ever-changing London scenery: the missing buildings, the barrage balloons, and people clearing debris from the latest bomb blasts. We dismissed it all and walked into the hotel as if we did it every day.

When the moment came to take the coat off, I was half excited and half frightened.

The woman who emerged from the coat was nothing like me; she was Janet's creation. Frank's eyes opened like saucers, and his face lit up in obvious delight. Had his reaction been anything less, I would have died of embarrassment. Janet would have said nothing and simply enjoyed the moment, but I flustered and babbled.

"For heaven's sake, tell me I look alright, Frank."

"Alright. Emma, you look … amazing."

My lovely Ken would have waxed lyrical with his flamboyant metaphors. He would have lifted me up and placed me on a cloud so high I would have had the world at my feet. He would have seen a butterfly and been dazzled. Frank thought I looked amazing, so why did I think of Ken? I couldn't answer that. We sat in the cocktail bar and drank an alcoholic concoction called a 'Ward Eight' - what else? Rye whisky, grenadine, lemon and orange. I'm not sure if it was the drink or the dress that made my head spin. When we went through to the restaurant, I felt slightly unsteady on my feet.

"This is another world, isn't it, Em?"

"As far from St Thomas's as it's possible to get."

"You wouldn't think there was a war on, would you?"

"What war?"

We talked, and we talked. I felt very relaxed with Frank. We talked about his childhood and how he loved football. He encouraged me to talk about my family, something I hadn't done since that awful night.

"For years, I didn't get on with my sister-in-law, convinced she looked down on me."

"Why on earth did you think that?"

"You haven't seen my sister-in-law. She's beautiful, she really is. She also dresses beautifully, and well, I'm none of those things, so I thought she looked down on me."

"I don't know what you mean, Em. You're a lovely woman."

"That's a nice thing to say, Frank, but we both know it isn't true."

"It is true; you are a lovely woman. The moment you walk into a room, it lights up. You have a way with people. You make everyone smile; your patients worship you. Beauty is more than skin deep. You're a beautiful person."

"Oh, Frank, that's the most wonderful thing to say. I'm speechless."

I honestly didn't know what to say or do. Situations like that didn't happen to me. He looked slightly embarrassed at his own words; they were as much out of character for Frank to say as it was for me to be the recipient. I reached across the table and held his hand; it felt like a wholly inadequate response, but I didn't know what else to do. We looked at each other, locked in an unspoken conversation. The dress made me feel exposed in more ways than one. The waiter approached the table with our next course, and the spell broke. We might have rekindled it, but I had to be certain. I thought committing to a relationship should be like a fledgling bird taking to the wing, an instinctive step into the unknown.

The war and its casualties dominated my life to the exclusion of all else. That day, I saw another world where war didn't exist, a world without fear. It made me feel as if I had been drowning and finally came up for air. It was a breath of normality, and it had never tasted sweeter. Leaving the hotel meant leaving that world behind and once again entering the war. We couldn't escape the bomb damage and the barrage balloons, but I took that breath of fresh air with me.

Frank parked the car and walked around to open the door for me. He effectively ambushed me, but I willingly stepped out and into his arms. We came together in a long, lingering kiss I didn't want to end. I felt like that fledgling bird spreading my wings in wonderment. He stepped back, and we looked at each other. I knew then that I had a relationship with Frank. I didn't understand what it meant or where it was going, but I welcomed it.

The hospital didn't greet us as two people in a relationship; we became doctors again the moment we entered the door. With everyone looking on, we went our separate ways but shared the same memory. Without the accommodation block, I had nowhere to change except our makeshift basement bedroom. The hotel felt a long way away as I walked down into the windowless world of pipes, cables, and girders. I stood there looking down at my mattress on the floor. I looked like a princess, but my coach had turned into a pumpkin, and my dress was about to become a white overall.

I'll never forget that wonderful day. It was the 15th of November, and the very next day, a bomb struck the Savoy Hotel just a short distance from where we had lunch. It killed two people and caused considerable damage, but like the hospital, it didn't close its doors.

Janet and the girls insisted on sharing my memory of that day, so it didn't just lift my spirits. Frank and I were no longer like ships that passed in the night. We found a mooring away from the raging sea. Weeks passed without another bomb hitting us. We settled into an uneasy routine. Thoughts of the Balham disaster were never far away; my nightmares alternated between my entrapment and that of my parents. When they finally recovered the bodies, it was as if they died again.

There were so many bodies during the Blitz that many had to be buried in mass graves. We were determined that wouldn't happen to our parents. Andrew took charge of arrangements with his usual businesslike efficiency. I couldn't have done it; I could hardly bring myself to think about it. When the day came, I realised that my apparent stoicism had been nothing more than denial. As long as there had been no funeral, they were not gone; I hadn't said goodbye. Frank came with me to offer me the support I so desperately needed.

Funerals were not like in peacetime - Andrew had to accept whatever arrangements they offered him. We limited the guests to just a few close family friends, and we had to fit into a short time slot. I told myself it was much better than a mass grave and one of the cardboard coffins. The ceremony at St Michael's Church was hurried, and the next group of mourners filed in as we left. The interment was at St Mary's cemetery in Wandsworth, where we stood at the edge of two graves on a cold, miserable November day. Words were spoken, but I heard nothing. The two coffins were just empty boxes.

I remained detached from it all as if it wasn't happening. It was only when my father's coffin was being lowered into the ground that the finality of the situation hit me. The reality of him passing from this world into the next hit me like a bolt of lightning. He was still there in that box, about to have the earth shovelled on top of him. I wanted to scream 'no' at the top of my voice. I wanted to stop the burial; I wanted him back. Maybe it would have been better if I had screamed. Perhaps it would have been the final act of goodbye. Instead, I fell to my knees and cried hysterically.

Frank, Andrew, and Patricia immediately came to my aid, but I wanted the one thing they couldn't give me. Even surrounded by them, they couldn't shield me from the pain within. They lowered Mum's coffin into the ground, and then both of them were gone. The small group of mourners turned away and walked solemnly towards the exit. We stood until the last of them had gone, clinging to the past. Then it was our turn to walk away, to turn my back on them. I walked a step at a time, gathering my thoughts. It felt as though turning my back was the last goodbye. They had not left me; I was leaving them. I let them down; I didn't remember any of the service and I hadn't said goodbye.

"I'm sorry, I have to go back. I have to say goodbye."

"We'll come with you," Andrew said.

"No, I have to do this alone. Can you wait? Just give me a minute."

"Of course," said Frank.

With a deep breath, I walked back towards the two holes in the ground. I didn't remember approaching the graves the first time; this time, I wanted to. The path through the gravestones was a constant reminder that this is all that's left when we're gone. The grey November sky joined seamlessly with the distant mist. Autumn leaves lay all around, yet one more reminder of the cycle of life.

It was a bleak place, offering no comfort, but despite everything, it existed in my world - the land of the living. My parents were no longer a part of that world. I approached the graves cautiously, not wishing to see the coffins. I'll never know if it was for me or them, but I had to say goodbye. I needed to thank them, if only in whispers.

"Goodbye Mum, goodbye Dad. Thank you for all the love and everything you taught me. Thank you for it all. I must leave you now, but you know I'll always love you. You know I will always try to make you proud. I can leave you knowing nothing has been left unsaid."

I stood for another minute, subconsciously letting them go. Only then did I realise you're never really parted from your parents. They live on in every cell of your body; you are only the latest chapter in the long story of life. I thought of all the wisdom my father so meticulously passed on to me. He described every scrap of knowledge as one more piece of the jigsaw puzzle. Well, now I had the complete picture; the wisdom of the ages was now mine to pass on. I turned and walked away from them, but I was not alone. They walked with me.

Frank and Andrew looked at me with concern. I think they thought I was going to be hysterical again. I assured them I was alright and I wouldn't embarrass anyone again. We had no formal wake, just a drink in the local pub before we resumed our lives. Before the war, my father would have had a huge memorial service with all the great and the good of academia paying homage. The war and the rationing put a stop to all that. More significantly, death had to exist in the shadows. Imagine London if every death had a funeral procession. We had no procession; we just drove back to the hospital.

"I'm sorry you had to meet my family that way, Frank."

"Yes, so am I. Your brother seems a fine man; it's a shame we didn't have time to talk."

"What did you think of my sister-in-law?"

"She's quite something, isn't she?"

"Now you understand why I used to feel so inferior to her."

"Once you get past the exterior, she seems to be a nice lady."

"I'm sorry it took me so long to realise that. Patricia's lovely; we're like sisters now."

"I wish I'd met your parents. You're always quoting things your father said; you talk about him all the time. He was really important in your life, wasn't he?"

"He was, he still is. I can't explain it; we were equally important to each other. I was always a 'daddy's girl'; now I know how unfair it was to Andrew."

"There's plenty of time to mend that."

"You're right, and we are. He's the head of the family now."

"It sounds as if your father will be a hard act to follow."

"I'm not sure anyone can fill my dad's shoes."

A silence followed that comment. I had inadvertently spelt out my greatest fear.

# Chapter Forty
# November 10th, 1940

Roger

*"Love is when you have to be together because being apart
is to be incomplete. It is when the love you share offers everything
you desire, but you only desire each other. It is when time
stands still because you want it to last the rest of your life."*

When I went to see Bartholomew, the hospital seemed less frenetic, although they still had plenty of casualties. I found him writing his notes at one end of the room near the dissecting table where a body lay under a sheet. He looked his usual self, obviously unfazed by his gruesome task.

"Good morning, Inspector; I've just finished my report on Alice Cox."

"Good morning, Doc. I really need something that's going to help me. Have you got anything?"

"Well, it's obviously the same man. The cause of death is almost certainly the cut to the throat. It's the same as last time: a single slash with an extremely sharp knife from left to right. It's been done so violently that it has almost separated the vertebrae. There were indications on Irene Newnham's body that the killer had some degree of anatomical knowledge. There's no doubt about this case. The body looks as if he's randomly sliced it open, but that's not the case."

"Are you telling me that the appalling mutilation I saw had been done methodically?"

"Precisely. It's been done in extreme haste, but the methodology is

265

unmistakable. The intestines were separated from their mesenteric attachments and laid over her shoulder. The uterus and the upper part of the vagina, as well as part of the bladder, are removed. He's taken those parts with him."

"What!"

"That's what I thought. You're dealing with a seriously depraved man, Inspector."

"How can you tell he has anatomical knowledge?"

"He has secured the pelvic organs with the single cut of a knife, avoiding the rectum. That requires precise knowledge."

"Is the knife the same?"

"Yes. It must be at least six inches long, maybe more. No more than an inch wide, and razor sharp. It must also be sharply pointed. It has a single cutting edge, so I would hazard a guess that he used something like a filleting knife, the same as last time."

"How much blood would he have on him?"

"I suspect he's careful to avoid it. This would fit with cutting the throat. I suspect he positioned the victim face down on the bed, and then kneeling astride her, he slashed the throat. That would avoid blood splatter. He then turns the body over and commits his mutilation post-mortem. In that way, he may confine blood to his hands and arms."

"He's going to continue doing this until I catch him, isn't he?"

"I think so. You're dealing with the worst kind of monster. He's quite mad, but somehow he retains a rational, methodical mind."

"My thoughts exactly. We're asking for more help from Scotland Yard. We have to find him."

"I wish you luck, Inspector. I'll send my full report over to you as soon as it's typed up."

"Thanks, Doc."

I left him, feeling deeply concerned. I had investigated many murders in my career, but never one like this. This man sent a chill down my spine. I could only describe his actions as those of the Devil, but he wasn't the Devil. He was just a man like me. Somehow, that made him even more sinister, even more frightening. There had to be something I had missed; I pondered over every scenario as I drove back to the office.

There was a message waiting for me on the front desk in Jack's handwriting. 'Doctor Stevenson rang to ask if you would be free this evening from 5 o'clock. She apologises for the short notice and says not to worry if it's inconvenient. Ring this number if you can'. I wondered if she would ring me. I wanted to talk to her, so I thought I would make the effort. Both Jeff and Alfie were out, so it gave me the opportunity to slip out early. I rang the number, and when someone finally answered, I left a message to say I would pick her up at 5 o'clock. My first port of call when I left was Jean's house.

"I'll come round for you at about 6:15, Jean. I've got to go out again for an hour first."

"Okay, Roger. Don't bother coming here, I'll go to your place, it'll be quicker. Are you doing anything exciting?"

"No, not really. Do you remember the doctor at the tube station, the one we both stood with for a while?"

"Vaguely, yes."

"Well, she wants to talk about it. So I agreed."

"I try not to think about it. Don't be late, will you?"

I just had time to prepare a bag for another night in the tube station before I set off for St Thomas's. Balham is near the hospital, but it gave me enough time to wonder why she wanted to see me. I assumed, like me, she wanted to talk about that night. When I thought about it, plenty of other people were there that night who shared a similar fate, but we didn't know them. Nobody else I could talk to would understand how we both felt. I arrived to find her standing there outside the hospital. She looked cold and lonely with her hands in her pockets and her shoulders hunched up against the cold.

"Where would you prefer to go, Doctor?"

"I don't know anywhere, Inspector. I'll leave it up to you."

"My local pub is pleasant enough; we can go there."

She wore a jacket above a skirt and jumper, the shiny patches on the elbows attesting to a lot of use. Her brown hair was tied back in a business-like bun, but bunches of hair had escaped and hung down the side of her face. She looked as if she had taken her white coat off and simply walked away from the hospital without glancing in the mirror. We exchanged small talk on the way to the pub, but it felt slightly awkward. We didn't really know each other, and we were both apprehensive about mentioning the one thing we had in common. The Fox and Hounds was quiet that evening, so I walked towards what I called 'my table'.

"What would you like to drink, Doctor Stevenson?"

"I'm not much of a drinker, Inspector, but my friends have taught me to drink beer."

"A small one?"

"No, one of those large glasses, not the dimpled ones, a straight one."

"You sound like a serious beer drinker, Doctor."

The smile on her face settled somewhere between laughter and bewilderment. "I have no idea what I'm talking about, Inspector. I'm only repeating what my friends tell me to say."

I liked her total absence of pretension; she didn't look remotely like a beer drinker, let alone a whole pint. As the barmaid drew our beers, I noticed how she lowered her head to look over the top of her gold-rimmed glasses. She gazed intently around the pub as if she hadn't set foot in one before. She raised her eyes and smiled as I returned with our two beers.

"You called this your local pub, Inspector; do you come here often?"

"Before the war, we did, yes. We used to call this table 'our table'."

"Did you come here with the same friends?"

"Yes, it was always the four of us. We did everything together."

"I assume that was with your wife?"

"Yes, my wife and my best friend and his wife. We were inseparable."

"Oh, I'm sorry, I think I understand. Your best friend is the man you mentioned that night. And the woman you comforted - is that his wife?"

"That's right, I've lost them both."

"What was your wife's name?"

"Marilyn, and Jean is Dave's wife."

"Tell me about your wife, Inspector."

"Dave and I met Marilyn and Jean at the Hammersmith Palais. We were both married for fourteen years. We have two children, John and Mary, named after our parents, and Dave and Jean have two kids as well."

"Where are they? Who takes care of them?"

"We evacuated them; they ended up in Cornwall, so they're safe."

"You must miss your children terribly?"

"I do; I hear their voices even though they're not there. I get a postcard from them every so often. It's not always legible, but I can tell from the drawings that they've settled in well."

"Can I ask, how are you coping with the loss of your wife?"

"It's been difficult."

"I can't imagine how bad it must be. I loved my father more than I can say, but losing a partner sounds even worse."

"I won't pretend that Marilyn and I had the perfect marriage - we didn't; it wasn't always plain sailing. We had our share of ups and downs - I don't suppose my job helped."

"Nevertheless, it must be awful going home to an empty house. I'm so sorry."

"It's not something you can imagine, is it?"

"No, you can't. My father was very frail. I knew more than anyone that his life expectancy was limited. I've seen enough death to know when it lurks in the shadows. I knew I would lose him, but I didn't anticipate what would replace him."

"I know what you mean. There's no such thing as a void, is there? It's the pain and emptiness filling the void you can't imagine."

"I have one blessing with my parents; I've no regrets, we left nothing unsaid."

"You're extremely lucky, Doctor; very few people can say that. The void is usually full of regret, and 'if only'."

"Is yours?"

"The questions torment me every night. We had frequent rows and upsets, but I miss her so much. Every memory cries out 'what if'?"

"Do you think the perfect marriage exists?"

"That's a good question, Doctor. I would like to think so."

"What would it look like, this perfect marriage?"

"I don't know, but it would have to be built upon love."

"I loved my father, but I suppose that's different. How would you recognise the love you talk about?"

"You ask some tough questions, Doctor."

"I'm sorry. It's just that I think you know the answers."

"Well, I suppose the moment comes when you realise that the person whose presence fills your entire body and soul feels exactly the same about you."

"That's a wonderful answer, Inspector. So, the love you recognise - how would you describe it?"

"Why are you asking such difficult questions of a stranger?"

"If I knew you well, Inspector, I wouldn't dream of asking. Strangers enjoy anonymity. But really, it goes back to that awful night. You understand these things; I know you do; I saw it in your eyes that night."

"And you're saying that you don't?"

"I'm not sure that I do. Perhaps you could tell me before you're no longer a stranger and when I'll be too embarrassed to ask."

I just said the first thing that came into my mind. "Love is when you have to be together because to be apart is to be incomplete. It's when the love you share offers everything you desire, but you only desire each other. It's when time stands still because you want it to last the rest of your life."

I sat in silent wonder, reliving the words she had elicited from me. Her smile spoke of wonderment, but it was difficult to read her expression. One minute, she appeared thoughtful and the next, she was mournful. Her smile came with generosity and warmth. Her questions initially sounded naive, but I quickly realised they were well-considered. I got the impression that what I saw was what she was - an unpretentious, profoundly honest woman who unashamedly wore her heart on her sleeve. I knew if I asked her why she was asking about love and marriage, she would tell me, but she changed the subject.

"Do you mind if I ask, Inspector, have you been able to have a funeral for your wife yet?"

"Yes, they recovered my friend Dave first, and then they found my wife a couple of days later. We had both funerals last week."

"Was it bad?"

"Second only to that night in the tube station."

"We buried my parents last week as well."

"I'm sorry. I know exactly what you're going through."

"I know you do - you know precisely. "

"Why are we here, Doctor? What do you hope to achieve from this meeting?"

"Oh, I'm sorry, I don't mean to pry, really I don't. It's just that when you told me there were no more survivors, my world collapsed. That was the single worst moment of my life. We were a close family; my father and I were extremely close. It's impossible to describe the pain I felt when you told me. I didn't think anyone could possibly understand. Then I looked at you, and I've never seen such sorrow in a man's eyes before. Despite that, you took me, a stranger, in your arms to share my grief. I owe you an enormous debt, Inspector. My friends tried to comfort me, but they didn't understand. How could they? We - you and I - both understood, didn't we? You gave me the strength to carry on that night, and I'll never forget it. I really don't mean to intrude, but I just wanted to know the man who had been so kind to me."

"That's generous of you to say, Doctor Stevenson, but I think it was the other way around. You took me in your arms, and you gave me the strength to carry on."

She peered over her glasses with a look of puzzlement on her face. I didn't know what to say, so I lit up a fag.

"You shouldn't smoke those, Inspector, they're bad for you."

"Too late now; I've been smoking for years."

"I disagree; you must try. It damages your lungs and shortens your life. If your wife knew how bad smoking was, she would have wanted you to stop."

"Well, if you put it like that, perhaps I should think about it. But what about you, Doctor? All this talk about marriage, but I don't see a ring on your finger?"

"No, I'm not married. I suppose I'm married to the job."

"Has there ever been anyone?"

"No, I'm afraid not. I'm a bit of a loner when it comes to relationships."

"Oh, I'm surprised to hear you say that. I would have thought the opposite."

"I'm sorry to disappoint you."

"Disappointment is a word I wouldn't associate with you, Doctor. By the way, who was that little girl I dragged out of the mud?"

"Alma. Did you know the flood killed both of her parents that night?"

"No, I didn't."

"She's a very special little girl. Alma's a polio victim, but she's doing very well. I'm hoping she will walk again with the right help. She's all alone in the world now; they've placed her in foster care in the countryside. I have a special relationship with her. I don't know what the future holds, but I always want to be a part of her life. If circumstances ever allowed it, I would even consider adopting her."

"That would be a wonderful thing to do."

"If you knew Alma, Inspector, I think you would say the same. She lights up my life every time I see her; she really is a special child."

"That says a lot about you, Doctor. You said you were close to your father; tell me about him."

Her face lit up with a sad smile. She spoke about her father's academic achievements and their relationship in glowing terms. While it was nice to hear of such a close-knit family, I couldn't help thinking a woman in her thirties should have established her own life. Batholomew described her as being unapproachable, a woman with a reputation for being shy and aloof. I saw a woman full of compassion, someone with the gift of human kindness; I found her quite charming. I suspect Bartholomew mistook that kindness for vulnerability.

We talked openly for two strangers, and I understood what she meant about it often being easier to talk with someone you don't know well. She was also right about what had passed between us in the Balham Tube Station that night. I didn't understand it, and neither did she. Whatever it was, it was very significant for both of us. I stubbed out my cigarette and sipped my beer while she looked on thoughtfully. We were no longer strangers; I wondered where our conversation would go next.

"I was trapped like you were, Inspector, when they bombed the hospital on the 15th of September; I know what you went through. Do you still see it every time you close your eyes?"

"It never leaves you, does it?"

"No, it's always there. We have lost so many friends and colleagues at the hospital, but somehow, we just carry on."

"That's all any of us can do. Did you lose close friends that day?"

"Yes, a surgeon colleague who'd become very close to me. I still see his face and hear his voice."

"I'm sorry. This must end one day, and when it does, only the living can keep the memory of our loved ones alive."

"That's a profound truth, Inspector. I'm living day to day, but carrying the memory of those we've lost into the future is reason enough to survive, isn't it?"

"That's what I keep telling myself."

"You speak fondly about your friend Jean. Do you think you might continue to support one another?"

"I promised Dave I would always be there for her. I can't imagine her not being somewhere in my life."

"Do you think you will eventually remarry?"

"What, to Jean?"

"It sounds possible."

"There were occasions when we'd had a row that Marilyn used to call Jean my girlfriend. When we first met that night at the Hammersmith Palais, Dave and I did that thing that men do in those circumstances. We agreed which of the two women we would each ask to dance. From the first moment, I felt I had made a mistake because there was a kind of spark between me and Jean. It's silly how an initial decision based on nothing more than the toss of a coin ended up being so binding. So yes, we had a soft spot for each other, it's true, but it's never been anything more than that. The silly thing is that what Marilyn said about Jean being my girlfriend would have been unthinkable. Everything's different now, of course. We're just friends who need each other."

"I've got a friend who's a bit like that. His name's Frank."

"I suspect he's more than a friend."

"Is that because you're a detective?"

"Probably, assessing people is a habit, I'm afraid."

"Well, maybe you're right about Frank."

"Do I assume your questions about love and marriage relate to Frank?"

"You're really being a detective now, aren't you, Inspector?"

"It's what I do."

"You're right. Frank wants a relationship with me, and I have to decide."

A stranger is no longer a stranger the moment the heart is laid bare, and suddenly she appeared to be vulnerable. She was right about many things that evening, including that talking to someone you don't know well can often be easier. The problem was, I no longer regarded her as a stranger. It suddenly felt inappropriate to ask her about her relationship with Frank. So I said what people say when they can't think of anything better.

"I'm sure you'll make the right decision."

"I hope so, Inspector; I really hope so."

That marked the end of our conversation. When it was time to drive back to the hospital, I felt sorry our evening had ended. She shook my hand when I stopped at the hospital and thanked me.

"Thank me for what, Doctor? I really enjoyed our conversation."

"I had to know the man who shared my grief and who saved Alma that night. You're an extremely thoughtful man, Inspector Pritchard. You're what I assumed you were; I hope we meet again."

"I'm sure we will, Doctor. Stay safe."

"And you, Inspector. Goodnight."

What a strange but pleasant hour we spent together. I rushed home, thinking about it all the while. The time was rapidly approaching 6:30, and we needed to waste no time driving over to the Clapham tube station. I could see a faint light shining from behind one of the blackout blinds in my house, so I knew Jean would be there, ready to go. I opened the door to find an enormous bunch of flowers on the hall stand.

"Where did these come from, Jean?"

"They were delivered; they're for you and me. The card says to Mrs Wheeler and Mr Pritchard. The message says, 'Please accept my sincere condolences for your tragic loss. I share your pain.' It's signed by Joey Katz. Isn't that nice, Roger?"

"What on earth is he doing sending us condolences, and where did he find cut flowers?"

"I don't think he can be as bad as you say he is. He's obviously very grateful for you helping Rachel; I expect he's just being kind."

"Joey Katz isn't kind, Jean; he's just trying to curry favour."

"I know Dave said that, but I'm not so sure. Rachel loves him; she won't hear a bad word spoken about him."

"Don't trust any of it, Jean. Rachel seems like a nice girl, I'll give you that, but I suspect she's taken in by his charm."

"Well, at least you've admitted he's charming. How long have you known him?"

"Joey and I go back a long way. I was just a young copper on the beat then."

"Has he always been charming toward you?"

"To be honest, yes, he has. It goes back to when his oldest boy, Aaron, was bullied by the local kids. I came across a gang of them beating the hell out of the boy. I stepped in and put a stop to it, but not before the boy had a bloody nose. Joey was grateful when I took him home, but that's not why I did it."

"Why did you do it then?"

"Well, apart from being my job, it's something I feel strongly about. It was the same with Rachel the other night. The Katz's are a proud Jewish family - they escaped persecution in Russia to come here, so it's not surprising that they're rightly sensitive about that kind of thing. I didn't want Joey intervening, so I watched over the boy after that."

"You're too principled for your own good, Roger. Isn't it obvious that Joey Katz feels he owes you a debt, and he's just as principled as you are? Why not accept his kindness?"

"I can't be seen to associate with a criminal, but maybe you're right. My guess is that he's taken a step back from all that; his wayward son Ezra is in charge now."

"Well, there you are then, you can stop being so principled. Now, take me to the underground station before the bombs fall on us."


ooOoo


Jean and I found Christmas 1940 very difficult. The memories were raw, and the empty seats were too painful to look at. Jean cooked us Christmas lunch, but corned beef is hardly comparable to a stuffed turkey. Gerry and his wife Margaret came round for a drink in the early evening, and Jeff and his wife Norma made a surprise visit. They were all being very thoughtful, realising it would be a difficult time for us. Having 'celebrated' Christmas day, we decided that caution was the better part of valour, and we would be wise to spend the night in the underground.

For us, the 'festive' had gone out of Christmas, but for many in the Clapham underground station, festivities were in full swing. To my surprise, it did much to raise our spirits. People were determined to maintain the Christmas spirit despite everything. Paper chains decorated the tunnel, bunches of holly adorned the walls, and candles added their own flickering atmosphere.

A small group of able musicians played music well into the night. Jean and I even danced together. For a fleeting moment, we almost forgot. We laughed and sang 'Roll out the barrel'. It's a powerful thing when the human spirit comes together with a common purpose. Those people were not about to let Hitler take their Christmas celebrations away, they wouldn't give in. They even lifted our spirits, if only for a moment.

For many people, Christmas provided a welcome distraction from the daily grind that the Blitz had become. But it didn't last. On the 29th of December, in a cruel attempt to break our spirit, the Germans launched one of the most devastating raids of the war. They dropped 100,000 incendiary bombs on the City of London. We were unaware of the scale of the fires as we sheltered in the underground station. It was only when we emerged, squinting our eyes into the daylight the next morning, that the magnitude of the event became apparent.

The fire that broke out in the City of London could be seen from miles around. The sky looked as if a terrible storm was approaching. It menacingly filled the horizon as far as we could see over the rooftops. What appeared to be towering thunderclouds were not clouds at all. What we saw became known as the second 'Great Fire of London'. Smoke blanketed the centre of the city and spread far and wide. The smell of destruction filled the air to Balham and beyond.

There was one saving grace as far as public morale was concerned. The dome of St Paul's Cathedral still stood defiantly above the carnage surrounding it. It may not have been of any strategic importance, but St Paul's, like the great clock tower of Big Ben, had become a symbol of resistance. Those iconic symbols of British history seemed to be possessed of the same spirit that galvanised the people. With every bombing raid that failed to destroy them, the invincibility of the British people grew. We could only pray they really were invincible.

The passing of the old year was fraught with emotion, 1941 was born of tears. There were shouts of 'Happy New Year' at the stroke of midnight; there were even cheers. People hugged one another and shook hands until one of our Clapham Station musicians lifted his violin. He played a single cord, and the station fell silent. The haunting melody emanating from those strings cut through the crowd like a chill wind. Voices joined in with the words almost reluctantly. There were no loud voices, no great enthusiasm, just sombre reflection.

*Should auld acquaintance be forgot,*
*and never brought to mind?*
*Should auld acquaintance be forgot,*
*and auld lang syne?*
*For auld lang syne, my dear,*
*for auld lang syne.*
*We'll take a cup of kindness yet*
*for auld Lang syne.*

There would hardly have been a person in that tube station who had not lost someone or knew someone who had. For Jean and me, and for so many others, we wouldn't be taking a cup of kindness for old times' sake. We celebrate those words in peacetime, but not so in 1941. Tears rolled down Jean's face, and she was not alone. New Year reminds us of the passage of time. For those wishing to escape the past, the passing of time is your friend. But the passing of time comes with one unavoidable caveat. Our loved ones belong to the past. They cannot come with you. For us, parting with 1940 was a bitter sorrow. We could not go back, not even for Auld Lang Syne, but our memories will always be brought to mind.

# Chapter Forty-One
# December 1940

Emma

*"Grief is an empty room where love once lived, a place where memories echo against bare walls, a room I felt compelled to revisit."*

December heralded the shortest day of the year, and the long nights had never felt longer. What remained of the hospital settled into a routine. The bombing continued relentlessly around us, night after night, and each morning, the casualties arrived at our door. Having lost so many of our medical facilities, we had to make do with whatever we had. We had to make do in our personal lives as well. Creature comforts disappeared with the loss of the accommodation block. Life for all the hospital staff had long since become intolerable, but somehow, we rose above it. Adversity brought out the very best in people.

Janet and I were inseparable; all of us in our basement bedroom grew closer with every passing day. Marion made a good recovery and joined us in our nocturnal existence. Before the war, a hospital Matron would never associate with the nurses outside of work. In our basement world, we were all just women as vulnerable to the falling bombs as anyone else. At night, Janet and the others called her Marion; during the day, they reverted to Matron. For her part, I think Marion secretly enjoyed it. It was a case of all for one and one for all. It was a great source of strength to know that we would stand by and support each other, no matter what. On December the 5th, Beverley came looking for me.

"Emma, there's a very elderly lady in admissions asking for you."

"Who is it? Is she a casualty?"

"She arrived by ambulance. She's not a casualty; she's got breathing difficulties and a temperature; I'd say it's pneumonia. Doctor Wiśniewski is insisting she be sent to another hospital. She says her name is Daisy and keeps asking for you."

"Oh no, not my lovely Daisy. I'll come immediately."

I found her left in reception, unattended. Beverley was right; Daisy had stage four pneumonia. She looked so frail - my heart ached at the prospect because I knew she wouldn't survive the night. When I took her hand, she slowly opened her eyes.

"You came; I knew you would."

"You told me you wouldn't come to the hospital, Daisy; you must feel poorly."

"I've only come here to be with my Herbert. I won't be leaving, will I?"

Daisy was a wise old lady; she knew it was her time. I would normally tell patients that there is always a chance and they must be strong. I knew Daisy so well, and she knew me - I wasn't about to lie to her now.

"No, you won't, Daisy, I'm so sorry."

"Don't be sorry, Doctor; my Herbert has been waiting for so long. I won't keep him much longer, will I?"

"No, I don't think you will. I'll make you as comfortable as I can. I'll be with you all the time."

"Bless you. I've had a good life, I'm ready now, and you're with me."

I struggled hard not to shed a tear. I didn't notice Doctor Wiśniewski walking up behind me.

"I'm transferring this patient, Doctor Stevenson. There's no point wasting your time here."

"I know this lady, Doctor; I'm not wasting my time."

"I think we both know that you are, please allow the porter to remove her."

"No. This patient is not going anywhere. We will show her some dignity and compassion in her last hours."

"I beg your pardon, Doctor Stevenson. Did you not hear me?"

"I heard you, Doctor Wiśniewski, and I'm ignoring you. This patient is staying in my care."

"How dare you? Who do you think you are to question my authority? We don't have space for this patient, and if you persist with this impudence, we will not have space for you either."

"You would dismiss me?"

"You are dismissing yourself, Doctor."

"Are you mad?" said an enraged Beverley. "She's the most caring doctor in this hospital. If you dismiss Doctor Stevenson, then you dismiss me as well."

"Then consider yourself dismissed, Nurse. Report to Matron immediately."

"Wait a minute, Doctor Wiśniewski," I said. "I think you're being hasty."

"I will not be spoken to by a nurse in that manner, and I can no longer tolerate your disregard for authority. My word is final."

Marion watched from afar until she could watch no more. The sight of the hospital matron marching imperiously towards you can be quite daunting.

"What seems to be the problem here?" asked Marion.

Beverley told her every detail before Wiśniewski could get a word in. Marion looked at me, and I raised my eyebrows.

"You actually used those words, Nurse Roberts? You told Doctor Wiśniewski he was mad?"

"No, Matron, I asked if he was mad."

"That is outrageous. Why would you say such a thing?"

"Dismissing Doctor Stevenson can only be described as an act of madness; how else could you describe it?"

"Well, yes, it would be disastrous, I agree. And you are prepared to be dismissed in support of Doctor Stevenson?"

"I am, Matron."

"Doctor Wiśniewski, I can't afford to lose Nurse Roberts, and I would suggest that you can't afford to lose Doctor Stevenson. May I suggest you apologise for your inappropriate remark, Nurse Roberts? And Doctor Stevenson, it's not my place to comment, but do you think a compromise might be found?"

"Thank you for your wise words, Matron. If Doctor Wiśniewski could see his way clear to reverse his judgment regarding this patient, then I think we can all apologise for raising our voices."

"I'm very sorry, Doctor Wiśniewski. I spoke in the heat of the moment," said Beverley with a look of defiance in her eyes.

"Well, yes, indeed," replied Wiśniewski, "perhaps it would be better if I didn't pursue this matter further. But this complete disregard for authority cannot continue, is that clear, Doctor Stevenson?"

"Absolutely, Chief, you're quite right. I'll try harder in the future."

"This isn't the first time, is it, Doctor Stevenson? This must not happen again. Right, well, I have work to do. I suggest we all do the same."

With that, he stormed off. Marion waited until he was out of sight.

"Well done, Emma and you, Nurse Roberts, well done indeed."

Marion walked away wearing a broad smile. I looked at Beverley, and we both burst out laughing. Before the war, such insubordination would undoubtedly have cost Beverley her job; I so appreciated her support. I realised that each of my friends would have done the same thing for me, and I would also stand by them, regardless. Wiśniewski might not have appreciated it, but our spirit of unity held us together during those dark times.

I kept my promise; I didn't leave Daisy's side. Her breathing became increasingly laboured as the end approached. People know when the moment comes. It was an effort for her to smile, but she made that effort. She looked at me and somehow found the strength to squeeze my hand. Her hand went limp, but her smile remained. That was the moment when she joined Herbert. I cried. I walked among death every day, but it never got any easier.

We were never complacent about the bombing, but we began to think our good luck might continue. That triumph of hope over expectation ended on December the 8th, when at 1 am, several incendiary bombs hit the hospital. They don't explode like high explosive bombs, so we were unaware of the danger until the fires took hold. By the time we ventured out under the night sky, the firemen had it under control. We were hit by incendiaries yet again on the 29th, and once again, the firemen saved us from even worse destruction. We stood there looking at an apocalyptic scene. Jets of water from the fire hoses rained down on our hospital, and the firemen stood defiant, silhouetted against the backdrop of London burning. I wondered how much more London could take.

In the distance, I saw a parachute as the canopy caught the light of a burning fire. My first thought was that it must have been a pilot, maybe a German pilot, who had bailed out of his aeroplane. I watched it as it descended closer to the light. It wasn't a pilot; it was a parachute mine. The bomb exploded right before my eyes with a blinding flash. The smoke rising from the hospital suddenly rushed away from the blast, only to come rushing back the other way a moment later. We all instinctively cowered in fear until we realised the bomb was just far enough away not to kill us. The sound echoed across the river and rumbled on like thunder. How much more, how much more, my thoughts echoed with the thunder.

As 1940 drew to a close, our thoughts should have been of Christmas and the New Year, but what cheer did Christmas hold for me? What cheer did the New Year hold for anyone? This would be the first Christmas I would ever spend without my parents. Grief is an empty room where love once lived, a place where memories echo against bare walls, a room I felt compelled to revisit.

## Chapter Forty-Two
# Betty Sullivan and Maureen Elkins

Roger

*One of life's greatest sorrows is that love survives death.*

1 941 brought us no respite from the bombing, continuing relentlessly, night after night. It wasn't only confined to London; the carnage was spread far and wide. Coventry suffered beneath 502 tons of high explosive bombs and 30,000 incendiaries in a single raid. The list went on: Birmingham, Manchester, Liverpool, Sheffield, Bristol, Southampton, and the south coast ports.

Maintaining law and order became increasingly difficult as the people became more desperate. Looting had a terrible effect on public morale. For most honest folk, it challenged our notion of solidarity. It undermined the social order and caused distrust, even between friends and neighbours. There were siren voices repeated in newspaper headlines demanding the death penalty for looters. Social order was being severely challenged.

The situation escalated dramatically on January 22nd when the Ripper struck again. A family member discovered the body the following morning. New Scotland Yard sent a detective constable to increase our number, DC Fleming, and he assumed that the case was not connected. It came to me via Jack that the local bobby, who'd been the first to attend the scene, thought otherwise. Jeff and I rushed over to Wandsworth to see for ourselves. We arrived to find a police photographer just about to leave and the detective constable standing with the local bobby, who had raised doubts about the killer.

"What's the story here?" I asked.

"It's a horrible murder right enough, Guv, but it doesn't bear the hall-marks of the Ripper," replied DC Fleming.

"But you think otherwise, Constable."

"Yes, Sir. It doesn't look like a random killing to me. The victim's been placed on the bed; it's been done methodically."

"Who is she?"

"Her name's Betty Sullivan. She's a midwife. Married, has no children, and her husband is serving in North Africa."

"Okay, let's go in and have a look."

Even before I saw the body, I could feel the presence of the Ripper in that building. Just like the previous murder, the ground floor was undisturbed, with no sign of blood or anything untoward. We went upstairs to the bedroom, and I took a deep breath before we entered. The victim was positioned on the bed where she had obviously been killed. She was naked except for a blouse that had been left open. Her throat had been cut, and the bedclothes were covered in blood.

"It's him, no doubt about it. Well done, Constable; your instinct was right."

"But she's not been mutilated, Guv. I thought that was his signature."

"Look at her throat, Fleming; what's that if it's not mutilation? Her position on the bed is identical to the other two. It's almost as if he wants us to know it's him. You saw the photographs; it should be obvious to you."

"Should we get the pathologist to come here, Guv?"

"Yes, good idea, Jeff, I'll see to that. Did you find an Anderson shelter in the garden, DC Fleming?"

"Yes, Guv."

"Does that not link it to the other murders?"

"Lots of people have shelters in the garden, Guv."

"They're not all murdered women, though, are they?"

I despaired; had the constable not spotted the obvious similarities, I might not have been called in. The Yard wanted to be involved, yet they sent me a rookie. I told him to stay there until fingerprints and the pathologist had attended the scene, anything to keep him out of my sight. What happened next turned the course of the Inquiry. Jeff and I walked out of the front door straight into two local reporters.

"Is this the work of the 'Blackout Ripper', Inspector?"

"What Ripper? What are you talking about?"

"Come off it, Inspector. Is this the third or the fourth victim?"

"Now listen, you two. I don't want names like that appearing in the newspapers. In fact, I don't want any of this in the papers."

"It's too late for that, Inspector. It's already going to print for the evening edition."

"Where did you get this information from?"

"We have our sources."

"You mean it's come from us? One of our lot has tipped you off?"

He wouldn't tell me, but it was obvious. They conjured up the name 'Blackout Ripper' between them, and the damage was done. The moment the evening paper hit the floor, the station telephone didn't stop ringing. The paper said a depraved killer was stalking the streets of South London in search of women victims; as if the women of London didn't have enough to worry about. We were never far away from mass hysteria, and this pushed many women over the edge. It was already bad enough with the evening rush to the underground stations or public shelters. The nights would now come with an additional terror.

The moment the killer was given a name, the newspapers also gave him an identity. The public's perception of a murderer is one thing; the 'Blackout Ripper' was something else entirely. Jeff and I agreed the killer wanted us to know it was him. That also implied that he would thrive upon his newfound notoriety. Jeff and I were both trying to dismiss the image in our minds as we drove back to the station to go through the witness statements already collected by the local constable. The pattern was the same - the people on the street at night saw nothing, the neighbours saw nothing. Our madman appeared to be possessed of demonic powers, no doubt an illusion reinforced by his new-found name. I knew otherwise; he was just a madman.

I couldn't conceive how the day could get any worse - what a mistake that was. We walked wearily into the station, where Jack stood grim-faced. I knew Jack well, so I waited for him to put words to his expression.

"The day's not over. It sounds as if he's struck again."

"What do you mean? We've just come back from dealing with it."

"This is another one, phoned in fifteen minutes ago. It's close to the last one in Wandsworth. You'd better get back over there. Here's the address."

We both looked at Jack incredulously. Surely not, it wasn't possible. My blood ran cold. The day was already well advanced, so we wasted no time and left immediately. The moment we sat in the car, it became obvious to me. The two Jack the Ripper victims in 1888, Elizabeth Stride and Catherine Eddows were both murdered on the same day, one closely followed by the other. Elizabeth Stride had her throat cut, but she hadn't been mutilated. Our victim, Betty Sullivan, suffered identical wounds. In 1888, the police assumed that the Ripper had been disturbed and couldn't complete his work. He left the scene presumably unfulfilled from his perverted perspective. The assumption is that he must have set out on a frenzied search for another victim to fulfil his demonic desire. He found poor Catherine Eddows.

"It's obvious, isn't it, Jeff? He's copying 'Jack' precisely. Except, of course, he wasn't disturbed. He planned it all."

"I hate to think what we're going to find."

"I know what we'll find, Jeff. He's carved her up the same as Catherine Eddows. You're going to need a strong stomach."

We arrived to find the now familiar scene in front of an ordinary terraced house on an ordinary road in Wandsworth. The PC standing at the door looked positively green. Family members were huddled together, almost hysterical in their anguish. I couldn't begin to imagine seeing a loved one in the condition that I knew the victim would be in. We hesitated to approach them, but we had no option. I beckoned the PC over.

"What can you tell me, Constable?"

"The victim's mother found the body about an hour ago, Sir. I went in to look, but I can't describe it. I came out and threw up in the garden."

"That's alright, Constable, I understand. Who's the victim?"

"Her name is Maureen Elkins. She's married. I knew her husband, he was serving in the forces, but he's been killed."

"We'd better go in, Jeff."

Jeff looked how I felt. The constable controlled the grieving family so we could get past them. Their combined grief was palpable. I could almost feel it like a physical barrier. As we stood in the hallway, their cries echoed through the building. We looked first downstairs, and as before, found no sign of disturbance or break-in. After spending more time than needed, we knew we couldn't avoid going upstairs. I went into the bedroom first, and I heard Jeff audibly gasp behind me. The victim was laid out on the bed, identical to the other victims. The mutilation of her body was truly horrific. This time, as with Catherine Eddows in 1888, her face had also been mutilated.

Jeff and I stood silently, unable or perhaps unwilling to comprehend what we saw. I made notes in my notebook as I silently walked around the bed. A part of me did my job, while the greater part raged between revulsion and anger. When Jeff said we should check the back garden, I seized upon the suggestion. We found the almost ubiquitous Anderson shelter, and it had obviously been used. The pattern fell depressingly into place. Our madman wasn't just poking fun at us. He was running rings around us. Our next job was to interview the family and the neighbours on either side. Jeff looked at me as if to say, I'm not interviewing the family. I didn't blame him; I knew it would be a harrowing experience. The victim's mother was incapable of words, but the victim's sister and her aunt told me everything I needed to know.

Mrs Elkins found her daughter at 3:15 in the afternoon. Maureen Elkins visited her mother the day before and left for home in the early evening. Her mother was the last person to see her alive. Jeff returned from speaking to the adjoining neighbours with the news that one side had gone into the underground for the night, and the other side spent the night in their Anderson shelter. They saw and heard nothing. The raid that night had been quite bad. Several bombs and incendiaries fell locally. One of those bombs fell at the end of the road at 2:30 am.

DC Fleming arrived at an auspicious time - we both wanted to leave the scene. I told Fleming not to touch anything and to wait until the local doctor, our fingerprint people, and the photographer were there. I also wanted Bartholomew to see the murder scene, so Fleming was in for a long night. We left, promising the family we would find the murderer, the words sticking in my throat as I said them. It was already nearly dark when we finally left.

I felt utterly drained and exhausted. It was too late to return to Balham; we would only end up sheltering in the cells. I asked Jeff to drop me off at home, where my car was. When we stopped outside my house, to my dismay, I saw Mr Hewitt standing on my doorstep. I felt so tired and preoccupied I could hardly find the words to speak to the man. My instinct was to tell him to go away.

"Good evening, Mr Pritchard. I have your finished suit ready for you, sir."

"You'd better come in, Mr Hewitt."

It wasn't Hewitt's fault; he was just in the wrong place at the wrong time. I put my hat on the hall stand, and it fell to the floor. Too tired to pick it up, I left it, but the ever-considerate Hewitt picked it up. My coat followed the hat, and I took off my loose tie.

"It's not my place to ask, sir, but are these stories in the paper true?"

"Broadly speaking, yes, I'm afraid so. Do you have a wife at home, Mr Hewitt?"

"Yes, sir, I do. Should she be worried?"

"No, tell her not to be concerned. This man only attacks lone women. I'm sure you will be with your wife."

"I'll tell her that, sir; she is rather worried about it."

"You're out late tonight, Mr Hewitt. You'll be going home in the dark. Let's get this done so you can be on your way, but first, would you join me in a glass of whisky?"

"That's very kind of you, sir, but your requirements come first."

I marvelled at Hewitt's dedication and sense of duty. He risked his life to see me after hours and took such pride in his work. I ended up feeling privileged to be given his undivided attention. I poured him a glass anyway, but first, I drank mine and poured myself another.

"You look as if you needed that, Inspector."

"I've had a long day, Mr Hewitt, a very long day."

Two glasses of whisky later, I was standing in my underwear, being dressed by Hewitt. The world felt a strange place at that moment. He stood back, looking at his creation with a very approving smile. Only when I looked at myself in the mirror did I take the whole suit affair seriously. What had been a distraction at best and a bribe at worst suddenly became something else altogether. I had never seen a suit like it. A lustrous dark grey with a faint pinstripe, it displayed perfection in every hand-stitched detail.

"I have to say, sir, I'm delighted with the finished result. You'll need an exceptional quality shirt to complement this suit. I could suggest the name of a shirtmaker I can thoroughly recommend, if you wish, sir. A fine Egyptian cotton shirt and a silk tie would be perfect. They say that clothes maketh the man, and that is undeniably true. From a tailor's perspective, however, the reverse is also true. You have the height and build to wear this suit to its full advantage, sir. It will give you years of service, and I hope, great pleasure."

I had never considered clothes to be things that gave me pleasure. Hewitt had introduced me to a hitherto unknown concept. Standing in front of the hall mirror, I found myself puffing up my chest and standing tall. Hewitt smiled in genuine appreciation.

"Mr Hewitt, you should be proud. This suit is magnificent. I feel you've gone above and beyond the call of duty on my behalf. I'm grateful to you."

"I can assure you, sir, all our clients receive the same personal attention at Slater and Fenwick."

Conscious of his journey home, I ushered him towards the front door, but only after he gave me the name of his recommended shirtmaker. I thanked him again and shook his hand. I realised that Hewitt would always go above and beyond for all of his clients, and he did it regardless of the bombing, and indeed, the threat to his life. I meant it when I said I felt honoured to have received his services.

The suit came with a polished hanger and a cover emblazoned with the name Slater and Fenwick beneath the Royal Crest. I couldn't imagine when, or even if, I might wear it, but I enjoyed placing it in my wardrobe. It was now nearly 9 o'clock, and I was supposed to take Jean to the underground before the bombing started. Having thrown on my regular jacket and trousers, I momentarily caught sight of myself in the hall mirror as I left. It was a very disappointing sight. I pulled the brim of my hat down to obscure my reflection.

Jean stood at her front door, waiting for me. As I stopped the car, the siren greeted me with its awful wailing. It's a sound you always remember. It conjured up terrible images and immediately filled you with fear. We looked at each other, not knowing what to do for the best. Dave installed an Anderson shelter in their garden, but it was low-lying and prone to filling with groundwater. We could make a dash for the Clapham underground station or one of the other less reliable public shelters, or we could chance our luck. Our area had been lucky so far, so, like a lot of people, we decided to stay put.

I thought it best not to mention Hewitt and the suit. Jean had prepared some food for me, and we sat down at the table as if everything was quite normal. We made a good pretence of it, but all the time, our ears were alert for the sound of approaching bombs. Our relationship had settled into a mutually beneficial arrangement without even talking about it. Spending our nights in a congested underground station deprived us of the opportunity to talk. In contrast, the silence of Jean's kitchen seemed to demand answers.

"You're quiet tonight, Rog. Are you alright?"

"Don't say anything, but the Ripper's struck again today - twice."

"Oh, good God. You mean he killed two women last night?"

"It's the worst thing I've ever seen. He's not just deranged. He must be possessed by the Devil."

"I knew you'd had a bad day. You smell of fags and whisky; do you need another one?"

"Anything to block out what I've seen today. Will you join me?"

We sat drinking whisky to the distant sound of falling bombs. Marilyn would have been angry with me for coming home late, accusing me of drinking with Dave. Jean was concerned for me, understanding that the whisky was anaesthetic, nothing more.

"Are you feeling any better?"

"Not better, just less."

"I know. You've taught me to enjoy this stuff."

"You'd best put the bottle away before I fall over."

"Yes, I've had more than enough. So, what are we going to do, Roger?"

"As you said, we'll stay here and chance our luck."

"No, I mean us, the future."

"I don't know, I find it difficult to think about."

"I do, too. I think I'm cheating on Dave if I even think about it. He never asked about you and me, not once. Did you know that?"

"I'm not surprised. It all goes back to that night at the Palais. We both wanted to be with you, but Dave won the toss. I only had eyes for you for those first few weeks, but I wasn't about to renege on an agreement with Dave. He knew it was all in the past and would stay there."

"You two were really close, weren't you?"

"I'll never have another friend like Dave. He literally saved my life. I'd no more cross him than I would jump off a cliff."

"I know. I liked that you were close. I think Marilyn did, too. Do you think they would mind us being together like this?"

"We aren't together, Jean, not in that sense."

"I thought you were a detective, Roger. I'm trying to ask if they would mind if we were."

"Is that what you want?"

"No, I'm not saying that, but I think about it, Roger. If it wasn't for Dave and Marilyn, it would have been us, wouldn't it? I mean, if we had met, just the two of us."

"Yes, it would. You were the only woman there when I saw you that night at the Palais."

"You've not told me that before."

"Didn't you feel the same?"

"You know I did. But that was a long time ago. I'm fifteen years older, and I've had two children."

"You haven't changed at all, Jean. You were beautiful then, and you're beautiful now."

"Do you still fancy me then, Rog?"

"Are you being serious?"

"I suppose I am."

"You're a lovely woman, Jean. I'd be crazy not to fancy you."

"I think that's your way of saying you do - that's nice to know. I thought you did, but I wanted to know."

"Why?"

"I'm as unsure as you are. I just want to be a bit less confused. There's no one closer to me now than you, Rog, so we can be honest with each other, can't we?"

"You're right; having it out in the open feels good, no more doubts. We need each other at the moment. I don't know what I would do without you. I'm grateful for that, Jean. You're right about a lot of things. We've always been fond of each other, and it feels good to admit it. Let's just wait and see what comes of it."

"That's what I hoped you would say. It's what I want. I feel as if they're watching me and that I need their approval. I feel guilty even talking about it. One of life's greatest sorrows is that love survives death. And it's strange, isn't it? Married people have affairs all the time, but somehow this seems worse. You've never had an affair, have you?"

"How do you know?"

"Because I know you, Roger. You haven't got a disloyal bone in your body."

"It seems I don't have any secrets either."

We laughed, something we hadn't done for a long time. I needed that conversation with Jean, but left to my own devices, I doubt I would have had the courage to mention it. I was sure from day one that Jean felt the same about me, but because we never acted upon it, a sliver of doubt remained. Hope and expectation are easily confused. With that doubt removed, we grew closer. I knew that, at the very least, she would be my closest friend for life. If those barriers melted away, then that would also be wonderful. Strangely, I almost didn't want to be a part of that decision-making process; I didn't want to influence the outcome.

At about 11:30, we heard the sound of explosions getting closer. Jean had prepared herself for bed, dressed in a nightdress and dressing gown. We sat listening as the explosions grew ever louder. When they were getting really close, we decided to sit under the stairs, just in case. With precious little room between buckets, mops and brooms, we huddled together in the corner. One or two bombs sounded very close, and Jean squeezed me tightly. We sat with our arms around each other; she smelt of toothpaste and soap and felt soft and inviting in my arms.

## Chapter Forty-Three
# February 22nd, 1941

Emma

*"Love is the tune we all dance to. When the music stops, it isn't the silence we grieve; we mourn for the love that dances alone."*

The new year brought us nothing to cheer about. Night after night, we slept in our nocturnal underworld, and night after night, the bombs fell. Someone else's misfortune became our good fortune because the bombs continued to miss us. The routine became precisely that; we became habituated to it - it became routine. The ever-present spectre of death was our daily companion, and it no longer filled us with dread. When that happens to you, it means you've crossed a threshold; you've sacrificed a part of your humanity in exchange for a way to survive.

When I heard about my friend Betty, the midwife, I immediately assumed she must have been a bomb victim. The local newspaper dispelled that assumption in the cruellest possible way. The headlines read 'Midwife is Blackout Ripper's latest victim.' I stared at the headline in complete shock and disbelief. I had become desensitised to the bombing but not to murder. I hadn't seen Betty for several months, but the prospect that a depraved madman had killed her filled me with horror. The bombs fell indiscriminately - we didn't think about the German pilots trying to kill us. We could somehow regard the bombs as no more than blind assassins.

Whoever murdered Betty was anything but a blind assassin. He did what the bombs could never do; he sought out his victims and only a certain kind of victim. It might seem strange that with the bombs killing people daily, people should worry about one more death. The murderer touched a nerve the bombs failed to reach. There would not have been a woman in South London who wasn't frightened. Without our hospital accommodation block, I'd gone home on one or two occasions out of necessity. My little terraced house had a coal cellar, and I once slept there among the cobwebs. It seemed illogical compared to the threat of bombing, but I decided, like a lot of women, not to go home alone again.

Even in the dead of winter, in February, the days were growing longer, and more importantly, the nights were getting shorter. We all needed an hour or two away from the hospital and, given the occasional opportunity, a drink in the Tavern before nightfall became a lifeline we all looked forward to. On the night of February 21st, most of the bombs fell on unsuspecting souls outside our area. This meant that for us, Saturday the 22nd was a quiet day. Pleasures had become such a rarity that the prospect of an evening in the pub filled the air with a sense of excitement.

Beverley had a new boyfriend, Leo's junior doctor friend, Maurice. I didn't see that coming, but I suppose I wasn't really tuned into those things. Surprisingly, the ever-flirtatious Shirley didn't have anyone to go with, so for once in my life, I wasn't the one without a boyfriend. Janet took it upon herself to remedy that situation. She had long decided that when the opportunity arose, Barry would bring a friend with him. Saturday evening became that opportunity.

We walked the short distance over the river as a group. Halfway across the bridge, I marvelled at the sight of us laughing and joking as if the surrounding devastation didn't exist. Beverley and Maurice walked side by side as if they were tied together in a three-legged race. They couldn't get physically any closer. Janet and Shirley held arms, sharing the same smile. I put my arm through Frank's on one side and Leo's on the other. I felt like a thoroughly modern, emancipated woman with a man on each arm. Behind us and all too visible from the bridge, our hospital lay partially in ruins, and yet, for us, our simple pleasure took precedence.

Barry and his friend Roy were there to meet us in the Tavern Inn, and Janet immediately melted into Barry's arms like butter on toast. I sat watching them all as Frank went to the bar. Roy was an RAF ground crew like Barry, and I must admit he made an instant impression dressed in his sergeant's uniform. With the same dark hair and boyish good looks, he and Barry might have been brothers. We all knew that Janet and Barry were matchmaking, and I would have found that situation difficult and embarrassing. Not so Shirley. She was an attractive woman with her blonde hair and curvaceous figure, and she was certainly not backwards in coming forward. Shirley looked at Roy as a seasoned housewife might look at a tray of vegetables on a greengrocer's shelf. She looked him up and down, and having decided he would do just fine, she reached out with both hands and made him her own.

When Frank returned from the bar, I sat, unable to take my eyes off my friends. I noticed Frank and Leo on either side of me were equally mesmerised and like me, slightly embarrassed. Janet and Barry sat intertwined in each other's arms. It would have been easier to see where one end of a ball of string began and the other ended. They were completely oblivious to the rest of us, their mouths locked together in a passionate exploration of one another. I imagined they were deep in an unspoken conversation that only lovers understood. Beverley and Maurice sat equally engrossed in each other.

Maurice and Leo went to university together and remained friends ever since. Both come from wealthy backgrounds and share the same expensive tastes. That's where the similarity ended. Leo wore today's expensive clothes with a swagger, while Maurice wore yesterday's expensive clothes with a relaxed confidence. Leo was dashing and charming; Maurice didn't feel the need to dash anywhere. I worked alongside him for several months without realising what an engaging man he was. Beverley said the same; they started talking one day and didn't stop.

Both couples were so engrossed in each other that they were oblivious to their surroundings. I had no doubt Shirley wanted what they had. It felt awkward as if we were intruding upon a very private situation. Suddenly disturbed by our silence, Janet opened her eyes and realised they'd become the centre of attention.

"Oops, sorry, we got a bit carried away. I love him, you see, I can't help it."

Our embarrassment turned immediately to laughter. Janet had a way of reducing any situation down to a fundamental level by expressing her feelings without the slightest concern. She loved him, therefore she couldn't help herself. Only Janet would say such a thing, which is why she's one of those people who brings joy into your life. The pair radiated love, and it was impossible not to share their happiness. I squeezed Frank's hand beneath the table, but of course, that hardly compared to one of Janet's unfettered declarations. Only then did I stop to consider how Leo must be feeling. What he shared with Gloria was no different to Janet and Barry. They were equally consumed with each other, two halves of the same person. Janet and Beverley must have been a painful reminder of what he had lost.

I caught his eye, and my expression must have portrayed my feelings because he turned his mouth down and closed his eyes before slightly bowing his head. I understood Leo's pain; it reminded me yet again that life is played out on the edge of a precipice. We dance to life's tune in the sure and certain knowledge that every day takes us closer to the great divide. Beyond lies only memories, ripples on a pond destroying our own reflection. I looked into Leo's eyes, and I realised something. Love is the tune we all dance to. When the music stops, it isn't the silence we grieve; we mourn the love that dances alone. I put my arm around him and kissed his cheek.

"It's okay, Leo; you don't have to hide your pain from me."

"Thanks, Em. I can have no secrets from you, can I? You see right through me, don't you?"

"I'm sorry, Leo," said Janet, "I wasn't thinking, was I?"

"And neither should you, any of you. If Gloria were here now, she'd want you to enjoy every second of your happiness. God knows it's in short supply right now."

"Let's all drink to that," I said. "Here's to happiness, past, present, and future."

We raised our glasses in praise of a single word. A word that held its own special meaning for each of us. I looked at Frank; his expression conveyed so much more than a mere smile. He didn't say it, but I knew he wanted much more from our relationship than I had been prepared to share. I sensed he wanted commitment. The words danced on his lips, desperate to become mine to share. Emotions were running high around our table, and in the heat of the moment, I felt my eyes widen in anticipation of what Frank was about to say.

"The papers are full of these 'Blackout Ripper' stories," said Roy, obviously keen to change the subject.

"What do you think possesses someone to do something as evil as these murders?" asked Beverley.

"I imagine that's a question people have asked ever since we first picked up a stone."

"That doesn't say much for the human race, does it, Frank?" said Barry.

"No, it doesn't," replied Frank, suddenly looking very serious. "We work day after day putting people back together, and the question those casualties would ask is - why? How can anyone value human life so little that they're prepared to destroy thousands of people's lives simply to impose their will upon us? What kind of utopian world does Hitler want to create where life has no value?"

"Frank's right," I said, "we work to save lives, so we can't understand why anyone would want to reverse that order."

"Our job is to defeat Hitler," replied Roy, "and that means killing the enemy."

"This is the question that decent-minded people have asked ever since that first stone that Frank mentioned. My father was a humanitarian in every sense of the word - he hated war and being a soldier. He described in graphic terms how he shot and killed German soldiers who were intent on killing him. He struggled, knowing that some or all of those soldiers were probably just like him; they didn't want to be there. The justification for that war was the same as this one: imposing one nation-state's will upon another. The justification for resisting that imposition is maintaining our way of life, our reason for living."

"So, do you think your father did the right thing?" asked Roy. "Do you believe we're doing the right thing, or do you think we should simply surrender?"

"My father and I struggled with that question. It amounts to asking if there's a greater and lesser evil because, as a doctor, I regard the killing of anyone as something inherently evil. My dad turned that question around the other way. He asked if I wanted to live in a country where I had no rights or freedom other than what the state saw fit to grant me. He asked if I could accept people being separated and persecuted on grounds of ethnicity alone. Could I bow to the rule of a corrupt dictatorship that would probably sink ever deeper into corruption?

I answered no, to which he asked if I would be prepared to die resisting it. I've learnt in life, as in medicine, to follow the logic of the evidence, to follow the path of cause and effect to its conclusion. Yes, I'm prepared to die for what this country represents, and so I have to reluctantly admit that there's a higher cause than life. So, the answer to your question, Roy, is no, we must never surrender. We must resist the greater evil with the lesser evil. If there's no other way to defeat Hitler other than by killing those who choose to further his cause, then that's the only option they present us with."

"If only the world's leaders had your insight, Emma, we wouldn't have any wars," said Janet.

"I only asked what possessed the Ripper," said Beverley, "but perhaps we're talking about the same thing?"

"Perhaps we are," replied Leo. "The Ripper murderer is obviously deranged. When we look at Hitler in those films of him addressing the masses, does he not sound deranged?"

"He does," answered Frank, "but the bigger issue for me is how does someone like him convince the people to support them in the first place?"

"That's the real question, isn't it?" I asked. "It's happened repeatedly. Disaffected people blame their condition on whoever is running their country. They support anyone who can point the finger of blame at someone else."

"But why?" replied Shirley. "Why did the people of Germany vote Hitler into power in the first place? Isn't it obvious that radicals and extremists always end in disaster?"

"It is when you look on from afar," I said. "It's a lesson that my father impressed upon me. We don't think objectively; we think emotively. If someone offers you a vision and a reason to dislike the alternative, we all have an unerring ability to believe what we want to believe. We simply don't allow the evidence to affect our judgment."

"I wish I'd met your father, Emma; he sounds a very learned gentleman. You often quote him. You must be very proud of him."

"I am, Frank. It's how I was brought up. Our house was constantly full of conversations, exactly the same as this. Except it was conversations between philosophers, historians, physicists and bishops."

"We must be a disappointing bunch in comparison."

"Actually, it's quite the opposite. It's all those people from academia who are disappointing. My father was one of the few exceptions. Most of them had a very narrow view of life. They would broaden their horizons in just half an hour talking with Janet."

"Why me?"

"Because you embrace life more than anyone I know – you're not limited by horizons."

"I'll take that as a compliment, then."

We had all drunk two or three pints of beer, and I was rambling too much. Janet seemed to be able to drink any amount without making a fool of herself. She remained the same, or more correctly, more of the same. She laughed and made everyone around her happy, while I always ended up reciting my father's wisdom.

# Chapter Forty-Four
# March 1941

Roger

*"There can be no greater pain than the death of a child. But however vast the unbearable emptiness, it will still overflow with a parent's pride."*

When I left Jean the following morning, she came with me to the door and kissed my cheek. The closer we became, the more awkward I felt in the presence of Marilyn and Dave, and they seemed to be present all the time. Nothing in life prepares you for situations like that. The four of us lived together in an uneasy harmony. I realised there was an inevitability about our relationship; we were behaving more and more like a married couple. The outcome might have been inevitable, but it wasn't obvious to me.

A bomb that Jean and I heard overnight fell only two streets away; I passed it on my way to the station. It must have been a big bomb, probably a landmine. Three houses in the terrace lay in ruins, and another two stood like skeletons devoid of all those things that make a house a home. I stopped to ask the ARP warden if there were any casualties, and his reply shocked me.

"We've recovered eight bodies so far; I'm expecting to find another one."

"Why were they not in a shelter?"

"People think, if their house hasn't been bombed, then perhaps it won't be, so they take a chance and stay at home."

"I did the same last night. It's not worth the risk, is it?"

"People are sick and tired of underground stations and Anderson shelters; I can understand it."

I could understand it as well, having just done it. As the fatigue set in, many people became blase; it's all too easy to be seduced by the thought that it won't happen to you. I thought about nothing else for the rest of the short drive to work. As I parked the car, my thoughts immediately turned towards the job in hand and our serial killer. Jack greeted me at the front desk with a cheerful face.

"Morning, Jack. Any disasters this morning?"

"Only the landmine on Chessington Road; that's been a bad one."

"Yes, I passed it on my way in. It's a terrible business, though I can understand why people push their luck."

"The tube stations are full; conditions are grim, aren't they? We arrested a bloke yesterday for selling a space on the platform. The 'droppers' claim an early space on the platform and then try to sell it to the desperate."

"How much are they getting for a space?"

"The bloke in the cells now was asking for half a crown. There's also been more looting and a couple of burglaries."

"I'll get our boys onto that. What about the Ripper; has anyone reported anything useful?"

"Not a bloody thing. All we've picked up is gossip. Mrs Elmbridge in Portland Street is convinced it's her neighbour because he's rude to her."

"God help us. We need something to go on; I'm getting desperate with this one."

"He'll make a mistake; they all do."

"Of course he will, but how many more will he have killed by then?"

I left Jack with that thought and went through to see Gerry. He was sitting looking at all the statements we'd gathered; the room was already thick with cigarette smoke. He continued to sit in silence as I placed my hat on the stand and took off my coat.

"This is useless, Roger; we don't have a single positive sighting."

"Yes, morning, Gerry."

"Oh, sorry, mate, this bloke's getting to me."

"I think that's the point of it for him. He means to torment us, and he's doing a good job."

"Have the relatives and friends of Betty Sullivan added anything about her movements?"

"No, her mother saw her the morning before the murder. Her sister found her the following afternoon; she lives a few miles away. The neighbour's statement says they saw her go into the house about 5 o'clock that evening, so that's the last sighting."

"I don't suppose the fingerprint report will show us anything; it could be weeks before we can exclude the husband's prints. Bartholomew might give us something, but I'm not holding my breath. As soon as he's ready, I'll see him."

Jeff and Alfie appeared, both looking tired and dishevelled. They'd been out late, interviewing ARP wardens. Jeff put his hat on the stand as if he didn't have the strength to lift it. We organised cups of tea and sat down together around the table. DC Fleming arrived for all the good he would bring to the day.

"Did you get anything useful last night, Jeff?"

"No, Guv. Damn all. I still think our man could be a warden or fireman. They're the people who are out and about during the raids."

"I agree; we can't rule anything out. I want to concentrate on his modus operandi because he's left us a calling card with each murder. We can't ignore that he's obviously motivated by Jack the Ripper. It's obviously not a coincidence that the mutilations are almost identical. He has deliberately set out to copy those murders. I didn't want to believe it, but now we have no option."

"You're sure about that, Guv?"

"Yes, there's no doubt about it."

"You're the expert on Jack the Ripper, Roger," said Gerry, "you should know."

Gerry's comment prompted a memory in the back of my mind; I jumped up and dashed to my office. In the dusty old filing cabinet in the corner, I had a file on Jack the Ripper. It contained just about every detail of the case from 1888. I suddenly remembered the murder that was not attributed to the Ripper, and I needed to check some details. When I returned, they all sat silently, wondering what I was up to. I thumbed through the pages until I came to the section I was looking for. I read the details until my cigarette ash fell on the page that had commanded my attention.

"Good God. He killed Margaret Thompson as well."

"The Clapham Common stabbing?"

"Yes, Jeff. We thought it was him, but this proves it. On the 7th of August 1888, Martha Tabram was killed in George Yard, Whitechapel.

She was stabbed 39 times, but because she wasn't mutilated, the police didn't think her murderer and the Ripper were the same, so he didn't get the credit for it. Margaret Thompson was also stabbed 39 times; that's not a coincidence."

"Bloody hell, it can't be a coincidence, can it?" said Alfie.

"So we're dealing with someone who has set out deliberately to follow in the footsteps of 'Jack', even to the point of copying the first possible Ripper murder. He murdered Irene Newnham and copied the mutilation of Mary Ann Nichols, the presumed first victim of Jack the Ripper. Then he moved on to Alice Cox and copied the Ripper's victim, Annie Chapman. Now we have two victims on the same day: Betty Sullivan, who is copying Elizabeth Stride, and Maureen Elkins, who is copying Catherine Eddows. That means he has one murder to go. He wants to copy Mary Jane Kelly, the last Ripper victim."

"That's chilling, Roger," Gerry said.

"Can I say something, Guv?"

"What is it, Fleming?"

"The names, Guv, look at the names."

"What about them?"

"He's trying to get close to, or at least have a link with the names."

"Oh, my God, Fleming, you're not as daft as you look. You're right. He killed Margaret Thompson for Martha Tabram. The initials match. We have Irene Newnham for Mary Ann Nichols. Then Alice Cox for Annie Chapman. Betty Sullivan gives us the initials of Elizabeth Stride; Elizabeth might be called Betty. Finally, Maureen Elkins, E, and Eddows are the same. He hasn't always got both initials right, but it's close enough. What the hell are we dealing with here?"

"This might just be a coincidence," said Alfie.

"It could be, but it looks very convincing to me. If it's true, how on earth does he select them? How can he find a woman living alone who also has the right initials? That's impossible."

"Each victim had a husband in the forces who was away from home. We already flagged that up as a connection."

"That's right, Jeff, but how does he know that, and how does he get the names?"

"It sounds impossible, Guv."

"Think about it, Jeff, who knows the names of everyone living in the area? The government does. The 1939 register was taken to produce identity cards and ration books."

"But it's confidential; we can't access it, it's not a public record."

"That's a good point, Alfie. So, how could he access it?"

"God knows. Unless, of course, he's a government official. Is there any other way he could find a list of people's names and addresses?"

"I'm not aware of any other up-to-date list. That's why the government needed the '39 register, Alfie."

"We need to talk to the local Registrar and find out who had access to it," said Gerry.

"You're right, Guv - we could finally be onto something here."

"As you said, Guv, he's left a calling card each time," said Jeff. "This looks like another deliberate clue. He's playing with us."

"He certainly is. He can only have gone to so much trouble in the hope we would find it. The newspapers have given him exactly what he craved; he's now compared to Jack the Ripper. So everything is going exactly as he wants it to. My guess is that he'll commit one more murder and then vanish, like Jack, and with all the notoriety he obviously craves."

"Why would he give us the initials of his next victim?" asked Gerry. "We could warn the public."

"Perhaps he's even more clever than we think he is. If we put out a public warning about the names, it'll confirm his place in criminal history. Then he could kill a victim with a different name just to make us look incompetent; we would lose all credibility while he gains more notoriety."

"In that case, we must make sure the papers don't get hold of this; we don't want to feed him what he wants."

"Good point, Jeff, this doesn't leave the office. Let's go and see the Registrar at the Wandsworth Register Office and find out what we can about the '39 register."

We left Alfie and Fleming with the unenviable job of cross-checking the statements and interviewing yet more people. For the first time in the investigation, I felt we'd moved a step ahead of the Ripper. We had something to follow up on. Jeff drove us over to Wandsworth, picking his way around the road closures.

"How's Norma, Jeff? Is she coping alright?"

"She doesn't like me being out at night."

"She's not staying at home, is she?"

"No, she goes to the tube station at Stockwell with her mum when she knows I'll be out late. I've told her never to be alone in the house."

"This bloke is affecting us nearly as much as the Luftwaffe, and he's just one individual."

"How about you and Jean? It must be really difficult for you both."

"You're right, it is. It feels as if Dave is still in Jean's house when I visit, and Marilyn is still in my house when Jean visits."

"I'm really sorry, Roger, it's tragic what's happened."

"Yes, thanks, mate, but we're not alone, are we?"

We arrived at the Register Office and were pleased to see it was still there. A starchy lady at the front desk said we needed an appointment to see the Registrar, so I quickly disabused her of that notion.

"This is an urgent police matter; I wish to see him right now; thank you."

A bespectacled middle-aged man, looking rather how I thought a registrar should look, approached us and invited us into his office. He introduced himself as Mr Wilberforce.

"Mr Wilberforce, tell me how the 1939 register was collated and who has access to it."

"That's a very confidential record, Inspector. It's only available to government officials."

"I'm not asking to see it; I want to know how it was compiled in the first place."

"Oh, I see, well, we were all prepared, you see; everything was already in place for the 1941 census. We recruited enumerators to go door to door to collect the information. We divided the enumeration districts into small units so that one person could cover an area over the allotted weekend. The information was collated and then centralised."

"So your enumerators visited every home in their allotted area, and they collected the names and personal details of every person at each address on the given weekend."

"Yes, of course."

"Am I correct to say that it didn't include members of the armed forces?"

"That's right, but of course, this was before conscription, so most eligible young men were still civilians and were counted."

"Do you have a list of your enumerators?"

"There will be a record, yes."

"I want a list of all the enumerators who worked on the register in South London."

"We would only have those that worked out of this office, and that information will be confidential."

"You're well placed, Mr Wilberforce, to organise that list for me. I want you to contact each Register Office in South London and explain the urgency of the situation. If you delay me, Mr Wilberforce, by demanding a Court Order, which I can get, you will be directly obstructing an urgent enquiry, and I'm sure I don't need to spell out to you what the implications will be for your career. I want those lists sent by messenger to Balham Police Station, and I want them yesterday. Do you understand, Mr Wilberforce?"

"Well, this is most irregular; I'm not at all sure about this. I need authorisation."

"Give me your telephone, Mr Wilberforce."

I dialled the station, and as soon as Jack recognised my voice, I employed a ruse I had used before. "Good morning, this is Inspector Pritchard, Balham. Can I speak to the Commissioner, please? Yes, it's important." Jack put me through to Gerry. "Good morning, Commissioner. This is Inspector Pritchard, Sir, Balham. It's about the investigation you ordered as a priority, Sir. I'm receiving no assistance from the Wandsworth Registrar. His name's Wilberforce. Yes, Sir, I'll pass him over to you."

Gerry caught on immediately and harangued Wilberforce. He must have given him a real dressing down because the disagreeable man turned quite pale.

"I've been told to assist you in any way I can, Inspector. The Commissioner threatened me with dismissal; can he do that?"

"You're a public official the same as we are, Mr Wilberforce. You're employed by the local authority. The Commissioner has the ear of the Home Secretary. I would jump to, if I were you."

We left the poor man scurrying down into his archives; I felt bad about it, but a woman's life was at stake. I didn't have the time to get the correct authorisation. Jeff thought it was hilarious until I reminded him that a woman had already been selected to take the place of 'Jack's' fifth victim. It was a long shot because our man might have been anyone involved in the register, even down to the printer who produced the ration cards. We couldn't trace everyone; the list of enumerators would be daunting enough. We went through it all at the station again, but until that list of enumerators arrived, we were left fishing in the dark. I finished up early that day; I wanted to pay Joey Katz a visit before I went home.

Mr Hewitt and the suit had been such an enormous gesture, I felt obliged to thank Joey. A part of me realised I was stepping over the line;

thanking a mobster is tantamount to admitting I was in his debt. I had a long history with Joey but was more conflicted about him that day than ever. If you could overlook the fact he sat at the top of a criminal empire, you would have to say he was a thorough gentleman in every respect. He had only ever shown me great kindness and respect and never asked for anything in return. In an unguarded moment, I might even have to admit that I liked him.

I arrived at his shop just as his staff were closing the door. The most senior of his staff, who was very elderly, recognised me and opened the door. He was a delightful old gentleman whom I had to assume Joey retained as an act of loyalty. I walked into the shop and directly into a suffocating atmosphere. It was instantly apparent that something awful must have happened. His elderly retainer had tears in his eyes, and another assistant sat with her head in her hands.

"What's happened?" I asked.

The retainer took a moment before he replied in an almost inaudible voice. "Mr Katz's son Aaron, he's been killed in action."

Aaron, by then Squadron Leader Katz, was everything a father would wish a son would be. Joey doted on him; he was everything that his son Ezra wasn't. As the news sank in, I looked at the reaction of Joey's staff. These were not just people who worked for Joey; they loved him, and this was a personal loss for them. I walked through to Joey's office uninvited; I felt compelled to. He was sitting at his desk, surrounded as always by his order books and rolls of material. The moment I entered, he stood up, looking like a totally broken man. Without thinking, I put my arms around him, and his eyes welled up.

"I'm so sorry, Joey. I share your pain."

"I've lived through this day a thousand times. Now it's arrived; it's even more terrible than my worst fears."

"Aaron is one of the finest young men I've had the privilege of meeting. You must be so proud of him."

"No man could have had a finer son. A part of me has died that can never be replaced."

"There can be no greater pain than the death of a child. But however vast the unbearable emptiness, it will still overflow with a parent's pride."

"You're a wise man, Mr Pritchard. It's true, there's no limit to my pride; perhaps in time, those proud memories will take his place. You're quite right; it's an unbearable emptiness."

"I wish there were words or deeds that would take your pain away, but we both know there's nothing."

"Nothing indeed. Nothing but the support of a valued friend. Can I call you that, Mr Pritchard?"

"My friends call me Roger, Joey."

"We've both lost those we loved. We tread the same path, you and I, Roger. I share your loss as you share mine."

"I believe you do, and I thank you for that."

"Aaron valued your friendship; did you know that?"

"Yes, he said as much. I thought he was a fine boy. That first time when I saved him from those thugs, he was more wary of the uniform. I think he would have preferred the thugs."

"He called you an interfering policeman."

"I bet he did. I bumped into him in the street a few months ago when he was home on leave. He nearly shook my arm off. I felt proud to shake his hand, Joey."

"And now you've extended your kindness to my daughter-in-law."

"I simply happened to be in the right place at the right time. Any decent person would have done the same."

"I agree, but the pub that night was full of people, yet there wasn't another decent person."

"The suit, Joey, you shouldn't have done that. It's too much."

"Are you telling me Rachel and our friendship are not worth a bit of cloth and the tailor's time?"

"No, I'm saying I'm not worth the tailor's time."

"Aaron would disagree, as would Rachel. I've always valued your good sense and judgment, so now is the time to value mine. I didn't misjudge you."

Joey had a way of talking to you. He spoke with a deep gravelly voice that added enormous gravitas to his words. Joey also had the wisdom of Solomon; when he said something, you listened. I convinced myself that he was no longer involved in criminal activity. I wanted to believe it because I liked and respected him enormously.

# Chapter Forty-Five
# April 10th, 1941

Emma

*"We are all our parents' future, but they only succeed
if we live a life they are proud of."*

The bombing had now continued without respite for nearly eight months. On April 6th, the hospital was hit yet again by incendiary bombs. Even as firemen struggled with the fires, a parachute landmine hit us with devastating effect. It struck two hospital blocks away from our basement world, but the enormous explosion threw us to the ground. We struggled to our feet, knowing that, once again, we had to face whatever horror lay beyond our basement. The worst moments are those before you reach the scene of an explosion. We had already seen enough; our minds needed no encouragement to conjure up images of devastation and carnage.

Another of our blocks had been destroyed. I braced myself for the sight of those imagined horrors. When the news came that the block was unoccupied, the terrible destruction became seen as good news. Two of our physiotherapists had been badly injured; imagine that: an entire block destroyed and only two injured. I wouldn't have wanted to be the person to tell their relatives the 'good news' that we only had two casualties.

Victims started arriving at our door within hours of the attack, and despite everything, we were there to receive them. However inadequate our facilities, we didn't once turn them away. I went through the days like an automaton, and the more dehumanised we became in the hospital, the more we wanted to embrace life whenever we had the opportunity. We were not alone in that sentiment. The entire nation adopted the attitude that we might not be here tomorrow.

Four days after the April 6th bombing, our local casualty rate had reduced, and everyone's thoughts turned towards themselves. On April 10th, a window of opportunity appeared for us to get out of the hospital, so we grabbed it with both hands. With daylight hours now significantly longer, we had the possibility of four hours before curfew. We debated where to go, and I suggested a pub where I had been taken once, called the Fox and Hounds. It didn't require debate; we were eager to go anywhere. We squeezed into two cars with people sitting on each other's laps.

We didn't stop laughing from the moment we piled in until we all tumbled back out of the open doors. Even the silliest of simple pleasures had become a treasured delight. We only found Leo's very expensive fedora hat after Janet had stopped sitting on it. For the fashion-conscious and impossibly stylish Leo, this amounted to a disaster. For the rest of us, it brought tears to our eyes. Only a year ago, I would have avoided going out with a group of people, and yet here I was, marching them into the pub, feeling like the leader of a bunch of hoodlums. I looked across the bar to where I had sat before, and to my surprise, I saw Inspector Pritchard sitting there with two women. Even the newly liberated me felt awkward talking to him, but he caught my eye and waved me over.

He looked the same as the last time I saw him. I suspected he was wearing the same tired and crumpled suit. Despite his bedraggled appearance, there was a spark about the inspector that I liked. He was actually quite handsome despite seeming to do everything to disguise the fact. Next to him sat a woman I thought I vaguely recognised. I assumed it must be Jean, the woman he'd spoken about. Opposite him sat a younger woman. She sat there looking every bit like Royalty, expensively dressed and absolutely beautiful.

"Inspector Pritchard, we meet again."

"Doctor Stevenson, how very nice to see you again. Are all these people with you?"

"I'm afraid so. This motley bunch are my friends and colleagues from the hospital."

"Why don't we pull these tables together and bring some chairs over?"

We did exactly that, and I introduced my friends.

"This is my friend, Jean," he said, "and this young lady is Rachel."

Janet jumped in with both feet. "What's your name then, Inspector? I'm not going to call you Inspector all evening, am I?"

"It's Roger."

"Delighted to meet you, Roger."

I marvelled at Janet; she asked the questions I would have asked if only I could be as confident as she was. She has no sense of reserve whatsoever, and people love her for it. If I did those things, I would be seen as being too forward. I stood back, just slightly envious, as she spread her magic. Rachel immediately attracted Leo's attention, or was it the other way around? The two best-dressed people there obviously had that much in common, at least. I sat next to Roger and Jean.

"I remember you, Jean, from that awful night."

"I'm afraid I remember very little of it, but Roger has spoken about you."

"Can I say how sorry I am about your loss that night; you've both suffered so much."

"I understand you lost both of your parents, Emma. That's awful."

"Yes, I don't think any of us will forget that night. Roger spoke a lot about you when I last saw him. You're very fortunate to have each other at a time like this."

"It's still difficult for us, but as you say, I think we are fortunate. Do you have anyone, Emma?"

"Frank and I have been kind of together for months now."

"I know what you mean. I hope it goes the way you want."

I liked her immediately. She was a little like Janet; she was very open, warm, and easy to talk to. Roger came back from the bar and sat next to me. Jean became involved in talking to Janet and Beverley.

"It's nice to call you Emma. I feel I know you now."

"Yes, I feel the same. Our paths haven't crossed that often, but it's always been memorable when they have."

"I really enjoyed our last conversation. It's good to talk with someone I can really engage with."

"I remember the last time we had such an interesting discussion. We talked about you and Jean. Now that I've met her, I can say you're a lucky man, Roger."

"She's a lovely woman, isn't she? What about ... it was Frank, wasn't it?"

"Yes, we're still what Frank calls a work in progress."

"Well, I hope you make progress and don't have to work too hard."

"Is that how it is with you and Jean? Is there progress, or is it proving hard?"

"It's both, really, and Jean would agree with me. These things are difficult, aren't they; life doesn't prepare you for events like this."

"I remember so well what you said when I asked how you would recognise if you had fallen in love. Do you remember? I've thought about that so often. I've decided I want to feel that way one day."

"So do we all, Emma, but I think it only comes to the lucky few."

"If only it were like a fledgling bird taking to the wing, we would all do it instinctively."

"I enjoy talking to you, Emma. I would probably feel ridiculous talking about these things with anyone else, but you have such depth of understanding. I feel we can talk about anything."

"Oh, Roger, that's a nice thing to say. I've spent my entire early life listening to such debates between my father and the great and good of academia. Now I enjoy taking part by myself."

"You talk about your father a lot, Emma. You're not living in his shadow, you know; you're your own person. A parent's role is to equip a child for the life ahead and then send them on their way. We are all our parents' future, but they only succeed if we live a life they can be proud of. If your father is looking down on you right now, Emma, he would be so proud. He'd tell you that you're no longer a fledgling bird, so spread your wings because he taught you to fly."

I looked at him, and tears rolled down my face. "Oh, I'm sorry."

"No, I'm sorry. I didn't mean to offend you."

"You haven't; really, you haven't. You've seen right through me. I hardly know you, and yet you understand everything about me."

"Are you alright, Emma? Is Roger upsetting you?"

"No, Jean, but he has a way of getting to the heart of things, doesn't he?"

"He does it all the time. You can't keep a secret from Roger."

"I realise that now."

"I like your friends; Janet's a real handful, isn't she? They're all so friendly. Your doctor friend, the handsome one who's making eyes at Rachel."

"Yes, that's Leo."

"He had best not think he's in with a chance with Rachel."

"Why? Is she married?"

"Tell her, Roger."

"Jean's right. She doesn't wear a wedding ring these days, but Rachel is most definitely married."

"I'll mention it to Leo. But actually, it's nice to see him interacting with another woman. The love of his life was killed by one of the bombs at the hospital."

"Oh no, how awful. Nevertheless, you'd better tell her, Roger."

"Tell me what?"

Roger whispered in my ear. "Rachel is married to a mobster and a particularly unpleasant one. If he thought Leo was making eyes at his wife, then God help him."

"Oh, my goodness. Leave it to me. What a shame though, look at them, the two most attractive people here - they seem made for each other."

We laughed about that, but I could see Roger was being deadly serious. I had a word with Leo between beers, and I think, at first, he thought I was kidding. Everyone got on remarkably well that night. Shirley and Roy seemed to hit it off immediately. Beverley and Maurice only had eyes for each other, and we all knew about Janet and Barry. Jean looked at me as I downed my second pint.

"What about you and Frank? Do you have any wedding plans?"

"I asked Emma that," said Roger, "they're a work in progress."

"A bit like us then, Roger," Jean said.

"Seriously, you two. I know the difficult circumstances, but you seem to be made for each other."

"We are," she replied, "I think a work in progress sums us up well."

"You shouldn't light that cigarette, Roger. They're seriously bad for you."

"I know, you told me that before, Doc. I should try."

"You should do it for yourself."

"I'm not sure I have the willpower, but I'll try."

I smiled at that comment. We had such a good evening together, though Frank seemed a little subdued, and Beverley was more preoccupied with Maurice than usual. Roger said we should do it again and there was a unanimous agreement. When it was time to leave, Janet hugged everyone as she always did. Leo put his arms around Rachel, and she responded rather warmly. Roger approached me a bit awkwardly, but I had drunk two pints of beer. I put my arms around him and kissed his cheek. He responded in kind, and I enjoyed it.

We climbed into our two cars, one on top of the other. It was getting dark, and we didn't have a sober driver between us, but at least the roads were empty. Frank volunteered to drive one car and Maurice the other. We dropped Barry and Roy off at the station, and probably more by luck than judgment, we made it back to the hospital in one piece. With time being of the essence, I turned towards Frank and kissed him goodnight. We stood in each other's arms for what seemed an eternity.

"Oi! Cut it out, you two," shouted Janet, "it's basement time."

We had time to spare that night; the Germans were in no rush. It was just as well because we didn't want to stop talking. Marion must have been appalled at us, gossiping like a bunch of schoolgirls.

"You have to make your mind up, Em, about Frank," said Janet. "He was very quiet tonight. You're going to lose him if you're not careful."

"Yes, he was quiet, I noticed that. Do you think he's getting fed up with me?"

"I think he is. You should sort it out between you in bed one night."

"Janet, really," said a shocked Marion.

As always, Janet spoke her mind, and as always, she had a point. We could talk about anything as a group and often did, but my doubts and fears about the bed issue were just too embarrassing. I wanted to change the subject.

"You've been preoccupied as well, Beverley. Is anything wrong?"

"Well, yes, there is. You'll all find out soon anyway, so I might as well admit it. I'm pregnant."

Sometimes, silence can express our thoughts better than words. In normal circumstances, the prospect of a new life entering the world would be a cause for celebration. For an unmarried nurse faced with all the uncertainty that the future held, it was unfortunate, to say the least. We looked at each other with imponderable questions flashing through our minds.

"What are you going to do?" asked Janet.

"Well, I can't have it, can I?"

"But you can't abort it," said Marion.

"I'll have to; I can't have a baby now. Who knows what the future holds?"

"You're not alone, Bev," said Janet, "you have us."

"You haven't said how stupid I've been."

"That goes without saying," replied Janet.

"Can you help me, Emma?"

"If you mean can I abort the baby for you, then no, I can't do that. You know I can't."

"What does Maurice have to say about this," asked Shirley.

"He doesn't know yet."

"Oh my goodness, why haven't you told him?" I asked.

"He wouldn't want me to have an abortion. I know he wouldn't."

Marion puffed up her chest and put her hands on her knees. We all silently looked in her direction.

"Doesn't that answer your question? I've seen dozens of young women in your position over the years. For some, I have to admit the responsibility of a new life can be a disaster. But for the majority, it's a blessing in disguise. Much depends upon the father. The last thing a new mother needs is to be thrown into a loveless marriage of convenience, and neither does she want to face motherhood alone in the world. It's perfectly obvious to all of us that you love each other, so why on earth would you risk throwing that all away? You'll go to Maurice tomorrow, and you will tell him he's going to become a father. His reaction might surprise you. The war will end, Beverley. You're standing on the threshold of a wonderful future, so step into it."

Once again, our silence spoke volumes. Beverley looked at Marion with tears in her eyes and rushed to put her arms around her. Marion patted Beverley's back like a mother patting a colicky child. When the voice of reason has spoken, only those who choose not to listen go on to make the wrong decision.

## Chapter Forty-Six
# April 12th, 1941

Roger

*"Arrogance may stand out from the crowd, but humility stands above it."*

I didn't anticipate that the list of enumerators and districts would arrive at the office in dozens of boxes. Wilberforce had certainly come up with the goods. We leapt on it and were quickly overwhelmed by the scale and complexity of what lay ahead. Each enumeration district had a unique four- or five-letter code. Each household had its own schedule number, and then each person in the household had their own sub-number.

The enumeration districts for South London were divided into area codes. Battersea, for example, was area code ABA, and Wandsworth was AXA. They confined districts to about 300 households, and enumerators were assigned only as many as they could get through in a weekend. The whole exercise was a long shot. Our man could have been anywhere in the system if he was there at all. We concentrated on the most likely scenario: our man worked as an enumerator. Perhaps he visited the victims; although he couldn't have visited beyond 300 households, he might also have had more access as they compiled the information.

It took us days to find the 300 household areas that covered the victims' addresses and to combine that with the list of enumerators. The names gradually appeared on a list; many were women. That reduced the list even further, and our daunting task gradually became more manageable. We started adding names who could conceivably have had access at the collation stage, but we resisted straying far from our area. The final list counted 42 men. We then reduced that further to 31 by excluding, for the time being, those who lived some distance away. We had to assume our man lived locally; he couldn't possibly be travelling long distances during the blackout.

"Well done, everyone," I said. "This might just be a red herring, but at least it's kept you out of mischief, Fleming."

"Cheers, Guv."

"Right, divide these names between you and get out there and interview them. Don't tell them why you're asking questions. Tell them there's been an irregularity with the register, and it's a routine check. The thing is to keep them talking; if you can get into the house, even better. Use your intuition and follow your gut feeling. This man might look perfectly respectable. He could be anyone. I'm going to St Thomas's to see the mortuary attendant."

"Don't you mean the pathologist, Guv?"

"I'm seeing him as well, Fleming."

"What's the mortuary attendant got to do with it?"

"You would be surprised, Jeff. It pays not to jump to conclusions about people."

I left them with that thought and set off for the hospital. I hadn't driven past the hospital since a landmine hit it on April 6th. Another block lay in ruins, with the debris spread far and wide. Workmen had cleared the road in front and erected barriers. It was a sad sight to behold, how they continued to receive patients I couldn't imagine. Now that I knew Emma and some of her colleagues, it all felt so much more personal. That evening in the Fox and Hounds, they seemed such a cheerful bunch of people; I had difficulty understanding how they maintained their good spirits.

Inside the hospital, it was a story of two halves. Even the undamaged parts of the building were disrupted, as all kinds of items and equipment had to be stored in hallways and corridors. It appeared to be completely dysfunctional. The other side of the story was that the staff continued as if nothing had happened. Nurses in crisp white aprons marched about in complete control of the situation.

They informed me that the pathology department remained intact. I would have to access it via a different staircase. I went the way of the dead while the living walked in the other direction. The mortuary had long since become one of the busiest places in the hospital. I went first to the mortuary to find the chief attendant, Mr Rawlings. He now had two assistants and was as busy as ever. He caught my eye and came over to me.

"Good morning, Inspector. Did you want to see me?"

"Yes, good morning, Mr Rawlings. I wanted a word with the professor." He understood what I was implying and looked around the mortuary. He took me to a quiet corner where we wouldn't be overheard. "I need your opinion, Professor. The serial murderer I'm looking for continues to elude us. I need to know what kind of man I'm looking for."

"I've already given the matter some thought, Inspector. From the details that Doctor Bartholomew has given me, your murderer presents some extremely unusual characteristics. Can you confirm he's copying the 1888 Whitechapel murders?"

"Yes, he is. He copies them almost precisely, even down to the point of finding women with the same initials."

"Really, that's interesting."

"He's obviously quite mad, but he's also very calculating."

"Your description, Inspector, is simplistic but accurate, although I wouldn't personally use the term 'mad'. Psychopathy is a mental disorder distinguished by the desire to manipulate and control others with little or no empathy or regard for the victim. They can exhibit a superficial charm, but it's far from genuine. Typically, they usually have an exaggerated sense of self-worth, they're narcissistic. They tend to be opinionated and glib; above all, they will lie instinctively. A psychopath can commit horrendous crimes because they have no remorse. They cannot empathise or accept any responsibility for their actions."

"So, if I'm routinely interviewing a man, what should I look for?"

"He'll try to appear normal, of course, so look for exaggerated responses. Look for stimulation-seeking behaviour in his background. Is he impulsive? Does he lose his temper easily? Ask if he has plans for the future because he'll lie about it. Away from the initial charm, he will be anti-social, so ask about personal relations because he's unlikely to have any proper relationships. Those that he has will be parasitic in nature. Look for the need to be praised for his intelligence."

"This is really helpful, Professor, but does the degree of planning in this case fit with your profile? He seems to have an ulterior motive?"

"You're very perceptive, Inspector. Your man will be everything I've described, but he's much more. Serial murderers are usually random killers. Any victim will fulfil their desire. This man is trying to fulfil more than one goal. He needs particular victims to show how intelligent he is, and he's prepared to go to extraordinary lengths to do that. This is significant because it shows a rational, calculating intelligence, and rationality is not something you would associate with this kind of personality."

"So what is he, then?"

"Your man is extremely unusual. He must function on different levels. This possibly indicates a psychosis, auditory or visual hallucinations, delusions."

"In layman's terms, he's mad."

"In layman's terms, yes. But you're also dealing with a rational intelligence, so there's probably a reason, in his terms, why he's chosen to kill women. He most likely has a hatred of women, and that will often go back to childhood, usually to the mother or some other childhood incident. That could also be picked up again in adulthood via another interaction with a woman."

"I suppose there's no chance he'll come to his senses?"

"Absolutely not. The rational aspect of his mind will completely deny the existence of the killer."

"But how can he deny it to himself while he plans the next one?"

"Definition of mental illness, Inspector. None of us would have personality disorders if we fully accepted the meaning of abnormal behaviour. We convince ourselves it's normal. Therefore, the condition does not exist."

"Yes, I can see that. So do you think he'll stop when he has copied 'Jack' down to the last victim?"

"That's a more troublesome question, Inspector. Normally, I would say no; he would continue until he's caught. In this case, I'm not so sure; I suspect he might stop. Unlike the normal serial killer, he's set himself a specific goal. You had best find him, Inspector."

"I can't thank you enough, Mr Rawlings. This information is really helpful."

"I trust you won't reveal its source."

"That was our agreement, Mr Rawlings, and you can depend upon it."

Professor Rawlings was a remarkable man. I had enormous regard for him. Although I didn't understand why he needed to maintain his anonymity, I respected it. I moved on to see Bartholomew, who was an entirely different character. They were obviously hard-pressed in the pathology department; I had never seen so many bodies. It was fortunate that Bartholomew had such an interest in forensic work; thankfully, he made the time.

"Good morning, Inspector Pritchard."

"Morning, Doc, what do you have for me?"

"I've studied the original autopsy reports from 1888 and compared the dissection to our latest victims, and they correlate closely. It's chilling, Inspector. God only knows what kind of man you are looking for. I can tell you he has dissection skills, that much is obvious, but he isn't a highly skilled surgeon or anatomist. With Maureen Elkins, he has removed part of the womb and taken it with him, as did the Ripper. The mutilations to Elkins' face do not precisely match, but they are close. Unlike the Ripper, who acted in a frenzy, I can see how he has dissected the victims methodically."

"I assume he used the same knife?"

"I would say so, yes."

"Can you give precise times of death for both women?"

"Yes, Betty Sullivan was killed at midnight, give or take a little. He killed Maureen Elkins at 2 am."

"You found no trace of the killer, I suppose?"

"He works methodically, Inspector. He's inside the victim's house. There is nobody around because of the air raids and blackouts. This man doesn't rush. He does everything methodically; I doubt he will leave you a trace. The footprint you found in the Irene Newnham case - I suspect he left it deliberately to link him to the previous murder."

"I thought the same thing. Did you notice that the Mary Thompson stabbing matched the 39 stab wounds inflicted upon Martha Tabram in 1888?"

"Damn, I should have; well done, Inspector. I only matched him to the canonical five accepted victims."

He seemed positively affronted that I had pointed out a shortcoming. I left him absolutely none the wiser while Professor Rawlings gave me a wealth of information. I began to understand why he wanted his anonymity. Bartholomew was a man who felt superior to just about everyone. He had some justification for that opinion, but not with Rawlings. As a psychology professor, I guess he understood the dynamics of that situation better than I did. It was another reminder that arrogance may stand out from the crowd, but humility stands above it.

Back at the Balham station, everyone was out interviewing potential suspects, so I sat and re-read the statements. Our only night-time sightings were of a tallish man wearing a trilby hat and an overcoat. Two of the sightings mentioned the possibility of a bag or briefcase. In the dark, we had no colour, no detail, nothing. It could be anyone who wears a hat and coat. Then I remembered the bomb that fell at the end of Maureen Elkins' road. I checked the time, and it fell at 3:10 am. She was killed at 2 am, so he might just have been walking past. I wondered if there was a remote possibility that our man had been close to it when it exploded. How convenient it would be if he'd been a victim. I made a note to follow up just in case.

# Chapter Forty-Seven
# April 14th, 1941

## Emma

*"If lust is the servant of desire, then love is the master of the servant."*

When Beverley told Maurice he was going to be a father, his reaction did indeed surprise her, just as Marion said it would. Janet and I watched from afar across the canteen as she told him. Beverley looked nervous, and although we couldn't hear what she said, Maurice's reaction was self-explanatory. He jumped to his feet and put his arms around Bev, lifting her off the floor. They stayed in each other's arms for ages.

"I think we can safely say he's happy about it."

"That's more than happy, Em. That's what I call over the moon."

"It's lovely, isn't it? Everyone's looking at them and smiling."

"Bev's going to be in the same position as me. If they get married, she'll have to stop being a nurse."

"She'll have to stop in a few months' time, that's obvious, but this thing about single women isn't a regulation, you know."

"Do you think it will change?"

"I think a lot of things will change, Jan. It seems ridiculous that you can't get married if you want to. It'll change, I'm sure."

"What about you and Frank? Has that changed?"

"You don't give me a moment's peace about Frank, do you?"

"You're wasting your life, Em. I don't mean being a doctor; I mean your love life. You've been going out with Frank for months. You can't keep holding him at arm's length; what's the point?"

"Is this another Janet Walters' lecture?"

"Yes, of course it is. I look at Bev and Maurice over there, and then I look at you."

"Don't spare my feelings, Jan, tell me straight."

"You love me, really."

"I don't have any option, do I?"

"You've got two options with Frank - you can take it or leave it."

"Do you think Frank is right for me?"

"Right for what?"

"Right to spend the rest of my life with."

"Who said anything about the rest of your life? You don't have to think that far ahead. We might not be here tomorrow."

"You don't think he's too old for me, do you?"

"He is older, but he's not exactly an old man, is he? Besides, you obviously prefer older men. Frank adores you, and you've got Bartholomew waiting in the wings. We all know what he wants."

"Why do your comments not shock me any more? Anyway, you can forget Alex. That's not going to happen; he tries it on with all the women."

"He tried it on with Bev once; she told him to piss off."

"It's my niece's birthday next week, they've invited Frank to the party with me. It's a long way. We would have to stay the night."

"Emma. I'm shocked."

"What do you mean?"

"I know what you're thinking, and I absolutely approve."

"I can't think of anything that would shock you. But you're right, maybe it's time."

"Emma, it was time ten years ago."

The bombs continued to miss us as we entered May. What we called our 'country branch' of St Thomas's Hospital opened in Godalming, Surrey. Several of our colleagues who found accommodation had already moved over to Godalming; it represented a safer location. It went on to have 360 beds. We could have gone there as well, but I decided not to. All of my little group decided to stay; this was our hospital, this was our area, and these were our patients. We didn't make any sort of announcement; we just stayed.

I mentioned Audrey's birthday to Frank, and he showed a limited amount of enthusiasm. I didn't dare to say anything else, so I confirmed it with Patricia, hoping we could make it. As the day approached, Janet worked behind the scenes, ensuring we had cover for the afternoon and the following morning. As the day approached, she grew more excited, and I grew more nervous. Our daily rush of casualties continued, but for the first time in ages, I also remembered I had another life. It gave me renewed energy, albeit nervous energy. Janet said nothing to anyone, but I'm sure Frank thought she was acting strangely, even for her.

On the day, we had an influx of casualties who desperately needed our attention. I looked at Frank across the ward and shrugged my shoulders. They needed me in the operating theatre. The time ticked by as I removed a piece of shrapnel from a man's abdomen. A crushed leg and a ruptured spleen later, and I'd finished. The kiddies' party would soon finish, but we could still join them for the evening. Frank came looking for me to say it seemed too late, but I said no, we should still go; I didn't want to disappoint the children. I desperately hoped he wasn't looking for an excuse not to go, but he agreed it was still possible.

We were both desperately tired, but nevertheless, I offered to drive us there. We just threw a few things into the back of the car and hastily drove off. My romantic getaway turned into a tired procession. I left London, heading towards Maidenhead. The further west we drove, the less bomb damage there was. We drove through Hammersmith and onto the Great West Road, heading towards Windsor. Even there, we saw bomb damage; only as we neared Maidenhead did England begin to look like England again.

Within fifteen minutes, Frank was asleep. I felt awake for reasons of my own, but Frank couldn't keep his eyes open. He slept with his head lolling from side to side and his mouth open. I couldn't think of anything less romantic. When I finally came to a halt on the gravel drive of Andrew's house, Frank didn't stir. I leaned across and kissed him. He woke with the most delightful smile, part pleasure and part bewilderment.

"What a nice way to wake up. Where are we?"

"We're here, in Maidenhead."

"I must have dozed off."

"Sweetheart, you've been sound asleep for an hour and a half."

He looked at me as if he had received a wonderful present from an anonymous benefactor, part delight, part puzzlement. I didn't usually call anyone sweetheart. That's what Janet calls people. His puzzlement quickly gave way to delight, and he kissed me again as if he were testing to see that I was real. We sat for a moment, looking at the view that my brother called home. The house sat on the banks of the river Thames. I couldn't think of a more opulent setting.

"You said your brother was prosperous, but not this prosperous."

We might have sat there longer, mesmerised, but my little niece and nephew ran out of the house to greet me, followed by Patricia. She hugged Frank as if they were long-standing friends while I cuddled the children. Frank looked a little overwhelmed. I couldn't tell if it was the children, the house, or being embraced by the ever-lovely Patricia. Patsy then turned towards me, and I was so pleased to see her. Young William called Frank 'Uncle Frank', which caught him even more unawares.

Andrew greeted us and showed us into the drawing room. After years of being distant from my brother, we were now close. It was only the second time I had been to their new riverside house, but I felt a part of the family. They treated 'Uncle Frank' as if he was also a part of the family. Andrew and Frank got on very well together, which was a surprise. Andrew is outgoing and always terribly smartly dressed, while Frank is quiet and not exactly a snazzy dresser. They both have sharp minds, naturally bringing them together, but cricket was the deciding factor. When one cricket fanatic meets another, they drift off into another world that might as well be on the far side of the moon as far as Patsy and I were concerned.

What was left of the evening was completely taken over by the children. The excitement of their afternoon party had done nothing to diminish their energy. I confess they totally exhausted me. They filled the house with noise as if their dozen party guests were still there. When the maid finally led them away upstairs, I missed them and welcomed their absence, all in one confused emotion. Frank slumped back in his chair with a sigh. We weren't used to children and probably looked overwhelmed, but Patsy and Andrew just sat smiling. There's no sense of pride greater than that between a parent and their child, but they hadn't been working seven days a week for months.

I think they took pity on us because we were pampered from that moment on. We drank wonderful champagne before dinner, and Frank went into a head spin about the red wine Andrew had served. That, of course, was music to Andrew's ears. Apart from cricket and interest exchange rates, there's nothing he enjoys talking about more than wine. I remained preoccupied all evening, and the longer I left it before I told Patsy about our bedroom arrangements, the more difficult it became. When the two of us retired to the quiet end of the room, I knew I had to pluck up the courage.

"You look really exhausted, Em. It's hard for you at the hospital, isn't it?"

"It's relentless, day after day, and each time another part of the hospital is destroyed, the worse it gets."

"You're so brave, both of you. I don't know how you do it."

"We don't think about it, Patsy. We just get on with it. Every day, the casualties arrive. What option do we have?"

"Well, at least you can relax here. I have two rooms ready for you both."

"We only need the one bedroom, Patsy."

I forced myself to say it while simultaneously trying to sound as if it was nothing. I desperately tried to think of a response to whatever comment she was about to make, but my mind became blank. She looked at me with a delightful smile, and I braced myself for the embarrassment to come.

"No matter, one of the rooms is a double room, anyway."

"Oh, good … I meant to say earlier … forgot to mention it."

"How serious is scarlet fever, Em? There are several children at school who've gone down with it."

"Oh, yes, scarlet fever. No, it shouldn't be a great cause of concern. There is a slight risk of it spreading further into things like ears or throat, but it should be self-limiting. I shouldn't worry, Patsy."

"Did you hear that, Andy? Em says we don't need to worry about the scarlet fever."

He and Frank used the comment as a cue to come and join us. My embarrassment disappeared, to be replaced by anxiety. I couldn't decide if she simply ignored the issue about the bedroom or if she did it intentionally to save my embarrassment. I didn't know how worldly-wise Patsy was. It's not the sort of thing we would have talked about. Frank described her as a 'sassy lady'. I assumed that meant she had a lot of experience with these things. I wished I had her experience to call upon.

"How long do you think the bombing will go on for, Andrew?"

"From what I hear, Frank, not very much longer. Not on the current scale, anyway."

"What makes you say that? Do you have any inside knowledge?"

"I have the banking network, and I get to speak to the Governor of the Bank of England occasionally. It's only hearsay, of course, but it begins to paint a picture. My guess is that Hitler will turn his attention towards Russia."

"Why? He has the Molotov-Ribbentrop Pact. They've already carved up Poland with the Russians."

"I know, it makes little sense, but Hitler has always been obsessed with ethnically cleansing the Jews and Slavs. It's all in 'Mein Kampf' - his primary focus has always been the non-Aryan land to the east. Stalin knows that; he's just created three military bases in the Baltic. He's preparing for a war with Germany."

"I read in the paper about Tobruk. This is the first time the German Panzer advance has been stopped. I wonder if it's a turning point?"

"We need it to be," I said. "I'm not sure how much longer Londoners can take it, and the same applies to the other big cities. There's been a million houses damaged or destroyed; if that's a turning point, I would hate to see what defeat looks like."

"We've got some friends in the RAF," Frank replied. "They tell us they have more planes now than they had at the start of the Blitz, including some new night fighters. When you look at our hospital, we may look defeated, but you never hear people say that. We deal with the broken of society, the ones the bombs have fallen on, and I can tell you we never hear talk of surrender, quite the opposite."

"I had to amputate a woman's leg the other week. She dismissed it as unfortunate, saying Hitler wouldn't stop her from getting around."

"Emma's right. I don't know where the courage comes from, but the British people will never surrender."

"Do you think we'll ever defeat Hitler?" asked Patricia.

"We have to," Andrew replied. "He wants to dominate a world that he considers to be ethnically pure, in other words, Aryan. Can you imagine living in a dystopian world where everyone has to prove their birthright in order to stay alive? This would be a society where the individual has no value. All that will matter is the perpetuation of the controlling elite."

"I remember what Dad said once. 'A totalitarian regime has to subjugate the people to its will. The people wouldn't have it any other way.'"

They laughed at the play on words, but of course, Dad was so right. The German people wouldn't have ushered Hitler into power if they'd known the truth. Our evening reminded us of the debates that were such a regular occurrence at home as we grew up. I tried to participate, but all I could think about was going to bed with Frank. I felt committed to my decision, and a part of me was excited, but I also wanted to be longing for it to happen, and I wasn't sure I was. The lovely wine was a great temptation, and I'm afraid I submitted to another glass. It offered the illusion of confidence.

As the evening progressed, our lively conversation inevitably submitted to our fatigue. Our eyelids became heavy, and the silences grew longer. That was when Frank announced it was time for bed, and my heart jumped in my chest. Patsy yawned and agreed we should all retire for the night. I'd drunk far too much wine, but the Dutch courage I hoped it would provide simply drained away like sand in an hourglass. I followed Frank up the stairs. We stopped outside the first bedroom, and he put his arms around me. We kissed.

"They're very generous with their hospitality, aren't they?"

"Yes, we all get on well together, don't we?"

"I'm absolutely shattered, Em. I can't wait to get into a proper bed. I'll see you in the morning."

"Where are you going?"

"Oh, sorry, I thought this was your room."

"No, it's our room, Frank."

The words came out of my mouth easily enough, but everything changed the second they passed my lips. The look on Frank's face said it all. His initial reaction was confusion. Had he heard me correctly? When I didn't correct him, his eyes widened in surprise. Perhaps he saw something in my eyes that prompted his next reaction because he took me in his arms as if to reassure me.

I had never felt such an intense feeling in my life; I realised I wanted this. Frank opened the door, and we walked hand in hand into the large bedroom. My head was spinning. I didn't know if it was the wine or passion, and I didn't care. Frank turned on a bedside light, so I turned off the main light. He stood at the far side of the bed, looking at me. I didn't know what the correct thing was to do, so in order not to appear hopelessly inadequate, I fumbled with the catch on my mother's pearls.

I slipped them from my neck and placed them on the dressing table. Frank placed his tie over the chair. He slowly undid his shirt buttons, one at a time. I thought I'd better do the same with my blouse. When he placed his shirt on the chair, I did the same with my blouse. My heart raced as I unfastened my skirt. We looked at each other as we continued with our unscripted erotic melodrama. I didn't know what I was doing; it just seemed to be the right thing to do.

I found undressing in front of Frank acutely embarrassing. I wasn't sure if I should reach for my nightdress or not; in the end, I slipped quickly between the sheets to hide my embarrassment. That first moment when our bodies came together felt like nothing I had ever experienced. I expected it to bring joy beyond my wildest imagination. In the grand scheme of things, I suppose our lovemaking was a little elementary; it certainly didn't last long. I confess I found it all rather anticlimactic. Perhaps if I hadn't drunk so much, the compulsion to fall asleep might not have overwhelmed me.

The morning arrived abruptly, with Audrey and William banging on our door. Before I knew it, they were both bouncing on our bed. I had to cling to the bedclothes to keep myself covered. It was Aunty Emma this and Uncle Frank that. Their energy knew no bounds. As much as I loved them, I didn't want them there, not that morning. Patsy eventually heard them and called them away, but it was hardly a romantic start to what I regarded as a new dawn.

Frank and I looked at each other in the light of a sober day. I wanted to do it all again; I wanted to experience every touch that the alcohol had diminished, but the house echoed to the sound of children and breakfast plates. We cuddled in each other's arms, and it awoke something in me that remained unfulfilled. I didn't know what it was I craved. I reasoned if lust is the servant of desire, then love is the master of the servant. Perhaps I wanted it all.

"We'd better get dressed and go down, Frank. It sounds as if they're waiting for us."

"It's bad timing, isn't it?"

Frank got up and put on a dressing gown to go to the bathroom. I felt even more self-conscious than I had the night before; I sat holding the bedclothes around myself. We were certainly not lovers acting with reckless abandon. It all felt a bit matter of fact that morning. I confess I dressed quickly before Frank came back. By the time I finished in the bathroom, it was already late.

Frank was sitting at the table when I joined them for breakfast. For a moment, I felt self-conscious, thinking that Andrew and Patsy would look at me with knowing eyes. When they didn't, I told myself they were deliberately trying not to embarrass me. It was slightly disappointing to realise that what was a momentous night for me was, in fact, just another night for everyone else.

Frank seemed unfazed by it all, or perhaps he was still in shock. I did rather spring it on him. Patsy looked at me and then at Frank; she knew things had changed between us. Her approving smile was reassuring. We had to leave; we had to get back to the hospital. In every other way, it was business as usual, but Frank and I would never be the same.

# Chapter Forty-Eight
# Burrows

Roger

*"It's not the lack of self-control that demonises a person.
It's what takes over from the self."*

I arrived at work rather late after interviewing two of the enumerators. May the 9th started no differently than any other day. We suffered the usual bombing the night before, but I expected our investigations to be continuing as usual. The news greeting me at the desk shouldn't have surprised me. Ezra Katz had shot someone in front of witnesses in the 'Turks Head'. When Jack told me, I just turned up the corner of my mouth and momentarily looked towards the heavens. I knew Ezra was always going to end up on the gallows. What concerned me was that Joey would inevitably lose his only remaining son so soon after losing his elder son, Aaron.

"Have you arrested him, Jack?"

"No, he's gone to ground, and we can't find him. We will do, all in good time."

"Who did he shoot?"

"This is the problem - he shot one of Jack Comer's men from the other side of the river."

"Oh, my goodness. That boy hasn't got an ounce of sense, has he? Is he hiding from us or from 'Spot' Comer?"

"Both, I suspect. We need to find him first."

"You say you've got a witness?"

330

"Yes, we've got a whole family of them. It was some sort of family celebration. Katz obviously assumed he could intimidate everyone in the pub into keeping quiet; he didn't reckon on it being the victim's family."

"He knows this, does he?"

"Apparently so - the family is out to get him, and he knows it."

"Keep me informed, will you, Jack?"

They were all sitting in the incident room discussing the interviews with the enumerators. I went in with an expectant expression, hoping for some good news.

"Well, do we have a suspect?"

"Not really, Guv, but maybe one or two possibilities," said Jeff.

He explained that most of them appeared to be happily married with children. We couldn't rule them out, but it made it less likely. Others presented well and didn't raise any suspicion. Only three made them suspicious, and only then because they were uncooperative. I read through the profiles, and nothing stood out.

"The two I've seen this morning are improbable, so let's work on these three for the moment."

"We're putting in a lot of time on this, Guv. We could be wasting our time."

"Yes, of course we could, Alfie, but what else do we have to go on? You could interview every man in South London who wears a hat and coat."

"If you're right, Guv," said Fleming, "we're waiting for him to recreate what 'Jack' did to Mary Kelly."

"That's right, Fleming, and that's not something I even want to think about. Let's get back out there and interview these three suspects again. You and Alfie see this man Atkinson again. Which one do you want, Jeff?"

"Let's go with Burrows, Guv."

"Why him?"

"I don't know; it's just something about him. He lives locally, and he works for the Wandsworth Council. He's rude and arrogant, but more than that, I didn't like the look of him."

"That's good enough for me, Jeff; get your hat."

We left without further debate and headed for the man's workplace. He didn't work directly for the Register Office but held a senior position in the housing department right next door. He volunteered to act as an enumerator. Needless to say, his department would be inundated with people who needed rehousing; I realised our visit would be unwelcome.

Jeff warned me that Burrows had been short-tempered and officious. A secretary in the outer office told us he couldn't be disturbed. The woman was a formidable obstacle. She eventually suggested that perhaps he might find us five minutes during his lunch hour. That sounded reasonable, so we waited. At 1 o'clock precisely, I knocked on his door despite the efforts of his formidable gatekeeper.

"How dare you interrupt me without an appointment; leave immediately."

He stood at his office door wide-eyed and indignant. A tall man in his fifties, he appeared to be someone used to authority. His receding hair was almost entirely grey. He wore thick, round-rimmed spectacles that magnified his eyes. That was unfortunate for him because eyes say a lot about a person, and his eyes were dead and devoid of expression. Like Jeff, I instantly disliked him, but that didn't make him a serial murderer.

"Sit down, Mr Burrows, or I will insist upon interviewing you at the police station."

"I've already answered this man's questions."

"Sit down, Mr Burrows. The more you try to avoid us, the more I must assume you have something to hide. Answer our questions now, or I will have to arrest you."

"What are you talking about? Arrest me for what?"

"Someone has disclosed information from the 1939 register for the purpose of producing counterfeit documents. Is that you, Mr Burrows?"

"Don't be ridiculous."

"As an enumerator, you were in the ideal position, Mr Burrows. It's in your best interest to convince us otherwise. So - first, tell me about your background, and remember, we'll check every detail you give us."

Like many puffed-up administrators, he was used to intimidating people. When he realised that wouldn't work, he diminished in stature. He sat down, looking very stern-faced.

"I have nothing to do with counterfeit documents, Inspector. Anyone with a grain of intelligence could see that."

"The law is blind, Mr Burrows. How long have you worked for Wandsworth Council?"

"Twenty-two years."

"Are you married? Do you have a family?"

"What has that got to do with anything?"

"Just answer the question."

"No, I'm not."

"So you live alone?"

"Yes."

"What, not even a cat or a budgerigar?"

"There's nothing wrong with choosing to live alone."

"No, of course not. What do you do in your spare time?"

"What? I read."

"Is that all? No interests outside of work?"

"I read, I'm a studious person."

"So you have no interests at all other than reading."

"I do the usual things."

"What, like a drink in your local pub with friends?"

"That sort of thing, yes. What has this got to do with anything?"

"What are your plans for the future, Mr Burrows?"

"I have no idea. Perhaps I'll retire to Bournemouth."

"Have you never been married?"

"No."

"Did you serve in the last war?"

"We all did."

"What did you do? Who were you with?"

"Cheshire Regiment."

"Rank?"

"Captain."

"Good war record?"

"Exemplary."

"So you won commendations?"

"I served my country."

"Were you awarded any gallantry medals?"

"What does that have to do with you?"

"Stop being evasive, Mr Burrows. Do as you're told and answer my question."

"How dare you speak to me like that. You have no right. I'm a senior Council official."

"As far as I'm concerned, Burrows, you're nothing but a jumped-up office clerk. What medals were you awarded?" I asked in a raised voice.

"British War Medal and the Allied Victory Medal," he shouted.

"Why not the Star?"

"Yes, that as well."

"That will do for now, Mr Burrows, but you may see me again."

"You haven't asked me anything about the register or these so-called fake documents. There will be no reason for you to see me again."

"That'll be my decision, not yours."

He glared at me with an expression I couldn't interpret. The veins on his forehead were prominent, his breathing was fast, and he held his mouth tight, forming a straight line. Usually, the eyes are the best clue to emotions, but not in his case. He infrequently blinked and seemed to look through you rather than at you. Above all, his eyes were expressionless. To say that I didn't like him would be an understatement. When we left, he closed the door firmly behind us. We didn't say a word until we were in the car.

"Bloody hell, Roger, you were incredibly hard on him."

"He's lying through his teeth, Jeff."

"Was all that shouting just to wind him up?"

"Yes, of course, and it worked."

"How can you be sure he's lying?"

"His service record for a start. He says he was a captain in the Cheshire regiment. He would have received at least some kind of commendation if he had been. Did you notice how he didn't want to disclose his medals?"

"Yes, why was that?"

"They were service medals; he got those simply for being there. Veterans at the time called them Pip, Squeak and Wilfred because they were normally awarded together at the end of the war. He might have served with the Cheshires, but that man wasn't a captain."

"We can check his service record."

"We'll do exactly that. I want you and Alfie to concentrate on this man. Check to see if he has a police record, talk to his neighbours and check out the local pub where he says he goes. Send someone they haven't seen to the council buildings. We need a friendly chat with some people who work with him. If anyone from there goes to the pub after work, then that'll be a good time."

"Do you think it's him?"

"We don't know, but he fits the profile perfectly. He doesn't feel right, does he?"

"I didn't like him the first moment I saw him."

We mulled it over on our way back to Balham. You must never let your emotions influence your better judgment. I've always been very good at assessing evidence rationally and joining the dots. This case had become personal, but I had to retain a rational mind. Burrows fitted the profile; he was certainly a suspect. We were both so preoccupied with Burrows that neither of us spared a thought for the Katz case. That changed abruptly the second we arrived back at the station.

"We've found him," Jack told us the second we walked in.

"Well done. Is he in the cells?"

"No, I'm afraid not. The stupid bastard is holed up in a house in Brixton."

"Why haven't you arrested him?"

"He's shooting at people, that's why. DC Fleming's there, and just about everyone Brixton can spare is there."

"He knows it's the end of the road, doesn't he? I suppose he thinks he has nothing to lose."

"He may not, but he's got a woman in there. He says he'll shoot her if we don't allow him to leave."

"Idiot."

"You know this boy and his family, Roger. Do you think you could talk him around?"

"Me? What does Gerry say?"

"He said, 'Ask Roger.'"

"Oh, for goodness' sake. This is the last thing I need."

"He might listen to you. It's worth a try before he gets more people shot."

"Have they got firearms there?"

"Yes, Brixton's issued handguns, and they've got a trained marksman there."

I walked right into that. Gerry obviously set me up for it. Jack even got the Webley revolver out of the cupboard to take with me. I wanted that even less than I wanted to see Ezra. Jeff came with me and drove me to the address. We arrived at an ordinary terraced road in Brixton, and uniformed police were everywhere. One of them was equipped with a Lee Enfield rifle. It looked as though we were preparing to reenact the gunfight at the OK Corral. Most of the coppers at Brixton knew who I was, so I approached the rifleman first.

"What are your orders, Constable? Do you intend to use that thing?"

"Yes, Sir, if he threatens anyone, I've been told to shoot him."

"How's he behaving?"

"Like someone who has nothing to lose."

I found Fleming, who was keeping his head down. He said the same thing: Ezra was behaving completely irrationally. He'd already fired two shots. They were not sure if he aimed at the police or not, but he didn't hit anyone. He obviously didn't think he would leave there alive. From what I'd been told, I tended to agree.

"Why is he here in this house? Do we know?"

"We don't know. I guess he must know someone here, and asked to be taken in."

"Even if I could talk him out, it would only be for an appointment with the hangman."

"That's why I can't see him coming out."

I always knew Ezra would step over the line one day. Rachel knew it, and so did Joey; I just didn't want to be a part of it. I went back to the rifleman, thinking he might be crucial for my safety. He had taken up a suitable position, and I didn't doubt his commitment.

"I'll try to talk to him, but only if I can see him first. If I can get him near the door or window, and he looks as if he is going to open fire, then, provided you can get a clear shot, take it. Are you a good shot, Constable?"

"I could hit a fly's testicles at a thousand yards, Sir."

"Aim for something larger, will you, especially if he points his damn gun at me."

"Don't worry, Sir, I won't miss."

"It's not a case of missing, Constable. It's a case of reacting quicker than he does."

"If he steps out of that door with a gun, his foot won't get beyond the doorstep."

With that reassurance, I crossed the road fifty yards further down and worked my way along the front garden walls. When I was behind the wall in front of the house, I shouted out to Ezra.

"Ezra, it's Inspector Pritchard. You know me, and I know your father. He'd want you to put your gun down and come out."

"Let me see you," he shouted.

"What, so you can shoot me?"

"If you've got something to say, I won't shoot. The old man says you're a good copper."

I took him at his word, and I stood up. I'm no hero in these situations; I wasn't like Dave. My heart raced as I stood up. I breathed a deep sigh of relief when nothing happened. I slowly approached the house. The front door opened just enough to talk around it. He said something, but I replied, saying that I couldn't hear. Ezra opened the door a little further until I could see him around it. I realised the rifleman wouldn't have seen him from his vantage point. I didn't know who the unfortunate woman was, but she looked absolutely terrified. Ezra had his arm around her neck with the gun pointing at her head.

"You know you won't get out of this, Ezra. All you can do now is dishonour your father even further."

"To hell with you, Pritchard. Get me out of this, or you and this woman are going to hell with me."

"What's the point? Show a bit of respect for your father, even if it's the last thing you do."

"Stop going on about my old man. You're not dealing with him."

"You're right there. For once in your life, do something honourable. Give him something he can respect you for."

"You think standing on the gallows is honourable?"

"Compared to killing that woman, yes. Let her go, Ezra. I'll give you an easy way out if you've got the guts to take it."

"What do you mean?"

"Let her go and point that gun at me."

I was absolutely terrified. His eyes were like saucers. He looked completely manic. I doubted he could think rationally at all. I made the immediate judgment that he had no intention of leaving that house alive. The only question in my mind, and probably in his, was how many others he might take with him. The best I could hope for was to save the woman.

I knew from conversations with Rachel that Ezra had a pathological hatred of anyone questioning his sanity. It obviously confronted him with reality, and that was not a place he wanted to be. He almost beat a man to death once because the man said he was mad.

"Come on, Ezra, she's got her whole life ahead of her. Don't take that away from her just to satisfy your madness."

"Don't you call me that, copper."

"I'll call you what you are, Ezra. You're insane; you're like a rabid dog. Someone has to put you down."

"I'll kill her."

"Why? There's no sense to it, but of course, you don't have any sense, do you? Anyone with half a brain can see you should point the gun at me, not her. You can't work it out, can you, you stupid idiot."

Ezra was renowned for his violent temper. It's what made people so terrified of him. It's not the lack of self-control that demonises a person. It's what takes over from the self. I knew if I goaded him, he would react, I could push him into shooting at me rather than the woman. That was when Ezra's demon took over what little reason he might have had left. He half-stepped around the door, still holding the woman. He raised the gun towards my head. A loud shot rang out almost instantaneously, and I saw the flash from his gun. He fell back into the hall behind the door, and the woman screamed hysterically. For a moment, I expected the lights to go out. I thought he'd shot me. Several seconds later, I was still standing with my ears ringing. Numerous uniformed policemen rushed forward. I looked behind the door, and Ezra lay on the floor motionless in a growing pool of blood.

I only heard one shot, but obviously, two shots were fired simultaneously. The woman remained standing, screaming hysterically. A bobby knelt to check if Ezra was indeed dead. Others helped the unfortunate woman away to a waiting ambulance. I vaguely remember many people slapping me on the back calling me a hero. Jeff could see I was a bit dazed by the whole thing, so he led me away. My ears were still ringing, but as I crossed the road, I started coming to my senses. I looked for the rifleman and went straight to him.

"It looks like I owe you one, Constable. How much of him could you see?"

"Between you and the woman, not much, but a lot more than a pair of fly's testicles."

"Well done. What's your name, Constable?"

"Gibson, Sir. Clive Gibson."

"Thank you, Clive, you did a brave thing there. You would have been in trouble if you'd shot the woman."

"I had no option, Sir, that bastard tried to shoot you. I saw what you did, Sir. That was the bravest thing I've ever seen. I hope that woman realises you probably saved her life."

"You played a large part in that, Clive. I hope they give you a commendation."

There would have to be all sorts of reports to be written, and goodness knows what else, but at that moment, I only wanted to leave and have a drink. Fleming came with us, and we walked back to the car together.

"I take my hat off to you, Guv. That was a hell of a thing you did there.

How did you know he would come at you like that?"

"Same reason he shot the man in the 'Turks Head'. Ezra was a hothead. He never applied reason to anything."

"How did you know the marksman would react so quickly?"

"Intuition, I suppose. He's a cocky sod, full of confidence, but I could tell it wasn't just bravado. I trusted him."

"You put your life on the line for that woman, Roger," said Jeff. "You deserve a bloody medal, mate."

"Forget the medal, Jeff, but I wouldn't say no to a drink."

# Chapter Forty-Nine
# May 10th, 1941

Emma

*"Respect and admiration are fickle beasts liable to run off in the night."*

I thought my life would change after that night with Frank. I would step onto the sunny upland where couples besotted with each other live in a state of bliss. That didn't happen, of course. I may have glanced in that direction, but we quickly returned to war-torn London. The days that followed comprised passionate kisses in hallways and glances across the ward. We had no real-time together, and our nights were spent in our respective basements. In many ways, it was as if nothing had happened between us. My sunny upland became a table in the canteen.

"Anyone doing anything tonight?" I asked.

"Yes," replied Shirley, "I'm going to see Roy's parents."

"Where do they live?" asked Beverley.

"Croydon, it's not that far. We're staying the night."

"Where will you take shelter?" I asked.

"They don't get as many bombs down there; I think we might stay in the house."

"Separate beds, I bet," laughed Janet.

"Yes, probably."

"What about you, Em? Anything exciting?"

"Yes, I've got an exciting night planned. I'm going to spend the night with my friends in the basement."

"That sounds fun, I might do that as well," laughed Janet.

Somehow, we all laughed. The bombing had continued relentlessly for over eight months. Over 42,000 people had already been killed across the country, including eight of our friends and colleagues. Over a million houses had been damaged or destroyed. It is perhaps a testament to the power of the human spirit that, after all we had been through, we still retained our ability to smile. Every obstacle we overcame gave us a little more determination to carry on. Every life we saved gave us another reason to rejoice. That spirit was everywhere to be seen; it smiled on the faces of my friends sitting around the table. Had we known the night of May 10/11th was to be the last night of the Blitz, we would no doubt have been celebrating. Had we also known it would be the worst night of the Blitz, I hope we would have had the strength to face it.

I was late arriving; no sooner had I joined them than they had to go. We were very fortunate in the hospital to still have a functioning canteen. It might have been relegated to a small lecture room in what was left of the medical school, but our rations were not as restricted as the general public. Fish wasn't rationed at all, but it was far from plentiful. What we had that day didn't look at all appetising. I looked up from it to see Frank coming to join me.

"You look far away this afternoon, Em. Is everything alright?"

"Oh, sorry, Frank, perhaps it's this fish. I've been chatting with Janet and the others; they all have so much going on. Shirley's going to stay with Roy's parents for the night; she hasn't met them before."

"That sounds ominous."

"That's what I thought. Things are getting serious between them."

"What about Beverley and Maurice? Have you heard from your brother about renting them your parents' house?"

"Not yet, but I'm sure he'll agree. I think it's wonderful how they've embraced the whole thing. "

"I hope it works out for them; it's certainly a brave decision."

"Look at Alex over there; where do you suppose his future lies?"

"Professionally or personally?"

"Well, both, I suppose. We all know he's a bit of a womaniser. I'm surprised that doesn't tarnish his reputation. Respect and admiration are fickle beasts liable to run off in the night."

"That's normally true, but consultants like Alex seem impervious to scandal. I suppose it's the nature of being at the top of the tree. The rest of us have no option but to look up at him."

"You make it sound like such a lonely place, Frank; perhaps that's why he's a womaniser. I wonder what his long-term prospects are?"

"What about us, Em? Do we have long-term prospects?"

I walked right into that, didn't I? Frank and I avoided discussing the future, but that didn't mean I hadn't thought about it. In truth, I was in a reflective mood that afternoon. My friends were each charting a route into whatever their future held. Looking at them, I saw a reflection of myself.

I saw Marion, who was content with her life, but it came with regret. Beverley and Maurice stood at the crossroads of life and chose the steep incline leading into the mist of the unknown. Shirley seemed to have chosen her path with Roy, and Janet, well, the entire world knew what her path was. A part of me wanted to share those thoughts with Frank. I had made my commitment, so I assumed we needed to embark on our future. It just didn't seem that straightforward. I blamed the war, the bombing, the intensive pressure at the hospital; I blamed everything other than myself. I didn't entirely walk into Frank's question - I intentionally moved towards it, but when the moment came, I faltered.

"Let's hope we have long-term prospects, Frank. The bombing must end soon."

"You know that's not what I mean."

"Yes, I know. I just find talking about it so difficult with all that's going on."

"I need to know. We don't have to rush into anything, but I must know if I have a future with you."

"Of course, we have a future together; what are you saying?"

"Well, it's just that you never mention it. You're sort of noncommittal about the future. I know the future generally has never been more un-certain, but as you say, that doesn't stop your friends from planning for theirs."

"I thought we had already chosen our path, Frank; now we have to see where the war takes us."

Having invited the question, you would think I might have used the opportunity to explore it, but I didn't. I closed the book, too frightened to read the next page. Perhaps I thought everything would change after our first night together and that I would be miraculously transformed into someone like Janet. When that didn't happen, I questioned all my assumptions. The only certain reality was the war and the relentless bomb-ing. None of us led a normal life; Frank and I spent our nights apart in separate hospital basements. We stole kisses in quiet corridors and devised secret liaisons.

We kissed that night in an improvised operating theatre before once again setting off in separate directions. It had all become a kind of torture. My shared basement bedroom felt oppressive that evening despite my friends continuing their good spirits. We settled in for the night as usual; I was so tired I quickly fell asleep. The bombs started falling at 11:15 pm, and the distant rumble woke me as it always did. My first thought was that it was business as usual. It wasn't long before we realised that this was going to be a really terrible night. The building shook time and time again as bombs fell close by.

"This sounds like a bad one," said Marion.

"It's one after another, and they're getting closer," replied Beverley.

"Lucky Shirley isn't here tonight," I said, "she would get really agitated."

"It's not just Shirley; my heart's racing already," replied Janet.

"I think it's the past more than the present. I relive that night every time I hear a bomb fall."

Just as I said that the hospital was hit again. Our basement shook violently, dust fell from the ceiling, and our light went out. It must have been two or three blocks away, but we instantly relived that terrible night when we were buried beneath the rubble. My hands shook, I felt as if I was gasping for air; I wanted to scream in panic. With our torches lit, we huddled together as the ground continued to shake beneath us. We each looked towards the ceiling, expecting it to fall onto us. When the next lull arrived, we collected ourselves with thoughts of helping those who must be injured.

"Let's get ourselves ready, ladies. There will be people who need us," said Marion.

We did precisely that. When the threat subsides, the panic is replaced with an urgency to help others. A sense of purpose was restored. No sooner were we about to set off when the bombs started falling again. Another direct hit followed several close explosions. It was an awful explosion that threw us off our feet. We felt the shock wave, followed by the crash of falling bricks and masonry. It must have been the block next to ours. We thought that at any second, our nightmare would reenact itself. I expected everything to collapse on top of us again. Too frightened to speak, we stared at each other wide-eyed in terror. Then, just as we thought it could get no worse, another bomb hit us. It must have been two or three blocks away, but our building shuddered violently yet again.

With bombs continuing to fall close to us, it felt as if this was the beginning of the end. We sat on the floor holding hands, expecting that end at any moment. The bombing continued until 5:15 am when the silence became as loud as the explosions. It took several minutes before we allowed ourselves to hope it was over. The moment the danger passed, we returned to being human beings again with all our human frailty. I burst into tears; we all did. It was part terror and part relief that we were still alive. We squeezed each other's hands in an expression of gratitude that we had been spared.

When we collected ourselves, our thoughts immediately returned to our colleagues, Frank, Maurice, and Leo. The terrifying question is always the same: did one of those bombs fall on our loved ones? I looked at Beverley, and a new terror lodged itself in my throat. If we could get out of the building, there would be people injured or dying who needed our help, but Frank filled my mind. Miraculously, our exit wasn't blocked, so we walked out into the early morning. Even before we stepped into the open, the air became increasingly laden with dust and acrid smoke. The fumes made our eyes sting, and it caught our lungs.

The early morning light of a new day revealed a vision of hell. The spectacle that confronted us hit me with all the force of a bomb blast. I gasped aloud. Our hospital had been devastated. Fires raged, and three more blocks lay in ruins. The destruction was too extensive to comprehend. We each stood in disbelief. Only then did I glance across the river. The heart of government, the Palace of Westminster, was ablaze. The iconic symbol of Britain's resistance had been bombed several times. Many fires raged, but the worst image was the massive column of black smoke rising from the very centre of the government. The House of Commons chamber had been destroyed, gutted by fire.

The four of us stood with our mouths open, immobilised by shock, unable to comprehend our surroundings. All around us, fires burned, and smoke billowed into the heavens. We stared with eyes that could no longer see and listened with ears that refused to hear. Eventually, our rock in life, Marion, brought us back into the hell we tried so hard to exclude. That was when my worst fear came true. Frank, Leo, and Maurice sheltered beneath one of those collapsed buildings.

# Chapter Fifty
# May 11th,1941

Roger

*"Achievement speaks with a loud voice.*
*Inspiration need only whisper its name."*

The night of May 10/11th was the worst single night of the Blitz. It had been a clear night with a full moon. 505 German planes followed the river up from the estuary and dropped 700 tons of high-explosive bombs and 86,000 incendiary bombs on London. This was the London we emerged into when Jean and I left the Clapham South tube station on the morning of the 11th. We could see fires in all directions. The air hung heavy with smoke and dust.

When the casualty figures were later released, it revealed that 1436 people were killed that night, and a further 1800 were badly injured. Another 12,000 Londoners were made homeless. It took time for us to realise that this had been the worst night of the Blitz; the government tried to suppress news which might upset public morale. Had we known the 10th of May was to be the last night of the sustained bombing, it would have been an enormous morale boost, but of course, we expected more of the same. I stopped for a cup of tea when I dropped Jean off at her house.

"Last night looks like a terrible one, doesn't it?"

"Yes, it does. I'll find out later how bad. What are you picking up from people, Jean? What are your mass observation diaries telling you?"

"I would say morale is declining, but considering what we're all going through, it remains remarkably high."

"What are the common gripes?"

"The state of the underground shelters is high on the list. Everyone wants decent facilities. And the looting features high on the list. It really enrages people."

"What about these Ripper murders? Are people talking about it?

"They are, especially the young women. Some of them are as frightened about that as they are the bombs."

"Does the government listen to all these observations?"

"I have to type it all up and make a proper report, so I hope so. It all goes to the Ministry of Information."

"It's good work, Jean; I know how much time you put into it."

She returned from the kitchen with a cup of tea, put her arm around me and kissed my cheek. I didn't know how to respond; it wasn't a hello or a goodbye kiss - an unsolicited kiss is something different. I responded with my arm around her waist and a brief hug. It was insignificant but marked a point when our relationship changed. We both continued to struggle in the aftermath of the Balham disaster, but as I left Jean that morning, I thought perhaps we'd turned a corner.

The events of the day before were weighing heavily on my mind. I didn't give a damn about Ezra; it was always going to happen, but it remained a horribly disturbing thing to have been a part of. I didn't think Rachel was about to shed many tears either, but my heart went out to Joey. However wayward, Ezra was still his only remaining son. I decided to pay him a call on my way to Balham.

I passed several fires and bombed houses along the way and realised the full extent of the overnight bombing raid. Some roads were blocked; if fire engines were not in attendance at fires, they were on their way to one. The moment I turned into Streatham High Road, I could see a column of black smoke rising into the air further down the road. As I drove nearer, I suddenly realised the smoke rose above Joey's shop and warehouse. Hundreds of rolls of material were going up in smoke.

Firemen were in attendance, and a crowd had gathered. I found Joey standing in the crowd with his trusted retainer at his side. He saw me approaching and stepped away towards me. He looked like a completely broken man. His eyes were red, and his face expressed the sorrow of a thousand ancestors. He put his arms around me without a word being spoken.

"I'm truly sorry, Joey. No man should have to suffer so much."

"Perhaps it's God's judgment, my son yesterday and this today."

"I can't believe God could be so cruel. The bomb that did this didn't have divine guidance."

"You're right. I just need someone to blame. Tell me what happened to Ezra."

"Do you want the truth?"

"Roger, you know me. I need the truth."

I did know Joey; he could deal with the truth, and he would have seen through anything less. It didn't provide him with a crumb of comfort, but he seemed to expect it. There was absolutely nothing I could say to make any of it better. He knew precisely what his son was and despised him for it. They didn't get on. I would go as far as to say he was ashamed of him. But none of it could make up for the fact that his only surviving son and heir was dead. I didn't doubt Joey remained financially secure despite his warehouse going up in flames, but he had lost his life's work. He once commanded respect as the head of a family and of a successful business, but now he had nothing. His wife Eva and his two sons were gone.

"I'm pleased you were there at the end, Roger. I know you would have treated him fairly."

"If I could have got him to surrender to us, Joey, I would, but it was his decision. He knew exactly what would happen when he stepped through that door. He wanted it to end his way."

He shook my hand and wished me well. I didn't kill his son, but I played a large part in it. He bore me no malice; he might have been broken, but he remained a man of enormous stature. I drove to the station, overwhelmed by the events of the last 24 hours.

When I arrived, everyone wanted to congratulate me on my handling of the shooting. Apparently, I was a hero. That's not how I saw it, wanting to put it behind me. What seemed far more important to me were the effects of the overnight bombing. The damage was becoming clear. When they told me about the House of Commons, it almost sounded like defeat. Jack said the Palace of Westminster had been hit several times, as was the hospital opposite. I could put faces to some of our politicians, as well as some of the staff at St Thomas's. The war was becoming ever more personal. Against that background, we had to continue to function as policemen, or the bombing would have been successful.

We had a tough day ahead; I wanted them to concentrate on the Ripper case, but everything was against us. The Ripper was affecting public morale in South London; I saw that as our priority. We always had plenty of other crimes to deal with, and accessing records was becoming increasingly difficult, and therefore, ever more time-consuming. We needed more detectives, but at least we had Fleming. I berated him, but he was trying. I sent them all out in search of records and information. Gerry came over and sat with me.

"You did really well yesterday, Roger. We all knew that boy had it coming."

"I won't shed a tear for him. I don't know who the woman is, but she didn't deserve to be terrified by that idiot. I couldn't allow it to go on."

"You invited him to shoot you instead of her, didn't you? You put your life on the line for that woman - you took a terrible gamble."

"To be honest, Gerry, I didn't think he'd pull the trigger."

"He did, though, didn't he? I'm not sure if you were brave or foolhardy. Either way, they'll give you an award for this, and you bloody well deserve it."

"Well, I'm not sure about that; I just want to get back to normal. Not that any of this is normal."

"How are you getting on at home? It must still be difficult for you?"

"We're coping; it's been eight months now."

"You're fortunate, I suppose - you and Jean have always been close, haven't you?"

"It's a mixed blessing, believe me."

"I still see Dave walk through that door sometimes; I have to look twice."

"I see him every day, Gerry. I think he's sitting next to me in the car. Sometimes I even look, expecting him to be there."

"It's not my business, Roger, but I'm pretty sure if Dave could give you advice today about Jean, he would approve of you two being together."

"I've asked myself that a hundred times."

"And?"

"I think he probably would."

"Tell me about this man Burrows that you have everyone investigating. How sure are you?"

"I'm not sure at all, Gerry. It's just that I have no one else. He fits all the criteria. I'm certain he's lying and - call it a copper's intuition - but I'm also certain he's a nasty piece of work."

"I hope you're right; I've just authorised our entire detective team to concentrate on him."

"I admit it's a gamble, and the odds are low. But if Burrows were a poker hand, I'd bet on it."

"You just did."

We laughed about it. What else was there to do? I had drawn the straw to interview Burrow's neighbours in Wandsworth, so I wasted no more time before setting off. After another disrupted journey around closed roads and bomb damage, I found Burrows lived in a rather impressive, detached house on a leafy road in the better part of Wandsworth. The neighbours were decent people; I spent a lot of time with them. It was mainly just chatting and hearsay, but that's often when people reveal something they might not realise is significant.

The important thing was that they saw little of him, and they thought he was a bit strange. I found out he drove a luxurious car, a Humber Super Snipe, aimed at the executive market. I immediately asked the obvious question: Did he ever come and go at night? They shrugged their shoulders. The one thing everyone had in common was that during the blackout, especially during the bombing, people didn't spend time looking out of their windows.

They described him as being secretive, evasive, and uncooperative. Burrows continued to fit the criteria. I thanked them for their cooperation and asked them not to say anything to anyone about it, especially Burrows. I left with my notes and my head full of details. The day still had a couple of hours left, so I gave in to a concern that had been troubling me all day. St Thomas's had suffered more bombing, and the reports made it sound especially bad. Emma Stevenson popped into my mind repeatedly that day; I didn't want to think she had been killed or injured. We weren't exactly friends, but I liked the woman; we had a good rapport together. I wanted to know if she and her colleagues were alright.

I couldn't park near the hospital; the damage was too extensive, and the road had been closed. It looked utterly devastated. Several of the blocks now lay in ruins so there had to be a lot of casualties. I didn't expect to see any medical activity going on at all, but to my profound surprise, I saw nurses in uniform and casualties being attended to. I shouldn't have interrupted them, but I did. One block, despite everything, had some activity going on, and so I approached them.

"Can anyone tell me if Doctor Stevenson is here?"

"Roger," came the reply. It was Emma's friend, Janet, I recognised her.

"Janet, thank God you're okay. Is Emma alright?"

"Yes, we walked away without a scratch, can you believe it?"

"There must have been people killed and injured?"

"Yes, we've suffered several injuries, and two of our people are dead. But when you look at this place, it's a bloody miracle."

"Do you know where Emma is?"

"Yes, she's in there. She set up a kind of emergency operating theatre in the lobby."

Janet appeared to be indestructible. They must have been to hell and back, and yet there she was, tending patients. I left her there and went in search of Emma. I followed the blood trail and found her at the end of it. Her operating theatre was nothing more than a trolly in the middle of the lobby.

She had a patient in front of her and another trolly covered in equipment behind her. The nurse with her recognised me. She was also at the pub that night; it was her friend Beverley. When I saw how preoccupied they were, I thought it best to leave and allow her to get on, but she pointed to a row of chairs. Fifteen minutes later, Emma walked over to me, looking as if she'd been dragged through an abattoir by her hair. Her apron was covered in blood, and there were smudges of it on her forehead where she had brushed her hair aside. She was holding her hair back with surgical tweezers.

"Roger, are you alright? You're not injured?"

"No, I came to see that you were alright."

"Oh, that's nice of you. Yes, we must have nine lives. Everyone I share the basement with walked away."

"What about your doctor friends?"

"It's been the most horrible irony. Alex Bartholomew thought he was safer sheltering in the basement of his club. He was killed last night. Frank and the others were in the basement beneath one of the damaged blocks, and somehow they all walked away with hardly a scratch. I honestly don't know how. There's a feeling that another miracle's taken place. It's not the first time that's happened. We can hardly believe it. That's not to say we didn't lose anyone here. Another member of staff was killed, and we've got five serious injuries."

"Oh, I'm so sorry. You say Bartholomew is dead?"

"Yes, he's been identified. It's just so awful."

"I often come here to see him; we've shared a pint together. I can't believe it, he's gone, just like that."

"I know, we just stood in shock when we were told. It just doesn't seem possible. He was such a brilliant man I would often seek his advice about patient concerns. It's true he could be a bit too high and mighty at times, and he had a habit of asking me out rather too often. But all that aside, he was our friend, he was one of us. I confess when they told us, I burst into tears."

"I'm not surprised; it's a terrible personal loss. What about the other person who was killed?"

"I didn't know her well, but yes, I knew her."

"You've lost people close to you but you're still working here. How can you function amongst all this destruction?"

"We don't function, we just carry on. As long as I'm still standing, this hospital will never close its doors."

Emma Stevenson sat there looking like an apparently insignificant, tired, and bedraggled doctor. However unprepossessing she might appear, beneath that war-jaded exterior, she possessed a spirit that stopped me in my tracks. It was the way she said the hospital would never close, the look in her eyes, and the strength in her voice. I was left in no doubt; this magnificent woman was a force of nature.

"You said that with such conviction. You people should be so proud of what you're doing here."

"We all do what we can, Roger; you're doing the same."

"I agree; we all do what we can, but some do more than others. You're an inspiration, you really are."

"I enjoy talking to you, Roger, you always make me think."

"I enjoyed our evening in the pub the other week. We must do that again sometime."

"I'd like that. Leo was very taken with your friend Rachel. He was mortified when I told him what you said."

"Well, you might tell him that her circumstances have changed somewhat. He might even be in with a chance now."

"Oh, how intriguing, I'll tell him."

She looked so tired and bedraggled that I thought she might fall asleep at any moment. Despite that, she retained an inner smile, a radiance I could feel rather than see. I saw it reflected in the faces of the people she worked with. It was easy to see where their inspiration came from. Achievement speaks with a loud voice. Inspiration need only whisper its name. I didn't take up any more of her time, but I left feeling better for having seen her.

# Chapter Fifty-One
# June 1941

Emma

*"It's all just baggage. Work out what's important in life and dump the rest. Sigmund Freud spent his life working that out."*

We came as close as we ever got to closing the hospital following the terrible night of the 10th. Nearly everything was lost. All but one of our remaining wards had been destroyed. Before the war, we had a complement of 682 beds. Now, we were reduced to just one basement ward and 12 beds. Had the bombing continued, we would not have recovered, but the lull allowed us to try at least. Work began immediately to utilise what little we had left. It is a source of enduring pride that St Thomas's didn't once close its doors at any time during the war.

We were all badly shaken by Alex's death. The absence of a friend and colleague is an empty space where voices echo in the dark. We all expected to see him or hear his voice, but all we saw were memories of the past. One by one, we lost colleagues and friends and had to carry on as if it didn't matter. We couldn't allow our personal feelings to weigh us down. The obstacles were so large, and the need so great, we just didn't have the capacity to grieve. Glasses were raised to Alex in the pub as if a man's life can be remembered in a single sentence. It reminded us that we are all nothing but specs of humanity. We view life in our own image, but life doesn't see us at all.

After eight months and five days, the Blitz finally ended on May 11th, but everyone lived in fear that it would start again. Only in late June, when Hitler moved the Luftwaffe towards the east, did our fears subside. There was no return to normal; life would never be the same. Buildings could be rebuilt, things could be replaced, but we had changed irreparably. We talked about it in the pub one night when we were all together.

"Do you think the worst is over, Barry?" I asked.

"The worst of the bombing looks as though it's over, but it's only the beginning for the RAF."

"It feels like this is going to go on forever," Shirley said.

"Barry's right," Roy replied, "it's only just beginning. I fear we're a long way from the end."

"How will it end?" Beverley asked.

"There's only one way this can end. Dictators like Hitler will never stop, not until they defeat us, or we defeat them," replied Maurice.

"I don't see how we can defeat him," replied Frank. "He has control of mainland Europe. How do we defeat him from our little island?"

"This all has echoes in history," I said. "Hitler is a latter-day Napoleon; he wanted to conquer Britain as well. Napoleon made detailed preparations to invade us. Thousands of men-at-arms stood ready just across the Channel. Villeneuve's fleet set sail to join the invasion force. He was met by the British fleet and defeated by Nelson at the Battle of Trafalgar. It has its parallels today with the RAF and the Battle of Britain. Both then and now, the outcome of those two battles made an invasion impossible."

"So how was Napoleon defeated in the end?" asked Janet.

"The Battle of Waterloo," replied Frank.

"There's another interesting parallel in history," I said. "Napoleon also invaded Russia and look at what a disaster that was."

"So how long did it take to defeat Napoleon then?" asked Janet.

"Twenty-three years," I replied.

That sobering thought put an end to the conversation. The prospect of the war possibly lasting many more years was depressing. We did what we always did when faced with a harsh reality - we ignored it. Roy bought another round of beers, and we were determined not to mention the war again that evening.

Apparently, Don Bradman scored 254 runs in his first test match against England in 1930 at Lords. A debate rapidly ensued about the greatest batsman of all time. My eyes glazed over, so I moved to the other end of the table with Janet.

"What are you and Barry doing about finding somewhere to live?"

"Haven't had time to look. We need to, Barry's flat's too far away. What will you do, Em? Will you both live in your house in Battersea?"

"It's convenient, but I'm not sure I want Frank to move in with me, not just yet."

"Why? I can't wait to move in with Barry."

"It's a commitment; it sort of makes things final."

"So what's Frank going to do now that we don't have an accommodation block in the hospital?"

"That's the problem, isn't it? If the bombing has ended, then he desperately needs to find somewhere, and I feel obliged to say come and live with me."

"You mean get married?"

"Well, that's what my parents would have expected."

"What about your parents' house in Balham? That's empty now, isn't it?"

"I wanted to talk to you about that, Jan. I know you and Barry are desperate to find somewhere, and I really wanted to offer it to you. The thing is, Beverley's also desperate for somewhere to live with Maurice."

"It's a kind thought and I love you for it, but Bev can't wait, can she? You must offer it to her."

"It's not my house to offer really, it's half my brother's. He did say we should rent it, so I'm sure he will agree. I wouldn't want you or Bev to pay me anything, but it's up to my brother; he's the banker."

"I wouldn't accept it rent-free, and I'm sure Beverley wouldn't either. You're too generous, Emma; you don't value money at all, do you?"

"Apart from the obvious at the moment, I don't want for anything."

"You're the most selfless person I know, you would give someone the clothes off your back, wouldn't you?"

"If the need was great, I suppose I would."

"No wonder your old patients call you the Angel of Balham. I think we should call you St Emma."

"You're making fun of me."

"No, Emma. I would never do that. You're an inspiration to us all. I'm just trying to tell you - I admire you more than anyone I've ever met."

"Well, I'm not sure I deserve that, but it's a really lovely thing to say."

"Do you remember when you first came to the hospital and I asked you for advice? You were shocked even to consider me living with Barry. Now listen to you, talking about living with Frank."

"I know, everything's so different now. We know how short life can be; what was important yesterday isn't important any more."

"So, what do you think is important now?"

"I'm still working that out. You're important to me, my work, and Frank, of course."

"You're evading the question, aren't you?"

"Am I?"

"I think what's important is to value the life we have. The trouble is that so many things get in the way. Life can be a struggle, especially now. It's easy to lose sight of what's important. I know that however bad my day is, it's still a day of my life, and I must make the most of it. It's Barry who's made me realise. I think about him all the time; he makes me so happy, and that happiness is always with me. Barry says I look at the world through rose-coloured glasses, and I do. You can find joy in anything if you know where to look. I can find joy in changing a bedpan. The joy is that I've done my job well, I've made a patient more comfortable, I've made a difference."

"Jan, you're amazing. You laugh and joke about everything, you never stop smiling, and then you say something as profound as that."

"That's not profound; that's just how it is. You have to carry the joy with you and apply it to everything you do. It was you who told me the whole world rejoices when a life is saved. I've seen you do that countless times, and I see it in your face every time. That's the joy I'm talking about."

"You're right; those are the best moments in my life."

"That's my point; living for the moment is fine, but what about the rest of your life? You have to capture the joy of the moment and take it with you. When I'm with Barry, I'm the happiest woman who's ever lived, and I carry that with me everywhere I go."

"You do, I can see you do. Does Barry realise how incredibly fortunate he is to have you?"

"Oi, Barry. Do you realise how fortunate you are to have me?"

"Every second of every day, Sweetheart," he shouted back, raising his glass.

Everyone laughed - that was typical of Janet. We all know her as the outspoken, carefree woman she professes to be. I wonder how many realise what lies beneath the carefree exterior. Knowing her changed my life; she showed me a world I didn't know existed.

"I can't be like you, Jan, but is it wrong to want what you have?"

"No, that's the whole point, I want you to have it. Perhaps you just need to work at it a bit harder."

"That's a Janet Walters reprimand, isn't it?"

"Well, maybe, just a bit."

"So, tell me then, how do I try harder?"

"Do you remember the shy, reserved Emma Stevenson who first arrived at the hospital?"

"I vaguely remember that person."

"You're still that same person. We don't change, we just discard a few things along the way."

"So I should discard some more things?"

"That's it. It's all just baggage. Work out what's important in life and dump the rest. Sigmund Freud spent his life working that out."

"You take for granted what the rest of us struggle to understand."

"There you are then; what did I tell you? I know these things."

I laughed, if only we could all be like her. Her simplistic view of life wasn't really simplistic at all. Janet's reasoning was flawless. We all go through life carrying the baggage that life has loaded onto us. Our past is there to inform us, not to weigh us down. If only it were that simple. The others had moved on from cricket; the conversation was now about Beverley and Maurice. Janet and I joined them.

"So, do you have wedding plans yet?" asked Frank.

"Well, he proposed, and I said yes. So I suppose that's a start."

"We can't leave it too long," said Maurice.

"You're not concerned about it all happening a bit quickly?"

"Not in the least, Frank. I was about to ask Bev to marry me, anyway. This just brings it forward a bit. What about you and Emma?"

"We're not rushing into anything, are we, Em?"

"No, hopefully, we can take our time. If Hitler takes his army into Russia, things might get a bit easier for us. For a while, at least."

Shirley and Roy hadn't known each other for all that long, but she sat looking at him with eyes that told their own story. Each of my friends had a well-defined path ahead of them. We didn't know what the future held, but they were looking forward to it anyway. I had so many things to think about and so many decisions; I envied the others for what appeared to be their clear vision of the future. Janet was so right. I needed to work out what's important in life and dump the rest.

# Chapter Fifty-Two
# July 1941

Roger

*"The cold light of day is that moment when you look back from a fresh perspective. It's when yesterday's expectation meets today's reality, two age-old protagonists that rarely sit comfortably together."*

It was the middle of July, and still, there were no more bombs. We regarded it as nothing more than a temporary respite, we just carried on as before. There was still circumstantial evidence to gather against Burrows, but we had enough to call a meeting and plan the way forward. It was a wet, gloomy day, befitting the subject matter. Jeff arrived late, hurrying in, clutching Burrows' war record. The rest of us sat in anticipation as he shook the raindrops off his coat and hat before placing them on the stand. Then he made us wait longer as he lit a fag and shook the smoking match in the air before discarding it in the ashtray.

"Come on, Jeff, what have you got?"

"You were dead right, Guv. Burrows wasn't a captain in the Cheshires. He joined the Cheshires but never rose above the rank of private. You'll never guess what he did."

"Oh, come on, Jeff."

"He volunteered as a stretcher bearer."

"What!"

"Yes, he volunteered immediately he was recruited."

"That doesn't sound right. It wasn't always the case, but stretcher bearers were often damn brave men; they just didn't want to take up arms. Are you telling me Burrows was a pacifist?"

"That's his war record. Mind you, it gave him contact with medical procedures. He would have seen a lot of surgery. Interestingly, he was medically discharged a few months early before the end of the war. Shell shock."

"Well, I didn't expect that. So we have a possible pacifist who saw so much of the last war that he broke down with shell shock. This doesn't sound like a psychopath, does it?"

"I've got something even more interesting," said Alfie. "Burrows also lied about not being married. He was married. He married Elizabeth Oldfield in 1913, about a year before the war. She died in 1919, a year after the war. The coroner's report says the cause of death was accidental. And get this, she fell from a first-floor window and succumbed to multiple injuries."

"Oh, well done, Alfie - that sounds more like our man. We need to find out about Elizabeth Oldfield."

"Already have, Guv. Her mother is still alive and living at the same address, so I found her quite easily. She doesn't believe her daughter fell by accident. She's adamant Burrows killed her. She didn't want to admit it, but eventually, she told me that her daughter had a child with another man while Burrows was away."

"Well, you know the next question, Alfie."

"No, the baby didn't survive beyond six months. It wasn't thought suspicious at the time. Infant mortality during that period was high partly due to the prevalence of feeding unpasteurised cows' milk. Obviously, it raises suspicion now."

"If you weren't so ugly, Alfie, I could kiss you. That's great work. What about you, Fleming?"

"I've spoken to several people he works with, and he's not liked. Two women described him as creepy."

"That fits with the neighbours that I spoke to. At least we can now keep a watch out for his car."

"What about friends, Fleming? Have you found any?"

"I've asked people in the local shops, in the three nearest pubs, and in the pub near the council buildings. I even asked the milkman and the postman. It's the same story as his work colleagues. This bloke is a loner."

"What do you think, Guv?" I asked Gerry.

"It's good work. He undoubtedly fits the profile. He's our number one suspect. We should bring him in for questioning."

"He's much more than that, Guv; he's our only suspect," replied Jeff.

"He's lied about just about everything, but that in itself isn't a crime. The thing is, from his perspective, he still has an outstanding victim; he wants to reenact the Mary Kelly murder. He'll already have a victim lined up for it. We need to let him know immediately that he's our chief suspect. He's not likely to admit it, but if he knows we're on to him, he might back off. We need him under surveillance."

"Bring him in today, Roger, for questioning. See if you can get a confession out of him."

"I think we should get an arrest warrant, even if we have to let him go. If we arrest him at his home address, we can search his house. He must be left in no doubt that we know it's him, and we'll be watching him. At least then he'll think twice about killing his last victim."

"I'll go along with that, but do it quickly, Roger."

We did it quickly, alright. We arrested him that evening, the moment he arrived home. Four of us then searched his house from top to bottom. The only remotely interesting thing we found were two books about the Whitechapel murders in his bookcase. I fully expected to find the list of names and addresses of his victims. We looked through every book and every hiding place but found nothing. His kitchen contained knives, but they were all blunt and not particularly pointed. His clothes didn't reveal a spot of blood. Everything was clean and tidy, far too tidy. I didn't believe it; he must have been ready for us.

Burrows protested like a scalded cat. We let him cool off in the cells overnight. Late that night, I drove home in complete darkness; it had been another incredibly long day. Jean was waiting at the doorstep of my house. There had been no bombs for weeks, but no one took it for granted. Many people continued using the shelters for the rest of the war. Jean was really anxious about the time and put her arms around me.

"Sorry, Jean, it's been a long day."

"What do you want to do? Shall we take a chance and stay here?"

"I know we shouldn't, but would you mind?"

"No, I hate it in that underground station. I've got a dried-up pork chop for you."

"That sounds exciting."

"Well, make the most of it. That's our meat ration gone for this week."

"Let's have a drink. I've got something to celebrate."

"What's that?"

"I've got a suspect in the cells for the Ripper murders."

"Oh, Roger, that's wonderful. I knew you'd catch him."

"I've arrested him, but we have no solid evidence at all. Unless he confesses, he'll be out again."

"Tell me about him."

"I will. I'll tell you everything, but would you mind if I didn't right now? I've had it all day, and I need a break."

Jean takes everything in her stride. She reached for my bottle of Johnny Walker Red Label without asking; I only had to smile, and she poured two glasses. I drank a large glass before the pork chop and another larger glass after. We sat on either side of my small kitchen table with our heads resting on our hands, elbows on the table. The washing up sat on the draining board, and the leaking tap dripped rhythmically into the sink. I was oblivious to it all. The whisky and the end of a long day combined to make me content just to sit and look at Jean. We talked about her day, observing the national mood. I leaned forward to ask a question, and she leaned forward to answer. I asked another question and slouched further across the table. Jean leaned forward until our heads touched. That was when it happened.

I don't know if I instigated it or she did. There is an indescribable look in a woman's eyes when she invites you to kiss her. I saw that look in Jean's hazel eyes. When you kiss someone for the first time, I mean really passionately kiss them, it's one of life's most special moments, and it has to be savoured. There can only ever be one first kiss; it should never be squandered. I looked into her eyes, and all the doubts melted away. At first, our lips did no more than touch, as if we were seeking each other's permission. Jean slowly closed her eyes as our lips came together in that long-anticipated first kiss. I explored every contour of her lips, and every second expressed what words were incapable of saying. It was a sublime moment; we were at the centre of the universe. Everything revolved around us.

Reluctantly, after what felt like an eternity, we broke apart. We looked at each other in silence; we had expressed everything that needed saying. I knew what that kiss meant, and so did Jean. Johnny Walker came between me and reason. I didn't stop to question any of it. We wanted each other, and we could answer those questions another day. I didn't say a word; I didn't want to lose the moment. We stood up, holding hands, and she led me towards my bedroom.

We were two people trapped in a whirlpool of desire. The passage of time drew us ever closer to the point of no return, to that place where the vortex finally separates us from all constraints. After months, perhaps years, we surrendered to the inevitable; we were consumed by desire. The moment I followed her through the bedroom door, I could no longer wait. I kissed her neck and enveloped her in my arms. I ran my hands intimately over her body and she arched her head back onto my shoulder. The feel of her was intoxicating. It is a fortunate couple indeed who can follow a sublime first kiss with a sublime first act of love. We were that couple.

Still half asleep the following morning, I turned my head expecting to see brunette hair spread over the pillow next to me. For just one waking second, the sight of Jean's blonde hair took me by surprise. It was a sudden jolt of reality. She opened her eyes with an inviting smile, and I instinctively kissed her. Marilyn was slightly built, you might almost say, skinny. Jean had what I considered the perfect female body. I found her impossible to turn away from; I had to embrace every inch of her.

We were late getting up; the day promised nothing that could entice me away, but eventually, we had to go down for breakfast. The cold light of day is that moment when you look back from a fresh perspective. It's when yesterday's expectation meets today's reality, two age-old protagonists that rarely sit comfortably together. I sat silently watching Jean slice the national loaf into thin slices. She looked at me without saying a word as she placed them under the grill. With a stroke of the flint, the gas ignited with a bang. A small square of butter and half a jar of marmalade waited on the table.

The kettle boiled with a whistle, and Jean poured the boiling water into the teapot. I silently watched her every move. She then dropped the burnt toast onto a plate, blowing the tips of her fingers. We exchanged glances as I poured the tea, but still hadn't said a word. She sat opposite me with her dressing gown more open than closed and her hair loosely held back with a large hair clip. Reality and expectation sat comfortably together that morning; there was no cold light of day. Jean was the first to speak.

"We waited a long time for that, didn't we?"

"We did. Are you sure it's what you want, what we both want?"

"Are you kidding? It was simply wonderful, Roger."

"Last night or this morning?"

"Both, you idiot. I don't know what I expected, but it was nothing like that."

"Yes, it was something special, wasn't it?"

"It was more than special, Roger. When do you think you'll be back tonight?"

"As soon as possible."

We did experience something extraordinary. I knew Jean thought about Dave, and we were both in Marilyn's bed. Despite the memories, what we had between us couldn't be denied. Jean is a very attractive woman. I admit I had occasionally wondered what it would be like. Before that night, I hadn't been sitting waiting fifteen years for Jean. But after that night, fifteen years felt like a long time to have waited. It seems we were two lost souls, united in mutual desire. I left her that morning with questions littering the house, but nothing was about to break the spell.

Gerry's face provided a poor substitute when I arrived at the station. I could still feel Jean's body in my arms. That was when the cold light of day really did stream in through the window. I had to interview Burrows. Jeff and I discussed our tactics.

"How do you want to handle him, Guv?"

"How sure are we that it's him, Jeff?"

"We can't be certain; we have no evidence, but it feels like him, doesn't it?"

"It does to me. I've seen a lot of murderers; you get a sixth sense for it, and I'm sure it's him."

"What if we're wrong?" asked Alfie.

"We could be in trouble. Against that is the possibility we might save a woman's life."

"I agree, the stakes are high. Let's try to force it out of him."

"My thoughts exactly, Jeff. We have to assume it's him."

I even felt uncomfortable walking into the same room with Burrows. He sat there expressionless, wearing the same suit we arrested him in. I doubt he slept well in the cell. In fact, I doubt he had any sleep at all. Knowing his temperament, I assumed he would be writhing in anger and struggling to control it. My job was to let that demon lose. He sat on one side of a bare wooden table in an otherwise empty room next to the cells. A single light bulb hung from the ceiling, and one of our largest uniformed PCs stood looking down at him. Jeff and I abruptly sat opposite him and thumped our paperwork on the table.

"I'm Detective Inspector Pritchard, and this is my colleague, Detective Constable Payne. You have had the charges read to you, so why did you do it, Burrows? Why did you have to kill all those women?"

"I didn't kill anyone, and that's all I will say until I've seen my solicitor. I've done nothing; therefore, you can have no proof that I did. You have no right whatsoever to hold me."

"We know all about you, Burrows. You lied to us about being a captain in the Cheshires, didn't you? You were a stretcher bearer. Were you a pacifist, Burrows, or just a coward?"

He tried hard to conceal his reaction, but the word 'coward' got a response. Having tried not to make eye contact, he instantly stared at me with narrowed eyes before averting his gaze again.

"You lied about not being married as well, didn't you? We know all about your wife. Played around, did she, while you were away? Made you look like a right fool, didn't she? You killed her as well, didn't you? Is that where you got the taste for it? Or was it the baby? Was that the start of it?"

He looked as if he was about to explode. The veins on his forehead pulsated, and his eyes stared right through me. His breathing rate visibly increased and sweat appeared on his forehead and palms. Burrows looked as guilty as hell. I goaded him about his war record and how weak he must be to be discharged with shell shock. I described how sick he was, getting his pleasure from carving up dead women. I had never seen so much obvious pent-up rage. The fact that he didn't crack told me he also had unnatural self-control. I tried another tack.

"Very clever, giving us clues by copying the Ripper murders. You need us to know it's you, don't you? And that clue with the women's initials, that's brilliant. You really hoped we would spot that, didn't you? What you didn't expect was that we would track you down through the Register. You want to be caught, don't you, so that everyone will know how clever you are? You want to be talked about in the same breath as Jack the Ripper."

He didn't flinch, so Jeff tried another approach. "You're finished, Burrows; you'll never get the opportunity to kill that last victim. There will be no Mary Kelly for you. You tried to copy Jack the Ripper, but you failed. People will see you for what you are, Burrows, a failure."

His eyes widened for a second, and he clenched his fist tighter. His self-control returned a fleeting moment later. It showed me that completing his list of Ripper murders remained important to him. I was sure he craved notoriety, but that involved being exposed. It was the only weakness he showed us. I remained convinced that he didn't crack because he still clung to his need to kill the last victim. Jeff and I persevered for hours, trying every approach we could think of. Occasionally, he answered with one or two words, denying everything. I had to demonstrate as much self-control as he did, and he was better at it than me. We eventually gave up for the day and returned him to his cell.

"He's as guilty as hell, isn't he, Roger?" said Gerry.

"He gives me the creeps," said Jeff.

"What do we do, beat it out of him?"

"If I thought that would get us a case in court, Roger, I'd say it was a good idea. He's almost inviting us to push harder, isn't he?"

"That's why it wouldn't work. Let's keep him as long as we can. Deprive him of sleep and try again, but he won't admit anything. We'll have to release him."

"I think you're right," replied Jeff.

"We need him under surveillance 24 hours a day, but we don't have the resources, do we? We must be as visible as we can. He must always suspect we're watching him, even when we're not. We need him to think we have people behind every curtain. He must suspect his neighbours and work colleagues of watching him. Let's question his neighbours and work colleagues again. Everyone needs to be suspicious of him."

"The newspaper can do a good job of that if we give them the go-ahead."

"Good idea, Alfie, get onto it. Nothing slanderous; report that a suspect will be released due to insufficient evidence. If a photographer by chance happens to be here when we release him, they might just get a photograph of the suspect."

"That might work, but there's a limit for how long."

Gerry was right; we couldn't watch Burrows indefinitely. We needed to find out as much as possible about Burrows. My research confirmed what Professor Rawlings told me. The key to Burrows' psychosis would lie in one or all of three areas: his childhood, his army service, or his wife and child. My guess was that aspects of all three came to fruition when he found his wife had been unfaithful. Very often during a criminal investigation, if it looks like a duck and quacks like a duck, then it's a duck.

The obvious conclusion about Burrows was that his wife, being unfaithful, triggered his psychotic hatred of women. It wasn't a coincidence that he killed young married women with husbands in the forces. Each of them likely represented a reenactment of his wife. In Burrows' twisted mind, mutilating those women provided revenge for his wife being unfaithful.

I left work that evening with an uneasy feeling about Burrows. I hadn't dealt with anyone like him before. He had to be quite mad, but that part of him coexisted alongside another person. I didn't get to Burrows the man; I could only question the thing in front of me. That thing was evil, leaving me very uneasy. My worst-case scenario was if he would continue to evade us, and worst of all, that he might get away with it. I made a pledge to pursue him for as long as it took. I would never let that monster get away with it.

When I left Jean that morning, all I could think about was getting back to her. I arrived home thinking only of Burrows. Jean wore one of her dresses that she knew I liked. It was a red polka dot dress with short sleeves. She had gone to a lot of trouble; she looked beautiful. The moment I opened the door, she threw herself into my arms. It was precisely what I dreamed of as I left that morning.

"What's wrong, Roger? Have I done something wrong?"

"Look at you, you're a dream come true, Jean. It's nothing to do with you. It's that man, Burrows. Give me time."

Jean lifted off my coat and then my hat, placing them on the hall stand. Then she led me by the hand and sat me down on the settee. She gently removed my glasses, followed by my tie, and loosened my collar. I heard the welcome sound of whisky being poured into a glass behind me. She returned, taking a mouthful before placing the glass next to me. Jean then leaned over and kissed me, sharing the taste of the whisky, wet and inviting on her lips.

This was not the Jean I had viewed from a distance for fifteen years. I didn't recognise this woman at all. Then she lifted the glass to my lips, and I sipped the whisky. She put the glass down and kissed me again, once more intimately sharing the taste with her tongue. A part of me was completely mesmerised by this beautiful, seductive woman that I hardly recognised. Burrows was already fading from my mind as she began undoing my shirt buttons. She undid the first and second buttons before offering the whisky glass to my lips again. I was only allowed a sip before her lips met mine again. She then returned to my buttons, looking up at me with an ever-increasing smile. I couldn't even remember who Burrows was.

# Chapter Fifty-Three
# September 1941

Emma

*"Friendship is like oxygen. A candle burns so brightly
in its presence, it lights up your life."*

The summer of 1941 was significant for three things. The continuous bombing of Britain's cities had ended. No matter how hard life remained in its aftermath, it was better than living beneath the falling bombs. The second significant thing was the reason the bombing had stopped. Hitler did as expected and invaded Russia. 'Operation Barbarossa' started on June 22nd with the largest land invasion force of the Second World War. We were relieved that it diverted Hitler's attention away from us, but as time went on, its significance became ever more crucial to the war's outcome. By late summer, German forces had crushed all before them, and it looked like a repeat of the conquest of Europe.

The third significant event was that Frank proposed to me. The poor man lived hand to mouth in the hospital while I had a home to go to. Perhaps it was inevitable; I didn't consciously decide to invite Frank to live with me. It just happened. One evening, we returned to my house on Birley Street as we often did, but this time he didn't leave. Janet is irresistibly drawn to Barry; when they're forced apart, she climbs the walls. I convinced myself that other people didn't behave that way. Frank and I didn't behave like that - he didn't knock down my front door to get to me. He just brought his toothbrush one evening and stayed. After about three weeks of us waking up together, he casually proposed one morning.

"Don't you think we should get married, Em?"

"Are you proposing to me, Frank?"

"Yes, I suppose I am. Living together like this isn't very conventional, is it?"

"Do we need to be conventional?"

"It is the accustomed thing to do in these circumstances."

"If my parents were alive, it certainly would be. You'd even have to ask my father's permission first. I'm sure he would have approved, Frank, but they're not here now. There's nobody to judge us, and everything has changed now."

"But wouldn't you like to be married?"

"At some point, yes, I'd like a family; I want it all, Frank. But now isn't the time, is it? I want to know we can live our lives in peace. I want to plan for the future with the certainty that there is a future to look forward to."

"Perhaps the uncertainty in the world is telling us we should enjoy what we have today."

"That's the point, Frank; we're enjoying what we have today without worrying about how uncertain the future is."

"That sounds like a 'no', then."

"Don't say it like that. It's not 'no', it's 'not now'."

Frank accepted that, and we settled, as did everyone else, into an uneasy post-Blitz period. Everything was in short supply, especially food, clothes and housing. Despite the hardships, the spirit that endured during the worst of times continued stronger than ever. Churchill told us the future of the British way of life depended upon us winning the Battle of Britain. He said the survival of Western Europe and Christian civilisation was at stake; he said we would never surrender. His words ran through the British people like the words in a stick of Brighton rock. To an outsider, Britain, as typified by the East End of London, might have appeared to be a defeated nation. The reality was quite different for those of us who survived the Blitz - we knew we had won.

We did what we could to bring order back to the remainder of the hospital; we made up for what we lacked in assets with determination. Medical provisions were in short supply, but with our capacity drastically reduced, we had enough for our needs. Nothing remained the same, and it would never be the same again. Society itself had changed. Nearly all the young men had enlisted, most of the younger women worked in ammunition or armament factories, and a huge number joined the Land Army.

We all had one thing in common: we survived the worst that Hitler could throw at us. In every aspect of society, the spirit of unity was stronger than ever.

The other change affecting us all was the dismantling of social norms. Before the war, I wouldn't have dreamed of living with Frank before we were married. People everywhere realised they had a life to live and a duty to live it to the fullest. Our re-emergent social life revolved around the pubs and one or two London clubs and theatres. Dance halls remained very popular, but Frank said he didn't dance. For me, it was a brave new world.

I spoke to Andrew again about renting our parents' house, and to my surprise, he agreed to a low rent for my friends Beverley and Maurice. Before the war, he would have used phrases such as 'optimisation of assets'. When I asked him, he just said, 'Yes, of course.' My brother had changed. When I told Beverley, her response lit up my life. She was so happy; it gave me joy far in excess of any amount of rent.

Their wedding day had been decided, and it seemed the entire hospital looked forward to it. Being slightly rushed, they agreed upon a brief ceremony at the Registry Office. A reception at the Highcroft Hotel in Westminster would follow that. Maurice knew this hotel, and it had the enormous advantage of still being there. About a week before the date in September, we all had an evening together in the Tavern. Our evenings out were different; we no longer felt the need to rush there and back in daylight.

We still walked across the bridge arm in arm as a group, but it was no longer fear which united us. Roy met Shirley at the hospital, and Janet and Barry came straight from the station and met us there. Barry hadn't had any leave for three weeks, and if Janet had been a spider, she would have been climbing the ceiling as well as the walls. They tore themselves apart early that evening especially to be with us at the Tavern. She arrived looking rosy faced with her eye makeup slightly adrift. Barry tried to appear calm and collected, while Janet puffed up her cheeks as if she had run all the way.

"You made it, Barry," Frank said.

"Yes, sorry, we were held up."

"Held up." Janet replied, "I don't remember you holding me up."

Anyone else would have tried to conceal what they had just been doing, but not Janet. We all laughed and I doubt I was the only one who felt just a little envious. Janet would usually be centre-stage most evenings, but that place had been reserved for Beverley and Maurice. It must have been difficult for them to plan everything so soon after the Blitz. With everything in short supply, relying on anything beyond the Registrar became impossible. We all helped where possible, but Maurice was fortunate to have a friend at the Highcroft Hotel.

"Are you confident everything is in place, Maurice?" asked Leo.

"No, the right word is hope. But we have grounds for being hopeful."

"What about guests?"

"We're keeping it small, only family and close friends," replied Beverley.

"Is that us?" asked Janet.

"Of course, it's you lot, dopey."

"Your family lives quite local, Bev," said Shirley. "What about yours, Maurice?"

"They live in Surrey, but I've arranged for them to stay overnight at the Highcroft."

"How did your mum take the news of her grandchild, Bev?" asked Janet.

"I've only just told her."

"But look at you," I said, "you're five months."

"I know. I kept putting it off because I knew what her reaction would be."

"Well, was it as bad as you thought?" asked Shirley.

"Worse. She's absolutely mortified. She says I've disgraced the family."

"Oh, I'm so sorry, Bev," I said, "is your father the same?"

"No, my dad was wonderful. He says Maurice is a fine young man, and they got on so well together when they met. He says we make a perfect couple, and as long as we're marrying for love and not convenience, then we have his full blessing."

"Oh, that's lovely," said Janet, "that's what fathers should say."

"So what about your mother?" asked Frank. "Is that going to be a problem?"

"I think my dad will talk her around. I hope so anyway."

"I shouldn't worry, Bev," I said. "I haven't met a grandmother yet who didn't melt at the sight of her grandchild."

"That's what I'm hoping, Em; I'm sure you're right."

"I expect your mother would be mortified to know that the pregnancy rate has skyrocketed during the Blitz. It's as if the entire nation has lived for the moment."

"I'm not sure it would help to tell her that, Leo."

"When will you leave the hospital, Bev?" asked Shirley.

"Matron has been brilliant; I can't believe how she has bent all the rules for me. I don't think I can go on concealing it much longer. Now that we have a place to live together, I can leave any time, but I'll hang on as long as possible. I'm really going to miss it."

"We work like dogs in appalling conditions, the Germans are trying to kill us, and you're going to miss it?" said Janet.

"Yes, it's been my life. I love working with you, Emma, with all of you. I'm going to miss you all so much."

"I'm not sure you'll have the time to miss us," said Frank. "I suspect you're going to be rather busy."

"You won't be free of us, Bev," I said, "we'll all be regular visitors."

"You promise?"

"Now, who's being dopey?" replied an indignant Janet.

I could understand how Beverley felt. The more adversity people face, the more they come together. We had been through hell together; we almost died together, and there was nothing we wouldn't do for each other. We had a friendship rooted in the dust and rubble of despair, and it's grown stronger every day. Friendship is like oxygen. A candle burns so brightly in its presence, it lights up your life.

# Chapter Fifty-Four
# December 1941

Roger

*"A new passion is like a pure mountain stream, rushing over rapids and tumbling into sparkling pools. It remains untainted by the many tributaries that will eventually transform it into a slow, meandering river."*

1941 came to a close in a maelstrom of mixed emotions. We had to release Burrows even though I knew he was the Ripper. We did everything we could to make him feel under pressure. His photograph in the Evening Standard wasn't ideal; he wore his hat with his coat collar turned up. The fact remained, however, that he couldn't be sure he wouldn't be recognised. Doubt is a seed that, once planted, takes root in the darkest recesses of your mind. It devours confidence, and its bitter fruit is fear.

If Burrows thought people were watching him, then the seed of doubt would confirm that they were. In his mind, his neighbours and work colleagues suspected him. Despite my certainty that he was the Ripper, we simply couldn't mount a continual watch on Burrows; we didn't have the resources. Our list of unsolved crimes had grown throughout the Blitz. Included in that list were many other murders disguised as bomb victims.

My life slipped effortlessly into two contrasting halves. By day, I waded through the swamp of lies and deceit that is the language of all criminals. By night, I was consumed by a passion I didn't even recognise in myself. Jean and I were like two twenty-year-olds, besotted with the first love of our life. A new passion is like a pure mountain stream, rushing over rapids and tumbling into sparkling pools. It remains untainted by the many tributaries that will eventually transform it into a slow, meandering river.

Neither of us had ever experienced anything like it before. It was both beautiful and mysterious. Beautiful because our passion was unambiguous. It had a purity about it. Mysterious because why had we not experienced this wondrous thing before? How could we have lived our lives to this point without it? We chose not to discuss our children or what would happen when they came home. Dave and Marilyn weren't discussed, either. We simply drank from that mountain stream. Intoxicated by desire, we allowed ourselves to be swept along by the current. In a world where fear and deprivation replaced any semblance of normality, Jean and I shared an oasis of pure joy.

We retreated away into our own little world. Gerry and Margaret shared an occasional drink with us, as did Jeff and Norma, but we had yet to stray far into the desert beyond our oasis. We had almost forgotten what it was like to meet other people. So, when at the beginning of December, Emma telephoned me at home, her voice came as a pleasant surprise. I hadn't heard from her for some time.

"Hello, Roger, it's Emma, Emma Stevenson."

"Emma, how nice to hear from you. How are you?"

"I'm well, thank you. Roger, do you remember when you told me your friend Rachel's circumstances might have changed? Well, Leo has asked me to ask you about her. He can't get her out of his mind."

"I can understand that. She's an incredibly attractive woman, isn't she? Her change of circumstances that I mentioned. Well, the fact is her husband died a few months ago."

"Oh, the poor woman, she must be distraught."

"Well, actually, no, they weren't close. Rachel was sort of expecting it."

"In that case, do you think she might want to meet Leo again?"

"I've no idea, Emma, but I can ask. Jean sees her quite often. I'll ask her to find out."

"I knew you'd sort it out, Roger. I would love for us to meet up again. Can we arrange something before Christmas?"

"Of course, I'd like that. Leave it with me, I'll telephone you back. Do you have a home telephone number?"

"Not yet, I'm still not reconnected. I suppose they have had one or two interruptions. Telephone me at the hospital; we have the line working again now. Evelyn will get a message to me."

I welcomed the prospect of a social evening with her and her friends. As for Rachel, Jean initially befriended her as much out of kindness as anything else, but now they had become good friends. Jean already knew the answer to Emma's question. Rachel had asked her about Leo, so I wasted no time telephoning Emma, and we arranged an evening at the Fox and Hounds. Jean immediately went into a spin about what to wear.

"What should I wear, Roger?"

"Don't worry, Jean, it's only a drink in the Fox. You look lovely whatever you wear."

"Do they know about us? Do they know we live together?"

"No, I don't suppose they do. Why? Does it matter?"

"Of course, it matters. It matters what people think of me."

"You are silly. Times have changed, you know. All they'll see is this lovely woman I can't stop smiling adoringly at, and they'll all know that we're made for each other."

"Roger, you always say the right thing; come here."

A date was set for Wednesday, December the 10th, and I was looking forward to it. With Burrows reluctantly placed on the back burner, we started to investigate the backlog of what, on the face of it, looked like domestic murders. Evidence gathering during the Blitz was haphazard at best, especially when the circumstances made the victim look like a bomb fatality. We only really discovered the most obvious cases. It would be fair to say that several domestic murders went undetected.

Some were blindingly obvious, such as the man who stabbed his wife six times and then laid her out on a nearby bomb site with which they had no connection. Others, like the ball pein hammer murder, required proper detective work. Most of them involved a split-second moment of madness after a couple's home had been destroyed. One woman seized the opportunity to rid herself of her husband as they stood in the rubble of what had once been their house. She hit him repeatedly with a brick, and it would have looked compelling had the incident not occurred in broad daylight after they returned home from a public shelter.

The looting stopped abruptly the moment the bombs stopped falling. It wasn't a moment too soon. Looting became ubiquitous; we even arrested one or two ARP wardens and firemen. For the majority, who wouldn't dream of stealing possessions from victims already traumatised by the bombing, looting incited enormous anger. There's something very disturbing about the human psyche that we can transform into predators seeking prey amongst ourselves. It provokes a primordial revulsion. There can be few things less attractive than a rabid dog that devours its own limbs.

We achieved some arrests on our patch, but it relied upon catching them red-handed or in possession of the stolen goods. Despite the difficulties, 4500 cases were tried at the Old Bailey. Now that the bombing had ended, for the moment at least, we were left with a long list of stolen items to watch out for. I found our lack of manpower and all the disruption deeply frustrating from a policing perspective. We needed to maintain law and order; public morale depended upon it, but we were severely limited in what we could do.

Our evening out with Emma and her friends was a welcome distraction; I looked forward to it. Jean continued to worry about what to wear as if she had lots to choose from. She eventually appeared in my favourite red polka-dot dress. On the evening of the 10th, she insisted we should arrive first so that she wouldn't be seen arriving in her coat. I thought it was a fine coat, but apparently not. We had barely arrived and taken off our coats before Emma arrived.

The last time I saw her, she looked as though she had been dragged through an abattoir by her hair. This time, she looked much more presentable. When she removed her coat, she was wearing a smart but modest navy-blue dress. Her hair was not loosely tied back with surgical tweezers holding it in place. It hung in waves down almost to her shoulders and stood up from her forehead with the nearly ubiquitous victory roll. She wore little or no makeup, in complete contrast to Janet, who looked as vibrant as the last time I saw her. You had to like Janet; her cheeky personality was genuine and warm. Shirley was another lovely woman, defined by a mop of naturally curly blonde hair and blue eyes.

Emma seemed much more outgoing than the last time we met in the Fox and Hounds. She walked straight up and kissed my cheek; I was taken aback. She did the same to Jean. Her boyfriend, Frank, shook my hand and reminded me of Barry and Roy's names. Leo wore a fabulous suit and a jaunty fedora hat worn at just the right angle. He was a very sophisticated-looking young man. They were all smartly dressed, and the RAF boys were in uniform. The only exception was Frank, who seemed to have the same dress sense I had. The women had gone to a lot of trouble, so perhaps Jean was right. She looked fabulous despite all of her worries about which clothes to wear. Although she was a bit older than the other women, you wouldn't have noticed. Unlike the others, Emma obviously didn't feel the need to compete.

I bought us an expensive round of drinks, and the camaraderie of the medics was infectious. They were a good bunch, determined to enjoy their evening. Janet seemed to be their cheerleader. They bounced fun and ideas off her. The evening had only just started when Rachel appeared at the door. She slipped off her stylish coat and hat to reveal a sight few in the Fox and Hounds would ever have seen. Her dress was royal blue and fitted everywhere. I don't understand fashion, but that dress would have looked captivating on a manikin. On Rachel, it was something else entirely. I probably only imagined it, but I thought for a second that the entire pub fell silent at the sight of her. In that period of acute shortages, of make-do-and-mend clothes, Rachel appeared to be an apparition.

She was a mere 22 years old, tall, dark-haired, and exotic. Had I been a 22-year-old man, my eyes would have been like saucers. As it was, Jean gave me a dig in the ribs. Then I noticed Leo's eyes; I recognised that expression. In that dress, Rachel walked, or more correctly, wiggled across the room. She came to me first, put her arms around me, and planted a kiss on my cheek. Anyone else would have said hello in the usual way, but not Rachel. She whispered close to my ear so that her lips touched me.

"It's lovely to see you, Roger. How are you?"

This silly 35-year-old suddenly started behaving like a 22-year-old. Jean saved me from further embarrassment with a hug for Rachel. Then Rachel went around each of our friends one at a time, resembling the Queen at a garden party. The RAF boys were like me, even down to the dig in the ribs from Janet. Lastly, she came to Leo, and the two stood looking at each other as if they were founding members of a self-appreciation society. She didn't leave his side for the rest of the evening. I instantly saw how ideally suited they were. Both young, both absurdly good-looking, and both fully in possession of whatever that elusive thing is they call style and sophistication. I looked at Emma, and we both smiled, thinking the same thing. Barry wisely changed the subject.

"How's Beverley and Maurice?"

"She's as stately as a galleon," laughed Janet.

I gave Emma a quizzical look, and she replied. "She's Mrs Hargreaves now and nearly nine months pregnant."

"Oh, I didn't know. That was quick work."

"Very quick."

Glasses were raised to Beverley and Maurice, with huge smiles to accompany them. Obviously, events had moved on apace, but they all seemed delighted about it, so I joined in wishing them good fortune. They described the wedding and the reception at a Westminster hotel. I could imagine all the difficulties with the rationing, but the accounts they gave made it sound like a wonderful day. There had been some kind of problem with Beverley's mother, and apparently its resolution became the high point of the reception. They reminisced between themselves until the conversation returned to the unavoidable subject of the war.

"What about the Japanese attack on Pearl Harbor? We didn't see that coming, did we?"

"It's immensely significant," replied Frank. "Now the Americans are involved, it's a different ball game."

"There's a lot of talk on the base about it," said Roy. "Frank's right; this will change the course of the war."

"I hope you mean for the better," said Shirley.

"This war is all about resources: food, fuel, ships, aeroplanes, tanks. You name it - it all requires industrial might," I said. "With the industrial might of America on our side, we can, for the first time, out-compete Germany."

The ensuing conversation was lively and well-informed. Hitler's costly war in Russia hadn't escaped their attention either. We entered the scenario of the ultimate defeat of Hitler, and was it going to be possible? Warrant Officer Barry Roberts was exceptionally well informed; he said there was already talk of us mounting an invasion of Europe. I didn't want to mention that I had met the Lord President of the Council and War Cabinet member, Sir John Anderson. Our conversation was confidential, and an invasion of Europe was not a part of my remit. My intention, to not mention it, failed.

"What did Sir John Anderson say about it, Roger?" asked Jean in all innocence.

"Do you get to talk to the Government, Roger?" asked Barry.

"Not as a rule, no, but lately, I have had occasion to speak to Sir John."

"Is that Anderson, as in the Anderson air raid shelter?" asked Shirley.

"The very same man. He's been really helpful, I must say."

"Tell them what you've done, Roger," said Jean.

"I've been constantly putting him under pressure via the Police Commissioner about the underground shelters. Finally, he bypassed the Commissioner and now talks to me directly."

"What have the shelters got to do with police work?" asked Janet.

"Nothing at all, other than I use them like everyone else. No, the thing is, I've seen the appalling conditions, and Jean shows me her reports for her mass observation diary. I've been able to inform the minister. We need to convert some of the deep underground stations into proper habitable shelters with decent amenities. He's taken that on board, and as promised, the work has already started."

"Well done, Roger," said an admiring Emma.

"I just put forward some suggestions, that's all."

"Did he say anything about invasion plans?" asked Roy, changing the subject.

"Well, actually, he did. He told me in confidence, but I can't see that something of that scale amounts to a state secret, especially when you and Barry say the same thing. Winston Churchill has told the War Cabinet that an invasion is now our chief priority."

"Bloody hell!" exclaimed Janet. "All this bombing and destruction, and he talks about invading Germany. Is that remotely credible?"

"Not now," I replied, "something of that magnitude will take years to plan and prepare for. It's the only way the civilised world will get rid of Hitler."

"Well, what a turnaround."

"We can thank Barry, Roy and the RAF," said Frank. "If we had lost the Battle of Britain, it wouldn't be us launching an invasion."

Frank was right, and it provoked enthusiastic discussion among the men. Janet sparked another debate about rationing and the shortage of food and clothes. The debate merged into two groups, with Jean telling them what she had learned about rationing from her mass observation study. Emma caught my eye and sat next to me.

"You and Jean look very happy together, Roger."

"We are, Emma. We've become very close recently."

"I can see that. She's a lovely lady, isn't she?"

"She is; we've found something I didn't expect to find between us, and we're enjoying being together."

"That's intriguing; what did you find, may I ask?"

"Well, you may ask, but it would be embarrassing to tell you."

"Oh, I'm sorry. Oh dear, yes, I understand. Good for you, Roger."

"You're not shocked?"

"Janet's my advisor when it comes to personal affairs. So, no, I'm not at all shocked. I think it's wonderful."

"You've changed, haven't you? I used to think you were very reserved."

"I was, I admit it, but now I'm trying not to be."

"Well, you don't have to try hard on my behalf; I liked you the way you were."

"You're a lovely man, Roger. I couldn't wait to come over and have one of our conversations."

"So tell me, the last time we spoke, you were unsure about your relationship with Frank. Is that all resolved now?"

She thought for a moment, looking at me over her glasses, before taking a deep breath. "We live together now. There you are, I've told you, and I'm not embarrassed. Well, not a lot, anyway."

"Wonderful, I'm pleased for you. How is it; are you enjoying your life together?"

"Yes, it's fine."

"That doesn't sound very enthusiastic."

"I don't know what to expect from a relationship. My problem is Janet. Look at her with Barry. They're all over each other, all the time. She constantly talks about it, and I think I should be like her."

"We can't be like someone else; we are who we are."

"I wish I could be sure. Who wouldn't want what she has - is that wrong?"

"What a question. Superficially, I would say yes, that's wrong, you're different people. But that's a nuanced question. When you say you want what she has, what you mean is you want to share the same experience that she feels with Barry. That's a different thing altogether because it takes two to create that. In those circumstances, a man and a woman can be more than the sum of their parts. Who knows what might result, but Janet's experience will always differ from someone else's."

"I enjoy our conversations, Roger. Who else could I ask such a question and receive such an answer? You see things so clearly."

"We do invariably end up discussing things I wouldn't discuss with anyone else."

"I agree, although this is probably not the time and place for it."

"No, you're right. We should meet up, just the two of us, perhaps lunch or something one day."

"Yes, sometime after Christmas; we mustn't leave it so long."

She was right, of course; it wasn't the time or place for serious conversations that invariably arise whenever we met. I found her to be such an engaging person; her blend of humility, combined with generosity and integrity, was a rare combination in my experience. Emma wouldn't even know what it was to be regarded with respect and admiration, but it surrounded her like an aura. She attempted to change the subject, asking me about our progress with the 'Blackout Ripper' murders, and everyone wanted to know about it.

"We've got a strong suspect, and we're keeping a close eye on him."

"Why don't you arrest him?" asked Janet.

"We have no evidence, but I'm pretty sure it's him. Now the bombing seems to have ended for the time being, I don't think we need to worry about him for the moment."

"Do you mean he's got away with it?"

"No, Leo. As long as I'm on the case, he hasn't got away with it. I won't rest until he faces justice. I can promise you that."

"You said that with a lot of conviction, Roger," said Rachel.

"Yes, I mean it. One way or another, I'll get him."

"When Roger says he's going to do something, it happens," said Jean.

Our evening continued with the conversation leaping from one topic to another. They were an engaging crowd; Jean seemed to get on well with them. Rachel and Leo probably didn't want any other company, but I felt I needed to talk to her about Ezra. I wouldn't mention it in front of Leo, but I wanted to give her the opportunity if she wanted to. I pulled a chair up next to them.

"How are you, Rachel?"

"I'm fine, Roger, really I am."

"How's Joey? I haven't seen him for a few weeks."

"You should come and visit him. He needs company at the moment."

"I will; it's been an awful time for him."

"He told me everything about Ezra. I know what you had to do. I want you to know that I don't blame you."

"I didn't want it to end like that, Rachel. If it could have been any other way, I would have taken it."

"I know that as sure as I know the sun will rise tomorrow. I trust you Roger, and so does Joey."

"Do you know about this, Leo?"

"Rachel has just been telling me. It all sounds incredible; it seems like another world to me."

"It is another world, Leo, which is why I'm delighted Rachel has met you."

"You really watch out for me, don't you, Roger?"

"Yes, I suppose I do."

"Roger means that, Leo, so you'd better treat me right."

We laughed about it, but there was a ring of truth about it. Joey doted on her, and that was good enough for me. Having left them to their own devices, I sat again with Jean. What Emma said about Janet and Barry became ever more apparent, they were inseparable. I doubted they loved each other more than any other couple might. The difference was how Janet demonstrated the fact. Emma and Frank didn't seem to have the same connection, but then she wasn't like Janet. Jean and I didn't behave that way in public either. I began to understand the influence that Janet had on Emma. But, as Emma said, who wouldn't want what Janet had?

When the evening ended, as we started putting on our coats, I looked at Rachel and Leo - they looked as though they had just walked out of a fashion parade. In that time of conspicuous shortages, they stood out from the crowd, something that had already got Rachel into trouble. On the surface at least, they were ideally suited for each other, and I was pleased for them. They had both been through hell and so it seemed fitting they might find happiness together.

Emma was the first to say goodnight; as we left, she gave me a hug. "Don't forget, Roger, we're going to meet up after Christmas."

"I won't forget."

"And stop smoking those cigarettes," she called back as she walked away.

"Yes, Doctor."

Then Rachel put her arms around me. "Bless you for getting me together with Leo, and thank you for being my guardian angel, Roger."

"You seem to get on well with him."

"Thanks to you and Jean, yes. Between ourselves, I think he's wonderful."

Janet had drunk too much; she hung off my shoulder until Barry relieved me of her. Shirley insisted we should all meet again soon, and I eagerly agreed. I shook hands with Leo, Barry, Roy, and finally Frank. He was a nice enough chap, but he kept himself to himself. He was about ten years older than me, so I wondered if that was the difference. I wasn't able to strike up any rapport with him. I suspected it was Frank's reserve that attracted Emma in the first place. They would have been two of a kind. Emma had changed, though. She was trying to be more outgoing; I wondered if Frank would join her on that path. Jean and I left arm in arm.

"I saw you drooling over Rachel, you silly sod."

"Very true, but did you see her drooling over me?"

"No, I don't need to worry on that score."

"Am I so past it, then?"

"You're not past it at all, but you're mine. So take me home."

# Chapter Fifty-Five
# Spring 1942

## Emma

*"A baby is a new beginning, a new human being who needs to be loved and nurtured and led by the hand into the world of the future. It's an onerous responsibility, especially the world of the future."*

1942 was perhaps the darkest year of the war. Having survived the Blitz, we thought we were over the worst, but the tightening grip of world war pushed Britain to the very limit. In the spring, the Germans launched another series of bombing raids across Britain, including historic towns such as Exeter, Bath, York, and Canterbury. Once again, we spent our nights sheltering back in the basement. The war in the Far East against the Japanese proved to be a disaster, with one major defeat after another. In North Africa, the fortress that was Tobruk survived eight months of siege, and now it fell to Rommel's Panzers in just two days. Winston Churchill found himself subject to a vote of confidence.

Rationing continued to tighten its grip upon society like a vice forever turning the screw. Many people struggled at little more than subsistence level. We made do and mended, but British society was being severely tested. Everything now came to Britain by sea via the Western Approaches. Ensuring our critical supply line continued became known as the Battle of the Atlantic; it would be the most protracted conflict of the war. In London and other cities, we were still recovering from the Blitz. Somehow, despite everything, including the latest wave of bombing, life continued. Above all, we were alive, which was something we no longer took for granted; we celebrated it.

Beverley gave birth to a beautiful baby boy. It doesn't matter how many babies I bring into the world; it always makes my heart sing. In a world where I saw so much death, a new life completes the circle, it brings meaning back into our lives. A baby is a new beginning, a new human being who needs to be loved and nurtured and led by the hand into the world of the future. It's an onerous responsibility, especially the world of the future. Unlike many, Beverley and Maurice's son, Robert, came into the world with every advantage; so many did not.

We visited them often in my parents' old house. I found it very difficult; the memories haunted me the moment the door opened, and my mother wasn't standing there. One day in May, Janet and I called in for an hour in the evening because Maurice was on the late evening shift. To say Beverley didn't look her best would be like saying a bombed house needed some tidying. Weeks with no proper sleep had taken its toll; the house had fallen into disarray, as had Beverley. Baby Robert clearly had a fine pair of lungs, and he used them to great effect. Janet immediately picked him up from his cot and attempted to soothe him. I sat Beverley down at the kitchen table and put the kettle on. The sink was full of washing up, with plates left on the table.

"How much sleep are you getting, Bev?"

"I don't know what sleep is, Emma. He gets me up every half an hour during the night, and he cries in between. I walk around during the day holding him to the breast, and I still fall asleep. If I try to nurse him in a chair, I can't stay awake. He just isn't feeding properly, but Maurice doesn't know what's wrong."

"I can see he's not feeding properly; he's underweight. And look at you; you're leaking milk everywhere. You must be in pain."

"I am. I'm at my wits' end, Em."

"Has Maurice really examined him? There must be a reason he's not feeding well."

"He's so tired as well. He sleeps down here, but he can still hear Robert crying. Neither of us has had any sleep."

Janet took one sniff of Robert and immediately set about changing him.

"This isn't enough, Robert; I hoped for much more. Why are you being so mean? Is this normal, Bev?"

"Yes, it's because he's not taking much milk."

"Let me have a look at him."

Janet handed him to me, freshly changed and smelling sweetly. She then cleared the kitchen table before putting his bedding on it. I placed Robert on the table, where he protested very vocally. He was clearly in distress, and his distress obviously became Beverley and Maurice's. He was underweight and agitated, so I looked him over as much as he would allow. His nose, ears and throat showed no sign of infection. His tongue was normal. Sometimes, babies can be tongue-tied when the lingual frenum is too short. I looked at his skin colour; he wasn't yellow or sore. As best as I could tell, without instruments, his heart and lungs seemed fine. I warmed my hands and began to feel and probe all over his tiny body, especially his abdomen. There it was, a small lump just below the stomach.

"How often does he vomit?"

"Every day, usually over me."

"Have you noticed wavelike contractions across his stomach?"

"Yes, when he's really upset, he does that. What is it, Em? What have you found?"

"I can't be sure, of course, but I would say this might be Pyloric Stenosis."

"Oh my God, Em, that sounds bad."

"It's not good, but it's certainly not as bad as you're thinking. When the valve that separates the stomach from the small intestine is enlarged, it can cause a blockage. It can be rectified with surgery."

"Surgery."

Beverley collapsed into a chair with tears welling up in her eyes, she looked terrified.

"I'm only telling you because you're a nurse and my friend, and I know you trust me. Robert will be alright, I promise you."

"Are you sure?"

"It's a known procedure, Bev. This is not unusual."

"Can you operate on tiny babies?"

"You can operate on a mouse if you had to. Please trust me, Bev. I promise you he'll be alright."

We had absolute trust in one another, and when I told Beverley I thought he would be alright, I meant it. The fact remained, however, that surgery on a tiny baby was a frightening prospect.

"Will you do it?"

"No, you need a specialist who's done it before. Robert must go to the Hospital for Children at Great Ormond Street."

"Are you sure, Em? There's nobody else I could trust to operate on him."

"If I'd done it before, just once, I would say yes, but strictly speaking, I'm not a qualified surgeon."

"Qualified, my arse," exclaimed Janet. "You're the best, Em. We all know that."

"No, I'm not. You need an expert. Ken used to know a surgeon who works at Great Ormond Street; I met him once, I'll ask him."

"If it's what you say it is, and if this surgeon will do it, I want you to be there, Emma. I have to know you'll be there."

"I can ask. If he says I can attend, then I certainly will. The hospital might object - I'm not RCS registered."

"This is awful. What's Maurice going to say? He'll be beside himself."

"I don't think he will be, Bev. He'll understand; he'll reassure you."

The conversation continued as we discussed the same fears repeatedly. There's no greater fear for a mother than when her child is in danger. Janet did her best to calm Robert while I tidied up. Given a moment when she didn't have to attend to Robert, Beverley fell asleep, too tired to continue worrying. Eventually, when the house was ship-shape, I took over from Janet while she put the kettle on for a cup of tea. Beverley enjoyed forty-five minutes of sleep, the most she'd had in weeks. She woke instantly the moment she heard Robert enter the room. A mother's instinct overrides all else.

Beverley was a nurse; she knew what to do with her excess milk. She knew how to take care of Robert. We had to leave her to continue her ordeal, but only for as long as it would take me to get Robert into Great Ormond Street. I was surprised Maurice didn't at least suspect Robert's condition. He was nearly as tired as Beverley; perhaps that was the reason. Or maybe he didn't press Robert's abdomen as hard as I did. It's very different when it's your own child. He was due home any minute; Janet and I left so they could be alone. I drove Janet to her new flat, which she had recently found in Battersea, near me.

"Come in, Em; I've got a bottle of gin in the cupboard. Barry brought it home, but he doesn't much like it."

"I should really get home, Jan. Frank will be home soon."

"You can make time, come on."

I took very little persuading; I suspect, given the opportunity, we all drank more than we should. If nothing else, it helped deflect the memories. Janet's flat was above a newsagent's shop. It wasn't Buckingham Palace, but she and Barry had made it home. I certainly felt at home there, immediately slumping into the armchair. Janet duly appeared, holding up the unopened bottle of Gordon's gin.

"Oh, I've forgotten the glasses."

"I'll get them," I said.

"I don't have tonic or anything else to go with it."

"Oh dear, I can't drink gin by itself."

"Put a bit of water in it. I've got a piece of cake, though. I stole it from the canteen."

We sat with our gin and water and piece of dried cake, feeling like members of the privileged class.

"You're sure Robert will be alright?"

"You know I wouldn't mislead Bev. It's not without danger, but it should be alright."

"She looked awful, didn't she?"

"So would we if we had no sleep for weeks."

Janet raised her glass. "Here's to young Robert. Here's to his thingamy, whatever it was you called it."

"Robert's thingamy."

We raised our glasses, and I found myself praying there would be a good outcome. It was not a routine procedure, but the surgeons at Great Ormond Street would have performed it several times before. I knew the chances of complete recovery were very good. It wasn't the probability of success that concentrated my mind. It was the unlikely possibility that it might go wrong. Gin and water is pretty awful when it's not your drink of choice, but we drank it just the same. A second glass and the troubles of the world, which were many, faded away.

"Did you see your policeman again?"

"No, I intended to, but I'm not sure that I should, not by myself."

"Why not?"

"It's not appropriate, is it? It wouldn't be right if Frank was going off to see a woman, would it?"

"Oh, baloney. He's just a friend, and you like him; you told me so."

"I do like him. There's so much more to him than meets the eye. We have these really deep conversations that I probably wouldn't have with anyone else, well, apart from you. He's really insightful. Perhaps it's his job; he seems to understand me better than I know myself."

"In that case, why not see him with Frank?"

"It wouldn't be the same. Frank doesn't discuss the kind of things we talk about."

"Then, if it makes you feel better, I'll chaperone you. We can go together, and he can bring Jean, his lady friend."

"We could, couldn't we?"

"Of course we could, but you really want to see him by yourself, don't you?"

"I just enjoy the conversations we have. He's really interesting."

"Then stop fussing about appropriateness and arrange to see him."

"It's what you would do, isn't it?"

"Of course, where's the harm? It's not as if you're both unattached, is it? He looks really happy with Jean."

"You're right, I'm being silly."

"Good, that's settled then. So, ask me if Barry still makes my heart skip a beat."

"What! I can't ask you that."

"Here you go again, being appropriate. Go on, ask me."

"No, I've not had enough to drink, I can't discuss personal things like that."

"Alright, does Frank make your heart skip a beat?"

"Janet, I know you too well. I've just fallen into a Janet Walters trap, haven't I?"

"Hook, line, and sinker. I didn't like to ask."

"And neither should you."

"Even if I worry that you and Frank don't really make the bells ring?"

"What do you mean?"

"You're my best friend in the entire world, Em, and it makes me happy to see you happy. The thing is, I'm just not sure you are, and it worries me."

"Oh, Jan. What did I do to deserve a friend like you? I'm not unhappy, it's just that I look at you and Barry, and I think maybe there's something missing."

"There you are; I told you, I know these things."

"I mentioned to my policeman that I wanted what you and Barry had."

"And what did he say?"

"He understands these things; he said we were different people, and people experience things differently. So what you and Barry have is special to you, and my experience will be, well, different."

"You really do talk to Roger, don't you? Well, he's right, of course, but here's the thing. I reckon if you and Frank couldn't get enough of each other, like me and Barry, then I would see that look in your eye."

"And you think I don't?"

"No, not really. We all knew when Bev hit it off with Maurice, didn't we? She looked like the cat that got the cream."

"She did, didn't she? Perhaps it's just me. I'm very shy about these things. Before I met you, I wouldn't have dreamt about talking like this."

"And yet you talk about these things with Roger, a man you hardly know."

"We don't just talk about that. We talk about many things."

"It sounds as if he enjoys talking to you, so for goodness' sake, meet him for a drink."

"You don't think it's inappropriate?"

"What the hell, who gives a f ... care."

We laughed. Gin can do that to you. She made me think as she always does. I wanted to see Roger again, so as Janet said, why shouldn't I? Then, just as I had made up my mind, another dilemma occurred to me. Should I tell Frank?

# Chapter Fifty-Six
# July 1942

Roger

*"We were lost in a desert of misery. Is it any wonder that we didn't turn away*
*from the shimmering mirage that became our oasis?"*

When our children were evacuated, we had no idea where they
were going or who they would end up staying with. It couldn't
be organised any other way; it was just one more distress we
had to endure. Jean and I were lucky; both of our kids could write home.
Many parents with young children heard nothing for the duration of
the war. We did at least know where they were. John and Mary were in
Cornwall, staying in a farmhouse with what John described as nice people
and good grub. They were doing jobs on the farm and going to the local
school. It sounded as if they were enjoying it.

Jean's kids were maybe less fortunate. They were staying in a terraced
house near Aberystwyth in a Welsh village with an unpronounceable
name. Irene, the oldest, described the house as tiny, with a toilet at the end
of the garden and no bath. They shared the same bed and had to wash at
a sink in a freezing cold scullery lit only by a dim gaslight. She hated it. In
subsequent letters, she said they were now going to the local school, and
they were understanding the strange accent. The old couple taking care of
them were very nice, and it was much better now in the warmer weather.

They were all making the best of it. My two seemed to enjoy living
on a farm, but every letter and postcard ended with, 'I wish I could come
home.' Being separated from your children is like an empty stomach. It

constantly gnaws at you, and there is only one way to satisfy the hunger. Jean and I had the additional anguish of knowing they had each lost a parent. Dave and Marilyn towered over us like two enormous floodgates. We assiduously avoided discussing it, fearing the consequences of opening those gates. When an issue is too painful to contemplate, we push our fears into a dark recess. Our mind protects us, but it's an illusion; there's no hiding from reality.

"I know we said we wouldn't tell them until it was necessary, Roger, but when will that be?"

"The government advises leaving them where they are until after the war, but when will that be? Every week that goes by is a long time for children, but I suppose every week will ease the pain?"

"You're right; they'll forget what we look like in a few years' time."

"Oh, don't say that, Jean."

"It'll make it easier for them, as you say. Perhaps it's right not to tell them until they come home."

"I think that's the kindest thing to do, Jean, but how can we live with a decision like that?"

"We've avoided it so far, Roger. We've only been thinking about ourselves, haven't we?"

"I know, but that's not wrong, Jean. You can call it self-delusion, but it's also self-protection. I couldn't have got through these past months without you. You lifted me from the gates of Hell and took me somewhere close to Heaven. We've found meaning in life where there was none before."

"You say the loveliest things."

"It's true, Jean, what we've found in each other has got us through this."

"I can still hardly believe it; I never imagined it could be like this. Was it like this with you and Marilyn?"

"I thought we agreed not to bring them into it."

"I know we did, but it's not possible, is it? I can't allow myself to think about Dave when we're together, and I know you're the same about Marilyn, but that doesn't make them go away, does it?"

"You're right; we can't face it, can we?"

"Perhaps we need to, Roger. If we can't face it, it means we feel guilty, doesn't it?"

"I suppose I do feel guilty."

"Perhaps it's just natural to feel that way. Someone outside looking in would tell us that life has to go on."

"People say that, but it's not their life, is it?"

"No, it's not. What we have now is so different from the past. I don't remember me and Dave being as passionate as we are. That's what makes me feel guilty. Was it the same with Marilyn?"

"No, I don't think it was."

"I suppose we didn't connect like you and I do, Roger. I thought we did, but it's only now that I realise we didn't."

"We're behaving like a couple of twenty-year-olds."

"Oh, Roger, we do, don't we? Why wasn't it that way before?"

"Perhaps it was; perhaps we took it for granted."

"I don't think so."

"Well, you know what they say. Youth is wasted on the young."

"Dave and I were really happy together. We loved each other; I thought what we had couldn't be any better. That's probably why I kept you at arm's length for so long when we started living together. I'm frightened to let them in, Roger. What will happen when we tell the children? Do we tell John that his Aunty Jean is now his mummy?"

"That's precisely what we will have to do."

Jean didn't reply. She just looked at me with a fearful expression. We had excluded the past from our minds, only thinking of ourselves. I consciously removed photographs of Marilyn from the bedroom, and I only left a couple of group photographs in the front room. I noticed Jean had done the same; we just couldn't bear to be reminded. Nothing in life prepares you for what we experienced. The disaster that was Balham Tube Station is a nightmare that will forever torment the minds of its victims. We suffered the terror of the Blitz, consumed by visions of Hell. Neither the past nor the future offered any solace. We were lost in a desert of misery; is it any wonder that we didn't turn away from the shimmering mirage that became our oasis?

It had been twenty-one months since that fateful night in the underground: twenty-one months of not properly grieving. To grieve is to allow those we've lost back into our lives. It means reliving that fateful night and admitting the relationship that had grown in their absence. Somewhere in a dark recess of my mind, a voice called out, telling me I had denied Marilyn's memory. I had done the one thing she falsely accused me of: I had betrayed her. They say grief is a process that evolves in stages. Jean and I finally started that process the moment we allowed Dave and Marilyn back into our lives. We didn't make love that night or the next.

It was a natural and overdue progression of our relationship. The same could be said for my approach to my job as a police detective. I became increasingly disillusioned with the seemingly endless procession of crime crossing my desk. No sooner did we break one local black-market racketeer than another took his place. Domestic murders declined after the Blitz, but they didn't stop altogether. The tensions created by rationing, combined with the thousands of traumatised homeless people living wherever they could, made many relationships impossible.

Our failure to convict Burrows tormented me more than anything else. The most notorious murderer since Jack the Ripper, and he was still free on the streets. He was obviously keeping his head down, and without the constant bombing to conceal his movements, he rightly felt exposed. A monster like Burrows doesn't reform himself. If he felt a moment of remorse, he could have confessed his evil crimes. I didn't for a moment expect that to happen. I knew he would wait for his opportunity to complete his fifth, and possibly final, murder. I doubted if anything would deter him from wanting to recreate the Ripper's last act of demonic madness. He needed to recreate the Mary Jane Kelly murder, and when he did, I would be there waiting for him.

My pledge to bring him to justice was something I remained determined to see through to the end. I might even have walked away from the job had it not been for Burrows. I wanted to make a difference; rather than arresting the perpetrators of crime, I wanted to address the reasons for those crimes. I watched with increasing interest the progress Henry Willink made with rehousing the homeless. He was a classic example of a Member of Parliament significantly changing things for the better. With hindsight, we now know that Willink's reforms ultimately led the way towards the modern Welfare State; he certainly left his mark. Jean's work with her mass observation study changed how we ran the country. Her work with the Women's Voluntary Service was invaluable to so many individual people's lives. They were making an enormous difference while I arrested criminals who would soon be replaced by others.

The summer months of 1942 continued to be Britain's darkest hours. There were highlights, such as Willink's housing and renovation programmes. But the burden of rationing and deprivation continued to wear the people down. People tried to put a brave face on it; the 'Spirit of the Blitz' remained alive and well, but beneath the facade, we were clinging on by our fingertips. Whenever people are at their lowest, they're also at their most vulnerable. This is when the morally corrupt step out of the shadows. Like vultures circling above a sickly animal, they wait to swoop and devour the carcass.

Billy Hill, the notorious London gangster, was especially involved in the black market. He preyed on the unfortunate, primarily north of the river, where he teamed up with the likes of Jack 'Spot' Comer, running protection rackets in the West End. They didn't often stray south of the river, possibly not wanting to tread on Joey Katz's toes. With Joey now permanently retired, Hill saw an opportunity. As always, it was Jack who had his ear to the ground. He greeted me with the news one morning.

"Morning, Jack; everything alright?"

"Morning, Roger. My knees are playing up again. How are you? I've not seen you for a couple of days."

"I've been avoiding you, Jack; I need cheering up in the mornings these days."

"I know what you mean; Doris was beside herself last night. She's run out of powdered eggs as if anyone will miss that."

"Actually, Jean said the same thing. There must be a shortage. She said it's important; it's used a lot."

"Is this going to be the final straw that breaks the country?"

"Let's hope not. I suppose counterfeit dried eggs will be next. Perhaps yellow brick dust would do just as well."

"Talking about the black market, you won't like what one of my boys has reported."

"This is why I need a cheerful face in the morning, Jack. You always give me bad news."

"Well, you won't like this. Billy Hill is taking over from some small-time black-market gangs on our patch."

"What did I tell you? I come in, and you ruin my day before it even begins. I take it one of your boys has picked this up on the street."

"Yes, he was tipped off by one of his less savoury informers. Hill's trying to muscle in, especially with drink and fags. There's even talk of him moving into the meat market."

"Smithfield Market is outside of our patch, so who's he approaching, the local butchers?"

"That's what we think, yes."

"We need to nip this in the bud, Jack. I don't want the likes of Hill taking over around here. Can you spare your blokes to have a word with all the butchers on their rounds and to keep an eye on them? If any of them are approached, we need to know. Hill will keep his hands clean, but if we can make some quick arrests, he might just back off."

Gerry wasn't pleased with the news, either. We had quite enough to do without that kind of organised crime on our patch. I thought we had seen the last serious organised crime when we broke the big petrol racket. Collectively, we were working on a couple of domestic murders and a recent spate of burglaries we believed were committed by the same person. It was very much business as usual. I didn't need Billy Hill; I didn't need any of it. Gerry summed it up perfectly.

"You look as though you've lost a pound and found a shilling, Roger. What's up?"

"Oh, it's nothing, Gerry. It's just getting a bit on top of me lately."

"You mean Burrows?"

"Well, yes, it's him, but it's all of it, really. Don't worry, nothing a pint and a packet of crisps won't put right."

"I can help with that. You owe me a pint."

By the strangest of coincidences, I had another invitation at almost precisely the same time. It was Emma Stevenson on the telephone. I hadn't seen or heard from her for eight months.

"Hello, Roger, it's Emma Stevenson."

"Emma, it's been ages, how are you?"

"I'm fine, Roger; how are you?"

"Yes, I'm well, thank you. What happened to the idea we would meet up for a chat after Christmas? Do you remember?"

"I do, and it's after Christmas now, so I'm phoning to ask when we are going to have that chat?"

She sounded bright and breezy, but I detected something behind her voice. I got the impression she needed a chat rather than wanted one. Either way, I was happy to see her. I always enjoyed our conversations.

"Will it be you and Frank; shall I bring Jean?"

"Well, we can if you want to, but I was thinking more of us having one of our cosy chats."

"That's fine. When did you have in mind?"

We planned for an evening in two days' time. I would pick her up at the hospital at five o'clock. I had to tell Gerry I had a better offer. When I told Jean that evening, she asked why she wasn't invited.

"I suspect from her tone of voice that she needs advice. She seems to only think of me when she needs advice."

"You have that effect on people, Roger, especially women. We all turn to you for advice; Rachel's the same."

"Perhaps it's the hypnotic charm I have with women?"

"I'll let you into a secret, Roger. It certainly would be your hypnotic charm if they knew you like I know you. As it is, they just want advice from a fatherly figure."

"That's boosted my ego no end. There was me thinking it was my charm."

"I liked Emma and her crowd; I'd like to see them again sometime. Rachel's crazy about her friend Leo. She's taking him to see Joey."

"Well, that'll be a baptism of fire."

"Give Emma my regards, will you?"

"I'll arrange for us to see them again as a group; it was fun last time."

"She's not making eyes at you, is she?"

"You're forgetting, she wants fatherly advice."

"Yes, but you do have a little bit of charm."

We made love that night for the first time in over a week. It was especially passionate, even by our standards. It felt as if we had been apart for a month; we fell asleep entwined in each other's arms.

# Chapter Fifty-Seven
# August 1942

Emma

*"When a man wakes up next to the woman he loves, the face he beholds in the first light of morning will belong to the most beautiful woman who has ever drawn breath."*

I thought about my conversation with Janet a lot. She didn't make me think so much as cast doubts into my mind. She certainly convinced me I had been silly about not seeing Roger. It was perfectly innocent; I simply valued his conversation. I always came away with new thoughts and often decisions that he had influenced, so why should it be inappropriate? I telephoned him at the police station the next day, and luckily enough, I found him there. He sounded a little surprised to hear from me. We had mentioned seeing each other after Christmas. Well, it was now eight months after Christmas, but I made light of the slight discrepancy. He accepted my invitation with detectable enthusiasm, which reassured me. We arranged to meet in two days' time.

My next conversion was with Gordon Bingham, one of the surgeons at Great Ormond Street. I'd only met him on one occasion with Ken, so I was pushing my luck to hope he would remember me. It took a while to get through to him, but he came to the telephone after three attempts. I cautiously introduced myself, and as I laboured over the circumstances of our meeting, he interrupted me.

"Of course, I remember you, Emma. Ken didn't stop talking about you. What can I do for you?"

I explained my preliminary diagnosis of baby Robert's condition, and he stopped me in my tracks. He immediately said that mother and child should go directly to Great Ormond Street and that he would do whatever he could. Then I approached what I thought might be the thorny issue of me attending the operation, and once again, he surprised me.

"Emma, I don't care if you're a fellow of the Royal College of Surgeons or not. I can assure you that your reputation has spread far beyond St Thomas's. When the Prime Minister said, 'So many owed so much to so few,' he could equally have been referring to you and your colleagues. I would be honoured to have you attend my operating theatre. If I can help you or this baby in any way whatsoever, then I'm at your disposal."

It took me a moment to respond; Gordon completely disarmed me. I thanked him for his very generous words and said I would ensure that mother and baby were at the hospital that same afternoon. As a woman, I struggled in the medical profession; every step for me has been steeper and higher. He would never understand what a revelation it was to hear a highly regarded surgeon treat me with such respect and courtesy. I walked away from the conversation with a spring in my step.

Gordon confirmed my diagnosis the same afternoon. Robert needed surgery, and Gordon carried it out the very next day with me in attendance. I walked out of the operating theatre with an uncontrollable smile on my face. Beverley and Maurice were sitting waiting for me to appear, and my face said it all. Their reaction is another of those joyous moments that gave my spirit wings. I will keep that cherished memory for the rest of my life.

I had a bottle of wine at home; I had been saving it for a special occasion, but a suitable occasion hadn't materialised. When I told Frank the good news, we opened it. The combination of rationing and my cooking didn't make for an exciting meal to go with our bottle. In the event, the wine was by far the better part of the occasion. After everything we had been through, a simple thing such as sharing a meal was an absolute treat. I don't know if the simple pleasure or the wine made me feel lightheaded, but I sat back on the kitchen chair, enjoying a warm glow.

"I'm meeting my policeman friend tomorrow, Frank."

"Oh yes, where are you going?"

"I thought we might have a cup of tea and a scone. I know this little tea shop that makes perfect scones."

"Sounds exciting."

"Well, I'm sure it will be fun."

"He seems a nice enough chap, Roger. Give him my best, will you?"

"Of course. You don't mind, do you?"

"Why should I mind? Enjoy your cup of tea."

We didn't discuss it anymore. All my fears about meeting a man by myself were, as Janet said, 'baloney'. Gordon Bingham made me think as well. Perhaps I didn't need to be so cautious with people. I would try to be more outgoing when I met Roger. I didn't feel the slightest need to be on my guard with him. I really looked forward to it. Most of all, I looked forward to our conversation. I could depend upon it being absorbing and thought-provoking.

When Roger arrived at the hospital, I completely surprised him by suggesting I take him to a little tea shop just over the river. Part of its charm was its position on a side road. You could look in either direction and not see a bombed building. This had become an exception, conjuring up images of peacetime normality. The little tea shop was that quintessentially English tradition, unspoilt by the war.

"This is delightful, Emma; do you come here often?"

"Once or twice, I keep saying I should come again. I'm reliably informed they make the best scones in London."

"Then I'll certainly have one. May I say you look nice this evening? That's a lovely dress."

I was doing so well until he said that. I only had to say thank you, but no, he embarrassed me, so I had to babble. "Oh, I'm not used to receiving compliments. I'll be honest, though; it's not mine. I borrowed it from Shirley. Sorry to disillusion you."

"That's the one thing you never do, Emma. It doesn't matter whose dress it is; you look lovely wearing it."

If only I had said nothing, but I babbled again. "I don't really have many clothes, I'm not used to wearing a dress like this, I feel a bit self-conscious."

"Why do you have such a low opinion about yourself when there's no reason for it?"

The more I babbled, the worse it got. "Wow. We've only just sat down, and we're already involved in one of our conversations. And it's about me."

"Oh, I'm sorry, forget I said it."

Then, of course, I had to regain some kind of dignity; I felt obliged to explain my reaction. "No, I'm not complaining. This is what makes our conversations so interesting. We never discussed my appearance as a child.

My father considered such things to be a pointless indulgence. I'm not especially pretty or anything, and so I suppose I've always continued with the idea that such things are, as my father said, a pointless indulgence."

"Am I permitted to say you're talking complete nonsense?"

"I would hate to think I was talking nonsense, so enlighten me."

"I've noticed your friends go to a lot of trouble with their makeup and hair. And I know how difficult it is now with all the shortages. You never do; you must be the only woman who holds her hair back with surgical tweezers. I've often wondered why you don't seem to care, and now you've told me. I hate to be the one to disillusion you, but you're wrong about yourself. You say you're not especially pretty. That's complete nonsense. You're beautiful."

What did he say? I really was out of my depth now. "You're very gallant, Roger, that's what I like about you."

"You don't believe me, do you? Trust me, you're a beautiful woman."

"So you think I compare to your friend Rachel, do you?"

"No, of course not. You're far more beautiful than she is. I don't know you as well as your friends do, but I can tell you I've never met a more beautiful person in my life. You're completely selfless, you're kind and caring, and you have a unique ability to inspire everyone around you. Your close friends love you. You're a beautiful person, Emma, and it shines through your eyes. Don't ever believe that you're not a beautiful woman."

I was in completely unknown territory; I didn't know how to respond to such an outrageous comment. "Why are you saying these things, Roger?"

"I'm telling you because your friends are too close to tell you. And I'm telling you because I hate to see anyone carrying the burden of feeling self-conscious."

"Is that what I am, self-conscious?"

"You told me you wish you were more like your friend Janet. You were reaching out and almost admitting to yourself that you want to be unrestrained and confident like her. Well, you can be; you just have to know how other people actually see you. They see what I see."

I felt the blood rush to my cheeks; I must have been glowing like a red traffic light. I went from not believing a word he said to suddenly wanting to. Roger did that to me every time we met, always making me see things differently. I grabbed a handkerchief from my handbag, not wanting him to see my tears or the traffic lights. Then, of course, I had to lower the handkerchief at some point, which only made my discomfort worse as I ceremonially unveiled it.

"Forgive me, Emma, I shouldn't be so outspoken. I've assumed too much of our friendship. I'm so sorry."

He looked mortified, which compelled me to come to his rescue by being completely honest. "I know I look nothing like Rachel, but you really think I do, don't you? That's the most wonderful thing anyone has ever told me. I don't think of myself as being pretty, or lovely, or anything else like it, so that's what I am."

"For such a wonderfully intelligent woman, you can also be really daft. I'm afraid your father might have been your guiding star as a youngster, but he was wrong about a woman's appearance being frivolous nonsense. Looking down from his lofty viewpoint, perhaps he was right; in the greater scheme of things, perhaps it is nonsense. But in the real world, a woman's confidence is partly shaped by her appearance. Jean spends ages with her makeup, and what she can't buy now, she makes herself with all sorts of clever ingredients; it's important to her."

"So what happens first thing in the morning when a man wakes up next to a woman? No woman is looking her best then."

"Now, that's a sneaky question, but it doesn't undermine my argument. Different rules apply in those circumstances. When a man wakes up next to the woman he loves, the face he beholds in the first light of morning will belong to the most beautiful woman who has ever drawn breath."

"Then that woman is incredibly fortunate, Roger. I'm not sure every man sees things the way you do."

"I'll still argue about your father being wrong to make you think that being concerned about your appearance is frivolous. Just try telling your friends, Janet, or Shirley."

"You're right; they would tell me I'm mad. I just didn't think it was for me."

A young lady came and asked what she could get for us. Roger followed my advice and ordered the tea and scones.

"Okay, then, let's start again, Emma. We just sat down, and I don't comment on your lovely dress."

"Hello, Roger, how nice to see you again."

"Yes, it's lovely to see you again, Emma."

"Roger, why do you always wear the same crumpled suit and tie?"

"Oh, well, I tend not to notice what I wear."

"What you mean is, you don't care what you wear."

"Well, yes, that must be the case."

"That implies you don't care what people think about you."

"Yes, it's not important to me, I suppose."

"You also smoke far too much, Roger. Apart from making you ill, it makes your clothes smell of tobacco. It's not very attractive, you know."

"Yes, I'm sorry about that, I mean to stop one day."

"I wish you would; it's a really nasty habit. Apart from that, you're a very nice man."

"Okay, Emma, I get it. You're absolutely right, and I was absolutely wrong. I have no defence; the evidence against me is overwhelming. The only thing I can offer in mitigation is my otherwise good character and the assurance that I had the best of intentions."

"What were your intentions, then?"

"I'm trying not to make the same mistake again, but I wanted to pay you a genuine compliment. When a well-intentioned gentleman compliments a lady, he does so in the hope and expectation that he's brought a little delight into her life. I just wanted to make you feel good, Emma. What I'm guilty of is questioning why it didn't work."

His comment immediately reminded me of the first occasion when I met Ken. He used a similar form of words to apologise for paying me a compliment. Once again, I railed against kind words when the problem lay elsewhere.

"Now, who's being daft? It did work, you big softy. I'm just not used to that kind of thing."

"You were very unkind about my suit."

"Yes, I'm sorry about that. In mitigation, it is an old and crumpled suit."

He sat back in his chair with a huge grin on his face. "I really enjoy our conversations, Doctor Stevenson."

"So do I, Inspector Pritchard."

Our tea arrived together with two golden scones still hot from the oven. We shared a small glass dish of strawberry jam and a knob of butter. It was about as indulgent as any luxury I could imagine. We hardly spoke for a few minutes, the scones demanding our full attention. He watched me intently as I lifted half the scone to my mouth. I raised my eyes to the heavens in delight and let out a deep sigh.

"These are seriously good, aren't they?"

"I told you, Roger, the best in London."

"So, if you can see your way clear to tolerate my bedraggled appearance, tell me your news, Emma."

"Well, the other day, Beverley's baby boy underwent surgery for an abdominal condition, and it was a complete success. Doctor Wiśniewski at the hospital reminded me once again that I am not a qualified surgeon in the eyes of the RCS. And so, I've decided when it's possible, I will ensure I get the qualification, and I shall become a fellow of the Royal College of Surgeons."

"I didn't know you weren't qualified."

"Everything has been different during the bombing. We all have to do whatever is required of us, and I did surgery. I studied anatomy and surgery at medical school. I've always wanted to be a surgeon, so this became my opportunity."

"I know how your colleagues regard you at the hospital, Emma, so I know you'll be a spectacular success."

"That's kind, I hope so. What about you, Roger, are you still catching criminals?"

"Yes, I'm afraid so, but I'll admit something to you I've told no one else. I'm thinking about life after the police force. I want to make a real difference, Emma, and I'm not sure I can do that chasing criminals."

"What do you want to do?"

"I've had some dealings with government officials, and I can see where the power to create change lies. I want to become a Member of Parliament."

"Oh, wow. That's tremendous, Roger, good for you."

"Do you think I could make a success of being an MP?"

"Well, first, you'll have to be elected, but beyond that, I don't have the slightest doubt about it. You are, in my opinion, eminently suited to become a legislator. I can think of no one more erudite and capable of thoughtful analysis than you, Roger. I think you've chosen your perfect career."

"Coming from you, that's immensely reassuring."

"In order to be elected, you might need to look a little more presentable."

"Point taken."

"How's Jean?"

"She's fine, working hard for the WVS; she makes a real difference to people's lives. I'm proud of her."

"That's wonderful; you two seem to have the perfect relationship. After all you've been through together, you deserve it."

"I'm not sure what the perfect relationship looks like. It certainly wouldn't come with the memories that ours does."

"What do you mean?"

"I'll be honest, we've both done our best to exclude the past, but we can't continue to do that. I just don't want the past to come between us."

"It must be really difficult for you. It's unusual circumstances, isn't it?"

"It is. We briefly discussed the children the other day but haven't told them yet. Jean said, 'What do we tell John? Do we tell him his Aunty Jean is now his mum'?"

"Oh, that's difficult. I remember you have two children, and Jean also has two?"

"That's right, that's four young children who will have to accept what will be a strange and harrowing situation for them."

"What about your late wife, Roger, she must always be there?"

"She is; it's hard at times. What's equally hard is Jean's husband, Dave. He was my best mate; we were inseparable. On a bad day, I feel I'm cheating on Marilyn, but it feels more like betrayal with Dave."

"I'm so sorry, but you mustn't let those thoughts come between you."

"That's exactly what's happened recently, and we both worry about how the children will react. Enough of my troubles, how are you and Frank, when are you getting married?"

"Nothing happening for the moment."

"Sorry, I just assumed."

"No, I would need to be quite sure before embarking on something as irrevocable as that."

"Which implies you're not sure. Is it not sure about the institution of marriage, or not sure about Frank?"

"I suppose I keep going back to Janet's example. She's made it worse recently by saying she's worried about me."

"I think I understand. Forgive me if I've got the wrong end of the stick, but I'm getting the impression that you and Frank rub along just fine, but you want something more than that."

"Is that wrong, Roger?"

"No, it's quite right. You want your heart to race and your head to spin. You want to feel elation in a kiss and rapture in every embrace. You want to touch Heaven and carry it with you always."

He did it again. He knew everything I wanted as if he could read my mind and he expressed it as only Roger can. I grew in confidence with him and didn't suffer my usual urge to babble. Instead, I just admitted he was right.

"You're right, that's what I want. So what would you say makes the perfect marriage?"

"What are the perfect ingredients to make a marriage?" He repeated my question with a quizzical look on his face. "I would say a spoonful of empathy, a pinch of consideration, a sprinkle of understanding, and all mixed with a large measure of love. If only it were that simple."

Roger amazed me. Sitting there in his shabby suit, who would have guessed how his mind works? My father always encouraged me to listen to people with something to say. His idea of 'something to say' was anyone who might inform or inspire me to appreciate a different perspective. Roger did all those things. On each occasion we met, he made me feel exposed and vulnerable one moment and inspired the next. He certainly threw me off guard. I didn't know anyone who could so reliably reduce my conversation to babble. His marriage formula did exactly that. I never realised I was babbling until after I said it, so I just said it.

"Jean is incredibly fortunate to have someone as lovely as you, Roger."

My cheeks reddened again. Too late, I'd said it. I just told him to his face that I thought he was wonderful. Why did I do that? I decided to shut up and not make it worse.

"That's what I keep telling Jean," he joked, "but I'm not sure she believes it."

I wanted to say she would be an idiot not to, but for once I kept quiet. I had several questions to which I knew he would have the answers, but I sensibly avoided exposing myself any further. Only then did I realise the time - we had been talking for an hour and a half, and it seemed only ten minutes. Wherever we had been during that hour and a half, it wasn't in war-torn London. I didn't think about rationing, or the shortage of medical supplies, or the bombed and destroyed buildings; it was as if they existed in another time.

"We must go, Roger; Jean will be expecting you."

"Yes, you're right. Let's not leave it for eight months next time. Perhaps we could get together with your friends?"

"The eight months were my fault, I'm afraid. So yes, I'll arrange something with them."

"Why was it your fault?"

"Oh, just me being silly. I thought it might be inappropriate to meet you alone like this."

"Unchaperoned. I understand, but your virtue is quite safe with a policeman."

"I was never in any doubt, Roger. It's all about other people's perception."

"Rest assured, I greatly value our friendship."

He drove me back to the hospital and opened the car door for me. We then entered that awkward moment when I didn't know if I should just walk away or shake his hand. I half offered my hand, and he reached out with both hands. So, without thinking, I put my arms around him and kissed his cheek. It amounted to nothing, but we had long since ceased to be casual acquaintances. At some point, we became close friends.

## Chapter Fifty-Eight
# January 1943

Roger

*"Racism fulfils a need. What better way to elevate your position than by looking down upon someone else and blaming them for all your woes? Superiority can be intoxicating, even when it's illusory."*

1942 ended with unaccustomed good news that the newspapers printed with great enthusiasm. In North Africa, the German army was in a full retreat following their defeat at El Alamein. This paved the way for the Allied invasion of North Africa, which was to prove so decisive. Perhaps even more significant, the Germans failed to relieve their army in Stalingrad. For the first time since the outbreak of war, Hitler was retreating on two fronts. What had been our darkest hours during the summer of 1942 suddenly saw the first tenuous rays of light heralding a new dawn.

It might have been a false dawn, but the country had become desperate for any news that wasn't bad. Rationing tightened its grip to the point where the pips squeaked. It all resulted in more and more black-market activity, which we were supposed to control. We also had to contend with a dubious practice instigated by The Ministry of Food and Local Authorities. They sent people out into the community, effectively trying to entrap shopkeepers into offering them an extra ounce of tea or a few ounces of butter. We then had to arrest the beleaguered shopkeeper over an ounce of tea.

Another more serious problem was claims fraud. Individuals would pose as bomb victims to receive money from the compensation scheme. Whatever scheme the government came up with to help people, there would always be someone trying to abuse it. It would be fair to say there were thousands of individuals who had been involved in some kind of criminal activity. It may only be an ounce of tea, but in the eyes of the law, they were criminals. I had the opportunity to complain to Sir John Anderson. Far too much police time was being taken up with what I regarded to be the persecution of ordinary, otherwise law-abiding people.

I also spoke to Henry Willink about it because fraudsters were taking advantage of some of his compensation schemes. We talked at length, and all the while, I knew that the power to do things lay in his hands and not mine. Willink was the MP for Croydon. Appointed as Commissioner for the Homeless during the Blitz, he transformed the plight of thousands of destitute bomb victims. I learnt that he had been a battery commander during the last war at the Battle of the Somme, where he received the Military Cross. Henry was a no-nonsense man who understood what organisation was and how to get things done. More than anyone else, he inspired me to want to become an MP. I returned home one evening in January, having just had a meeting with him.

"How did it go?" asked Jean.

"Really well; he invited me to call him Henry. He was disappointed to hear about the claims fraud and immediately said he would put additional measures in place. I sounded him out about my becoming an MP, and he was encouraging. He said if he heard of a seat becoming vacant, he would tell me."

"Is he Labour or a Conservative MP?"

"He's the Conservative MP for Croydon."

"You voted Labour last time."

"I won't hold that against him. I'm not sure which party I'd like to stand for, or I could be an Independent."

"You're serious about it, aren't you?"

"I am, Jean. I really admire what Henry has achieved. That's exactly what I want to do."

"You're going to succeed, aren't you? I know you will."

"How can you be so sure?"

"I know you, Roger, when you set your mind on something, it always happens."

"I set my mind on convicting Burrows, didn't I?"

"And you will."

"We've pushed him as far as we can, and he isn't putting a foot wrong."

"He will, you told me he would."

"Yes, he will, but when?"

"Just be patient, Roger, don't let him get to you."

"He did that a long time ago. Anyway, forget Burrows, what delights do we have for dinner?"

"You're in for a real treat tonight. We have a powdered egg omelette and a sausage each. As a special treat, you could have it as a sandwich in your favourite national loaf."

"You must have read my mind. That's my absolute favourite. What other treats go with it?"

"I could offer you the omelette dressed only in my sexy underwear."

"This is turning into a wonderful meal."

"Forget it - it's too cold."

"I thought there'd be a catch."

By the end of the year, there were many catches like that. Our bubbling mountain stream had been joined by one or two tributaries. It was inevitable, probably perfectly normal, but once you have been swept along in a mountain stream, you never forget it. We were both very passionate people; our stream had always been a torrent.

We lived primarily in my house but also spent time in Jean's home. Inevitably, we shared our lives with Marilyn and Dave, and always in the back of our minds, we were accompanied by four children. Not that we were drifting apart; we were simply not so close together.

"I've invited Rachel and Leo to dinner one evening, and she asked if she could bring Joey?"

"What!"

"I thought you'd like the idea."

"I like Rachel, but we don't know Leo that well. As for bringing Joey into our house, I'm not at all sure."

"Come on, Roger, you like him."

"I know I do, but that doesn't make it right. Anyway, how do you propose to feed five people when we struggle to feed two?"

"Well, it was really Rachel's idea; she suggested everyone could bring as much food as they can, and we'll make one big stew out of it."

"Do I have a choice?"

"Of course you do. I can cancel the whole thing if you want to."

"If I do that, you'll never serve dinner in your underwear again, will you?"

"No, that's right."

"Well, you leave me no option. I have to agree."

We laughed; we had never disagreed about anything, but I wasn't comfortable with the idea. I wondered what Gerry would say about Joey Katz coming into my home. What if someone like Sir John Anderson or Henry Willink found out? Me consorting with a known criminal would take some explaining. Joey might be retired from that life, but it would still look bad. Despite that, I couldn't help but like the man. He must have been about seventy years old, but he had lost none of his ability to either impress or intimidate people. You paid attention when Joey spoke.

I also wondered about Leo. We met him and Rachel a few times recently, including just a few weeks before when he was a part of Emma's group. Despite having met him, I didn't really know the man. He wasn't much older than Rachel, and I certainly didn't share their obsession with fashionable clothes. It would be fair to say we didn't seem to have much in common. The more I thought about Jean and Rachel's arrangement, the more concerned I became. I didn't see how Leo, a smart, professional young man from a wealthy background, could feel comfortable with a retired gangster.

When the evening arrived, I put a brave face on it, not wishing to upset Jean. I even put on my best V-neck jumper. It was a kind of burgundy colour, very flamboyant for me. They arrived together, with Joey sitting in the back of Leo's car, looking like Royalty. We were totally unused to entertaining people; Jean had been in a flap all day. Even our best china came out, that tells you how important this was to Jean. My contribution amounted to a few bottles of beer. They collectively arrived at the front door looking like a fashion parade. The gentlemen wore immaculate suits, while Rachel was dressed in a shimmering creation beyond my description.

Rachel wrapped her arms around me and kissed my cheek as she always did. Being kissed by Rachel is quite something I can tell you. I could never prevent a juvenile smile from spreading across my face. Looking over my shoulder at Jean, I knew she would raise her eyes to the heavens as a rebuke for my child-like reaction. I shook hands with Joey and Leo, feeling significantly underdressed. They had two bags of food at their feet.

"Good evening, Roger," said Joey. "Thank you for inviting me this evening. I consider it a great honour."

"Joey, you haven't met my ... friend Jean."

"My dear, it is such a delight to finally put a face to your name. Roger speaks of you in exalted terms, and now I understand why."

"It's a pleasure to meet you, Joey. Rachel speaks about you so often."

"Take your coats off and make yourselves at home. I didn't realise we intended to make this a formal evening; I would have dressed more appropriately."

"I asked Rachel about what to wear," said Leo. "She said I had to wear my smartest suit."

"Rightly so, Rachel," said Joey. "We are guests in your home, Jean and Roger. It's a great honour, especially meeting you for the first time, Jean. The least we can do is dress accordingly."

Joey hadn't been standing in the hallway for more than two minutes, and Jean had already fallen under his spell. He had a way of complimenting people, such that the recipient considered it an honour to be on the receiving end. My V-neck jumper had no doubt been fashionable at some point in time, but compared to Joey and Leo, I looked like a rag-and-bone man's collection bin. I directed them towards my front room. Jean insisted we gentlemen go ahead while she and Rachel sorted out the various food contributions.

I felt distinctly uncomfortable entering the room with two men, neither of whom had been in my house before and who seemed to be incompatible with each other. I was only doing it because Jean wanted me to, and I knew Rachel had talked Leo into it. Joey seemed to be the only one who probably didn't feel uncomfortable. He'd always been a jovial, charismatic character. I had to assume that the incongruous association of a police officer and a gangster hadn't escaped Leo's attention. They both accepted a glass of beer and as I poured Leo's glass, he confirmed my assumption.

"How long have you two known each other?"

"Joey and I go back a long way, Leo."

"If you want to know something, dear boy, never be afraid to ask the question," replied Joey. "You're wondering why Roger has invited me to his home when my reputation and his might appear to be at odds with each other."

"No, I didn't mean to imply anything like that. I was just wondering how your friendship with Roger started."

"It's a long story, my boy, perhaps as old as the Jewish people themselves. My distant family were Polish, but we ended up in Russia when the country was partitioned between Russia, Austria, and Prussia in the late 1700s. Repressive restrictions and persecution made their life increasingly difficult. When the expulsions began in 1821, my family came to this country trying to escape persecution. This is who we are, Leo, shaped by our past.

When I learned that my eldest son Aaron was being bullied at school for no other reason than his Jewish heritage, you cannot begin to understand the depth of my despair. Then one day a young police constable turned up at my door holding Aaron by the hand. My boy had been badly beaten, and the policeman no doubt saved him from further injury. Any other policeman would have sent Aaron on his way, but not this policeman. He helped him get home that day, and then he took it upon himself to watch over him until Aaron was old enough to take care of himself."

"I assume the young policeman was Roger?"

"It was, and I asked him why he had gone to so much trouble for a little Jewish boy. Roger said he despised racism; he said it generated hatred simply because it provided the illusion of power to those who have none. I asked him to explain what he meant, and I'll never forget his reply. 'Racism fulfils a need. What better way to elevate your position than by looking down upon someone else and blaming them for all your woes? Superiority can be intoxicating, even when it's illusory.'

You cannot imagine what those words and deeds meant to me. I'm in Roger's debt, and it gives me the greatest pleasure to repay that debt whenever I can."

"I just did what was right, Joey. You don't owe me anything."

"I believe I do, Roger, and I thought if I lived long enough, I might manage to repay you. Then you intervened again when Rachel was persecuted. You protected and befriended her, so I owe you again, Roger. I suddenly realised I couldn't live long enough to repay such a debt."

"Rachel told me about that, Roger," said Leo. "She calls you her guardian angel."

"Any decent person would do the same, and don't forget my partner, Dave, had a lot to do with it."

"There were few decent people in the pub that night; only two stood head and shoulders above the rest."

"Well, be that as it may, I don't want you to think you owe me anything, Joey. You've been incredibly generous; let that be the end of it."

"I can exchange the debt for friendship. One serves the purpose of the other."

Joey meant every word he said; the debt, as he perceived it to be, was a lifelong commitment. I didn't mention the suit, which took pride of place in my wardrobe, and neither did Joey. It took me a long time to accept that his generosity came with no ulterior motive. I had spent too long dealing with people whose word was meaningless to recognise honour and integrity when it stared me in the face. If debt and friendship served the same purpose for Joey, then I would accept friendship.

"I hear that after the war, you are considering a career change, Roger?"

"News travels fast, Joey."

"I have far-reaching connections in my local constituency. I'm chairman of the Conservative Association. If you're serious about this, Roger, it would be my pleasure to put your name forward."

"You would do that for me?"

"Of course, and with the greatest pleasure. I can't think of a more suitable candidate than you."

Such a connection would almost guarantee me a foot in the door. I thanked him without sounding too effusive, but it was an offer I wasn't about to forget. I changed the subject.

"How are things at the hospital, Leo?"

"Working in a bomb site has its limitations, but things are improving. Rachel has generously donated a large amount of money towards the repair of one of our wards."

I could guess where that money came from. Joey neither confirmed nor denied it, but I knew Rachel didn't have that kind of money. The donation had Joey written all over it.

"How's Emma? Is she working as hard as ever?"

"If she could work twenty-four hours a day without a break, she would. Do you know that Florence Nightingale worked at St Thomas's? Well, the joke now is that she's come back. If I had my way, I would name the ward we're trying to rebuild, the Emma Stevenson Ward."

"I think you could name it after any of you. Joey, did you know Leo has been awarded the George Medal in recognition of his 'conspicuous gallantry' when rescuing the victims trapped in the hospital's basement after one of the bombings?"

Joey looked at Leo with an initial expression of astonishment. That quickly changed as the implications of the award sunk in. He obviously knew that the George Medal and Cross are the two highest civilian awards and only rarely awarded for the most outstanding gallantry. I knew what

Joey was thinking; like me, he had misjudged Leo. There was so much more to him than just his good looks and expensive clothes.

"No, I didn't know. Leo, I've not had the privilege of meeting anyone who has been so highly honoured. It would be a privilege to shake your hand."

"I just helped my friends, Joey; I didn't think about it. I don't deserve an award."

"That's the essence of courage, my boy. You didn't think about yourself. You thought only about your friends."

Leo looked a bit embarrassed. Emma had told me about Leo receiving his award when we met them all a few weeks previously when Jean and I enjoyed another evening with them in the Fox. I warmed towards him, and the award only confirmed what I had begun to suspect. The girls marched into the room just in time to save Leo from further embarrassment. They both wore aprons and carried a casserole dish in front of them, which created an implausible sight in Rachel's case.

"Your banquet awaits, gentlemen."

"What have you managed to create?" Leo asked.

I doubted Rachel had much experience in the kitchen, but she looked rightfully pleased with whatever they had concocted between themselves.

"I think we've done rather well, haven't we, Jean? It's called an 'all-in stew,' and there's a wonderful starter course."

We all marched into the kitchen with Rachel acting as maître d'. I don't doubt we made a slightly ludicrous sight with them all dressed up to the nines in my little kitchen. Jean had laid the table earlier. Her finest tablecloth was emblazoned with my best china plates; the dresser looked bare with them missing. The silver cutlery was Jean's, and I had never seen it come out of the box before. Rachel instructed us to sit down so she could present the first course. Jean took off her apron and sat next to me.

"Did I say you look lovely tonight?" I whispered.

"No, you didn't, but now will do."

Rachel then placed a small plate in front of each of us containing a thin slice of toast covered in caviar. It was something I recognised but had never eaten. I didn't need to ask where it came from. Caviar wasn't an item in the ration book. Joey sat with a smile as Rachel returned with a wine bottle and proceeded to fill our glasses. Jean whispered in my ear.

"It's fish eggs, apparently very expensive."

"I know what it is. I just haven't tried it before."

Joey then contemplated the wine bottle. "I wanted us to share something very special from my wine cellar. I have been saving my finest bottles for a special occasion, but since losing those dear to me, that occasion has never arisen. So please, make me a happy man and share this with me."

I looked at the bottle - 1929 Domaine de la Romanée-Conti Montrachet. I knew just enough about wine to know this was incredibly special. We all raised our glasses to Joey, and I had experienced nothing like it in my life. It had an almost creamy texture, with flavours of vanilla and butter and fruits such as apricots and pears. Personally, I found the fish eggs slightly underwhelming, but the wine was a wonderful experience. Leo, no doubt, had experience of both; his expression was pure delight.

Rachel followed that with the 'all-in stew', and Joey produced another bottle of wine. This time, a 1921 Château Cheval Blanc. Rachel poured a sip for Joey to taste before she poured the rest of the glasses. I hadn't realised that he was a connoisseur of wine, but that quickly became apparent as he described the wine to us. Apparently, 1921 had been an outstanding Bordeaux vintage, produced during one of the hottest summers in a generation. His pleasure was a joy to behold and quickly shared by the rest of us. The superlative wine and the 'all-in stew' combined to produce the finest meal I had eaten since the war started.

Everything came together to create that most valuable gift - a memory that will stay with you forever. Our conversation didn't stop. We laughed one moment and were serious the next. Whatever the subject, Joey offered us wisdom that only age can command. We couldn't avoid the one recurring subject, one inescapable reality. The war affected everything; it shaped our past and would shape our future. The reason our evening together proved to be so memorable, and the 'all-in stew' so delicious, was that the war had denied us everything else.

"It's just sheer madness," said Jean, "is it worth destroying everything we've spent generations creating? Is Hitler going to achieve anything worth the life of one individual, let alone hundreds of thousands?"

"You're absolutely right, Jean," replied Joey. "Of course, it's madness. Mankind has only existed for the blink of an eye. Life existed before us, and it will continue after us. Darwin told us that evolution is the survival of the fittest - those best able to adapt and survive. Every common sense tells us that mankind can best adapt when we cooperate. The more we come together, the more we share, the more we ensure our survival. We've departed from that evolutionary principle. We created our own evolutionary process. One population cooperates and builds, and another does the reverse and destroys. One group works together to create and thrive, while the other works to destroy what's been created. Of course, it is madness. Darwin would see it as an aberration within the natural order, the opposite of survival of the fittest."

"Do you not see a future for mankind, Joey?"

"Ask yourself a simple question: is there any other life form that succeeds by destroying itself? Is there a bird that thrives by building a nest and then tearing it down? I fear for the future, Roger. Our only hope is that this is the war to end all wars. We thought that was the last war. Perhaps it will be this one."

"That's something we can all agree on," said Leo, "the war to end all wars."

We raised our glasses. Were we being naive or just hopeful? We had to be hopeful because Joey made an inescapable point: our cycle of creation and destruction was not sustainable. We had seen first-hand what the end of civilisation looks like. It was a sobering moment. When Joey had to leave the table to answer the call of nature, Rachel was eager to say something.

"Thank you, Jean and Roger, for agreeing to host this evening; it's been truly wonderful. I wanted to do something for my father-in-law because he is so special to me, and he is in so much pain. He has never recovered from losing his beloved Eva, then Aaron, and now Ezra. I don't think he's been out of the house since the warehouse burnt down. He's the father I never had, and I would do anything for him. I knew he would come tonight if I told him he was coming here with me, and I'm so glad he did. I can't remember when I last saw him smiling as he is this evening. So, thank you both for showing him your friendship."

I hadn't seen that side of Rachel before; she was holding back tears. Jean rushed to comfort her. She had barely recovered before Joey returned, and I used the opportunity to propose a toast.

"May I first propose a toast to Jean and Rachel for creating the wonderful and aptly named 'all-in stew.' Thank you both. It was a triumph. Thank you, Joey, for sharing the caviar with us and, of course, the wonderful wine we are still enjoying.

Lastly, I want to acknowledge the empty chairs that sit in this room. For us, those chairs are not empty. We see the occupants as clearly as we see each other. Their memory is in our care. Their past is now our future.

Their hopes and dreams are now our hopes and dreams. It is our sacred duty to keep their memory alive and to live the life they were denied. We must make them proud; they would want nothing less. So, I give thanks to Marilyn, Eva, Dave, Aaron, and Ezra, and all those who share their journey with them."

My little speech was met with silence as the names continued to echo in everyone's mind. Jean held my hand and took Joey's hand with the other. Rachel held my other hand and joined with Leo, who joined Joey. We sat hand in hand, sharing a profoundly moving experience. It was perhaps the first time I really came to terms with Marilyn and Dave's deaths and the implications of their enduring memory.

## Chapter Fifty-Nine
# August 1943

Emma

*"Hope is the lifeblood of the oppressed, just as peace
is the foundation of civilisation."*

There was a slight but perceptible feeling of optimism in the air in 1943. Shortages were even worse, and rationing was ever more restrictive. Even sausages were rationed in 1943. Clothes coupons continued to decrease in number as the war progressed. We literally had to make do and mend. Despite all the hardships, we were like moths attracted to the light, and no light shines brighter than hope. Hope is the lifeblood of the oppressed, just as peace is the foundation of civilisation. It was the Americans who helped engender that feeling of optimism. They were everywhere. You couldn't walk over Westminster Bridge without seeing a few uniformed American soldiers.

The newspapers made much of the German surrender in North Africa and their ongoing retreat in Russia. Recent newspaper headlines were full of the air raids on Hamburg that took place at the end of July. Our initial reaction, having suffered months of continuous bombing during the Blitz, was that it was an overdue taste of their own medicine. That opinion became slightly tempered when, after a quiet day at the hospital, we took the opportunity for a quick after-work drink in the Tavern where Barry and Roy joined us.

"The air raids on Hamburg sound as if they must have been devastating," commented Frank.

"I read that," I said. "The papers are full of it."

"They are," replied Barry, "it's been a terrible retribution for the Germans."

"Do I sense a 'but'?"

"Well, perhaps you do, Emma. Our previous Wing Commander, Johnny Albright, is now flying reconnaissance missions. Johnny flies mainly over the French coast but he flew over Hamburg the other day. He told me he had seen nothing like it. The bombing continued over several days and nights, us by night and the Americans by day. Something like 9,000 tons of bombs were dropped, and thousands of incendiaries. The result has been a firestorm that's destroyed over 60% of the city."

"So we did to them what they did to us during the Blitz," said Leo.

"We did, but we did it in just a few days, not months."

"Do we know how many civilians were killed, Barry?"

"We don't, Emma, but Ministry experts will have worked out estimations. The people Johnny serves with have made estimates based on population and the amount of destruction, and he told me it was probably in the order of 40,000."

"That's as many as died during all the months of the Blitz but in just one city and in only a few days."

"That's right, Frank. It makes you think, doesn't it?"

"Oh, my God. All those people."

"This is an all-out war, Jan. This is the whirlwind Hitler has sown."

"I thought we were fighting against tyranny," I replied. "I thought we were fighting to maintain our way of life. Killing 40,000 people in just a few days isn't our way of life."

"You're right," replied Roy, "but we can only defeat Hitler if we fight him on his terms."

"But this is a regime whose war aims include conquering nations of people it considers racially inferior. It's all in Mein Kampf. He said, 'All who are not of good race are chaff.' He said the elimination of the Jews, 'Must necessarily be a bloody business'. Look at what they did to the Jews in Poland. They're committing terrible atrocities as a deliberate strategy. This is not a regime that values any form of human life other than its own. We must think carefully before we fight Hitler on his terms."

"That's unfair, Emma," replied Barry. "We didn't start this war, and we didn't dictate how it would be fought. Hitler did that. I agree it raises questions, but we're fighting fire with fire."

"This is the sheer utter madness of war, isn't it?"

"What would you have us do, Leo, surrender?"

"I am a Jew, Barry. That means nothing to any of you around this table, but for Hitler, that's sufficient to have me killed. Do I think we should surrender to that kind of barbarism? No, not just for the Jewish people, but for anyone who wants to live in a decent civilised country. So no, I agree we must fight. There's no other option, even if our actions cross the boundary into madness. But I agree with Emma, we must not allow ourselves to sink into barbarism."

"Well said, Leo. I wish Alex were here to listen to you make that pronouncement."

"I wonder what he would have said, Em?"

"I very much doubt he would have said, 'Oh shut up, Leo'."

"He did say that, didn't he? He really intimidated me, Alex."

"He intimidated a lot of people," said Frank.

"He intimidated a lot of nurses, I can tell you," said Shirley.

"I'll be honest," replied Janet, "I don't miss him putting his arm around me, but I keep expecting to see him, and he's not there."

"I actually miss him a lot," I said. "He gave me a lot of help and advice."

"That's because you refused to accept his proposals, Em."

"I guess you're right, Jan. He was a terrible womaniser, wasn't he?"

"Beverley had the right approach," said Shirley. "He touched her bum once, and she really gave him what for. She told him to bugger off. She said he was a creep."

"Oh dear, I can't imagine Beverley saying that. I don't know why he behaved that way. It's not very becoming, is it?"

"I think it was a power thing with Alex," replied Frank. "His position as a senior consultant, not to mention a revered expert, gave him the power of authority. I'm sorry to say he misused it."

"Roger misses him terribly. He had been incredibly useful to his investigations. He was quite a forensic authority."

"How is he, Roger? I've not seen him for a while."

"I met him only a few weeks ago; he's fine, Jan," replied Leo. "He always sends his regards when I see him."

"I think he's really nice," said Janet, "not like your average policeman. Not that I know many."

"Rachel and I have seen him and Jean a few times recently. Rachel and Jean are really close."

"Your ex-Wing Commander, Barry, is it usual for such a senior officer to go into reconnaissance?"

"No, Emma, it's very unusual. We're good friends, always have been. He was the most decorated Battle of Britain fighter ace we had on the base, and then overnight, they transferred him into reconnaissance. I assumed he had been transferred to RAF Medmenham. That's the big photo recon base, but he said no, it wasn't them. I asked him where he'd been stationed, and apparently, it's all very top secret. He can't tell me who they are, but he let slip that Fiona, his girlfriend, is a part of it. It's all very intriguing if I'm honest. Whoever they are, they have an awful lot of clout to get someone like Johnny to up sticks and join them."

"You say he flies mainly over the coast of France. That's interesting."

"Forget I said that, Frank. It was a slip of the tongue."

"Come on, Barry, this is us. You know all the talk is about an invasion of France; why else are all these Americans here?"

"Well, yes, it does kind of sound as if it might have something to do with that."

"Can we actually do that, launch an invasion across the Channel?"

"Of course we can, Jan. The question isn't, can we do it? The question is, can we do it successfully? It'll be no good just capturing a beach somewhere. We have to get the largest amphibious invasion force that's ever been assembled, ashore and inland, against what will be stiff opposition. We'll need to supply and reinforce the initial invasion for what will become the bloodiest battles of the war in France and later Germany. Can you imagine how much planning such an operation would require?"

"Not just planning, but also aerial reconnaissance of the French coast. Your mate Johnny has told you more than you're letting on, Barry."

"Emma, you always do that. I'm keeping my mouth shut, and don't any of you repeat a word. I mean it, anything to do with an invasion is so secret, you're not even allowed to dream about it in your sleep."

"Don't worry, Barry, you haven't told us anything that a mind like Emma's couldn't deduce by herself. Anyone for another pint?"

"I'd love to, Frank, but Roy and I must go; we've got a train to catch."

It was time to go. We had only intended to have a quick drink. As usual, we walked back over the bridge together, arm in arm, but we were surprisingly quiet this time. A seed had been planted in our minds. The prospect that we might invade Europe and finally push Hitler back to his defeat had ceased to be speculation; we created our own expectations. It offered a path towards peace. It would be a path lined with unimaginable suffering, but it offered us hope where none existed before. You can't imagine what it's like when everything you know and love is threatened by a degenerate monster with the power to enslave you in his own likeness. We lived in that hellish nightmare since 1939—no wonder we were entranced by the prospect of vanquishing the monster.

Frank and I discussed it over our evening meal at home.

"It's the prospect of an end to it. Don't you find it exciting, Frank?"

"It's just a prospect, don't get your hopes up."

"Oh, why can't you show some enthusiasm, Frank? You must have some hope for the future."

"You also have to be a realist; we live in the here and now, and look how we live."

"Do you mean what we're eating?"

"That's part of it."

"It gets us by. I don't have time to queue at the shops for our rations. I scrounge any leftovers I can from the canteen and buy whatever is left in the shops."

"This is what I mean, look at it."

"I know it's not much, but there are many people for whom this would be a banquet. You should be more grateful, Frank."

"I see it for what it is, not some fanciful vision of the future. Sometimes, it just rains. There are no rainbows."

"There's always a rainbow. You have to want to see it."

"And I don't, I suppose."

"No, you don't. I try so hard, but you refuse to make the best of it."

"I'm sorry if I disappoint you, Emma, but I just don't have your eternal optimism."

"Well, I'm going to continue to hope. I need to believe there's an end in sight. This war can't go on forever."

Frank didn't answer; I suppose if your glass is half empty, then that's how it is. We were all under intolerable pressure; I suppose it wasn't surprising when it weighed us down. We finished our meal, such as it was, and Frank sat with his newspaper. I would have preferred to talk about what we were trying to do at the hospital or the much-rumoured invasion of Europe. Rather than disturb Frank, I listened to the wireless in the kitchen until my eyes started closing, which didn't take very long.

"I'm going to bed, Frank. Are you coming?"

"Yes, I'll come with you."

Frank used my little bathroom first, so when I returned to the bedroom, he was already in bed in his pyjamas, reading his book. I slipped off my underclothes beneath my nightdress with my back towards him. Not that Frank would have bothered to look up from his book, but I remained very modest about those things. We were both tired, as always, so Frank put his book down after just a few minutes. He kissed my forehead.

"Night, Em."

"Night, Frank."

# Chapter Sixty
# 21st January 1944

Roger

*"They said Florence Nightingale still walked the corridors of St Thomas's in a lonely vigil to inspire the next generation of doctors and nurses. She wasn't lonely any more."*

Jean and I were clearing up after dinner when we heard the siren. Since the Blitz, there had been numerous air raid warnings, mostly false alarms, but there had been some small-scale German incursions. Despite the false alarms, we looked at each other with growing apprehension. I peered around the blackout blind but could see nothing. Once you've experienced the terror of being beneath falling bombs, it becomes a part of who you are. Your heart jumps into your throat the moment you hear that sound. This is why so many people spent the entire war sleeping in the deep underground shelters. Jean and I considered it, but with me so often coming home late, we opted to 'take our chances'.

"Can you see anything, Roger?"

"No, but I'll just pop outside and listen."

I went rushing back moments later. "Under the stairs, Jean, quickly. This isn't a false alarm."

It certainly wasn't a false alarm; I could see and hear distant bombs exploding beyond the rooftops. The night sky had that same ominous glow we became accustomed to during the Blitz. Distant clouds were illuminated with flashes of yellow and orange, and columns of smoke became visible against the reflection. The sudden terror we experienced had less to do with the bombs searching for us - we instantly relived the memory of the Blitz, and Balham tube station came back to torment us.

The bombing grew louder and closer; it was the Blitz all over again. We clung to each other, stripped bare of the reassuring illusion that the bombing was over. We didn't leave the under-stair cupboard until the all-clear had been sounded. The sound of German bombers filled the sky, but we were spared any close hits; our luck had held out.

"We should have stayed in the underground shelters, Roger. All those people were right, weren't they? Is this the start of another Blitz? I can't go through that again. I just can't."

"It's over for now, Jean. Try to calm down. Let's put the kettle on."

"What do you mean, it's over for now?"

"We can't be sure. They might be back, guided by the incendiaries."

"Oh no, please God, no."

"I'll make you a cup of tea, Luv. Remember what we used to do - concentrate on your breathing."

"It brings it all back. It's as if it's all happening again. That night, when we walked to the shelter with Rachel and Barbara; just five seconds earlier, that bomb would have killed us."

"It didn't, though, did it? We were lucky, and we're going to stay lucky."

"Dave and Marilyn weren't lucky, were they? When we heard that roaring sound in the tunnel, Dave grabbed my hand. I saw it. I could see it coming towards us."

Jean was getting more and more agitated. Her eyes were wide open, but it wasn't me she could see. Reliving the terrors of the past is every bit as real as a present danger. She buried her head on my shoulder as we shared the memories of Balham Station.

"It's in the past, Luv. We have to put it behind us."

I knew it was a glib thing to say; I had those same memories over and over again. For Jean, it was the look of horror in Dave's eyes as his grip on her hand slipped away. For me, it was knowing I couldn't be with Marilyn during that last second. I didn't have a last image to cling to, only the very worst my mind could imagine. We stood holding each other as if we were back in that tunnel, clinging to life. Except in Jean's mind, it wasn't me she was clinging to. The terror passed, as it had done dozens of times before. We had plenty of experience to call upon; what pulled us through it before would pull us through again. The battle between fear and courage is won by the brave.

"I'm sorry, Roger, I lost it a bit there. I'm alright now. What should we do?"

She wasn't alright, of course, and neither was I. The sudden return to bombing became our worst nightmare coming true. You can endure all manner of hardship when there's no alternative. When you live with the alternative, the mental resilience you held onto for so long begins to crumble.

"I think we need to stay here. We don't want to get caught outside if they come back."

We tried to sleep, but all the while, we waited for the sound of the siren. That ghastly sound dictated our very existence. Just before dawn, it started up again. We were dressed and under the stairs within a few minutes. Then the bombs started falling again. The pattern was familiar. The German bombers used the same tactic they used during the Blitz. They followed the Thames up from the estuary, so we heard the distant bombs being dropped on the East End of London first, but we knew they would progress west towards us. We could feel the ground beneath our feet shake as they drew closer. The danger is most imminent when you can hear the bombers' engines. You don't know if their bomb bays are empty or full. You only know they're above you. We just held each other, powerless to do anything other than think that every second could be our last.

A bomb fell very close, and the glass in my rear kitchen window shattered. The light went out as the electricity was cut off. Then, as quickly as the bombers passed over us, they were gone. They came in waves during the Blitz, so we braced ourselves for worse to come. We cowered in the cupboard illuminated with a torch for another fifteen minutes, but nothing happened. Then we heard the all-clear, the only friendly sound the siren made. The relief was palpable. Looking at Jean, holding her in my arms, every second of simply being alive became a treasured moment. I made a silly comment.

"I told you our luck would hold out, didn't I?"

"You did, and you were right this time, but we're spending the night in the shelters from now on."

"We don't know if this is a one-off or the start of something else, but I agree, we can't rely on luck."

That was the start of what the Germans called Operation Steinbock, or what we ended up calling the 'Little Blitz'. Had we known it would continue until April only to be replaced by something even worse, I'm not sure how strong our resolve would have been. We picked ourselves up and dusted ourselves off, just as we had done so many times before, ignorant of what lay ahead. My kitchen window had been blown in by a bomb falling on the adjacent road. An entire family was killed, including two children. Our only damage was the window glass lying on the floor, partially held together by the adhesive tape that criss-crossed all our windows.

The Blitz taught us to carry on regardless, so that is precisely what we did. Jean knew how vital her work with the WVS that morning would be. There would be hundreds of people in desperate need. I envied her work; she helped forlorn people in their hour of greatest need. I also helped them by protecting them from those who would take advantage of their desperation and by maintaining public order. The difference was that Jean came home celebrating all that's best about human nature. I came home feeling despondent, having seen the very worst of human nature.

There was another aspect to the renewed bombing which hadn't escaped my attention. We knew from experience that some aspects of crime increased during the Blitz; I expected it to be the same this time. I went into the police station that morning, weighed down by the whole experience.

"Morning, Jack. Any casualties this morning?"

"Yes, I'm afraid to say PC Hastings bought it last night, him and his wife."

"Oh, I'm so sorry, Jack. He volunteered to come back in, didn't he? The poor sod thought he'd retired."

"They were at home; it was a direct hit. He wasn't on police duty."

"We've lost one of our own; he was a good man."

Jack didn't dwell on it, and neither did I, but I knew he and Walter Hastings were friends from the last war. It must have hit Jack hard, but he would be the last person to buckle under emotional pressure. He would maintain the morale of the station, regardless. His telephone didn't stop ringing, so I left him to do what he did best.

"Morning, Jeff, this is bad news about Hastings; is everyone else alright?"

"Yes, Guv, I came in with Alfie, but there's no sign of the Inspector."

"Not like Gerry to be late. I hope to Christ he's okay."

"What do you make of it, Roger? We didn't expect that last night, did we?"

"It was a big raid in two waves, just as during the Blitz. I can't help but think it's the start of another campaign."

"That's what I think. If that's the case, it'll bring out the usual suspects. There have already been two reports of looting."

"As if it's not bad enough having to contend with the bombing. Doesn't this get you down, Jeff?"

"Human nature, you mean? I joined the force because I wanted to do good in society. I naively thought when war was declared that I would be protecting society from without, not from within."

"War can bring out the worst in people as well as the best. I didn't dream there would be such a large element who'd turn in on themselves. It doesn't make sense. You'd think everyone would be united against the common enemy."

Jack came in looking very grim-faced. "Gerry's been badly injured. Both he and Margaret have been rushed to St Thomas's."

"Oh no, not Gerry. How bad is it, Jack?"

"I don't know. That's all I've been told."

I must have looked badly shocked because Jeff spoke immediately. "You go to the hospital, Roger. Me and Alfie will deal with things here."

"Thanks, Jeff; keep me informed if you can."

You realise the true value of your friends when you think you might lose them. I rushed to St Thomas's as quickly as I could. The roads were disrupted by the bomb damage, with fire crews and ambulances still dealing with incidents. As I approached the river, the destruction grew worse. The air became laden with smoke. I half expected to see the hospital in flames, but a column of smoke rose from the other side of the river. The Palace of Westminster, the seat of government, had been hit again. I walked into a war zone; injured people lay on the ground where ambulance crews had to leave them. I looked around for anyone I recognised. Janet saw me and rushed over.

"Janet, do you know if a police chief inspector has been brought in with his wife?"

"Yes, a constable came in with them. I think he's in surgery now with Emma."

She pointed towards the operating theatre down in the basement. I had no business being there, but I wasn't thinking. Two porters carried a victim on a stretcher towards the operating theatre, so I followed them down the stairs. The injured were lined up, waiting to be wheeled into surgery. Among them lay Gerry and Margaret. He was unconscious, but Margaret saw me. Her face was contorted in pain. She had an obvious injury. I could see bone protruding through the flesh of her lower left arm, and she had several injuries caused by flying shards of glass.

"Roger, how is he? Is he alright?"

"I don't know, Margaret, but you're in expert hands, I can promise you."

Emma burst through the door into the hallway and glanced over at the human misery demanding her attention.

"Roger, what are you doing here? Are you injured?"

"No, this is my Chief Inspector and his wife."

She looked at me with that knowing look I had become accustomed to. "They're close friends, aren't they?"

"They are very close friends. Gerry looks bad to me. Please, Emma, do what you can for him."

She immediately looked at Margaret and dismissed her as a minor injury. Then she examined Gerry. I watched in complete wonder as she felt and probed; her eyes seemed to see every bone and organ. She shouted instructions to the nurse before turning towards me.

"He's got serious injuries. There's a lot of internal bleeding. It's probably caused by the flying glass. I can see no sign of a crush injury. He's concussed as well."

"Can you save him?"

"I don't know, but if it's possible, then yes, I will. I'll do everything I can."

She wasted no more time talking to me; she vanished as quickly as she appeared. I turned to Margaret, who was distraught about her husband, not knowing what was going on.

"He's been taken into surgery, Margaret. He's got internal injuries, but the surgeon will take care of him. I'm sure he will be fine."

"Are you sure, Roger? Is he in good hands?"

"That's why I'm sure of the outcome, Margaret. He's in the hands of someone who won't rest until she's delivered him safely back to you."

"How can you be so sure?"

"I know this woman. I would trust her with my life. If it's a miracle we need, then she'll deliver it, I promise you."

Margaret almost managed a smile, but as much as I had reassured her, I couldn't relieve the pain she suffered from the gaping wound on her arm. A nurse came and gave her some morphine before loosening the tourniquet above the wound.

"Don't worry," the nurse said confidently. "This looks bad, but Doctor Stevenson will have it fixed in no time."

I didn't doubt her. Emma's presence filled that hospital. They said Florence Nightingale walked the corridors of St Thomas's in a lonely vigil to inspire the next generation of doctors and nurses. Well, she wasn't lonely any more.

## Chapter Sixty-One
# February 1944

Emma

*"Love is one of life's most elusive gifts. It doesn't always announce its presence; it can arrive with a whisper and depart in a tear. Allow that first fleeting moment to slip through your fingers, and you can spend the rest of your life regretting it."*

As soon as the air raids started again, Frank and I found ourselves living separate lives as we reverted back to a nocturnal existence in the bowels of the hospital. We faced the impossible situation of reduced capacity, diminished staffing levels, and a sudden dramatic increase in casualties. With no other option, we were on call twenty-four hours a day during the emergency.

I discharged Roger's friend Gerry after two weeks. Removing shards of glass from bomb victims was one of the most common injuries we had to deal with. In Chief Inspector Higgins' case, a large piece of glass had perforated his bowel, and to a lesser extent, his liver. It caused considerable internal bleeding. I repaired his bowel, and the liver has extraordinary powers of self-generation. Typical of bowel injuries, it was the infection that almost killed him. Roger visited him and his wife every day while he remained critical.

I'll never forget when I came out of surgery and told Roger the operation on his friend had gone well. The look on his face was a joy to behold. He completely forgot himself. Roger instantly put his arms around me and kissed me on the lips. He then spent the next ten minutes apologising.

I reassured him there was no reason to be concerned. He hadn't offended me; we were close friends. I learnt something rather special about Roger that day. The kiss was nothing more than a spontaneous outpouring of emotion. It was how he expressed himself. But then later, after discussing his friend, he apologised again and said something very meaningful.

"I wouldn't have kissed any of your colleagues, Emma."

"No, I don't expect you would."

"That's precisely why I'm apologising. I allowed myself to cross a boundary uninvited, and that's unforgivable."

"You're making a fuss about nothing, Roger. Actually, it was rather nice. Perhaps that boundary you're so concerned about doesn't really exist."

Why did I say that? I meant it, but why did I have to blurt it out? Of all the occasions to admit such a thing, I chose the moment when we were standing in a hospital corridor with me dressed in a surgical gown covered in blood. Roger took a step back, and his expression changed.

"Boundaries between people, especially between a man and a woman, are very important, Emma. I live in a world where those boundaries are violated on a daily basis. That isn't my world. That isn't who I am. If you had invited me to kiss you, it would have been an entirely different situation."

I felt like saying kiss me now; I am inviting you. Thank heavens, I managed not to be so silly. Instead, when we said goodbye, I did something slightly more dignified. I kissed his cheek very correctly and then threw it all away with what I said next.

"You would never offend me, Roger. You're the perfect gentleman, and I love you for it."

I understood and deeply appreciated what he meant about boundaries after living for so long behind an immensely tall boundary of my own creation. Roger was unlike all the other men I had ever known. I didn't once feel anything other than completely relaxed in his company. If that boundary existed at all, then he made it seem totally redundant. He always made me feel as if I was the centre of his attention. My needs were his concern.

That evening in the basement, Janet had a field day at my expense. Shirley saw Roger kiss me, and of course, they made the most of it.

"You kept that very quiet, Emma."

"Kept what quiet?"

"Your romantic affair with Roger," Janet replied.

"Don't be silly. I'm not having an affair with him."

"Oh, it's just sex, is it? I don't blame you; he is a bit of a dish in a scruffy kind of way," said Shirley.

"You know that's not true, so don't go repeating it. What if Frank overheard?"

"Don't worry, Em, your secret's safe with us."

I didn't think for a moment that Janet would repeat it in front of anyone else, but even the thought of it made me feel guilty. I desperately wished I didn't blush at the slightest provocation. Marion took one look at me and whispered a more pertinent observation.

"Perhaps you're wishing you were having an affair with him."

"You're becoming as bad as the rest of them, Marion. I'm wishing no such thing."

"A word to the wise, Emma. I speak as someone who let love pass me by. Love is one of life's most elusive gifts. It doesn't always announce its presence; it can arrive with a whisper and depart in a tear. Allow that first fleeting moment to slip through your fingers, and you can spend the rest of your life regretting it."

I stood in stunned silence. I didn't anticipate for a second that Marion was about to say something so profound. Her words cut through me like a knife. She saw in me something I dared not even think. Roger was a lovely man. I liked him and really enjoyed our conversations. Actually, he was so much more than that; I had never met a man like him. He had all the masculine qualities I recognised in men such as Alexander Bartholomew. He was intelligent and authoritative, but he also possessed the great charm and eloquence of Ken. Quite unlike Alex, he combined those qualities with extraordinary warmth and empathy, especially towards women. He understood me in ways that Frank never did. It would be very easy to fall in love with him.

## Chapter Sixty-Two
# Marjorie Knowles, D-Day June 6th, 1944

Roger

*"4414 men died on the beaches of Normandy that day.
We are the future they died for."*

The renewed bombing rekindled a miserable time, a return to the Blitz in all but name. Jean and I spent our nights back in the claustrophobic subterranean world of the Clapham underground. During the day, I negotiated my way through the morass of crime following in the wake of people's misery. The nights offered no relief, as we sacrificed privacy, comfort, and clean air for safety. I counted the straws, thinking we must be approaching the final one. When you think things can't get any worse, they usually do. The overnight bombing raid had already defiled a bright sunny morning when Alfie rushed into the room.

"Morning, Guv, there's been a vicious murder in Battersea. There's nothing to say it's Burrows, but the PC who called it in sounds badly shaken up. It's a young female victim."

"I'll get straight over there. Grab your hat, Jeff."

Jeff and I were silent as we walked to the car, both thinking the same thing. Could this be Burrows? We were still keeping an eye on him, but with our limited resources, it amounted to only a token effort. He'd kept his head down for a long time, but I knew he was only biding his time. The renewed bombing once again provided him with the cover he used to his advantage during the Blitz. We approached the address in Battersea with considerable apprehension. A tragedy awaited us, whatever the circumstances. A young woman's life had been cut short. I prepared myself for the worst. The constable who called it in stood at the front door of a typical red brick terraced house in Battersea.

"Morning, Constable, what's the story here?"

"The victim's in the back garden, Sir. She's been stabbed dozens of times, including wounds to the face. It turned my stomach over."

"Who found her?"

"The next-door neighbour found her this morning. She says she heard a disturbance last night and looked out the back window to see what was happening. She saw nothing, so she called out to the woman, but there was no reply. Perhaps she scared the killer off."

"What time was this?"

"Middle of the night, after the siren had sounded. Then the air raid started, so she obviously didn't pursue the matter. You don't think this could be the Ripper again, do you, Sir?"

"What's the victim's name, Constable?"

"Marjorie Knowles."

"And there's a rear alleyway leading to the garden, and her husband is a serving soldier?"

"Well, yes, that's right. Does that tell you anything, Sir?"

"It does, Constable; it tells me this is the work of the Ripper. Does she have family, anyone local?"

"I believe so, Sir. They tell me her family all live locally."

"Have you made a note of the names and addresses?"

"Yes, it's all in my notes, together with the neighbour's statement."

"Well done, Constable. Thank God I won't be the person who has to go around there and tell the woman's parents. Show us where the body is."

We entered a small but lovingly tended garden at the back of the house. Flower borders bursting with colour surrounded a perfectly manicured lawn. The garden spoke of loving care and attention. In the middle of the lawn lay the body of the gardener. The victim had self-evidently been stabbed many times. Her fully clothed body lay in a pool of blood where Burrows killed her.

My initial interpretation of the murder scene became our working hypothesis. Burrows followed his modus operandi to the letter. He probably selected the victim months or even years previously. Her initials were MK, shorthand for Mary Jane Kelly. She was in her late twenties, had no children, and her husband was away serving in the forces. Burrows took advantage of the air raid, knowing the woman was in the habit of using the Anderson shelter in the garden. He no doubt lay in wait, possibly in or near the shelter. When the victim came out of the house to spend the night in the relative safety of the shelter, he pounced on her. Had his intentions gone according to plan, no doubt he would have taken her into the house, where he intended to reenact Jack the Ripper's terrible mutilation of Mary Jane Kelly in 1888.

There would have been a momentary scuffle before Burrows subdued his victim. Before he could take her into the house, the next-door neighbour disturbed him. In Burrows' psychotic mind, every aspect of what he intended to be his masterpiece had to be played out exactly as he fantasised. Being disturbed would have enraged him. The knife wounds to the victim's face and body could only be described as frenzied. Burrows clearly went berserk with rage.

We interviewed the neighbour, who said only what I already knew. I also doubted that the pathologist over at King's College Hospital would add anything new, either. Our only hope lay in a door-to-door investigation and with the local ARP wardens. It was just possible someone might have seen him come or go. However, we knew from experience that all those efforts would likely come to nothing. During the blackout, especially during an air raid, Burrows remained as elusive as an autumn daffodil.

As soon as I had put everything in motion at the murder scene, Jeff and I pursued our best line of enquiry - Burrows himself. I telephoned ahead and asked Jack to have two of his uniform boys go to the Town Hall and bring him in for questioning. My instructions were to arrest him on suspicion of murder if he didn't cooperate. I then wanted his neighbours interviewed in case they saw him come or go during the night. We had no evidence against him, but I wanted him shaken up. Jeff and I mulled over the case as we drove back to the station.

"It comes back to the same thing, Jeff. How does he come and go without ever being seen?"

"We have a few sightings of a tall man wearing a coat and hat."

"That's really helpful, isn't it? I don't suppose he drove his car. That's too obvious. So what does he do? Does he walk everywhere?"

"He must do, but it's a reasonable distance."

"Every murder has been within a twenty to thirty-minute walk from his house. It's perfectly possible."

"It's possible but very risky. Don't forget he's carrying at least one knife and possibly blood-stained clothing."

"We didn't find a murder weapon at his house, did we? He could have hidden it well, but why risk taking it home? Think about it, Jeff. It's far too risky from his point of view. Much safer to have a place he uses on his route home where he can store incriminating evidence."

"That's a good idea, Roger. That's worth following up. I very much doubt he has an accomplice, but it needs to be nothing more substantial than a good hiding place. Something such as a garden shed or a garage."

"A lock-up garage would be ideal, wouldn't it?"

"It'll be like looking for a needle in a haystack. It could be anywhere."

"Let's start with the lockups."

We drove on in silence, both deep in thought. Burrows waited all that time to strike again. I mulled over what that told me about the man, and it sent a shiver down my spine. The meticulous planning, combined with a resolute determination to succeed, spoke of a highly motivated individual, not the description of a madman. But clearly, Burrows was insane. The more I tried to understand my adversary, the more terrifying he became. I needed to change the subject to protect my own sanity.

"Talking about being locked up, how are you and Pam coping in the underground at night?"

"It's much better than last time. We've got decent facilities now. Everyone certainly puts a brave face on it. How about you and Jean?"

"As you say, it's much better now. It's the lack of privacy that gets Jean down."

"Yes, Pam hates that; it's certainly not good for your sex life."

"What sex life?"

"Some people just don't care, do they; it can be quite entertaining at times."

"Jean's mass survey diary shows people are generally in good spirits about it. It surprises me; I suppose the fact is, it's a lot better than the alternative."

We waited back at the station for Burrows to appear, and I confess that I felt anxious. He had that effect on me, and I wasn't alone. It was probably all in my mind, but I really felt as if I was in the presence of something evil. Jeff and I debated about how he would arrive. Would he be calm and controlled, or would he be spitting blood? An innocent man would present a mixture of bewilderment and anger. I knew Burrows. He might be superficially calm while trying to appear indignant, but beneath the surface, he would be seething.

Two PCs escorted him to a chair in our interview room, where we left him for ten minutes. He came directly from his place of work in the housing department. Burrows didn't look like your average murderer. He was dressed in a smart suit and tie and didn't conform to the usual stereotype. It all added to the discomfort I felt in his presence. The moment Jeff and I walked in, his eyes narrowed as he stared at me. He didn't waste any time; he started complaining in the strongest possible terms. It was all bluster, a futile attempt to appear outraged. I let him rant on until he ran out of steam.

"I've had enough of this charade, Burrows. We've just come from your latest sadistic murder. You really are a sick bastard. Where were you last night?"

"At home as usual, and I spent a large part of the night in my garden shelter."

"Anyone who can corroborate that?"

"You know I live alone; besides, I don't need to prove my innocence."

"All that research and all that planning, but you couldn't account for the unexpected, could you? That didn't accord with your fantasy, did it? You were denied fulfilment, and you couldn't cope with that, could you? You lost it, Burrows, didn't you? You lost control of the situation. You like control, don't you, Burrows? How did it feel to lose it completely? You behaved like a demented savage. Is this what you are, Burrows?"

He squirmed on his chair, desperately wanting to deny what he would have considered a shortcoming. In Burrows' twisted world, control gave him power, and the lack of it implied weakness. The psychotic part of him wanted to deny any hint of weakness, but the more rational part remained silent. I couldn't get inside the head of a monster like Burrows. Understanding him would mean entering his world, which would be a terrifying prospect. His silence spoke volumes.

"Let's end it here, admit what you've done, and grab your moment in the limelight."

"Don't be absurd. How dare you accuse me of these crimes? You have no evidence to connect me to any of it. I'm the victim of your personal vendetta. You can rest assured I will complain to the highest authority. I'll ensure there are implications for your career."

"You're a sad excuse for a human being, Burrows. Do you seriously think the Commissioner is going to listen to you? Don't delude yourself. You're in no position to threaten me. If it's a threat you want, I can promise you one thing. I will get you, Burrows. I'll see you hang; I can promise you that."

I'll never know if I got through to him or not. There were times when his denials appeared to be perfectly genuine as if one part of him deluded the other. Then, on other occasions, the manic look in his eyes and the menace in his voice were enough to make my blood run cold. Jeff and I questioned him for the rest of the day. He admitted nothing, and we didn't have a scrap of evidence against him. We had no other option but to thank him for helping us with our enquiries. I went home that night thoroughly depressed.

I remembered times when Jean had the power to turn a bad day into something heavenly - those days appeared to have gone. She greeted me with a kiss and a warm embrace, but the fire that used to ignite between us had dwindled to a smouldering ember. We just had time for a quick meal of rationed misery before rushing over to the Clapham underground for the night. It wasn't so much that the romance had seeped away from us; it had been stolen.

We lay in our separate bunks that night amongst thousands of others. Row upon row, three deep. There was always snoring, coughing or talking. Then there's the constant smell of people, the great unwashed of London. Some nights, it represented the triumph of the human spirit as we collectively overcame adversity. On other nights, it amounted to nothing more than squalid dehumanisation. I didn't feel in the slightest triumphant that night. I longed for clean sheets and the warm, soft body of a woman. Not just any woman; I wanted the woman in the bunk below me, but she began to feel a long way away.

The weeks that followed had only one significance. The bombing had stopped, for the moment at least. Experience taught us to re-enter the world of light with caution. So often, we would emerge to find death and destruction. The following morning was unlike any other morning - it was the most significant date of the European war. The largest invasion force the world has ever seen landed on the beaches of Normandy. It was June 6th, 1944, D-Day.

The news emerged slowly, but when it did, it brought with it something we had almost lost sight of. Without hope, the human spirit has no future. 4414 men died on the beaches of Normandy that day. We are the future they died for. The enormity of their sacrifice was not lost on those of us whose job it was to hold society together.

Chapter Sixty-Three
# June 14th, 1944

Emma

*"We allowed ourselves to dream of normal things, and now those dreams lay crushed beneath the rubble. We were left to mourn their passing."*

D-Day changed everything. There hadn't been an air raid since April, and now the Allied armies had a foothold on mainland Europe. We finally had reason to hope that the bombing might finally be over. Renewed optimism filled the air. It reflected in peoples' faces. Like many people, Frank and I dared to return home at night to enjoy a brief taste of normality. After all we had been through, the prospect of clean sheets and a toilet was intoxicating. It didn't last.

On the 13th of June, a report on the wireless spoke about an enormous explosion in Bow where six people had been killed and dozens made homeless. We didn't know what had caused that explosion. It just sounded as if it was another huge bomb. Everything changed the following day. Shirley saw it first; she thought she could see a fighter plane flying low towards us. It appeared sufficiently unusual for her to shout out for us all to look. At first, it looked like a small aeroplane, but the noise it made was unlike anything we had seen or heard before. Even through the hospital windows, the rasping sound became alarming. We looked in astonishment at the flame trailing behind it. As quickly as it appeared, it disappeared as it flew over us. That was our first sighting of a V1 flying bomb.

It didn't take long for us to realise the seriousness of this new threat. Our introduction to the damage it could inflict came that same day when an extraordinary incident occurred at the hospital. It began an event that no one involved has ever forgotten. An ambulance arrived carrying four seriously injured men. I met them directly from the ambulance. Two soldiers were in uniform, one a private and the other a four-star general. A third man I recognised as a Member of Parliament. The fourth man, who I didn't recognise, wore a beautifully tailored suit. He had a very nasty head injury, and they all suffered from blast injuries.

I took care of the many cuts and abrasions and fixed the broken arm of one gentleman. The man with the head injury looked to be in a bad way, but he remained conscious when he arrived, which was a good sign. He told me his name was Edward Sinclair, and then he promptly lost consciousness soon after. I bandaged his broken ribs and closed the open wound on his head, but I didn't like the look of his condition. When I had done everything possible for them, Doctor Wiśniewski decided they should be placed under observation in ward 5. We still called it ward 5, even though it was our only functioning ward. That proved to be the start of the most extraordinary day.

I remained concerned about Mr Sinclair. My initial diagnosis pointed towards an intracranial hematoma. That being the case, he would likely die without surgery. I disagreed with Wiśniewski's demand that he should only be observed. The man's condition worsened; he needed the kind of surgery we were not capable of providing. In my opinion, we needed to send him to another hospital where they could carry out the brain surgery I thought he needed. Later that morning, I risked Wiśniewski's wrath by sneaking into the ward to check on Mr Sinclair. He had slipped into a deep, unresponsive coma. I was right about his condition. That's when the most extraordinary woman appeared.

A woman in her thirties, very smartly dressed in a navy dress suit, with a great shock of auburn hair, she immediately grabbed my attention. I could see the fear in her eyes as she looked along the row of beds, obviously searching for someone in particular. When she came upon Mr Sinclair and found him unresponsive, she almost collapsed onto the bed. For a moment, the poor woman was catatonic. I then saw her physically struggling to compose herself. She stood up, straightened her clothes, and appeared to summon a hidden reserve of strength. I saw her take a deep breath before she shouted for help. Shirley was the nurse on hand.

"I need to speak to the doctor who is tending this patient. I want to see him now," the woman demanded.

"That's not possible. Who are you? You shouldn't be here," Shirley replied.

"I'm not going anywhere."

Shirley didn't know what to do. Later, she said the woman seemed to stare right through her. I could understand what she meant; the woman had piercing eyes that seemed to analyse everything she looked at. Shirley called for Marion, who promptly marched down the ward towards whom she regarded as an intruder.

"I'm staying with this man," the woman said, very defensively.

"I don't know how you got in here, but I'll have you removed if necessary," Marion said.

"The Luftwaffe couldn't do that, so you certainly won't. I'm staying here. You can beat me to the ground and drag me out screaming, and I'll come straight back. I'll never leave this man's side, do you understand?"

"Who are you? Who is this man to you?"

"I love him. That's all you need to know."

"That explains a lot. In that case, you had best have a chair, my dear; it may be a long wait." Marion beckoned to Shirley. "Nurse, fetch this lady a chair."

"Thank you, Matron, I'll cooperate with you," the woman said. "I'll not be in the way, but I'm not leaving. Can you explain to me what this man's condition is?"

"He has broken ribs and multiple minor injuries which will heal, but he has a serious head injury; he's in a coma."

"When will he come out of the coma?"

"I'm sorry, my dear, but he might not come out of it."

The woman's legs buckled beneath her at the news. She had to grab the bed end to steady herself. When I saw her reaction, I wanted to step forward to help her, but Doctor Wiśniewski came into the ward, and I did not want to antagonise him. One of the other patients in the ward had developed what I suspected to be a thrombosis in the blood vessels of the spleen. Doctor Wiśniewski finally agreed I should attend the patient with a view towards surgery. With a reason to be there, I could keep an eye on our uninvited guest, who so intrigued me.

"Thank you for being honest with me, Matron," she said, "but I can assure you he will come out of the coma and make a full recovery. I need to speak to whoever is in charge of his treatment."

"That's Dr Wisniewski; he's with another patient. Would you like a nurse to fetch you a cup of tea? You look as though you need it."

"That would be greatly appreciated, thank you. What's your name, Matron?"

"Mrs Horworthy."

"And your first name?"

"I'm known as matron, my dear, but my first name is Marion."

"Thank you again, Marion, I'm Mrs Heywood, Lily Heywood."

Marion became transfixed by whoever Mrs Heywood was, as indeed we all were. Mrs Heywood then walked over to one of the other casualties who came in with Mr Sinclair, and she promptly addressed him as General Ashton. She spoke in whispers. Something very unusual was going on. She then took Marion to one side, and Marion later confided in me what had happened. Mrs Heywood asked Marion if she understood the meaning of a state secret - she said she had to confide in someone.

The mysterious Mrs Heywood seemed to be involved with state matters at a very high level. She instructed Marion to change the names on the admission papers for the casualties who came in with Mr. Sinclair. They were apparently too important to be named. Then she commandeered Evelyn's office and sent her out while she made some phone calls. Everyone fell under the spell of the mysterious Mrs Heywood and did as they were told. Everyone, that is, except Wiśniewski. Marion has told the story of what followed a hundred times. Doctor Wiśniewski stormed up and addressed Mrs Heywood.

"Now look here, Mrs Heywood, or whatever your name is. Matron has spoken to me and tells me you're from some sort of government department. I'm not releasing hospital records to you or anyone else. I deeply resent timewasters like you walking into an emergency like this and expecting cooperation. Who the hell do you people think you are? Why don't you leave it to those who actually get things done?"

Marion told me with obvious delight what happened next. Mrs Heywood looked at Wiśniewski with disdain, and obviously, realising his Polish background, she gave him a real dressing down.

"Your ignorance of this situation is perfectly understandable, but that's no excuse for such arrogance. Let me explain something to you, Dr Wiśniewski. There are people in this ward who have contributed enormously to the invasion of Europe, and I'm proud to count myself among them. Allied soldiers are fighting for our freedom in Normandy right now. The people of Poland know better than anyone what German occupation means, and yet they continue to fight through their magnificent resistance movement. I'm asking you to do something for this country. If you don't value what we're fighting for, then shame on you. You're a disgrace to your brave countrymen."

"Are you threatening me, Mrs Heywood?"

"Yes, I am."

I would have given anything to have been there. Apparently, the look on Wiśniewski's face was a joy to behold. I doubt he had ever been spoken to in that way before, and certainly not by a woman. Mrs Heywood was quite right; he was arrogant. I can only think he realised he had met his match because, for once, he backed down.

"Perhaps I do need to know more about this situation. I too have been fighting today. I've been fighting to save lives, but I apologise for appearing arrogant."

"I've also had a traumatic day, Doctor. I would normally be far more courteous," Mrs Heywood said. "The men in this ward serve this country at the highest level. I mean no disrespect to you or your staff, but I will forward their medical notes to higher authority. The well-being of these people is not for you to decide. I'm particularly concerned about this man. Explain to me what his condition is."

Wiśniewski had finally accepted my diagnosis of Mr. Sinclair's condition. He had to explain that he had a serious condition requiring brain surgery and that we didn't have the expertise to perform the operation. When she asked who did, he told her about a surgeon called Cairns at the Military Hospital in Oxford. Mrs Heywood promptly made a series of phone calls. Before we knew it, arrangements had been made to transfer Mr Sinclair to St Hugh's Hospital in Oxford. Whoever Mrs Heywood was, she was a force of nature. I spoke to her briefly as they were leaving for St Hugh's in an ambulance. She must have been under tremendous stress, but somehow, she retained her composure.

"I know something about Hugh Cairns at Oxford," I said. "He's a world-leading authority on brain injury. You couldn't be taking Mr. Sinclair to see a more competent person."

"Oh, thank God. That's the first reassurance anyone has given me. I have everything organised. Mr Cairns will be there personally to receive us and perform the surgery as soon as we arrive."

"I can't begin to imagine how you've arranged all this, but I wish you all the luck in the world, Mrs Heywood. You must love this man very much."

"I do. You obviously realise his name isn't Mr Sinclair. I wish I could tell who he is and why I love him so much. He has to survive; the country needs him, and I need him. I couldn't face the future without him."

I had never seen a woman remotely resembling her. Not before or since. She came into the hospital to find the man she loved in a critical condition. That alone would send most women into a tailspin. She then calmly took control of everything to do with the man and his colleagues. Everyone did as she requested, and she achieved it all by sheer force of character. It was only right at the end, as she left, I saw tears welling up in her eyes. That was the first hint that this extraordinary woman was human, like the rest of us.

She left a deep and lasting impression on me. Whoever Mr Sinclair was, he must consider himself deeply fortunate to be loved by a woman like her. I would love to know who they were and what they did that was so vital to the war effort. They were two people about whom I knew nothing. They were parallel lives existing next to mine but with paths that had now crossed. I prayed that his operation would be successful. I had absolutely no doubt that if Lily Heywood had any say in the matter, his future would be assured.

We were later told that his injuries, and those of the others with him, were caused by a V1. We still had no concept of what this weapon was or what its effects were going to be. The V1s were unlike anything we had seen before or anything we might even have imagined. The era of the missile descending upon an unsuspecting population had begun. A new terror fell among the people. Within days, they became a familiar sight above our heads. We quickly learned that when the dreadful rasping sound stopped, it would fall out of the sky. As the sound approached, we prayed it wouldn't stop. Your heart would race every time you heard one; we prayed they would continue onwards and effectively kill someone else.

Casualties rapidly started arriving at our door. People lived in constant fear because this was not like the Blitz. The V1s didn't arrive only at night; they arrived arbitrarily at any time. Each one had the capacity to kill dozens of people and destroy entire streets of houses. Within a week, there were thousands more homeless, and we were turning away ambulances, sending them to other hospitals. Just as one lot of casualties had been taken care of, another lot would arrive. We had no idea when they might come or how many. The optimism that D-Day offered us lay dashed beneath the rubble. During the Blitz, we had a reasonable certainty that we could tend to patients during the day without fear of being killed. Now,

I fought to save victims with awful injuries while listening out for the V1 that might kill us all.

All of our functioning facilities were now in the hospital's basement. The operating theatre had an array of pipes running across the ceiling and down the wall. A massive steel girder spanned the ceiling, supporting the floor above. There were no windows, no ventilation. I didn't see daylight for days at a time. The hardest part was that we had briefly tasted the fresh air of hope. We allowed ourselves to dream of normal things, and now those dreams lay crushed beneath the rubble. We were left to mourn their passing.

After three weeks of not leaving the hospital and listening to the constant threat of the V1s above my head, I found myself sinking into a dark place of my own making. I didn't recognise the symptoms that I now frequently diagnosed in others. I told patients to stay in touch with people, try to remain active, face their fears, and try to keep to a routine. All the things I no longer did. Janet recognised those symptoms, and as always, she didn't shy away from watching over me.

"You need a break, Em."

"I know, so do you."

"You shoulder all the responsibility for the patients, Em. Is it any wonder you're worn out?"

"I am feeling tired, Jan, but I'll be alright."

"No, you're not alright. I want you to take an afternoon off. I want you to arrange to see your friend Roger."

"Why Roger?"

"Because you always come back smiling when you've seen him, and you need to smile again. Please, Em, I'm worried about you."

She stopped me in my tracks. I listened to Janet; we trusted each other implicitly. When she spoke seriously that way, I knew I had to listen. My whole life had become the hospital. Frank and I shared our lives in hospital rooms and corridors. Janet was right; I needed to take my own advice, and my only friend outside of the hospital was Roger. I hesitated to telephone him; it had been several weeks since I last saw him, and it always felt like trying to renew an old friendship.

Janet, bless her, led me by the hand to Evelyn's office and put the telephone into my hand. With little other option, I telephoned the police station. At least the station was still there. Thoughts like that were my constant companion. They told me he wasn't there, but he would receive the message. I just said, "Tell him Emma called."

Later that afternoon, Roger called me back. He called at a bad time; I had just lost a patient in surgery. The poor woman had horrific injuries. She had no real prospect of surviving, but I tried desperately to save her. When she slipped away from me, it came as it always did, as a personal tragedy. I no longer shed tears. She simply became another empty space inside me. I had forgotten about Roger; when I heard his voice, it took me by surprise.

"Oh, hello, Roger."

"You telephoned me, Emma. It's lovely to hear from you. How are you?"

"Oh, yes, of course I did. I'm sorry, Roger, I'm not feeling myself."

"What can I do for you, Emma?"

"Nothing really. I just called to say hello, that's all."

Janet was standing behind me, and without further ado, she took the telephone from me. I was too surprised to respond.

"Hello, Roger, it's Janet. Emma's had a terrible day; she's not thinking clearly. She's really feeling down, and you're the only person who can lift her spirits. She won't come right out and say it, but she needs you, Roger. Be a good chap and arrange an afternoon or evening to see her. I'll hand you back to her."

"Roger, I'm so sorry. What are you thinking, Janet?"

"Emma, I would love to see you; can we arrange an evening?"

"Well, yes, I'd like that. Janet gets a bit carried away. You have to ignore what she says."

"I'm a detective, Emma. I listen to what people tell me. You're very lucky to have someone like Janet in your corner. Tell you what, how about tomorrow at the Fox and Hounds? I can get away by six. Shall I come and pick you up?"

"I can't really plan in advance. I never know when a patient needs me."

Janet stepped forward again, and we both had a hand on the telephone. "Whatever you're planning, Roger, it's yes," she said. "I'll make sure she gets away."

"You're a good friend, Janet; make sure Emma gets away before six tomorrow."

"I'm here, you know, I can talk for myself. I'll drive there, Roger. Janet says I can be there by six."

"I owe you one, Janet. Tell Emma I'm looking forward to seeing her."

"You can tell her yourself, you know."

"See you tomorrow, Emma. Thank Janet for me, bye."

I looked at Janet, and the relief I felt turned into laughter. I couldn't remember when we last laughed, but the pair of us just stood there in fits of laughter. Evelyn came back into her office wondering what on earth was going on. When I recovered from my embarrassment, I gave her a hug and thanked her.

"What must Roger think of me when I need a chaperone to act for me?"

"You'll find out. If he thinks less of you, then you never need to see him again, do you?"

"He isn't going to think less of me, is he?"

"No, of course not; he really likes you. I know these things."

The following afternoon, Janet ensured everyone, including Frank, was prepared to stand in for me. He asked where I was going, and Janet had no option but to tell him. Once again, I felt awkward, and the moment I saw Frank, I started blathering.

"I just have to get away, Frank. It's all getting on top of me."

"Why Roger; why is it always him you have to get away to see?"

"I don't know anyone else outside of the hospital. I feel very safe with him - he's virtually married to Jean, and he's a proper gentleman. You don't mind, do you?"

"I need a break as well, but no, I don't mind."

He did mind, but I wasn't about to cancel our arrangement. I don't know what I would have done if he had objected; I think it might have caused a considerable rift. When the hour approached, Frank was one of the doctors who stood in for me, which, of course, made me feel even worse. My car hadn't been started for ages, and to my horror, it didn't start. The battery was flat. I sat with my head in my hands, but one of the hospital porters I knew saw me and immediately came to my rescue. He made the entire problem seem a non-event. Within ten minutes, my car had started.

"I'm so grateful, Stan, what would I have done without you?"

"It's a real pleasure, Doctor Stevenson. Any time I can help, don't hesitate to ask."

He was a lovely man, Stan. He probably should have been retired, but he kept an eye open for me. I was so grateful. Rushing off, conscious of the time, I didn't anticipate the amount of damage to so many buildings caused by the V1s. I had to divert around a closed road. Workmen were busy trying to clear debris. As I approached the Fox and Hounds, I could hear a V1 in the air. I instinctively slowed down and tried to see where it was coming from. Just as I caught sight of it, the loud rasping sound stopped.

It appeared to be coming straight towards me. I froze in terror. There was nothing I could do. I braked hard and stopped seconds before I saw the V1 plunge into the buildings ahead of me. A massive flash of light preceded an enormous blast that ripped through the buildings. The houses furthest away blew up like balloons seconds before they were reduced to flying debris. The entire row of houses instantly shattered like so many matchstick models. Glass and roof tiles flew in the air like confetti. For a fraction of a second, I saw the blast wave coming towards me. It hit the car with a terrible bang, as if I had driven into a wall. My lungs recoiled, and the windscreen shattered.

# Chapter Sixty-Four
# July 21st, 1944

Roger

*"Love means giving the greater part of yourself to another person. There is no going back. If love is lost, then that part of you is lost forever."*

I sat in the Fox and Hounds, waiting for Emma, looking at my watch. She was only a few minutes late, but we were always worried when someone was late. I'd heard three V1s so far that day, one of which fell close enough for me to hear the explosion. Then, as I looked at my watch again, I heard another one. As the sound increased, it caused alarm in the pub. When the pulse jet engine stopped, seemingly directly above us, the alarm turned to panic.

People started rushing about or clambering under tables. For a split second, I heard the sound receding away from us before it cut out; I already knew enough about the V1 to be reasonably sure it wouldn't fall on us. Within seconds, it exploded with tremendous force. The blast shook the pub violently, and several windows blew in.

We all picked ourselves up, and apart from the windows, the pub didn't appear badly damaged. One or two people close to the windows had some minor cuts, but we appeared to be relatively unscathed. It took a moment to regain my senses, but as soon as I did, I rushed outside. The choking fumes were oxidised Amatol, the chemical explosive in the V1. As the choking dust settled, I saw smoke rising above the side road opposite the pub.

When I looked down from the end of the road, the full extent of the destruction had to be seen to be believed. The V1 appeared to have fallen in the middle of the row of terraced houses. At least five or six houses on either side of the epicentre lay in ruins or were badly damaged. The houses opposite suffered a similar fate. I hurried down the road, stepping between bricks and debris. There were no cries for help. That's when I saw what I thought might be Emma's pale blue Morris Eight car. To my horror, the windscreen had been blown out. Then, as I ran towards her, I saw Emma sitting behind the steering wheel. My heart leapt in my chest. She appeared lifeless. For several seconds, she just sat there with her eyes closed.

"Emma, can you hear me? Emma, it's Roger."

"Roger, is that you?"

"Are you injured? Can you move?"

"Yes, I can move; am I bleeding anywhere, Roger?"

"I can only see some minor cuts and abrasions."

"Are any of them pumping blood?"

"No, nothing like that, you look alright. If you can move everything, I think you should be able to walk away. Just sit calm for a moment and compose yourself. You've had a very close call."

"Where were you when this happened?"

"Sitting in the Fox and Hounds waiting for you, thank God you were late. I came running the moment the bomb went off. A hundred yards in either direction and one of us would have bought it."

"My car wouldn't start; if I had been a bit earlier, I would be dead. I'm shaking and feeling cold. Help me out, Roger. I need to get away from here. I need to sit with my head between my knees for a moment, and I need a cup of tea."

"You're coming home with me, Doctor."

Emma struggled out from the remains of the windscreen. I helped her out of the car, and she stood without assistance. She was covered in pieces of glass, but the Triplex windscreen had saved her from serious injuries. I walked her to my car, which luckily remained undamaged. We arrived at my house within ten minutes, and I sat her down in an armchair. I offered her a choice between a mug of tea or a glass of whisky. She started with the tea.

I sorted out my first aid kit and cleaned up her cuts and abrasions. Emma asked me to fetch her a mirror. She looked into it, almost afraid to look at her own reflection. All she saw were the minor cuts and abrasions I described, most of which didn't even require a dressing.

"You've done a good job of cleaning me up, Roger. I've been incredibly lucky, haven't I?"

"We both have. There must be nearly twenty houses destroyed or damaged on that road. Those things cause terrible destruction."

"There must be so many casualties. I need to go back and help the injured."

"You'll do no such thing. For once in your life, Emma, let other people take care of it."

Alcohol is not the ideal medication for shock, but it sufficed well enough. Emma drank another one as her problems drifted away.

"Janet said you needed my company; that's nice to know, Emma."

"I know, she's terrible, isn't she? I was feeling a bit down. It's been really difficult recently, and she watches over me like an old mother hen."

"I think that's wonderful. Most people don't have such a great friend."

"You're right, I'm very lucky. I love her like a sister; there's nothing I wouldn't do for her, and she watches over me."

"That's like my mate, Dave, we were inseparable. I still miss him all the time."

"We both need people, don't we? You miss your friend Dave, but you also enjoy the company of women, don't you?"

"Do I?"

"You know you do. I've seen you when we've all been together. The other men talk about cricket, and you migrate towards the woman. I think it's lovely."

"Perhaps I just migrated towards you."

"What are you saying, Roger?"

"I'm just saying that I enjoy your company. Janet said you needed me - well, I want you to know that I'm pleased to be the one you can turn to."

They say a fool and his money are easily parted. Well, the same can be said of best intentions. I wanted to make her feel perfectly comfortable. I wanted her to know I really liked and wanted to be with her. Even in my own house, I struggled not to make a fool of myself. Emma looked at me with those beautiful, thoughtful eyes of hers. She saw the fool in me.

"Where's Jean? Why isn't she here?"

"She's just got her house back. She invited a homeless family to live there, and after four months, they've finally been re-housed."

"Isn't she living with you any more?"

"It's not like that; she just wanted her own space for a while."

"You make a lovely couple. She's beautiful, isn't she, and you're ... well, you just seem to be perfect for each other."

"We have a complicated relationship, but you're right. Jean is a really beautiful woman in every respect."

"I'm a bit envious. Oh dear, I've had too much to drink, haven't I?"

"Other people's relationships are never as uncomplicated as they appear, Emma."

"We had a complicated relationship in the hospital last week. A woman just walked in looking for a patient, the man she so obviously loves. She then reorganised the entire hospital around him. I've never met anyone like her. I think she would have given her life to save him."

"It sounds as though he's one hell of a lucky man. What happened to him?"

"I don't know. She rushed him off to a hospital in Oxford. I pray he survived. She said she couldn't live without him, and she meant it. Love can be a source of great pain, can't it?"

"Love means giving the greater part of yourself to another person. There is no going back. If love is lost, then that part of you is lost forever."

"That's a lovely way of expressing it, Roger. It certainly applies to our mysterious intruder. I found myself willing the man to survive because I feared the consequences for her."

"Yes, I can empathise with that."

"Are you speaking from experience?"

"I suppose I am. Commitment in love is a double-edged sword; sublime happiness on one side, and exquisite pain on the other."

"Are you talking about Jean or Marilyn?"

The fool and his best intentions had been parted. I used to think of Emma as a reserved woman with no experience of life. I saw her as an exotic flower reaching out in search of sunlight. She might have been some of those things, but she was so much more. The fool in me wanted to open my heart to her, but she would see through anything that wasn't completely honest.

"We're doing it again, Emma. We're having one of our deep and meaningful conversations."

"Yes, I'm sorry. I've had two glasses of whisky, and I'm prying."

"Don't apologise, Emma, not to me. I hope we can say anything to each other. How are you feeling now? You've had a shocking experience."

"I'm feeling much better, thank you. Those V1 things are terrifying, and there seem to be more and more of them. We're getting increasing numbers of casualties."

"It's spreading alarm among the public. People can't live in shelters all day. The powers that be are concerned about public unrest."

"We coped throughout the Blitz. I expect we'll cope with this new threat."

"I hope you're right, Emma. Gerry and Margaret are doing well, by the way. He especially asked me to thank you."

"There's no need, really. I did my job, that's all."

"Your patients are not just your job, and you know it. I watched you with Gerry. You saved his life."

"I could see how important he is to you."

"You do the same for all your patients. I know you do. They're eternally grateful, and so am I. How are things at the hospital? Is that what's been getting you down?"

"Yes, it's been relentless. I realised the other day that I couldn't remember when I last saw daylight."

"I'm sure people don't realise the sacrifices you and your colleagues make. You all deserve a medal. It must be hard on your relationship with Frank."

"It is. We don't have any time together. We spend day and night in the hospital basement, and when I attempt to go outside, one of those things nearly kills me."

"It takes a special courage to sacrifice your personal life in the service of others. It must come at a significant cost."

"You make it sound as if I were extraordinary. I'm not extraordinary, Roger. I'm just the same as anyone else. We just keep going; that's what we all do."

"I agree. Courage isn't in short supply at the moment. But believe me when I say what you're doing is extraordinary, and I've no doubt about the personal cost."

"You're really kind, Roger. Janet has only been home a few times when Barry's been on leave, and Shirley's the same with Roy. Maurice can only get home occasionally to see Beverley and his son."

"What about you and Frank?"

"We haven't been home together for a while. What about you and Jean?"

"We spend most nights in the Clapham underground. We have to run the gauntlet of these buzz bombs during the day, but at least we're safe at night."

"What's that like?"

"Jean hates it. It's much better than it used to be, and there's a tremendous community spirit. But to be honest, it's awful."

"And then you do everything you can to maintain public order during the day. We're all doing what we can, Roger."

"We do. That's what annoys me the most when a minority does the exact opposite."

"I'm philosophical about it. As long as I'm still making sacrifices, it means I haven't had to make the ultimate sacrifice. If I survive this war, then I'll be one of the privileged ones."

"When people talk about the spirit of the Blitz, they're talking about you, Emma."

The fool in me was desperate to tell that woman what I really thought about her, but the grizzled detective in me applied the voice of sound judgment. It's always the circumstances, those arbiters of reason, that come between you and that step into the unknown. She laughed even though I was being perfectly serious. Emma dismissed the notion that her determination was in any way heroic or extraordinary. It was time I took her back to the hospital before the fool in me said too much.

"What can I do about my car, Roger?"

"Leave your car to me. I'll have it taken to the garage that takes care of our police vehicles. When it's repaired, I'll see you get it back as good as new."

"Oh, that's wonderful, thank you."

"It's not like saving a life, but it's the best I can offer."

"And it's gratefully accepted."

Having delivered her back to the hospital, I walked around the car to open her door. She looked at me with a lovely expression. I bowed to those arbiters of reason and remained determined to do the right thing. I kissed her cheek, and we hugged each other. Perhaps I held her in my arms slightly longer than protocol dictated, but the fool didn't disgrace himself.

# Chapter Sixty-Five
# August 10th, 1944

Emma

*"The V1 and V2 missiles rained death upon a traumatised nation. In Europe, every mile of the race to reach the launch sites was being paid for with Allied lives."*

On August 10th, Barry and Janet attended Barry's previous wing commander's wedding in Kent. Janet returned absolutely full of it. It was, by all accounts, a lavish affair by wartime standards. We hung on her every word. In our basement world, what she described sounded like a fantasy, an impossible dream we were desperate to share. Wing Commander Johnny Albright married Fiona Robinson at St Michael's church in Middlebourne, Kent. Barry was a part of the contingent from RAF Hendon, Johnny's previous station before he was moved on to some top-secret surveillance operation.

Johnny Albright had been Hendon's top fighter ace during the Battle of Britain. Apart from being a long-standing friend of Barry's, Johnny remained revered by his comrades. So much so that against all regulations, and obviously without permission, Barry organised a low-level flypast of five Spitfires to fly over the congregation. Janet became reduced to tears as she described it. As the planes flew over, Barry and his colleagues stood to attention and saluted the bride and groom. Everyone cheered as memories of the Battle of Britain came flooding back. Janet didn't stop talking as we sat in the canteen one evening.

"The entire village must have been outside the church; I've never seen so many people at a wedding. Then we went to the reception in the village hall. It was amazing; there were Lords and Ladies there. One woman caught Barry's eye. When she saw us dancing, she realised how good Barry is at swing. Well, I ask you, the cheeky woman asked Barry to dance. It turns out her name was Elizabeth, Lady Elizabeth, no less. You should've seen her, she looked like a film star, and wow, could she dance. Everyone just stopped dancing and watched. Barry was in his element. She must have been a professional dancer or something. She was absolutely amazing."

"What about the bride?" Shirley asked. "Did she look beautiful?"

"Oh, she really did. She had on a wonderful white silk gown, and she really was beautiful. She looked just like Ingrid Bergman; she had the same hair. Barry danced with her as well."

"Who were the Lords and Ladies? Does Fiona have aristocratic connections?" I asked.

"No, apparently she works for Lord Middlebourne. I think that's the connection. I don't know who they are. There were some very aristocratic-looking people there. It was the best wedding I've ever attended, and I hadn't even met them before."

"I bet you gave Barry what-for, deserting you to dance with another woman," said Shirley.

"To be fair, she asked him, and he couldn't really refuse. Besides, they were the best two dancers there. I couldn't compete with Lady Elizabeth."

"I'm pleased you had such a good time. You both deserve it," I said.

It obviously made a deep impression on Janet. Apart from the lavish occasion and the fly-past, it provided a glimpse of normality - an opportunity to exist for a while away from the war that had now ratcheted up to a new level. The V1 flying bombs were wreaking havoc over a large swathe of South East England. The noise of the pulse jet engine caused instant terror, and the 1800 lbs of high explosive produced devastating destruction.

They fell from the sky at any time and anywhere. The threat was constant, as was the fear they created. We were neither blasé nor heroic. We just needed to maintain our sanity. So, when all the usual gang could meet up at the Tavern one evening, we carried on as usual. We marched across the bridge arm in arm for the first time since the new threat emerged. Barry and Roy were there to meet us. Janet had already given us her description of the wedding that they attended, and now it was Barry's turn.

He described it all again, and Lady Elizabeth featured more than once.

We had come to our second pints when Barry produced some photographs from his pocket. We were all keen to put a face to Lady Elizabeth, so we took a keen interest. When he produced the photograph of the bride with her bridesmaids, I stared in disbelief. I showed it to Shirley, who also instantly recognised one of the bridesmaids.

"That's her, that's our mysterious woman."

I couldn't believe it. There she was, the woman who made such an impression on me. Then, as I looked at some group photographs, I saw the man she had been so desperate to save.

"Who is this man, Barry?"

"I think that's Lord Middlebourne."

"And who is this woman with him?"

"Her name's Lily. She's Fiona's best friend and colleague."

"We already know what her name is; what does she do?"

"I've got no idea. Johnny won't even tell me what his wife does. One thing you can be sure of - it's top secret, so you had best forget you ever saw her."

And so that was that. The mysterious woman became even more mysterious. Frank insisted that Shirley and I were exaggerating about her, but he didn't see her. Our conversation returned to the usual topic of the war, particularly the V1. And so the mysterious woman became one more footnote in our collective memory. We had much to discuss. The Allies had finally pushed past Caen in Normandy, opening the way for the advance into the rest of France. The cost of lives and equipment had been enormous, but this amounted to success in the language of war. We left the pub that night torn between hope and fear.

Something even more sinister happened in September that would seriously affect public morale. The Germans launched a new weapon. The first one hit Chiswick in West London on September 8th. This was something no one had ever seen before. It became known as the V2 rocket, the world's first ballistic missile. The implications were terrifying as the news of its arrival became widely known. The V1 flying bomb was a crude, low-flying missile that became vulnerable to anti-aircraft fire and fast fighter planes. The V2 rocket was totally undetectable. It would plunge out of the sky at supersonic speed, unseen by anyone. Its 2,200 lb warhead would explode deep in the ground, creating a devastating seismic shock wave. It caused dreadful damage, and most terrifying of all was that we had no defence against it. Once they had been launched, we were powerless to stop them.

If one hit the hospital, it would penetrate right through the basement and destroy the entire building. The newspapers reported it as a new unseen weapon, but Barry said our intelligence services were well aware of its development. But that didn't make it any better for the people of London, who were the primary target.

The war entered its final and bloodiest phase. The V1 and V2 missiles rained death upon a traumatised nation. In Europe, every mile of the race to reach the launch sites was being paid for with Allied lives.

# Chapter Sixty-Six
# January 1945

Roger

*"The human spirit at its best can inspire an entire nation and make you weep with joy. At its worst, it just makes you weep."*

Jean and I emerged from the Clapham underground every morning to a scene of increasing carnage. It was the Blitz all over again, except even the reassuring predictability had been removed. If a V1 had your name on it, you had a moment to watch your life flash before your eyes. If it was a V2, you had no such warning. One moment, people were going about their business, and the next, they were gone or horribly injured. If we accepted that reality, day-to-day life would have become impossible so we lived in denial; it wouldn't be us. It wasn't our time. Denial is not restrained by reality and not even by moral or ethical considerations. That's why we found it so comforting. In our world, provided they were not our nearest and dearest, it would always be someone else that death would rain down upon.

There was a feeling of desperation among those who had suffered the most. For those among us who dwell in the twilight zone, where morality and empathy no longer exist, one person's suffering becomes another's opportunity. The looting we suffered during the Blitz rose to the surface again, like oil on water. Domestic murders increased, as did the ever-present black market. Left unchecked, this is the road to anarchy and social breakdown. There were times, many times, when holding the line felt almost impossible. At its best, the human spirit can inspire an entire nation and make you weep with joy. At its worst, it just makes you weep.

The fact that life can be cut short without warning affected us all. The notion that you should live for today because you may not be here tomorrow became prevalent. The birth rate notoriously increased, but so did crime. It was fostered by the belief that if you delegate responsibility to an uncertain future, then perhaps it will no longer be your responsibility to accept. I had to believe that also applied to Burrows.

I knew he wasn't the devil incarnate. Despite all the evidence to the contrary, he was a human being. As such, he shared many of the same reactions affecting us all. In his twisted mind, his killing spree had purpose and structure. For him, if tomorrow never came, then he would fail to complete his fantasy. It would all have been for nothing. I knew, for him, the impulse to murder again was overwhelming. He had the motivation, the night-time blackout, and the renewed reign of terror provided his cover. I felt impotent, simply waiting for him to slaughter another inno-cent victim. Jeff and I stopped off for a pint late one evening on our way back from yet another crime scene. As we sat there, an old friend walked into the pub.

"Hello, Ray, I haven't seen you in ages; how are you?"

"Roger. Yes, I'm fine. It must be eighteen months or more."

"More like a couple of years. Jeff, this is an old mate of mine, Ray Collins."

Ray and I went back a long way to when we were young PCs together. Ray eventually moved over into another line of work, and we had a lot to catch up on. During our conversation, Ray asked about the Ripper case and whether we had a suspect. I told him everything, and he understood my frustration completely. His approach to that kind of situation was completely different from mine. Ray worked for MI5.

"Why don't you set this bastard up with a victim, lure him out into the open?"

"That's fine for your lot, Ray - on my side of the fence, we call that entrapment."

"Precisely, it's my stock in trade. It's what we do."

"I would be so tempted, Ray. I want this monster, but he's not like your average German spy who you can turn the other way. Burrows is like a venomous snake; expose him, and he will bite. We couldn't risk putting an innocent woman in that kind of danger."

"That would depend upon who would be in danger, the woman or Burrows."

"What do you mean?"

"I've just been working with a woman who's quite unlike any woman I've worked with before. She's not strictly MI5; she's from another outfit. I can't tell you anything about her, but trust me, if she came across Burrows, I wouldn't want to be him."

"Are you being serious, Ray?"

"Deadly serious, mate. I made a bit of a fool of myself when I underestimated this woman. That's not a mistake I'll make again. I'm not saying she would offer to do it. This would be totally unofficial; she isn't MI5, not yet anyway. If you're interested, I could ask her. She's just done an unofficial job for us, but she got approval right from the top."

"Are you saying the boss of MI5, Sir David Petrie, sanctioned the use of this woman?"

"I couldn't confirm or deny that, even though I was in the room at the time."

I could trust Ray completely. What he said was very appealing. Gerry would also find it appealing, as would the Commissioner, but neither of them could officially sanction such an operation. I would be out on a limb with a saw in my hand. If it went wrong, it would be me who would fall. Before we parted company, Ray left me a phone number where I could leave him a message. Jeff and I left the pub, deep in conversation.

"Ray's right, you know, Roger, this is how they turn agents all the time."

"But Burrows is so dangerous. If he realises we've trapped him, this woman is likely to be dead."

"What if Ray's right? What if it's Burrows who's in danger?"

"Precisely - what if? I can't take the risk - can I?"

"Burrows is going to kill again; we know he is. I think we should at least talk to this woman."

"Yes, I suppose we could talk to her."

I didn't realise that our conversation would put in train such an extraordinary chain of events. I went home that night as usual, unaware of what I had initiated. It had been another bad day for V1 attacks; I had heard and seen about a dozen. On some days, as many as 200 would hit in and around London, as well as several V2s.

I quickly picked up my overnight things and went straight to Jean's house. Even on that brief journey, I passed the end of a road where a V1 had struck. During the Blitz, a 250 kg bomb could destroy a house and damage several others. A V1 could destroy a dozen homes. Just a glance down that road told its own story of lives cut short and traumatised survivors.

Jean gave me a welcome hug. We sat down to a meal of sorts while, a few streets away, people would never share a meal again. This was the reality we lived with; the wartime mentality that said - there, but for the grace of God, go I. So I ate a scrappy meal of corned beef, a couple of small carrots and three potatoes. It sufficed; roast beef and Yorkshire puddings had long since faded from memory. It had all been replaced with a thin gruel we called hope.

1945 opened with a potential breakthrough in the Allied advance in France. We were only told some of the news, but our daily gruel suddenly contained genuine hope. The newspapers spoke of a reversal of the German advance in the Ardennes in what became known as the Battle of the Bulge. With the Allies now pushing the German forces back, it sounded like a decisive breakthrough. It would prove to be the German army's last major ground offensive. If the Allies could finally advance across France and into Germany, the universal hope was that the V1 and V2 launch sites and manufacturing centres would be overrun. That kind of hope was difficult to suppress. We finished our meal and wasted no time before setting off to the shelter.

The deep underground shelters at Clapham and elsewhere were a vast improvement upon what we had to tolerate during the Blitz. We had every basic amenity that you would expect above ground. Thousands of people spent their nights and even their days in the safety of the deep underground. We had purpose-built toilets and canteens where they served sausage rolls, meat pies, and plenty of hot drinks. We ate better in the shelters than we did with rationing at home.

Despite all the improvements, you could never escape the fact that we were sleeping in endless rows of three-tier bunk beds, offering not a scrap of privacy. Shelters were ventilated, but the resulting foul air is inevitable when you confine 8000 people in a tunnel. In terms of public morale, the deep-level shelters were a godsend. The indiscriminate nature of the V weapon threat meant that people were constantly aware of their own mortality. It created obvious tensions. Camaraderie in the shelters was a direct release of that tension. Jean and I settled ourselves in for the night. She had the bottom bunk while I was above her. In the bunk next to me, slept a young woman in her early twenties who hardly ever spoke.

The poor woman lost her parents during the bombing and had been traumatised ever since. She was not alone. We were surrounded by traumatised people who had no option but to cope as best as they could. We all recognised the vacant expressions, the nervous reactions, and the isolation. We also had those habitually happy, extroverted people who lifted our spirits every night. These people told us to keep our chins up and look on the bright side. They were the first to start a sing-along or to entertain us with their hilarious stories.

The majority of us were in between those extremes. People like me and Jean, people who were traumatised but managed to cope. People who had learnt how to smile again and were always prepared to offer a helping hand. We were all the same. We were just people trying to survive. When thousands of people are collected together like so much detritus, all that remains is the irrepressible human spirit. I saw that spirit triumph every night in the shelter. Despite the comfort of safety, the following day, people were prepared to leave the shelter and face it again during daylight hours. This was to be a happier day for me at least; Gerry would be back behind his desk after recovering from his injury.

"How are you, Gerry? Are you sure you're up to it?"

"Don't you start as well, Roger. I've had Margaret nagging me about coming back. Of course, I'm alright and I have a lot to catch up on."

"Where do you want to start: the recent unsolved crime file or the one before that?"

"Is it as bad as that?"

"It is. Official statistics say crime has increased by 60%. It's just more of the same. Looting has raised its ugly head again; domestic murders and some organised crime are cashing in on the chaos. Billy Hill left us his calling card, but I think Jack's boys have put a stop to that."

"It's as if I haven't been away. What about Burrows, anything there?"

"He'll kill again; I know he will. We still have nothing to connect him to his last victim. That inquiry's getting nowhere, same as the others. There's just one thing that might be worth thinking about."

I told him about Ray's suggestion, and Gerry's reply was predictable. "It sounds like a great idea. I wish I could sanction it."

"What if you weren't told about it, not officially, I mean?"

"You mean - you put your neck on the block if it went wrong?"

"Yes, that's about it."

"I don't know, Roger. We could probably get away with entrapment, but if this woman was injured or, heaven forbid, killed, we would be in big trouble."

"I'm tempted to see this woman. My friend knows what he's talking about. He wouldn't suggest it unless this woman had been highly trained."

"Who is she? What training has she had?"

"He didn't say. He just said she wasn't MI5."

"You're going to see her no matter what I say, so go ahead, but keep me informed - unofficially."

I did exactly that; I got a message to Ray, and eight days later, he set up a meeting. She suggested a tea shop that I hadn't heard of before. I noticed it was very close to Charing Cross Station, so I guessed that might be the reason for the choice. I have to admit, I was intrigued, and so was Jeff. It said a lot about her that this woman was prepared to come and discuss it. She chose three o'clock in the afternoon when it might be quiet. Jeff and I were there about ten minutes early, so with nothing else to do, we both ordered a cup of tea. Ray appeared with the woman at precisely three o'clock.

My imaginary image of our mysterious lady would have been an elegant, well-dressed woman of intrigue. A fashionable hat with a veil and an extravagant cigarette holder. She looked nothing like that; she wore a uniform. At first, I thought the uniform was ATS, but then I realised it was a FANY uniform. What really caught my eye was that she had the parachute wings insignia stitched to the top of her left arm. She was tall, about five feet ten, with short dark hair. She walked towards us with a broad smile and eyes that would stop the traffic. Beneath the unflattering uniform, there was a decidedly female body.

"Gentlemen, this is the lady I was telling you about," said Ray. "This is Detective Inspector Roger Pritchard and Detective Constable Jeff Payne."

"Hello, gentlemen. Raymond has told me about your little problem." She spoke with a broad Cockney accent.

"Thanks for coming," I said, "what do we call you?"

"I don't know, what should they call me, Raymond? You understand these things."

"What about Daphne?"

"You're bloody joking. Surely you can come up with something better than that."

"Perhaps I could make a suggestion," I said. "Our killer is looking for a woman with initials that match Mary Kelly, so how about Margaret?"

"Hang on, Inspector, I didn't say I was taking this job."

"No, no, of course not, it's just a suggestion."

"As long as we understand that. Okay, I'm Margaret, you can call me Maggie."

"How much did Ray tell you, Maggie?"

"He said you've got a nutcase who kills women, and you want me to trap him for you?"

"Is that all he's told you?"

"Pretty much. A man of few words is our Raymond."

"The man in question doesn't just kill women, Maggie. The newspapers call him the Blackout Ripper."

"Oh, shit. I've heard of him. Really nasty bastard."

"He is a nasty bastard, Maggie. He's the nastiest bastard I've ever had to contend with. I don't want you to be under any illusions about what's at stake here. Before we go any further, I'm going to show you some photographs of this man's handiwork."

I handed her the photographs and deliberately watched for her reaction. Most women would be horrified and shocked. Maggie was horrified, but she wasn't shocked. Whoever she was, she had seen a lot of things during this war. Her eyes narrowed as she looked at each photograph, and a frown formed on her forehead.

"This man carves up his victims and leaves them for you to find, like this?"

"That's precisely what he does."

"He's a monster. This man's a lunatic."

"He is, but he appears to be sane and respectable. He's also very clever at covering his tracks."

"But you know who he is. Are you sure?"

"Absolutely, I know everything about him."

"And you think I can trap him into exposing himself? Whereupon you rush in and arrest him."

"Something like that."

"What if he tries to assault me but then denies the murders?"

"Yes, I'm not saying this is the perfect solution. We need to have evidence. We think in the right circumstances, he'll bring his tools of the trade with him. That might be enough."

"You mean knives."

"At least one knife, possibly an overall."

"How does he approach his victims? I mean, when he kills them?"

"We think he grabs them from behind with a stranglehold and renders them unconscious. Then he cuts their throat."

"He doesn't cut their throats first?"

"Each victim showed signs of bruising around the neck. One victim who survived described a stranglehold with the arms interlocked."

"Does he cut their throats from behind or from the front?"

"From behind. We believe he's right-handed. We think the victim is lying flat, and he must be kneeling astride her. He slashes the throat from left to right."

"Why does that mean he's right-handed?"

"The pathologist has established that from the other wounds and mutilations."

"What's your suspect's build?"

"He's tall, 6 ft 1 in. He's 54 years old, and about 14 stone."

"So he's a big bloke, past his prime, with a knife he thinks he knows how to use?"

"When you put it that way, yes."

"Has he had any special combat training? What's his army record?"

"You won't believe this. He was a stretcher bearer during the last war."

"Are you sure you've checked his war record?"

"Of course."

"What is it about me you think will entrap him?"

"Your name. Margaret Kennedy."

"Nothing more. I don't need to have a special hair colour or build?"

"No, it's just the name, and we think a husband away in the forces might be another motive. The victim has to live alone."

"Is there anything you're not telling me?"

"In terms of the dangers, no."

"So why Margaret Kennedy?"

"He's copying the 1888 Jack the Ripper murders. He selects victims with the same initials so that we'll be in no doubt it's him. There's one victim left, and that's Mary Jane Kelly. Jack the Ripper mutilated Kelly almost beyond recognition. It was his most frenzied attack. This is the last and most important victim for our man. Without it, he hasn't completed his ambition."

"He really is a monster, isn't he?"

"He is, and that's why I'm concerned. I have to ask, why is Ray so sure you could handle a man like Burrows?"

"That's his name, is it, Burrows?"

"Yes."

"If this bloke is as you say he is, and he tried to strangle me, I would make absolutely sure he didn't do it again."

"That's all very well, but what if he came at you with a knife?"

"The same thing applies. I would take the knife from him, and he wouldn't do it again."

"How can you be so confident about that?"

"Let's just say I'm highly trained and I practise the martial arts in my spare time, just for fun."

"So, will you do it?"

"I need to know exactly what I have to do and how long it might take. I would need complete control of the trap, and I need to know what happens if I kill him?"

"Are you serious? I'm not asking you to kill him."

"I don't want to kill him, but you have to understand something. If my life is in danger, I will meet that danger with whatever it takes. Very often, the quickest and surest way to ensure my safety is to employ a blow or a manoeuvre that can be fatal. Be in no doubt, Inspector, if this bastard threatens me with a knife, I'll likely kill him. I'm on Civvy Street now; I'm not supposed to do that kind of thing."

I nearly choked on my tea. She was being deadly serious, and I believed every word she said. Ray said nothing. He just sat with a smug expression that said, 'I told you so'. I noticed again the wings sewn on her shoulder and the comment about Civvy Street. Whoever she was, she really was highly trained. Not only did she exude confidence, but she also had tremendous feminine charm and charisma. I was eating out of her palm, and I had only just met her. Burrows could not resist her.

"It would be self-defence, whatever you did."

"He doesn't understand, does he, Raymond? I can't end up in court and go on the public record. I have to stay out of it."

"She's right, Roger," said Ray.

"I didn't realise that. I'm sorry, I should have thought."

"Don't worry, Roger," she said, dropping the Inspector. "I'll do it, provided you keep me out of it, regardless of what happens. Can you do that?"

"I'm not sure how, but yes, I'll give you my word."

"Okay, let's get him."

"Will you be armed?" asked Jeff.

"Has Burrows ever carried a gun?"

"Not as far as we know. He certainly hasn't used one. But he obviously carries a knife."

She then put her hand inside her uniform jacket and produced a deadly-looking knife. "I always carry this, even to see policemen. Burrows might be good at carving up dead bodies; let's see how good he is with live ones."

"When can you start?"

"I've got a couple of weeks right now."

And so it began.

## Chapter Sixty-Seven
# February 1945

Emma

*"Guilt is a faithful companion. It waits for you in every thought and action."*

The war in Europe had turned decisively our way. The Germans were now retreating on both fronts. To the east, the Russians had expelled them from their homeland. The Red Army advanced towards Germany itself. Following the German defeat in the Ardennes, the Allies marched towards Germany in the west.

With the V1s and V2s constantly falling from the sky, our boost in optimism had no practical foundation. Just the suggestion of ending the war sufficed to lift our spirits. There were days when the flying bombs killed and injured people in districts further away from us. Those days were not days to celebrate, but they occasionally offered a rare opportunity for us to venture into the outside world. At short notice, it would be nothing more than our usual after-work drink in the Tavern, but it felt more like a big night out. I telephoned Roger; I wanted him to join us; Rachel would be there with Leo.

Our triumphant march across Westminster Bridge instantly lost its attraction when we saw smoke rising from various parts of London. We pretended to ignore it and marched on, arm in arm, to the Tavern. It was just another evening in the pub, exactly the same as so many others during the war. Except this wouldn't be just any other evening. This was the day that changed my life.

Barry and Roy were there as usual, and then Rachel arrived with

Leo. Roger didn't ring me back, so I imagined it was too short notice. I welcomed my first pint like a veteran beer drinker. Then, just as I began to see the bottom of my glass, there he was, standing just inside the door with Jean. I waved like an excited schoolgirl, and they came over and sat with us. With no vacant chair beside mine, he sat next to Rachel, and Jean sat next to Janet. We all knew each other, and the conversation flowed from one topic to another. Leo made us laugh with tales about awkward patients. Barry told us what he could about the missions being flown out of RAF Hendon. Jean told us about her work with the WVS. All the while, Roger sat quietly.

"You're very quiet, Roger," I said.

"Yes, I'm sorry; I've got a lot on my mind at the moment."

"Then you've come to the right place," replied Janet.

I knew Roger well by then. I could normally look into his eyes and tell what he was thinking, but not that evening. He smiled at me, and Jean followed his eyes to mine. I looked away, feeling as if I had committed a mortal sin. Janet noticed and raised her eyebrows. Frank typically noticed nothing, which was just as well. As the evening progressed, each time Jean and I looked at each other, I felt she was disapproving. What she was disapproving of, I wasn't sure. I may have been guilty of being attracted to Roger, but I hadn't as much as mentioned those thoughts, let alone acted upon them. For me, the evening descended into a strange atmosphere. Nobody else would have noticed it, but in my mind, I stood before a judge and jury, pleading guilty to improper thoughts.

I had nearly finished my second pint of beer when the inevitable call of nature demanded my attention. Thinking I would quietly disappear, it came as a surprise when I saw Jean follow me. Guilt is a faithful companion. It waits for you in every thought and action. I scurried into a cubicle and slammed the door. It reminded me of my first and last cigarette in the girls' toilet at school. Other women came and went, and I hoped Jean would be one of them. When I opened the door, she stood in front of me.

"I need to talk to you, Emma."

"Have I done something wrong, Jean? I'm sorry if I have … I have never…"

Jean cut me short. "We need to talk, just the two of us."

"It's about Roger, isn't it? Nothing is going on between us. It's not like that, Jean, really it isn't."

When I babble, I jump in with both feet and make a fool of myself. I did a wonderful job of it on that occasion. I told myself to shut up before I made the situation even worse.

"Yes, it's about Roger. I'm not sure this can wait, Emma, but not here, please."

I nodded and followed her back into the bar. The others must have wondered what was going on as I marched behind her with my head bowed. If I had a gold coin, it would have been in my hand, ready to give to the executioner to ensure a swift end to my misery. Jean sat at a table close enough to the others to not look strange but far enough away to have privacy. I picked up what was left of my pint and sat beside her.

"This isn't easy for me, Emma, but I need to say this. I love Roger with all my heart. I think I always have."

"I know that Jean…"

"Just let me say this, Emma, please. I think we fell in love all those years ago when the four of us first met. Fate stepped in, and he married Marilyn, and I married Dave. Roger is the most honourable man I've ever known. He wouldn't have dreamed of being unfaithful to Marilyn, so we never mentioned it again. Dave and I were really happy; I loved him, but I never forgot my feelings for Roger.

We were suddenly thrown together when that terrible night happened in the Balham Underground. It was months, Emma, months before he as much as kissed me. We were both remaining faithful to Dave and Marilyn. When it finally happened between us, it wasn't the two people you see here tonight; we were those twenty-year-olds again. It was as if we stepped back in time and started again."

"Jean, that sounds wonderful."

"It was more than wonderful, Emma. We behaved like twenty-year-olds, and we made love like twenty-year-olds. In amongst all that death and destruction and all that hardship and - sorry - we found Heaven."

"Oh, Jean. I'd never take that away from you."

"I know you won't, Emma. Roger will never leave me. When he said he would always be there for me, he meant exactly that. He will always be there. Only death will part us."

"I don't understand, Jean. Nothing has happened between me and Roger, and as you say, it never will."

"You don't understand, Emma. It wasn't two twenty-year-olds who fell head over heels in love. Both of us thought it was, but I've got two children, and so has Roger. We have memories of another life. We are the people who will step into the future, not those two twenty-year-olds."

"I still don't understand, Jean. What are you saying?"

"I'm saying there will always be the four of us. Marilyn and I grew up together, and then our kids grew up together. I was Dave's wife; I loved him, and I don't want to forget him. My kids are his kids; how can I tell them Uncle Roger is now their daddy? How can I tell his children that I'm no longer Aunty Jean, I'm their mummy? Roger and I share our relationship with two absent parents and four children. We can never be those twenty-year-olds again. I thought we could, Emma. I wanted to be them, but they just slipped away. The truth is, we fell in love with who we were, not who we are. It's not real, Emma."

Tears rolled down her face and dripped unashamedly into her lap. These weren't tears of sorrow but the bittersweet tears of memories never to be lost. I offered her my handkerchief, and she took a moment to compose herself as she let that memory slip by.

"Why are you telling me this, Jean?"

"Roger worships you, Emma. He makes no bones about it. I've lost count of the metaphors he uses to describe you."

"He tells you this?"

"Every time he sees you, he tells me."

"I'm so sorry, you must hate that."

"Not at all. I recognise how he describes you. You're everything he says you are, Emma."

"Then you must hate me."

"I don't hate you, Emma. It's important to me that we remain the closest possible friends. I can't marry Roger. There's too much from the past that comes between us. He can't marry me for the same reason. We can't remain together, but neither can we be apart. We haven't made love together for nearly a year but we remain devoted to each other. Can you possibly understand that, Emma?"

"I'm trying to, but I've no experience with these things."

"I don't know when liking someone turns to love, but Roger really likes you. You feel the same about him; I know you do. Perhaps you love him. I'm not angry or jealous because he isn't mine to have and hold. We each need to find our own path in life, a fresh path that doesn't involve our past. I think for Roger, this might be you, Emma. I hope it is you because he's right; you're a wonderful person, and he deserves someone like you."

"Why tell me this now, Jean?"

"I don't want Roger's chance of happiness to slip by. He said he would always be there for me, and I know he will. He will never make an advance towards you because of his promise to me, at least not without my blessing, and I want to give that to him. Who knows, perhaps you don't have a future with him either; I know you live with Frank. But just in case, I want you to know everything. Roger and I will always be there for each other. We will always love each other in our own way. Whoever he spends the rest of his life with has to understand that I will never come between you. I'll always be a part of his life, and he will be a part of mine, like a brother and sister."

"I don't know what to say, Jean. I admit I think about Roger all the time, but I would never have said or done anything to come between you. I felt guilty and stupid even thinking about it."

"That's exactly how Roger feels about you. Can't you see how silly that is? I need someone in my life as well, Emma; we all need to move on."

"Do you have someone in mind?"

"No, I won't look at another man until Roger is happy. I won't allow anything to come between us, which is exactly what he's doing. I have to release him from what he believes is his vow to me, so that we can both finally move on."

"This is a lot to take in, Jean. My heart's racing, and I don't know what to say. What usually happens at a time such as this is that I babble and make a fool of myself."

"You won't make a fool of yourself in front of me, Emma. Just babble."

"I want to. I think you're incredible. I've heard no one express their deepest feelings with such passion. You love him, but you'd let him go. You would be happy to see him in my arms. I mean, theoretically; I don't know if he would ... you know ... in my arms. I can't think of any greater sacrifice than to love someone enough to let them go. I'm very fortunate to have two wonderful friends I admire and wish I could be like. My friend Janet can fill any room with joy. I wish I could be like her. I have another friend who has wisdom and understanding beyond her years. She's feminine and beautiful; she's kind and understanding. She has so much love to give. I wish I could be like her."

"You mean me?"

"Of course I do. Roger described you as a beautiful person in every respect. He's right, Jean, you are. There's someone out there who will see the lovely woman that Roger described. That man doesn't know how blessed he's going to be. I've babbled, haven't I?"

"Would you give me a hug, Emma?" Everyone looked at us, but we just ignored it all. Janet was the one who smiled, and Frank was the one who thought we were a pair of over-emotional women. "Is Roger wrong about you and Frank?"

"I don't know what he's said, but I can guess. Frank's a lovely man; he's kind and gentle. What you see in Frank is what you get. He isn't spontaneous, he's not romantic or passionate. I'm not sure that he really understands me."

"You mean he's dull?"

"No, that would be cruel. When I listen to Janet, it makes me think something is missing in our relationship. Perhaps it's just me; I'm not like you, Jean. I don't excite men, you know, not in that way."

"I suspect Roger would disagree. Trust me, Roger has the keys to Heaven when it comes to passion."

"This is such a strange conversation, Jean. You shouldn't be telling me things like that."

"Don't you see, Emma? I have to let him go; this is me trying to do that."

"Yes, perhaps I do see. Perhaps that's why I've told you Frank isn't passionate. I've told no one that before. Not even Janet, and I tell her everything."

"Do you want to leave him?"

"I don't know. It all seems so painful and hurtful. I don't even want to think about it. But I have thought about it, haven't I?"

"You have, and I understand."

"Will you tell Roger about this conversation?"

"I tell him everything. Will you tell Frank?"

"No, I'm not ready for that."

"I think you should, Emma, regardless of our conversation."

Roger looked on with, I suspect, more than an inkling of what was being said between us. I caught his eye, but he didn't return my smile. He made a half-hearted gesture, but I could see he remained consumed with his thoughts. It's only when a wild fantasy becomes a possibility that you truly come face to face with it. I longed to be in Roger's arms, but could I really be a passionate, desirable woman like Jean? Would I even know what to do with the keys to Heaven? My longing suddenly slipped through my fingers and took to the air on the wings of wild fantasy.

# Chapter Sixty-Eight
# February 24th, 1945

Roger

*"Love never dies. It reluctantly dips below a distant horizon clinging to the crimson sky. Love hasn't gone; it just fades gently from view."*

My conversation with 'Maggie' haunted me. There was something about her. Even dressed in uniform, she was immensely attractive in an unconventional way. When she smiled, her big brown eyes were mesmerising. But there was something else in those eyes; just occasionally, she had the look of a predator. I didn't question Ray's assertion that it would be Burrows who would be in danger. I somehow knew it instinctively. I threw caution to the wind and started to formulate a plan. Jeff completely agreed with me; he wanted to involve Alfie and the others, and I reluctantly agreed.

When I picked up Emma's message about meeting that evening, my mind raced in all directions. Had anyone else asked me, I would have said no, but this was Emma; I couldn't refuse her anything. Jean wanted to go, desperately needing a break from her WVS work and the constant threat of the flying bombs. If I had been sitting with Emma and had my mind not been full of other matters, I'm sure it would have been a wonderful evening.

I watched Jean and Emma from a distance; they were obviously deeply involved in conversation. I could tell from the occasional glance that they were talking about me. It felt slightly surreal, the two women I admired the most talking to each other about me. We left the pub in high spirits despite the sound of a V1 somewhere in the distance. I put my arms around Emma and kissed her cheek, desperately trying to avoid her lips, and then I put my arm around Jean as we walked out together. The magnitude of my guilt was only matched by my ineptitude. Life doesn't prepare you for situations where your heart says one thing, and your head says another. Jean said very little as we approached my car, but I sensed that was about to change. I opened the door for her, and she looked at me with tears in her eyes.

"I've spoken to Emma."

"Yes, I saw you both deep in conversation."

"I'm letting you go, Roger."

"What do you mean?"

"You know what I mean. It's time, isn't it?"

I knew precisely what she meant. I just didn't have the strength to vocalise it myself. We both stood back from that impossible decision, but no amount of pretence would make it go away. It was as if our tragic story had been foretold. We knew how that story ended without saying the words. Neither of us said anything as we drove away. We didn't need to express our pain; we felt it. Only as we neared Jean's house did she break the silence.

"I love you, Roger. I always will, but we have to let each other go."

"I know we do, but that doesn't make it any easier, does it?"

"I've told Emma. I won't come between you."

"There's nothing to come between, Jean."

"I think you'll find there is. Emma's one of those exceptional women you might meet only once in a lifetime. She thinks the same about you, Roger, and she's right."

"After everything we've been through together…"

"Don't say it, Roger. It isn't the end; it's just a new chapter. You're my best friend, and that will never change."

"No, it won't, and it mustn't change for the kids. When they return, they must continue to grow up together, and we must grow old together. You're a part of my life that I can never replace, and I don't intend to. Love never dies. It reluctantly dips below a distant horizon clinging to the crimson sky. Love hasn't gone; it just fades gently from view. Our love has simply changed into something we can all live with."

"Do you think Emma can live with that?"

"She may not intend to leave Frank. I don't know if we have a future or not. If we do, then she has to understand that you occupy a place in my life."

"She already knows, Roger. I told her she has my blessing, and she knows I'll never come between you."

"You discussed it? What did she say?"

"We did. I feel very close to her; perhaps we share something in common. All she said is that she thinks about you all the time. Other than that, she's walking on eggshells the same as you."

"You're a remarkable woman, Jean. This is an impossible situation, and how you've dealt with it is quite amazing."

"We both have to. If I have to see you being happy with someone else, then I hope it will be Emma, someone I like and can respect."

"You're assuming a lot. I like her immensely, but there's nothing to say we have a future together. She's still with Frank."

"I know that but call it a woman's intuition. She's an extraordinary person. When this war's over, you're going to become a Member of Parliament, I know you will. You'll do great things, Roger, because you're also an extraordinary person. You need a woman like Emma. She's all the things that I'm not."

"But is she all the things that you are?"

I couldn't believe I said that. Jean would understand precisely what I meant, and it wasn't something a gentleman should have mentioned. I was already extremely uncomfortable talking about another relationship. She managed a smile.

"She's a woman. With you, she will be."

"I hope when the situation is reversed, I can deal with it as well as you. You deserve someone exceptional, someone worthy of you. I think I could cope with it if I thought you had found the right person."

"Why is that important to you?"

"Because I'll always love you, and your happiness is my happiness."

"Don't you see? That's why I'm not jealous of Emma. I think she's the right person. She hasn't come between us; she has my blessing."

Jean is a remarkable woman. She would give me her blessing for whatever I did. It's very hard to even think about your one-time lover in the arms of another without feelings of jealousy and regret. I had to accept that there would be someone else in Jean's life. Someone who would love and desire every soft curve of her body. Someone who would hold her in his arms each night. There can be no greater love than to give to another what you hold dearest. We started that process months ago, but as long as the decision remained in the future, I could pretend it wasn't happening.

The moment that decision stepped into the present, the full magnitude of its implications fell onto my shoulders. We looked at each other and were both unable to say another word. I took her in my arms, and we kissed as we used to as lovers. I remembered the exquisite passion of our first real kiss. The first exploration of paradise found. We re-lived that kiss, and a thousand like it. I wanted to remember everything because we would never share such a kiss again.

## Chapter Sixty-Nine
# March 2nd, 1945

Roger

*"The limit of human endurance is a point in time that we constantly redefine and push further into the future. After nearly six years, it had never been closer."*

Ray organised another meeting with Maggie at the station. We intended to discuss the plan that Jeff and I proposed. We wanted to see if Maggie would be receptive to the idea. Even before she arrived, there seemed to be a sense of finality. Gerry agreed to turn a blind eye while still wanting to attend the meeting. We were desperate for a result with Burrows, but it hadn't escaped my attention that we were going down a dangerous route even to consider using a woman as bait. She arrived alone and walked into the station as if she owned the place.

"Look at all these lovely policemen. Morning, boys."

Jack looked up with a dumbstruck expression. She wore a white blouse, a black skirt, and a smart red jacket. Combined with her short black hair, heavily mascaraed eyes, and red lipstick, she instantly silenced the entire building.

"Can I help you, madam?" Jack finally uttered.

"Of course, you can, Luv. I'm here to see Roger, you know, the good-looking one."

"It's okay, Jack. I'm expecting this lady."

"Roger, I bet you've been missing me. How do I greet a policeman; do I shake your hand, or do I give you a kiss?"

"I think a kiss, don't you, Roger?"

"Yes, thank you, Jack. Just come on through, Maggie."

I introduced her to Gerry and Alfie, and she was all over them. She had an infectious smile that made men behave like idiots. It was impossible not to like her cheeky personality. My impression when we first met was that she was a typical East End barrow girl. She disillusioned me of that false impression within the first minute. Gerry and Alfie had only a few seconds left to go with their initiation.

"Oh, I can see Raymond, he's arrived. Lovely chap, but he's of more use to Mrs Collins than he is to me. He has connections, though, with that bunch up at St James's Street."

"I thought you were a part of that bunch," said Gerry.

"Me, no. I'm not going to keep calling you Chief Inspector. What's your name, Luv?"

"Gerry."

"No, well, you see, Gerry, I did a job for them a while ago. A sort of subcontractor and Ray was supposed to hold my hand."

"So, who are you with, then?"

"I can't tell you that; I had to sign the Official Secrets Act. I'd have Winston himself putting the cuffs on me if I uttered a word."

"But you've had proper training - you can defend yourself?"

"You don't have to worry about me, Gerry. I can more than take care of myself."

"What if Burrows attacked you with a knife, Maggie?"

"I've told Roger he wouldn't pose a threat to me. My concern is what happens if I injure him, or worse, what if I kill him?"

Gerry took a deep intake of breath, his reaction much the same as mine. Ray saved Gerry from any further tricky questions. I introduced him and then quickly set about detailing my proposal.

"Burrows is the housing officer for Wandsworth. He wouldn't normally interview homeless people, but nevertheless, his work presents us with a way of getting to him. What I propose, Maggie, is that you present yourself at Wandsworth Town Hall as Margaret Kennedy. You're married with a husband serving in Europe. A V1 has partially destroyed your home, but you were safe in your Anderson shelter. You're living in dreadful conditions and need the Wandsworth Council to rehouse you. I have a house in mind, near to where Burrows lives. You have the right initials to fit Mary Kelly. If we can get you in front of Burrows, then when he sees Margaret, I don't think he'll be able to resist you."

"That sounds plausible, Roger. So I hook him, but what happens when I bring him to the net?"

"He waits in the garden, and when the victim goes to their Anderson shelter, we're fairly sure he jumps them from behind with a stranglehold. He renders them unconscious and takes them into the house."

"What kind of stranglehold?"

"Interlocked arms with a hand behind the head."

"He doesn't cut their throat in the garden?"

"There's never been any blood in the garden except for the one occasion when he was disturbed."

"I can't allow him to render me unconscious, so what do I do?"

"This is where my plan is a bit patchy. You need to get him into the house, where I'm hoping Ray can provide us with some sort of recording equipment."

"You're presuming a lot, Roger," replied Ray.

"Can you do it?"

"No, not unofficially. You need official approval for an MI5 operation. In that way, Maggie would be excused from testifying in court."

"Would we get approval?"

"No, this is a civil, criminal matter."

"I'll get your approval," she said. "I know some very influential people."

"You continue to amaze me, Maggie. I should be flabbergasted at that suggestion."

"Flabbergasted - that's a good word; I must make a note of that," she replied.

Who was this woman who casually talked about killing people and had contacts in high places? Ray just smiled. He obviously had the answers to my questions but was not about to tell me. Despite the holes in my plan, Maggie agreed to do it. She spoke as if the official approval was just a formality. The mystery surrounding her deepened. Gerry was also happy. An official MI5 operation relieved him of responsibility.

"You need to get him into the house, Maggie, and you need to get some sort of confession out of him. He's obsessed with his own fame as the new 'Jack the Ripper,' and he has a violent temper if his fantasy doesn't go according to plan."

"That's good, I can use that against him. I need to know everything about him so I don't take any unnecessary risks. I have to be in complete control of everything, including Burrows."

Her confidence was contagious. I went from being concerned for her to being concerned for Burrows. Not that I gave a damn about him, but I didn't want our case against him to be derailed. I also didn't want her to deny him his appointment with the hangman. It was important to me that justice was seen to be done. We talked well into the afternoon as I showed her everything we had on Burrows. By the end of the day, she knew everything that I did, and she'd seen the photographs of every crime scene and victim. None of it concerned her; if anything, it added to her determination to get him. She left with Ray, full of the same high spirits she arrived with. She left me with two bright red lips planted on my cheek, much to everyone's amusement.

I left that evening for another night with Jean in the Clapham South deep underground shelter. Those nights had become increasingly difficult to bear. The limit of human endurance is a point in time that we constantly redefine and push further into the future. After nearly six years, it had never been closer. That evening was no different, but my mind remained full of other matters. Jean and I were not like a divorced couple; we had no animosity between us. We were two people who had lost a mutual friend; we consoled each other in our hour of need.

## Chapter Seventy
# March 1945

Emma

*"The journey from denial to acceptance is but a*
*short step from the dark into the light."*

My conversation with Jean left me in a state of shock. I felt as
if I had been living in another age and Jean opened the door
into the here and now. Everything I believed about myself had
been an illusion. I told Jean I thought about Roger all the time. I couldn't
believe I said that; the words formed on my lips, and I just said it. The
journey from denial to acceptance is but a short step from the dark into
the light. Our walk back to the hospital from the pub no longer seemed
familiar. I looked at the River Thames as if I hadn't seen it before. Frank
remained oblivious to my emotion, but Janet was so perceptive she knew
something had happened. As soon as we were alone in the basement, she
pounced on me.

"What did Jean tell you that was so important?"

"How do you know she said anything important?"

"You looked like a rabbit caught in the headlamps. And now look at
you. Your eyes are sparkling."

"Are they?"

"It's about Roger, isn't it?"

"You're right. She confirmed what we thought: their future is not
together, and she told me Roger really likes me."

"I already know that. So what does it mean?"

"I don't know. My head's spinning: I don't know what to think."

"You're crazy about him, aren't you?"

"I didn't want to admit it, not even to myself, but I am; I can't stop thinking about him."

"I already knew that as well; I've just been waiting for you to realise it. You know what my next question is, don't you?"

"Yes, I have to tell Frank; it can't go on, can it?"

"No, it's not fair to either of you."

"Do you think I'm doing the right thing?"

"It will be the best thing you've ever done. Frank's a lovely man, but I've always known you want more. I know you do."

"It's all so painful; how do I tell him?"

"Just tell him the truth. Something is missing from your relationship, and it's not fair to either of you."

Marion arrived in the basement. "Have I interrupted something?"

"No, not at all. Emma was just saying how she intends to break up with Frank."

"Janet. You mustn't tell everyone."

"It makes it real, though, doesn't it?"

"Janet's right, Emma. You've been thinking about this for a long time; I know you have. Every journey starts with the first step, and you've just taken it. Well done; we're all here for you."

"I've been unlucky in love, but I'm lucky to have friends like you. I don't know how I would manage without you all."

Shirley then joined us, and it started all over again. My friends knew everything about me, which is more than I did. Janet was right, though; talking about it made it real, and it would happen. My heart raced at the prospect of telling Frank, but I knew it was the right decision, regardless of Roger. As daunting as it was to have to tell Frank, I suddenly realised I also had to face Roger. He liked me; Jean told me he did, but what did that mean? After finally admitting to myself that I thought about him all the time, what if he only liked me as a friend? The thought filled me with the fear that I might lose him. He wasn't mine to lose, but still, the prospect terrified me.

We felt the building shake during the night. It was very sudden and violent; it felt different to the bombs we were used to. The following day, we woke to the news that a V2 rocket had struck near the hospital. I had every intention of telling Frank as soon as I saw him, but that all changed as casualties poured in the door. The injuries were horrendous, but even more frightening was the number of victims who didn't have a mark on them, yet they arrived dead. The shock wave from a V2 could destroy internal organs without causing external damage. Organs such as the heart could rupture, and the lungs collapse. We worked all day, and the senseless procession of human misery seemed to be never-ending.

Late in the afternoon, the usual confusion of doctors and nurses shouting for help or assistance suddenly stopped abruptly when the reception hall became filled with a scream that made me shudder. A young woman in her twenties had discovered her loved one lying dead on the floor. Her grief was all-consuming; it filled the hospital like a malign entity. I ran to her and grabbed her in my arms before she collapsed. I felt her body trembling violently as she struggled for breath. She screamed again as if she expressed the pain of the entire nation. We did what we could to relieve her heartache, but nothing we could do would bring her husband back.

I lost count of the number of grieving men and women I had seen during the war, but none made the same impression on me as that woman did. Her agony was irreconcilable. She cried for the nation, and she cried for me. She expressed everything I had suppressed for so long. Frank gave her a sedative, and I had to walk away. The poor woman invoked a terrible fear in us all. There can be an awful price to pay for being human and loving someone. For every casualty that day and every other day, there is someone somewhere who has paid that price. I felt utterly drained when I finished with the last of the injured.

Frank came and suggested we have a cup of tea together. We sat at a table in the canteen amongst a sombre crowd. Janet and the others didn't join us. I thought of that poor woman's pain, and mine seemed insignificant in comparison. Weary and depressed, I just wanted life to be easier. I sat looking at Frank, confused and uncertain, consumed by the words I was about to say to him. All the while, I could still hear the bereaved woman's scream echoing in my head.

"I'm so sorry, Frank, I can't go on. We're not right for each other, are we? Please don't think badly of me, Frank, but I think it's already ended between us, hasn't it?"

"You're right, Em. I've felt it for some time but didn't have the courage to say anything."

"You don't hate me?"

"Of course I don't. I'm sorry as well. You're such a wonderful person, Em; I wish I could have made you happy, but it's not working, is it?"

"Did I make you happy?"

"You did but seeing you unhappy has been destroying me. Is it your policeman friend; is that what this is all about?"

"No, it really isn't. Nothing has happened between me and Roger, absolutely nothing. I don't know what the future holds, but I want to look for it, Frank. I want to find whatever is waiting for me."

"I think what you'll eventually find is yourself, Em. I hope you find it, and I hope you share it with someone like Roger or whoever the lucky man is."

"I didn't expect you to say something like that; what a wonderful thing to say. Will we remain friends? We can, can't we? I never want to lose you, Frank; I'll never forget what we had together."

"After everything we've been through, how can we not be friends?"

I kissed him; I don't know why, I just did. I thought he would make a scene and hate me, but he didn't. Frank rarely showed his emotions, much less expressed them, so I certainly didn't expect his response. It was like drinking a glass of whisky; the tension drained from my body, and I felt heady with relief. We held hands across the table, and strangely, I had never felt closer to him. Frank and I hadn't lived together since the V1s started falling on us. We drifted apart a long time ago. I felt happy we were spared a traumatic breakup; we could still be kind to each other.

I walked towards the basement that evening like a weary soldier retreating from the battlefield, except I had discarded my heavy burden. It had been a day of contrasting emotions, a rollercoaster of lives saved and grief shared. I told the others, and they understood my tangled mix of emotions as I knew they would. My day ended with one last burst of adrenaline when Marion arrived.

"I haven't had a chance to tell you, Emma. Evelyn took a message from your friend Roger this afternoon. He asked if he could see you, and he'll phone back tomorrow morning at 8:30, so could you be by the phone?"

"Yes, of course, I'll be there."

My weariness overwhelmed me, and I fell asleep almost immediately. Four hours later, I woke up thinking it might be half past eight. When it wasn't, I just lay there, and all I could think about was what Roger was going to say in the morning. I didn't get back to sleep despite feeling desperately weary. I stood outside Evelyn's office even before she arrived. What if she was late? What if I couldn't get into the office when the telephone rang? I would have to break the glass to get inside. Evelyn was never late, and she arrived five minutes early as she always did.

"Morning, Emma. Did Marion give you your message about the phone call this morning?"

"Yes, she did, that's why I'm here."

"Tell you what, I'll go and get a cup of tea and leave you to it, shall I?"

"There's no need to do that, Evelyn."

"Oh, I think there might be. Besides, I'd like a cup of tea."

There were times when I thought the entire hospital knew everything about me. Nevertheless, I was grateful. If I had to make a fool of myself, I thought it best to do it privately. The telephone rang at precisely 8:30, and I grabbed it immediately.

"St Thomas's Hospital, can I help you?"

"Is that you, Emma?"

"Roger, you rang."

"I said I would. I hope it's not inconvenient."

"No, I was working close to the office, anyway."

"It's a bit awkward, isn't it? Jean's kind of dropped a spanner in the works, hasn't she?"

"We had a difficult conversation. She's remarkable, isn't she...? Are you still there?"

"Yes, sorry, Em. She is remarkable. What do you think about what she told you?"

"I thought it was incredibly brave of her."

"Well, yes, it was, but I meant what she said about us."

"She told me she wouldn't come between us, and I said there was nothing to come between."

"Is that how you feel, Emma?"

"No, that's not how I feel, but it's true, isn't it?"

"You told her you couldn't stop thinking about me. Is that right?"

"I'm sorry, I didn't mean to say that. You know me, I babble."

"Is it true, though?"

"Well, I said it. She also said you liked me. She said you didn't stop talking about me."

"Oh, God, Emma, this is difficult. You're with Frank; I shouldn't be saying this. It's all wrong, but Jean's right, I do like you. I think about you from the moment I wake up until the last moment before I go to sleep. You're always in my mind. What am I going to do?"

"I'm not with Frank any more. I've been awake half the night waiting for you to call me."

"Stay where you are. I'm coming over."

He put the phone down, and I just stood there with my heart pounding. I was still standing there when Evelyn came back.

"Did your friend call?"

"Yes, he did, thank you, Evelyn. He's coming over to see me."

Only then, when I told Evelyn, did it become real. He really was coming to the hospital. I looked terrible, or was it just how I always looked? Either way, I looked awful. I had to put some makeup on and do something with my hair. I panicked, but I had no time. Roger might be here in fifteen minutes and I had already wasted five.

As I rushed back towards the basement, I came face to face with the day's casualties arriving. Leo, Frank, and Maurice were already there treating patients. Janet waved desperately at me with one hand while the other pressed against a wound, pumping blood. I instinctively stepped in and worked with Janet to stem the blood loss.

The casualty, a middle-aged woman with blast injuries, was what we politely called a bleeder. We had only a few precious minutes to save her life. It was touch and go for a moment. As I closed the last of her wounds, Janet smiled approvingly. We stood looking at each other. The end of a crisis is always a moment to savour. We could finally breathe normally again; our hearts could slow down. Janet's eyes suddenly looked behind me. I turned, and there he was, standing on the other side of the hall.

My only thought for the previous twenty minutes had been saving that woman's life. Now, my only thought was Roger. I stepped from one world into another. My shabbily dressed policeman stood smiling at me with his hat in his hands. I walked towards him, wiping the blood from mine.

Conscious that everyone could see me, I fought desperately against the temptation to run towards him. He passed his hat from hand to hand as I pulled my loose hair back with the aid of my surgical tweezers. I felt the eyes of my previous world upon me.

"You came, Roger."

"Yes, I came immediately. We need to talk ... is there somewhere private that we can go?"

"I wish there was. Oh, Roger, how I wish there was. Look at all these casualties; I can't leave them."

"It's alright. I didn't think; you have that effect on me. I just had to see you. I had to be sure."

"And are you?"

"Yes, I'm quite sure."

"So am I - I'm sure."

"Am I going to see you later, then?"

"You will."

"I must go, Emma. Later, then, I'll see you later?"

"I'll be waiting."

We didn't mention a time; we didn't need to. People make arrangements to secure a piece of the future. We didn't need that assurance. I had never been more sure of anything in my whole life.

# Chapter Seventy-One
# March 1945

Roger

*"The unobtainable resides in a greener field where we covet its perfection. Open that gilded cage, and what will step out is an impossible dream of your own creation."*

The revelation that Emma had broken her relationship with Frank removed an insurmountable obstacle for me. My impulsive rush to St Thomas's to see her said more about my state of mind than it did my common sense. When the object of your desire is beyond reach, it simply becomes more desirable. An obsession can so easily become a fantasy.

The unobtainable resides in a greener field where we covet its perfection. Open that gilded cage, and you might find an impossible dream of your own creation. My relationship with Emma, if that's what it was, remained exactly that: an impossible dream. Except this was no longer a dream. There she was, walking towards me. Achingly weary, bloodstained, dishevelled, and the most gloriously wonderful woman I had ever seen.

I wanted more than anything else in this world to hold her in my arms. I needed to know that my impossible dream wasn't a fantasy and that Emma shared the same vision. The hospital was full of casualties; all the staff were there. We stood centre-stage, the only actors in the spotlight. I wouldn't have been there at all if I had applied even a semblance of common sense, but there was nothing rational about my feelings for Emma. There was so much to say, so much to confirm. In the end, the spotlight became too intense. I submitted to it and resorted to uttering meaningless words. I said I needed to be sure, but sure of what I didn't say. Emma replied, saying she was sure. Suddenly, the need to prevaricate melted away. We both knew what we were sure about, even if our words didn't. The look on her face mirrored my own. 'I'll see you later' expressed a thousand words. I walked away, smiling like a Cheshire cat.

I'd left Jeff outside in the car, wondering what the hell was going on. We should have been on our way to check out the empty terraced house in Wandsworth that I knew would fulfil Maggie's cover story.

"You look as if your horse just won."

"I think it did, Jeff."

"When am I going to meet this doctor friend of yours?"

"I'll let you know. Let's get on our way to Wandsworth and look again at that house. We just have to be sure Maggie, or whatever her name is, can actually spend some nights there."

"Time's the problem, isn't it? We can't expect her to stay there for weeks. I had an idea about her cover story. She could say the landlord wants her out within the week to carry out repairs. This would explain why she would make such a song and dance at the Town Hall."

"That's a good idea, Jeff. That will put pressure on Burrows to act while he still can."

When we arrived, we found the blast had not only broken all the glass in the front windows but also damaged the frames and some surrounding brickwork. The rooms in the back of the house were not damaged beyond some fallen ceiling plaster. Amazingly, the tiled roof had only suffered damage at the front of the house. It was plausible that Maggie could theoretically live there. The kitchen, one bedroom and the toilet were functional. The family who'd previously lived there decided they could take no more, and with Jean's help, moved in with relatives.

"The problem with this, Roger, is where are we going to be?"

"I agree. Our only option is to talk to the next-door neighbours and see if we can get the use of a room."

"What if they say no?"

"Then we're buggered."

We did precisely that and had two possibilities, one on either side. Good fortune shone on us that day. The first house we knocked on took a bit of convincing, but they agreed. The next step was the slight issue of MI5's official involvement. Jeff and I went back to the station, where I telephoned Ray. A woman answered the phone, a secretary or a telephonist - I didn't know which. It took some time and a lot of explanation, but eventually, Ray came to the phone.

"What's the news, Ray; do you have official sanction to use Maggie?"

"She's been true to her word. I've been given the go-ahead."

"How, how can she achieve that?"

"I wish I could tell you, mate, but trust me, that woman's not what she seems."

"Okay, good enough. The house I've found is ideal, and we have a room in the adjoining house we can use."

"Excellent. Give me all the details, and I'll have our technical people over there to install the listening equipment."

"I need to brief Maggie again. Can you organise that?"

"Yes, that's not a problem. You can trust this woman, Roger, I promise you. I recently worked with her on a job where she was confronted by a bunch of Jack Comer's boys, including Jack himself. It was something to witness, I can tell you."

"I hope you're right. If not, this will come down on me like a ton of bricks."

We got as far as we could go that day; I needed to wait for Maggie to make contact. A part of me was excited about the prospect, while another part remained terrified. I juggled a dozen thoughts at once, but only one dictated my actions. Late afternoon and early evening had become one of the same; Emma might be free. I left early and drove directly to the hospital. When I arrived, things had obviously calmed down. The frenetic pandemonium of the morning had given way to a more orderly procession of walking-wounded. A V1 flew overhead, reminding me that another rush of casualties could arrive at any moment.

I sat waiting for an hour, and then there she was. No longer dressed in her surgical gown, she walked towards me wearing a skirt and jumper. Emma never seemed bothered about her appearance, but I could see she had gone to considerable trouble, which instantly made me feel even more shabby than usual. I stood up as she walked towards me. Although I hadn't so much as kissed her, we had an understanding. We longed to be together; she knew it, and I knew it. The need to dance around each other had gone. She held out both hands, and I took them in mine.

"What would you like to do, Emma?"

"Why don't we try to get a bite to eat somewhere? Let's try the nice little tea shop just over the bridge, they also do basic meals. They were still there a couple of weeks ago."

We walked side by side, talking about her day and then mine. All the while, I could feel her hand in mine. The little tea shop was still there. I had no idea how they managed to continue with both food and customers in short supply, but I was pleased they did. Only one other couple sat at one of the tables. We sat opposite each other, looking at the dinner menu, which comprised sausages and mash or vegetable soup. She looked up from the menu and surprised me, as she always did.

"Does this mean we have a relationship, Roger?"

"If that's what you want, then yes, I think we do."

"It is what I want, but can we take our time? I'm not used to these things. I don't know what you expect."

"I expect nothing, Emma. I just know I have to be with you."

"I feel the same about you, and for once in my life, I'm not embarrassed to say it."

"That's a good sign, isn't it?"

"It is. I feel confident when I'm with you."

"Emma, can I lean across this table and kiss you?"

"I'll meet you halfway."

Exquisite moments in time are few and far between. Our lips coming together was such a moment. A passionate kiss is both a declaration and an exploration. That kiss expressed a thousand unspoken words, and suddenly, I knew Emma, the woman. I knew the softness of her lips and the touch of her cheek. I didn't want it to end, and neither did she. When we finally sat back in our respective chairs, she looked overwhelmed. She took several seconds to gather herself before smiling at me.

"Is that what normally happens when you kiss someone, Roger?"

"No, it's not. I've never kissed anyone like that before."

"Not even Jean?"

"No, never. I feel as if I've opened a gilded cage, half expecting to find an impossible dream, but this isn't a dream, is it?"

We kissed again until the waitress appeared, using words designed to break magic spells.

"What can I get you, then?"

"Oh, yes. What do you think, Emma, sausage and mash or soup?"

"I've not eaten all day."

"That will be two sausages and mash then."

We sat looking at each other as the waitress walked away. I thought

Emma would be embarrassed that we'd been caught kissing, but a huge smile appeared on her face, and we both laughed. My heart said one thing while my head said another. I couldn't deny that, over time, I had become infatuated with her. I knew enough to realise fantasies don't always come true. Jean and I embarked on a journey together, both thinking it was a dream come true. I didn't want to make the same mistake again. There was no one I admired and respected more, and I didn't want her to have a single regret.

"I've made mistakes in the past, as you know, and there's no way I ever want to think of you as a mistake, Emma. I agree with what you said about taking our time. I want you more than anything else in this world, and I want nothing to spoil that."

"This is why I feel confident with you, Roger. You understand me so well."

The waitress walked towards us carrying two plates of sausages and mash. She took a few steps before becoming frozen to the spot as the sound of a V1 filled the air. Emma and I both looked towards the ceiling as if we could see it. The sound increased as it drew closer. It sounded as if it was coming directly towards us. The pulse jet engine sputtered and stopped. We looked at each other wide-eyed. The other two diners stood up, not knowing what to do.

"Quick, get under the table," I shouted. "Turn your back to the window."

Fifteen seconds can feel like a lifetime. I held Emma close to my chest, expecting the worst. When it came, the explosion was close, but not that close. The building shook, and dust fell from above, but everything remained intact. We struggled out from beneath our table, and I rushed outside. I couldn't see anything from my vantage point, so the V1 had obviously fallen one or two streets away. I returned to the restaurant to find the waitress clearing the sausages and mash she had dropped on the floor. The other couple sat back at their table as if nothing had happened.

Emma's instinct was to rush towards the bomb site and tend to the injured, but I convinced her she had done enough that day. The waitress apologised for dropping our plates as if it had been her fault. She said she would replace them as quickly as she could. We sat down at our table like the other couple. For us, it was business as usual. Just streets away, people would be lying beneath the rubble, killed or injured. For those unfortunate people, life would never be the same. This was the cruel reality of our daily existence. I was never sure if we were being strong in defiance or weak in denial, but somehow, we knew we had to carry on.

## Chapter Seventy-Two
# April 4th, 1945

### Roger

*"An illusion is a blank canvas where we paint our own picture. The vision is complete when we see what we are intended to see."*

Mystery creates its own intrigue, and Maggie was no exception. She didn't fit the usual profile of an MI5 agent like Ray, but she was a highly trained individual. Her broad Cockney accent and flirtatious manner only added to her intrigue. She arrived at the station precisely on time and immediately became the centre of attention. Her personality filled the room until we came to the details of her cover story. The bubbly character disappeared to be replaced by the experienced professional I knew she was. Her attention to detail was impressive. She studied Burrows' file meticulously and stared intently at his photograph. She wanted to see where he worked at the Town Hall before she encountered him, as well as the Wandsworth property.

I was the one who had doubts, but I found her confidence immensely reassuring. I asked her if she would carry a gun in addition to the knife I knew she carried. She replied, saying she would have a Colt 38 in her handbag. According to Maggie, there were only two things that could go wrong. It was vital Burrows would see her when she made a scene at the Town Hall. And secondly, she had to get him into the house while not allowing him to strangle her in the garden. Her attention to detail even went as far as the phase of the moon. She wanted to go ahead as soon as possible because, in three days, it would be a full moon, which would give her the best chance of night vision should she encounter Burrows in the garden.

It all felt slightly rushed, but everything was in place. We had a clandestine trip to the Town Hall so she could familiarise herself with the layout, and then we went to see the Wandsworth house. The state of the place didn't put her off. Ray's technical man had installed the listening equipment, so I put the plan into effect.

I met Maggie on the morning of the operation, and she appeared perfectly calm and collected. I hadn't given her choice of clothing much thought, not really my department, but self-evidently she had. Everything from her coat to her shoes spoke of an impoverished woman living in terrible conditions. She wore no makeup, and her hair, although short, was unwashed and unkempt. The weather was cold even for April, so I didn't look out of place with my hat on and my collar turned up. I entered the Town Hall first and mingled with several other people.

Maggie followed me, playing her part to perfection. Somehow, she looked utterly broken and desperate. She had to queue in line with the other people desperately seeking accommodation. When her turn came, I didn't doubt that the young woman was trying to help her, but Maggie played the part of the irate victim to perfection. In reality, Margaret Kennedy's character would have been no more deserving than anyone else, but they didn't all protest as loudly as Maggie. The duty manager was called but to no avail. He couldn't pacify Mrs Kennedy. The people queuing behind her were becoming irate, just as she intended. Maggie chose precisely the right words and attitude to antagonise the crowd, and they started shouting and pushing. I could hear her asking who was in charge and demanding to see him. The crowd of people behind her played right into her hands. She almost started a riot. An illusion is a blank canvas where we paint our own picture. The vision is complete when we see what we are intended to see.

The duty manager had little option but to escort Mrs Kennedy to see the man in charge. I couldn't help but smile; her performance was flawless. With Maggie bursting into his office, Burrows would certainly pay attention. She was in there for nineteen minutes, far longer than he would typically give any other homeless person. When the door opened again, I desperately watched for a sign. She appeared very relaxed and smiling. Burrows offered his hand, and Maggie shook it enthusiastically. I almost forgot myself and punched the air. Maggie calmly left the Town Hall as imperiously as she had entered, and I followed soon after.

"That went well, Roger."

"How well?"

"He was very aggressive and unpleasant until I told him my name. His attitude changed immediately. He offered me a seat and couldn't have been nicer."

"Do you think you've got him hooked?"

"Of course. He wanted to know about the Anderson shelter and did the garden have a rear entrance? He asked where my husband was serving. He did everything apart from inviting himself over."

"He'll scout the place out first, probably tonight or tomorrow. I'll have a few bobbies well-hidden so we can confirm he's been there. Probably best if you spend the nights in the shelter immediately."

"Are you sure he will only reconnoitre?"

"No, but I'd bet on it."

"I'll be ready either way. It's exciting, init."

"Do you really find something like this exciting?"

"You've gone to a lot of trouble. We baited the trap, and he's going to fall into it. Of course, it's exciting. He's a horrible piece of work. I could see it in his eyes, Roger. I'll get him, don't you worry."

"I am worried. Just take care of yourself."

"Don't be daft. You're a sweet policeman, but you don't have to worry about me."

I did worry about her despite her unfailing confidence. She had a suitcase of personal effects with her, and I had already made sure the larder had at least some basic provisions. The plan was that she should approach the house alone so as not to raise any suspicions. Jeff and I loosened one of the garden fence panels to gain quick access from the rear of the house without being overlooked. I dropped her off a few streets away and parked the car around the corner from the house.

The elderly couple in the house next door were there, but I also had a key. Ron and Doris were a charming couple and probably enjoyed the attention. I told them we were involved with police surveillance, which was true. They wanted to be helpful, but I had to dissuade them from bringing me a constant stream of tea and cakes. I told them several other men would arrive after dark because I didn't want them to be noticed. It was probably one big adventure for them, but I felt nervous. I gave it half an hour before sneaking into the garden and through the fence. Maggie sat waiting for me with two cups of tea.

"How did you know I would come at this time?"

"Because you're a really lovely man, Roger. It's not in your nature to leave a woman alone when she might be in danger. I figured you couldn't wait more than half an hour."

"So, are you settled in?"

"If you call this settled in, then yes. Thank you for providing me with clean sheets. That was thoughtful."

"I've tried to think of everything."

"Stop worrying, Roger. This is luxury as far as I'm concerned. You would understand if you could see some of the places I've had to call home. This is easy, trust me."

"What are you comparing it with, Maggie?"

"I've recently spent an age in a damp cellar beneath a pigsty. I can still smell it. At least that was out of the weather."

"Was that in occupied France?"

"That's cheeky, Roger, you're prying. You know I can't tell you."

"Sorry."

I was so intrigued; she was obviously MI6, SOE, or possibly some other secret organisation, but she was far too professional to tell me. We went through our plan time and time again. She would go out to the Anderson shelter after her evening meal. Although there was no particular time that the buzz bombs and rockets might fall, most people chose to sleep in a shelter. Ray's technical man, Brian, had connected the shelter via a wire to our adjoining room. We couldn't communicate with Maggie, but she could talk to us. The house had a microphone in each room. Our only blind spot was the garden. We could see part of it from the rear window of our surveillance room, but we could hear nothing.

Brian drilled an inch-wide hole through the party wall that separated the two properties. Placed behind a framed photograph, it was sufficient for us to talk to Maggie if she put her ear next to it. If all else failed, we had the failsafe option of banging on the wall. I couldn't think of anything we hadn't considered, but more to the point, Maggie was happy with the setup. I fully accepted by then that she knew far more about this kind of thing than I did. When I asked if she could cope in the unlikely event that Burrows produced a firearm, she opened her shoulder bag and waved the Colt 38 at me. I left her for the night, feeling Maggie was very much in charge.

Ray and the communications expert, Brian, arrived after dark. Jeff was only a couple of minutes behind them. We had barely settled in for the night when Doris knocked on the door with a tray of tea and cakes. It wasn't ideal - she must have noticed the recording equipment; it was impossible to avoid it.

The rear entrance to the back garden was via a communal alleyway running between the houses. It was only accessible from one end, which was very helpful. I had two of Jack's boys sitting in a car with a pair of binoculars and a good view of the alleyway entrance. Brian supplied us with a field radio so that they could communicate with us. Our boys weren't used to using the kit; it caused a bit of fun and eased our tension.

"Observation car, observation car, this is watchtower, over," Brian said.

"Hello, this is PC Butler speaking. Can you hear me? Am I pressing the right button?"

"Just use your call sign and talk normally; don't shout into the microphone."

"Do I need to say my name each time, sir?"

"Your call sign is 'observation car', not PC Butler, and stop shouting. Now, you call. watchtower, over."

"Hello, can you hear me?"

"The man's an idiot," said Brian. "He's still got his finger on the button, and I can't talk to him."

"Hello, are you there, over?"

"Observation car, observation car, this is watchtower. You don't say, can you hear me? You use the call sign twice to indicate who you are calling, followed by your own call sign. Then you speak, and when you're finished, say 'over', and take your bloody finger off the button."

"I've got it, sir, sorry ... over."

It was a light-hearted moment in what was otherwise a very tense situation. We settled down for what we expected would be a long wait.

# Chapter Seventy-Three
## April 6th, 1945

Emma

*"A woman might face the world with a smile, but a woman in love wants to embrace it. For her, the world holds no fear. She has the power of love and the strength of two."*

The unknown can be frightening, a place that harbours our worst fears. It can also be where good news hides from view. There was news which would have been cause for celebration had it not been concealed behind one of the worst tragedies of the war. Just days previously, on March 27th, a V2 rocket hit an apartment complex in Stepney, East London. The apartments were occupied by many Jewish people who had escaped persecution in Europe. 134 people were killed, and 120 of those were Jewish. Another V2 fell on Orpington in Kent the same day, and that killed one person.

How could we possibly know that such a devastating event was also the harbinger of wonderful news? The number of casualties arriving at the hospital suddenly declined abruptly. We waited, as always, for the tidal wave of misery to come flooding towards us. It didn't come, and neither would it. What none of us knew was that March 27th was the last day that a V2 rocket would fall anywhere in England. Two days later, the last V1 fell without causing casualties in Kent.

Despite everything, it would have been a cause for celebration, but the unknown is always just out of reach. It was serendipitous that Roger and I opened a new page on the unfolding story of our relationship just days before that event. The lack of casualties was timely because my head remained firmly in the clouds. Had I known the civilian war was effectively at an end, I would have viewed my life through fresh eyes. We continued to spend our nights in the basement, living one day and one night at a time.

"When are you seeing Roger again?"

"I don't know, Jan, he's currently tied up with a very important case. He's out all night on some kind of surveillance operation."

"He's not giving you the runaround, is he?"

"No, I trust him completely, Shirley. He would never do that."

"Emma's right, Shirley. I know Roger. He has this thing about gallantry, especially towards women. It doesn't apply to many men, but you can take what Roger says to the bank."

"I'm pleased for you, Emma," said Marion. "I'm pleased for all of you. I've watched from afar as your relationships have ebbed and flowed, and I can tell the moment when you can no longer be parted from them."

"How do you know?"

"It's hard to describe, Janet. A woman in love has a certain glow about her. A woman might face the world with a smile, but a woman in love wants to embrace it. For her, the world holds no fear. She has the power of love and the strength of two. I begin to wonder if a woman without love is incomplete."

"Oh, Marion, that's a sad thing to say. You're not incomplete just because you're not married. There's not a person in this hospital who doesn't love and respect you. You'll never be alone in this world. Hundreds of us will always be there for you."

"Emma's right, Marion," said Janet. "We don't jump to and tidy up our uniforms every time you walk into the ward just because you're the hospital matron. And we don't do it just out of respect, either. We do it because you're the one we can all turn to. You're the one who supports us through thick and thin. We do it because you care about every one of us, and we love you for it. I would do anything for you, and so would Shirley. So would any of us."

I thought Marion was about to burst into tears; she buried her face in her handkerchief for a moment. "You're very kind, and you're right; I do care about you all. I like to see my nurses happy. A happy nurse is a good nurse. Thank you for what you said, Janet. That means a lot to me. I'll always treasure those words. So, tell me about Roger. Apart from when he was a patient, I've only seen him from afar."

"Then you know he's always scruffy, he doesn't always shave, he smokes, which I hate, and he mixes with people I wouldn't want to meet."

"Yes, but?"

"Well, he's all those things, but he's also the most empathetic man I've ever met. He's caring, especially about women. He intuitively understands me; if I'm unhappy or concerned about something, then he's unhappy and concerned. You asked if he might give me the runaround, Shirley. Janet's right. I think he's incapable of being disloyal. I think for Roger, being disloyal to a woman or abusing her in any way should be a capital offence."

"And he's good-looking," laughed Janet.

"Perhaps he is in his own way. I just think he's lovely, and I can't wait to see him again."

"It sounds as though you're thinking about a long-term future with him, Emma."

"I'm trying not to, Marion. I'm trying to be very sensible and take it one step at a time."

"Is it working?"

"No, Shirley, it's not."

Being forced to sleep in a small basement room for months on end, sharing with other women, might sound like an awful experience. However, deprivation and hardship were the midwives of friendship for many during the war. I had never really had girlfriends such as Janet, Beverley, Shirley, and Marion, and having shared so much together, we were inseparable. Despite six years of war, I lay in bed in that smelly basement, thinking how lucky I was.

Roger made it clear that he couldn't see me in the evenings for the time being, but he was desperate for me to get away for half an hour during the day. I said I would meet him in the tea shop at 1 o'clock, and the following morning, I counted the minutes. Not a single casualty arrived. We only had to attend to those we had taken care of before. My friends rallied around me, and I got away in good time. Despite being early, I almost ran across the bridge. I sat waiting for him, constantly checking the time. I intended to remain calm and controlled; I didn't intend to do or say anything rash. When he finally arrived, he looked harassed and physically drained. My intention to remain demure vanished in a second. I threw myself into his arms.

"How are you? You look exhausted. Have you had any sleep?"

"I grabbed two hours of sleep this morning. I have to admit, I'm struggling a bit."

"Have you eaten anything, anything substantial?"

"Not really. I bought a sandwich at the baker's yesterday."

"Can you tell me what's going on?"

"It's to do with the Ripper inquiry. We have a house under constant surveillance, but he hasn't shown up so far."

"Why do you think that he might?"

"I shouldn't be telling you, but we've set a trap for him. We have a potential victim waiting for him."

"What, an actual victim, a woman?"

"I know it sounds bad, but trust me, this is no ordinary woman."

"I'm sure you know what you're doing, Roger. Give me your wrist; I want to take your pulse." His heart was racing, he was obviously highly stressed, and I knew his blood pressure would be high. "How many cigarettes are you smoking?"

"It's far too many, but they keep me awake."

"How long is this surveillance thing of yours going to last?"

"Not much longer, just another few days."

"It's important to you, isn't it."

"This man has killed five women, and he wants to kill another. I can't rest until he faces justice. I have to get him, Emma, I have to."

"Why is it so important to you? It's not just because he's a murderer, is it? Is it because he kills women?"

"Yes, it is. I can't stand by and allow him to get away with that."

"You're very protective towards women, Roger. I think that's an enviable quality, but is there a reason for it? Has anything happened that has made you feel that way?"

"I've never spoken about it, Emma, not even to Marilyn."

"Can you tell me?"

"When I was a kid, my father was a brutal man. He would take his belt to me for the slightest thing. But it wasn't just me. He did the same to my younger sister and even to my mother."

"You've never mentioned your family once."

"No, it's not something I talk about."

"How did it end?"

"He came home one night, drunk as usual. My sister Elsie came home late after seeing a friend, and he went into a terrible rage. I think he might have killed her if I hadn't stepped in. I hit him with a milk bottle."

"What happened?"

"Elsie couldn't take any more. She eventually ran off with her boy-friend. I couldn't live there any more, not with him, so I left home. I was sixteen years old."

"Do you still see your family?"

"No, Elsie didn't know where I was, and I didn't know where she was. I think she wrote to our mother, but she disowned me when I left home."

"What about your parents now?"

"They're both gone now; mother went ten years ago, and dad died soon after. I didn't even go to the funeral because I didn't know."

"I'm so sorry, Roger, that's a horrible story. Have you ever tried to find your sister; she would be so proud of you."

"I did once, but I suppose in truth I didn't try very hard. It's all so painful; I didn't want to face it again. I've always blamed myself. I was the oldest; I should have done more to protect her. "

"I'm pleased you've told me; it explains a lot. The past always shapes the future, but it doesn't have to control us. Look at you; you're not remotely like your father. You're a kind and gentle man. You have a successful career, and now you have the ambition to become a Member of Parliament. I think you need to be free of this murderer, Roger. You need to close that book and embrace the future."

"Is that Doctor Stevenson's diagnosis?"

"I'm sorry, you're right. I've jumped to all sorts of conclusions. Ignore me, Roger."

"No, I don't think I can. You see, you're right about everything. I will get this man. His name is Burrows, and when I do, I want my past to die with him."

"If it's what you want, then that's what will happen."

"Shall we have the sausage and mash again?"

# Chapter Seventy-Four
# April 10th, 1945

Roger

*"A single seed of doubt is all that's required to take root. Invite it into the light, and it will grow into your every thought and deed."*

I had become desperate; we were nearly a week into the operation, and there was no sign of Burrows. Maggie took it all in her stride. She was the counterbalance to my anxiety. We had established a routine. She went out into the garden each evening at about 10 o'clock and spent the night in the shelter. Each morning, she would go back into the house and then go out during the day, ostensibly to the cleaning job she told Burrows she had. She bought food; the milkman delivered milk, and we ensured the postman delivered mail. In every respect, her appearance was in accordance with her cover story.

A single seed of doubt is all that's required to take root. Invite it into the light, and it will grow into your every thought and deed. Had Burrows seen us entering the next-door property? Had he spotted the plain-clothed bobbies in the observation car? The buzz bombs and rockets were no longer falling. We still had the blackout, but Burrows had lost the cover of exploding bombs and chaos. I could think of a hundred reasons why he had not fallen for the trap. Ray became ever more anxious about extending the operation further, and I had to agree. The chair I sat in grew increasingly uncomfortable as my tension increased. The first light of dawn marked the end of another fruitless night's surveillance. I stretched and yawned, trying to ease the pain in my back. As I walked out into the hall to light up a fag, the radio crackled to life.

"Watchtower, watchtower, this is observation car, over."

Still half asleep, Brian woke up with such a start that he knocked over what was left of his cold cup of tea. "Observation car, observation car, this is watchtower. Go ahead. Over."

"It's him, sir, I'm sure of it. A tall man with a trilby hat and a long coat with the collar turned up. He's entered the alleyway. He's coming your way, over."

"Standby, observation car, well done, over."

"Bloody hell, it's him. What's he doing here at this time? Maggie's probably asleep."

"It's okay, Brian, he's checking the place out, that's all."

"Roger's right, Brian," said Jeff. "We just didn't expect him to come at first light."

We all rushed to the rear window, desperate to catch sight of him. In the half-light of dawn, we saw only the suggestion of a shape standing by the garden gate. As elusive as the swirling mist surrounding him, he disappeared back into the cold, damp air.

It might have been an early morning dog walker; not everyone had disposed of their dogs. Our visitor might have had any number of innocent reasons for being there, but I didn't need to consider any of them. This was Burrows; I didn't have the slightest doubt. He left as silently as he arrived. A creature of the mist, he simply evaporated into thin air. The boys in the observation car caught just a fleeting glimpse of him as he left. We stood in silence, not sure if we should celebrate or panic. Burrows had fallen for our trap.

Maggie greeted the news with unnerving enthusiasm. She pointed out that we had set the trap, hoping Burrows would fall into it. His appearance should be regarded as a success. She was right; Burrows had fallen for it, and we should celebrate. The problem was that we didn't have Maggie's nerves of steel.

I spent the day like a coiled spring, unable to do anything but equally unable to wind down. As usual, Burrows went to work at the Town Hall, behaving perfectly normally. We didn't have the manpower to follow him for months on end, but we certainly followed him that day. Alfie had the onerous task of watching his house that night and following him when he left. He had the strictest possible instructions not to be seen. I would rather he lost Burrows in the blackout than raised his suspicion.

We settled in for what would be an incredibly tense evening, knowing that Burrows would come. It was especially exasperating that I couldn't talk directly to Maggie. I could hear her via the headphones, but she could only hear me through the hole in the wall. She would often keep us informed with comments such as 'I think I'll make a cup of tea, boys,' which did nothing to calm my nerves.

At 9:45 pm, we rapidly approached the critical moment when Maggie would go outside to the Anderson shelter. She would have been drying the twigs in the oven. They had to be dry and brittle before she spread them on the grass in front of the Anderson shelter. She did that methodically every night so an intruder would unwittingly step on one and snap it.

"Watchtower, watchtower, this is observation car. Over."

"Observation car, observation car. This is watchtower. Go ahead. Over."

"A tall man wearing a trilby hat and long coat has just entered the alleyway. It' him; he's carrying a briefcase. Over."

"Well done, boys, keep your eyes open. Over."

My heart nearly burst out of my chest. "Quickly, Jeff, tap on the wall. We need to tell Maggie before she goes outside."

We heard her say she was coming via the microphone. I breathed an enormous sigh of relief when she lifted the photograph, and a shaft of light shone through the hole.

"He's coming, Maggie, wait there."

We sat every night in total darkness so that our eyes were accustomed to low light. I even left the room to light a fag. We had a little moonlight, just enough to see from the rear window. Then suddenly, there he was. He walked silently along the rear hedgerow like a prowling hyena. He then crouched next to the Anderson shelter. Having satisfied himself that Maggie was not there, he concealed himself in the undergrowth next to the shelter. My heart pounded. This was it. He had walked into the trap.

"It's him, Maggie. He's hiding in the undergrowth to the left of the shelter. He presumably intends to grab you from behind when you try to enter it."

"Then I had better not disappoint him, Roger. Anything else I need to know?"

"For God's sake, be careful. We can be there in about thirty seconds if you need us."

"Stop worrying, Roger. I know all about him, and I know where he is. He knows nothing about me. I would say that gives me the upper hand, wouldn't you? My only doubt is about talking him into the house. It wouldn't be a problem with most men, but he's not most men, is he? Wish me luck."

Ten minutes later, she appeared in the garden. She wore a dressing gown with her bag hanging on one shoulder. I noticed the dressing gown was wide open at the top, and although I couldn't see, I suspected she had little on underneath it. Her intention was obvious. She employed the oldest trick in the book as far as men are concerned. I could hardly breathe as she walked across the garden. Burrows made his move as she approached the shelter entrance. Her reaction was instant. She casually turned to face him, and Burrows stopped in his tracks.

We were desperate to hear the conversation that we assumed must be taking place. Maggie faked embarrassment about her dressing gown being open. She covered herself up, and they appeared to talk like old friends for several seconds. She then calmly walked back into the house with Burrows following. The hyena had suddenly become an obedient dog. I could hardly believe my eyes. We huddled together, each desperately trying to see out of the small window. If we could have seen each other's faces, we would have shared a collective expression of amazement. The second Maggie stepped into the house, we rushed back to the headphones, desperate to hear what was being said.

"Come in, Mr Burrows. I'll make us a cup of tea."

"That's very kind of you, Mrs Kennedy. I was just out on my evening walk when I realised I was passing by. I really shouldn't impose myself on you at this time of the night. Perhaps just a quick cup."

"I think it's the least I can do. Do you always check on your homeless people at this time of the night?"

"No, indeed not. I just wanted to know how you were coping, living in these conditions."

"Have you found somewhere else for me? Is anything available?"

"Not at this moment, but you won't be here much longer."

His hidden meaning sent a chill down my spine. Then, we heard the sound of a kettle being filled with water and the sharp sound of cups being placed on saucers. I tried desperately to combine all the sounds and visualise the scene. Maggie drinking tea with Burrows. It seemed so improbable. The conversation continued with everyday small talk until Burrows suggested she should sit down. A kitchen chair scraped the floor as it was moved. When he suggested she sit down again, I realised he must have offered her the chair as a gentleman might offer a lady. I could just visualise Burrows standing behind the chair, waiting for Maggie to sit in front of him.

Instantly realising his intentions, she refused, saying she had been sitting for hours and needed to stand. He sounded slightly agitated. Burrows had an immutable fantasy that compelled him to reenact every detail precisely. In his twisted mind, he had to strangle Maggie from behind. He needed her unconscious but not dead. We saw before what happened when his meticulous plan was thwarted. He lost control, and his rage took over. I prayed Maggie was prepared for it. We heard a chair move again, and a cup was returned to a saucer. I assumed she was keeping him at arm's length.

"What are you doing, Mr Burrows?"

"I just need something from my briefcase."

"Why do you need a knife, especially a long knife like that?" Maggie obviously spoke for the benefit of the microphone, describing Burrows' actions. "I think you need to stay there, Mr Burrows. You're frightening me."

"Should we go in?" said Jeff.

"No, she's leading him on. She's not frightened," said Ray.

"Well, I'm bloody terrified," I said as I gripped the arms of my chair.

"It's alright, my dear. Don't be frightened. It will all be over in a second." Burrows' voice sent a chill down my spine.

"What do you mean, it will be over? You're not going to hurt me, are you?"

"If you make the slightest sound, I can kill you in a second with this knife. I want you to walk towards your bedroom quietly. If you do as I say, I will spare your life."

"You're going to rape me?"

"Or, I can kill you. Which is it to be?"

"You're the Blackout Ripper, aren't you? And you'll kill me, anyway."

"Why do you think that?"

"You don't deny it then. I know who you are. You're even more famous than Jack the Ripper."

"You're right, I am. People will talk about Jack and me in the same breath. Everyone will soon know my name. You're about to discover why I'll be even more famous than Jack."

A chair scraped the floor again, followed by the brittle sound of china shattering. There were more sounds of movement as Burrows must have rushed forward. A commotion ensued. There were breathless voices followed by a sickening thud. A scream of pain filled the headphones. I couldn't take it a second more. We jumped to our feet and ran as fast as our legs would carry us out into the garden and into the house. Burrows lay on the kitchen floor, obviously in tremendous pain. Maggie stood over him with her hands on her hips. His right arm was bent across his body at an alarming angle, obviously broken. He could hardly move. He just lay there in shock.

"Are you alright, Maggie?"

"Yes, of course. Did you get it? He admitted he was the Ripper."

"We got it. Did he try to kill you?"

"He certainly did. He came straight at me with this knife."

"Get up, Burrows, you're under arrest."

"I think he might have hurt his back, and I broke his arm."

"I can see that. Let me help you, Burrows."

He screamed again in pain, obviously unable to straighten his body. He didn't say a word.

"Put the handcuffs on him, Jeff."

Jeff grabbed the twisted arm and wrenched it behind him. Burrows almost fainted with pain. His face turned an ashen grey. After all the murders and all the years of pursuing him, there he was. A sad, pathetic figure who knew he faced an ignominious death on the end of a rope. I thought I would feel like celebrating, jumping for joy or punching the air. In reality, I felt no such thing. My only reaction was relief that Maggie was alright and an overwhelming sense of admiration for her. Burrows said only one thing.

"Who are you?"

"Someone you wish you hadn't met," she replied.

"Take him away, Jeff, and do everything by the book."

Alfie arrived breathless as he rushed into the kitchen.

"You've got him. You've got the bastard."

"And we've got a confession, Alfie. He said he's the Ripper."

"We've also got his hiding place. I followed him; he's got a lockup he uses a few streets away."

"Looks like we've got it all, Burrows."

He remained silent. He looked like a man who was in both physical and mental pain. For a man governed by his psychotic fantasy and illusions of absolute power and control, his demise must have been shattering. I confess I enjoyed his discomfort. The two bobbies arrived, and they bundled Burrows into the back of the car, still groaning in pain. Only as the car drove away did I accept his reign of terror was finally over. I returned to the house to find Ray and Maggie preparing to leave.

"Where are you going?"

"This is it, Roger, job done. I'll take Maggie back with me. Her job's over."

"But I'll need statements from you both. There's so much more that we need to do."

"That's your department, Roger. I thought you understood. We were never here."

"How do I explain all this?"

"MI5 will provide a confidential statement which will be presented to the Court with the recording."

"And that's it?"

"That's it, Roger," said Maggie. "I'm not used to it either, but this is how it works. Give me a kiss before I go."

She put her arms around me and kissed me full on the lips. What an extraordinary woman. A notorious murderer had just attacked her, and she dismissed it all as a day's work. I probably made something of a fool of myself trying to thank her. There are only so many ways you can tell someone how incredible they are. Ray shook my hand with a wry smile as if to say, 'I told you so.' A few minutes later, she was gone.

Brian said he would return in the morning to remove the rest of the listening equipment and provide me with the recording. They left me to gather the evidence, Burrows' knife and briefcase, and the photographer would need to attend in the morning. There were still so many questions to be answered. It was the calm after the storm, that strange eerie silence that continues to invade the senses. I made my way back into the adjoining house to be presented with yet another tray of tea and cakes.

"Is it over?" Doris asked.

"Yes, it's over."

# Chapter Seventy-Five
# April 11th, 1945

Emma

*"I just held him. We didn't need to say anything,*
*he was mine, and I would mend him."*

R oger emerged from his long conflict with Burrows like an injured
man learning to walk again. He came straight to me and put his
head on my shoulder. His only words were, 'It's over.' I just held
him. We didn't need to say anything, he was mine, and I would mend
him. We were not alone in starting our lives again. There was a palpable
sense across the country that the end was in sight. On the 18th of April,
370,000 German troops surrendered in the Ruhr. The newspapers celebrated it as the beginning of the end. We finally accepted that the last
bomb had fallen. It was April, and the daffodils had returned, looking for
the sun.

The girls and I said goodbye to our basement bedroom. We collected
our few belongings and looked back with an unexpected sadness. Each of
us felt the same emotion. It had been a terrible and traumatic period of
our lives, but we knew it was a part of our lives that would live forever.
Something that started as an occasion to celebrate became an occasion to
reflect.

"I can see Alice, Joyce and Catherine standing here," said Shirley.

"I can see Gloria and Ken."

"They're not alone, Emma," replied Marion, "we've lost ten of our
own."

"Ten of our colleagues who can't be here. Why were we spared?"

"Why is anyone spared, Janet? We've all seen so much death. That's the tragedy of war. We have to live the life that they were denied. Anything less would be a betrayal."

"Emma's right," said Marion. "What frightens me is that a whole generation will follow who will not understand that."

"Perhaps it's always the same. My parents tried to tell me, but I didn't want to believe it. My father used to say, 'The wisdom of the ages dies with each generation'."

"We must always remember this moment. We're closing the door on a piece of history only we can re-tell."

"Do we really want to relive what we've been through, Marion? Can you go through all that pain again?"

"The time will come when we have to. As you said, Emma, anything less would be a betrayal."

"It's quite a moment, isn't it?" said Janet. "Shall I close the door?"

She did, and we walked away. We each left a part of ourselves in that basement, the part that stayed with those we left behind. It was a strange time. For us, the war was over, but for the Allied troops in the Far East and those now fighting their way towards Berlin, it was far from over. A new chapter awaited us, but for now, we had to remain with the sad reflections of the final page.

Roger and I were trapped on that last page. We wanted to move forward; we wanted to do normal things, but the country remained at war. I moved back to my little house in Battersea. It survived the bombing. In fact, the whole road remained unscathed. Roger and Jean no longer went to the shelter at night. Having a home to go to without fear is something that only we understand, and something we relish. Roger invited me to dinner one evening, something that might sound like an everyday event, but during six years of war, it was anything but ordinary.

"What have you managed to buy, Roger?"

"Not very much, I'm afraid; it's more a token gesture."

"I'm sure it will be the best token gesture I've ever eaten."

"I can offer you a glass of sherry or whisky. That's it, I'm afraid."

"Sherry would be lovely."

We sat sipping our sherry, smiling at each other across the half-full glasses. True to his word, we took our relationship one step at a time. Like any series of steps, they were going somewhere, and there was an inevitability about the destination. A part of me wanted to go to bed with Roger, but I was not ready. We didn't discuss it, but that prospect had become a frightening obstacle for me. We drank our sherry and then some whisky. Roger's attempt at 'toad in the hole' was admirable. He made the best of the only two ingredients available. Food and alcohol are a heady mix; they combine to dull the sensibilities. I found the courage to ask those questions that frightened me most.

"How's Jean, Roger?"

"She's fine. It seems strange not going to the shelter at night. Jean especially hated it, but in a funny kind of way, I almost miss it. All the people, the camaraderie."

"We've said goodbye to our basement bedroom, so I know what you mean."

"Jean has her house, and I have mine. She still very kindly does a bit of shopping for me. She was washing my shirts, but I said I must be self-sufficient."

"Do you still, you know... fancy her?"

"No, not like that. I wouldn't be sitting here with you if I did."

"She told me she would always be a part of your life. Where does that leave me?"

"I know it's a bit unusual. Jean and I have known each other for so long and have been through so much together. It leaves its mark, Emma. She's my best friend in many ways, but not in the way you suggest."

"I'm finding it difficult, Roger, I really am. You were lovers here in this house, probably here on this settee. Jean's everything that I'm not. Look at her; she's beautiful, and she's really sexy. Even I can see that. I can't be her, Roger. I wish I could, but I can't."

"I don't want you to be. What we had was an illusion. We saw what we wanted to see in each other, like two twenty-year-olds meeting for the first time. I wanted the woman you described, but that's not what Jean is. We both found out the hard way. It's been a painful lesson in life, but it's over. What's left is the woman, not the illusion. The woman who has always been a part of my life and my kids' lives."

"You'll always be comparing me to her, and I don't compare, do I?"

"My darling, Emma. Will you always be comparing me to Frank?"

"No, of course not, that's different."

"Why is it different?"

"Frank's no longer a part of my life."

"But he's a friend, isn't he? You've been through too much together to lose that friendship."

"I don't... you know... desire him. I don't think I ever did."

"People move on; we have to. Of course, you don't compare to Jean. No one does; we are all different. It's not about the person; it's about how we feel about them. Jean and I were infatuated with the idea of each other. I admit it, but that's not how I feel about you."

"I would like someone to be infatuated with me."

"I'm completely infatuated with you. I think of nothing else but you. But with us, it's different. Between me and Jean, that's all it was, but you and I have something far greater."

"What do we have that you didn't have with Jean?"

"I wasn't ready to spell it out, not here, not like this. I wanted the occasion to be right."

"Tell me, Roger, I need to know."

"I love you. I am completely and utterly madly in love with you."

"You are?"

"I am, and so are you. You know you are. I see it in your eyes every time we kiss."

No other words in the English language can affect you as much as the three Roger used. I knew he loved me. I could see and feel it, but when he said it, my heart leapt with an indescribable joy.

"I do, I do, I love you. I'm exactly what Janet says I am. I'm crazy about you, but I'm frightened by all of it, Roger."

"I know you are, but there's no need to be. We have all the time in the world now. You know, when a man plucks up the courage to tell the woman of his dreams that he loves her, she's supposed to throw herself into his arms."

"She is, isn't she."

I realised in that moment that I had never truly felt desire before. I wanted him so badly that evening, but not there, not where Jean had been. I couldn't understand why Roger put up with me, even though I wanted him to. There were issues to be resolved. Jean remained one of them. The other was Roger's two children. Their mother was dead, and there was I, standing by their father's side in her place. The prospect of meeting them terrified me. Stepping into their world filled me with dread. However daunting, the alternative was unthinkable. For the first time in my life, I knew I had found what I always wanted. I love him with every fibre of my being; best of all, he loves me for who I am.

April ended with such growing optimism that it became difficult to suppress it, not least between Roger and me. The news arrived on the 30th that Hitler had shot himself with his own pistol. As my father said, 'Few people rejoice when a life is lost, much less a thousand, but the whole world rejoices when a life is saved.' What does that say about a person when the whole world rejoiced at the news of his death? My father's generation saw it coming, but I didn't. Dictators, by their very nature, erode a nation's freedom to their own ends. Their rise and fall throughout the ages is clearly marked by a trail of death and destruction. We allowed one man to usher the world into the worst conflagration it has ever seen. His legacy is the death of over 70 million people.

## Chapter Seventy-Six
# VE-Day, May 8th, 1945

### Roger

*"There will be another war generation, and they will see what we have seen. They will see the gradual decline of their democracy. They will see the power slipping through their fingers and into the hands of the new self-proclaimed saviour. There will be an inevitability about the outcome, but like us, they will choose not to see it because it will be too terrible to believe."*

Burrows failed to complete his evil fantasy, but he nevertheless gained the notoriety he craved. The newspapers heralded him as some kind of satanic monster. I regarded him as an aberration. Had he been possessed by the Devil, we could have employed an exorcist to redeem his soul. The reality was far worse. The evil in Burrows didn't come from without; it came from within. He reminds us we are all the architects of our own demise. Burrows was one manifestation, and Hitler another. I concluded there are no depths to which mankind is not prepared to descend.

He was my last case; I saw it through to the end, but I had nothing left to offer the police force. When you stand side by side with the worst that human nature can offer, it demands a price from you. I paid that price, and it left me bankrupt. It's difficult to see your feet when your head is in a dark cloud. It's even harder to see a path out of it. Emma offered me that path. It seemed almost impossible for something so wonderful to rise from the ashes of war. It might be a statement of the obvious, but when I told her I loved her, my world changed. She offered me what six years of war had taken away.

When she invited me to her house on May the 4th, I knew she had decided. I wanted her so much; the prospect made my heart race. For the first time in my life, this had nothing to do with lust or desire. I needed her; we were two halves of the same person. Without her, I remained incomplete. Emma's concerns about Jean were understandable, even though they were misplaced. She understood the implications of her decision; it was a commitment to the future. There was no need for her to ask if I wanted that future. I was desperate to take her there.

"Flowers, how lovely, thank you." A kiss is such an intimate expression; it says so much. We must have stood in Emma's hallway for five minutes, locked in each other's arms. "Where did you find them?"

"If ever there was a sign that peace is almost here, it must be a woman selling flowers from a stall on Balham High Street."

"They say it might be any day now. It seems almost too good to be true."

"People are preparing for it. I think it's going to be the biggest street party of all time."

"Everyone's so excited about it. There's talk about rebuilding the hospital."

"Half of London needs to be rebuilt."

"This is the future, isn't it? We can start again, but we can't replace all the people we've lost. Will we ever really recover?"

"No, I don't think we will, but our children will."

"We need to talk about them, Roger; your children, I mean. There's so much to talk about. Would you like a drink? I've got a special bottle of wine, it was Father's. He would want me to share it with you."

"Then I would be honoured."

Emma flitted from one subject to another and then went back into the kitchen. She couldn't stand still. When she poured the wine, her surgeon's hand revealed a slight tremor. Considering the rationing, Emma produced a surprisingly good meal - lamb chops had become like hens' teeth. Add mint sauce and roast potatoes, and the meagre ration became a banquet. The wine was sublime, and our intimate conversation seemed to have no end. Despite having all the ingredients for the perfect evening, our minds were elsewhere. We sat opposite each other, both consumed with the prospect of making love while playing the charade that perhaps we might not.

Emma still couldn't relax, adjusting the knife and fork on her empty plate and moving them again to a more perfect position. She raised her wine glass and put it down without drinking from it, only to replace it again a few inches away. She repeatedly stroked the same strand of hair away from her face. Had she been a suspect I was interrogating, I would know she had reason to be nervous. I ached for her, but it had to be on her terms. I wanted it to be an unforgettable experience, a defining moment we would each remember for the rest of our lives. This wasn't how I wanted it to be.

"I don't want to be late leaving tonight, Emma. I've still got work to do at the station tomorrow."

"You're leaving ... I thought ... well, I mean ... why are you not staying?"

"I love you, Emma, and I want us to make love more than I've wanted anything in my life. I desperately need you in my arms. I have to feel like a whole person again, but not now, not here."

"If not now, when?"

"It has to be perfect for you, for both of us. I want to take you to the best hotel in London. I want you to dress up in the finest dress you can find, and I want us to share the most wonderful meal we've ever eaten. We'll sit in opulent surroundings, and I will drown in your eyes. During every glass of wine and every morsel of food, we will only have each other in our minds. You'll know that every second, I will want nothing but you. When you decide the time is right, that's when we will make each other complete."

I have to admit, I had half rehearsed my thoughts beforehand. It was something that felt right, something I thought would make it perfect for Emma. What I didn't expect was her reaction. She burst into tears, not sorrow, sheer joy. She jumped to her feet so fast that her chair fell back to the floor. We were both in danger of joining it when she threw herself into my arms. Emma may not have even realised, but with her fears removed, she had been replaced by an intensely passionate woman. I had never been in any doubt.

I telephoned the Savoy Hotel first thing the next morning and booked the next available night. That was May the 7th. Events and decisions are the signposts that change the course of destiny. How could I have known the significance of that date? I knew it would be a day like no other, but I was only thinking of us. On the day, I drove to Emma's with all the anticipation and excitement of a child on Christmas morning. When she came to the door, I couldn't believe my eyes. No more surgical tweezers holding her hair back, no more blood-stained surgical gowns, no more baggy jumpers. She wore a beautiful olive-green dress, a matching jacket and high-heeled shoes. With her chestnut brown hair pulled into an elaborate French twist, she looked positively regal. And her eyes; I had never seen her wearing makeup to such effect.

"Emma. I don't know what to say. You look wonderful."

"I think that might be a slight exaggeration but thank you. By the way, who are you? I was expecting to meet a scruffy policeman."

"Do you like it?"

"I think we're both lost for words. This dress suit came from a second-hand shop, and the makeup is courtesy of Janet. But that suit didn't come from a second-hand shop, did it?"

"No, this was tailored for me personally by the King's tailor."

"Are you being serious? It's wonderful."

"I am, but let's not worry about me. Let me look at you."

"Don't embarrass me, please. I feel very self-conscious."

We entered the Savoy with our overnight cases, feeling like Royalty. What's more, they treated us as if we were. The black and white tiled floor seemed to disappear away into the distance, punctuated only by its magnificent pillars, hanging chandeliers, and soft furnishings. This was so far removed from the war-torn London that I knew; this was another world. It was even more impressive because I knew the Savoy had suffered a direct hit in 1940. I booked us in as Mr and Mrs Pritchard with Emma standing by my side. I looked at her for a sign of approval, and she put her arm around me.

We were shown to our room and stood there looking at each other, with a large double bed in front of us. Emma's usual self-conscious expression would have been incompatible with the dress and the makeup; I think she had little option but to abandon it. As we kissed, there was almost a moment when we fell into that bed. It took considerable self-restraint, but I wanted everything to be perfect for her. We walked hand in hand down the stairs and sat in the central atrium, where they were honouring the age-old British tradition of afternoon tea.

The maître d' immediately offered us a table. A glorious array of cakes appeared on a three-tier cake stand. As well as cakes, there were sandwiches, all neatly cut into squares. We both requested tea, which arrived complete with a silver tea service, bone china cups, and saucers. This was indeed another world; the past six years didn't exist here. If we were ever to forget those years, if only for one night, then it would be here.

I tried to enjoy it all but could only concentrate on Emma. The afternoon melted into the evening without either of us noticing it passing. Nearly everyone had left, so we decided we should do the same and prepare for dinner. Even the carpet beneath my feet felt different; with Emma's hand in mine, I saw everything as if for the first time. From our room, we could see across the river, and despite the ravages of war, the Thames had never looked finer with the evening sun dancing across the surface. We stood together at the window with the world seemingly at our feet.

"I had better change for dinner, Roger."

"Change? I don't have anything to change into."

"I think you might find that a lot of the gentlemen will wear a dinner jacket and bow tie."

"Oh dear. Will this do?"

"You couldn't be wearing a finer suit; I think it will do just fine. I'll pop into the bathroom and change."

Twenty minutes later, the bathroom door opened, and Emma stepped away from her former self like an emerging butterfly, her metamorphosis complete. Nothing in all of nature's glorious creation could compare to the vision standing before me. She took my breath away. There wasn't sufficient oxygen in the room to revive my senses. I know nothing about the intricacies of women's dresses. I only knew that her plum-coloured cocktail dress was close-fitting, revealing, and absolutely stunning. A double row of pearls with a ruby clasp sat in the hollow of her neck. Her hair, her eyes, her lips, she was that rarest of women for whom there is no shade. Above all, what really took my breath away was the curvaceous, sensual woman she had become. I couldn't take my eyes off her. This was my gloriously wonderful Emma, as I had never seen her before.

"What do you think?"

"Think? I can hardly think at all. Where has this Emma been hiding? You look incredible; you're beautiful; you look sensational; I'm lost for words."

"Really? Do you mean that?"

"Have you not looked in the mirror? You're simply breathtaking."

"No one has ever said I look lovely and meant it, much less breathtaking."

"Then either you've kept that person hidden, or you've been living in the land of the blind. Let me touch you to see if you're real."

"Don't you dare smudge my lipstick."

No woman could look like Emma and not enjoy it. It might have been an unaccustomed experience for her, but she stepped into the part with more confidence than she realised. She took my hand and led me towards the restaurant. She was right about the bow tie, but one or two gentlemen wore suits and ties. I wondered how many of those had been constructed by the King's tailor. We were shown to our table, and I just sat, momentarily looking at the surrounding opulence.

We were surrounded by ladies adorned with diamonds and pearls. Yesterday's bustles and trains looked enviously at today's slender chic. Gentlemen wore Savile Row's finest, some fresh from the fitting like mine, some with the patina of past indulgence. They all had one thing in common: power and wealth. I recognised two Members of Parliament, and for a second, I allowed myself to wonder.

"I've never seen so many beautiful women and dresses in one place before," said Emma.

"Neither have I. Did you notice how many heads you turned when we came in?"

"I did, didn't I?" She dipped her head, raised her eyebrows and giggled as if she had just let slip a secret. Every time I looked at her, I fell in love again. "You have to tell me about the suit."

"It's a long story. Let's just say it was a present from Joey Katz."

"Oh my goodness, I won't ask. It is fabulous though, isn't it? It looks perfect on you. When you become an MP, this is how you need to look."

"You're right; I need to smarten myself up."

"I think you've achieved that. And what about that wonderful shirt? I've not seen that before?"

"I had this made for me; it's Egyptian cotton."

"You haven't smoked a single cigarette this afternoon either."

"I've stopped."

"You said you couldn't do without them."

"I didn't have the motivation to do it for myself, but I can do it for you." Her face beamed approval across the table. "Tell me about the dress and the pearls."

"The pearls were my mother's; I've only worn them once before. The dress came from Janet's friend, who runs a couture business. There's been little call for haute couture recently, so she also takes in her wealthy clients' second-hand clothes."

"Why would anyone part with such a dress?"

"I don't think it's ever been worn; perhaps it didn't fit."

"You mean the unfortunate woman didn't have a body like yours?"

"Oh, Roger, stop it. I'm already self-conscious."

I diverted her attention towards the menu. This truly was another world. Whatever happened to rationing? I decided upon the lobster soup and the turbot with brown shrimp, mussels, and shellfish. Emma looked up from the menu.

"What have you decided upon?"

"The soup and the turbot."

"I've not had turbot before; what's it like?"

"I have no idea, but it sounds wonderful. What are you having?"

"As I can't see the menu properly without my glasses, I'll have what you're having."

We both laughed aloud, and she looked so confident and happy. The maître d' came to the table resembling a starched penguin wearing a bow tie. He spoke with a heavy French accent, lapsing into French when it suited him. It's one of those affectations that I find pretty annoying in restaurants. He spoke perfect English when he was of a mind to. To my surprise and delight, Emma answered him in French. I looked at the wine list and shuddered at the prices, but being a good detective, I had already done my homework. I ordered the 1934 Batard-Montrachet. The maître d' nodded approvingly. My suit already impressed him, so this elevated us to a new level.

"Can we afford the 1934 vintage? That's the vintage of the decade."

"I didn't know you were a wine expert as well as everything else."

"I'm not. These are the kind of facts I picked up in my formative years. You don't live in the school Principal's house without some of it rubbing off."

"You were close to your father, weren't you?"

"I know, I'm always quoting him; I'm sorry."

"Don't be. Is that what attracted you to Frank, him being quite a bit older?"

"Oh, I don't know. Maybe you're right."

"We haven't talked much about you and Frank, have we?"

"It was a mistake; I know that now. Frank's a lovely man, but he's very reserved, and I'm very reserved. So between us ... well, we didn't ... you know ... we didn't exactly light up the sky."

"Are you talking about sex?"

"Oh, God. It's that word. Yes, that had something to do with it. I came to Frank knowing nothing and left pretty much the same. This is why it all frightens me, Roger."

"That's all in the past, Emma. Trust me, you'll never feel that way again."

The Sommelier made a tremendous fuss about pouring our wine. I nodded approvingly and couldn't avoid looking delighted. He poured Emma's glass, and she looked at it in anticipation. We touched glasses and savoured the straw-coloured wine.

"Oh, Roger, I've tasted nothing so wonderful. It seems to touch every sense I've ever experienced."

"They say enjoying a fine wine is like making love, and that's how you've described it."

She looked at me, deciding if she should be embarrassed or enthralled. She smiled, and I noticed the little vertical creases on each side of her mouth. The spell broke when one of the staff rushed into the restaurant, making his presence known.

"Ladies and gentlemen, may I have your attention? There has just been an announcement from the BBC. Tomorrow, at 3 o'clock in the afternoon, the Prime Minister, Sir Winston Churchill, will address the nation. My Lords, Ladies and Gentlemen, tomorrow will be Victory in Europe Day."

The Savoy restaurant, in all its long history, would never have seen a moment like it. Everyone jumped to their feet and started clapping and cheering. We all knew the day was coming soon, but I doubt anyone realised the full extent of their pent-up emotion. After six long years of war, the outpouring could no longer be contained. The people went wild with joy, including us. We hugged everyone in sight. I found myself being kissed by women I had never seen before and shaking hands with their husbands. Several men hugged me. Elegant ladies in beautiful dresses stood with their mascara running down their faces. Men were in tears.

One of the most elegant women in the restaurant, a most impressive auburn-haired lady, kissed me, saying, 'Isn't it wonderful.' I would have agreed with her, but she had already fallen into the arms of another. When our usual British reserve returned, our circumstances appeared slightly embarrassing. This was the Savoy restaurant. The cheering subsided, and we gradually returned to our tables, but the high spirits were irrepressible. Emma came back, desperate to tell me something.

"Roger, that woman with the auburn hair, that's her."

"What do you mean?"

"That's the woman I told you about at the hospital. She's the mystery woman. That's Mrs Heywood, and that's the man who had the head injury."

"Are you sure?"

"Yes, I knew he would recover; she simply wouldn't allow him to die."

"Why don't you say hello?"

"She looked at me for a second, but she's not going to recognise me, is she?"

"I don't recognise you."

"You remember Barry and Janet met them at their friend's wedding? Isn't it incredible that our paths keep crossing like this? She's something important in the War Ministry, and I'm sure he is, too. I bet she has an incredible story to tell. I bet everyone here has a story to tell about their part in the war."

"You're right. Will our children believe any of this?"

"Our children, you mean your children."

"I wasn't thinking, a Freudian slip. But the thing is, I don't see a future that doesn't contain us together, so who knows, perhaps it might be our children."

"Are you proposing to me, Roger?"

"Well, no, I wasn't planning to, not right now. When I do, I'll make a much better job of it."

She looked at me with wide eyes, and soon those little creases reappeared at the side of her mouth. The waiter arrived with our first course, and the thought hung in the air like the heavy scent of lavender. Emma didn't mention it again, but those creases kept reappearing. We drank the wine and ate the food in an indescribable atmosphere of elation.

The war was over. Finally, after six long years of suffering, we once again breathed the fresh air of freedom. It was impossible not to be intoxicated by it. We were drunk with joy, passion, and not a little alcohol. The waiter offered us the dessert menu, and Emma pretended to look at it. After a few seconds, she put it down and looked me straight in the eye.

"Take me to bed, Roger."

I didn't answer; I felt incapable of speaking. She took my hand and led me away. In normal circumstances, the diners in the Savoy would have been invisible to each other, and we would have left them in complete anonymity. Not that night, people, including us, raised their glasses at any excuse. They said goodnight. The auburn-haired Mrs Heywood raised her glass to us. I don't remember the walk to our room. I don't even remember opening the door. My next memory is when Emma turned her back to me and asked that I undid her buttons. I slipped the dress off her shoulders, dropping it to the floor. She turned to me and opened her arms. I walked into them, and the spark of passion ignited between us.

I have never experienced such spontaneous elation in my life. It was as if I had waited all my life for that moment. I couldn't get enough of her, and she of me. We scaled heights where the air was too thin to breathe and only slowly fell back to earth. We lay there, ravaged by the storm. Emma turned her face towards mine with a smile I had to kiss.

"That was the most wonderful moment of my life. Will it always be like this, Roger?"

"God, I hope so. Perhaps it might even be better."

"Is that possible?"

"I don't know, you've just taken me somewhere I haven't been before."

"I took you?"

"Yes, didn't you notice? Don't you realise the power you have over me?"

"No, but I'm finding out. I didn't know making love could be like this. I just had no idea."

"Neither did I. But then again, I've never been in love this way."

It had been an experience like no other. Two souls united in love, lifted by the combined joy of the entire nation on that day of days. Our emotions were stretched to exhaustion. We fell asleep in each other's arms until the early morning. I woke to find her head still resting on my shoulder. Gently lifting her with my other hand, I carefully placed her head back on the pillow. Her chestnut brown hair lay in stark contrast to the white bed linen. I marvelled at the sight of her, the smell of her, the smooth touch of her skin, and the inviting soft contour of her body. She filled my senses to overflowing. I was in no doubt: no man could love a woman more than I loved her.

Her eyes opened, and we instantly returned to where we were before sleep denied us. We kissed and continued kissing for the next two hours. We answered the question, could it get even better, and yes, it could. Had this been just another day, I doubt the world would have had anything to offer us. But this was a day like no other. This was the day of days. We were consumed with each other to the exclusion of all else, but the moment we left our bedroom, we stepped into VE-Day. We walked down to a late breakfast, clinging to each other. The hotel echoed to the sound of rejoicing, and we could hear the cheers coming from the masses of people outside. The atmosphere enveloped us as it had everyone else. Our breakfast was not so much a meal; it was a part of the celebration.

"Look at the crowds, Roger; there must be thousands outside. Where are they all going?"

"I'm not sure they know or care. Some will go to Buckingham Palace, and others will go to Whitehall. We all want to hear the Prime Minister speak to us."

"We have to be there, Roger; we have to hear him address the nation."

"I'm not sure where that will be, but my guess is Whitehall."

"Then we must go there."

Emma's mystery friend, Mrs Heywood and her husband, if that's who he was, sat at a table near us, and like us, they looked so happy. He wore a wonderful suit, which might even have come from the King's tailor. I would like to have spoken to them, but none of us were masters of our destiny that day. We were standing on a bridge between the past and the future. Our lives that day were as sticks dropped into the raging torrent below. By the time Emma and I left the hotel, we became a part of that torrent. People of every age, from every part of town, were there to celebrate. It wasn't just London; the entire nation and the world were filled with the same euphoria. Passing strangers hugged us, pretty girls kissed me, and elderly men danced like boys. The nation had become intoxicated. Many people had celebrated all night, and nothing was about to stop them.

When human beings come together in happiness and joy, it is a force like no other. Hours vanished like minutes, and nobody wanted it to stop. The great tide of people swept us along until we found ourselves in White-hall opposite the Ministry of Health building. There was anticipation that Winston Churchill would address the nation. When he appeared on the balcony, the outpouring from the crowd instantly became focused towards the man many regarded as the nation's saviour. He appeared with his famous black hat and his victory sign. Beside him was Sir John Anderson, with whom I'd had dealings, and Ernest Bevin. I thought nothing could silence the crowd, but when Churchill spoke, the nation listened.

*"My dear friends, this is your hour. This is not victory of a party or any class. It's a victory of the great British nation as a whole. We were the first, in this ancient island, to draw the sword against tyranny. After a while, we were left*

*all alone against the most tremendous military power that has been seen. We were all alone for a whole year.*

*There we stood, alone. Did anyone want to give in? Were we downhearted? The lights went out, and the bombs came down. But every man, woman and child in the country had no thought of quitting the struggle. London can take it. So we came back after long months from the jaws of death, out of the mouth of Hell, while all the world wondered. When shall the reputation and faith of this generation of English men and women fail?*

*I say that, in the long years to come, not only will the people of this island but of the world, wherever the bird of freedom chirps in human hearts, look back to what we've done and they will say "do not despair, do not yield to violence and tyranny, march straight forward and die if need be - unconquered." Now we have emerged from one deadly struggle - a terrible foe has been cast on the ground and awaits our judgment and our mercy.*

*But there is another foe who occupies large portions of the British Empire, a foe stained with cruelty and greed - the Japanese. I rejoice we can all take a night off today and another day tomorrow. Tomorrow, our great Russian allies will also be celebrating victory, and after that we must begin the task of rebuilding our health and homes, doing our utmost to make this country a land in which all have a chance, in which all have a duty, and we must turn ourselves to fulfil our duty to our own countrymen, and to our fallen allies of the United States who were so foully and treacherously attacked by Japan. We will go hand and hand with them. Even if it is a hard struggle, we will not be the ones who will fail."*

(Winston Churchill's address to the nation from the balcony of the Ministry of Health building in Whitehall. May 8th, 1945.) *

Winston Churchill turned the English language into both a weapon of war and a rallying call. Standing before him, we felt the full force of the blast. He even led the densely packed crowd in a chorus of "Land of Hope and Glory". We sang the words 'mother of the free' at the top of our voices. I stood there like everyone else, with tears running down my face. Churchill was right when he said we would come back from the jaws of death and out of the mouth of Hell. After six terrible years, it was finally over. The good people of Germany didn't celebrate on the streets when Hitler invaded Czechoslovakia. They didn't stand with tears of joy when Hitler invaded Poland. Only a fool celebrates the outbreak of war, but the entire world rejoices when it's over.

A nation of people stepped into the future as the 'greatest generation'. If we are worthy of that accolade, then it is because we as a generation retain the memory of the worst disaster the world has ever seen. We know what future generations can never know. We know that democracy is the voice of the people. We know that those seeking to circumvent democracy do so for their own ends, not ours. Above all, we know that those who seek to impose their will are those who will wage war.

Humanity's greatest tragedy is that the wisdom of the ages dies with each generation. There will be another war generation, and they will see what we have seen. They will see the gradual decline of their democracy. They will see the power slipping through their fingers and into the hands of the new self-proclaimed saviour. There will be an inevitability about the outcome, but like us, they will choose not to see it because it will be too terrible to believe.

Emma and I stepped into that uncertain future together. Some say we represent the triumph of the human spirit, two of the greatest generation; while others might say we were just lucky to survive. We were all those things, but perhaps our story confirms what I had always wanted to believe - that love conquers all.

# The Story Continues

The story of the greatest generation will be retold for as long as we value our freedom. The mystery woman, Lily Heywood, who made such an impression on Emma, does indeed have a story to tell. Her story has captured the hearts of readers around the world. Lily is just one more victim of the Blitz, lying beneath the rubble of her home. An unbreakable spirit, this is not the end for Lily; this is merely the beginning. Defying the expectations of her background and social class, she embarks upon an incredible journey that will take her from the ashes of the Blitz to the very top of the British wartime establishment. Shortlisted for the Book of the Year award by both the Independent Author Network and the 'Selfies' award, Lily tells her story in:

## "None Stood Taller"

ooOoo

The second book in the 'None Stood Taller' series continues Lily's story from D-Day to VE-Day. Britain faces a new threat with the arrival of the V1 and the V2 rocket. Lily's life is plunged into despair when Edward falls victim to a V1 flying bomb and is rushed to St Thomas's Hospital. Her story continues in:

## "None Stood Taller -The Final Year"

ooOoo

"Maggie", the mysterious but highly trained woman who became Burrow's nemesis also has an incredible story to tell. Her training and operations in occupied France and Germany are meticulously researched. It is a story that will astound you, and her exploits will leave you breathless. She survived, but 15 of the 39 female SOE agents who served in occupied Europe did not return to tell their story. The true cost of our freedom is a price "Maggie" continues to pay. She tells her incredible story in:

**"None Stood Taller -The Price of Freedom"**

ooOoo

# The Final Word

It is my greatest wish that this book has enlightened and inspired you as much as it has me. As a self-published author without the marketing reach of a publishing house, the success of my books has been entirely due to the support of readers. We cannot exist without your support. So please, spare two minutes of your time and place a review on my Amazon or Goodreads page. Share your thoughts and comments with me through my website or email me directly. Now, it's time for me to move on to another adventure - come with me.

peterturnham.author@gmail.com

# Principal Characters

Emma Stevenson - Doctor

Albert Stevenson - Emma's father

Marjorie Stevenson - Emma's mother

Andrew Stevenson - Emma's brother

Patricia Stevenson - Emma's sister-in-law

William Stevenson - Emma's nephew

Audrey Stevenson - Emma's niece

Hamish McPherson - Emma's GP Partner

Roger Pritchard - Police Detective Inspector

Marilyn Pritchard - Roger's wife

Elsie Pritchard - Roger's sister

John and Mary - Children of Roger and Marilyn

David Wheeler - Police Detective Sergeant. Roger's best friend

Jean Wheeler - Dave's wife

Raymond and Irene - Children of Dave and Jean

Gerry Higgins - Police Chief Inspector

Margaret Higgins - Gerry's wife

Jeff Payne - Police Detective Constable

Norma Payne - Jeff's wife

Alfie Chambers - Police Detective Constable

Pamela Chambers - Alfie's wife

Bob Hughes - Police Detective Constable

DC Fleming - Police Detective Constable

Angela Meadows - Victim

Rose Jackson - Victim

Mary Thompson - Victim

Irene Newnham - Victim

Alice Cox - Victim

Betty Sullivan - Victim

Maureen Elkins - Victim

Joey Katz - One-time mobster

Aaron Katz - Joey's older son, RAF pilot

Ezra Katz - Joey's mobster son

Rachel Katz - Ezra's wife

Helen - GP practice secretary

Mrs Bottomly - GP practice benefactor

Daisy - Emma's patient

Nobby Clarke - Emma's patient

Scotty Henderson - Emma's patient

Alma Wilson - Child patient of Emma

Doctor Wisniewski - Senior hospital doctor

Marion Horworthy - Hospital matron

Evelyn - Hospital administrator

Frank Cooper - Hospital registrar

Kenneth Osborne - Surgeon

Leonard (Leo) Jordan - Junior doctor

Maurice Hargreaves - Junior doctor

Alexander Bartholomew - Senior consultant pathologist

Janet Walters - Nurse

Gloria Cummings - Nurse

Beverley Roberts - Nurse, later Beverley Hargreaves

Shirley Anderson - Nurse

Barry Roberts - Janet Walters' boyfriend. Warrant Officer RAF

Roy Woodward - Shirley Anderson's boyfriend. Sergeant RAF

Burrows - The Blackout Ripper

George Rawlings - Professor of psychology and mortuary attendant

Barbara - Friend of Rachel Katz

Mr Hewitt - Tailor

Ray Collins - MI5 agent

Maggie - Pseudonym of mystery agent

Brian - MI5 communications agent

# Historical Characters

**Winston Churchill.** Sir Winston Leonard Spencer-Churchill, KG, OM, CH, TD, DL, FRS, RA. Prime Minister of the United Kingdom 1940 - 1945, and 1951 - 1955. Popularly accepted as Britain's greatest ever leader, and the most inspirational voice of World War Two.

**Gordon Cummins.** The mass murderer Gordon Cummins, known as the "Blackout Ripper" served with the RAF at the junior rank of leading aircraftman, although he aspired to be a pilot. In February 1942, Cummins murdered four women and attempted to kill two others. He is also suspected of other killings and was hanged on the 25th of June 1942.

**John Anderson.** 1st Viscount Waverley. GCB, OM, GCSI, GCIE, PC(Ire), FRS. He was part of the government War Cabinet and also held the portfolio of Home Secretary and Minister of Home Security jointly with Herbert Morrison, a position in which they served under Winston Churchill. John Anderson was the inventor of the Anderson shelter, widely used in World War Two. He went on to be Chancellor of the Exchequer 1943-1945. (Wikipedia)

**Henry Willink.** Sir Henry Urmston Willink, 1st Baronet, MC, PC, QC (1894 – 1973) was a British politician and public servant. A Conservative Member of Parliament from 1940, he became Minister of Health in 1943. During his time in power he was appointed Special Commissioner for those made homeless by the London Blitz and was involved with the production of the Beveridge Report.

**Sir Hugh Cairns** KGB, FRCS. An Australian who spent most of his life in England. Set up Nuffield Department of Surgery in Oxford. A key figure in the development of neurosurgery as a speciality, the formation of the Oxford University Medical School and the treatment of head injuries during WW2. Instrumental in the creation of the hospital for head injuries at St Hugh's College Oxford.

**Jack 'Spot' Comer**. Son of Polish immigrants, born Whitechapel. Notorious East End gangster.

**Arthur Neville Chamberlain** FRS (1869 – 1940) was a British politician who served as Prime Minister of the UK from May 1937 to May 1940. He is best known for his foreign policy of appeasement, and in particular for his signing of the Munich Agreement on 30 September, 1938, ceding the German-speaking Sudetenland region of Czechoslovakia to Hitler's Nazi Germany. Following the invasion of Poland on 1 September 1939, which marked the beginning of the Second World War, Chamberlain announced the declaration of war on Germany two days later and led the United Kingdom through the first eight months of the war until his resignation as prime minister on 10 May, 1940. (Wikipedia)

**Ernest Bevin**. Transport and General Workers' Union from 1922 to 1940. Served as Minister of Labour and National Service in the wartime coalition government.

Made in the USA
Monee, IL
10 October 2024

67568538R00322